Wicked Beauty

Susan Lewis is the bestselling author of twenty-six novels. She is also the author of *Just One More Day* and *One Day at a Time*, the moving memoirs of her childhood in Bristol. She lives in Gloucestershire. Her website address is www.susanlewis.com

Acclaim for Susan Lewis

'One of the best around' *Independent on Sunday*

'Spellbinding! . . . you just keep turning the pages, with the atmosphere growing more and more intense as the story leads to its dramatic climax' *Daily Mail*

'Mystery and romance *par excellence*' *Sun*

'Deliciously dramatic and positively oozing with tension, this is another wonderfully absorbing novel from the *Sunday Times* bestseller Susan Lewis . . . Expertly written to brew an atmosphere of foreboding, this story is an irresistible blend of intrigue and passion, and the consequences of secrets and betrayal' *Woman*

'A multi-faceted tear jerker' *heat*

Susan LEWIS

Wicked Beauty

arrow books

Published by Arrow Books 2010

4 6 8 10 9 7 5

First published in Great Britain in 2002 by
William Heinemann
Random House, 20 Vauxhall Bridge Road,
London SW1V 2SA

www.randomhouse.co.uk
Addresses for companies within
The Penguin Random House Group can be found at:
global.penguinrandomhouse.com

The Random House Group Limited Reg. No. 954009

A CIP catalogue record for this book
is available from the British Library

ISBN 9780099534389

Penguin Random House is committed to a sustainable future for
our business, our readers and our planet. This book is made from
Forest Stewardship Council® certified paper.

Printed and bound in Great Britain by Clays Ltd, Elcograf S.p.A.
Typeset by SX DTP, Rayleigh, Essex

For Pamela

For Pamela

Acknowledgements

I should like to extend my sincere thanks to Diane Bodle and Nicole O'Flaherty who so very kindly guided me through the maze of political and parliamentary procedures. Also I warmly thank Jocelyn Jane, Nigel Legge, Tonks, Sharkey and the fishermen of Cadgwith who so willingly gave of their time and knowledge to help me create the fictional village of Killian. I hasten to add that the characters I have created are all fictional too.

A huge thank you to Julian Mounter, a treasured friend and expert pilot who helped me with the flying scenes, as well as lending considerable moral support. And to Nick and Monica who made our stay on Virgin Gorda so easy and pleasurable.

Prologue

The door of the small gallery opened, the overhead bell chimed and in swept the winds of change; the curious, capricious stalker called fate. The door closed, and in several different parts of the world the destinies of a handful of people who didn't yet know each other began their inexorable journeys towards the events that were ultimately to bind them together.

The owner of the art gallery, a strikingly handsome man in his late thirties, was watching his new visitors – two grey-suited men with expensive raincoats and an air of mild self-importance that seemed to suggest disdain for the paintings they were viewing. The taller man wore horn-rimmed glasses and an expression of weary impatience. The other's steel-grey hair curled over his collar, and flopped randomly over one eye, lending him a look that might once have been rakish, but had, in middle-age, deteriorated to merely unkempt. At first glance, the owner had assumed them to be interested buyers, or maybe rival dealers, but now he didn't think so. In fact, he was starting to become uneasy, for there was a discernible change creeping into the room that, whilst no more menacing than a sheathed weapon, seemed to discharge the same underlying potential.

The tall man was the first to speak, while taking a sideways look at a surreal interpretation of a human brain. 'I believe congratulations are in order,' he commented pleasantly.

The owner stared at him, his dark, sunken eyes showing more wariness than surprise.

The man turned round and smiled, thinly. His voice and appearance portrayed culture and a high degree of education, though the look in his eyes suggested many darker shades of the image. 'Marriage can be a haven or a hell,' he commented. 'In your case, I'm sure it will prove the former.'

The owner still said nothing, though alarm had punched him like a fist. Why mention his new wife? Were they about to threaten her in some way? Use her as leverage to make him do something illegal? The art world was a smorgasbord of criminal cunning; this wouldn't be the first such approach . . .

'It seems to be a good time for you,' the tall man continued, turning back to the carefully slected display of figurative works by unknown artists. 'A new wife. A new client.' He paused to scrutinize a circular arrangement of multi-coloured squares. 'A very important client, we're told.'

The owner heaved an inaudible sigh of relief. Of course, the client. He should have realized sooner, for such a man would naturally be of interest to anyone able to distinguish a Picasso from a Matisse, or even a gun from a sword.

'A Modigliani nude, I believe,' the tall man said.

The owner didn't confirm it; there was no need when they obviously already knew.

The other man suddenly spoke. 'You have pilot skills,' he stated.

The owner's eyes moved in his direction. Tension was

building inside him, causing a small muscle to twitch in his temple. Yes, he had pilot skills, but he was suddenly wishing he hadn't.

'This client,' the tall man said, sliding his hands into his pockets and perching on the edge of a table. 'He's an interesting individual, wouldn't you say?' When he received no reply, he said, 'We'd like to know more about him.'

The owner considered a facetious referral to a businessmen's almanac, or the Internet, but as he was now beginning to get an idea of precisely who these men were, he held on to his silence.

'We all need to play our parts,' said the man with the silver hair. 'As your father's son, I'm sure you understand that.'

There was his confirmation, they were who he suspected, and now he wished he'd stayed at home today. 'But I'm not my father,' he said mildly, though fear was definitely starting to factor in with the anger and hostility now.

Appearing surprised the tall man said, 'There was a time when you were eager to follow in his footsteps.'

'I was much younger then. I know better now.'

As though he hadn't spoken the tall man said, 'You received a good training. Your record in the field is exemplary, though not extensive, I grant you.'

'It was a long time ago,' he protested.

'It won't take long to bring you up to date. We need you to start building trust with your client right away.'

The owner looked at him. He could and would protest some more, though he knew already that it would do him no good.

The tall man smiled again, showing his expensively capped teeth. 'It won't be difficult for a man such as yourself,' he told him amiably. 'Educated, civilized, charming . . . In fact, I can already feel my own trust starting to grow.' He let the compliment bask in its glow of sarcasm, then said, 'If we begin now, it should all be over by the end of the year.'

That had been three years ago and so much had changed during that time, the deception and duplicity had become so deeply ingrained in his life that it *was* his life. How gullible he'd been back then, for he'd truly believed it was all about art. How naive and short-sighted, when he'd always known that nothing with these people was ever what it seemed, and now gone was the art dealer who got his kicks from mentoring; the amateur musician who liked to sing and fool around in the local pub; the new husband who couldn't get enough of his dazzling Titian-haired wife. He was different now in ways that often made him unrecognizable, even to himself, yet perversely, wholly irresistible to his wife. His only escape was the time he spent with her, when their passion burned even hotter than the early days, when, after only a month of knowing each other, they'd managed to tumble out of bed long enough to get married. Did she have any idea who, or what, he really was now? How his gallery had become a front for a whole other kind of culture that was as malign as art was benign? Did she even care? He doubted it, for the mystery of his sudden departures and frequently pro-longed absences was as addictive to her as the erotic games they played were to him. She was a woman like no other – as unusual as she was beautiful, as uncon-ventional as she was unpredictable. He couldn't imagine ever loving or desiring another woman, but nor could he have imagined the events that were about to crash into their lives and change them as irrevocably, yet much more catastrophically, than that short visit to his gallery had, three years ago.

Chapter 1

Jubilation exploded skywards. Champagne corks flew along with multi-coloured streamers, as confetti showered the triumphant faces like kaleidoscopic rain. Shouts of congratulations and laughter made up the chorus behind an orchestra of clapping hands and party hooters, while cameras flashed and rolled as news reporters shouted into microphones and mobile phones. Like everyone else, they were electrified by the elation as they transmitted this widely anticipated victory to the nation. No last-minute upsets here, no surprises either, but the joy was as great as if the charismatic Tim Hendon had been a rank outsider.

Rachel Hendon's smile was ecstatic. The press loved her and followed her every move almost as closely as her husband's. Some said it was thanks to her that her husband enjoyed the kind of popularity most politicians only ever dreamed about, for it was widely known that she consulted frequently with his team of advisers, and kept his image as polished as any icon's. But the famous

1

Hendon gravitas and intellect were as much his own as the famous mass of blond, wavy hair and casual Armani chic. Not many political couples were so photographed or written about as the Hendons, and since his appointment to the Cabinet, eighteen months ago, their profile had attained an almost celebrity-style status, while their credibility remained a source of head-thumping frustration for those who were out to destroy it.

Rachel's slight, impeccably dressed figure moved through the crowd like a beacon of light. All eyes followed, everyone wanted a piece of her, for they all knew what a powerhouse she was, how ready her wit and generous her laughter. Being around her, her husband had once said, was as intoxicating as happiness. Her lustrous brown eyes shone with gratitude and friendship as she grasped the outstretched hands warmly, and thanked and hugged those who'd worked tirelessly alongside her and Tim during these past hectic weeks. And now tonight, the Government, their party, was back in power. No Opposition bench for Tim Hendon. His seat would once again be beside the Prime Minister, as a member of the Cabinet – maybe even as the youngest, and possibly most controversial, deputy leader in the party's history. Such an elevation for the thirty-eight-year-old Hendon would, it was claimed by some, only happen over certain dead bodies, but Tim's supporters weren't too concerned about that. Politics was a divisive and dangerous business, with dirty tricks, jealousy and rabid ambition forming the major opponents in the game.

Rachel was nearing the door. Poppers and

blowers continued to explode and trumpet with the laughter. Those who needed to express their joy were still circling her, elbowing their way through the crowd to clutch her hands or embrace her. No one noticed the children's drawings and poetry pinned to the walls, or the gold and silver stars that gleamed around them. The everyday purpose of this school hall meant little tonight.

Across the room she could see Tim being interviewed by John Wakeham, a reporter she knew well. After John would come Janet Crispin, then Steve Chalmers, then . . . The list was endless, and she didn't want to think about it now. She wanted only to slip away quietly, with Tim, so that they could indulge in a celebration of their own.

But that couldn't happen tonight.

'Rachel! Tell us how you're feeling right now.'

'You must be thrilled!'

'How certain were you of victory?'

'It was a landslide.'

'Have you spoken to the PM?'

Scores of reporters, well-wishers, party members. Was there anyone here she didn't know? A few maybe, but not many. She felt profoundly moved by their loyalty; and blessed by their friendship. It was no hardship to give them the soundbites they needed, or to return their embraces with as much affection as they offered. She did it willingly, joyously, and not a little emotionally.

Katherine Sumner was with Tim now, taking part in one of the interviews. His arm was loosely round her shoulders as they both leaned in to the mike and shouted over the din. As campaign manager Katherine had done an excellent job. It had been Rachel's decision to bring her in, even though Tim hadn't thought it necessary, considering the safeness of the seat he was standing for. But Rachel wasn't leaving anything to chance. Her husband's enemies could be lethal and Katherine's reputation, on her own side of the Atlantic, had been right up there with Stephanopoulos and Carvel, before she'd left the States – and politics – to start a new life in Europe. This would be her last campaign, only agreed to as a favour to Rachel, whose powers of persuasion were as irresistible as her frankness, Katherine had declared, and as admirable as her belief in her husband. So Katherine's new life had been put on hold until after the election, when she intended to embark upon a journey that was still a secret to most.

From the corner of her eye Rachel watched Katherine step back to allow Tim the limelight, in much the same way as Rachel often did herself. Katherine's stylish blonde hair and perfectly formed features reflected her inner poise as effectively as the cameras captured her beauty. There was nothing in her manner now to suggest the anger she'd shown earlier, when she and Tim had appeared, from the distance Rachel had been at, to be arguing quite violently. Rachel still had no idea what it had been about, she'd had no chance yet to ask, but whatever it was, they seemed to have made up now. Indeed, at the moment the results had been announced it was to Katherine Tim had turned first; after Rachel, of course. Rachel wanted to be over there with Tim now, but working the room was expected of her in a way it wasn't of Katherine.

Then Katherine was coming towards her, face glowing with delight, arms outstretched for yet another embrace. There was so much noise around them that probably no one else heard as Katherine said,

'This is as much your triumph as anyone's, Rachel. You've been an inspiration to us all. I really want to thank you for talking me into it.'

'It's for me to thank you,' Rachel replied, returning the pressure of her hands.

Katherine's expression was softened by affection as she gazed down into Rachel's face. Her height almost made her ungainly next to Rachel's petite femininity, yet Rachel felt diminished by it. And there was a radiance to her blondeness that seemed to dazzle Rachel's duskiness into uneasy submission. 'You're very special,' Katherine said, her words issuing sincerity. 'You and Tim both. I'm really going to miss you.'

'We'll miss you too,' Rachel assured her. It wasn't a lie, but nor was it meant in quite the way Katherine presumably thought.

'I hope we stay in touch,' Katherine said, and after pulling Rachel into another embrace, she turned back into the crowd.

For a moment Rachel watched her, tall and slender, confident almost to the point of arrogance, graceful almost to the point of regal. In many ways she was a shining ambassador for her nation, generous of heart and spirit, lively of wit and dedicated to her cause, which, for the past three months, had been the re-election of Tim Hendon. There was no doubt she had captivated them all with her zeal, as well as her willingness to adapt to their ways. She had, in fact, very quickly become an integral part of the team, which was certainly going to feel incomplete once she'd gone, but Rachel wouldn't be sorry to see her go.

She was very close to the door now, so close that it was possible to reach out and touch it. She was still smiling. No one would know that behind her mask of laughter and delight was an exhaustion she could barely support. It was making her dizzy, almost nauseous. How long had it been since they'd slept for more than three hours at a stretch? At thirty-four she should have the energy to withstand the pressure and lack of sleep. During her time as a news producer it had been almost a way of life.

Catching Tim's eye, she mirrored the raise of his eyebrows and felt the warmth of their connection reviving her. It was one of the ways they spoke, when words weren't possible. Katherine, she noticed, was talking to a reporter from CNN. The rest of the core team, sporting their colourful rosettes and 'Vote Hendon' T-shirts, had spread out through the hall, filling paper cups with champagne and happily donning the Union Jack hats and garlands that were being passed round the room.

The door was right there. She could feel its pull as though it were the persistent undertow of a tide, telling her that no matter how hard she swam now it was going to carry her away. She turned her back on it, only to find her hand moving up behind her, and her palm filling with the cooling brass of the handle.

'They're calling you the ultimate wife,' someone shouted.

'The power behind the throne.'

'She's our very own Helen of Troy,' another voice piped up, and everyone laughed, though Rachel wondered which Helen? the *Iliad*'s or the *Odyssey*'s. Either way she could never claim such beauty.

Across the room a commotion was breaking out around the temporary bank of TV screens. Everyone turned to see what it was, then began surging forward. Rachel's hand tightened on the doorknob. Quickly she turned, stepped back and seconds later she was walking swiftly along a dimly lit corridor, the noise receding behind her like a waning storm.

She took the back way out, letting the doors swing creakily behind her. There seemed to be no one around. The night air was clear and cool. She inhaled deeply, one hand on her heart as though to steady its rapid beats. Then suddenly she was bent double, throwing up in a gutter.

She felt better afterwards, though her vision was blurred by tears. She should go back inside, but knew she wouldn't, because already she was walking to her car. Tim would understand. He'd call on the mobile soon, wondering where she was, why she'd left. If she told him the truth she knew that the celebrations would come abruptly to an end. He'd want to be with her, she knew that, because given the choice, he always did.

Normally it was a half-hour drive from the school hall, at the heart of their North London constituency, to their town house in Hampstead – at two in the morning it took less than ten minutes. As she passed through the familiar Victorian terraced streets she wondered about the people behind the curtained windows. How many had stayed up to watch the election? What percentage had actually gone out to vote? Scenes such as the one she'd just left were being repeated all round the country. She envisaged them like a starry night sky, random bursts of light and merriment surrounded by a slumbering mass of indifference and darkness.

Not until she was standing in the kitchen, staring blankly at the answerphone's flashing green light, did she allow herself to start thinking again. For hours, days, weeks, she, Rachel, the private individual, had been switched off, packed away, put on ice, in order to give full stage to her public persona. Platitudes, homilies, promises and rhetoric had buzzed around her brain and out through her mouth in a ceaseless flow of loyalty and confidence. All that neural commotion. All that persuasive hot air. And now, at last, she could be quiet, take time to think and plan; to deal with the issues that, of necessity, were pushed aside by the perfect publicity machine.

She wondered if she was going to be sick again. Her stomach felt unanchored; and so did her mind. Both were spinning in a turmoil of confusion that even the stillness of her body and withdrawal from the fray didn't seem to be quelling. She was breathing too fast, and the sweat on her skin was turning chill. She knew, without looking in the mirror, that her normally olive-toned face would be pale and anguished. Her short, mahogany hair, that had triggered a small craze with its Meg Ryan-ish layers, felt limp to the touch, and she was finding it hard to see. Tiredness was making her emotional. More than anything she wanted to talk to Tim.

She started as the telephone rang. Then hearing her sister's voice on the speaker she snatched up the receiver.

'Anna, I'm here,' she gasped. How wonderful it was to have Anna back in her life after a silly year-long rift. How on earth had she let it go on so long?

'Rachel?' Anna cried. 'I was expecting to leave a message . . . '

'I came home. What are you doing up at this hour?'

'We watched the results, of course. I was just calling to . . . The hell with that. Why aren't you with Tim?'

'I didn't feel too good. I needed some air.'

Anna was immediately concerned. 'Are you OK now?' she demanded, in the bossy way that Rachel had once resented and now loved again.

'I think so.' Rachel's hand was trembling as she pushed it through her hair. 'Things aren't . . . Katherine was there – obviously. I don't know what's going on, Anna, but something is.'

Anna didn't answer right away, though Rachel knew, because they'd had this conversation at least a dozen times in the last few weeks, that she wasn't leaping to the obvious conclusion. 'Have you mentioned anything to Tim?' Anna finally said.

'No.' Rachel's mind was so tormented that it was hard not to drag Anna into yet another analysis of the mysterious phone calls he'd been receiving, both here and at the office; or of his recent edginess that was so much more noticeable in a man who was known for his easy, relaxed manner, especially when stressed. And though she couldn't exactly accuse him of becoming secretive, there was something he wasn't sharing with her, she was convinced of it, and she wasn't sure whether she was more upset by the thought of him holding back, or by the fear of what it might be.

'Are you going to?' Anna prompted.

Rachel could feel herself stiffening. 'I'll have to, now the election's over,' she answered, dread welling up inside her, for there was nothing worse than asking questions you didn't want to hear the answers to.

There was a beat before Anna said, 'I'm sure he's not sleeping with her . . .'

'No.'

Anna paused again. 'I take it you haven't told him about the baby yet?'

Rachel's head fell forward to rest against one of the glass-fronted cabinets. To be encumbered with a pregnancy now, at least in the physical sense, was truly the last thing she wanted, when she needed her energy and a calm, rational mind. Yet somewhere, just beyond her reach, she adored the total happiness and completeness that came with knowing she was going to be a mother, that she was carrying Tim's child . . . Nothing could be more important than that.

'He wants that baby more than anything,' Anna reminded her.

'He's very ambitious,' Rachel responded.

'So are you. The baby won't change that.'

'But something's going to change,' Rachel replied. 'I feel it so strongly. Maybe the feeling will go when Katherine does.'

Anna sighed. 'You're tired. You need to get some

sleep. Everything always looks bleak at this time in the morning.'

Rachel's eyes closed as tears threatened to spill out of them. 'You're right,' she finally managed. 'Everything'll be all right once we get away on holiday.'

'When do you go?'

'In three days.'

'The Virgin Islands,' Anna murmured dreamily. 'What I wouldn't give.'

A tightness in Rachel's throat stopped her from answering, for the very thought of just her and Tim being remote from the rest of the world, and together in a way that these past weeks hadn't allowed, made her so weak with longing that she could scarcely remember when she'd felt such a need for him. 'The villa's quite big, there's plenty of room,' she finally managed. 'Why don't you bring the girls for the half-term week?'

'Robert's schedule won't allow,' Anna answered. 'And I have to be here for him.'

'Of course,' Rachel responded, wondering, not for the first time, how much of Robert's success, as a playwright and director, was actually down to Anna, since she was even more ambitious for Robert than Rachel was for Tim.

After saying good-night and promising to call in the morning, she put the phone down, unplugged it and walked upstairs to the master bedroom. The earlier detritus of hastily taken showers and wardrobe changes had been magicked away by the redoubtable Lucy, who'd been with them for the past two years as personal assistant to Rachel, and occasional housekeeper to them both. Normally the latter duties were carried out by Winnie, who came

11

every morning, but since Lucy lived in the basement flat and worked in the office next to the kitchen, she had become, in a respectful yet almost familial way, such an integral part of their lives that no real boundaries existed any more.

'God bless you, Lucy Ryall,' Rachel murmured, sinking into the plush indigo and mauve pillows that had been plumped and perfectly arranged on the big, four-poster bed. Gazing up at the diaphanous folds that drifted between the tops of the posts like waves in a friendly ocean, she could feel guilt starting to burden her, but there was just no energy left in her to go back. Maybe she should call to let Tim know she was all right, but she didn't really want to talk to Gordon or Dennis, his personal aides – or to Katherine, who'd be sure to have taken charge of his phone. However, she should turn on her own phone so he could get through if he tried.

Dragging herself up from the bed again, she rummaged in her bag for her personal mobile, and had barely switched it on when it rang.

'Darling? Where are you?' he said. 'This is the third time I've called. Are you all right?'

She could hear the noise going on around him, and was easily able to picture him, turned away from the crowd, blocking one ear in order to hear her. People would be tapping his shoulders or tugging his arms, but she knew the polite yet firm way he had of making them wait. Quite suddenly her heart was so full that her words came out with a sob. 'I'm fine,' she laughed. 'I just had to get some air, and then I was so tired . . . I'm sorry. I should have told you.'

'It doesn't matter, as long as you're all right. Everyone's been asking where you are.'

'I'm sorry,' she said again. 'I'm at home.'

'Do you want me to come?'

To think he'd leave the celebrations now, at their height, just because she might need him, caused her heart to swell with the full strength of their love. 'Yes, of course I do,' she whispered, 'but you can't.'

'They can get drunk without me.'

She smiled. 'No. Stay there. I just need to sleep.'

There was a pause before he said, 'Are you sure you're all right?'

'Yes, I'm sure. Are you?'

'We won,' he reminded her.

Knowing that the question had been too subtle to elicit any other kind of response she said, 'Have you heard from Andrew?'

'Yes, about ten minutes ago. There's going to be a Cabinet reshuffle.'

The elation in his voice filled her heart with relief, for it was the call he'd been waiting for, a few words to reassure him that his portfolio was going to change. He'd never been comfortable in Defence, it wasn't his area of expertise or passion. Nor, with his business and economics background and total lack of military experience, had he ever been welcome. In fact, he'd been sorely resented, to the point that almost every day saw another flare-up as his efforts to drag the Ministry into the twenty-first century and to introduce some much-needed transparency to their murky and shadowy dealings were fought on every front. Thank God it now looked as though that was going to pass to someone better suited to the task. 'Did he say what's next?' she asked.

'No. But we're meeting on Saturday.'

Knowing he had high hopes of the Foreign Office, or even the deputy leadership, she said, 'You've served your time, he'll give you what you want now.'

'I think so,' he agreed.

Wishing she was with him, so she could put her arms around him, she pressed the phone in tighter to her ear as she said, 'I love you, Tim Hendon.'

'Not as much as I love you, Rachel Hendon,' he murmured.

She smiled, and was still smiling when a few minutes later she slid between the sheets and fell almost instantly asleep.

Franz Koehler came awake without a start as the phone next to his bed rang with an early morning wake-up call. Though it was only four-thirty, he was almost instantly alert as he reached for his glasses, then threw back the covers. He was a tall, upright man, with tight, wiry grey hair, a disciplined manner, and sternly handsome features. His pale green eyes, distorted by the thick lenses of his glasses, seemed to bulge to the full roundness of the frames, giving the impression that they could see a great deal more than many would want him to.

He was in a sumptuous, old-English-style suite at London's Dorchester Hotel, where he'd spent just one night and was now making an early start back to Zurich. Before going into the bathroom he turned on the TV to check the markets in Tokyo and Hong Kong. No financial news yet, just more

14

about the landslide election. He knew already that Tim Hendon had won, and since he had no interest in anyone else, he went off to shower.

By five he was downstairs settling his bill as Rudy, one of his personal aides, was pulling up outside in a Daimler. Sliding into the passenger seat as a doorman dropped his bag in the boot, Koehler turned on the radio. More about the election.

Rudy eased the car away from the kerb and U-turned out into Park Lane. Thanks to the early hour there was almost no traffic; the rising sun was casting a warm, fiery glow over the park. They were in plenty of time to make the flight so Koehler didn't object to Rudy's leisurely pace as they clockwised round Hyde Park corner and headed down towards Knightsbridge. He wouldn't be sorry to leave London; he'd never enjoyed doing business with the Brits, they were too secretive, devious almost to the point of downright dishonest, and yesterday had proved no exception.

After finally getting an update on the financial news he turned off the radio and they travelled on in silence.

'So,' he said, as they passed the Royal Barracks and drove on towards Kensington, 'what interesting sobriquet have you chosen for our friend from the art world today?' His voice was smooth, cultured, and subtly accented.

Rudy's cheerful face broke into a grin. 'Vincent,' he answered. 'As in Van Gogh.'

A gleam of humour glowed in Koehler's eyes, then vanished again. 'Are we picking him up, or is he meeting us at the airfield?'

'He's meeting us there.'

Koehler's owlish gaze moved to the passing town houses and exclusive garden squares. A minute or two later his mobile phone rang.

'Yes,' he said into it.

He listened, said nothing, then flipped the phone closed.

He didn't speak again, only looked out of the window as they approached the street where Katherine Sumner's rented flat was located. He'd seen her on the news with Tim Hendon last night, celebrating Hendon's victory. Not the hardest election battle she'd ever fought, by any means, but it was certainly going to be her last. She'd been quite decided about that, even before going into it, and the phone call he'd just received had told him that she now had absolutely no choice but to remain true to her word: there would be no going back after this, not for her, not for any of them – and for one uncharacteristic moment he wanted to laugh, for the sheer pleasure it was going to give him to watch the smug and superior British Establishment reel in the wake of the scandal that was about to break was, for him, supremely better than sex.

'Mrs Hendon. Mrs Hendon. It's time to wake up.'

Rachel's eyelids flickered.

'There's someone here to see you.'

Rachel frowned as the voice penetrated through to a part of her brain that grudgingly received it. 'Lucy?' she mumbled.

'There's a cup of tea here,' Lucy responded, in her soft Australian tones. 'Winnie brought one earlier, but you let it go cold.'

'What time is it?' Rachel said, putting a hand out to block the streaming sunlight as Lucy dragged open the curtains. 'Has Tim gone already?'

'It's ten past eleven,' Lucy answered, her homely features blanked by the sun. 'There are two men downstairs. They want to see you.'

Rachel yawned, and forced herself to sit up. 'My God, how could I have slept so long?' she groaned, checking the clock. Then registering Lucy's words she said, 'What men?' But before Lucy could answer, her stomach churned so horribly that all she could do was make a dash for the bathroom with barely enough time to close the door behind her.

'What men?' she repeated, a few minutes later, dabbing her mouth with a towel as she came back. She looked at the bed, and felt suddenly uneasy, for it was plain that only her side had been slept in. 'Where's Tim?' she said, expecting to hear that he'd slept in the spare room so as not to disturb her.

'I don't know,' Lucy responded, folding back the duvet to air the sheets. 'The visitors are in the conservatory. Winnie's making coffee.'

Rachel's eyes were on her mobile, as last night's victory, her suspicions and exhaustion regrouped at the front of her mind. 'Who are they?' she demanded, her unease starting to grow. Nothing was quite making sense. Then her heart turned over in fear. 'Oh my God, has there been an accident?' she cried.

Lucy stopped plumping the pillows. 'I don't think so. Why do you say that?' she responded, her young eyes showing as much concern as bewilderment.

17

Rachel didn't know, but something felt wrong. Not that Tim hadn't come home, because he might have stayed with Gordon or Dennis, but that he hadn't called to say so. Then she remembered he'd almost certainly have had a lot to drink, so was probably still sleeping it off.

'I'll leave you to get dressed,' Lucy said. 'I'll be in the office if you need me.'

The instant the door closed behind her Rachel snatched up her mobile. Its display showed nothing – no messages, voice or text. Her heart twisted with another jolt of unease, as quickly she dialled his number.

A recorded voice told her his mobile was out of range.

She clicked off, aware of a rising panic. But it was OK. Out of range could mean out of power. But where the hell was he? Maybe she should try Gordon or Dennis, but if they didn't know where he was . . . Frantically she looked round the room. Katherine was the one she should be trying and she knew it, but she was afraid to. Forcing herself to dial the number, she returned the phone to her ear and listened. Five rings, then an announcement to say that Katherine's mobile was out of range too. Next she tried Katherine's Kensington apartment. On the third ring a male voice, not Tim's, answered.

'Hello, is Katherine there?' she asked.

'I'm afraid not,' he answered. 'Who's speaking, please?'

'It's uh . . . Just a friend. I'll call back.' Before he could say any more she rang off.

So what conclusions was she going to torment

herself with now, she wondered angrily. No Tim and no Katherine. Did that mean they were together somewhere, sharing out the spoils of whatever corrupt enterprise they were engaged in? Was she seriously going to put herself through that on the morning after his election victory, when his future couldn't be more dazzling, or his need for scandal less vital? When she believed totally in his love, and had just heard another man altogether answer Katherine Sumner's phone, no doubt because Katherine herself had popped out for bagels? So maybe the most sensible idea right now would be to pull herself together, slip into a pair of jeans and a T-shirt, and go downstairs to find out what her visitors wanted.

Twenty minutes later she walked into the conservatory where the two men were sitting amongst the plants, either side of a small mosaic-topped table, apparently absorbing the garden's early summertime colours. 'I'm sorry to have kept you,' she said, her voice sounding perfectly natural as she tried to gauge from their appearance who they might be. 'Did we have an appointment?'

'Mrs Hendon.' The taller and bulkier of the two stretched out a hand as he got to his feet. 'William Haynes. I'm sorry to barge in on you like this.'

She shook his hand, feeling the warmth of it enclose the iciness of hers.

'George Flynn,' the other man told her.

She took the hand Flynn was offering, and met his sober grey eyes with a cautious stare. A sixth sense was telling her who they were, and she was now prepared to give anything not to have stepped into this glass prism, where the many shards of light were like a maniacal display of her inner fears.

'We're from the 17 Division,' Haynes informed her. 'We have a few questions we'd like to ask you.'

A buzzing started in her ears: 17 was the Specialist Operations division assigned to Westminster. But now? The morning after an election win? His enemies really knew how to play their hand.

'Shall we sit down?' Haynes suggested. He was indicating a chair, as though he were the host.

Obediently she perched on the edge of it, then her anxiety doubled as Flynn went to close the kitchen door before coming to sit down too. Obviously, whatever they had to say wasn't for Winnie's ears, which wasn't so surprising, it was just . . . unnerving.

Haynes folded his hands on the table and waited for her to look at him. 'When did you last see, or speak to your husband?' he asked in a neutral tone.

Rachel's heart jolted. 'Why?' she countered, trying not to run with the thoughts that were already terrifying her half out of her wits. 'Where is he? What's happened?'

'Please, just answer the question.'

She stared at him hard, wanting to refuse, but knowing she couldn't. 'I spoke to him on the phone, at about two-thirty this morning,' she said.

'And where were you at the time?'

'I was here. Tim was still at the celebrations.'

'How do you know that?'

'I could hear them going on in the background.' Her eyes darted between the two men. 'Please tell me what this is about,' she said, politely but firmly. 'Why are you . . . ?'

'You say you were here at two-thirty,' Haynes interrupted. 'Did you go out at all after?'

'No!' she cried, shocked by the question.

His tone became almost apologetic as he said, 'We're just trying to get things straight, make sure we know where you were.'

She blinked, and felt her heartbeat jar against another onrush of dread. 'I was here,' she said shakily. 'Now obviously there's a reason for these questions, so please tell me what it is.'

She was staring at them with harsh, yet fearful eyes, waiting for one of them to speak, but for the moment neither did. She tried hard to muster some calm, to find a way of dealing with this that was less defensive and antagonistic, because it wasn't helping. She couldn't think why she was behaving this way, for she had nothing to hide, but she was terrified that Tim did.

'Where's my husband?' she demanded. 'Do you know where he is?'

Haynes's gaze wavered towards Flynn, but came back before reaching him. 'Mrs Hendon,' he said quietly, 'is there a member of your family you can call? Someone who lives nearby?'

Rachel's heart stopped beating. She knew very well why that question was asked, and she wanted this to end *now*, before anyone said any more.

'Perhaps we can make the call for you,' Flynn offered.

'What's happened!' she suddenly shouted. 'Where is he? Just tell me where he is.'

Haynes's face had turned a shade paler. 'I'm sorry to have to tell you this, Mrs Hendon,' he said, 'but your husband is . . . dead.'

21

The breath left her body as shock struck her a staggering blow. But no, she hadn't heard right. She couldn't have. Her hands went up, as though to protect her from any more, but the words were there in her head and she couldn't get them out again. She stared at Haynes. She tried to speak but no sound came out. Then it was as though her brain stopped functioning as it should. It was slow, tangential and so full of horror that it was impossible to think. 'What are you talking about?' she finally managed. 'Was there an accident?' Before anyone could answer she continued. 'He's just won an election. Last night. You must have seen it on the news.'

Haynes's regret was apparent as he looked at her.

She looked back, then suddenly she was pressing her hands to her head. 'He can't be dead!' she cried. 'It's just not possible. Don't you know who he is?' She spun away from Haynes as he tried to reach her. 'I'm telling you, he's not dead,' she shouted, backing into the plants. 'He's *not dead.*'

'We should call someone from your family,' Haynes insisted. 'If you could give us the number . . .'

'I'll get it from the housekeeper,' Flynn said quietly, and left the conservatory to go back inside.

Rachel's eyes moved from nothing to nothing. Her head was pounding hard, but it was as though it was happening to somebody else. Haynes came up to her and put his hands on her shoulders. She looked at him strangely, then allowed him to lead her back to the chair.

'I'm very sorry,' he told her earnestly.

Her pale, dry lips opened, then hung loosely apart as in her mind's eye she saw Tim through the crowd last night, his eyebrows raised in that small, familiar gesture they shared to convey their love when it couldn't be spoken. That was the last time she'd seen him. She closed her eyes as a terrible emotion wrenched at her soul. Please God no, that couldn't be the last time she'd ever see him.

'Mrs Hendon?'

Her vision half focused on Haynes. 'How?' she said. 'Was it the car? He shouldn't have been driving . . . '

'It wasn't the car.'

She looked away, then back at him, and wanted to beg him to say he was lying. That he'd come here about something else entirely, and she was misunderstanding . . .

'Your husband was . . . shot,' he said, awkwardly. 'In the head.'

Rachel sat very still, unable to move. This wasn't happening. It couldn't be. She had to make herself wake up . . .

Haynes was speaking again. She watched his lips, but it was a moment before she registered what he was saying.

'. . . so we need to be clear about where you were between two-thirty and six o'clock this morning,' he said.

'Why?' Her voice was like the dry clatter of a stone falling to the ground. Then realizing why, her head started to swim. 'You think I . . . ' She couldn't say the word, she just couldn't.

He had the grace to look embarrassed. 'I'm afraid I have to ask,' he said.

She looked out at the garden and felt a dreadful numbness spreading through her like a fog. There were a hundred questions she should be asking, dimly she knew that, but she couldn't think what they were. He was dead! Someone had killed the man she loved more than her own life. 'I was here,' she said, her voice croaking with the strain of holding back. 'I left the party around two and came straight here. I don't have an alibi.'

'Why did you leave so early?'

Her eyes were wide and staring again as she thought about the baby. Then she was picturing how Tim's face would look when she told him he was going to be a father. His laughter and tenderness, his shouts of joy and pride . . . It all felt so suddenly real that it might actually have happened. Then from a place that seemed strangely remote from their surroundings, she could hear a sound like an animal wailing. Her shoulders were shuddering, and great racking sobs started to choke her.

'It's all right, Mrs Hendon,' Haynes assured her, putting a hand out to steady her. 'You don't have to do this now.'

Behind her Flynn opened the door, then closed it again quietly. 'Your sister's on her way,' he told her.

Haynes was passing her a handkerchief. 'Can we get you something?' he offered. 'Water? Maybe something a little stronger?'

'The housekeeper's making some tea,' Flynn told him.

'We're going to the Virgin Islands on Sunday,' Rachel said drying her eyes. She gazed out at the weeping ash that bowed over the small, flagstone patio. She must remember to fill up the birdbath, and reset the sprinklers to water the beds every day before they left. 'We've rented a villa. We want to be private.' She didn't know what she was saying. All she knew was that the world was trying to trick her because it still looked the same, even though it was another place now, one she didn't want to be in, ever.

'Where does the sister have to come from?' she heard Haynes saying quietly to Flynn.

'Primrose Hill. She shouldn't be long.'

'You don't have to wait,' Rachel told them.

Neither man attempted to move. After a while she became aware of some kind of commotion going on elsewhere in the house, but only later did she learn from Lucy that it was officers from the Anti-Terrorist Branch, searching Tim's study and removing most of the contents. It was just a precaution, they'd insisted, but it had to be taken.

Winnie bustled in with a tray of tea. 'I make toast as well,' she told them tersely. 'Mrs Tim have no breakfast. She hungry.' Whether she had any idea why Haynes and Flynn were there Rachel didn't know, but the strain in her sallow cheeks showed that she was aware something wasn't right. As she set the tray down the smell of the toast wrenched so hard at Rachel's stomach that she only just made it to a flowerpot in time.

After taking the water and towel Winnie fetched from the kitchen, she watched the portly old woman leave again, then turned her gaze back to Haynes.

'Sorry,' she said, exhaustion cracking her voice.

25

'It'll be the shock,' he told her.

She nodded and sat down. She didn't know what else to do.

Haynes spooned sugar into her tea then passed the cup. 'It might help,' he said.

She took it but didn't drink. 'Where is he?' she said. 'I have to see him.'

'Of course. As soon as the coroner's finished.'

Coroner! Oh please God, please, this wasn't happening. 'You said he was shot,' she said.

Haynes nodded.

'Where? How?'

'In the head,' Haynes repeated.

It wasn't what she'd meant, and she flinched, almost as though she'd been shot too. She stared at him, her eyes glittering with tears. The image in her mind was so devastating she doubted she could handle any more. 'Where did it happen?' she asked.

She turned round as the doorbell rang, so missed the glance Haynes threw at Flynn.

She could hear voices in the hall, then the door opened and Anna was there, her face almost as white as Rachel's.

As they embraced, Anna's husband, Robert Maxton, introduced himself to Haynes and Flynn. He was a slight, wiry man with large brown eyes, receding hair, and a manner that exuded enough confidence for Haynes and Flynn to appear relieved to have another man on the scene.

'When did it happen?' Robert asked.

'We think some time around five or six this morning,' Haynes answered.

'Do you know who? Or why?'

Haynes glanced at Rachel. 'Not yet,' he answered.

'Where did it happen?' Robert said.

'At a flat in Kensington.'

Hearing Rachel groan, Robert put a hand on her arm. 'Katherine's?' Rachel said.

Haynes's expression showed sympathy for her distress. 'If you mean Katherine Sumner, then yes, it was a flat she was renting,' he confirmed.

Robert looked at him. 'And what about Katherine?' he asked. 'Where is she?'

Haynes shook his head. I'm afraid we don't know. Her clothes are still there, but her personal effects, wallet, passport . . .' Again he shook his head. 'I'm afraid she's disappeared.'

Rachel pressed her hands in tighter to her face. 'Oh God, Anna, I can't stand this,' she sobbed. 'I just can't stand it.'

'It's all right,' Anna shushed, pulling her back. She turned to Haynes, her dark eyes showing confusion. 'You are looking for her, I take it,' she said.

'Of course,' he replied.

'What about witnesses? Did anyone see or hear anything?'

'It's still very early in the investigation,' Haynes reminded her. Then somewhat cryptically added, 'At this stage we're ruling nothing out.'

Anna was about to speak again when someone rang the doorbell. A moment later Winnie could be heard shouting over a chorus of other voices.

'I would imagine,' Haynes said, glancing at his watch, 'that the press has got hold of it. We kept it back as long as we could.'

'I should go and help her,' Flynn said.

After he'd gone, Haynes turned to Rachel. 'We can take you away from here,' he told her. 'We have places where the press won't find you. Your sister and her family can come too.'

Rachel hardly heard what he was saying.

The door opened and Lucy came in. Her small face looked pinched and uncertain, the redness of her eyes showed she'd been crying. She handed the phone to Rachel saying something that Rachel wasn't quite hearing. Then understanding, Rachel put the phone to her ear.

She listened dutifully to the voice at the other end, and gave the answers that seemed to be required, though not much of what was being said managed to penetrate her mind, except she was dimly aware that maybe she should feel heartened to learn that their leader had such confidence in Tim's integrity as a politician, if not as a husband. Later she would feel intense anger at the assumption of an affair, and of the careful manipulation that seemed to be pushing her towards admitting it was no more than that. But for the moment, the fear and magnitude of what she was facing now was making it hard to feel anything, beyond the utter disbelief and devastation of the loss – or even to recognize the subtle warning that she was very probably about to be ostracized even by those her husband had considered friends.

When the call was over she handed the phone back to Lucy and turned to Haynes as he spoke her name. Was he really going to subject her to questioning now? She supposed he had to, and she could feel herself resisting. A voice of utter despair and denial was crying out inside her. This wasn't happening. It couldn't be. He wanted to know about Tim's relationship with Katherine. What could she tell him? What did she really know?

Robert put an arm around her and she leaned gratefully against him. 'There was no relationship,' she heard herself say. 'At least not in the sense you mean it.'

Haynes said, 'Then in what sense?'

She closed her eyes and allowed herself to sink deeper into the comfort of Robert's reassuring presence. She so desperately didn't want to do this now. Why wouldn't Haynes just go away and never come back? Almost without thinking she began apologizing to Robert for making him come here when he had other much more pressing commitments elsewhere in London – a cast of actors, a crew, a schedule that come what may had to be met. As she spoke she was wishing she could plunge herself into the fiction of his world, lose herself in the fantasy rather than deal with the brutal reality of her own.

The door opened and Flynn put his head in. To Haynes he said, 'Bartle and his team are here.' Then to Robert, 'Can I have a word?'

After Robert had left with Flynn Rachel turned back to Haynes, who was still sitting at the table. 'Their relationship was purely professional,' she said.

'Then maybe you could tell me about that,' he said.

Going to the table, she sat down opposite him and clenched her hands in front of her. 'You think Katherine did it, don't you?' she said.

29

'Do you?' he countered, his eyes fixed unerringly on hers.

'Was anyone else at the flat?'

'Not that we know of, at this stage.'

Her eyes fell away.

'Do you know of any reason why Katherine Sumner might have done it?' he prompted.

She looked at him again. 'No,' she said. 'None whatsoever.'

Beside her Anna only blinked.

Chapter 2

Sir Thomas Kelsey put down the phone and stared hard at the woman seated opposite him. His pale grey eyes were unfocused as he absorbed the information he'd just been given, while his long, bony fingers ran a path over his down-turned mouth. They were in his private office at Vauxhall Cross, in the building some called Ceaucescu Towers. As one of the most senior ranking officers of this intelligence unit he had just been given the task of monitoring, not conducting, the investigation into Tim Hendon's murder. It was going to be an extremely delicate operation, which was clearly going to require the utmost discretion and careful handling that his agents were trained to provide. Already he knew who he would call upon; he was now merely deciding how much to tell them before they began.

His eyes drew focus on Jean Dowling, his personal assistant. She was a small, neatly dressed woman in her mid-fifties who'd been with him for over twenty years. There were few he trusted as completely, and certainly none in that exclusive little group that belonged to the intelligence gathering unit of the Ministry of Defence. Since she knew already that the call had been about Tim Hendon, he dispensed with any preamble and said, 'Katherine Sumner's connection to Franz Koehler is a priority. The police will be interviewing him in the next few hours. We won't be interfering with their investigations, we will merely be taking steps to ensure that nothing, but nothing, is revealed to the press, or anyone else, before it has been through this office.'

Jean Dowling nodded, while typing fast into the laptop computer she'd set up on the far side of his desk.

'Rachel Hendon is already causing some concern,' he continued. 'The combination of her personal involvement and news background puts her in a high-risk category. We need to keep a close eye on her, to know what she's doing, who she's talking to at any given moment. It could prove embarrassing, to say the least, if she were to uncover something crucial before we did, and for the time being we'll be working on the presumption that there is something to be uncovered. We also need to know if she's playing a role that has so far failed to come to our attention.'

Jean was still typing as she said, 'Does anyone actually know where Katherine Sumner is, or might be?'

'No,' he answered.

'Or why she might have done it?'

'It looks like an affair,' he responded, 'so that's the line they'll be taking.'

Jean's blue eyes came up as she named the agents she assumed he'd want to begin briefing as soon as she could get them here.

He nodded.

Getting to her feet, she picked up her laptop and started for the door.

'Under no circumstances is the press to find out that we're involved,' he told her. 'They will surmise and speculate, of course, but there will be no confirmation.' His eyes suddenly sharpened. 'Get the American Ambassador on the phone,' he said. 'Let's find out what he knows about Ms Sumner and her association with our friend Franz Koehler.'

The shocking news of Tim Hendon's murder was gripping the nation, sweeping through it in a tidal wave of horror and suspicion. It seemed everyone had an opinion and no one knew where it would end. Was it really just an affair gone wrong, or something more sinister – or both? What kind of fall-out was there going to be over this? How was the Government going to handle such a serious blow? The speculation was rife, in the media, in the street, in pubs, cafés, supermarkets and office blocks. Few were moving far from their TVs, though very little new information was coming out to accompany the shots of the large Regency house in Kensington where the murder had happened, or of the smart town house in Hampstead where Rachel Hendon was reported to be under sedation. Someone had said, a while ago, that Robert Maxton would be coming out soon to make a statement on behalf of his sister-in-law, but there had been no sign of him yet.

In the darkened interior of a West End theatre the cast and crew of Anna and Robert Maxton's film, whose day's shoot had been cancelled as a direct result of the murder, were grouped around a TV that had been set up on the stage. With Tim Hendon being related to their producer and director, they were experiencing a sense of importance and involvement that, they believed, set them apart from the average pundit, even though none of them had ever met Tim Hendon in person, or had any real idea of the inside workings of his office. It was enough that he'd held the position he had, and that the whole world knew how much he'd loved his wife. At least the whole world had assumed that until today, but now it seemed that the perfect marriage had had some cracks, which the scandal of an affair was already seeping through – and what, they were all wondering with no small relish, was going to follow?

In the shadowy emptiness of the stalls Stacey Greene stifled a yawn. It wasn't that she had no interest in the murder; on the contrary, she was probably even more fascinated by it than her colleagues, for unlike them she had actually met one of the key players in this tragic ménage. However, a few moments ago Katherine Sumner's position at the front of her mind had been usurped by an urge to speak to her husband, whose love-making the night before was still rippling through her body like the tremors of an aftershock. As it turned out, his mobile was turned off, so she merely sat for a few moments, ignoring the intrigue on the stage, while admiring her magnificent sloe eyes in the light-ringed mirror of a compact. She narrowed them slightly, which seemed to fan the lashes and increase the sensuality that exuded from the mesmerizing depths of their colours. They were a deep, smoky grey, flecked with mauve and cerulean blue. In certain lights they glinted like amethysts. Running the tip of her tongue over the luscious fullness of her lips, she watched the light playing on the amber waves of her hair, turning it into rivers of flame that cascaded to the tops of her perfect breasts. Like small buds in a forest, her nipples protruded through the tresses; while pale as a snowy landscape her skin warmed to the headiness of her exposure. Had anyone noticed? She had no idea, nor did she particularly care.

Closing the compact, she slipped it back into her bag, refastened the buttons of her blouse and stretched out her long legs to rest them on a chair back in front. Ordinarily she'd have been irritated at having the day's filming cancelled so abruptly, but today it would be singularly inappropriate to be thinking of herself, not to mention insensitive, for how could her own mild inconvenience even begin to compare with what poor Rachel Hendon must be going through now? And poor Robert and Anna Maxton too, who were only just into their second week of directing and producing this screen version of Robert's stage play, *The Geddons*. Obviously this terrible business was going to cause havoc with the schedule, but what could that possibly matter, when Anna's sister had been so cruelly bereaved? Actually, it was only in recent weeks that Stacey had learned Rachel and Anna were even related, for Anna had never mentioned it before. Still, whatever silliness had caused the rift between them, it was apparently behind them now, thank goodness, because Rachel was surely going to need Anna in the weeks and months to come, in a way she'd probably never needed anyone before.

'So where do you suppose this leaves us?' she said to Bryn Walker who was playing Arnie Geddon, as he came to sit down beside her. 'Without a producer, is my guess.'

'We probably won't be seeing quite so much of her,' he agreed. 'But there's always someone waiting in the wings, just dying for the chance to shine.'

Stacey's eyes narrowed. 'Do you think one of the financial backers will try to step in?' she mused.

He shrugged, and scratched his lightly bearded chin. 'I don't even know who they are, do you?' he said.

She shook her head. 'Only vaguely. I wonder how Robert's going to find it, not having Anna to keep him grounded, and on schedule.'

'The production managers will do it,' Bryn assured her. 'If they need to. We still don't know what's going to happen yet. Did you ever meet Tim Hendon, by the way?'

'No, but I was hoping to, at Robert's fortieth party.'

'He was there.'

'I heard, but he and Rachel arrived after I left. Weren't they on a late flight from Scotland, or somewhere?'

'Bryn!' the art director shouted from the stage. 'Are you out there?'

'Over here,' Bryn shouted back.

'Is this your mobile?'

'Looks like it,' Bryn replied, getting up. 'Answer it, will you?'

Stacey watched him trot down the aisle and swing back up on to the stage. Then taking out her own phone, she dialled her husband's number again. Not really expecting to get through, she left her buttons fastened, though idly stroked her nipples through the thin flowery chiffon of her blouse as she waited.

'Darling,' she murmured in surprise, when his voice came down the line. 'At last. I've been trying for hours. Where are you?'

'Going through some tricky terrain,' he responded, 'so I might lose you.'

Her voice was a soft, guttural sound from the base of her throat as she said, 'You know you'll never do that.' Letting her head fall back, she increased the pressure of her fingers and imagined they were his. 'You didn't kiss me before you left this morning,' she chided gently.

'You were asleep.'

'Then you should have woken me. What time did you go?'

'Around five.'

'And we probably didn't get to sleep until two. You must be exhausted.'

'Exhilarated,' he corrected.

She laughed softly. 'When will you be back?'

'In a few days.'

'I wish you were here now,' she grumbled. 'Filming's been cancelled, and I'm just in the mood to expand on last night.'

'Why's the filming cancelled?' he asked.

'You haven't heard the news? Where are you? On Mars?'

'The landscape does seem unfamiliar,' he responded drily. 'So what's happened?'

'Stand by for a shock,' she warned. 'Tim Hendon's been murdered.'

Silence.

'Are you still there?' she said.

'I take it we're talking about the same Tim Hendon,' he said. 'Secretary of State . . . ?'

'. . . for Defence, yes. And Robert and Anna's brother-in-law, which is why the filming's been cancelled. They're saying Katherine Sumner did it, the campaign manager. You might remember seeing her on the news. The American woman.'

'Yes, I do,' he said. Then incredulously, 'She murdered him?'

'That's what they're saying. Shot him in the head, apparently.'

'Hang on, I've got another call.'

As she waited, Stacey let her mind roll back over the brief but memorable encounter she'd had with Katherine Sumner at Robert Maxton's fortieth birthday. Evidently Katherine hadn't been in Scotland with the Hendons that day, or she'd managed to get an earlier flight back. Whichever, she'd certainly arrived before them, and alone, as Stacey recalled, though she couldn't really be too sure about that. What she did know was that they'd hit it off immediately, and would probably have quite happily discussed their mutual passion for the artists Max Ernst and Jackson Pollock all night. But they'd just reached the point of envying Peggy Guggenheim, who'd had the means to mentor such talent, and who had obviously been as turned on by it as they were, when Anna had thrust someone else on them, forcing them to mingle. However, the conversation, as well as the woman herself, had lingered in Stacey's mind for days after, until finally picking up the phone, she'd called Katherine to invite her down to the country house for a weekend, once the election was over. They'd made an arrangement to drive down together, this weekend in fact, which Stacey had quite been looking forward to until this morning, for it was clearly highly unlikely to happen now.

'OK. I'm back with you,' her husband said.

'I wish you were,' she sighed, sliding further down in her chair. 'I miss you when you're gone. If it weren't for the reunions, I swear I'd never let you go. Which country are you in?'

'Switzerland,' he answered, surprising her more by the fact that he'd told her, for he generally didn't, than by how fast he'd managed to get there. 'When are you likely to start filming again?'

'We haven't heard anything yet, so I guess we'll just have to wait and see what happens. What are you doing in Switzerland?'

'Running a test.'

'Which means absolutely nothing,' she responded, yawning, and waving to Bryn as he broke from the group on the stage and disappeared into the wings. 'Next time you call, be naked,' she murmured to her husband.

There was silence from the other end, telling her they'd been cut off, so she cleared the line, then stared down at the phone, trying to decide whether or not to call Robert. Would it seem intrusive? Or merely genuinely concerned, which she was. She wondered if Bryn had tried to call, since his friendship with Robert went back to Robert's break-out success with *Donna Jean in Paradise*. She doubted it though, for knowing Bryn he'd be boasting about it by now. And she was certain that Gloria, who was playing the third lead, wouldn't have tried, for she'd only just joined the production, having been cast at the last minute, after the actress who'd played Alma Geddon in the stage run had, quite literally, broken her leg.

In the end, realizing how unlikely it was that she'd get through, she dialled the number anyway, and began rehearsing a message.

'Robert Maxton,' his voice said after the second ring.

'Robert, darling,' she purred into the line. 'I'm so sorry. I've just heard. How utterly terrible for you all.'

'Stacey,' he said, sounding extremely tense. 'It's good of you to call. I'm sorry I've had to let you all down today.'

'Oh darling, please. Your sister-in-law needs you. How can any of us possibly matter? How is she?'

'Not good, I'm afraid. She's taken it hard.'

'And who can blame her? Such a dreadful, dreadful thing to happen. Please send her my condolences, and if there's anything I can do. Anything at all . . . '

'That's very kind of you.'

'Not at all. But listen, I'll clear the line now, because I'm sure you're expecting much more important calls than mine.'

'I'll be in touch,' he told her.

'Any time. You know where to find me,' and after sending him an affectionate kiss down the line she rang off.

The next mobile number she tried was Katherine Sumner's, but this time she didn't get through. It would have more than surprised her if she had, so dropping the phone back into her bag, she took out an emery board and glided it gently round her already perfectly manicured nails.

'So, dear Katherine, dear Katherine,' she hummed quietly to herself, 'where in this big, bad world are you, my dear?'

'Talking to yourself, sweetie?' a voice said behind her.

Smiling she let her head fall back on the seat and stretched up her arms to Petey, the pale skinned, ebony-haired androgyne, who was her very own dresser-cum-personal assistant-cum-personal masseuse. 'Mmm, the very person,' she responded, as he stroked her arms. 'My husband's away, and now faced with all this free time . . . '

'Speak your heart's desire,' he said gallantly, 'but before you do, remember the words of the great Sir George, *"There are two tragedies in life. One is not to get your heart's desire. The other is to get it."*'

Her eyes were suffused with humour as she gazed up at him, and twirled her fingers around his face. '*And tragedy*, as we know, *requires testicles*,' she responded.

Laughing delightedly he said, 'Voltaire,' then bowing the gesture for her to walk on ahead of him, he was about to pick up her bag and follow when Gloria Sullivan called down from the stage,

'Stacey, Robert's about to make a statement. Don't you want to hear it?'

Stacey turned back. 'Of course,' she responded, and moments later she was folding her willowy frame into the space the pretty young Gloria had made for her in the group around the TV. She smiled her thanks, then turned to the screen, masking her distaste for Gloria's flushing cheeks and shyly lowered lids. As far as she was concerned the jury was still out on the cute little starlet, though right now she was more interested in their director, who was looking extremely tired and overwrought as he stepped up to the bank of microphones that had been erected outside his sister-in-law's elegant house in Hampstead.

It was now almost three hours since the news of Tim Hendon's death had been made public, so it was hardly surprising that Robert Maxton, standing on the threshold of the Hendons' home, should find himself facing such an enormous and voracious crowd of cameras and reporters. The house's proximity to Hampstead Heath allowed for a great deal more parking – albeit illegal – than many other locations might have, so in both directions, as far as the eye could see, were countless numbers of news-gathering vehicles, satellite dishes and all manner of broadcast paraphernalia from the world over.

Since this was going to be the first statement from the family, Robert's appearance was causing quite a stir, though he knew that despite having a job to do, many of those he was confronting had a genuine and personal concern for Rachel. They'd want to know how she was, and in some cases what they might do to help. Of course, they'd all prefer it to be her standing here now, but he guessed that none had really expected it.

As the police helped to get everyone into position he talked quietly to Chief Inspector Bartle from the Met. Apparently the inspector was now in charge of the case, so quite where Haynes and Flynn fitted into the picture, Robert was no longer sure. The various ranks and departments of Scotland Yard and its affiliates always had been a mystery to him, and he was quite happy for them to remain so, just as long as they did their jobs and solved this terrible crime.

Before coming out here he'd spoken briefly with Rachel, then separately with Haynes and Flynn, to decide what should be said. Haynes and Flynn had left now, but would return tomorrow to speak to Rachel again. In the meantime, she'd gone up to the bedroom with Anna, not wanting to take any more calls, even from the various ministers of Tim's department, or other Cabinet members, in fact not from any government officials at all. As of an hour ago not even close friends were managing to get through, which was making poor Lucy's life more hellish than ever, so he could hardly blame her for the outburst he'd happened to overhear, when she'd screamed at someone down the line that if they could see how devastated Mrs Hendon was, they'd understand why it simply wasn't possible for her to deal with anyone right now.

'OK, it seems everyone's ready,' Bartle said, next to him.

Robert's eyes returned to the sea of faces. An

intrinsically shy man, he wasn't finding it easy to confront so many cameras and microphones, but his grave, dignified expression showed nothing of how anxious he was feeling – or perturbed to find himself thinking about Stacey Greene at such a wholly inappropriate moment, for the call earlier had unnerved him to a degree that even this crowd couldn't.

Leaning towards the microphones, he clutched his notes in his hand and spoke softly, but clearly, his tone conveying how deeply he was feeling the loss of his brother-in-law. 'I know,' he began, 'that you will all understand what an extremely difficult time this is for my family, my sister-in-law especially. I'm afraid that right now we don't know much more than you, so there's nothing I can tell you, except that Rachel, as you might expect, is still trying to deal with the terrible shock this has been for her. The police are doing everything they can to find Katherine Sumner, and we would ask if anyone out there has any information that might help in the investigation, that they either contact Chief Inspector Bartle at the Yard, or their local police.' He glanced down at his notes. 'I would also ask those of you in the media to do everything possible to respect Rachel's privacy in the difficult time ahead. As you know, she, more than most, appreciates the pressures you will be under to get as much information as you can, but please be patient, and try to understand what a very great loss her husband's death has been.' He looked up. 'Thank you,' he said, awkwardly, then, not sure what to do next, he turned to Bartle.

'Robert!' someone shouted. 'Will you answer some questions?'

Dismayed, he turned back to the microphones. He could feel himself perspiring, despite the coolness of the late spring day, and wished Anna was with him, for she was so much better at this sort of thing. 'If I can,' he responded.

A tidal wave of demands swept forward from the crowd.

'No, I'm afraid I've no idea where Katherine Sumner might be,' he said to one. 'No, Rachel hasn't either. Yes, Katherine is American, but I don't think her nationality has any bearing . . . Yes, this was to be her last campaign. No, I don't know what she was intending to do next. The Prime Minister spoke to Rachel this morning. He expressed his sadness and regrets at the loss of a friend. It's too early to be talking about by-elections, but of course there will be one. Rachel and Tim have been married for four years, together for five. Yes, Rachel did leave the celebrations early last night. She was extremely tired after having very little sleep these past few weeks.' The pregnancy was to stay under wraps for the moment, so he made no mention of it.

'Has Mrs Hendon been cleared from inquiries?' a woman near the back shouted.

Shocked, Robert tried to find the source as a terrible hush fell over the crowd. The idea that Rachel Hendon might have done it was unthinkable, but someone had to ask.

Robert dabbed his neck with a handkerchief, and wondered how Rachel, who was watching this inside, was feeling right now. 'Naturally, Rachel is doing everything she can to assist the police with their inquiries,' he said. 'As for any suggestion that she might in some way have been involved . . . Frankly I find the question so abhorrent I'd rather treat it as though it hadn't been asked.'

Bartle stepped forward. 'Mrs Hendon is not a suspect at this time,' he told them.

'Is anyone, besides Katherine Sumner?'

'Not at this time,' Bartle answered.

'Is there any truth in the rumours that Tim Hendon and Katherine Sumner were having an affair?'

'We still don't know the answer to that,' the inspector responded. 'Yes,' he said in answer to another question, 'Mr Hendon's offices have been sealed off and documents have already been taken. It's normal procedure.'

'Is it true that the Anti-Terrorist Branch are involved in the investigation?'

'Mr Hendon's position makes that a normal procedure,' Bartle replied blandly.

'Robert, can you tell us anything about your brother-in-law's recent showdown with the Prime Minister?'

Robert looked startled. 'I think that's already a matter of public record,' he responded. 'As we all know, Tim could be outspoken on issues that he feels are being neglected . . . But I want to say, *I want to say*,' he shouted over a sudden surge of noise, 'that he often clashed with his colleagues . . . '

'Was he going to rejoin the Cabinet?' someone cut in, loudly.

'I'd say it was likely,' Robert answered.

'He was being tipped as deputy leader.'

Since it wasn't a question, Robert didn't respond.

'How long had he known Katherine Sumner?'

'I believe since the beginning of the election campaign.' Robert turned to Bartle. He'd had enough. He wanted out of here now.

Bartle stepped forward again. 'OK,' he said, leaning in to the mikes. 'We can give you no more at this time. For those of you who are going to insist on camping out here, please have some consideration for the neighbours who have nothing to do with this and would like to get on with their lives.'

A new voice called out from the sidelines. 'Is it true you're investigating the possibility that someone else might have been in the flat at the time of the murder?'

Bartle ran a finger under his collar. 'We're not ruling it out,' he answered. 'But so far there's been no evidence to suggest it.'

'Are there any signs of a forced entry, or a struggle?'

'None so far,' Bartle replied.

'Robert, do you have any idea why *anyone* would want to kill him?'

Robert's face was bleak. 'None at all,' he replied.

'What do you say to all the conspiracy theories that are bounding around?'

'I'm not aware of them.'

Bartle put a hand on his shoulder, and they turned back to the front door.

'Robert, my condolences to Rachel,' someone called out.

'Hear, hear,' several voices echoed.

'If you're listening, we're here for you, Rach,' a woman shouted.

'Anything we can do, babe,' said a reporter from her old news team.

Inside the house Rachel was sitting with Anna in the bedroom, watching the broadcast, fresh tears starting in her eyes as her old colleagues expressed their support.

'This is when you find out who your friends are,' Anna murmured, squeezing her hand. Tears were shining in her own eyes, which were so like Rachel's that were it down to that feature alone it would be almost impossible to tell them apart. But Anna's lips lacked some of the fullness of Rachel's, and her shoulder-length hair was a much lighter brown. She was also taller than Rachel, and heavier, rather more like their mother in fact.

Looking down at their hands, Rachel's voice caught on a sob as she said, 'He handled them well.'

'He's better in these situations than he realizes,' Anna responded.

Rachel's smile was tremulous as she thought of how loyal and supportive Anna was, not only to her husband, but by nature, and how strong she was too. Tim had had enormous respect for her, and a lot of affection too, which was why he'd gone out of his way to bring about their reunion after the rift had gone on much longer than it ever should have. In truth, it was what both sisters had wanted almost since it had happened, but each of them had had too much pride to be the first to back down. It was so like Tim to know how to go about setting things right. 'I know I've told you this before,'

Rachel said, 'but I'm sorry for all the terrible things I said when we . . .'

'Sssh,' Anna soothed. 'It's over, forgotten. And anyway, you were right. I am overbearing, and I do worry and fuss too much. And what's more I know I can't ever replace Mum, the way I was trying to . . .'

'You only did it because you care,' Rachel said, her voice strangled by emotion. 'I always knew that.' She looked into Anna's face. 'You're so like her,' she said, as more tears fell. 'Oh Anna, I'm going to miss him so much,' she said, her face crumpling. 'I don't know if I can stand it.'

'It's all right. We're just going to take it a day at a time,' Anna assured her. 'I'll be here whenever you need me.'

'But you have to think about the film. And the girls . . .'

'I've got a very good nanny, and the shoot can happen whether I'm there or not.'

'But Robert . . .'

'Ssh, Robert can cope. You just think about you and the baby, and I'll take care of everything else.'

They looked up as Robert came into the room.

'Thank you,' Rachel said, reaching for his hands. 'I couldn't have faced it.'

Pulling her into his arms he held her close and rocked her as she cried. 'The police are still down-stairs,' he said, stroking her back. 'Poor Lucy's tearing her hair out.' His eyes met Anna's. 'There are so many damned rumours,' he said, almost angrily.

'There are bound to be,' she answered.

Rachel stepped back, and blew her nose. 'I

49

wonder if it's true that I'm not a suspect,' she said, reaching for another Kleenex.

'Oh Rach, no one thinks you did it,' Anna protested.

Rachel's eyes were still bright with tears as she said, 'I don't have an alibi.'

'But what reason would you have?'

'The oldest one in the book: he was having an affair.'

'You don't know that.'

Rachel looked at her. 'Everyone else obviously thinks so.'

'But you just told Haynes . . . You don't believe it.' Anna was shaking her head. 'You don't know anything for certain.'

'Except that he's *dead*.'

Anna inhaled deeply, and immediately Rachel was sorry. It was one thing to try bludgeoning herself with reality, but Anna didn't need it.

'Are the phones never going to stop?' Robert complained, responding to the incessant ringing coming from elsewhere in the house.

'BT are setting me up with a new number that I can give to family and close friends,' Rachel said, then realizing she wouldn't be giving it to Tim, she felt herself buckling inside and buried her face in her hands again.

Anna's arms went round her, and the three of them sat quietly in an embrace as the sheer awfulness of everything stole over them again.

'I don't know what to do,' Rachel said eventually, her voice clogged with tears. 'I feel I should be doing something . . .'

'There are a lot of arrangements to make,' Robert

said. 'We need to find out from someone where he is, and when they're likely to release the body.'

'We'll take care of all that though,' Anna assured her, stepping in quickly to try to lessen the impact of referring to Tim as a body.

Rachel nodded, but her mind seemed to be elsewhere.

Someone knocked quietly on the door and DCI Bartle put his bald head round. 'I'm leaving a couple of officers outside,' he told them. 'Some of the reporters have gone, but there're still quite a lot out there. We don't expect any kind of trouble.'

'It might be a good idea to take you over to our house,' Robert said to Rachel.

Her eyes went down. 'I can't leave here,' she said. 'This is our home.'

'Then I'll stay with you,' Anna told her. 'Cecily can manage the kids, and I won't be far if they need me.'

Bartle cleared his throat. 'There's a Nigel Bingham outside,' he said, 'asking if you'll see him.'

'Oh yes, tell him to come in,' Rachel said. Then to Anna and Robert, 'We should go downstairs now.'

A few minutes later she was wrapped in Nigel Bingham's arms, feeling the strength of his embrace almost crushing her. He was a producer with the news programme she'd left four years ago, and the man with whom she'd shared three years of her life until she'd met Tim. She loved him like a brother now, so it was only right that he should be here.

'He was a good man, Rach,' he told her gruffly, his taut, unshaven face showing how deeply he felt the loss too. 'One of the best. Don't let anyone tell you otherwise.'

'Thank you,' she said. 'You don't know how much that means right now.'

Keeping an arm around her he reached out to shake hands with Robert, then to include Anna in the embrace. They'd known each other for a long time, and though it had been hard for Nigel when Rachel had fallen for Tim, they'd all managed to remain friends. 'We're going to get to the bottom of this,' he said fiercely. 'Because something's not right about it, that's for sure.'

Robert and Anna both looked at Rachel.

'I'm glad you think that too,' she responded, a faint trace of colour staining her cheeks. 'I was afraid I might just be in some kind of denial.'

He was shaking his head. 'You heard the questions they were asking outside,' he said. 'No one's buying the rejected mistress thing – not yet, anyway.' With his arm still around her he led her to the sofa. 'So who's questioned you so far?' he asked.

'Two men from "Special Ops",' she answered, drawing quote marks round the words.

'Do you know which division?'

'Westminster. Their names are Haynes and Flynn.'

'OK, I'll get them checked out. Have the regular police interviewed you yet?'

She shook her head. 'I think I'm an exclusive for the big boys.'

'Makes sense. So what have you told them? Anything?'

'Not really. It was all too much, after they told

52

me . . .' Her breath caught. 'I went to pieces. They're coming back tomorrow. Everyone keeps insisting I'm not a suspect, but I know they're not ruling it out. After the Ashby case they'd be fools to.'

Nigel glanced at the others. 'You remember that case?' he said.

'Of course,' Robert answered. 'A couple of years ago. Colin Ashby, the Downing Street press secretary. His wife killed his mistress, then managed to get Ashby arrested for it, and no one ever even suspected her because they were so busy trying to cover up their own rotten crimes. If it hadn't been so tragic, it'd have been farcical.'

'Well, just because a wife was guilty once, doesn't make it the case now,' Anna protested. 'And besides, it's not the mistress who's dead, if that's what she was, which I don't happen to believe . . .'

'Do you have any idea where Katherine might be?' Nigel said to Rachel. 'Or why she might have done it?'

'None at all,' she answered. 'Apparently her passport's gone, so she might not even be in the country any more.'

'Where would she be likely to go? Back to the States?'

'I don't know. As far as I was aware she'd left America for good and was about to start a new life in Europe. She never said where, but I got the impression it would be France or Spain.'

'Do you know any of her friends here in Europe?'

'She never mentioned any. The only connection I knew about was with Franz Koehler.'

'The Swiss guy?'

She nodded. 'But the relationship was over. He was only mentioned in her profile as someone in her past.'

'Did Tim know him?'

'Not personally. At least I don't think so. He'd know of him though, he couldn't not, considering who Koehler is.'

'Who is he?' Anna asked.

Nigel turned to look at her. 'He's the head of the Phraxos Group,' he answered. 'A Zurich based private equity firm that's probably one of the richest companies in the world. It specializes in defence industry investment, which is why Tim would certainly know of the man, even if he didn't know him personally.' To Rachel he said, 'Who put you in touch with Katherine in the first place?'

'No one,' she answered. 'I just read in one of the US papers that she was giving up politics and coming to Europe, so I contacted her through the British Embassy in Washington and asked if she'd be interested in running one last campaign.'

Nigel's eyes narrowed as he thought. 'I hear there's no sign of a break-in at the flat,' he said, 'or of a struggle, which obviously doesn't rule out someone else being there, someone who might have been an accomplice of some kind, or who could have had a key and let him or herself in.' He was shaking his head, unsure where to go with that yet. 'The most important question,' he declared, 'is why anyone, whether it was Katherine Sumner, or someone else, would want Tim dead?'

Rachel's heart turned over. 'I wish to God I knew,' she said, 'but something was going on before he died . . . I don't know what, but I saw them arguing, just yesterday, and for several weeks now he's been receiving phone calls on the mobile phone that I thought only I had the number to. They were from a man with an accented voice. He'd never give his name, but on the occasions Tim wasn't available he'd ask for Katherine.'

Nigel's eyes were wide. 'Obviously you asked Tim who it was?' he said.

'Of course, but he just said that it was nothing to worry about, he'd tell me about it later.'

'But he never did.'

She shook her head.

'What kind of accent was it?' Nigel asked.

'I don't know. It wasn't that strong, and from the little he ever said to me he sounded fluent in English.'

'Have you told the police any of this?'

'No. I needed time to think, because if he was involved in something . . .' She took a breath. 'I just don't feel I can trust anyone right now. Even the PM, when he called earlier, seemed a bit too keen to keep it "domestic".'

'You think he might know something?'

'He might, who knows. He's probably just looking out for his own skin, though. He and Tim were pretty close, despite their occasional clashes, so if there was something . . . shady going on, if it ever comes out, his enemies are going to have a field day. It could even cost him the leadership, so make no mistake the race will already be on to find out what really happened. What scares me the most is how things can be twisted, or covered up, or manipulated to create as much political gain as any of them might need to get the results they want, and to hell with Tim and his reputation. So if it suits them better to keep this as a purely domestic affair, they'll do it, regardless of truth. Or, if there does turn out to be some other kind of scandal, and they can't keep it under wraps, they'll just work it to make him the fall guy in order to protect themselves.'

They were all thinking of the men in grey suits and decorated uniforms who populated the remote, shadowy corridors of the Defence Department, those who'd resisted Tim on every level from the day he'd taken office, and who, every one of them, were now retreating far behind the veil of secrecy that shrouded the Department.

Rachel turned her tormented eyes to Nigel. 'Do you think there was an affair?' she said quietly. 'Tell me honestly. Haynes said . . .' She swallowed, and her voice became more strained than ever as she said, 'Apparently he wasn't just found in her flat, he was found in her bed, so . . .' Her body tensed as a fresh wave of pain closed in on her heart. 'I don't think that's public knowledge yet,' she said.

'I'm afraid it is,' he told her, not adding that Tim had been naked too, for she probably already knew that, so wouldn't need to hear it again. Taking a breath he said, 'Obviously it looks like there was, but maybe that's what someone wants us to think. I mean, no one's been allowed near the crime scene, which I grant you is normal, but how do we *know* he was in the bedroom?' He glanced at Robert and Anna, who appeared to be waiting for him to answer the question himself.

'Can you find out?' Anna said.

'Probably. What about the gun?' he said. 'Has it been found?'

Rachel shook her head. 'I don't know,' she answered.

'I'll check. Now back to the phone calls. How many were there, that you know of?'

'Half a dozen, give or take.'

'And what did this foreign voice say?'

'He just asked to speak to Tim, and if not, to Katherine.'

'Did you ever overhear their end of the conversation?'

'No. They always moved out of earshot.'

He chewed his lip thoughtfully. 'And where's the phone now? With the police, of course.'

'They've taken just about everything,' Rachel said. 'Files, address books, computers. I spoke to Gordon a couple of hours ago. It seems the offices in Whitehall and at the house have been cleared too, and no one's allowed near them. Not even me. Or probably, especially not me.' An acute sense of despair swept over her. It was unthinkable that as recently as yesterday he'd been here in this room, discussing the election, and teasing her about some small gaffe she'd made earlier at the polling station. Then last night he'd regained his parliamentary seat, and now tonight, he was . . . never coming back.

Anna was looking at her, noticing how horribly pale she had become. 'Why don't we resume this tomorrow?' she suggested. 'It's been a long day.'

Nigel's eyes closed in dismay. 'I'm sorry,' he groaned. 'I should have realized . . . I just thought it might help to get you focused, make you feel like you were doing something.'

'You were right,' she told him. 'It did help, and we have to do this. It's just . . . I'm still trying to get used to the idea that he's not going to be here . . . That everything we planned . . .' She squeezed her hands tightly together and took a breath to try to get herself past the pain. 'I think you should know that I'm going to have a baby,' she said, her voice faltering. 'Tim didn't know. I was going to tell him when we were on holiday. If I'd told him last night, when he called, he'd have come home. I know he would. And he'd be alive now instead of . . . Oh God, Tim, *please, please come home,*' she begged, covering her face with her hands.

As she broke down, Nigel drew her into his arms and held her tight.

'Where is he?' she sobbed. 'I want to see him.'

'We'll find out,' Nigel assured her.

'Come on,' Anna said, taking hold of her. 'You've had enough for today, you should try to get some rest now.'

After they'd gone Robert walked over to the drinks cabinet and took out two tumblers.

'Make mine a large one,' Nigel said.

Pouring two generous measures of Scotch, Robert carried them back to the sofa and sat down. 'It's a damned peculiar business,' he commented, almost to himself. 'Damned peculiar indeed.'

'Do you have any theories?' Nigel prompted.

'Not really,' Robert said. 'I only met the woman a couple of times, but for what it's worth I never thought there was an affair. Nor did Anna, and she's usually got an instinct for those things.' He took a sip of his drink. 'But naked in her bed,' he said, shaking his head again. 'It's hard to think anything else now.'

'It could have been just a one-night stand,' Nigel said. 'The euphoria of winning, mixed with alcohol and the fact she was about to say goodbye.'

'That wouldn't explain why she killed him,' Robert pointed out.

'No,' Nigel responded.

Robert sighed. 'You know, what gets me is, naked in her bed or not, I just don't see him putting everything – his marriage, leadership ambitions, integrity – in jeopardy for the sake of a quick roll in the hay.'

It didn't seem very probable to Nigel either, though Tim certainly wouldn't be the first man who had everything to screw up his own life that way. 'What about the phone calls?' he said. 'Do you have any theories about them?'

Robert took another sip of his drink. 'I knew about them,' he said, 'because Anna told me, but I'm as much in the dark as you are.' He shrugged. 'A man in his position, it could have been anyone.'

'Except they were coming in on his private line, which was a number Rachel thought only she had,' Nigel pointed out.

Robert sighed again. He really couldn't offer any explanation for that, and nor could Nigel, so they sat quietly staring at the muted TV screen for a while, where pictures of Tim were repeatedly being shown as the wall-to-wall coverage continued.

'I dread to think how messy this is going to get,' Robert commented finally.

Nigel was about to respond when the doorbell

rang. 'One of my colleagues?' he said, getting up to look out of the window. Since the sitting room was on the first floor, it wasn't possible to see down into the porch, but he could hear Lucy dealing with it, then recognizing the voice of one of Tim's senior aides, he walked over to the door.

'Up here, Gordon,' he shouted. 'Is Dennis with you?'

'Yep, I'm here,' Dennis Callaghan responded.

Robert was already filling two more glasses by the time Gordon and Dennis came into the room. Both men were in their early fifties, though Dennis was much greyer, and more weathered than Gordon, whose lanky frame never quite seemed to fill out his suit. Both looked in dire need of the drink.

'What a day,' Gordon groaned, slumping into an armchair. 'I just can't get my head round it. One minute we're celebrating a victory, the next . . .' He stared blankly at the TV, as though it were broadcasting some kind of madness that ought to be stopped. Then looking up he said, 'How's Rachel? Where is she? I spoke to her a few hours ago. She sounded . . . Not good. Not good at all.'

'She's upstairs with Anna,' Robert told him, handing him a drink.

He took it, downed it in one go, then said, 'Before anyone asks, neither of us knew anything about an affair, though I suppose we now have to assume there was one, unless you can tell me what the hell else he was doing in Katherine Sumner's bed at five o'clock in the morning.'

'Did he leave the party with her?' Nigel asked.

'We all did,' Dennis answered. 'There was a car

60

and driver waiting outside to take him home, as you'd expect, so he gave us all a lift. Gordon was dropped off first, then me, and as far as we knew Tim was going to be next. Katherine lived the furthest away so it made sense she'd be last.'

'Was it his usual driver?'

'No. Martin had the night off, so it was a replacement. The police have been talking to him all day.'

'Have you managed to yet?'

'No. But he was no stranger. He had clearance, and we've used him before.'

'What time did you all leave the celebrations?'

'Around four. I got in at four-fifteen, so they'd have been at Katherine's by four-thirty, a quarter to five at the latest.'

'Was he drunk?'

'He'd certainly had a few. We all had. We were celebrating, for God's sake.' He shook his head in disbelief. 'What a long time ago that seems now,' he said, sounding as exhausted as he looked. 'By the way, Michael Jarrett's here. He stopped in the office to use the phone.'

'Michael Jarrett?' Nigel frowned.

'Tim's lawyer,' Robert answered, glancing up as Jarrett let himself in the door.

After greeting Robert and the others, Jarrett went to help himself to a Scotch. 'How's Rachel?' he asked, his jowly face as strained as everyone else's. 'I've been trying to call, but it's impossible to get through.'

'It's been a madhouse,' Robert told him. Then because no one else seemed inclined to speak, he said, 'I don't suppose you can throw any light on matters?'

Jarrett bowed his head and stared down at his drink. After taking a generous mouthful he said, 'Not exactly, but I had a phone call earlier . . .' He stopped and started again. 'It was a bit of a shock, I don't mind telling you, especially coming right on top of everything else.' He looked up, then said, 'I don't know if Rachel already knows, but . . . Well, confidentiality and all that, I should tell her first. I'm sure you understand.'

Chapter 3

Seventy-two hours had now passed since the world had become a place that Rachel no longer wanted to be in. She'd spent most of the time being interrogated by Haynes and Flynn, while DCI Bartle and an ever-increasing team of detectives continued to question everyone who had ever had any contact with Tim Hendon or Katherine Sumner. There seemed to be no limits to the investigation, both at home and abroad, and no new information either. Katherine was still missing, and since no ransom note, or body, or even evidence of any further crime, had materialized, the general opinion all round was now leaning heavily towards an affair that had gone wrong.

Other than to go and view the body, when she'd all but collapsed to see her handsome, vital husband looking simply as if he was sleeping, as if he could easily be woken up so that they could get on with their lives, Rachel hadn't left the house. Now she felt that she never wanted to again, for the viewing had taken such a toll on her that the mere thought of the funeral, and all the nightmarish security arrangements – not to mention the grotesque self-interest of those who weren't sure how much damage it might do them to be seen at the funeral – was filling her with so much dread, she was starting to doubt she had the courage to go. As it was, she hated even coming out of her bedroom, for the house always seemed so full of people all wanting to talk to her, question her, forcing her to go over and over the minutest detail of conversations, meetings, schedules, her and Tim's personal lives, who his friends were, his enemies, anything he might have said, or done, that could lead to an explanation of what had happened. Then there were those who came to comfort her, to make sure she was eating, sleeping, still breathing even. She knew they were trying to be kind, that she was fortunate to have so many friends who were willing to take care of everything for her, but though she thanked them, and did her best to reassure them, even put on the occasional show of eating to keep them happy, in her heart she longed for them all just to go away. She wanted only Anna and Robert and Nigel, because between them they would find out the real truth of what had happened. As soon as she could she was going to throw herself into this investigation like she'd never thrown herself into one before, because no one, but no one, was going to get away with attempting some kind of spin, or cover-up, or web of lies that would leave a slur on Tim's name. And they were trying, she knew that already, which was why she so desperately wanted the house to herself again, so that she and Nigel could really get to work. It was all that had kept her going these past few days, knowing that she had a way to sustain herself, a purpose that would bring some sense to this insufferable madness.

Then Michael Jarrett broke his news.

She'd known since the day Tim died that Michael wanted to talk to her, but this was the first opportunity they'd had, and now he'd finished she could only stare at him in utter horror and wonder how much worse things could get.

Her eyes moved to Anna, who was looking equally stunned. They were in the conservatory, where dazzling blades of sunlight were making Jarrett's fleshy face seem, perversely, more holy than lawyerly, and a breeze, wafting in through an open window, was carrying the clean, invigorating scent of freshly mown grass. It felt like a day for happiness.

'Four million US dollars?' she echoed, finally.

Jarrett nodded. 'In a Swiss bank account.' Then added, as though it might help, 'The Dresdner Bank, Zurich.'

'But where did it come from?' she said.

His eyes showed his dismay. 'I was rather hoping you might be able to tell me that,' he answered.

Rachel was shaking her head in disbelief. 'There has to be a mistake,' she said. She looked at Jarrett. 'There has to be,' she insisted. 'Tell me what this caller said again.'

'He just gave me the account details, told me how much was in it, and that I should inform you of its existence and urge you, for the sake of Tim's reputation, not to mention it to the police.'

Rachel turned to Anna. 'I don't understand it,' she said, knowing it was really a case of not wanting to understand it.

Anna looked at Jarrett. 'When was it put there?' she asked.

'I'm afraid I don't have that information,' he answered. 'All I know is what I just told you. The call came the day Tim died. About five or six hours after.'

'But who was he?' Rachel broke in. 'Did he give a name?'

'I asked, but he just rang off.'

'Then what did he sound like? Was he English?'

Jarrett looked surprised. 'Actually no, I don't think so,' he said. 'There was a slight accent, but don't ask me what. I'm no good at those things.'

Rachel's face was draining of colour as she turned to stare out at the garden. She'd hardly slept the night before, and now, hearing this, she felt so depleted of energy she could hardly make herself think. 'So what are we going to do?' she said finally. 'Four million dollars is a lot of money. We can't just pretend it's not there.'

Anna turned to Jarrett, hoping he might have an answer.

'Well we at least have to find out where it came from,' Rachel cried.

Anna said to Jarrett, 'Do you have any theories, or even a wild guess, anything that might give us some kind of clue?'

He inhaled deeply. 'I wish I did,' he said, 'but I'm as mystified as you are.' Then after a pause, 'I suppose the only good thing about it is that you don't have to declare it – unless you bring it into the country of course. Then you really could have problems.'

'You don't seriously think I'm going to touch it?' Rachel protested.

Jarrett didn't answer. Clearly he didn't know.

Suddenly she was on her feet. 'OK, I've had enough!' she declared. 'Enough, do you hear me? I want to know who made that call, where the money came from and how the bloody hell I'm supposed to deal with any of this when he's not here to answer any damned questions.'

Though she was close to tears, she wasn't there yet, and Anna knew better than to try and calm her, for more than anything right now, she needed to work up some anger.

'Well to hell with his bloody reputation,' she suddenly raged. 'I'm not damned well covering up for him. Wherever that money came from it didn't get there legally, so fuck him! Do you hear me! *Fuck him!* I don't give a damn any more,' and thrusting Anna aside she slammed out of the room.

A ringing silence followed her exit, until finally Jarrett said, 'Are you going to go after her?'

Anna shook her head. 'She needed to do that, and with any luck there's more to come, because she can't go on pretending he was some kind of saint, when it's plain to everyone that something was happening before he died – and if nothing else this . . . *money* confirms that it was a lot more involved than a mere love affair. No, don't look at me like that because I'm not even going to hazard a guess at what it was – he moved in circles that were far too elevated for me to begin to understand, and frankly I don't think even Rachel has a full grasp of it all. Who does, when it comes to men at that level, particularly in that field?'

'But he detested that department,' Jarrett reminded her. 'He couldn't wait to get out of it, so it doesn't seem likely that he'd have got himself involved in anything . . . untoward that might be going on there.'

'No it doesn't,' she agreed. 'Unless he was staging some kind of brilliant cover-up to throw everyone off the scent.'

Jarrett filled his cheeks with air then blew out slowly. 'Robert told me about the phone calls,' he said after a while. 'The ones on Tim's personal mobile.'

'Yes, well, if we knew what they were about, or who'd made them, we might be in a much better position to know why he isn't with us any longer,' Anna said. 'In fact, given the coincidence of the foreign accent, we might even have an idea where the money had come from.'

'The police have all the phone records, I take it?' he said.

She nodded. 'They didn't waste a second. The whole house was cleaned out faster than you could say Mr Sheen.'

Jarrett pursed his lips sombrely. 'So what do you think she'll do with the money?' he asked. 'Will she tell the police?'

'I'm not sure. She's obviously angry at the moment, but when she calms down . . . Well, she's very protective of him, so my guess is no, she won't tell them, at least not yet.'

'Withholding evidence is a crime,' he reminded her.

'I know you had to say that,' she responded. 'But I hope you're going to keep her confidence.'

'I can claim lawyer–client privilege,' he said. 'She can't, but she knows that.' He picked up the coffee that he'd allowed to grow cold. 'I'm afraid for her, Anna,' he said frankly.

'Tell me about it,' she murmured. Then, bringing her eyes back to his, 'You knew him as well as anyone. How do you think he made it?'

'God knows, but considering the comment about his reputation it doesn't look good. And in my profession I'm constantly being reminded of the weakness of man and the seduction of power, and I don't think anyone would doubt that Tim was power hungry.'

'But he already had it,' Anna pointed out, glancing furtively at her watch. The talk of weakness and seduction had made her think of Robert, but remembering that Stacey Greene wasn't on the set today, she relaxed and said, 'Did you read the *Observer* yesterday?'

Jarrett nodded.

'All that speculation and they didn't even know about the money,' she said.

'You wouldn't have to to know that Katherine Sumner could have provided an extremely useful bridge to someone as powerful as Tim. And considering the nature of her Swiss connections . . . I imagine the police must be examining them quite closely by now.'

'It would be interesting to know exactly *what* the police are examining,' Anna responded. 'Because for all the information they're collecting, they seem to be giving out precious little. In fact, so little that we could easily believe they've made no progress at all since the day Tim died.' Her eyes moved to Jarrett. 'And if you believe that,' she said, 'you'll believe that my husband is going to be appointed Secretary of State to replace him.'

Ernesto Gomez's studio was tucked away in the heart of Chelsea, on the top floor of the spacious, though sadly neglected Edwardian house where the great artist occasionally resided. But he cared nothing for material displays, or the bourgeois pettiness of domestic routine; his interest was solely in his art, and the subjects he so lovingly reproduced, on canvas in oils, or as a sculpture cast in bronze. Some were of animals, exotic and tame; while others – those that commanded the highest prices of all – were of the women whose husbands could afford it.

This was Stacey Greene's fourth sitting for the small, wiry man, whose trim goatee beard and flowing white ponytail had been caricatured to form the logo for a calling card that had no need of a name, for the design itself sufficed. However, few were privileged enough to receive one, which meant that they had become almost as collectable as his art, a great deal of which was cluttering the studio now, for he couldn't always be persuaded to part with his highly stylized creations.

The sculpture he was currently crafting, of Stacey, had been commissioned by her, as a gift for her husband, whose father, it could be said, was responsible for Ernesto's early success, for it was he who had brought Ernesto's talent to London, and the discerning eye of collectors. The son Ernesto didn't know quite so well, though he was certainly a man he might envy, were he of the heterosexual persuasion, for the way his wife was posed now, standing with her back to him, legs crossed at the ankles, as she rested her elbows on a makeshift bar in front of her, was as tempting as the fourth deadly sin. The position was highly flattering to her beautifully rounded buttocks, while the tapering length of her most exquisite limbs was also enhanced by the gentle lean forward. What wife, he wondered, had the style, or imagination, to come up with such a magnificent idea – of having her legs and back cast as a bronze table in the shape of a figure 7? It was going to be a masterpiece, and he could tell how deeply it was thrilling her already, just to think of her husband's wonderfully male hands caressing the alloy curves of her likeness as erotically as he no doubt stroked the peachy warmth of reality.

As Ernesto worked, Petey, the dresser-cum-factotum, was perched on a stool just out of the master's periphery, relating all the messages that had come in for Stacey the day before, while she was otherwise engaged. As she listened she occasionally inhaled on a fat, marijuana-filled cigarette, her eyes fixed on the portable TV where Tim Hendon's funeral was currently dominating the Sky News broadcast.

'So what shall I tell this writer about his script?' Petey prompted, his narrow, sleepy eyes drifting to the TV as for the third time the commentator announced the imminent arrival of Mrs Hendon.

'Tell him I loved it,' Stacey responded. 'Then

71

send it to Micky Frost. He's good with first time writers.'

'But sweetie, it's a heap of junk,' Petey protested.

'Says you. Someone else might not think so.'

Rolling his eyes at her inability to crush anyone's ego, no matter how minimal their talent, Petey duly noted his instructions, then moved on to the next. 'You've been invited to take part in a sponsored run, for breast cancer,' he said. 'I thought you'd be interested, because it's a celebrity thing.'

'No, because it's for a good cause,' she corrected.

Knowing he'd got it right first time, for she absolutely adored the idea of being famous, which she wasn't in any big way, just in a West End-ish type of small time, he said, 'It's on the second Sunday of next month. Currently you're available, but we might find ourselves shooting that day, now we're falling so behind in the schedule.'

'Then explain the situation to the organizers, and if they're happy about me giving an answer last minute, sign us up,' she told him, taking another puff of her cigarette.

'You're on your own, ducky,' he told her. 'I don't run.'

Laughing, she tossed her long wavy tresses back over her shoulder and returned her eyes to the screen. 'Ah, there's Robert,' she purred, as the camera panned to him getting out of a funeral car. 'Remind me to tell him how distinguished and dignified he looked,' she said to Petey. Then tilting her head to one side, she said, 'What an absolutely darling man he is. And there's Anna. Oh my, she looks so tragic, poor thing.' Her heart contracted as Rachel Hendon, all in black, stepped out of the car and tried to keep her face averted from the cameras. 'Can you imagine how difficult this must be for her?' she said soulfully. 'You did remember to send flowers, didn't you, Petey? Good boy,' she said when he gave the thumbs up. 'To Robert and Anna too?'

Petey's thumb stayed up.

Her eyes remained full of tragedy as she turned back to the screen where the camera was now following Robert as he joined the pallbearers ready to receive the coffin. 'He looks so tired, doesn't he?' she said. 'I think he was genuinely very fond of his brother-in-law. Who're the others carrying the casket, do you know?'

'If you listen, darling, they'll probably tell us,' Ernesto piped up from behind her.

'You just concentrate on my ass,' she scolded playfully.

Chuckling, he reached out for his own joint, inhaled deeply, then returned to smoothing out the clay curves of her cheeks. 'This is excellent dope,' he told her. 'Excellent.'

'Petey, didn't we bring Ernesto a special little box?' she said.

'He's already given it to me,' Ernesto assured her. 'And I've put in an order for a dozen more. Tell me, where did you find those darling boxes? The carvings are superb.'

'They're hand crafted by one of the locals, near our country home,' Stacey told him. 'Divine, aren't they? So perfect for gifts.'

'Especially when they're full of the finest hashish this side of Bangkok,' he commented wryly.

Laughing, she threw a kiss over her shoulder,

then returned to the TV as Petey answered her mobile.

'Stacey Greene's message service,' he announced. 'Who's calling please? Oh, I'll see if she's available,' and putting a hand over the receiver, he said, 'Gloria Sycophant.'

Slanting him a reproachful look, she said, 'I take it you mean Sullivan,' and trying not to laugh at the way he mimicked Gloria's pouty expression, she beckoned for the phone and put it to her ear. 'Gloria, darling, how are you?' she gushed, ignoring Petey's pantomime throw-up.

'Oh I'm fine, Stacey, how are you?' Gloria responded eagerly.

Stacey's eyes returned to the TV. 'What can I do for you?' she said.

'Well, actually, I'm having a bit of a problem with the scene we're supposed to be shooting at the end of next week,' Gloria confessed. 'The big one, you know with the mirror, and transitions . . .'

'I know the one,' Stacey said.

'Well, I was wondering, hoping, that we might go over it together, in advance, if you have some free time.'

'If I haven't, I'll make some,' Stacey promised. 'Petey will call you by the end of the day to set something up. Is there any time that doesn't work for you?'

'Oh, no, I'll fit in around you,' Gloria assured her.

'Marvellous,' Stacey said, smiling sweetly, and without saying goodbye, she passed the phone back to Petey. 'Try my husband's mobile again,' she said, not taking her eyes from the screen. 'Oh my goodness, has she collapsed?' she gasped, as

74

those flanking Rachel Hendon closed in around her.

'No, she just staggered a bit,' Petey responded, pressing out the number. 'I wonder what her eyes are like behind those dark glasses. Mashed beetroot, I'll bet.'

'Poor, poor woman,' Stacey murmured. 'What a way to find out her husband was having an affair.'

Petey handed the phone back. 'It's ringing,' he told her.

Taking it, Stacey listened, then smiled and moaned softly as Ernesto came up behind her and ran his hands over her buttocks. 'Oh darling,' she said into the phone as her husband answered. 'At last. You're proving very hard to get hold of these days. Are you still in Switzerland?'

'Yes,' he answered. 'And it doesn't look as though I'll be home by the weekend, if that's why you're ringing.'

'You read my mind,' she told him, pouting with disappointment.

'Actually, you left a message last night,' he reminded her.

She gave a sultry smile. 'Did it excite you?' she asked.

'What do you think? Where are you now?'

'At Ernesto's. He's fondling my bottom, as we speak, and I rather think he's enjoying it, the old rascal.' Laughing as Ernesto spanked her, she said, 'So when will you be home?'

'Monday or Tuesday. Are you filming those days?'

'I think so, which means I'll be in London. I might go down to the house for the weekend, though. Now you've spoiled me with all my new equipment, which apparently has finally been installed . . . Maybe I can talk Ernesto into coming to give me some lessons. What do you say, Ernesto? Can you teach me to be an artist like you? I've got a brand new studio, completely kitted out . . .'

'Impossible, darling,' he told her loftily. 'And I'm not free this weekend.'

'Such a grouch,' she commented.

'Look! Look!' Petey suddenly declared. 'It's the Prime Minister!'

Stacey looked up. 'We're watching Tim Hendon's funeral,' she told her husband. 'It's so tragic. His poor wife looks utterly wretched.'

'I read in the paper this morning that someone's claiming to have seen Katherine Sumner in Milan,' he said.

'Milan?' she repeated. 'Not quite as far afield as Manila, which was where she was supposed to have been two days ago. Seems she's having quite a little globe trot, doesn't it? By the way, I didn't realize she was an ex-girlfriend of Franz Koehler's, did you?'

'Mm, yes I did,' he answered.

Opening her mouth to receive the truffle Ernesto was popping in, she said, 'Have you ever met her?'

'Once or twice. It was a while ago.'

'What's Franz saying about it?'

'Not much, actually.'

Swallowing her truffle, she changed the subject: 'I'm considering keeping you a prisoner so that I never have to miss you or share you with anyone, ever again.'

'You'd soon get tired of me,' he laughed.

'Never,' she assured him. 'Tell me you love me.'

'I love you.'

'That you never look at other women.'

'There is only you.'

'Come home as soon as you can,' she murmured softly, and rang off.

Behind her Ernesto had returned to his model, while Petey was still glued to the TV. 'You always have to tell him what to say?' Ernesto queried. 'Does he not know how he feels? Or is it you who doesn't know how he feels?'

Stacey's eyebrows arched dangerously as she cast a look over her shoulder.

Chuckling, he said, 'I believe I have hit a nerve.'

'No, just a wrong note,' she responded. Then with a sudden restlessness she said, 'OK, that's enough. Can we finish for today?'

'Sure, we finish whenever you like.'

Immediately Petey jumped up with her clothes.

'Here,' she said, passing him the phone, 'call Gloria back and invite her down to the house at the weekend. She's right, it's a big scene and we do need to rehearse, especially now Robert's got so much on his mind. We should do our bit to help him by making sure we're prepared.'

As Petey made the call she tied a tan georgette skirt around her waist, then pulled a beige silk vest over her head. After fluffing out her hair she was about to check her reflection in the mirror, when the TV commentator announced that Robert Maxton was now stepping up to the podium to read from the Gospel of St John.

Dutifully she listened to the solemn timbre of his voice as it resonated around the cathedral, carrying solace to the bereaved and spiritual comfort to those who believed. She wondered how much it was helping Rachel Hendon, or was it Robert himself who was giving her more strength?

'I imagine he's been like a saviour to her,' she murmured, as Petey came to stand next to her.

Petey arched his carefully plucked eyebrows, then lifting her glorious mane of golden red hair he began lovingly to brush it. 'All set with Gloria,' he told her. 'I think she peed herself with excitement when she heard she was being invited on to hallowed ground.'

Stacey's eyelids went down. 'Did you find out if she's having an affair with that rather gorgeous young spark?' she said.

'Apparently he's dumped her,' Petey responded.

'Mm, pity. We could have invited him too.'

Petey looked surprised. 'Don't tell me you've got designs on him?' he said.

'Not me, darling,' she replied, 'but I know you have. I'm totally faithful, remember?'

He grinned. 'Tell that to Robert Maxton,' he responded, then quickly ducked as she spun round to cuff him.

Stacey's husband was sitting in the driver's seat of a rented Audi Quattro, surveying a small airfield on the outskirts of Zurich. His dark, sunken eyes conveyed only wariness, though the shadows around them, and the rough stubble on his chin, were those of a man who'd hardly slept in days. He was parked just inside the airfield's perimeter fence, about two hundred yards from the customs check-in, and an equal distance from the runway. It was just coming up to two in the afternoon. Conditions were clear. The flight, he'd just been informed, was due to arrive on schedule.

Because of his connections to the art world his partner, Rudy Forester, who was elsewhere in the airfield, seemed to gain some pleasure from naming him after a different artist each week. This week he was Vincent, as a tribute to Van Gogh, which Rudy, having been educated in America, pronounced Van Go. Last week, Rudy had chosen Pablo, and no doubt by next week he'd have delved back into his A–Z of artists' names, to come up with something maybe mildly less predictable, such as Corot or Lievens.

He continued to look around. Everything appeared as it should. There was no reason for anything to go wrong, but things always could. Catching a movement from the corner of his eye, he charted the progress of an armoured bank van as it entered the airfield and headed towards customs. The walkie-talkie in his left hand abruptly squawked into life.

'Do you see what I see?' Rudy said.

'I see what you see,' he confirmed, ducking his head to look up at the sky.

'I see it too, if anyone gives a shit,' another voice said.

'No one does,' Rudy told him.

There was a chuckle, then everyone fell silent as an S500 Mercedes entered the airfield and began heading towards the bank van.

'Is that Dexter?' Rudy asked, over the airwaves.

'Looks like it,' he answered.

'It had better be,' Rudy said, 'or we're fucked.'

'It's him. He's making contact.'

All went silent again as two customs officials came out of their terrapin hut carrying clipboards and two-way radios. The bank van pulled up in front of them, the Mercedes right behind it.

A few minutes later Rudy said, 'Here she comes.'

Van Gogh's namesake looked up at the crystal clear sky, and after a moment he too saw the moving black dot that was starting to emerge as an aircraft. He turned on a short wave radio on the seat beside him, and listened as the Lear was given clearance for landing.

'Did you get confirmation of how many are on board?' he asked Rudy.

'Two, plus the pilot,' came the answer.

By now the plane was no more than a couple of hundred feet off the ground. The landing gear was visible, the nose tilted up ready for contact. Confirmation had been received hours ago that the cargo was safely on board, so no last-minute hitches were expected there.

The jet made a perfect landing, speeding along the runway and coming to a halt five or six hundred yards from where the bank van and Mercedes were waiting.

For several minutes nothing happened. He could feel the tension like steel in his limbs. Apart from the Mercedes and bank van no other vehicles had driven in or out of the airfield in the last twenty minutes. No other planes had landed or taken off. All attention was now focused on the Lear jet, as they waited for the passengers to deplane.

Finally the door sprang open, and a stairway was lowered. He put on his sunglasses and reached for the ignition key. He wouldn't start the engine until the people were clear. A minivan from airport ground services was heading towards him, then suddenly it veered off and carried on towards the plane. A flash of humour shone in his eyes, as he pictured the minivan's driver.

Moments later the pilot and his two passengers, one male, one female, were descending the steps and getting into the van. He reflected on how much less complicated certain lives would be were the woman Katherine Sumner. But that was another issue, for another day; hopefully never for him.

As the van pulled away his eyes returned to the jet. It was unmanned and unprotected now, with sixteen million dollars in hard currency on board. It would have been twenty, but the other four had taken an earlier flight and had already reached their final destination.

He waited for the minivan to stop and those inside to enter the airport building. Then bringing the walkie-talkie close to his mouth, he said, 'OK, time to unload.'

Half a dozen or more vehicles started moving sedately towards the aircraft. He remained where he was, his engine idling, though not yet in gear. Adrenalin was pumping into his veins. The bank van was heading for the plane too; the Mercedes hadn't moved. The first vehicles to arrive kept the stairway clear, so that the bank van could back in, then half a dozen men were bounding up the steps into the body of the jet.

He noticed that the customs officials had disappeared, then spotted one lying on the ground behind the Mercedes. He had a gun clasped between both hands, but so far no one had fired. His own gun was still in the glovebox, along with the mobile phone he used to speak to his wife.

'Bingo!' Rudy shouted over the airwaves, telling him that the steel boxes were there. Moments later he saw them being passed down the human chain on the stairway, and thrown into the back of the armoured bank van. The rear doors of the van were sealed shut, the driver leapt back into his seat and he waited only until the Mercedes had fallen in behind the van before sliding his own car into gear ready to depart the scene.

Thanks to fog at the originating airport it had all happened three days later than planned, which had played havoc with everyone's nerves, but it was over now, and he was just wondering if anyone had ever acquired sixteen million dollars with such ease when a sudden eruption of gunfire behind him caused his eyes to jerk up to the rearview mirror, and his foot to slam on the brake.

Chapter 4

It was barely more than a week since the funeral, but already Tim's enemies were at work on the press, not exactly vilifying him, but planting the kind of suspicions that questioned his honesty, both in business and in politics, while also reminding the public of what a playboy he'd been before his marriage. The implication was that the partying and womanizing had never stopped, even though there was absolutely no evidence even to suggest that he'd ever been unfaithful. He hadn't, Rachel knew that in her heart – until Katherine, of course, but despite everything, she still wasn't prepared to believe that yet either. Nor was she even going to attempt to deal with the way she too was being criticized for the 'soulless ambition' that had 'pushed her husband to the top and then into the arms of another woman'. It would do no good to try to address it, because this was just the beginning, and getting into the mudslinging would only demean her, and worsen the situation to a degree she probably wouldn't be able to stand.

Now, as she sat on the sofa in the drawing room, her face was pinched and agitated as she watched Anna pour the tea that Lucy had just brought in. On her lap were the notes she'd made in the early hours of that morning, when, unable to sleep and consumed by grief, she'd tried to distract herself by scribbling out some reminders to help them get started on this, their first strategy meeting. For the moment only she and Anna were present, but Nigel would be here soon, and possibly Gordon and Dennis too, if they could make it.

'So,' she said, tapping her pencil against the page, 'we now know that there was no semen on the sheets, and no used condoms, which means that unless Katherine took the condom with her, which hardly seems likely, there's a very good chance they didn't make love.'

Anna lowered her eyes to hide her dismay, for this was the third time in less than an hour that Rachel had made the point. It was almost as if she was trying to convince herself, while deliberately ignoring the fact that Tim had been naked, that the condom could easily have been flushed down the toilet, and that the forensic tests were still incomplete. But she could see that Rachel was in no mood to tolerate a dispute, so she merely passed her tea, saying, 'Is Haynes coming here again today?'

'I don't think so,' Rachel answered. 'I hope not.'

Anna picked up her own cup and went to sit on the armchair next to the sofa. 'I know you don't trust him,' she said, already feeling anxious about how Rachel might react to what she was going to say, 'but I'd like to know, just for my own information, if you're hoping to achieve some kind of cover-up of your own by not telling him about the money and the phone calls?'

Even before Anna finished the question Rachel's heart was turning over, for the subject of Haynes and the money distressed her almost as much as the subject of Katherine. 'I know it might look like that,' she said, 'but what I'm trying to do is get to the truth. I mean the real truth, not a version of it that someone has spun into . . . No, listen,' she said, as Anna started to interrupt. 'Whoever made that phone call to Michael Jarrett obviously doesn't want me to go to the police, so maybe I can use that to help us find out who he is and how Tim got the money. A trade-off, as it were – my silence for his information.'

Anna was looking very uncertain. 'That's presuming he gets in touch again,' she said.

'If he doesn't, then I'll go to the police. I just want to give it some time before I do. See what we can find out ourselves.'

Anna was still frowning.

Suddenly Rachel's patience gave out. 'We're on our own now,' she cried. 'Don't you realize that? We have to forget the privileges I had as Tim's wife. They're over. We have none of the power or even the back-up. That was made abundantly clear to me the very day he died. Mud's flying and no one wants it sticking to them, least of all the PM – the one person I really thought was a friend and ally. It's obvious to everyone now that he's distancing himself. They all are, which makes us the little people, and that's exactly how they're going to treat us if we allow it. In fact they're already doing it, because they're telling us nothing about what they've found in Tim's private papers, and they're refusing to let me have any of them back.'

Anna sat with that for a moment, wishing that someone who knew about all the complex aspects of Tim's office were here to advise, but Rachel was right, his colleagues, even his so-called friends, had given her such a wide berth since the funeral that it almost broke Anna's heart to think of how ostracized her sister now was. Even Gordon and Dennis were starting to show signs of discomfort around her, and Anna wouldn't be at all surprised if they failed to turn up today. 'Do you think,' she said, returning to the subject of the money, 'that this anonymous caller is the same person who called Tim and Katherine on the mobile?'

Rachel shifted uncomfortably. 'He could be,' she answered, looking up as Nigel came into the room. 'The foreign accent makes it possible, but there are a lot of foreigners out there.'

'Who are we talking about?' Nigel said, giving her a hug. 'Are you OK?' he asked, showing concern as he looked down into her swollen eyes. 'Still not sleeping?'

'Not very well,' she answered. 'The doctor's given me some Valium, but I can only take a small dose.' She tried to smile, but it didn't quite happen.

As she poured him some tea Anna filled him in on what they'd been discussing before he'd arrived. 'So what's your opinion?' she said, offering him a biscuit as he sat down. 'Should we tell the police about this money?'

'Mm, it's a hard one,' he responded ponderously, 'because although the immediate answer is yes, of course we should, when you start getting into how he might have made the money, and who else was involved . . . Well, frankly, I think Rachel's right, it's great bait for getting to a truth that someone somewhere might rather we didn't have. On the other hand,' he continued, looking at Rachel, 'I guess you realize that by not telling the police you're allowing them to build on the theory of it being an *affaire manqué*.'

'They'd do that anyway,' she responded tersely. 'But whatever they try to make of it, they won't get away with it being just that, because to paraphrase Rupert Bloch in the *Times* today, whether Katherine Sumner's in Timbuktu or Tehran, someone must have helped her get away, and someone must know where she is. So *affaire manqué, crime de coeur* or whatever other French epithet you want to put on it, she didn't act alone.'

Nigel nodded. 'Do you know if the police have spoken to her old boyfriend yet?'

'You mean Franz Koehler? I've no idea. They don't tell me anything. But I think we should try speaking to him ourselves.'

'From what I hear no one seems to be having much luck on that front,' he told her, dunking his biscuit. 'What about her connection to Iran? Tell me about that again.'

'Her father was posted there, back in the seventies. He worked for the American Bureau of Intelligence and Research. She went to the International School in Tehran for a while, but after her father was killed her mother took her and her brother back to the States. She would have been about eleven at the time. Since then there's no record of her going to Iran again, so as a connection I'd say it's pretty tenuous now.'

'It was obviously pre-Revolution, that she was there?' he said.

'Yes.'

'How was her father killed?'

'He was shot during what was thought to be an assassination attempt on Amir Hoveyda, the Prime Minister at the time. It happened at Ramsar, a Caspian Sea resort, where they were all on holiday. Hoveyda survived it; so did everyone else, as far as I'm aware. Everyone, that is, except her father who died from his wounds a couple of days later.'

'Was Katherine there when it happened?'

'Apparently, yes.'

'Did she tell you about it, or was it in her dossier?'

'Both. She didn't talk about it much. It was a long time ago, twenty-seven years, and it's hardly the sort of thing you want to keep bringing up.'

'Where's her mother now?'

'In the States. She has Alzheimer's.'

'Did the mother ever remarry?'

'I don't think so.'

'And the brother?'

Rachel frowned. 'I'm not sure what happened to him. Presumably he's still in the States too.'

Nigel glanced at Anna as she said, 'He could be the one who's helping her.'

'I'm sure the police will have spoken to him by now,' Nigel said, 'but it's worth checking. What about marriages, or serious relationships for Katherine?' he said to Rachel. 'Do you have anything on that?'

'She's never been married. There was a bit of a scandal when she was in her early twenties over a relationship with some senator – or was it a congressman? I can't remember. It's in the file, anyway, if we could get our hands on it. He was married, of course, or there wouldn't have been a scandal. She never mentioned it, but it was so long ago it would have been surprising if she did.'

'Did she ever talk about Franz Koehler? Tell you about how it ended, or even how it got going?'

'No. I never heard her mention his name.'

'What about any more recent relationships?' Anna prompted.

Rachel's eyes flicked to hers, and Anna's heart sank as Tim's name seemed to scream between them. 'No one she ever discussed with me,' Rachel said, feeling herself fill up with hurt and anger as she recalled the times she'd seen Katherine and Tim together, their apparent ease and enjoyment of each other, the thrill of the campaign trail, the intellectual sparring and moments of triumph they'd all shared. Then there were the phone calls, that she, Rachel, had been excluded from, and that last day when they'd obviously been rowing. Would she ever find out what that was about now?

'What was she planning to do once the election was over?' Nigel asked. 'Wasn't there some talk of a career change?'

Rachel's laugh was derisive. 'Apparently she was intending to go on some kind of spiritual journey, to nourish her soul and find the right path for her life.' Her expression was loaded with bitterness as she looked at them. 'I don't suppose she'll be sending any postcards, do you?' she said.

Rachel's eyes had become almost feverish, but Anna could sense the underlying bewilderment and despair, and all the other emotions too, that ranged from blaming herself for bringing Katherine Sumner into Tim's life, to the terrible, wrenching pain of his death.

'Of course, what we really need,' Rachel suddenly said, 'is someone over there in the States, talking to the people she knew.' She was staring at Anna, though Anna could see her mind was elsewhere. 'Who do we know over there?' she demanded, looking at Nigel now. 'There must be someone we can trust.' She took a breath, then realizing that this time the queasiness wasn't just going to pass, she excused herself and left the room.

'She's having a pretty rough time with morning sickness,' Anna explained, just in case Nigel didn't connect with why the departure had been so abrupt.

He smiled briefly, then stared thoughtfully down at his cup. After a while he put it back on the table, and turning to Anna said, 'You know, she shouldn't be doing this, and I shouldn't be encouraging her. It's too much for her to deal with. She's too close. She's pregnant, bereaved . . . For God's sake, the funeral was only just over a week ago, and we both know what a strain that was on her.'

Anna nodded gravely. 'She held together well until we got home.' She sighed as she recalled just how painful it had been witnessing and trying to soothe the sheer depth of Rachel's grief during those hours after the funeral. Looking at Nigel again, she said, 'You're right, it is too much for her, but she's seeing it as some kind of therapy, or duty, and until she's ready to give up and hand over to the police, I don't know what to do but go along with her.'

In the silence that followed Anna watched him get up and go to stand at the window. There were still a dozen or more reporters camped out on the Heath, but she didn't think he was looking at them, or the view either; it was more that he was deep inside his own thoughts in a way that appeared to be unsettling him. She was about to ask if he was all right, when her mobile rang. Seeing it was Robert, she clicked on to answer.

Though she tried to keep the conversation short, Robert seemed determined to update her on what was happening with the shoot, and knowing how helpful he found it to run things by her, she listened, and encouraged, and wondered at the back of her mind how on earth she was going to split herself between those who needed her in the weeks ahead.

When finally he rang off she put the phone back on the table next to Rachel's, and said to Nigel, who was still standing at the window, 'Why am I getting the impression that there's something you're not telling us?'

His smile was wry as he turned round to face her. 'Typical Anna,' he commented, 'always seeing through the façade and looking for the subtext.' Then looking worried again, he said, 'But you're right, there is something. I had a call from Phyllis at the police labs this morning, she's the contact Rachel and I have used for years. Rachel spoke to her yesterday about the sheets on Katherine's bed?'

Anna nodded, her throat turning dry for she could already guess what was coming.

'There *was* semen,' he said. 'Phyllis couldn't bring herself to tell Rachel, so she's asked me to.'

Anna's heart contracted, for she knew only too well what a crushing blow this was going to be to Rachel. Then understanding that Nigel was hoping she would offer to tell her, she was about to ask more about it when, to her dismay, she realized Rachel was standing at the door. From the expression on her face there could be no doubt that she'd heard.

'And you're prepared to believe it was his,' Rachel said hoarsely.

Nigel took a breath, then letting it go, merely shook his head.

'Rachel,' Anna said softly.

Rachel's eyes were turning livid with pain and anger.

'Look, I know how hard it is to accept that he might have been unfaithful,' Anna started.

'He wasn't! There was no affair!'

Anna turned to Nigel.

Looking as inept as he felt, he said, 'Rachel, honest to God, if I thought they were lying . . . But the circumstances, where he was found, how he was, and now this from Phyllis . . . The evidence is there . . . That's not to say something else wasn't going on . . . The money proves something was, but . . .'

'Have you seen it?' Rachel challenged. 'With your own eyes? Do you really know that evidence exists?'

'Rach, you know Phyllis as well as I do, she wouldn't lie about something like that.'

'But did she say it was Tim's? Did she actually come right out and say that?'

Nigel ran a hand over his face, then back through his hair. 'No,' he conceded, 'she didn't actually say it was Tim's. But . . .'

'But you're willing to believe it was!' Rachel cried again, half sobbing, half shouting. 'Without waiting for the test results, you're willing to believe it was his. Well, I'm sorry, but I'm not.' She came further into the room. 'Now, we've got a job to do here, so I suggest we get started.'

Nigel glanced at Anna, then looking at Rachel again he said, 'I'm sorry. I know how much this means to you, and how convinced you are – we all are – that there's a whole lot more to it. I just don't think you're the one who should be doing this. No, hear me out. I agree that the investigation needs a journalistic watch on it, and God knows it's got enough of them, but you're too close, Rachel, and frankly, if you could be even sporadically objective at a time like this, then you're not the woman I know.'

Rachel looked as if she was about to argue, then turned abruptly away. After a moment she took a breath to speak, wanting to insist that it *had* to be her; that she was Tim's wife so it was her place to do it, but there was too much emotion blocking her throat.

Nigel put his hands on her shoulders, and tried to look into her face. 'I can't do it either,' he confessed. 'Marsha's having a problem with it. She thinks I'm using it to be close to you, and she could have a point. And if she does, then that's not right either. It's not what you want, and it's not what she deserves. So I've got to back out. I'm really sorry. You know how much I want to be there for you, and you know I'll do anything I can, I just can't go full on the way I wanted to.'

Rachel's face was still averted. Her heart felt like a stone splitting in two; her world like a place that no one wanted to be, even the baby, for she'd lost some blood earlier this morning, and again just now, so maybe she was going to lose Tim's child too. If that happened then maybe nothing would matter any more anyway. 'It's OK,' she said, brokenly. 'I understand.'

'This isn't me saying you should give up on it,' he told her. 'I just think you should let someone else take over. Someone who's every bit as good as you, but detached in a way you can never be.'

'Hear, hear,' Anna said softly.

'You know who I'm talking about?' Nigel prompted.

Barely listening, Rachel shook her head.

'Rose Newman,' he said. 'You know her even better than I do, and her programmes always go right to the heart. I think you'd agree, she's one of the best in the business.'

Rachel felt dull and weak inside, but there was no denying the vague flicker of something, too remote to really distinguish, that was starting to respond to his words. It was like being exhausted and finally told that soon you could sleep. Or finding that God might not be quite ready to give up on you after all.

'I haven't talked to her yet,' he said, 'but I will, if you want me to.'

Drawing back from his embrace she went to stand at the window that looked over the small back garden. She watched the rain drizzling down on to the flowers, and in some kind of parallel universe she could see the happily married couple who'd struggled to carry the mermaid fountain into place. She remembered how they'd laughed that day, and how thrilled they'd been when they'd actually got it to work. They'd celebrated with champagne, and by making love on the grass. How long had they been married then? Two years? Sometimes she'd wondered just how long the honeymoon could last, for theirs had seemed to just go on and on – right up to the day he died . . . And now she missed him with an ache that was impossible to contain. As each day passed it got worse. She didn't want her life to go on without him; she wished she was dead too, or she had until this morning. Now she knew that she wanted this baby more than anything else in her life. It was her only link to Tim now, and one so precious that she must do everything in her power to protect it. Just please God it wasn't already too late.

'Shall I talk to Rose?' Nigel said gently. 'I could at least find out if she's free.'

Rachel's eyes drifted up to the pale, cloudy sky, as though she might find some kind of sign that would tell her whether she should follow it through herself, or hand it over to somebody else. But there was only the colourless expanse of cloud, no thunderbolts or lightning, not even a small chink of blue. However, in her heart she knew

Nigel was right; all these unanswered questions should be shouldered by someone who could be more objective, someone who had both the emotional and physical strength, because for her it was like standing in front of a mountain and finding she had no legs, or heart, to climb. 'OK,' she said finally. 'Yes, please talk to Rose, but if she can't do it . . .' She broke off as one of the mobile phones on the coffee table started to ring.

'It's yours,' Anna said, picking it up and handing it to Rachel.

Rachel simply stared at it.

'What is it?' Nigel said, seeing how white she had become.

'There are only two people who have the number to that phone,' she said. She looked at Anna. 'You and Tim.'

Suddenly everyone's eyes were on the phone. Nigel snatched it from Anna and clicked it on. 'Hello?' he said.

No one responded.

'Hello! Is anyone there?'

There was still no answer, yet he was certain someone was at the other end.

'*Hello*,' he said again. 'Katherine? Is that you?'

Rachel's hand went to her mouth. Anna moved to her side.

Nigel was shaking his head. 'They've gone,' he said, cutting the line.

'But you said Katherine,' Anna cried.

'It was just a guess,' he responded. 'I don't know who it was, but I don't think any of us seriously thinks it was Tim.' He looked at Rachel. 'Is there a chance Katherine might have the number?' he said.

'I don't know,' she answered, the shock still visible in her trembling limbs and ashen face. 'Did a number show up to say where the call came from?'

Looking at the display, he shook his head.

'What made you think it was her?' Rachel said.

'I don't know,' he confessed. 'She was just the first to come into my mind.'

Rachel's heart felt as if it was turning inside out, as the constantly shifting sands of her emotions suddenly changed her despair to fury and her grief to hate. 'I'm going to find her, Nigel,' she declared. 'With or without you, or Rose, or anyone else, I'm going to find that woman. And when I do . . .' She grabbed up the phone and spoke to it as though it were Katherine herself, 'I'm going to kill you,' she raged. 'Do you hear me, you bitch? I'm going to find you and I'm *going to kill you.*'

'He's coming,' Stacey cried, running into the house. 'Elwyn! Felicity! He's on his way. He'll be here in less than ten minutes. Oh, Elwyn, there you are,' she laughed, bumping into the young caretaker as he came out of the kitchen. 'Saddle Athena, will you? I'm going to ride out to meet him.'

With a jaunty salute, and an even wider grin than normal, Elwyn took off for the stables, while Stacey, hair flowing in her wake, skirted the kitchen's large central island and disappeared out into the hall.

From where she'd been abandoned, on a sun-dappled garden terrace, with its spectacular views of open countryside and the shimmering sea waves beyond, the diminutive, yet curvaceous, Gloria

Sullivan stared after her, virtually quivering with intrigue and delight. What an added bonus to the weekend this was going to be, meeting the elusive Mr Stacey Greene, who, it seemed, was about to make an unexpectedly early return from wherever he'd been.

'I take it you've met him before,' she said to Petey, who appeared unmoved by Stacey's euphoric departure, as he lay half dozing in a hammock strung between a towering beech and a pillar of the gazebo.

Not bothering to answer such a ridiculous question, he merely yawned without troubling to cover his mouth, and pulled the cord to set himself rocking again.

'Is he as gorgeous as I've heard?' she pressed eagerly.

'Oh dear,' Petey groaned, irritated by her persistence and grating lack of finesse. 'Yes, I suppose so,' he answered, yawning again. 'If you like that sort of thing.'

Fingering the script they'd been studying before the phone call had erased everything else from Stacey's mind, Gloria glanced back in through the french windows, not sure what she was expecting to see, and indeed seeing nothing more than an elegantly furnished sitting room with walls covered by an eclectic collection of art. 'So maybe,' she said, a hopeful gleam starting in her eye, 'now he's home it won't only be you having all the fun tonight.'

Petey's eyebrows formed two incredulous arches, for her unsubtle reference to his little dalliance last night with the German sailor he'd met in Tesco's, who'd come for dinner and stayed for breakfast, was almost as startling as her delusional assumption that things were going to hot up for *her* now that Stacey's husband had returned.

Turning pitying eyes on her, he assessed her pert, though rather brassy appearance, then assumed a mildly withering tone as he said, 'Gloria, sweetie, you really shouldn't believe everything you hear about what goes on in this house.'

Flushing at his patronizing, and – considering her position in the cast – disrespectful manner, she was still trying to think of a suitable put-down when he said,

'Stacey gives a lot of different impressions about herself, and her life, some of which are true, and some are false. It's for you to distinguish between the illusion and reality, but this much I will tell you, just so's you don't get it wrong again: no matter what she leads you to believe about bacchanalian orgies and decadence *par excellence chez elle*, she shares her husband with no one. And by that I mean *no one*. So, if you came here believing all those deliciously lurid tales of weekend parties where inhibitions get checked at the door, and games like hide-and-seek and hunt the thimble have rather more adult variations on the theme, then I'm afraid, little sweetie, that you're on the wrong flight.'

Colouring to the roots of her hair, Gloria turned away and snatched up the script in a ludicrous attempt at a snub. Inside she was shrinking with humiliation, for his disdain had made her feel gauche and disgustingly obtuse. What was worse, she just knew that he'd use her blunder to turn her into a laughing stock with the rest of the cast. It was excruciating, unthinkable, the way she'd so foolishly exposed her own sexual, as well as social, aspirations, and despising him for being a party to it she began desperately trying to think of a way to repair it without inflicting any further damage.

Upstairs, in the master suite, Stacey had already removed the long chiffon dress she'd been wearing, leaving it, and her espadrilles, in a trail up the wide, curving staircase for Felicity to gather. The sun was streaming in through the open french windows of the large yet cosy bedroom, where the exquisite hand-embroidered silk bedspread and drapes made a sumptuous Oriental contrast to the antique black iron bedstead and rough stone walls. As she padded across the carpet to the dressing room, her beguiling lavender-blue eyes were warming with pleasure, for her state of nudity, combined with the image of her husband's expression when he saw her, was, for a woman with her acute sensitivity, almost as potent as the reality.

Pulling open one of the closet doors she stood a moment to gaze at her reflection in the full-length mirror. Her long, glorious waves of hair were cascading around her shoulders like a shimmering fountain of gold; her flawless, alabaster skin seemed to glow with the heat of arousal. Touching her fingertips to her lips and tongue, she dampened them, then rolled the hard, crimson buds of her nipples, inflaming them with sensations that flashed through her like fire. Already she could feel his fingers taking the place of her own, the erotic moistness of his breath as his mouth hovered over the peaks before he sucked and bit them until she could take no more. Her eyes dropped to the smooth, flat contours of her tummy, the female flare of her hips, and the fiery triangle of hair that was neatly trimmed to show a clitoris already rampant for love.

At the door Felicity, the young housekeeper, stood admiring the beauty of the woman she adored, a small, secretive smile curving her cupid's bow mouth. Catching the girl's eye in the mirror, Stacey watched her with a catlike intrigue, then laughed as Felicity produced a riding hat, crop and boots from behind her back.

Neither of them spoke as Stacey pulled on first one boot, then the other, though their eyes kept meeting in a laughing, conspiratorial way. Then Stacey stooped so that Felicity could put the black, peaked hat on her head, and draw the strap tight under her chin.

'Athena's ready,' Felicity told her, in her soft, countrified tones, and passing over the crop, she watched the most magnificent filly of all stalk proudly from the room.

Elwyn was leading the mare across the cobbled courtyard as Stacey came out of the house. From the terrace above Gloria watched, stupefied, for the young man showed no surprise at Stacey's nudity, nor did she show any embarrassment. He merely brought the horse round, steadied her, then cupped his hands to help his mistress into the saddle. Gloria didn't hear what Stacey said, but she saw the youth laugh before he stood aside to watch the spectacular vision of a thoroughbred mare carrying a splendidly naked woman out to the wide open fields of the estate.

101

As she left the house behind Stacey's pulse began racing with the same power as Athena's galloping hooves. The breeze on her body was like a stream of intimate caresses, touching her beneath the arms, between her thighs, over her bare breasts and the entire length of her legs. The growing lust in her loins was an ache of almost unbearable intensity, continually pummelled and piqued by the fall and rise of her hips. How easy it was to imagine riding him this way, up and down on his cock, feeling it pumping in and out of her, while he grabbed her hips and watched her breasts bouncing and swaying in the mayhem. Flicking the mare's rump with the crop, she raised her buttocks higher as they sped on across the pastures, soaring over low wooden gates and babbling streams, heading for the peak of the rise, where she'd be able to see his car approaching.

When she reached the point she reined the horse in, circled round once or twice, then panting and painfully aroused, she leaned forward to stroke the mare's mane. As she waited she absorbed nothing of the landscape around her, that dipped and rose in a vast carpet of wilderness, where swathes of ragged green grass and brittle scrubland formed the billowing pastures that drifted randomly out to the horizon. There were almost no trees in this part of Cornwall, and the flowers, wild and colourful, clustered in shy yet defiant clumps around crumbling stone walls and petrified tree stumps. Behind her, out of sight and far from her mind, was the village she deliberately avoided, while all around this hauntingly bleak but beautiful peninsula the sea crashed and foamed over giant boulders and rocks, heaving its legendary might into the caves and gullies that turned the towering cliffs into sentries of mystery and danger. But she had no eyes or thoughts for anything beyond the narrow strip of road that snaked through the rugged terrain to the open gates at the other end of the meadow that marked the entrance to their land.

Her wait wasn't long, for very soon the glint of sunlight on a windscreen flashed like a silent firework in the distance, signalling his imminent arrival. Impatient as she was to see him, she remained where she was, watching the car come closer, and knowing that at any minute he would see her, an exotic outline on the horizon; an erotic force in his mind. Her heart was thumping with excitement as the car kept on coming, until finally it entered the gates and slowed to a stop. A second or two passed, then the driver's door opened and he got out. A sharp pang of lust tore through her, for she knew he'd seen her, yet still she didn't move, merely watched him closing the door then leaning against it, arms folded, legs crossed waiting for her to come.

Urging Athena forward, she started down over the gently sloping pasture, thrilling to the warm, salty air on her skin and pulsing sensations in her crotch. His eyes never left her, making her feel wanton and reckless and almost feverish with lust. By the time she reached him the yearning between her legs was so extreme that she almost feared the first moment of his touch. Then she was responding to the sternness of his expression that did nothing to disguise how greatly he approved of his welcome.

103

He nodded briefly towards the ground, then watched as obediently she dismounted and came to stand before him. For a long time they only looked into each other's eyes, reading, understanding and sharing the profound desire that was slaking their bodies.

'You must be the lady of the house,' he said finally, his eyes sweeping almost insolently over her breasts.

'And who might you be?' she replied haughtily.

He lifted a hand and grazed his palm over her right nipple. 'Whoever you want me to be,' he responded.

Catching her breath with the pleasure of his touch, she looked down at his hand and said, 'I don't recall giving you permission to touch me.'

'I assure you, it's not the only liberty I intend to take,' he responded, keeping his hand where it was.

She looked up at him, amethyst eyes smouldering with desire, her lips quivering as she said, 'Even strangers must undress before coming on to my land.'

His eyes darkened, and she almost cried out as he pinched her nipple hard. Reaching for her crop, he used it to flick the hair back over her shoulders. She gazed defiantly into his face, keeping up the pretence as he drew a trail with the crop over her arms, her breasts and her tummy. Then the crop descended to the join of her legs, where he held it very still, touching her very lightly, yet with enough pressure for her to feel the probing hardness of its tip. She looked down at the long, slender stem, and watched as it began to disappear slowly and exquisitely into her most intimate place. Then raising her heavy-lidded eyes to his she held his gaze again, telling him wordlessly, yet earnestly, that she was willing to do anything he wanted.

Moving away from the car, he walked round to the boot, threw in the crop and took out a rolled-up blanket. Ignoring her, he began to wade through the long, cow parsley grass to a shady corner of the field, where he spread out the blanket then removed all his clothes.

By the time he was naked she was beside him, still in her hat and boots, and looking down at the powerful erection that bulged from between his thighs. He waited for her eyes to come to his, then, putting a hand on the top of her head, he pushed down gently, until she was on her knees and leaning forward to take him deep into her mouth.

As she pleasured him he stood with his hands on his hips, regarding the scenery he adored, taking in the verdant spring coating of ferns and gypsy flowers, the ragwort and prickly teasel, behaving as though it were the most natural thing in the world for him to receive this kind of attention as he surveyed his land. Then looking down as she freed him he stared into her magnificent eyes, watching as she licked the moist redness of her lips, while the breeze on his cock seemed to turn it harder than ever. Bringing her back to her feet he removed her hat, then wrapping his arms around her he crushed her beautiful mouth with his own.

They were still kissing as he drew her down on to the blanket, his tongue deep inside her mouth, his fingers pressing in hard between her thighs. She spread her legs wide, moving her hips up and down in response to the rhythm of his hand.

'Now,' she murmured, as his mouth descended to her breasts. 'Fuck me now.'

Turning her over, so that she was on her hands and knees, he lifted her bottom high and guiding his cock to her opening he plunged all the way in.

'Yes, oh my God, yes,' she gasped as he drew back and drove in again. He did it again and again, then grabbing her hips he rammed her with short, sharp bursts, as though stoking her full of his own lust, harder and faster and more brutal than she could stand, though she kept panting for more. He knelt over her and she turned her face for his kiss, but he pushed her head down and pounded even harder. Then he was lifting her up, so that her back was pressed tight to his chest, while his hands grabbed her breasts and smothered her nipples.

'Yes, yes, *yes!*' she cried, as his fingers moved between her legs. Her head fell back on his shoulder as he began rubbing her savagely, then his tongue was in her mouth feeling the vibrations of her moaning as he continued to pound her. He pushed her forward again, keeping his hand between her legs, chafing her with the roughness of his fingers, and feeling the exquisite softness that enveloped him starting to tighten and pulse in a way he could never mistake.

'Do it! *Do it now!*' she demanded, pushing her bottom higher. 'I can feel you, all the way inside . . . Oh Christ!' she gasped, as the first explosion of her climax erupted like a meteor shower. 'Oh God, oh God.'

Grabbing her hair, he pulled her mouth to his

and pushed his tongue harshly inside. His hips were pummelling her violently, rocking them both in a way that was beginning to thrust the seed from his body into hers. He held her tight, taking them both into a crashing tidal wave of sensation that finally weakened her limbs so that she sank to the ground beneath him, panting and whimpering and clutching his hands in her own.

For a long time they lay as they were, allowing their heartbeats to steady and breath to quieten, while the sun warmed their bodies and the breeze flowed around them like whispers. The heady scent of grass and drone of insects mingled with birdsong and the distant roar of the sea, while far overhead a plane trailed a thin white line in the sky.

Eventually he rolled on to his back, causing her to murmur a protest as he withdrew from her body. She turned to look at him, then moved in closer, throwing a leg over his and resting her head on his shoulder as he raised an arm to embrace her.

'I missed you,' she whispered.

He glanced down at her, then kissing the top of her head, he said, drily, 'I thought I was a stranger.'

She grinned. 'You are. My very own stranger who fucks as beautifully as he makes love.'

Hugging her, he tilted her mouth to his and kissed her again. Then his eyes held hers as, pushing a hand into her hair, he looked searchingly into her face, almost as though he couldn't quite believe her beauty. After a while he brought her mouth back to his, and kissed her so tenderly and passionately that the strength of his own feelings was like a tightening force around them both.

'How long are you home for?' she asked, settling

more comfortably into his shoulder when finally he let her go.

'A week. Maybe longer.'

'Will you come to London?' she said, knowing that he'd want to spend as much time here as he could, for it was the one place that he could relax and be himself in a way he so rarely could while he was working.

'Maybe,' he answered. 'When are you leaving?'

'Tomorrow. Early.'

'So I have you for tonight at least,' he said, hugging her. 'Is there anyone else at the house?'

'Only Petey, and Gloria, one of the cast. No one you have to see if you don't want to.'

'I don't mind being polite,' he told her, his eyes shining with mirth.

'But you look tired. Exhausted, even. And I want you all to myself.'

After kissing her again, he turned his gaze back to the sky and thought of how preferable that would be to having to deal with anyone or anything else at the moment, even himself. Closing his eyes he thought back over all that had happened in the past few days, things that were sure to haunt him for some time to come, for after the débâcle at the airport one man was dead and another might not make it. But only he seemed to be seeing that as an issue: for everyone else all that mattered was the successful transfer of the sixteen million dollars, which, in the end, had happened.

'What are you thinking?' she asked.

Keeping his eyes closed he hugged her briefly and said, 'Believe me, you don't want to know.'

'Try me,' she suggested.

For a moment he was tempted, but to let the words out here would be like violating a sacred place, and besides, he needed to protect her from the truth, not burden her with it. But it was hard, so damned hard, living day after day with the lies and the guilt, allowing her to know only a part of the story, while he was sucked deeper and deeper into an existence he despised, and should have had the courage to turn his back on right at the start.

'Tell me about the film,' he said, reaching for her hand.

Slipping easily into his escape route, she watched her fingers link round his, as she said, 'We've got some difficult scenes coming up this week. That's why Gloria's here. We've been running lines, and rehearsing.'

'What are the scenes?'

'They're new. They weren't in the original stage play, so you won't know them.' Then, after a short sigh, 'You know, I think poor Robert's finding it hard to focus again, after his brother-in-law's death. It's obviously been a terrible time.'

He shifted slightly to make them both more comfortable. 'Still no news on the mistress's whereabouts?' he asked, having had little time to read the British papers these last few days.

She was still gazing at their hands, loving the stark yin and yang contrast between them. 'None that I've heard,' she answered, turning her mouth to his neck and biting him gently.

His eyes drifted closed again, and once more they lay quietly, absorbing the twittering sounds and feeling the joy of being together as though it were an elixir.

Eventually, realizing he was almost asleep, she rolled on to him, then pushed herself up so that she was sitting astride him.

His eyes came open, and as he looked up at her she could feel her desire starting to stir again. Was there no end to her need for this man? No limit to what she would do for just one kiss, one gesture, one small, unprompted reassurance of how deeply he felt? She leaned forward to plant her hands either side of his shoulders, and a slow, tempting smile curved her lips as his fingers circled her throat.

'Just how dangerous are you?' she murmured, her eyes narrowing as they tried to probe the shadowy depths of his.

'It depends,' he responded with an ironic flick of his eyebrows, his thumbs pressing down on her trachea.

She sat watching him, as though waiting, even daring him to choke her, until finally his hands released the pressure, and descended to her breasts.

Feeling him growing hard beneath her, she raised her hips to take him into her again, then watching his face as she rode him gently, insistently, she felt her love growing and growing in a way she knew she'd never be able to express.

'Come here,' he said gruffly. Drawing her to him he held her tight in his arms, and gazed into her eyes as they moved slowly but inexorably towards another shared release.

It was a long time later that he pulled her to her feet and playfully waggled his eyebrows as she watched him dress. Then with his arm round her shoulders, and hers round his waist, they walked back through the field to the car.

'I think I'll get rid of the others so we can have the whole evening to ourselves,' she said, putting her hat on again.

'You should do that,' he told her. Then brushing her hair back over her shoulders he said, 'Incidentally, I spoke to Ernesto on the way here, who tells me you've been very generous with your boxes of magic, as he called them.'

She grinned sheepishly. 'Didn't we agree that I'd continue my little private enterprise while you disapproved in silence?'

Laughing, he said, 'OK, that was the deal. So what about the studio? Are you pleased?'

Pulling his mouth down to hers so she could kiss him, she said, 'You spoil me, and I love you for it. And now you're here I think you should be my first model, which means we get to christen it together.'

Slapping her playfully on the rump, he helped her back into the saddle and watched as she turned the horse round. 'I'll meet you at the stables,' he told her.

'Do you want to eat or shower first?' she said.

'I think shower,' he answered.

As she rode away, graceful and resplendent, he was wondering how many men were fortunate enough to receive such a homecoming and how many marriages could survive the pressure theirs was almost constantly under, with so much need for secrecy, and such frequent separations. Only a woman like Stacey could handle it the way she did, turning it into a kind of game that seemed to enrich their relationship and make them closer than ever.

111

He truly was blessed and determined never to forget it.

Ten minutes later, arms around each other again, they were crossing the stable-yard to the kitchen, totally oblivious to Gloria, who was standing on the terrace above, watching with amazement and envy the perfect and erotic picture they created, him fully dressed, and her in only long leather boots and a riding hat.

Petey was watching too. 'I'd say it's time for the little playmates to leave,' he murmured in her ear, as their hosts disappeared into the kitchen.

Gloria failed to hide her irritation. 'But we all came in the same car,' she reminded him tersely.

He smiled. 'That was before the *mad and savage master* returned,' he said, knowing she wouldn't have the faintest idea what he was quoting from, mainly because she didn't seem to have the faintest idea about anything.

She turned back to where Elwyn was unsaddling the mare, her view partially blocked by the silver Mercedes that had been abandoned at the centre of the yard. She wondered if Stacey and her husband had already made love, and felt certain they had – not only because of the time Stacey had been gone, but because surely no man in his right mind would be able to resist a woman who rode to greet him like that.

'I've just realized I don't know his name,' she said to Petey.

'Really?' he responded.

Feeling gauche again, she pursed her lips and tried to sound superior as she said, 'What does he do?'

Petey's thin nostrils flared with boredom as, sighing, he propelled her back towards the sitting room.

Wanting to slap his face, she shrugged him off, and stomped on ahead. They were perfectly normal questions that anyone would ask, but that creepy little faggot had once again made her feel about as sophisticated as cod and chips. Anyway, she didn't need him to tell her what was going on around here, because with her own eyes she'd seen enough marijuana to keep a whole city jazzed for a month. In fact, now she came to think of it, she might be doing herself a favour if she reminded him of exactly what she *had* seen in this house, for it could have the happy result of making him think twice before trying to turn her into a joke with the cast.

Suddenly emboldened, she said, 'You know, I really do want to meet him, Petey, so why don't you go off and set it up, while I wait down here in the lounge?'

Petey stopped, and looked at her, clearly surprised, though no less condescending than before. 'Sophocles,' he said finally. 'The *mad and savage master* is from Sophocles, in case you didn't know. He was speaking of lust.' With wickedly gleaming eyes, he added, 'Is that what you're feeling now, sweetie, after seeing them together like that?'

Immediately Gloria's cheeks coloured, for it was true, it had turned her on.

Laughing delightedly he said, 'You aren't the first, but be warned, as I told you earlier, she'll share him with no one.'

'But what about him?' Gloria challenged. 'Does he share her?'

Petey's eyes glowed, but he took his time answering, looking her up and down and appearing increasingly amused. 'No,' he answered. 'They're as exclusive a couple as you'll probably ever meet – and you, sweetie, are treading on *such* dangerous ground that if I were you, I'd go upstairs, pack my bags and be at the car in ten minutes flat or this little flight of fancy you seem to be on is going to have a very bumpy landing.'

Chapter 5

Rachel and Anna were just returning from a walk on Hampstead Heath when they spotted William Haynes amongst the small clutch of journalists that was still camped outside the house.

Rachel's mouth instantly turned dry. 'Are we expecting him?' she muttered, almost resentfully.

'No,' Anna answered, tightening her link on Rachel's arm as someone pointed Haynes in their direction.

Neither of them spoke as he crossed the road to meet them, nor could he be in any doubt from Rachel's expression that the mere sight of him was enough to turn her heart over with the pain of why he was in her life at all, never mind the dread of what he might be about to tell her now.

'Mrs Hendon,' he said, smiling pleasantly. 'Mrs Maxton.'

Rachel looked at him, and struggled with the urge to scream at him to go away. 'I hope you're here to tell me you've found Katherine Sumner,' she said shortly.

His expression showed regret. 'I'm afraid not, but I do have some other news,' he told her, falling in beside her. 'Initial tests are showing that there *could* – I stress *could* – have been someone else in the flat at the time your husband was murdered.'

Rachel's footsteps faltered. 'What kind of evidence?' she asked, her voice partially drowned by a passing lorry.

'Skin cells, hair, footprints in the carpet,' he answered.

She wanted to ask about the semen on the sheets, but knowing that the DNA results were still at least two weeks away, she bit the question back.

'All we can be certain about at this stage,' he said, as they began to cross the road, 'is that someone else, with a smaller shoe size than your husband, and much darker hair, certainly visited the flat at some point around that time, though we have no way of knowing yet whether he, or she, is in any way related to the crime.'

Rachel's heartbeat was unsteady as they pressed through the journalists to get to the front door. She didn't speak to them. She had nothing to say.

Once they were safely inside Haynes turned to Anna, saying, 'Perhaps you could rustle us up some tea, if you wouldn't mind.'

Realizing he wanted to speak to Rachel alone, Anna glanced at her sister, then after giving her arm a reassuring squeeze, she went off to the kitchen, as Rachel and Haynes started up the stairs to the sitting room.

'I'm expecting a friend,' Rachel told him, waving him towards an armchair. 'She should be here any minute.'

'This shouldn't take long,' he assured her.

Too anxious to sit down herself, she walked to the fireplace then turned back to face him.

'Does the name Franz Koehler happen to mean anything to you?' he asked.

Her blood started to turn cold. 'Isn't he something to do with the Phraxos Group?' she said guilelessly.

He nodded. 'Do you know him?'

'Not personally.'

'Did your husband?'

'Not that I'm aware of. Why? Do you think he's the other person who was at the flat?'

'The small shoe size makes it unlikely,' he said. 'Mr Koehler is a tall man, quite well built.'

'Then why are you asking about him?'

'Mr Koehler's company is heavily involved in defence industry investments,' he answered.

She looked at him, holding firmly to his eyes, though her mind was starting to reel as she tried not to think where this might be going. 'But mainly in the US,' she replied. 'Not here.'

He agreed, then said, 'Mr Koehler and Katherine Sumner were involved, on a personal level, for a number of years,' he stated. Then when she didn't respond, 'I take it you knew that when you hired her?'

'Of course.'

'Did she ever discuss Mr Koehler, or the Phraxos Group, with either you or your husband?'

'No. At least not with me.'

'What about with your husband?'

'If she did, he never mentioned it.'

'Do you know any of the other Phraxos directors, or shareholders?'

'If I do, then I'm not aware of it,' she replied. Her hands were bunched tightly together, while her whole body was turning rigid with dread. 'I'd like to know why you're asking all these questions,' she said. 'What have they got to do with what's happened?'

His smile was thin. 'We'll know that when we have the answers,' he responded. Then after a beat, he said, 'Are you absolutely sure you have no idea where Katherine Sumner is now?'

Her eyes widened with shock. 'Do you seriously think I'd keep that kind of information to myself?' she answered tightly.

'Frankly, I'm not sure,' he responded.

Her mouth fell open.

'There are those,' he informed her mildly, 'who believe you know considerably more about your husband's relationship with Katherine Sumner than you're telling.'

Rachel was offended and enraged by his words, but they were also starting to frighten her now, for their implications were almost impossible to gauge. 'Why should I hide anything?' she countered. 'My husband's dead. Don't you think I want to find the person who did it?'

'That person being Katherine Sumner?' he said, making it a question.

Her eyes were starting to show panic. 'Well who else?' she demanded. 'He was in her flat, and she's the one who's missing now, so isn't it reasonable to think she did it?'

He nodded as though agreeing. 'Where did you

118

go when you left the party that night, Mrs Hendon?' he said suddenly.

Her face instantly drained. 'What?' she said, her voice barely more than a whisper.

'Where did you go when you left the party?' he repeated.

'I came home,' she answered, shakily. 'I've already told you. I came straight home.'

'But you have no alibi.'

A cold sweat was breaking out on her skin as she looked at him. Footprints of a smaller shoe size, dark hair . . . 'You said . . . DCI Bartle said that I was not a suspect.'

His smile was small.

She stared at him in horror. The tide was turning. 'Why . . . why do you think I would do it?' she stammered. 'I loved my husband . . .'

'I'm sure you did.'

'It's the truth!' she cried.

'What is your shoe size?'

'Five,' she answered, her eyes bulging with fear.

He continued to look at her, then, treating her to an almost avuncular smile, he said, 'If Miss Sumner were to contact you, you would tell us, wouldn't you?'

She stared at him in amazement. 'Why would she contact me?' she said, her voice rising with incredulity.

'Or if Mr Koehler were to get in touch. You would let us know, I'm sure.'

A horrible sense of foreboding was starting to smother her mind, making it hard to think, though she was in no doubt now that they knew a great deal more than they were telling. 'Why would he get in touch?' she demanded. 'I don't know him, I have no reason to believe my husband did either, so maybe you could tell me *why you're asking these questions.*'

Getting to his feet he said, 'I'm doing everything I can to help you, Mrs Hendon, but you're not making it easy.'

'What on earth is that supposed to mean?' she cried angrily.

'I mean that you're holding back on your husband's connections to the Phraxos Group,' he stated.

'I'm telling you that I didn't know he had any,' she said through her teeth. 'But if you're telling me he did, then I want to know what they were, because it sounds to me as though you're making some very serious insinuations.'

'Indeed I am,' he agreed, 'because it would be highly irregular, to say the least, for a man in his position to have any financial connections at all to a company that specializes in defence investments. But I'm sure you know that.'

'Of course I know that,' she said bitterly.

'Though it was you, I believe, who introduced Katherine Sumner to your husband?'

Her head was spinning. 'And just what are you insinuating now?' she demanded.

His eyes were almost hawk-like in their intensity as he said, 'That is the case, isn't it?'

'As far as I knew, Katherine Sumner's relationship with Franz Koehler had ended over a year before she joined us,' she told him hotly. 'But even if it hadn't, there's no crime in using a professional campaign manager to do the job she

120

does, regardless of who she's involved with or related to.'

His expression showed cynicism, but after a few more tense moments of staring directly into her eyes, he obviously decided not to take it any further and said, 'You know where to get hold of me if there's anything else you'd like to tell me.'

He was almost at the door when she realized she hadn't asked the most obvious question of all. 'I take it you've contacted Franz Koehler to find out if he knows where Katherine Sumner is?'

He looked back over his shoulder. 'Certainly we've been in touch with Mr Koehler,' he replied. 'Though he's claiming that he doesn't know where Katherine Sumner is either.'

'And you believe him?'

'Would I have any reason not to?'

She stared at him, stunned by the question. 'I have no idea,' she said.

His smile effectively conveyed his disbelief, then after wishing her a good day, he left.

Half an hour later Rachel was sitting in the conservatory with Anna and Rose Newman whose crinkled, rather stern, features were magically transformed into a vision of loveliness whenever she smiled. However, at that moment, the piercing shrewdness of her pale grey eyes was dominating her expression, as she considered what Rachel had just told them about her meeting with Haynes.

Anna was watching her closely, waiting for her response, while carefully masking how shaken she was by the way Rachel had been informed that she might actually be a suspect herself now. In the end, unnerved by Rose's failure to take the umbrage she'd expected, she said to Rachel, 'They can't seriously think you had anything to do with it. It's absurd. It doesn't make any sense at all.'

Coming out of her reverie Rose said, 'Actually, they probably don't.' She looked at Rachel. 'But I think you understand why they're not going to eliminate you entirely from their inquiries?'

'The Ashby Affair,' Rachel said.

'Not quite the same thing as we're talking about here, it's true,' Rose conceded, 'but it's still a case of *cherchez la femme* and as they were burned once by a wife, they're not going to let it happen again.'

Rachel glanced at Anna, then back to Rose as she continued.

'The fallout from that scandal is still being felt, as we all know, because it virtually devastated the party, and it's really only thanks to the weakness of the Opposition that they're still in power – and, of course, to the likes of Tim, and our current leader, who were promising to bring new hope and new focus to the future.' She took a sip of her tea, then replaced the cup carefully in its saucer. 'I've lost count now of how many fortunes were lost, and careers ruined thanks to the party's involvement with that syndicate of billionaire powerbrokers,' she said, 'and God knows how many of them have been sent to prison already. The amazing thing was, that it never seemed to occur to any one of them, until it was too late, that far from being a politically motivated murder that was going to expose their corruption, it was no more complicated, and indeed no less tragic, than a wife reaching the end of her tether with her husband's infidelity. So they'll never make the mistake of ruling the wife out again – especially when this particular wife, namely you, Rachel, doesn't have an alibi.'

'Or a motive,' Anna pointed out, still bristling in Rachel's defence.

'The mistress,' Rose reminded her. 'I'm sorry,' she added, seeing Rachel blanch, 'but that's the way they'll be seeing it.'

'But I wasn't there, so there can't be any evidence even to suggest it,' Rachel said.

'It sounds as though your shoe size counted in your favour,' Rose said, 'and they've obviously got your DNA anyway, so they'll run tests, because they have to. Then this little bit of nastiness should be over.' She gazed meditatively down at her teacup. 'In my opinion,' she said, 'based on everything you've just told me, what it's really about is Tim's connection to this Franz Koehler, whatever that might be.'

'The police have all his files,' Rachel said, 'and all our computers, even Lucy's, so it's not going to be easy to find out. We should have new laptops within the next couple of days, so I should be able to get online to do some research into the Phraxos Group – and who else, if anyone, in that impenetrable department Tim detested so much, has links to it, because I'm damned sure we're going to find that someone does.'

Rose was nodding distractedly. 'You know, what I'm finding particularly curious,' she said, 'is the fact that they seem to think either Katherine, or this chap Koehler, might contact you.' Her eyes came up to Rachel's. 'I take it neither of them have.'

'I don't know,' Rachel answered. 'There was a call, on my personal mobile, a few days ago, but Nigel answered and whoever it was rang off without speaking. And then there was the call to Michael Jarrett, our lawyer, about the Swiss bank account. We still don't know who that was from.'

Rose pursed her lips as she thought some more.

'What about telling the police about the money?' Rachel said after a while. 'Do you think I should?'

'I must admit, when you first mentioned it I thought so,' Rose told her, 'but you're right, it does give you some good bargaining power, should this anonymous person contact you again, so I'd be inclined to wait a while, see if that happens, and then take it from there.'

Rachel glanced at Anna again, then back to Rose as she continued.

'I'm intrigued by this other person who was supposed to be in the flat,' she said. 'We know it wasn't you, and apparently the shoe doesn't fit Franz Koehler, so who was it? Surely not someone from Tim's department.' She frowned as she looked at Rachel. 'Do you think they'd go that far?'

'I don't know what they're capable of,' she responded.

'Did Katherine have a particularly close friendship with any of them, that you know of?'

Rachel shook her head.

'What about her brother,' Anna piped up. 'Might it have been him at the flat?'

Rose looked at her in surprise. 'The brother's dead,' she stated. 'He committed suicide about six years ago. I thought you'd know that. It's been in the papers.'

Rachel looked shocked. 'I don't remember seeing that in the file,' she said. 'And Katherine certainly never mentioned it.'

Rose shrugged, then looked at Anna's mobile as it started to ring.

'It's Robert,' Anna said, reading the display. 'I'll be right back,' and getting up she went outside into the garden.

'Would you like some more?' Rachel offered, as Rose drained the last of her tea.

'No, that's fine, thanks,' Rose replied, putting her cup down. Then after watching Anna stroll over to the fountain, she turned back and looked directly at Rachel. 'Before we go any further,' she said, 'there's something I should have told you at the outset, about me and the programme's current commitments, and, I guess, its current dynamics.'

Rachel's face started to drain.

Rose smiled. 'It's OK,' she assured her. 'We're certainly going to help you, there's no question about that, it's simply that I, personally, have already committed to an Amnesty project that's going to see me in South East Asia for most of the summer. However,' she rushed on, 'make no mistake, if I thought I could do a better job than my partner, I'd arrange a swap right now and take this on myself. But she's exactly the person you need on this. In fact I can't think of anyone more suited. I don't think you've ever met her, in fact I know you haven't, because she told me so. You'll have heard of her, though, and I'm only sorry that she couldn't come with me today. She wanted to, but there was just no way she could get back in time.'

Rachel's eyes were closing, at the crushing

disappointment of losing first Nigel and now Rose. It felt as if everyone was deserting her, and she hardly knew where to turn next.

'OK, from your lack of enthusiasm I can see that you really don't know who my partner is these days.' Rose said, chirpily.

Rachel was not sure she even wanted to know.

'If I said the name Laurie Forbes, would that mean anything to you?'

Rachel's eyes immediately widened. 'You mean *the* Laurie Forbes?' she said. 'One of the lead reporters on the Ashby case?'

Rose nodded. 'She's been with me for about eighteen months now, in fact, more or less since the whole Ashby thing erupted, so who better to take this on?'

Rachel was still taking it in, finding it hard to adapt to the idea of confiding in someone she didn't know, even if it was the woman who, together with another legendary reporter, Elliot Russell, had exposed more than a dozen corrupt politicians, and sent at least a handful of billionaires to jail with their earth-shattering exposés of currency and investment scams. And it had all come to light thanks to Laurie Forbes's dogged pursuit of the truth.

'Is she willing to take it on?' Rachel asked.

Rose smiled. 'Of course. Show me a reporter who wouldn't be.'

Rachel's eyes remained on hers as more details of the Ashby affair began resurfacing in her mind. After a while it started to make her feel strangely light-headed, almost as though she was losing her nerve. 'In the Ashby case,' she said quietly in the end, 'as we all know now, it turned out to be the wife who'd committed the murder.' Her eyes were still very intently on Rose's. 'I swear to you, that didn't happen here.'

Rose reached for her hand. 'I know,' she said gently. 'In fact, what concerns me more is how prepared you are to find out that your wonderful husband might not have been the paragon we all took him for.'

A cold vacuum opened up inside Rachel as she almost physically shied away from the notion, even though she knew already that she'd probably have to face it, especially the way it was all starting to look now.

Rose's voice was solemn, but still firm, as she said, 'There's something missing from all we've discussed so far, and though it pains me even to mention it, it can't be ignored.' She waited for Rachel to look at her. 'You know what I'm talking about.'

Rachel took a breath. 'Terrorism,' she said.

Rose nodded.

'I know there are a thousand theories abounding in the press,' Rachel said, 'but there's truly not been anything even to suggest it. Or nothing that I know of anyway, and it doesn't exactly bear any hallmarks, does it?'

'Maybe not, but I read that it was the Anti-Terrorist chaps who emptied his offices.'

'His position would dictate that,' Rachel responded.

Rose was willing to concede that point, since it would be true of any senior-ranking politician in such circumstances. 'Has anyone from the Anti-Terrorist Branch questioned you?' she asked.

'No. Which is why I'm presuming that there's nothing to worry about.' She looked at Rose again. 'Katherine doesn't exactly fit the profile of a terrorist,' she reminded her.

'And since she's been so close to so many US politicians in her career,' Rose continued, 'she's probably had more background checks than half the Senate put together. But I had to bring it up.'

'Of course,' Rachel said. Her eyes and heart were growing as heavy as the intrigue itself as Anna came back inside.

'Are you OK?' Anna said.

'Just tired,' Rachel answered. Then to Rose, 'I'm pregnant,' she told her.

'Oh my dear,' Rose murmured, her expression showing how deeply she felt for the joy and tragedy of that news. 'I had no idea. My goodness, what a very difficult time this is for you.'

Rachel looked at Anna. 'How's Robert?' she said.

Anna forced a smile. 'Fine,' she answered. Then to Rose, 'So where are we? What do we need to do next?'

After telling her about Laurie Forbes, Rose said, 'This is probably where I should bow out to go and prepare a report for Laurie who's in the States right now, so has probably already made a start, knowing her. She's due back at the beginning of next week, by the way. In the meantime, I don't want any of us to underestimate the kind of brains that could be at work here, because they'll be so convoluted, and brilliant, they'll make a chess-master's look about as cunning as a tiddlywink.'

Rachel's face was losing its colour, as the dreaded fatigue began smothering her like a fog.

'I'm sorry,' she said, putting a hand to her head as a dizzy spell blurred her vision. 'I'm just . . . It comes over me like this sometimes.'

'Don't worry, I understand,' Rose assured her. 'How far along are you?'

'Fourteen weeks. I went for a scan yesterday.' Her heart was suddenly heavier than she could bear as she recalled her first glimpse of Tim's child. That he hadn't been there to share such a special and momentous occasion was probably one of the hardest, and cruellest, moments she'd known since his death. 'When can I meet Laurie Forbes?' she asked, clinging to Anna's hand as it closed over hers.

'As soon as she's back,' Rose answered. 'But I can give you her contact numbers if you want to get in touch before.'

Rachel looked at her sister.

'OK,' Anna said, getting to her feet. 'I think that's enough for today.'

Having no will left to resist, Rachel stood up too, then embraced Rose warmly. 'Thanks for coming,' she said.

Rose smiled, and touched her cheek. 'Take care of that baby,' she said softly, 'and leave the rest to us. Or I should say, to one rather gifted reporter.'

It was early the following evening when Anna let herself quietly into Rachel's darkened bedroom and went to sit on the edge of the bed.

'Are you awake?' she whispered, her heart turning over at the sight of her sister virtually wrapped in her dead husband's clothes.

'Yes,' Rachel answered, not moving.

Anna put a hand on her shoulder. This was the first time she'd left her alone for a day, and now, seeing her like this, the guilt and concern were crushing.

'How are the girls?' Rachel said.

'They're fine. They send their love. How are you?'

Rachel's voice was shredded with pain as she said, 'I can't get rid of his things, Anna. I just can't. I was going through them, and I could smell him . . .'

'Ssh, it's OK, you don't have to,' Anna assured her, stroking her hair, as she bunched one of Tim's shirts in tighter to her face.

Finally she rolled on to her back, allowing Anna to see the utter devastation of her face. 'All this talk, all this scheming with Rose, and Laurie Forbes, it's getting us nowhere,' she said. 'We still don't know where Katherine is and she's the key to it all.' She gasped and sobbed. 'I'm becoming consumed by her, Anna,' she confessed. 'I can hardly think about anything else. Even when I'm thinking about Tim, she's there, destroying my memories, making a mockery of everything we had. I just can't bear it that she was the last one to see him, to touch him, to . . . I hate her, Anna. I hate her like I've never hated anyone in my life.'

Anna pulled her into an embrace, holding her tight and wishing she knew how to ease the pain.

After a while Rachel turned away. 'I'm sorry,' she said. 'I'm trying to be brave, but . . .' She bit her lip in an effort to stop herself crying again. 'I miss him so much. It's as though that's all there is in my life, missing him and wanting him, and talking to him as if he's here. I think I might be driving myself mad.'

Anna's eyes were full of sympathy as she said, 'How have things been with the baby today?'

In spite of the terrible sadness in her heart Rachel felt a small glow of relief trying to steal its way through all the layers of bleakness. 'No throwing up and no bleeding,' she reported.

Anna smiled. 'That's good. But you still need to rest more.'

Rachel's laugh had no humour. 'That's all I can do,' she answered. 'I've just got no energy. Were you like this when you were pregnant?'

'Definitely in the early stages,' Anna answered. 'And I wasn't having to deal with everything that you are, either.'

Rachel's eyes drifted as she tried to stop herself resenting the world and everyone in it. She and Tim should be in the Caribbean now, wallowing in the sunshine, counting the stars, making love on a moonlit beach, and talking about names for the baby. Then realizing how hard she was making this for Anna, she turned back and reached for her hand. 'Did you go to the set today?' she asked.

Anna nodded.

'So how was it?'

'OK. They're still behind, but not disastrously so.' Her eyelids dropped to disguise how concerned she really was. Then attempting to make light of it, she said, 'Robert's having a bit of a confidence crisis. It's not serious. He just doesn't seem to know how to handle a couple of the actors. Well, actually, one in particular.'

'Which one?'

'Her name's Stacey Greene. She was in the stage play, if you saw it.'

'Yes, we saw it,' Rachel told her, squeezing her hand. 'I wish we'd seen it with you though.'

Anna smiled. 'Robert'll be pleased you went.'

'So which one was Stacey Greene?' Rachel said.

'She played the part of Anita Cairn. Beautiful, redheaded. It's one of the leads.'

'Yes, I remember. She was very good. So what's the problem, is she being a bit of a prima donna?'

'No, not really. In fact, if anything, she's quite amenable, which you'd think would make life easy. But you know Robert, he's always been self-conscious around beautiful women, particularly when they exude the kind of sensuality Stacey does. It'll settle down, I'm sure.'

'What was he like with her during the theatre run?' Rachel asked.

'Shy, I suppose, and yes, awkward, though not quite to this extent. But I was directing then, so he wasn't quite so hands on. Anyway, he often goes through these phases of self-doubt, even when he's not directing, as you know.'

Rachel nodded, and squeezed Anna's hands again as she thought of how incredibly strong and capable her sister was in the way she handled Robert's phases, or crises, or artistic dilemmas as she sometimes called them. It made Rachel wonder what he, or indeed any of them, would do without her, for they all leaned on her so heavily, and sitting up to hug her, she said, 'You've got so much on your plate right now. I'm sorry I'm adding to it when you need to be concentrating on your film, and your family.'

'You *are* my family,' Anna reminded her firmly.

'But you're so torn between us all. Even now, you're here, taking care of me, when really you ought to be at home with the girls, or watching rushes with Robert.'

Looking into her face, Anna said, 'You matter every bit as much as Robert, and the girls, you know that. I'm just afraid that I'm going to let you down in some way.'

'No don't,' Rachel protested. 'You've got to stop trying to be all things to all people.'

'Then so have you,' Anna stated.

Rachel looked confused. 'Me?'

'Yes. You. I want you to let Laurie Forbes sort out all this mess with Katherine, and whatever's been going on, while you do what's right for you and the baby.'

Rachel smiled with affection. 'Why do I get the feeling that you're about to tell me what's right?' she said.

Despite the light-heartedness Anna was concerned, for she didn't want to appear controlling, or bossy, when it had caused such problems between them in the past. 'Why don't you go down to the house in Cornwall?' she said gently. 'Get away from London, if only for a few weeks, so that you can get past these early stages and recharge. Lucy and I can take care of anything that comes up here, and Beanie will be right next door to take care of you. She calls every day to find out how you are . . .'

Rachel's eyes were closed. Beanie. Wonderful, adorable, precious Beanie, with her fluffy grey curly hair, mischievous blue eyes and unfailing ability to make the world a better place, no matter how bad it really was. 'But I can't be that far away,' she said brokenly. 'I need to help Laurie Forbes . . .'

'There are phones and email, and besides, I just told you, you should be letting her do it all. In fact, she'll probably be quite relieved to know you're not going to be in her hair every minute of the day.'

The thought of the exquisite old cottage that Tim had inherited from his grandfather, sitting high above a picturesque fishing cove that was so full of people she knew and loved, sank so painfully, yet nostalgically, into her heart that more tears started from her eyes. There was a very good chance that the baby she was carrying had been conceived in that cottage, for they'd stolen a quick weekend there just over three months ago, before the real hoopla of the election had got under way. Could she bear to be there without him now, when they'd shared so much love and laughter under that quaintly thatched roof, and with the local fishermen and their families?

'I could drive you down there myself on Sunday,' Anna said, 'and stay a couple of days. I've talked it over with Robert, and we've got the children covered.'

Though she didn't want to say no, particularly when it would make life so much easier for Anna to have one less person to worry about, for some reason Rachel still couldn't quite bring herself to say yes.

'We could go Saturday,' Anna said, 'but Robert's invited Ernesto Gomez, you know, the artist, for dinner that night. You'd be welcome to join us, if you felt up to it.'

Rachel shook her head. Cornwall and having to deal with her memories was one thing; making social chitchat with someone she'd never met, and pretending her husband hadn't just been murdered, was another altogether. Forcing a smile, she said, 'Ernesto Gomez. That's quite a coup.'

Anna rolled her eyes, but it was plain to see that she was pleased. 'Robert wants to try to talk him into using the poems from the play, now film, as some kind of inspiration for a joint exhibition.'

'Sounds a wonderful idea,' Rachel commented, guessing it had probably been Anna's, for she was always devising new ways to promote Robert's talent. Then the thought of how much she and Tim would have enjoyed such an evening told her quite brutally that she really wasn't up to facing it without him.

'So what do you say?' Anna pressed. 'Shall I call Beanie and ask her to get the cottage ready for Sunday?'

Once again Rachel's throat closed with emotion, but the peace and comfort Beanie and the cottage offered was too tempting to resist. 'OK,' she said finally. 'Yes. I should go. But I'll need to talk to Laurie Forbes first.'

'Why not invite her down to Cornwall?' Anna suggested. 'I know it's a long way, but looking at it from her point of view, it's certainly a story worth travelling for. And I'll try to stay long enough to be there too when she comes.'

'Thank you,' Rachel whispered.

Anna hugged her, and carried on hugging her as she swallowed the guilt of not telling her that Robert had insisted she should stay in Cornwall as long as Rachel needed her. Of course it was what she wanted, to be there for her sister, but the oddness of Robert's behaviour lately, coupled with his nervousness around Stacey Greene, was making her afraid that the generosity of the gesture had rather more to do with getting rid of her than with a concern for Rachel.

Chapter 6

Stacey Greene had ceased to exist. Everything that made up the entirety of her being had been taken over by the hauntingly seductive persona of Anita Cairn. Anita's beauty was golden and earthy; her eyes glittered like vivid blue jewels, while her troubled spirit seemed to shroud her in a vaporous light. Her reflected image in the mirror was slowly fading into shadow; the room around her appeared to undulate in the floating clouds of a soft grey mist.

No one spoke or moved. The moment was as spellbinding for the crew as for the three performers enacting the scene. As yet only Anita was visible, a still, yet potent, figure in the midst of a fantasy turning to nightmare.

Robert Maxton's breath was shallow, his chest tight with suppressed emotion, as the power of the transition reverberated through him in profound, physical tremors.

Anita's eyes moved upwards as a man stepped in behind her, his face appearing above hers in the

137

thick, silvery haze. Her lips parted, but not to speak, only to breathe. The two watched each other's reflection, bound by the torment that raged in their eyes.

'Save me,' she whispered finally. 'Don't let me go.'

He no longer seemed to be seeing her, was somehow detaching from the invisible bonds that held them. When he spoke, it was to an absent listener, or to the sadness in his heart. '"*All her bright golden hair, Tarnished with rust, She that was young and fair, Fallen to dust.*"'

'You speak the words of Oscar Wilde,' she said, 'but your own are more honest, more pure.'

'It's too late,' he responded. 'Your flattery has lost its power.'

The dull, rosy lights dimmed around them. 'Without me you'll be nothing,' she warned, her voice threaded with emotion.

'But with you I am a madman.'

'Do you really believe it can be this easy?'

The mist thickened around him, swallowing him into its amorphous heart.

Anita's gaze returned to her reflection and saw that it was no longer her own face staring back. Her features had changed beyond all recognition; her hair was short and blonde, her eyes a glowing emerald green and her mouth a small, quizzical line of fear mingled with contempt.

'Is this who I am now?' she murmured.

'You are no one now,' the reflection told her. 'It's over. You have ceased to exist.'

'Then how am I still here?'

'You sit in front of a mirror, but is this your reflection you see?'

'Are you his wife?'

'Yes.'

'Then you saw how he loved me. Doesn't it make you wish to be me?'

'Are you really such a fool? It was the fantasy he loved, not you.'

The reflection stood. So did Anita. A breath of wind blew through the mist that shrouded their bodies. Their nudity had no real definition, for the detail was blurred by the skin-toned mesh that encased them.

'Come here,' said the reflection.

Anita stepped forward, in through the mirror as though through an open door. The reflection received her, arms open wide. As their bodies met the mist returned, swirling around them, shrouding them in its dense grey breath.

'Look,' the reflection said.

Anita turned to look back at the place she had left.

'You see, you don't exist any more,' the reflection whispered. 'You are me now, and I you.'

Long moments ticked by. The mist continued to eddy gently around the set, while the lights slowly faded to black.

More seconds passed, until finally Robert said, 'Cut,' and the working lights came on to reveal the dozens of crew, crouched in amongst the equipment, and hidden in the wings of the stage.

'Wow,' Stacey breathed, half laughing, half trembling.

Gloria, who was playing the wife, or the reflection, appeared equally moved. 'Where's Bryn?' she said, looking round for the actor who was playing her husband.

'Over here,' he answered, wiping his neck with a towel. 'I'm scared,' he suddenly shivered. 'I know what's coming next. You've got to let go, woman,' he said to Stacey. 'You're not real. OK? Got it? You don't exist, lovey.'

The others laughed, which helped break some of the tension that had repeatedly built up during the three takes they'd already done of this scene.

As he joined them Robert was talking to the cinematographer. 'The effect's really working,' he was saying. 'No actual mirror in the frame was the answer, and keeping Gloria in shadow at the beginning meant we had no idea it wasn't Anita's reflection we were seeing. We just need to turn it all around now, to focus on Anita's face. We need her in big close-up so we don't run into any problems with the smoke. I think the others are clear for the day.'

'No, hang on,' the first assistant jumped in. 'Before we go for the reverse, don't we need a shot of Gloria, standing full length, looking out of the mirror?'

Robert frowned, trying to think why.

'It's the last shot of the scene,' his assistant reminded him, 'when we see that Anita has melded totally into Alma, so that there is only one woman.'

'And then we go in on Alma's eyes and see that they're actually Anita's,' Robert finished. 'Of course. You're right. OK, everyone, stay where you are. We've got more to do from this angle.'

'I take it you were happy with that,' Stacey said, sauntering up behind him and putting a hand on his arm.

'Yes, it worked well,' he told her. 'You can stand down for a few minutes while we do this next shot. Then we've only got the close-up and you'll be finished for the day.'

Despite his brusqueness she smiled. 'I'm in no hurry,' she said, her voice soft and throaty.

Keeping his eyes averted he sought out the designer, who was helping props with the dry ice. 'Ken,' he said, going towards him, 'I want to do a wide shot that has only dry ice. We'll do it last. And is there any way you can put the mirror back in the frame? I need another shot with it in, but only after we've done this one of Alma.'

'No problem,' Ken replied. 'We'll be ready when you are.'

Robert moved on to the costume and make-up teams, talked with them about the coloured contact lenses Stacey and Gloria were wearing, then to the electricians who, because he was the director, didn't tell him to get out of the way, though they'd have liked to, and finally to the camera operator, who would have preferred him to wait to look through the viewfinder until the focus was actually set. He then joined the unit publicist who was sitting in the fifth row of the stalls, explaining to her new assistant what the film was actually about.

Feeling sufficiently distanced from the stage, and confident that Stacey would have at least put on a wrap by now, he dared to look back at the set. As it should be, it was overrun by technicians getting everything ready for the next shot with, mercifully, no sign of Stacey, dressed or undressed.

Breathing more easily, he allowed himself to

141

relax for a moment, and vaguely tuned in to the publicist as she continued her précis.

'So basically it's the story of Arnie and Alma Geddon,' she was saying, 'he's a poet and she's his wife, as well as his muse; then there's Anita Cairn, who's the mistress. The whole thing's a parody really, a kind of marital version of Armageddon, hence their names, Arnie and Alma Geddon, with Anita being the Antichrist who seduces them both, then tries to turn herself into Alma to destroy her and Arnie's lives. Alma resists, but Arnie isn't quite so strong, and we see, mainly through his poems, how obsessed he becomes with Anita, while Alma battles on, trying to save her marriage, and her husband from his own weakness and passion. The scene we just saw happens quite near the end of the film, where Alma finally starts to win the struggle.'

'Not bad,' Robert commented when she finished.

The publicist glowed.

He left her to it then, to take himself off to a darker corner of the audience seating where he could see what was happening on stage, but hopefully not be interrupted while he attempted to psych himself for the remaining shots of the day. Just thank God that the rushes so far showed no indication of his inner disquiet, nor had anyone on the set cast so much as a glance of curiosity or concern his way. If anything, even at this early stage, spirits seemed high, and the camaraderie was settling in with all the ease of an expected warm front. So he really had to try to keep things in perspective, find a way to detach himself from this unnaturally morbid dread he had that everything was going to go horribly wrong. If he didn't he'd end up passing the feeling on to the cast and crew, and then disaster really would start to loom.

Feeling himself starting to perspire, he used the script to fan himself, while silently thanking God for the invisibility of his thoughts. It was crazy, what was really going on in his head. If it weren't happening to him, he'd swear someone was making it up, because the sheer weirdness of what he was experiencing made him even stranger than the damned characters he'd created. It was like being some kind of freakish divinity whose own little cosmos was turning into the stomping ground for all manner of delusional ravings, not to mention perversions.

But no, it wasn't as bad as that. He had to be careful not to overstate this. He just had to think it through rationally, work out exactly where fantasy was overlapping with reality, and make sure it stopped. After all, the poet he had created for the play, and now film, was just that: a creation. He wasn't any more real than Anita Cairn. So there was no parallel obsession going on here, Arnie and Anita, him and Stacey, just an unusually close bonding between writer, actor and character. And of course director, which, ironically, was where it had all started to lose focus, for he hadn't felt this unnerved by Stacey during the stage run, maybe because Anna had been in charge then. He felt so much more comfortable when she came to the set.

Leaning forward to rest his head on his arms, he tried to recall when it had first started to overwhelm him like this. Of course he'd always been attracted to Stacey – what man with hetero-sexual blood in his veins wouldn't be, when there was probably no more sensual creature alive? But knowing and accepting an attraction was quite different to the intensity of feeling he was suffering now. And its power had built so quickly that already it was as though both she, and his thoughts, had become the tools of some iniquitous Sadean plot where he, a naturally shy and conservative man, was fantasizing about doing things to her that ordinarily he'd never dream of doing to any woman. It was as though she'd become his very own Anita Cairn, tempting him into all manner of decadence and depravity, turning him into a lecher, a defiler, a human being of the basest kind. Just thank God she had no way of reading his mind, for he didn't even want to think about the offence he would cause, particularly when he knew she was no more interested in him, as a man, than he was in her, as a reality. He was a happily married man, for God's sake, who adored his wife and would never do anything to hurt her, but there were too many moments now when the clashing giants of lust and morality were making it hard for him always to remember that.

'OK, Robert, wherever you are, we're ready to go,' the first assistant shouted from the stage. 'Cindy, go and call Gloria back to the set, will you? And make sure Stacey's not too far away for when we do the last close-up.'

By the time Robert sprinted up the steps from the orchestra pit, Gloria was coming on stage, and the dry ice was already leaking out over the set. 'I want to do some close-ups of Gloria's eyes and mouth before we get to Stacey,' Robert told them all. 'You understand,' he said to Gloria, 'we'll be mixing through the images, so that your eyes will become Stacey's and Stacey's mouth will become yours, and vice versa for everything, so that in the end poor Arnie doesn't know whether he's going completely mad, or hallucinating, or dreaming, or what he's doing.' He wasn't even going to allow himself to think about the way the peculiar horror of this was starting to play itself out in his own life.

'It's fine. I get it,' she told him.

He smiled and squeezed her arm. Thank God she didn't resemble Anna or he'd probably never get through this with his sanity intact.

The final two hours of the day passed swiftly, and with much less strain on his conscience, and libido, than he'd feared, considering that the last fifty minutes was spent looking at nothing else but Stacey Greene's mesmerizingly beautiful face. Could he dare to believe he was regaining some control? Was there some room to hope that the past week's prurience had been no more than a passing aberration that was now, mercifully, on the decline?

After calling a wrap he thanked everyone, including Stacey, then before anyone could waylay him he went swiftly through to the front-of-house where the manager's office had become his while they were shooting here. The other offices had been taken over too, mainly by the production and design teams, while the caterers had set up around the bar, and he probably couldn't have welcomed any gin and tonic more than the one that was thrust into his hand as he passed through.

He knew, as the door closed behind him, that his solitude would be brief, but he would take it anyway. This was the aspect of directing he found hardest – the seemingly irreversible tide of people that constantly demanded his attention. Yet in a way he enjoyed it too, for there was an electrifying immediacy to the process that didn't happen when it was just him, at home with his computer. He just wished he could settle into this shoot the way he needed to, for there was an enormous amount of money at stake, not to mention his and Anna's reputations.

Taking another fortifying sip of his drink, he was about to reach for the phone to call her, when someone knocked at the door.

'Are you in here?' Stacey said, putting her head round.

'Yes, of course. Come in,' he said warmly, though behind his smile the first stirrings of panic were already starting to bite. They shouldn't be alone in this room. There was very little light, the ambience exuded seclusion and seduction; the setting was too reflective of scenes in the film.

'Are you OK?' she asked, her beautiful head tilted to one side, as she closed the door and leaned against it. When had she found time to dress? What did it matter? Just be thankful she had. 'You seem . . . distant. Are things not going as well as you'd hoped?'

Aware of the dozens of photographs that crowded the walls, he spoke as if to them, using them as some kind of audience, or chaperon, projecting his voice slightly, so that it wouldn't enfold her in the way hers had enfolded him. 'Everything's going perfectly,' he replied. 'You're doing a wonderful job.'

146

She smiled ruefully. 'Thank you,' she said, 'but I didn't come for compliments. I came because I'm concerned.'

He didn't know what to say. The confusion of her words, and his thoughts, was already beginning.

Her smile was vaguely bemused. 'Is it your brother-in-law?' she said. 'Are you finding it hard to get over his death?'

'It hasn't been easy,' he said, his voice somehow squeezing itself from the tightness in his chest. Why was this happening? Why wasn't it possible for him to look at her without desiring her so intensely?

He was still smiling, and praying that the habitual twinkle in his eyes was masking the turbulence, as she came towards him like a nymph from the sea, hair tumbling randomly down over her shoulders, her flowing white dress pressed to the contours of her slender body. Knowing she wore nothing beneath it caused his eyes to drop, as his hand tightened on his glass.

'Would you like me to sit on your cock?' she said softly. 'Would that make you feel better?'

His head came up, as the blood drained from his face. He knew she hadn't said those words, that he'd imagined them, but . . . Her smile was almost angelic, her eyes slightly sleepy, though focused fully on his. 'I'm sorry,' he said. 'What did you . . . ?'

'I said, would you like to talk? Tell me what's on your mind.'

He swallowed hard, and gave a laugh that was twisted with relief and anguish. 'No, really, there's nothing,' he said. 'It's just been a difficult couple of weeks. Tim's death,' he added, seizing a truth she had handed him again.

'I heard you reading from the gospel, at the funeral,' she said. 'It was very moving. How is your sister-in-law?'

He shook his head. 'It's been hard for her,' he answered.

'For Anna too, I'm sure,' she said. Then added, 'You know if there's anything I can do . . .'

'Thank you. Actually, she asked me to thank you for the flowers. That was very thoughtful.'

She waved a dismissive hand.

It was on the tip of his tongue to invite her to dinner on Saturday night, but he bit it back, even though Anna herself had suggested it. Could he really do that to his wife, allow her to entertain the woman who was turning his mind into a cesspit of lust? Yet it would make sense for Stacey to be there, not only because she was a friend of Gomez's, but because he didn't want to be the one to suggest her as the model for their joint project. He'd stand much more chance of Gomez doing it if she were there. So why not just ask the question? *Would you like to come for dinner on Saturday night?* Why was he just sitting here, submerged in frustration, drowning in guilt, while his penis strained so hard it might be trying to burst from its skin.

He watched her as she walked round the desk, and came to stand beside him. Then raising her dress to her waist she bent over the desk to expose the tender, rosy flesh of her buttocks. 'Go ahead and beat me,' she said, over her shoulder. 'It's my fault that you're feeling this way, so punish me, and punish me hard.'

148

His eyes closed. His heart was a dull, painful throb that resonated like a drum in his head, and an instrument of torture in his loins.

'Robert?' she said softly.

He opened his eyes. She was standing next to him, a hand on his shoulder, her dress still hanging loosely around her knees.

'Would you like to be left alone?' she asked. 'Are you just too polite to say?'

He swallowed hard. 'Actually, I need to call my wife,' he said. 'If you don't mind.'

Leaning forward she pressed her lips to his forehead. 'Can I come to rushes tonight?' she asked.

'Of course. I think they're at seven. Someone out there will know.'

After she'd gone he let his head fall back against the chair and waited for the desire to subside. How was he doing this, allowing himself to see and hear the base thoughts of his unconscious mind; to almost trick himself into believing that those moments were real? This wasn't the first time it had happened, and though he was terrified of the next time he couldn't deny that he longed for it too. But he had to keep it under control, stop himself responding to the words he imagined her speaking, for if he'd put his hand out a moment ago, where would he have touched her? The thought of his fingers connecting with her thigh, even with a dress obscuring it, caused a renewed surge of desire that made him press down hard on his groin so that the threatened ejaculation could find no escape.

A moment later the door opened and the telephone rang at the same time.

'Need a lift to rushes?' the production manager offered.

Robert shook his head. 'I've got my car, thanks,' he answered. Then into the phone, 'Robert Maxton.' His face was blood red, his breath slightly ragged.

'Hello, darling, it's me. I take it you've wrapped if you're in the office.'

So much love and relief rushed through him that for a moment it was hard to speak. This woman meant more to him than anyone else alive; he'd rather die than even think about living without her. 'I was just about to call you,' he responded. 'How's your day been? Are you with Rachel?'

'She's in the other room, watching TV with the children. Shall we expect you for dinner?'

'Yes. Around nine. Is that too late?'

'We'll give them a snack to keep them going. How was your day?'

'I think it went well. All to schedule.'

'Did you invite Stacey tomorrow night?'

'Not yet. But I will if you want me to.' How desperately he longed for her to say yes, but how he dreaded it too.

'It's up to you,' she told him. 'You sound tired.'

'Yes, I am a bit.'

She hesitated, then said, 'Are you sure you're going to be OK while I'm in Cornwall?'

Guilt pared the shield from his conscience, as though to expose the miserable unworthiness of his motives. He'd told her to stay as long as she liked, because he'd known Stacey's husband was away again, but now he didn't want her to go at all. She was his only protection, without her here, he was

150

afraid of what he might do. 'I'll be fine,' he heard himself saying, while already envisaging himself offering Stacey anything she desired in exchange for one small kiss of her vulva. 'I'll miss you,' he added, ignoring the voice that was screaming for her to stay.

Her smile was audible, as she said, 'I like you better as a writer, you're less maudlin.'

He laughed, perhaps too loudly, but the sound was like a new wave of energy that seemed to wrench him from the depths of his ramblings. 'Less maudlin as a *writer!*' he challenged.

She laughed.

'I love you,' he said gruffly.

'I know,' she whispered.

After putting the telephone down, Anna stood staring into space, her mind taking her to where he was, trying to envisage how he looked, and what he was doing. All she saw was him, sitting at the large, old-fashioned desk, surrounded by decades of black-and-white photographs, his eyes staring into space like hers, as the turmoil in his mind and heart simmered silently on. He was such a sensitive man, so affected by his work and unsure of his talent, even though he'd received the kind of critical acclaim most writers hardly dared even dream about. He should be much more confident, but he was so easily hurt by criticism, and frequently confused by his own responses, such as those he was experiencing to Stacey. They were the cause of his anxiety now, she was sure of it, but though she longed to soothe him, it had never been her way to force him to talk. He would when he was ready, she knew that, she just hoped that it wasn't a mistake to be going off to Cornwall this weekend, when he clearly needed her here.

But she wouldn't have to stay long. Beanie was just dying to take care of Rachel, and as soon as they'd tracked down the local doctor, got in supplies from the supermarket, and made sure the old Fiesta was working, Anna could return to London. So she should be back by the end of the week, maybe even sooner, and what could happen in a few days? Stacey was hardly going to eat him, and though he couldn't bring himself to admit it, he was handling her much better than he realized. In fact, she hoped he did invite her tomorrow, for spending some time with her, away from the set, might help him get things into a better perspective. It would also give her, Anna, the chance to watch them together without the distractions of a crew or, more significantly, the complications of the actor/ director relationship that could distort reality even for the most grounded of people, never mind someone as profoundly reactive as Robert.

Through the vast picture windows of a palatial ocean front condominium the spectacular view of soft, white sand, tropical trees and rosy, sunlit waves was slowly starting to fade. The men gathered inside the all-white and chrome-furnished room were largely a sombre, business-suited bunch, who'd flown to Florida from many different parts of the globe, and would be leaving again tomorrow, secure in the knowledge that this particular shareholders' meeting would go unrecorded.

Later, when the women and stimulating substances arrived, the celebrations were likely to become much more raucous, but for now, as they unwound from the intensity of the past forty-eight hours, a variety of cocktails and fat Cuban cigars were suiting them fine. Indeed, despite their varying nationalities and occasional awkwardness with each other's languages, they all appeared as pleased with themselves as if they'd just won a fifty million dollar lottery, which, in effect, they were probably about to.

'Hey, Henri,' Rudy said, coming to join him. Today Rudy was honouring Matisse. 'Are you staying for the party, or heading home?'

'I think I'll stay,' Henri responded, his eyes moving through the crowd to where a large, ebony-skinned man, with a round moon face, immaculate dentistry and Savile Row tailoring, was talking to Franz Koehler and several others.

Rudy followed his gaze. 'Dr Bombola himself,' he murmured. 'Franz wasn't sure he'd turn up.'

'He's never let us down before.'

Rudy's eyebrows rose, then turning his back to the room, he said, 'Did you get how ticked Franz was at being hauled in by the London police again?'

'Did he tell you anything about it?'

'Not a word. You heard them talking about Katherine earlier?'

'Mm.' Then mimicking one of the Americans present, he said, '"The Limeys have got her holed up somewhere."' He took a sip of his drink. 'Interesting thought,' he commented. Then, 'Look out, Franz is on his way over.'

Affecting a cheery grin, Rudy turned round.

'Gentlemen,' Koehler said, his shrewd eyes seeming to read the short exchange that he couldn't possibly have overheard. 'A good meeting, I think.'

They both nodded agreement.

To Rudy he said, 'Give us a moment, will you?'

Obediently Rudy took himself off into the crowd.

'We need the money back from Mrs Hendon,' Koehler said quietly.

His expression didn't change, though this was the first he'd heard of any money being connected to Mrs Hendon.

'I will contact her myself and tell her what to do.'

He waited, presuming there must be a point to telling him this, but whatever it was, it seemed that Koehler wasn't going to reveal it yet, for he changed the subject, saying, 'Katherine is my absolute priority now. I'm putting together a team of private detectives to help find her. It'll be announced in the *New York Times* tomorrow. Hopefully, it'll do something to alleviate the suspicion that's surrounding me.'

There were many questions he'd like to ask now, but knowing the answers would only come when Koehler was ready, he maintained his silence and drained his glass.

They discussed a few details of the meeting then, and the next stage of the Phraxos Special Project, which had dominated the agenda for the past two days. Politically, financially and socially, it had been worse than Orwellian, but these Special Project meetings always were, so it was much less the moral aspects of the project that were concerning them now, than the sheer practicalities of circumventing embargoes while staying on the right side of the law.

'We'll be convening again in Paris, a month from now,' Koehler told him, then slapping him on the shoulder he returned to the body of his guests.

Going over to the bar, he poured himself another large vodka, and was about to disappear into an adjoining room, with the idea of calling his wife, when he was approached by one of Dr Bombola's men, who wanted more details on the government licences, or certificates, that were required for the weapons transactions that concerned their particular clients.

After explaining as much as he knew, which was considerably more than he'd known a year ago, he took himself off to a bedroom where he closed the blinds and set his drink down on a nightstand next to the bed. A quick check of the mobile showed that Stacey had left a couple of messages, one of them in text, which was so intimate he could actually feel the stirrings of arousal.

Speed-dialling her number, he put the phone to his ear, and sipped his drink. When he got a recorded message, he waited for the tone then, knowing she'd enjoy the joke, said, 'Hi, it's Henri Matisse. I guess you're at the Maxtons', having dinner. I'm still in Florida, should be home tomorrow night, Monday at the latest. I've got a couple of meetings in London, then can you get down to the house for the weekend? Love you and miss you.'

Just after he rang off the sound of female laughter told him that the evening's light entertainment had arrived, so downing the rest of his vodka he went back out to the bar for a refill. He had no personal interest in the kind of girls that were brought in for these parties, but he was always fascinated by how loose-lipped the men became in their presence, which was why he was staying around. If any more was going to be said, or surmised, about Katherine Sumner, or anything else come to that, he wanted to hear it.

'Monsieur Matisse,' a voice behind him said, as he recharged his glass.

He turned to find himself staring into the direct, inquisitive gaze of Dr Bombola himself, whose official role in the world was that of visiting lecturer at several prominent European and American universities on the subject of international trade and finance in developing countries. Unofficially he was head of the Demand Section of the Phraxos Special Project.

'I can't say parties are really my cup of tea,' Bombola remarked, in the deep, chocolatey tones that revealed his predominantly British education, 'so I was hoping you might consider joining me for dinner. Just the two of us. I think you'll find we have a lot to discuss.' He smiled, charmingly. 'Should I continue to call you Matisse, by the way? Or would you prefer I use your real name?'

Surprise caused his eyebrows to arch. 'Do you know it?' he said.

Bombola smiled again, this time showing a few gold teeth that glinted amongst his pristine white ones. 'Of course,' he replied. 'It's no secret, is it?'

He shook his head.

Bombola's eyes were almost overpowering in their intensity. 'But I'm rather entertained by your friend's artful use of pseudonyms, so perhaps I'll stay with Matisse,' he said.

'Oh, Henri, please,' he insisted, and after catching Rudy's eye across the room, he returned his full glass to the bar and allowed the good professor to lead him away.

Chapter 7

After just twenty-four hours of being in Cornwall there was a softness, almost a glow, to Rachel's skin that had been absent since even before Tim died, for the early stages of pregnancy and the strain of the campaign had seemed to dull the inner radiance that gave her her own kind of beauty. But now, being in a place she loved, surrounded by the stirring splendour of the cliffs and moors and the soothing rhythm of the waves, the natural blush was returning to her dusky cheeks, and a warm light was showing in her eyes, despite the sheer awfulness of being here without Tim.

It was late in the afternoon, and she and Anna were pottering about in the small garden at the front of the cottage, clearing weeds from the flowerbeds that hugged the whitewashed stone walls, and mowing the overgrown lawn, while Jake, a local handyman, repaired the mesh that protected the thatched roof from the birds. Hers was one of the two cottages that sat high up on the headland, and looked down on the secluded cove of Killian, where the village nestled quaintly in the deep U of the bay, and fishing boats cluttered the tiny pebble beach. From where she was standing now, she could see the narrow road that descended into the cove, snaking steeply down the rugged hillside to loop like a giant horseshoe around Killian's sprinkling of stone cottages, before making an ascent on the other side to the closest village, three miles away. At that moment she was absently watching a tractor as it chugged down the hill, following its progress round past the Killian Arms and the winch house, towards the beach, where several fishermen in rubber boots and oilskins were working on their boats and smoking the roll-ups they never seemed to be without. She was too far distant to make out their faces, but guessed that she'd probably know them all, if not by name, then certainly by sight.

Her eye was caught then by a lone figure, emerging from between the two cottages that were perched out on the todden, which was what the locals called the small outcrop of rock that divided the mouth of the bay like an uvula, with a tiny, black sand beach on the far side, invisible from where she was, that was used for bathing and swimming during the hot summer months.

'Isn't that Nick, Beanie's nephew?' she said, shading her eyes from the sun.

Anna winced as she stood straight. 'Looks like him,' she replied. 'But it's hard to tell from here.'

'I'm sure it is,' Rachel said, and waved just in case.

'Must be someone else,' Anna chuckled, when

the man continued strolling out to the end of the todden and didn't wave back.

Surprised that she was wrong, Rachel went to sit on the low, stone wall that paralleled the grassy footpath outside and provided some small privacy for her and Beanie's cottages. Looking back at her own, with its mullioned windows and white lattice porch draped in wisteria and roses, she felt her heart twist with longing. There wasn't a single inch of this place that didn't bring back at least a dozen memories, so just how easy it was going to be staying here, after Anna had gone, she could hardly dare think about. But as difficult as she knew it would be, now she was here, the mere thought of London, and all it had come to represent, was enough to make her shrink from the idea of ever going back again, never mind any time soon.

Inhaling deeply the warm, salt-tinged air she turned to gaze out at the sea. 'Do you know what I find so special about this place?' she said to Anna. 'Its separateness from everywhere else. Even from Roon Moor. The world as we know it seems to end up there, doesn't it? It's as if we've tipped off the edge of Dante's Inferno and come to rest in this lovely little cove, that sits here basking in its own sea of tranquillity, so real and uncomplicated and . . . I don't know, resistant, I suppose, to any kind of change, other than in the little ways that suit it.'

'Mm,' Anna responded, smiling. 'It is special, isn't it?' Then with mischief in her eyes she added, 'And here comes something else that makes it so. Beanie and her decadent teas.'

Smiling, Rachel turned to watch the stout little woman with soft grey curls and the warmest sky blue eyes coming up the footpath towards them. 'Here, let me,' she said, reaching out to take the overloaded tray from Beanie's hands.

'Careful, it's heavy,' Beanie warned. Then satisfied that Rachel had it, she plonked herself down on the wall and swung her legs over.

'This could do with a lick of paint,' she commented, eyeing the rickety iron table Rachel was putting the tray on. 'Jake can do it tomorrow.'

'What's this?' Rachel demanded, peering into the milk jug.

'Whisky,' Beanie responded, as though it were the most natural ingredient for a milk jug. 'Just in case anyone fancies a drop. You still there,' she called out to Jake, up on the roof. 'There's some tea down here, if you want some. Fresh crab sandwiches too. Got the crab from your dad, this morning.'

'Mmm, heaven,' Anna murmured, catching a whiff of the alcohol as she came over to join them.

'Half tea, half Scottish milk for me,' Beanie said, waggling her eyebrows at Anna as Rachel picked up the teapot. 'It's gone half-past four, so it's all right,' she assured her.

'I thought it was supposed to be half-past five,' Anna grinned.

'That's according to you foreigners,' she retorted. 'You're in Killian now, and you know what they say – when in Killian, do as the Killians do, which is make it up as you go along.'

Anna burst out laughing. 'Then half tea, half Scottish milk for me too,' she said to Rachel.

'Is there any of the cow variety for those of us undergoing forced abstinence?' Rachel demanded, searching the small flowery pots and plates.

161

'Just a drop, in the bottom of one of the cups,' Beanie told her. 'That one's yours, and you don't want to go spilling it now, or the fairies'll be moving in, and you know what that means.'

Rachel slanted her a look, which made the old lady chuckle with delight.

'What does it mean?' Anna asked.

'I don't know, and nor does she,' Rachel answered. 'She makes it up as she goes along.'

'Oi! Bean! Stand on the bottom of the ladder, will you?' Jake shouted down.

Beanie immediately went to balance on the first rung, then gripped the sides as though some unearthly force was about to swing her off into orbit. 'I been baking today,' she told him, as his bandy legs began their descent, 'so there's a nice bit of herring pie for you to take home to your dad. He's partial to a bit of herring, is Jake's dad,' she informed Rachel and Anna.

'Partial to you, more like,' Jake told her, chucking her under the chin as he reached the bottom. 'And who can blame him, you little cupcake, you.'

'You behave, young man,' she chided, her eyes glowing with pleasure. 'I'm too old for all that. Or I will be by the time your old dad gets round to anything,' she added, with a bawdy wink at Rachel and Anna.

'He's working up to it,' Jake assured her, making a beeline for the sandwiches.

Rachel was laughing, but as she picked up a sandwich too, a wave of memory intruded on the moment and swept her appetite away.

Noticing her put the sandwich back, Beanie said, 'I've got some nice red mullet for your tea, which you can have with the new potatoes I picked from my garden and the green beans I got from yours. Nice and healthy for the baby.'

Rachel rolled her eyes and shook her head. 'You don't have to go to all that trouble,' she scolded gently. 'We should be cooking for you.'

'Oh, no thanks,' Beanie said, starting with alarm. 'Not one of your strong points, cooking, as I recall. Don't know about Anna, though. Are you any good?'

'Not a patch on you,' Anna replied. 'But I'm Delia compared to her.'

Sticking her nose in the air, Rachel turned to Jake whose quirkily elfin features were so mobile in their munching that they made her smile. 'Are you going to have whisky in your tea?' she asked, as his dirty fist reached for several more crab and cucumber triangles.

'Got any rum?' he replied, his words mumbled by the food.

'There should be some,' Rachel said. 'I'll go and have a look.'

As she disappeared round the side of the house to go in through the kitchen, Beanie's four-year-old black Labrador came sailing over the knobbly stone wall to join them.

'Oh, woke up at last, have you?' Beanie said hoitily, as the excited beast made straight for Anna.

'Romie!' Anna cried, grabbing the dog's face and ruffling her up. 'You smelt the sandwiches, you greedy old thing?'

Wolfing down a crust, Romie took off to greet Jake. 'Cor blimey, Rome!' he grunted, as she landed her front paws dangerously close to his tenderest parts. 'Haven't you grown out of that yet?'

Her answer was to give him a thorough licking, before going off in search of Rachel.

'Oh, there's our Nick over on the todden,' Beanie declared, starting to wave. 'What's he doing, wandering about by himself? Wonder if he wants some tea?'

Anna watched in surprise as Nick waved back. So it was him. Of course there was a good chance he hadn't spotted Rachel waving just now, so taking umbrage at his failure to respond might be out of place. However, she couldn't ignore the fact that there had been other incidents like it since they'd arrived, with people seeming to go out of their way to avoid them, or barely muttering a reply when they said hello. It saddened her to think it, but she guessed the wariness stemmed from a general awkwardness with the nature of Rachel's bereavement, for it was hard to know what to say to grieving relatives when the death was normal, so when it was as shocking and scandalous as murder, it wasn't really surprising that people found themselves at a total loss how to handle it.

Helping herself to another sandwich, she smiled, and laughed as Beanie took a noisy slurp from her teacup then put her head back and declared, 'Nectar,' to anyone who might be passing over-head. What a blessing Beanie was at this time, Anna was thinking, so practical, and motherly and wise, yet mischievous and eccentric too. She had one of the most beautiful auras Anna had ever sensed in another human being, for there were times when she emanated such a soothing inner calm that it was hard to imagine anything ever going wrong around her. And then there were other times when her sense of merriment, or of the absurd, was so hilariously enchanting that it seemed as though nothing ever had a right to be anything but fun.

With a pang Anna realized how very much she'd like to spend some time with Beanie now, to have her own anxieties smoothed over by the old lady's gentle perspicacity, but Rachel's need was much greater, and besides, Robert's difficult spell would probably pass soon anyway. She just wished she hadn't had to come away the very day after the disastrous dinner party on Saturday night, when Robert had been so embarrassingly rude to Stacey that Anna had called her early the next morning to apologize. In typical Stacey fashion, she'd merely laughed, and assured her that she hadn't taken it personally; she understood that he was under pressure and sometimes things didn't come out quite the way one intended.

Well, Anna didn't know about that, but she did know that Robert certainly hadn't deserved the enthusiasm that both Stacey and Ernesto Gomez had shown for the joint art and poetry exhibition, when he'd all but ridiculed their interest from the moment they'd shown it. And even now, she could feel herself cringing at the way he'd scorned Ernesto's suggestion that Stacey should be the model. It was almost as if he was trying to sabotage the project before it began, though that hardly made any sense, when she knew very well that he was all for it.

Taking another sip of her nicely potent tea, she

glanced at her watch and saw that it was still too early to ring him yet, but the children would be expecting a call any minute, so she'd just wait until Rachel returned with the rum then go inside to use the phone. Come to think of it, Rachel had been gone rather a long time. Maybe she should pop in to check she was all right. But before she could even put her cup down Rachel came round the corner of the house holding up a half-bottle of rum.

'I knew we had some somewhere,' she declared, as she handed it to Jake. 'Take as much as you like.'

Despite the sunniness of her smile, it was plain to them all that she'd been crying, and Anna's heart went out to her.

'So when's this famous reporter supposed to be coming?' Beanie demanded, pouring more tea from the teacosied pot into Rachel's cup.

'The day after tomorrow,' Rachel answered. 'Which reminds me, we should book her a room at the pub.'

'We'll do it when we go down after dinner, or tea, as Beanie likes to call it,' Anna replied, teasingly.

'What reporter's that?' Jake said, his hand pausing en route to another batch of sandwiches.

'Her name's Laurie Forbes,' Rachel told him.

He frowned. 'What's she coming here for?' he asked.

Rachel was about to answer when Anna said, 'She's coming to write all about you, Jake Tucker. She's going to expose all your naughty little secrets to the world at large, so you'd better watch out.'

Jake's face was turning red. 'I got nothing to hide,' he told her gruffly.

'Pppfff!' Beanie snorted. 'If you've got nothing to

hide then I got nothing up here,' she told him, tapping her head.

'Then, it's like I said, I got nothing to hide,' he responded, guffawing at his own joke.

As they laughed, the phone started to ring inside the house, and Rachel's heart seemed to fold in on itself as Anna jumped up, because of course, it would be for her. For one awful moment she thought the grief was going to rise up and claim her again, but mercifully she managed to hold it back, though what she really wanted to do was sink to the ground and sob with despair, or worse, hurl herself down over the cliff onto the rocks below and into the sea.

'Rachel! It's Lucy for you,' Anna called out through the window.

Surprised, for she'd only spoken to Lucy an hour ago, Rachel finished her tea and got up. 'Did she say what it's about?' she asked Anna, as they passed in the kitchen.

'No,' Anna answered.

Hoping it wasn't going to be yet another irritating insurance glitch, Rachel descended the single step under the arch into the sitting room, and went over to the TV table to pick up the phone. 'Luce?' she said, wishing she could stop herself expecting the worst every time Lucy rang. 'Is everything all right?'

'I'm not sure,' Lucy's rhythmic Australian voice replied. 'There's a message on the machine. It must have come in while I was down in the flat . . . I think you should hear it.'

Rachel's heart was already filling up with dread. 'Who's it from?' she asked.

'I don't know. You need to listen.'

A moment later another voice came down the line. 'Mrs Hendon?' it began, and her insides turned to ice, for the accent was unmistakably foreign. 'Your husband has a certain sum of money that I'm afraid does not belong to him,' the caller informed her. 'We would please like you to return it. You will receive instructions through the mail in the next day or two, telling you what to do. Please follow them exactly.'

Rachel's thoughts were in chaos as she heard the sound of the line disconnecting, then a beep to signal the end of the message.

'Did you get it?' Lucy said.

'Yes,' she answered weakly. Quickly pulling herself together, she said, 'Has anyone called since? Can you dial 1471?'

'I've already tried,' Lucy told her. 'It didn't work.'

Rachel put a hand to her head, trying to think what to do. 'Play it again,' she said. 'I need to hear it again.'

Dutifully Lucy reran the message. By the time it finished Rachel felt more agitated than ever, for there was something different about it, something that didn't quite fit with the other calls.

'Should I erase it?' Lucy said.

'No! No, keep it for now, but don't let anyone else hear it, OK?'

'OK,' Lucy answered.

After putting the phone down, Rachel took a couple of steadying breaths, then found herself staring at Tim's handsome face, which was smiling back from its frame on the round fireside table.

'I can't stand this,' she sobbed angrily. 'Do you hear me? I just can't stand it. I want to know where that money came from! I need to know.'

Her only answer was the sound of the grandfather clock ticking monotonously on in the corner, and the distant sough of the waves.

She stared at his photo again and felt almost consumed by the frustration that was raging inside her. Four million dollars was such a lot of money, and the fact he'd never told her he had it was almost as bad as knowing it existed at all. But worse was having to decide now what to do about it, for though there had been no threat in the phone call, she didn't imagine whoever it was would appreciate having his instructions ignored.

'The trouble is,' she said to Anna later, as they walked down to the pub, 'if I simply do as he says, and give it back, I might never find out where it came from.'

'That's obviously the general intention,' Anna responded. 'But what about the voice? You said it was different.'

'The accent was much stronger,' Rachel told her. 'More discernible.'

'As?'

'German.'

Anna turned to look at her.

Rachel looked back. Franz Koehler was from Zurich, where the Swiss spoke German.

Anna turned to walk on, passing old Tom Drummond's cottage at the end of the footpath, where lavish quantities of geraniums and towering gladioli were doing their best to disguise the smug, round saucer of a satellite dish – the only bloom on the block that didn't give a hoot about seasons, fertilizer or aesthetic pleasure. 'So are you going to tell Haynes about the call?' she said, finally.

'I don't know,' Rachel answered. 'I'm still trying to decide.'

Anna looked distinctly uneasy. 'If you don't, you could be biting off a whole lot more than you can chew,' she warned. 'Just from what we've found out already we know this Franz Koehler is an extremely powerful man, so if it was him who made that call . . . Well, we're in no position to mess around with people like that.'

Rachel stayed silent as she watched a cat trot out from behind the neat row of cottages they were passing and start down to the beach.

'Face it, what you're doing is attempting your own cover-up,' Anna stated bluntly.

'If that were true I wouldn't be asking Rose Newman and Laurie Forbes to help me,' Rachel retorted.

'You would, because you need them.'

'But they wouldn't assist me in the cover-up of something criminal, you can be sure of that.'

'OK. So why won't you tell Haynes about it? Just so that I've got this absolutely straight in my head.'

'Because I don't know who he's taking his orders from,' Rachel answered, starting up the steps to the pub's terrace where a couple of backpackers were sipping beer and studying a map. 'If the Phraxos Group has been trying to buy its way into defence policy here in the UK, the way it presumably has in the States, then whoever's acting as the go-between, singular or plural, is not going to want it to come out. And since we've got no idea how highly placed that person, or persons, is, we've got no way of knowing how much influence they might have on the investigation, or on Haynes himself. And I'm afraid corruption is corruption, whether my husband was involved or not, so it has to be exposed. Now, we should change the subject before we go inside. This place is haunted, did you know that?' she said glancing back over her shoulder as she pushed the door open.

Anna pulled a face. 'Then just make sure you don't tell Laurie Forbes,' she warned. 'She probably won't want to stay.'

Rachel smiled, perhaps a little too brightly, but she wanted to show a happy face to everyone inside, in the hope of making them feel more at ease. But to her dismay, the instant they saw her their conversation dwindled into silence, as though some kind of witchery was stilling their tongues and turning their eyes in other directions.

Feeling a hollow of misery opening up in her chest, she struggled with the urge to turn back, and made herself walk across the room to the bar. 'Hello Pinkie, Todd,' she said, addressing two fishermen who were perched on stools in front of the beer pumps.

'Evening,' Todd grunted, obviously wishing he didn't have to.

'Would anyone like a drink?' Anna piped up, looking round at the watchful, wind-roughened faces. Her eyes alighted on Jake, who was sitting over by the empty fireplace, under a painting of his own great-grandfather, and Beanie's father-in-law, the legendary Jack Cormant. 'Rum?' she said.

Jake's face turned crimson. 'No, I'm all right thanks,' he said, holding up his glass.

She looked round again. 'Anyone else?' she offered.

When no one answered Rachel turned to the rotund, and normally jovial landlord, Dapper Lynch. 'Hello Dap,' she said. 'A lemonade for me, please. And a vodka tonic for Anna.'

Saying nothing, the landlord set about serving the drinks.

Rachel glanced at Anna.

'Keep smiling,' Anna said through her teeth, wanting to strangle the whole lot of them.

Rachel said, quietly, 'I think we should take our drinks outside.'

Anna nodded. It was obviously too much to expect Rachel to sit through any more of this atrocious silence, though Anna would have liked to, just to make them stew in their own cowardly ridiculousness.

The uneasiness continued as Dapper put their drinks on the bar, took the fiver Rachel offered, then handed her the change. A dozen pairs of eyes then escorted them back across the room to the door, and only when the latch clicked behind them did the voices start up again, though with markedly less animation than before.

'Don't,' Rachel said, seeing that Anna was about to explode. 'This isn't easy for anyone, and getting angry's only going to make it worse. They'll come round. You'll see. They just need time.'

'But you're the one who's suffering,' Anna seethed, banging her glass on the table and climbing inside the bench.

'Let's just leave it,' Rachel said. 'It'll be all right.'

'But what the hell's it all about? I mean, it's hardly your fault your husband died the way he did.'

'They obviously don't know what to say.'

'Sorry. Condolences. Anything I can do? How are you? It's not difficult,' Anna retorted, hotly. 'And I can hardly go back to London leaving you in an atmosphere like this, so it has to be dealt with.'

'It will be, but not by confronting it head on, the way you're intending. I'll find a way to handle it, I promise,' she said, as Anna started to object again. 'But deciding what to do about the money is more pressing right now.'

Reluctantly shifting focus, Anna tore her eyes away and poured the tonic over her vodka. She'd talk to Beanie before she left. She'd know what to do.

'He said I should get the instructions on how to return the money in a couple of days,' Rachel was saying. 'But it'll be longer than that, because Lucy will have to forward the letter, so I probably won't get it until the end of the week. Which is worrying on the one hand, in case he gets heavy if some kind of deadline isn't met, but good on the other, because it'll give me time to discuss it with Laurie Forbes. Since she's not personally involved in it all, the way we are, I'm hoping she might have a clearer idea what to do.'

Anna looked bleakly down at her drink, for the mention of Laurie Forbes in that context made her feel horribly as though she were shirking her responsibility, handing everything over to a stranger, when she should be trying to sort this out herself. But what else could she do? She had no experience of investigating *anything*, never mind something like this, so it made total sense for an expert to do it. And it wasn't as if she was just abandoning Rachel. She'd always be at the end of a phone, would come down to visit as often as she could, and was even going to stay on an extra day to overlap with Laurie Forbes, just to reassure herself that she really was the right person for the job. In fact, since speaking to Robert earlier, she'd been toying with the idea of staying till the weekend, for he'd sounded quite buoyant, and in control, and the fact that he'd been on the point of going over to Stacey's for the evening, to have dinner with her and her husband confirmed, to her relief, that no grudges were being held over his ugly display on Saturday night. Anna just hoped he didn't do anything to disgrace himself again tonight.

'Sorry, what did you say?' she said, suddenly realizing Rachel had spoken.

Rachel smiled. 'Only that it's really good to have you here, even though you're obviously miles away.' She put a hand on Anna's. 'No, don't apologize,' she said, 'and please don't feel you have to stay, because you're obviously much more worried about the film, or Robert, than you're letting on, so that's where you should be.'

Anna inhaled deeply, then slowly let it go as she gazed out at the twilit sky and towering black cliffs. The undercurrent of mysticism that was so rife in these parts, combined with the feeling that past and future were mingling with the present, was never more persuasive than now, at this time of day, when the light seemed to turn the cove into some kind of netherworld, where nothing was quite what it seemed. 'How well we read each other's minds,' she commented, finally. 'And how strange the world feels, at this moment, with us two, sitting here, on the tip of England, while God only knows what roils on behind us.'

'This is Cornwall, everything's strange,' Rachel quipped. Then, nodding towards the inside of the pub, 'Including the people.'

Anna picked up her drink. '*Especially* the people,' she corrected, and clinking her glass noisily against Rachel's, she waved out to Beanie who was just coming to join them.

Robert was standing alone in the middle of Stacey Greene's spacious and eclectically furnished sitting room, where the huge, inwardly sloping windows that formed the entirety of one wall looked down from the penthouse apartment on to most of central London. But his attention wasn't focused on the view, he wasn't even interested in the impressive collection of modern art that was hanging from the red brick walls, he was seeing only the exceptional and extraordinary creation that was a bronze table, shaped like a figure 7, which Stacey herself had posed for as a gift to her husband. It was like nothing he had ever seen before; so exquisitely crafted and erotically styled that he felt sure that if he touched it, it would be like touching the woman herself.

As he walked around it, he felt vaguely light-headed, for on seeing it the blood had rushed instantly to his groin, engorging his penis and making him wonder why she had left him alone to admire the magnificent, yet extremely intimate, view of herself that surely was meant for her husband alone. Was she watching him from the kitchen where she was supposed to be cooking? Did she want him to caress the smoothness of the sculpture; run a finger down the line in her buttocks; toy playfully with the small mound of her vulva? It was what he wanted to do, but he wouldn't. He would merely help himself to another of the marijuana cigarettes she kept in a box on the table, as she'd told him to, and try to stop hoping that this was a mere prelude to a private view of the real thing.

Shaking out the match, while pulling deeply on the cigarette, he held his breath for a long, sweet-feeling time, allowing the palliative qualities of the drug to penetrate his brain and begin to soothe the savagery of his erection. He felt much more in control of the situation than he might have a week ago, but that was because things had changed since then, in a way that even he, who was ready to believe in any or all of life's peculiarities, was still finding sublimely remarkable.

It had happened at the dinner on Saturday night, when he and Stacey had recognized the existence of a connection between them that no one else had seen, or even suspected. Indeed how could they, when he'd masked it so cleverly with a manner that had been shocking, even to him. At one point Anna had actually gasped at the way he'd ridiculed Stacey's likening of the proposed art and poetry project to the Pre-Raphaelite Brotherhood's depictions of the works of such poets as Tennyson and Keats, for the comparison wasn't only flattering, it was valid. But Anna, in her dismay, had failed to register how Stacey was telling him, with her refusal to take offence, that she could see through the charade, and was willing to forgive his insults because she understood the complexities of his mind on a level that even Anna had never quite attained.

At first it had alarmed him to think that she could so easily read the truth behind his false words, for it hadn't been his intention to reach her that way. To the contrary, he had been trying to save himself, and her, from the unworthy motives of the project, to do all he could to destroy any interest she might have in taking part, in order to shield her from the monstrous desire that was using his talent like a Trojan horse to smuggle itself into her graces.

He wasn't sure at what point he'd finally cleared his head of the resistance and allowed himself to acknowledge the bond that was forming between them. It could even have been the following day before he'd fully realized what had happened, but however long it had taken, there was no doubt now that the first true meeting of their minds had taken place that night. Of course, he must credit the marijuana cigarettes she'd brought with her for freeing his inhibitions, and allowing him to see what he'd been afraid of in his normal, cowardly state: that something fundamentally profound existed between them. So she had ignored his rudeness and continued to lavish on his idea all the charm and nourishment he secretly craved. Not even his insufferable disdain of Ernesto's claim that she was as beautiful as Rossetti's Maria Zambaco, had provoked anything more than a humorous surprise in her sultry oval eyes, for she'd known, unlike the others who'd reddened and even muttered in embarrassment, that his contempt was for Ernesto, who hadn't seen that her beauty could never be equal to Zambaco's, when it was far, far superior.

So now, as he joined her in the kitchen, still smoking one of her special cigarettes, though he couldn't quite boast the confidence she exuded as she moved about the magnificent stainless-steel environment, preparing a meal with her own exquisite hands, he could say that he was certainly less nervous than he had been, and that he probably had a much greater understanding of the subtext that was flowing back and forth between them as they conversed. Whether she actually shared any of his more physical feelings, he had not yet decided, but for now, it was enough to know that she understood them, and was unafraid, even willing, for him to be the first to set eyes on the exquisitely erotic table.

'How can I express how honoured I feel,' he said, going to sit at the central island.

She smiled, almost coyly. 'You liked it?'

'How could I not?' He might have told her that her husband was an extremely lucky man, but he was too jealous of him even to acknowledge he existed – except when telling Anna that he'd be here tonight, of course, but that was far from his mind now.

'You know, I sometimes feel quite transparent to you,' he told her, as she carried a chopping board to the centre island, and began to slice a red pepper.

Her eyes were suffused with merriment as she glanced up at him. 'Why do you say that?' she asked.

'Because you, as an actor, go deeper into a writer's psyche than anyone else. There's a place, on a level that no one else understands, or even reaches, where we meet and virtually become one.'

Her lovely head tilted to one side as she considered that. 'Is it we who become one?' she asked finally. 'Or do we create another that stands alone?'

'Our creation would still be us,' he responded. 'Like parents who are reproduced in a child by the combining of their genes, our creation has been fertilized by our joint intellect and visceral understanding of what is needed to bring it to life.'

She nodded slowly, and he watched as her long fingers scooped up the narrow strips of pepper and placed them randomly, though deliberately, over a crispy green mound of salad. Behind her two fillet steaks sizzled slowly in a pan, their mouth-watering aroma drifting around the kitchen as sensuously as the Offenbach that came from the CD. Beyond the sinks and drainers were wall-to-wall windows that, like those in the sitting room, looked out over lights that were starting to twinkle in the dusk.

She lifted her eyes and as they gazed deeply into his own he could feel the gentle but insistent power of their attraction coiling around him. He longed to know how intense the chemistry was for her, but he wouldn't ask, for they hadn't yet reached a point where they were ready to articulate anything of what was happening between them. Indeed, were it not for her reaction on Saturday, and now this invitation tonight, while her husband was away, he might not be daring to presume that she felt anything at all.

She turned back to the stove, still saying nothing, but the smile hovering playfully on her lips told him more clearly than words that he was right, he was transparent to her, and that she was enjoying the idea of cerebral copulation as much as he was.

Chuckling quietly he lifted his cigarette from the ashtray and took another long and satisfying pull. Were it possible, he'd be happy to sit here for ever, admiring the swan-like grace of her movements, the exquisite shape of her bones and bunched chaos of her hair, snared as it was at the nape of her neck. He could allow himself to envisage her as Prosperina, or Delia, with himself as Tibullus. Or he could imagine what it was like to be the man she had married, to be with her every day in this kitchen, knowing she wore nothing beneath the long, crêpe-de-Chine dress and apron, and that she was his to embrace, or ignore.

'Tell me who you really are, Robert Maxton,' she said finally, her tone imbued with a tease. 'I want to know what drives the writer inside you. Where do your ideas come from? How do you decide which direction they should take?'

Fortifying himself with another heady pull on the cigarette, he let the smoke go slowly, then said, 'If I could answer those questions, it would suggest that I'm in control of the process, and I never truly believe that I am.'

She glanced at him in surprise.

'I am, as we all are,' he said, 'an amalgam of

180

characters, a paradigm of emotional tests and conflicts. So there is no one me, just as there is no one you. We're like prisms, with more sides and angles than we can imagine, and where the light catches the prism today determines who we are, and how we respond, today.'

'Fascinating,' she murmured. 'Go on.'

'We all have a coexistence of anger and peace; love and hate; loyalty and deceit; depravity and morality. The capability of each is in us all, so if the issue is a crippled child, and the light catches pity, that is how we will respond. But it could equally catch indifference, or revulsion, because maybe the circumstances in our lives are such at that moment that we can't feel for another. So on any given day we could have a totally different response to any given situation. That doesn't change who we are, it merely illustrates our complexity.'

'But aren't we generally creatures of habit, governed by prevailing aspects of our natures?'

'Of course. I'm just saying that no one is as predictable as we might suppose them, and that we have the ability to surprise even ourselves.'

She regarded him with a careful expression. 'I like that,' she said.

The phone rang. She took the call in front of him, holding his eyes with her own as she spoke to the person at the other end. From the few words she uttered it was impossible to guess who it was, but as she clicked off the line, she said,

'Gloria.' She moved over to take the steaks from the heat and brought them to the centre island. 'Tell me what you think of her performance,' she said, grinding a little more pepper into the sauce.

Curious as to why she was asking, and ever mindful of an actor's devious intent, he said, truthfully, 'I think she's outstanding. Better even than I'd hoped.'

She smiled, and the sheer loveliness of it made his soul want to drink it. 'I'm glad you think so,' she said. 'But would it be too presumptuous of me to ask you to tell her?'

Surprised, he said, 'Does she need the reassurance? Does she feel I'm neglecting her?'

'I'm not sure,' she answered, pensively. 'I just think she's feeling . . .' She shrugged as the word eluded her, then smiled again. 'It never does any harm to tell someone how much they're appreciated,' she said, regarding him playfully from beneath her brows.

He watched as she lifted the steaks on to plates, then said, 'Does that mean I should be telling you how appreciated you are?'

Her smile deepened as she said, 'No. I think I know that already.'

He waited, anxiously, yet expectantly, for her eyes to come back to his, but she turned away, placing the pan in the sink and twisting on the water. Suddenly he was unsure what to say. It was as though the mood had undergone a subtle change, and he couldn't think what had caused it. Was she glad of his appreciation, or embarrassed to hear him express it? Perhaps this silence was her way of trying to stop him taking it any further. He attempted a smile, as though it might restore him, but his mouth only trembled. Then mercifully he found his voice, which came out with an unexpected warmth and assurance. 'I know how hard you and Gloria have rehearsed,' he said, 'so my praise for her performance is as much for you, as her director.'

Her golden eyebrows were arched sardonically, as she glanced over her shoulder.

He smiled and inclined his head, as though to reiterate the compliment. 'I can tell that she's deeply indebted to you,' he said. 'In fact she seems very attached to you.'

She sighed heavily at that and gazed out of the window. 'I'm afraid you're right,' she said. Reaching for a towel to dry her hands she came back to the island. 'I invited her to the country house a couple of weekends ago,' she confided, 'and now I'm rather regretting it.'

'Oh?'

'Well, at first she was snubbing those who've never been, as though she'd been afforded some special kind of privilege.'

'Maybe she had,' he teased.

She laughed. 'No, that's going too far,' she protested, passing him a plate. Then she continued, 'And now she's behaving rather badly towards poor Petey,' she said.

He drank some more wine, then deciding he didn't want to talk about either Petey or Gloria, he said, 'Where's your husband tonight?' Of course, he was putting himself on unsafe ground by asking such a question, but for some reason he was willing to risk it.

She smiled, wickedly. 'Where's Anna?' she countered.

'You know where she is. In Cornwall.'

Her eyes were still on his. 'Does she know you're here now?' she said, darkly.

His voice sounded hoarse as he said, 'Yes.'

A moment or two elapsed, as they continued to regard each other, then she surprised and dismayed him as she said, 'Did your sister-in-law know her husband was having an affair?'

Picking up his cigarette again, he relit it and shook his head. 'No,' he answered, exhaling a small cloud of smoke.

'Did you know? I mean before it all happened.'

'No.'

She regarded him closely, then said, 'I was introduced to Katherine Sumner at your party. On first impressions, I rather liked her. Did you know her very well?'

'It was only the second time I'd met her,' he answered.

As she mulled over his reply, her eyes slanted away. 'It seems everyone's starting to believe that's all it was about now, an affair, doesn't it? The theories of more dastardly elements appear to be dwindling.'

'Yes, they seem to be,' he agreed.

Her eyes came back to his. 'It's extraordinary that they haven't found her, isn't it?'

He nodded.

'Do you think she's dead?'

'I have no idea. Do you think she is?'

She shrugged. 'I have no idea either,' she responded. 'She was supposed to be spending a weekend at the house with me, but then it all happened, and I ended up inviting Gloria instead.' She sighed wearily. 'What a mistake that was,' she murmured. 'She keeps angling to come again, and I'm running out of excuses. That's why I thought maybe you might be able to help, by telling her how wonderfully she's doing, which she is, and kind of intimating that we don't need to do any more private rehearsals.'

'That shouldn't be a problem,' he assured her, taking the salad servers she was passing after stubbing out his cigarette again.

He was hoping that might be an end to Gloria, and that they could perhaps return to the subject of the erotic table, or some further analysis of her character, Anita Cairn, but as Stacey removed her apron, before climbing on to a stool the other side of the island, she said, 'I'm afraid she's started to become a little too intimate.' She spanned a hand over her breastbone and pressed it in tight. 'She holds her body against mine much longer, and even more closely than necessary, and during the kiss we shot yesterday she actually used her tongue. Now, I have no objection to anyone's sexuality, whatever it is, but since mine doesn't happen to be of that nature ... Well, I'm sure I'm telling you more than you need to know, and no doubt running the risk of making you respond the way most men do to the idea of two women together.'

His eyes remained on his plate as he served himself with salad. The image of her and Gloria embracing on the set was sharp in his mind, with an explicitness that had not occurred during the shoot. Was that why she'd said it? To let him know that she was happy for him to respond that way?

'Would you like to fuck me and Gloria together?' she said.

He looked up, his mouth turning dry as his head started slowly to spin.

She cocked her head curiously to one side. 'You did say medium rare, didn't you?' she smiled.

It was a moment before he nodded, then smiling too, he said, 'Yes. Perfect. Thank you.'

Picking up his knife he sliced off a small, succulent chunk of the meat. He knew very well that she hadn't said what he'd imagined, but he couldn't help wondering if it was the subtext to what she'd told him about Gloria. His erection was so hard he didn't dare to move.

'The flowers are beautiful,' she said.

He wondered if he should tell her they were Anna's idea, but decided not to, for to get Anna mixed up in this now could prove beyond disastrous. 'I'm glad you like them,' he said.

'Irises,' she murmured. 'Aren't they one of Ernesto's suggestions? I think for one of the poems about the Irish goddess, Macha.'

'To symbolize her close association with the soil,' he responded.

'And in the next she's racing against the horses of Conchobor, while pregnant.'

'That's correct.' He returned to his food, wondering what ideas Ernesto might have for showing her running with the horses, and pregnant.

'I sometimes like to ride naked on horseback,' she said softly.

His fork paused as the breath seemed unable to reach his lungs.

'I expect Gloria's told you that,' she said. 'She's told everyone else.'

Yes, he'd heard that, and yes she really was

186

saying these words, conjuring the image of her unclothed body, the motion of her hips and sway of her breasts as the wind streamed past her, her hair trailing behind like ribbons of fire.

'Is that how you'd like to see me for the poem?' she asked.

His throat was closed; his penis tighter than an angry fist. 'She's racing the horses, not riding them,' he finally managed.

'Of course,' she said, and lowered her eyes to her plate.

She continued to speak, but he was no longer listening. The table, the horse, Gloria – it had all suddenly become too much. He didn't want those images in his mind, for they were no longer imbued with the lustre of romance, or the benign playfulness of promise. Gone too was the illusion of superior minds and the exclusive understanding of artists, for the images he was seeing now were wholly degrading to her as a woman, whose beauty he revered, and whose friendship he cherished.

'I'm sorry,' he spluttered. 'I have to go.'

Her eyes widened with astonishment as he got to his feet. 'But you haven't eaten,' she protested. 'Robert! Are you OK?'

'No. I don't think so,' he answered, pressing his napkin to his mouth. 'I shouldn't have come. I – I . . . Please forgive me.'

'Robert!' she cried, going after him. 'Don't go like this. Please, tell me what I said . . . I'm sorry if it was wrong.'

When he turned back she almost gasped at his expression. 'It wasn't wrong,' he growled, 'it was exactly what I was thinking, hoping – that you

187

would offer to reveal yourself to me. But I'm afraid of it, don't you understand? I've never wanted a woman the way I want you. I look at you and see so much beauty that it tears right through my soul. Yet there's a monster inside me, a demon that makes me . . . No! Please don't touch me.'

'I'm sorry,' she said, pulling back. 'I – I don't know what to say. What can I do? I don't want you to leave like this.'

'Then what do you want?' he demanded, his eyes bright with the challenge. 'Tell me what you want.'

'That we should remain friends,' she replied. 'That we should try to work through this, whatever it is, and not let it come between us.'

How can we do that when all I want is to push you to your knees and thrust my cock into you so hard it'll make you scream, a voice inside him was snarling.

'I want to do it,' she said quietly. 'I really do.'

His eyes flew open with shock. Had he spoken aloud? Was she agreeing to his desire?

'I want to be a part of your project,' she said. 'Please don't shut me out.'

He stared at her, not knowing what to do, or say. His breath was laboured, his heart thundering in his chest. His cock was still hard, and she was so close. Too close. He took a step back, and found himself against a wall. 'I'm sorry,' he choked. 'I'm so sorry.'

'No, please, don't say that,' she cried. 'There's nothing to be sorry for. I'm flattered that you desire me. Truly.'

His head was moving from side to side, but he said nothing, for he knew, even before she did it, that she was going to put her arms around him.

And when she did he let her, wanting more than anything to inhale her powerfully female scent, while feeling the slenderness of her body pressing against his own.

'You know everything about me,' he said miserably into her hair, 'because you've reached into that place and become me.'

'Sssh,' she soothed, 'that's Arnie from the script speaking, not you. Not either of us. We're who we are. Separate, yet understanding of each other in ways that maybe other people don't quite comprehend.'

His hands were still hanging loosely at his sides. She'd acknowledged their special understanding, so maybe he should be saying something about it too, but he was afraid to make his mind work, in case those terrible images returned and forced him to act them out.

Finally, she pulled away to look at him, and without thinking he raised his hands to cover her breasts.

Her eyes continued to gaze affectionately into his.

'Doesn't that disgust you?' he said.

Her answer was to lean forward and press a kiss to his lips. 'Does that disgust you?' she responded.

His eyes closed as slowly he shook his head.

For a long time neither of them moved, as he cupped the soft mounds of her breasts, with their hard peaks pressing into his palms, until finally, folding his hands between her own, she said, 'We need to talk and it would be wrong for you to leave here before we do.'

Chapter 8

Laurie Forbes's ash blonde hair was gleaming in the sunlight as it fell in a fine, glossy bob to her shoulders, partially masking one of her lovely blue eyes. Her mouth was small, yet full-lipped, and her casual style of dress – distressed blue jeans and a black leather jacket – did little to dress down a very natural femininity. Indeed, the look was drawing more attention to her long, slender legs and surprisingly full bust than if she'd donned a slash neck and miniskirt.

She was sitting in the front garden of Rachel's cottage, barely registering the warm sea air and sunshine, as she studied the notes she'd taken during the past hour as Rachel filled her in on all she could. After a while she lifted her head to gaze out at the picture-postcard view, though it was clear from her expression that she wasn't really seeing it. Earlier, however, she'd been entranced by how dramatic the landscape was here, for she'd never been to Cornwall before, much less travelled down as far as the Lizard. She'd simply had no idea there were such wonderfully haunting expanses of moorland, or palm trees and pale sandy beaches, and so much sun on this small but magnificent peninsula that it might almost be Mediterranean. But despite the pleasure of the surprise, it was the vibrancy of the history that seemed to resonate throughout the shores like a living force that had moved her the most.

'You can just see the smugglers rowing to shore in the dead of night, can't you?' she'd murmured dreamily, gazing out at the evocative spectacle of a shimmering blue sea, pregnant with mystery, and rugged black cliffs that were pocked with shadowy caves and hidden trails. 'And the revenue men's horses thundering over the downs. The place is so full of secrecy and romance – I don't think I've ever been anywhere where the past feels so alive. It has to be haunted. It is, isn't it?'

Rachel had nodded, but didn't elaborate – there would be time later for the folklore.

Now, as she waited anxiously for Laurie to voice what she was thinking, and then, hopefully, to reveal what she'd managed to learn before coming here, she was feeling a profound relief at how easy Laurie had been to warm to, for it would be impossible to go any further if she weren't. Even so, she had to confess that Laurie wasn't quite what she'd expected, for the pictures she'd turned up on the Internet, and the interviews she remembered seeing at the time of the Ashby affair, had shown a much less worldly, even slightly awkward young woman. No doubt the Ashby experience, as well as the fame and the passing of time, had helped mature her, but for all the poise and subtle glamour she had attained in the past eighteen months, there was still an air of freshness about her that made her appear younger than her thirty years, and a guilelessness in both her smile and her eyes that, as a reporter, would be one of her greatest assets. People wouldn't only find her easy to open up to, as Rachel just had, but there would be no delayed horror at having said too much when she'd gone.

Finally, as she turned her ocean blue eyes to Rachel, her expression started to relax as she came out of the depths of her thoughts. 'OK, let's tackle the money first,' she began. 'It's true you have some good bargaining power there, but they're stymieing it by just giving instructions and not making any actual contact. However, I still don't think you should give it back too readily. We'll be in a better position to judge when the letter arrives. I take it there haven't been any more calls about it?'

Rachel shook her head.

'Then we just have to hope that they're not asking you to do anything too soon, or at least not before the letter has a chance to get here.'

Rachel's shrug belied just how worried she was about that. 'There's nothing I can do,' she said. 'They left no names or contact numbers.'

'Just a message on the machine in London, which suggests they don't know where you are – or didn't when they made the call. Do the police know you're here?'

'Yes.'

'Of course,' Laurie responded. Then after shrugging off her jacket and draping it over the back of her chair, Laurie said, 'Now to Katherine Sumner.'

Rachel immediately tensed.

'I've got several contacts in the States who're putting a profile together on her,' Laurie continued. 'We'll get to what they've found out so far in a minute, but for the moment, let's deal with her connection to Franz Koehler, because I'm certain that's where the crux of all this lies.'

Though Rachel agreed she said nothing, merely waited for her to continue.

'My initial chats with people in Washington were interesting,' she said, 'in that they more or less confirmed the relationship was over, at least on a personal level, but some of her friends and colleagues said they'd seen her with him several times since the break-up.'

Rachel was surprised.

'No one seemed to know him very well though,' Laurie continued. 'I got the impression he doesn't enjoy socializing.'

'Did you read what I emailed you about him?' Rachel asked.

Laurie nodded, and paraphrased the profile: 'Swiss businessman, living in Zurich, but with several other homes around the world. Personal fortune estimated at around five billion US; fifty-nine years old, divorced twice, not currently married, has an extremely valuable art collection, a doctorate in political science from Princeton, and another in social anthropology from the University of Berne. Not a bad bio, by anyone's standards, but it's when you start getting into the detail that it really gets exciting, particularly his early years in Africa when he was apparently keeping some very dubious company. I suppose it doesn't set him very far apart from a lot of intellectuals and radicals of his era, but considering who he is and what he does now, we can probably assume that a lot of seeds were sown at that time. Your email mentioned only that he's the founder and chairman of the Phraxos Group. How much do you know about the Group's activities?'

'I know it's a private equity firm with some ten billion dollars' worth of investments, mainly in the defence industries, and the kind of global reach that even BT might envy.'

Laurie nodded. 'And what about its stellar cast of senior executives? Are you familiar with that?'

Rachel's face was becoming strained as she said, 'I know that an ex-president of the United States is the chairman of Phraxos US, and that an ex-British prime minister is a senior adviser to the company in Europe. There are also ex-defence ministers from a handful of countries, policy advisers, a former secretary of state . . . Top executives who have come from the telecom or pharmaceutical industries . . .'

As she listened Laurie was tracking the flight of a red admiral as it flitted from the valerian growing along the wall to the recently planted pansies in the beds. 'A truly astonishing collection of power players, wouldn't you say?' she commented. Then, turning back to Rachel, 'Tim's name didn't come up during my search into the board members,' she said, 'but I can't say I really expected it to. However, if he *was* on the Phraxos payroll – and the fact that we've got four million dollars in a Swiss bank account makes it fairly certain that he was on someone's payroll – then it's probably not going to be easy to trace the connection, particularly when

194

his government position was current, rather than ex, as in the case of the other top officials.'

'Meaning?'

'Meaning that even the most indirect connection to an organization that makes such a vast profit from the manufacture and sale of arms and munitions would be totally forbidden, on any level, to a man in your husband's position, as you obviously know. It's a definite conflict of interests, and might even be illegal, I'll have to check. However, let's presume, for the moment, that there is a connection, that Tim did become a member of this elite group of investors. We can be certain that his status, or interests, would be extremely carefully disguised behind some kind of holding company, or in the directorship of some obscure subsidiary of an offshore affiliate. In fact the possibilities are endless, and as the police have all his papers and his computer, I'm not entirely sure where to start with that. However, I've got access to a red-hot research team, which I'll tell you about later, so we'll work it out. Now, what about the name Phraxos? Does it mean anything to you?'

Rachel looked surprised. 'Only in a literary sense,' she answered. 'It's what John Fowles renamed the Greek island of Spetses in his book *The Magus*, isn't it?'

Laurie seemed pleased with the answer. 'I wasn't sure if you'd read it,' she said, 'but since you have, don't you wonder if it tells us anything about Mr Koehler? Does he fancy himself as another Maurice Conchis, a raving megalomaniac, who, amongst other things, was a reclusive millionaire with a very impressive collection of art?'

'He also played some hellish games with people's minds – especially the main protagonist's,' Rachel commented. 'What was his name again?'

'Nicholas Urfe.'

Rachel nodded. 'It might be worth rereading the book.'

'It might,' Laurie agreed. 'But now let me give you what else I've managed to dig up on our friend, Mr Koehler. First, it turns out he was in London the day of the election, i.e., the day prior to the murder. He attended a meeting with some high rollers in the City, which ended around six, when he apparently returned to the Dorchester where he spent the night. The records show that he ate dinner there, and had an early check-out, around five the next morning, apparently to get a flight: but to where, or if he made it, are questions that still need answers, because checks with all the major airlines have so far turned up nothing. Of course a man of his means could very well have his own jet, and I'm working on that too.'

Rachel's chest was starting to feel tight. 'So if he left the hotel at five in the morning . . . Do you think . . . Maybe he *is* the other person the police are saying was in the flat.'

Though Laurie nodded, her expression was doubtful. 'He could be,' she responded, 'but apart from the shoe size being wrong, I just don't see a man in his position sullying his own hands with the business of murder. So no, if he is involved, I'd be more willing to believe that he was waiting downstairs to drive Katherine away after the deed was done. Did you know, by the way, that the police have interviewed him on three separate occasions?'

'I knew they'd spoken to him,' Rachel answered, experiencing another jolt of unease, 'but not three times. There hasn't been anything about it in the press.'

'Probably because after the initial obvious inquiries, they've kept the other two interviews under wraps. I found out through a very convenient family connection I happen to have inside the Yard.'

Rachel's face was pale. 'If they've spoken to him that many times then they must have found something on Tim's computer, or in his files,' she stated dully.

'Possibly,' Laurie responded. 'Or Koehler himself told them something during his first interview that they're following up on. Anyway, I'd say the real problem we're facing here is the Group's extremely complicated structure which makes it nigh on impossible to find out who's involved in the actual running of its operations, never mind who's on the boards of all its subsidiaries and affiliates and associates, or whatever they want to call themselves. The high-calibre players – pardon the pun – you mentioned just now are probably there, as much as anything, to give the company kudos, as well as to open doors to various corridors of power, for which they'll be handsomely rewarded. Do you recall anyone from the Group ever lobbying Tim, by any chance?'

Rachel shook her head. 'If they did, he never mentioned it, but maybe Katherine herself was doing it.'

'That's the most likely scenario,' Laurie agreed. 'There's no evidence at this stage of an order from the British Government going to a Phraxos-owned manufacturer, but it could very well have been in the works, which would be why they snapped up all his papers and computers so fast.'

Rachel's eyes drifted unconsciously towards Beanie's cottage. 'It just doesn't fit with his character,' she said, her voice seeming to echo in her ears. 'I mean, I know I'd say that, because I'm his wife, but if you knew how much he loathed that department . . . He was only there to try to force some transparency, to drag it into the twenty-first century, and he was resisted at every turn. So if there was something going on with any of them, some plan to put multimillion-pound orders in the way of Phraxos, I just can't believe he was involved.' Her eyes went down. 'Except the four million dollars tells me I'm wrong, doesn't it?'

'He could,' Laurie said, 'have stumbled upon the scheme and threatened to expose it.'

'That still doesn't explain the money,' Rachel responded.

'They did say it didn't belong to him,' Laurie pointed out, making another attempt to dilute the suspicion.

Rachel's eyes were barely focused as she watched a young cormorant perch on the wall, keeping its wings outspread to dry in the sun. She could feel the heat on her own skin, and the terrible chill in her heart, as she listened to the gulls screeching overhead and around the cliffs, to the low growl of the sea, the buzz of insects. She felt the distance of normality, and prescience of fear. Until, in the end, knowing that she had no choice but to voice what she was thinking, she said,

'The real and brutal truth behind an investment group like Phraxos is that it relies on conflict and war for its profits. In other words it *needs* civil unrest or rebellion or all-out military combat to create the million-dollar returns for its investors.' Her eyes closed as the horror of it seemed to fill up her heart. Surely Tim wouldn't have abused his position in such an unconscionable way, to profit from arms deals that were designed to stimulate a conflict, or keep a war going, rather than to end it.

Realizing she probably needed to lighten the load a little, Laurie said, 'That's the worst-case scenario. It might turn out not be anywhere near as bad as we're thinking, we just need to explore every avenue.'

Rachel's smile was small. She felt so over-whelmed by tiredness, and displaced from normality, that she wasn't sure whether she was reacting to the baby, or to the fact that she just couldn't bear to go where this seemed to be taking her. All those millions of refugees all over the world, the abuses of human rights, the starvation, the incalculable misery . . . For any company at all to reap any kind of profit from such horrors, never mind on such a scale, was, to her mind, immoral to the point of evil, and what made it even worse was the fact that those companies were legal. At least on the surface they were, but God only knew what went on behind the respectable façades of those organizations, what lengths they would go to to keep those multimillion-dollar defence orders rolling in . . . So if it turned out that Tim had been on a secret Phraxos payroll, part of some insidious scheme to generate revenue for the fat cat arms dealers and investors with total disregard for innocent lives, then maybe he deserved to be dead.

'We should know more once I've managed to get to the bottom of Franz Koehler's interviews with Special Ops,' Laurie said. 'I'll be interested to find out which particular branch it was, Intelligence, Anti-Terrorist, Protection, which includes Westminster and your friend Haynes, or some other section that might surprise us. I'm also trying to set up a meeting with the man himself. I've put in a call to his office in Zurich, but needless to say, no one's got back to me. At this moment in time, I can't even tell you exactly where he is, but that's just a temporary blip, because someone of his stature doesn't just vanish off the face of the earth.'

'Katherine Sumner's managed it,' Rachel reminded her. 'They could be somewhere together.'

'They could,' Laurie agreed. 'Though a spokesman for the Phraxos Group has announced in the US press that they're putting together a team of private detectives to help find her. That could, of course, just be a smokescreen – and frankly I'm inclined, right now, to think it is, but we can always re-evaluate later if need be.' Switching direction slightly she said, 'Tell me, do you know who reported the murder?'

A wave of dismay coasted through Rachel's heart. 'No,' she said, realizing that her failure to ask such a basic question at the outset showed how very much she needed Laurie's help with this.

'No, I don't know either,' Laurie said, 'which

bothers me, because I don't seem to be able to find out. But I will.'

Rachel turned to stare out to sea. It all felt so bizarre, so utterly unreal, to be sitting here, discussing such iniquity in the face of such beauty. It was like staring at a masterpiece, while the gallery around it was being massacred by madmen. Or like taking a last look at the wonderful wide world on the eve of the Apocalypse. She was feeling so alone, and afraid, that she wished she could just disappear into the vast blue beyond and never return. Then pressing her hands back through her hair, she said, 'I thought I was prepared for this, but it's so much worse . . . I can hardly take it in.'

Laurie's expression was full of sympathy as she watched Rachel's eyelids drop again, obviously to hide her pain. 'Like I said, we don't know anything for certain yet,' she reminded her gently.

Several moments elapsed before Rachel said, 'Did you ever meet him?'

'Yes, a couple of times actually, but I can't say I knew him.'

Rachel's heart was too full for her to say any more, so Laurie waited for the worst to pass, before saying,

'There is something we haven't discussed, which we probably should.'

Rachel forced herself to look up.

'It seems to have been known in advance,' Laurie said, 'that Tim would be going back to Katherine's flat that morning, so if the murder was pre-meditated . . .'

Rachel was shaking her head. 'Even Tim didn't

know he was going there,' she said, 'so it was impossible for anyone else to.'

Laurie started to press the point, then didn't. It was understandable that Rachel should still be in denial over that, so she said, 'OK, but we do know that even if it wasn't a prior arrangement, he did go into the flat willingly, because the chauffeur, who was driving them that night, swears there was nothing unusual about their behaviour when they got out of the car and went into the building.'

Rachel's eyes darkened. 'You've spoken to the chauffeur?' she asked huskily.

Laurie nodded.

'Did you ask if there was anything that appeared . . . intimate?'

'Yes, I did, and apparently there wasn't, or not that he saw. But obviously they'd have known he was watching, and since they didn't ask him to wait, we can only assume that Tim was intending to spend some time there.'

Rachel's face was white, her hands clutched tightly together.

'I'm sorry,' Laurie said softly. 'I just don't want to hide anything from you.'

'No, no,' Rachel said. 'Please don't do that.' Her eyes moved to the empty cups and plates on the table between them, and rather than think about what Laurie was telling her, she thought instead about how absurd the quaintly convivial ritual of tea really was. It conjured images of those who played music as ships went down, or prayed at the foot of an erupting volcano. What was the point, she wondered, for no matter the spirit, or faith, or how fierce the determination, disaster was still on the horizon, with fate guiding everyone inexorably towards it. *So what the hell was the point?*

'You must be tired,' Laurie said.

Rachel didn't respond.

'Rose told me about the baby. I hope that's all right.'

Attempting to pull herself together, Rachel said, 'Yes, of course. No, that's fine. In fact, maybe it could be your first exclusive in all this.'

Laurie smiled, and wondered how acceptable it would be to reach for Rachel's hand. Deciding it might not be appropriate this soon in their acquaintance, she injected as much warmth as she could into her voice, as she said, 'Thanks, but you don't want every Tom, Dick and Harry with a lens racing down here to take shots of you and your expanding waistline, so if I were you, I'd keep it a secret as long as you can. Does anyone in the village know?'

'Yes, Beanie, my next door neighbour. You'll have to meet her. She's quite a character.'

Laurie's eyes started to dance. 'Actually, I think I already have,' she said. 'Does she ride a motorbike, with her dog in a trailer?'

Rachel smiled. 'Yes, she does. When did you see her?'

'On the way here, as I was walking down from the car park. She chugged past me at about twenty miles an hour. Her name's on the back of her jacket.'

Rachel gave a quiet laugh. 'The motorbike belongs to her grandson,' she explained. 'She's looking after it while he takes a year off to travel the world, and he said she could use it. I don't imagine

203

he thought she would, but of course she is. Tim always said it was only a matter of time before someone made a trailer for Romie, the dog.' Her smile faltered, then forcing herself to go on, she said, 'Would you like some more tea before we go down to the pub? I'm sorry we didn't book the room in advance, we meant to, but other things came up. There won't be a problem though, there're hardly any tourists around at the moment.'

'Tea sounds fine,' Laurie replied, getting to her feet and stretching, 'but wine sounds better. I brought some with me, just in case. Anna put it in the fridge before she went out.'

As they walked round to the side of the house Rachel paused to pick up a watering can and put it under the tap, while Laurie gazed out to sea again, and gave a sigh of pure pleasure. 'I can understand why you'd want to come here to get away from it all,' she said. 'It's idyllic.'

Rachel looked out to sea too. 'Oh, here comes Zac and his multi-coloured dreamboat,' she smiled, pointing out the red, yellow and green vessel that was slowly bobbing its way coastwards. 'They call him that because he writes poetry and songs and sweeps all the girls off their feet when they come here on holidays. He's quite good, actually. My brother-in-law's helped him get a couple of things published in the past.'

'You mean Anna's husband, Robert Maxton?' Laurie said, following her into the old-fashioned kitchen, where hand-painted mugs of Cornish scenes hung from the overhead beams, and an assortment of herbs sprouted from clay pots on the windowsill. Two stainless-steel drainers opened like wings either side of a big square porcelain sink, while a small alcove behind the kitchen door housed the washing machine, raincoats and a collection of Wellington boots.

'Yes,' Rachel answered, taking the wine from the fridge. 'He writes poetry himself from time to time, which probably won't surprise you if you've seen *The Geddons.* He's devising some kind of an exhibition now, with Ernesto Gomez providing visual interpretations of the poems in the play.'

Laurie looked impressed. 'Certainly sounds like something worth seeing,' she commented.

'Could you pass me the corkscrew from the drawer in front of you?' Rachel said, pointing to a small pine chest that sat snugly between the stove and a corner.

'Isn't he turning *The Geddons* into a film at the moment?' Laurie said, passing the corkscrew over.

'That's right,' Rachel said. 'Anna's one of the producers, actually, which is why she can't spend as much time here as she'd like to.'

Laurie watched her as she tugged out the cork, then took a glass from a cupboard over the fridge. 'Aren't you having any?' she said. Then remembering, 'Oh no, I don't suppose you can.'

'I'm trying not to,' Rachel grimaced, 'but I can tell you it's been hard, because I've never wanted one more than in the past few weeks. And with only the very lowest dose of Valium and strictly no sleeping pills at all . . . Well, let's not encourage the self-pity,' and reaching into the fridge again she took out a large carton of tomato juice. 'My only vice,' she said. 'But Anna will join you when she gets back from Helston. She went to Tesco's to make sure I'm all stocked up before she returns to London.'

Laurie waited until they were both holding glasses, then after clinking she took a sip of wine, and said, 'I take it you won't mind me talking to your family about what's happened.'

'No, of course not. They're expecting it.'

'Does Tim have anyone?'

'No. He was an only child whose parents drowned in a boating accident when he was a boy, so his grandparents brought him up. His grandfather died about ten years ago, and his grandmother just five years ago. This was their cottage, actually. I always wished I had met them. Tim adored them.'

'So he grew up in Cornwall?' Laurie said, surprised.

'No. In London. His grandmother grew up here though, in this very cottage, so it's been in the family a long time. She moved to London when she married, so the place has really only been used as a holiday home since *her* mother died back in the thirties.'

Laurie looked around at the low, wooden ceilings, rugged stone walls and terracotta tiled floor. Opposite the stable door they'd come in through was another with a stained glass window and ornate brass handle that opened into a bathroom, and adjacent to that was an archway over a step down to the sitting room. 'If you don't mind me asking,' she said, 'what are you going to do with all your time while you're here? Apart from reread *The Magus*?'

'To be honest, I don't know how long I'll stay,'

Rachel answered. 'But I've promised myself a couple of weeks, at least, and the way I feel about London right now I wouldn't mind never going back. So, unless I get horribly lonely, I'll probably stay at least until I've sorted this place out, which is something Tim and I had been intending to do for ages. And though I blush to admit it, I'm thinking about writing a book. I know, everyone says that, don't they? I'd write a book if only I had the time. But my brother-in-law insists now is an excellent time, because, so he says, intense emotion can be very productive for a writer. And knowing him as well as I do, I have every reason to believe him.'

'He's an extremely talented man,' Laurie remarked. 'I wish I'd seen *The Geddons*. The reviews were glowing.'

'Yes, we're all extremely proud of him,' Rachel said. 'But talk to Anna, she'll tell you what a handful he can be, especially when he's going through one of his phases.'

Laurie looked surprised.

Rachel's tone was droll as she said, 'I'm told a lot of creative people go through them, so maybe that's what I've got to look forward to, if I do write a book – huge self-doubt, fear of losing my talent, or going unrecognized. In Robert's case, he's hardly got anything to worry about, when he has Anna behind him, and not only for moral and wifely support, because she produces his films, directs his stage plays, which is how they met, actually, while they were both at university where she directed his first play. She promotes him and his work, raises the finance for it all . . . She's amazing, because she does all of that while he whips up all manner of conflict and havoc in order to help himself create. It's probably all a sub-conscious thing, because when it's happening, she says, he truly seems to believe that he's going insane, or being possessed, or whatever. And then it all just calms down again and life goes on as normal.' The corners of her mouth went down in a grimace. 'Try living with that, two small children, a sister whose husband has just been murdered, and staying sane yourself.'

Laurie laughed. 'Well, she certainly looked it, when we met,' she said.

'She's a saint, and frankly I don't know what any of us would do without her.'

Laurie's smile turned almost wistful, and sad. 'That's what we used to say about my sister,' she said. 'And then we had to learn.'

Rachel's heart contracted. 'You're talking about your twin?' she said. 'The one who committed suicide?'

'That's the one,' Laurie said, adding, not without irony, 'You've obviously been doing your home-work on me too.'

'Of course,' Rachel admitted, 'that's what people like us do, isn't it? So I also know that you have a difficult man of your own to deal with. That's presuming you and Elliot Russell are still together.'

'Yes, we are,' Laurie replied, 'but I sometimes wonder why – or how. He's hardly been in the country this past year, which was why I was in the States, so I could actually get to see him.' She pulled a face. 'But you don't want to hear about that. You've got enough to think about. He knew your husband, did you know that?'

'I know they met a few times,' Rachel said.

'Mm, just a shame not more recently, otherwise Elliot might have been some help with this. He probably will be anyway. Certainly I'll be making use of his research team. They're the ones who helped crack the billionaire syndicate behind the Ashby affair.' As she finished they both turned at the sound of the gate banging open.

'Hi, I'm back!' Anna declared, coming to dump the shopping on the doorstep. 'Oh great, the wine's open. Pour me one, will you? I'm just going back to the car for the rest of the bags. Has Robert called yet?'

'No, not yet,' Rachel answered.

Anna immediately wheeled back. 'No?' she demanded. Then, glancing at her watch, 'I hope they haven't allowed him to go into overtime.' She pointed at the groceries. 'Those are the things for the freezer, so don't let them sit.'

Rachel looked at Laurie. 'You could be forgiven for thinking she's my mother, because believe me, she definitely sounds like her. In fact, that's why we didn't speak for almost a year, she just couldn't stop bossing me around, and one day I flipped. Now, I love it so much, I can hardly get through a day without it.'

Half an hour later, having left Anna trying to get hold of Robert, Rachel and Laurie wandered down the footpath towards the pub, passing a few neighbours on the way, whose mumbled greetings told Rachel that they were no less awkward with her now than they'd been two days ago. She wondered if Laurie was noticing their gruffness, but if she was, she didn't mention it, so Rachel didn't either.

Apart from a handful of tourists and Dapper, the landlord, who was chalking that night's menu on to a blackboard, the bar was empty when they walked in, so Rachel introduced Laurie to a few portraits of the heroes of the old Killian lifeboat that were hanging on the wood-panelled walls. She felt her mouth begin to water as Dapper hung the board and she read: Crab Salad, Lobster Thermidor, Monkfish with Lemon and Capers, and Hog's Pudding Pasty.

'Hi, Dap,' she said, when he finally put the chalk down. 'This is a friend of mine, Laurie Forbes. We'd like to book her a room for a couple of nights.'

Dapper's round face started to turn red, as his button eyes shifted off sideways. 'Got no rooms,' he grunted, starting to polish the pumps. 'Fully booked.'

Rachel felt her own face starting to colour, for it was such an obvious lie that she could hardly believe he was saying it. 'Are you sure?' she said. 'There don't seem to be many people around at the moment.'

'No. We're full,' he retorted, avoiding looking at Laurie as he finally directed his eyes defiantly at Rachel.

'Oh well, OK,' she said, angry enough to get into an argument, were she only emotionally equipped for it. 'Then I don't suppose we'll be having a drink either,' and turning to Laurie she said, 'Shall we go?'

Outside, on the terrace, Laurie put a hand on her arm and found she was shaking. 'What was all that about?' she said. 'There's a board in the window that says vacancies.'

'I know . . . I'm really sorry,' Rachel responded. 'I feel so embarrassed. But it doesn't matter, you should stay with us anyway. We've got the room, it just means three of us sharing a bathroom, if that's OK.'

'Of course it is. But don't you want to know why he said there were no –'

'No, please, let's just drop it. Where's your car?'

'Up the hill, in the car park.'

'Yes, of course. There's nowhere to park in the village. But you can probably squeeze it in next to mine, in the little clearing at the side of Beanie's cottage. Her motorbike and trailer don't take up quite so much room as the old Citroën she used to drive. And once Anna's car's gone there won't be a problem at all.'

As they walked on down through the village, along the top of the beach where sand and pebbles had been scuffed out on to the road, they passed half a dozen or more fishermen, standing around their boats, and several more villagers either going in or out of the small handful of shops that seemed to sell mainly postcards and handicrafts. All of them appeared almost hostile to their presence. In fact the atmosphere was so strained, and even strange, that Laurie wasn't sure she liked being here at all, for though everyone watched them, they were careful to avoid any eye contact, and the faint sound of whispering might have been almost comic had it not been so bizarre. Then, to her amazement, when she stopped to admire an assortment of hand-carved wooden boxes laid out on a table at the side of the gig house, the owner, and presumably artist, suddenly spread her hands over her wares saying 'It's not for sale.'

Laurie blinked. She hadn't even got as far as touching anything, so it wasn't possible to know what had taken her fancy. But she said nothing, merely followed Rachel on past Tucker's Crabbe Shoppe, up the hill towards the phone box that was at the road end of the todden, then into the narrow leafy lane that led up past the rose-covered chapel, until finally they climbed over the stile into the car park.

By the time they got there Rachel's distress, far from being under control, was pushing its way past her defences so that Laurie could see it was hard for her to speak.

'Please don't tell Anna about any of this,' she said, shakily. 'She'll only feel she has to stay, when I know she's worried about the film.'

'But what's it all about?' Laurie pressed. 'Surely they're not always like that? You wouldn't come here if they were.'

'No, of course they aren't. I just think . . . Anna thinks they're finding it hard to deal with what happened to Tim.'

'And you aren't? Anyway, they're Cornish. Half of them crew lifeboats, so for heaven's sake, if they don't know how to handle death, then no one does.'

'But murder's different. It has a stigma attached to it . . . Look, it doesn't matter. They'll come round, I know they will, and I have to stay because I just can't face going back to London right now. So please, not a word to Anna.'

It was a promise Laurie would have preferred not to make, for she'd have liked to hear Anna's take on what this strange behaviour was all about, but Rachel was obviously so worried about becoming even more of a burden to her sister that she had no choice but to agree.

Rachel smiled, obviously relieved. 'OK, so which is your car?' she said, looking around at the handful that was parked on the rough patch of ground.

Laurie grimaced. 'I'm afraid it's the Porsche,' she confessed. 'It's Elliot's. He's letting me use it, while he's in the States.' She looked around. 'Actually, it doesn't look quite as flashy as I'd feared, with these Range Rovers and Volvo estates. I thought the fishing industry was supposed to be in a decline. Or I guess they belong to the tourists we saw in the pub.'

'Probably,' Rachel answered.

'Which means,' Laurie said, pulling another face, 'we have to drive down through the village in this, with everyone staring at us the way they were just now.'

Rachel looked at her, then quite suddenly their eyes started to shine, and moments later they were laughing. 'The hell with it,' Rachel declared. 'Let them eat cake.'

Still laughing, Laurie pulled open the passenger door and waved Rachel to her seat. It was good to see her laugh, for it had brought some colour back to her face, and life to her eyes, though Laurie guessed it would be only fleeting. No doubt because of how all-consuming and debilitating her grief was Rachel was failing to see that the villagers' peculiar behaviour might not be quite as straightforward as she was presuming. In fact, Laurie wouldn't mind betting that it had much less to do with the stigma of murder than with the outside attention, as Tim Hendon's widow, that Rachel was bringing to the village. For there was no mistaking the fact that they didn't want Laurie here either – no room at the inn, no goods for sale – and for a village that surely must be even more dependent on tourism than it was on its catch, it just didn't make any sense not to want publicity, no matter how it was attained. So if she was right, and it was the limelight they were trying to avoid, then it quite naturally begged the question, what, in this quaint little piece of paradise, did they have to hide? And if she couldn't work that out, she had no business calling herself a reporter. However, it wasn't why she was here, so she'd just turn a blind eye and hope that time would prove they had nothing to fear from her, or more importantly, from Rachel.

Robert was pacing his study at home, tapping the blunt tips of his fingernails against his teeth, while casting anxious, fervid glances at the phone. In the room next door the girls were watching TV with Cecily, their nanny, the volume turned up too loud for him to work, but he wasn't going to complain. They should be in bed by now, but he wasn't going to do anything about that either – at least not until he'd made this call. He wanted it out of the way, off his mind, so that he could concentrate fully on his daughters as he read them a bedtime story and assured them that Mummy would be home soon –

though maybe not as soon as they expected. However, he wouldn't know that until he'd made the call, telling Anna not to worry about rushing back, to stay as long as she liked in Cornwall.

He looked longingly at the exquisitely crafted wooden box on his desk that contained a dozen fat cigarettes. Stacey had given them to him the night before last – a gift to commemorate the first of many precious evenings they'd promised to spend truly getting to know one another.

'And may each hour we share take us more deeply, more satisfyingly into each other's souls,' she had said, when she'd given him the box, and his hands had shaken as he'd taken it, for the desire to penetrate her fully, from every angle, in every place, for every moment, of every day, was as constant as the beat of his heart.

How desperately he wanted one of those cigarettes now to help him relax and feel convinced that everything was going to be all right. But no matter how strong the craving, he couldn't smoke dope while the girls were in the house.

He continued pacing. Back and forth. Back and forth. The dilemma was clashing around in his head, a deafening cacophony of vice against virtue, while his conscience retained full claim on his heart. Was it really only forty-eight hours since she'd pulled him back from the brink, and insisted he stay to talk? It seemed so much longer. But time's only relevance was in the knowledge that, from now on, nothing in his life would ever mean as much as the sacred moments he could be with her, holding her, touching her, feeling the tremulous whisper of her breath on his skin, the rhythm of her heart beneath his cheek as she cradled his head, the tearing ecstasy of joy as her eyes gazed so tenderly into his. He could see their cerulean beauty now, flickering with emotion, as he'd unburdened the might of his passion, and then he'd known the liquid lightness of relief as she'd told him she understood his need, and adored him for it. She even welcomed his love and rejoiced in his lust, for no one, she'd said, could put it into such words as he – words that were forming the poems for Ernesto to turn into art. And the demons that raged inside him, goading him towards acts of violence and obscenity, she was willing to embrace them too, in the hope of soothing, quieting and eventually conquering them, so that he no longer had to be afraid.

What a rare and sensitive woman she was. Had anyone ever shown a man such kindness, such faith? She had opened her arms to embrace him, and offered her face for his kisses, even though she felt no passion of her own, and was unable to give him her love. The agony of his unrequited madness was like a dagger in his heart, but one of creation not destruction, for when he'd returned home he'd sat in this room until dawn penning line after line of desperation, rage, ardour, and such rapture as he had never felt before in his life.

Then today, in her dressing room, after she'd read his verse, meant only for her eyes, she'd sent her assistant away so that they could be alone. She'd let him hold her, and kiss her, just as she had that night. She saw how it energized and inspired him, and how in turn his euphoria boosted the cast and crew. So the day had been a pleasure for them all, right up to the moment of leaving, when she'd smiled at him secretly across the set, making him feel they were as inextricable as dream and dreamer.

Now Ernesto had the poems and this weekend she would do her first sitting. He didn't know yet if he would be invited to watch, though he knew Ernesto intended to discuss his portrayals with them both before making his final decisions. He trembled with the excitement of seeing her disrobe for the portrait, of becoming the woman he had created in verse, whose lover was no more than a shadow. Could he be that shadow? Could it be his male form that covered her naked body, the ghost of his lust spreading over her breasts, her belly, and her thighs? Would he have the courage to suggest himself? Might Ernesto? Would she allow it? Or would she feel the intimacy to be too incendiary for his passion?

He should call her. He needed to ask the question, because he couldn't allow Ernesto to witness his rejection, should he have to suffer it. Would she mind him calling her now? She'd said he could, any time.

'Robert, darling,' her voice purred down the line. 'How are you?'

Already he was hard, and he knew that if she granted his request he would have no choice but to submit himself to the sublime humiliation of self-satisfaction.

She was still speaking. 'I'm so sorry, darling, but my husband has something here that needs urgent attention, can we speak in the morning?'

Hot colour flooded his face, as self-disgust

rushed like ice through his veins. 'Yes. Of course,' he mumbled, and dropped the phone as though it were a camera that might convey the truth of his misery. But disconnecting the call did nothing to cut him off from the images her words had evoked, for he could see her now, submitting to her husband in a way she never would to him. And even if it were only a document that needed signing, in his mind she was naked with her husband's hand on her bottom; or if it were a meal that was almost ready, she was cooking wearing only an apron; or if it were an injury that required tending, she would soothe it with her exquisite hands while his erection grew in anticipation of the same loving attention. So it would be her husband's shadow she'd want gliding over her naked body, his eyes absorbing her beauty ...

Jealousy was writhing in his chest like an awakening monster. He had to have her, he just had to. One kiss, one feel of her breasts, one deep and wonderful penetration. He pictured her, on her knees, looking over her shoulder with that wickedly sultry smile on her lips as he prepared to take her. A moment ago his erection had lost its might, but now it felt so big he could be Priapus himself, sitting in his chair, ripping open his trousers so that he could thrust the engorged organ of his lust into her lusciously open ...

His breath was ragged, his hands shaking as he dialled Rachel's number in Cornwall. 'Anna?' he gasped when she answered.

'Darling, yes. I was just about to call you.'

'Anna, come home. Please. You've got to come home.'

Chapter 9

Stacey was lying face down on a massage bed in the
stylish, white marble and granite bathroom
adjacent to the penthouse's master bedroom, where
her husband lay sleeping. It was just after nine in
the morning, and Petey had come round to give her
a massage before driving her to the set in time for
her eleven o'clock call. His hands were as good as
an expert's as he kneaded, pressed, pulled and
gently punched all the tension from her limbs,
while the fragrant oils permeated her senses in
other ways, so that she was being quite blissfully
lulled into a state of semi-sleep. This really was
such a perfect way to start the day, better even than
when her husband performed the massage, for the
touch of his hands never failed to arouse her, and
there were times, like now, when she preferred just
to relax.

But it didn't seem she would be allowed to this
morning, for this was the fourth time her mobile
had rung in the past ten minutes.

'Hello?' Petey said into the mouthpiece.

219

Stacey opened one eye to look up at him.

'Oh, I'm sorry,' he said, looking back at her, 'she's in the shower at the moment. Can I take a message? No. OK. Thank you for calling,' and he rang off. 'Gloria,' he told her.

Stacey groaned, and closed her eye. 'Actually, I won't be going down to the country for a while,' she said, almost happily, 'because the weekends are going to be tied up posing for Ernesto.'

'And Robert,' he reminded her.

She smiled tenderly. 'Yes, and dear Robert,' she said. 'Which reminds me, he called last night. I wonder what it was about.'

'I take it I'm invited to these weekend arty parties,' Petey retorted, raining little slaps on her back.

'Of course, darling, you're invited everywhere, you know that.'

'Except into the bathroom while I'm here,' her husband said, appearing in the doorway.

Stacey turned her head to look at him: the short black terry robe did nothing to disguise his magnificent physique. She inhaled deeply, then let it go in a murmur of pleasure. 'Darling,' she said. 'Good morning. Did you sleep well?'

'It's OK, you can stay,' he said to Petey, as his own mobile started to ring.

Back in the bedroom, he leaned across the low, king-sized bed to retrieve the phone from his nightstand.

'Gauguin, my man,' Rudy chirped down the line, 'not too early, is it?'

'Hardly,' came the reply. 'I wasn't expecting to hear from you for a couple of days.'

'Me neither. But a few things have come up I thought might interest you.'

Lying down on the bed, he folded a hand behind his head and listened.

By the time Rudy had finished he was back on his feet, standing at the vast picture window, staring down at the meandering grey strip of river that separated them from the cluttered roofs and soaring tower blocks of south London. He was frowning hard, for he now knew the reason why Franz Koehler had spoken to him about Rachel Hendon while they were in Florida, and he didn't like it – in fact he didn't like it one bit. It was much too close to home, which was why Koehler was using him of course, but proximity and personal connection – even at one or two removes – did not make it any more acceptable. If anything, it made it totally abhorrent.

Feeling his wife's arms sliding round his waist, he turned to take her into a loose embrace. She was wearing only towels, around her body and her hair, and her skin looked flushed and tender after her invigorating massage.

'Was that Rudy?' she asked.

He nodded.

'And what is he calling you today?'

He had to think for a moment, then it came back to him. 'Gauguin,' he answered.

She smiled and so did he.

'I've been meaning to ask you,' she said, gazing directly into his eyes, 'the little item I heard on the news, a few weeks ago, about an incident at an airfield in Zurich, was that anything to do with you, by any chance?'

His eyebrows went up. 'Why on earth would you think that?' he responded.

Her eyes remained intently on his, then laughing delightedly she twirled out of his arms and flung her towels on to the bed. 'I simply can't imagine,' she said. 'What a very silly thing for me to think.'

Which indeed it was, for she had no reason in the world to connect him with that, other than the fact that he'd been in Switzerland at the time. But it was a game she liked to play, pretending that he was some kind of mobster, or hit man, a gun runner, or smuggler of precious art – it didn't matter, as long as it was criminal and involved a lot of money. It added an extra *frisson* to their lovemaking, she claimed, to think she was giving herself to a man with no scruples, a villain who could be wanted by the police, a sociopath who might turn violent at any moment. And he certainly wasn't going to deprive her of the thrill, for it was as erotic to him as it was to her.

'So what did Rudy want?' she said, half an hour later, as they lay side by side on the bed, with Petey still hiding in the bathroom. 'Please don't tell me you're going away again yet.'

His eyes remained closed as he reached for her hand. 'How can I, when I'm taking my beautiful wife to dinner tonight?'

She smiled and rolled against him. 'Will you be Gauguin, or shall we invent someone new?'

He thought for a moment, then said, 'We could just be us.'

Her eyes narrowed as she regarded him suspiciously. 'Does that mean you're getting tired of our games?'

'That's like asking me if I'm tired of living,' he responded with a laugh, 'and married to you, that's just not possible.'

Pulling his mouth down to hers she kissed him lingeringly. 'I have everything in you,' she told him softly: 'a boss, a beast, a friend, a lover and even a romantic.'

'But slave and voyeur we'll leave to your friend in the bathroom,' he said, as something smashed into the sink, and finally remembering Petey, they burst out laughing.

'This is making for some fascinating reading,' Laurie commented, her eyes riveted to the printout of an email she'd received a few minutes ago, containing a profile of Katherine Sumner.

Engrossed in her own copy of the email, Rachel didn't look up. Her muscles were tight, as though she was tensing herself for a blow, but as yet nothing had come up to alarm, or even upset her. But that wasn't to say it wasn't there, waiting, either on the page, or lurking in the subtext, as if each word was a shadow, and each new sentence a corner for some appalling truth to hide behind.

They were in the long, low-ceilinged sitting room of the cottage, seated either side of the dining table that was pushed up against the wall of the wood-panelled stairwell. The windows and doors were open, as it was still mild outside, despite the rain that had drenched them earlier while they walked along the cliffs to Kennock Sands. The clouds were gathering again now, turning the sky a dramatically leaden purple, and exciting the seagulls to a frenzied chorus of screeching.

'Here's all the stuff about her father being shot in Iran,' Laurie murmured. Then a few seconds later, 'It doesn't sound as though her mother was very happy with the investigation into the shooting.'

'It seems to have dragged on for years,' Rachel commented. 'Used up all the family funds and drove the mother to drink. What a life, because she has Alzheimer's now.'

'Tragic about the brother too,' Laurie murmured. 'I wonder why he did it.'

Remembering Laurie's sister, Rachel glanced up, but Laurie was still reading.

'She certainly has an eclectic bunch of friends,' Laurie remarked. 'They seem to be from all political persuasions, and quite a diversity of nations.'

'Obviously from all the travelling she's done,' Rachel remarked.

Laurie made some notes, then almost simultaneously they turned over to the second page.

A moment or two later Laurie said, 'Did you know she went to Stanford?'

Rachel nodded. 'Sounds as though she was a bit of a radical – all these marches, and sit-ins, and protests she was involved in.'

'What about this affair with a married senator?' Laurie said. 'Did you know about that?'

'Yes. He's not a senator any more. He's got some kind of top level job at the Pentagon.' Her heart sank as she said it, for it proved another connection to a defence department. 'I'm sure it'll say here somewhere.'

'Yes, here it is,' Laurie said. 'Patrick J. Landen. Senior official at the Pentagon during the Bush Senior era. Now serving as a senior executive in the

Department of International Defense Strategy.' She looked at Rachel. 'How ominous is that?' she said darkly.

Rachel shook her head, and trying to overcome the quaking in her heart, she went back to the email. 'It says here that he and Katherine have "remained in contact, despite their differing political affiliations,"' she read. 'He's also been interviewed by the FBI since Tim's death, but there doesn't seem to be anything here about what was discussed.' Her unease was becoming more acute than ever.

They carried on reading to the end of the page, and once again flipped over almost simultaneously.

'Oh God, here we have it,' Laurie murmured. 'The relationship with Franz Koehler; the political campaigns she managed during the four years she knew him; Koehler's chairmanship of the Phraxos Group; the hobnobbing with senior executives of arms and munitions dealers, social engagements with high-ranking US military . . . It's all there. And who's this?' She frowned. 'Someone called Xavier Lachère, with a question mark after his name.'

Rachel read the next paragraph aloud. '"This name came up a couple of times, talking to her friends,"' it said. '"No one seems to know who he is, exactly, but apparently she talked about him as someone she could trust. 'Sometimes he feels like my only true friend in the world,' was what she told one roommate when they were back in college, but she was still talking about the guy as recently as January this year, when she announced she was leaving Washington, and told Gillian Fowles (see above, friend and news anchor for ABC affiliate) that one of the best parts of going to Europe was that she'd be closer to Xavier."' Confused, Rachel looked at Laurie.

'She obviously never mentioned him to you,' Laurie said.

Rachel shook her head, then looked down at the page again.

'The name sounds French,' Laurie said. 'Or maybe Belgian. He could be someone she met at Stanford, if she was talking about him back then. I'll ask Max to check the records,' she added referring to the sender of the email.

'I wonder if the police know about him?' Rachel said.

'I think we can assume they do,' Laurie answered. 'If her friends are telling Max, then why wouldn't they tell the police too?'

They read on through more details of the Phraxos Group and the many companies it owned, either in part or outright. Rachel felt certain she was about to be slammed with some terrible connection that she hadn't, even in her worst nightmares, begun to consider. 'Here's the link between Franz Koehler and Patrick J. Landen,' she said, pointing to a spot near the bottom of the page. 'It says, "Koehler and Landen have continued to meet frequently, despite Landen's *resignation from the Phraxos board,*"' she glanced at Laurie, '"in January of 2002. Landen is also known to be an occasional visitor to Koehler's luxury homes in Florida, Locarno, the French Riviera, and . . ."' Her eyes froze on the next few words, as the blood seemed to stop in her veins, '"the British Virgin Island of Gorda."' She felt suddenly light-headed and nauseous.

'What's the significance?' Laurie asked, watching her closely.

'Tim and I were due to go there, straight after the election,' she answered croakily. 'We were staying in a private villa.'

Laurie's face showed her dismay. 'Do you know who owned it?' she asked.

'No. But I think Katherine was the one who suggested it.'

'Who made the arrangements?'

'Actually, I did, after Tim gave me the contact details. But I was dealing with an agency, or a manager, not the owner.'

'Do you think Tim knew who the owner was?'

'I don't know. I never asked. I mean, we've often rented villas through agents without knowing who actually owns the place.' She was looking at the email again, though hardly seeing what was written there now.

'What about the other places where it says Koehler has homes?' Laurie said. 'Locarno. Florida. The Riviera? Has Tim ever been to any of them? Are you OK?' she said, noticing how haunted Rachel looked. 'Are you feeling sick again?'

'It's OK.' She took a breath. 'He's been to Florida and the Riviera,' she said, 'but I was with him, and each time we stayed at a hotel.'

'Do any of these hotels in Africa ring a bell?' Laurie asked, going back over some of the places Katherine had visited, with Koehler, in the past four years.

'We've been to Nairobi and Cape Town, but none of the others,' Rachel answered, closing her eyes as another wave of nausea swept through her.

She got up and went to sit in one of the window seats, where the cooling breeze wafted in the scent of roses along with the pungency of the day's catch. 'Tell me about Max Erwin, who put all this together,' she said. 'Do you know him personally?'

'He was an integral part of the Ashby story,' Laurie replied. 'He went undercover and got right inside the billionaire syndicate, to the point that I doubt we could have fully cracked it without him. Elliot's with him at the moment. They're working on another project that's so secret even I don't know all the details, which is why it's taken a few days for Max to get back to me on this. But what I do know is they've spent a lot of time in Africa this past year, and that's the continent that appears to keep coming up here.'

Rachel was feeling so weighed down by everything that she wanted only to sleep. But somehow dredging up some energy, she said, 'Well, their contacts should certainly be helpful.'

Laurie smiled, then realizing Rachel needed some time to regroup, she went back to scan the email again, making notes of the most salient points.

'OK?' she said finally, looking up to make sure Rachel was ready.

Rachel turned to look at her, and nodded.

'All right. The points of most interest to us here,' she said, 'are, (a) that Katherine Sumner, a known Democrat now, was apparently a radical right-winger back at college when she had an affair with a right-wing senator. Spin forward a decade or so and her political allegiance has swapped sides, yet her association, or relationship, with the

Republican senator is suddenly back on again, though now he's a senior official at the Pentagon.'

She glanced over at Rachel, who was staring absently out of the window, but clearly listening. 'Next,' Laurie continued, 'we have the mysterious Xavier Lachère, whom she's known for at least fifteen years, who it seems lives in Europe, and who – I've only just thought of this – could turn out to be the unidentified visitor to the flat, which means he could even be the owner of the semen on the sheet.'

The mere mention of it sent Rachel's heart into free fall. Her eyes closed, for everything seemed so much more complex and crowded with people now that she almost felt lost in the mêlée. Her hand went to her head, as a frightening vision of Tim, mocking her from inside a mass of strangers, felt strikingly, and hideously real. But it passed, leaving her with an image of him trying to reach out and grab her, as though pleading with her to save him from being swept away by the crowd.

'We have to find this Xavier Lachère,' she said.

Laurie picked up her mobile.

'It won't work here,' Rachel reminded her.

Putting it down again, Laurie reached out for the land phone. 'I need to speak to Elliot's researchers,' she said. 'If anyone can dig out information on this Xavier fellow, they can. And while they're at it, I'll get them to put some pressure on their contacts in the force, to find out if anyone there knows the man exists. I'm willing to bet a great deal that they do, though why they've never mentioned him to you, or why even keep his name a secret . . .' She indicated for Rachel to look behind her. 'The postman,' she said, as he came in through the gate.

Rachel's heart plummeted into yet another black hole of dread. She was afraid of all communication now, because no news ever seemed good. 'Over here, Reg,' she called, as the postman magicked a biscuit from his pocket and tossed it back over the gate to Romie.

'Bit of a handful here today,' he said, trudging across the lawn to the window as he dug into his bag. 'Looks like rain, too, and your washing's still on the line. Just in case you forgot.'

'Thanks,' she smiled, taking the letters. 'I'll go and get it in.'

'Anna gone now, is she? I noticed her car wasn't there.'

'She left first thing this morning.'

'Nice Porsche,' he said, peering in at Laurie. 'I expect that's yours, is it?'

'Oh, yes. Well, my boyfriend's, actually.'

'Good cars. Our Jason's thinking about getting himself one. Second hand, like. Three years old. That's my nephew. You know Jason, don't you?' he said to Rachel.

'Of course,' she said. 'And his family. Please say hello from me next time you see them.'

'Oh they're down in the cove all the time, now they've moved back into the village,' he told her. 'Managed to buy back our old gran's house, they did, so you'll probably see them before I do. Anyway, got to get on. Tell Beanie that dog of hers is getting fat.'

'Because you keep giving her biscuits,' Rachel chided.

She watched him walk back to the gate, holding the mail in her hand and desperately not wanting to look at it. Such a bunch could only mean that it had been forwarded from London.

'At last a friendly face,' Laurie commented, when she was sure Reg was out of earshot.

'He doesn't live in Killian,' Rachel said. 'He lives in Lizard. Maybe that's the difference.' She looked down at the letters, then leafed carefully through. 'Oh my God,' she murmured, drawing out a long white envelope that bore no markings other than her typewritten London address. 'This could be it.'

At that moment Laurie got through to Elliot's office, but instantly disconnected. Experiencing probably only half of Rachel's nerves, she watched as Rachel opened the letter.

'Yes, it is,' Rachel said, putting a hand to her head as she leaned back against the wall. A sudden rush of bile rose to her throat, and dropping everything she made a quick dash to the bathroom.

Picking up the letter Laurie read the few typed lines, then sat down on the sofa to wait, feeling her own senses responding to all that was happening here, for it was turning out to be much bigger, and infinitely more dangerous, than she'd expected. She knew she'd have to discuss it with Elliot, for there was probably no one more suited to dealing with something so entrenched in politics, arms deals and high-level corruption than he; she just had to make sure that she wasn't using it to put off facing the problems in their relationship, which she'd been doing for too long.

'I'm sorry,' Rachel said, a few minutes later as she came back into the room, dabbing her face with a towel. 'I thought that was all over with, and now today it's happened twice.'

'Would you like some water?' Laurie offered.

'No. I've just had some, thanks.' She looked at the letter in Laurie's hand. 'What does it say?' she asked, feeling light-headed again.

Laurie lifted it up and read aloud. ' "Transfer of funds to be made by July the second from your account to," then we have the details of another bank, also in Zurich,' she finished.

'No names?' Rachel asked, swallowing hard. 'Or contact details?'

Laurie flipped the single page over. 'Nothing,' she said. Her eyes went back to Rachel's. 'The second is next Friday. That gives us the weekend and maybe Monday to decide what to do, if we allow three days for the transfer.'

Rachel's insides were in chaos. She had no idea what she wanted to do now the letter was here. The prospect of clashing with someone as powerful as Franz Koehler was becoming too horrifying even to contemplate.

The phone rang, making her jump.

For a moment they both stared at it, then pulling herself together Rachel said, 'It'll be Anna, letting me know she got back all right,' and picking up the receiver she said, 'Hello?'

'Hi. Is that Rachel?'

It was a male voice she didn't recognize, but there was no discernible foreign accent. 'Yes,' she answered, turning to look at Laurie.

'It's Elliot Russell here,' he told her. 'Is Laurie still with you?'

'Oh yes. Yes. She's right here.'

After handing the phone over, Rachel left them to speak privately and went outside to start taking in the washing. To her dismay, she was so close to tears that she wasn't at all sure she'd be able to hold them back, or indeed finish the task at hand, for she was already clinging to the sheet she'd taken from Anna's bed, as though it were her sister herself. She loved Robert, absolutely adored him, but she *wished* he wasn't having one of his crises right now.

Pressing the sheet tighter to her face, she struggled even harder to fight back the tears. Perversely, it wasn't the email or the letter that was pushing her over the edge, but the phone call from Elliot Russell, for it was hearing his voice, asking for Laurie, just like Robert's when he asked for Anna, that reminded her Tim would never be asking for her again. It was strange and cruel the way those little things crept up on her, and they did all the time. Maybe she was going to need more than just a few moments to get herself together, because the despair was suddenly so black and overwhelming, that she was starting to sob, and right now it felt as though she might never be able to stop.

When Laurie came outside some five minutes later, it was to find the washing half collected in the basket, and no sign of Rachel. She looked around, then finally spotted her, at the very tip of the headland, sitting on a grassy bank next to the tiny hewer's hut, staring out to sea.

Laurie's heart went out to her, for she could only begin to imagine how terrible her inner torment must be. She guessed, too, that it might have been the call from Elliot that had finally tipped her, for she remembered only too well just how awful it was when friends received calls from the men who loved them at times when she had no one. Not that it could be compared to the agonizing loss Rachel was having to deal with, it was simply that Laurie understood, and almost wished she could tell her, that the call truly wasn't one she'd have wanted.

Deciding to leave her in peace for a while, Laurie went back inside and curled up with her notepad and the email in the window seat. The view down over the small bay was restricted from here, but she could still see the dramatic rise of the headland opposite as well as several cottages that sprawled up over the hillside. Not wanting to think about Elliot, she found her mind veering away from the email too, as she reflected on what she'd learned about this tiny fishing cove in the past couple of days: which was that there was undoubtedly some kind of smuggling operation going on. There had to be, for them to be able to afford the cars and expensive coastal cottages whose prices had been vastly inflated by Londoners buying them up as holiday homes. In fact, considering what a hard time it was for fishermen all round now, she really didn't blame them for trying to supplement their incomes, she just hoped it was only booze and cigarettes from across the Channel, and nothing more exotic from further afield, though she rather suspected it was, given the amount of money they seemed to be making. The real problem, however, at least as far as Rachel was concerned, was how leery they were of having her in their midst when her circumstances made her such a magnet to the very people the locals were trying to avoid, the police and the press. It was clearly why they were snubbing her, trying to force her out, for they were understandably afraid that she was going to jeopardize their newfound livelihood.

Noticing that the rain had started again, and remembering the washing, she leapt up from the window seat and ran outside to finish bringing it in. By the time she'd dumped the basket on a draining board, and turfed out an umbrella, it was threatening to turn into a downpour, so grabbing her leather jacket and a large plastic raincoat from a peg in the washing-machine niche, she set out along the footpath to where Rachel was still sitting, staring out at the darkening sky and swelling, grey sea.

'Here,' Laurie said, putting the raincoat around her.

Rachel smiled, and drew the back of her hand across her eyes. 'Sorry,' she said. 'I just needed to be alone for a while.'

'Please, don't apologize,' Laurie insisted. 'I'll go again now, I just wanted you to keep dry.'

'No, I'll come with you,' Rachel said, getting to her feet. 'I can't sit here for ever willing him to come back.' Her red-rimmed eyes met Laurie's and she forced a smile again. 'Come on,' she said, hooking Laurie's arm. 'I've been a terrible hostess since you arrived, so let's forget about everything else for a while and go and brave the village for a coffee. There's a nice little place next to the pub, where they used to take all the pilchards for pressing and salting, back in the eighteen hundreds. Then maybe we can take a walk on the beach and have a look at the boats. Or stroll up to the Devil's Frying Pan. That's always worth seeing.'

As they started back down the footpath the rain was already beginning to ease off, and by the time they reached the cottage it had stopped altogether. 'We should pop in and get some money,' Laurie said, as Rachel made to go past.

Rachel stopped, then turned to follow her inside. 'I didn't think about money,' she confessed, as they went in through the kitchen. 'We never used to while we were here. If we didn't happen to have any on us, we'd always pay later.' She was staring blindly down at the emails, still spread out on the table. 'I don't suppose I should rely on that now.'

Laurie was about to answer when someone knocked on the open back door.

'Hi,' he said, as they both looked round. 'Mrs Hendon? Rachel?'

Rachel frowned, not quite able to see the man with the sunlight glaring behind him.

'Chris Gallagher,' he said, introducing himself. 'I live over by Kynance Cove. I met your husband a few times, and I heard you were here. I wanted to offer my condolences, if it's not too presumptuous.'

'No, no, not at all,' Rachel said, glancing at Laurie. 'Uh, please, come in.'

He stepped up into the shade of the kitchen and Laurie almost felt her jaw drop, for though the voice had certainly been deep and alluring, she hadn't expected anyone quite as attractive as this. Indeed, with his beautifully chiselled features, jet black eyes and eyebrows, and mop of silvery black hair, he was so good-looking that she could almost

236

feel herself blushing at the way her basic feminine instincts were responding to the strong sense of his maleness.

'I-I'm sorry,' Rachel stammered, 'what did you say your name was?'

'Chris Gallagher,' he repeated, holding out his hand to shake. 'I hope I'm not barging in at an awkward time. I was just down at the beach, and I saw you up here . . .'

Rachel looked at his hand, then back at him as she took it. 'Have we met?' she asked.

The warm texture of his eyes seemed to deepen as he smiled. 'No, I don't believe so,' he answered. 'But I've read a lot of your op eds in various newspapers, and I have to admit, I'm quite a fan.'

She was still looking at him, then becoming aware that it was time to let go of his hand, she withdrew her own and tried to think of something to say.

'Each time I ran into your husband,' he said, 'you never seemed to be around. Actually, I was with him when he commissioned that painting, from Nick Cormant.' He nodded towards the watercolour of the cove that was hanging on the stairwell wall. 'It was for your birthday, he said.'

Rachel swallowed, and nodded. Then suddenly remembering her manners, she said, 'I'm sorry, this is Laurie Forbes, a – friend of mine.'

He turned his darkly magnetic eyes on Laurie, and took her hand. 'Being a bit of a news junkie,' he said, 'I confess I already know who you are.'

'Please don't believe all you hear,' she warned, then immediately felt foolish, despite his laugh. It was amazing, she was thinking, just how profound an effect he was having, and not just on her, she was sure of it, for Rachel definitely seemed flustered too. Then quite suddenly they were saved by a whirlwind appearance from Beanie.

'Chris Gallagher! Is that you?' she demanded, charging up the garden path. 'Yes, it's you!' she squealed with delight, as he turned to greet her. 'I thought I saw you go past.'

'Beanie!' he laughed, stepping out into the garden and swinging her round like a child. 'Did you think I'd forgotten you?'

'I know you never would,' she crowed happily. 'Oh, it's so good to see you. Give me another hug.'

Still laughing, he embraced her again. 'It's only been a fortnight,' he reminded her. 'I wasn't gone long.'

'It's always too long for me,' she said, flirtatiously. 'And now I hear that you're going to be singing with Zac in the pub tomorrow night.'

'I am?' he cried in surprise.

'Oh, yes,' she assured him. 'He's written some new tunes, and lovely they are too.' To Rachel and Laurie, she said, 'This man here has got one of the best voices this side of Truro. He's even better than Wilson and Foggie.'

Laurie's face was a picture. 'Than who?' she said.

Both Chris Gallagher and Rachel laughed. 'Wilson and Foggie,' Chris informed her, 'are the ghosts who sing in the cove on dark winter nights, and warm summer nights too, come to that.'

Laurie looked at Rachel, whose eyes were dancing, then back to Chris. 'You're kidding, right?' she said.

'Uh-uh,' he replied, shaking his head and looking at Rachel.

'Uh-uh,' Rachel echoed.

Laurie rolled her eyes. 'All right, I'll go for it,' she said. 'So who are they? Or perhaps I should be saying, who *were* they?'

'They're a couple of fishermen who used to live here – and stumble out of the pub on Saturday nights to sing in the cove,' Beanie told her. 'Excellent tenors, both. Fill your heart right up, they did. Still do.' She turned back to Chris, 'So we shall expect to see you. Eight o'clock. I'll let Zac know, unless you see him yourself,' and without so much as a by your leave, she went beetling off again.

Chris was still laughing, and his smile, Laurie decided, should be licensed, or rationed, or whatever was needed for something that was so devastatingly effective. 'So, I hope you ladies will be there too,' he said.

'We wouldn't miss it,' Laurie assured him, jumping in before Rachel could protest.

But Rachel did anyway. 'I'm afraid I might spoil it,' she said, surprising Laurie with her frankness. 'No one's very comfortable with my presence at the moment, and I don't want . . .' She stopped as he began shaking his head.

'Just leave that to me,' he said. 'I've got a pretty good idea what the problem is, so it should be all sorted out by tomorrow.'

Rachel looked at him in surprise, though Laurie could see that her cheeks were reddening. 'But I think it's about Tim and –'

'Don't worry,' he told her gently. 'I promise. It'll all be all right by tomorrow.'

Rachel and Laurie stood watching him as he walked away, their eyes following him down the footpath, their minds going in a thousand different directions.

'Who on earth is he?' Laurie finally managed.

'Chris Gallagher,' Rachel answered. Then pulling herself together, she said, 'Very good looking, isn't he?'

'Really?' Laurie responded. 'I hardly noticed.'

As they both laughed, and turned back into the house, Rachel caught a glimpse of herself in the small, beech-framed mirror. 'Well, don't I look a picture?' she said, grimacing at her red-rimmed eyes and blotchy face. 'I think I'd better go and do something about myself before we go for that coffee.'

Still smiling, Laurie returned to the sitting room to start tidying up the table. Further discussion of the email and letter could wait for a while, though she was willing to bet that not more than another hour would pass before they'd be fixating on them again. So why not just enjoy this small respite of an attractive new neighbour arriving just when Rachel needed him most, for if he really could make things easier with the locals, he would be a godsend indeed.

'I just can't imagine how you've managed to miss him until now,' Laurie commented, as they strolled into the cobbled courtyard of the Caves, where a young waitress was serving a couple of tourists with a traditional Cornish tea. 'Beanie's obviously mad about him.'

'Beanie's mad about everyone,' Rachel responded, picking up a menu.

Laurie picked one up too. Perusing it, she said, 'I wonder what he does?'

Rachel shrugged.

'He wasn't wearing a wedding ring.'

Rachel's eyes widened as she lowered the menu to look across at Laurie.

'I'm just saying, he wasn't,' Laurie told her.

Rachel's eyes were shining with laughter. 'I thought you and Elliot . . .' she began.

'We are, and . . . I just noticed, that was all.'

'A lot of married men don't wear wedding rings,' Rachel warned, though teasingly.

'I know. I just . . . Tell you what, let's just order, shall we?' Laurie said, laughing, though wishing she'd never got into this, for she'd actually been thinking about Chris Gallagher as a much-needed friend for Rachel, not her.

'So back to the money, and the letter,' Rachel said, after the waitress had taken their order. 'I've been wondering, what do you think might happen if I just don't make the transfer?'

Laurie's expression became sober.

Rachel continued. 'I mean, harming me in any way isn't going to get them the money, is it?' she said. 'It'll just create some unwelcome press, and police, attention when we make the matter public.'

'Do you want to do that?' Laurie said. 'Make it public?'

'Not yet. I want to find out what it's all about first, and while the money's still there, we've still got our bargaining power.'

Laurie waited as the waitress set down a cappuccino for her and a herbal tea for Rachel, with a small plate of home-made biscuits. 'Would you mind me discussing it with Elliot?' she said, when the waitress had gone. 'I'd like to get his opinion.'

'No, of course, not,' Rachel assured her. 'I was hoping you might. Presumably he already knows about the email Max Erwin sent, if he's with Max now?'

'Presumably,' Laurie agreed. 'But he didn't mention it when he called. He just wanted to ask me to do a couple of things for him before he comes home, and to know if I was going to be back in London in time to pick him up from the airport.'

'Will you?' Rachel asked.

'Probably. He's flying in on Tuesday. I was planning to drive back on Monday.'

Rachel's eyes dropped to her tea. Saying goodbye to Laurie might just prove even harder than saying goodbye to Anna, because once Laurie went, she'd really be on her own. But there was always Beanie, and if this Chris Gallagher really could make it all right with the villagers by tomorrow night, there would be everyone else too. It seemed a very tall order, getting everyone over their embarrassment and prejudice that quickly, but he'd sounded confident enough, so maybe she should just have faith. Yes, why not? Just believe he could do it, if for no other reason than she needed to believe that something was going to go right somewhere in her life, because God knew everything else seemed to be going very disastrously wrong.

Chapter 10

It was now thirty-six hours since Anna had arrived back to find the house empty, and a note from Cecily saying she'd taken the girls to their music club. Robert was still on the set, shooting, though he rang immediately they wrapped to check she was home. He'd sounded calm, pleased to hear her voice, and not in the least like the man who'd called, so desperate for her to come. And their reunion, when he'd finally returned from rushes, had been both tender and passionate, with an assurance to his lovemaking that bore no signs of the self-doubt or paranoia that occasionally rendered him impotent.

Afterwards, Anna had fallen almost instantly into a deep and dreamless slumber, only to wake with a start around two in the morning to discover the bed empty beside her. Going downstairs, she'd found, more or less, what she'd expected: a light shining from under his study door, with the occasional laboured breath or grunt that was the general sound of Robert working. Before disturbing him she went to make tea, then without tapping on the door, for he'd surely heard her around by now, she walked into the study and almost jumped as hard as he did when he looked up to find her there.

'What are you doing?' she'd asked, smoothing over the surprise with casual interest as she put his tea on the desk. His cheeks were flushed, and his eyes seemed guilty, which unnerved her, when there was no apparent reason for the discomfort.

'Just writing. Brushing up the poems for the exhibition,' he said.

She glanced down at the pad in front of him. It was covered in his scrawl with lines and crosses and annotations all over it. He never created on the computer – that only came later, when either she, or his assistant, typed it in, in order to present a neat and legible finished product.

'Can I read anything?' she asked, perching on the edge of the desk.

Though his composure was returning she could tell by the awkward positioning of his hands that he was trying to hide the words on the pad. 'It's not quite ready yet,' he answered, managing to slide the pad under some papers as he reached for his tea. 'Thanks for coming home,' he said, smiling up at her.

Her eyes remained on his. 'What made it so urgent?' she asked gently.

At that his expression became sheepish. 'I was missing you,' he confessed. 'I always function so much better when you're here.'

Though she knew that was true, she knew too that there was more, but she didn't press it; she'd learned that it simply wasn't the way to get anything out of him. So they drank their tea, talked about the girls, the film, and about Rachel, then returned to bed around three.

Now, here they were on Saturday morning, *en famille*, at Camden Market, loaded up with knick-knacks, as they wandered over to their favourite place for ice-cream and coffee. Some friends who were just back from Sardinia bombarded them with snapshots, and insisted Robert and Anna should try the Costa Smeralda too. They had all the details should the Maxtons be interested, which Robert certainly seemed to be, though it was his way to make everyone feel as if they had something exciting and worthwhile to contribute. Anna's mobile rang then, with a call welcoming her back to London and inviting her and Robert to dinner that night. Not sure whether it would be a good idea to go out, she said she'd get back to them, then passed the phone to Emily, their eldest, who needed to call a friend. Around noon Robert drove them all home, where they sent emails to Auntie Rachel, before going to play badminton in the rambling, slightly overgrown back garden, while Anna watched from the kitchen as she prepared a chicken salad for lunch.

Though she smiled as Robert looked round to catch her eye and wink, her heart tripped with unease, for that happily married, contented-looking persona he was showing to the world was as transparent to her as if it were a glass bubble he was shutting himself up in. And just like a bubble she knew how easily it could burst, which was why she was so torn about whether to take the girls to their friends' for the afternoon, or to keep them here. As they hadn't seen her for almost a week, and were so obviously enjoying having both their parents at home, she really wanted them to stay, but she knew how much it upset and frightened them to see their beloved daddy during his 'difficult periods', as they called them. And because she knew all the signs, Anna was very much afraid that one was simmering away beneath that oh so jovial veneer.

In the end, she picked up the phone and spoke to a couple of other parents to make arrangements.

They ate outside, on the stone patio. It concerned but didn't really surprise her to see how little Robert ate, nor did he put up much of a protest when she announced that she was taking the girls to their friends'.

'Please be here when I get back,' she murmured, as Justine hung back from getting into the car. She, more than Emily, always seemed to sense when something was wrong; which was why it made Anna's heart ache to see her anxious little face glancing back at her daddy, but it was better than having them witness a scene.

'Of course I'll be here,' he said, seeming surprised by her words. 'Where would I go?'

She didn't want to remind him of the times he'd run away from her in the past in case it prompted him to do so again, so she merely kissed him and left.

She was gone for almost an hour, but to her relief he was still there when she got home, slouched on a sofa in the TV room, watching cassettes of the rushes.

'Would you like to see them?' he offered, as she came to sit beside him.

'Of course,' she answered, snuggling into the arm he was holding out.

For several minutes they watched the same scene over and over, shot from different angles, with four or five takes of each. It showed first Anita (Stacey), then Alma (Gloria), walking down the same dark staircase, speaking the same lines. There were full-length shots, mid-shots, then both medium and big close-ups of their faces. The lines were clearly being spoken to the poet (Bryn) who was at the foot of the stairs, though he appeared in none of the shots.

'"Am I who you want?"' Anita/Stacey was demanding harshly. '"Or is it her? What can she give you, that I can't? What does she really mean to you, you fool? You have reality and you want to turn it into fantasy. You have fantasy and you turn it into reality. Don't you understand, you can have both? With me you can have everything. Capture me on canvas, create me with your pen, turn me into a goddess or a demon, but I will *never* be your wife. I will *forever* be your wife."'

'Do you see how this is going to be put together?' he said, glancing at Anna.

She nodded. 'You'll fade in and out of the shots, presumably, transitioning between their faces, so that we can see how the poet doesn't know which of them is coming towards him. The wife or the mistress.'

'Do you think it's going to work?'

'I think it'll be very effective.'

'What about scary?'

'Well, considering it's going to look as though

247

they're almost demonically possessed by each other, I'd say it'll be a lot more than just scary.'

Pleased by the answer, he stopped the video, then got up to turn off the TV. 'It's already giving me nightmares,' he confessed, jokingly, as he came back to the sofa.

'Then I suspect we should be grateful that Gloria and I don't look anything alike,' she commented wryly.

'A thought that has crossed my mind more than once,' he assured her, his eyes still showing only laughter.

As he settled down next to her again, she snuggled back into his embrace, noticing that a few light raindrops were starting to spatter the window. 'By the way, how did your evening go over at Stacey's?' she asked casually, as he pressed a kiss to her hair. 'You never mentioned it.'

'Oh, it was fine,' he answered. 'It would have been better if you were there.'

'So what did you talk about, the two of you?'

'Three of us,' he corrected, then something suddenly struck him and he leapt to his feet. 'I have a surprise for you,' he told her. 'Wait there. Don't move.'

He was gone less than a minute, before returning with a small, beautifully carved wooden box, which he put into her hands, saying, with a mischievous twinkle, 'Not exactly a Pandora's box, but it could be.'

Anna was frowning curiously as she looked at it. 'It's beautiful,' she said.

'It's from Stacey. A gift, for both of us. Look inside.'

Opening up the lid, she parted the white tissue paper, then her eyes dilated with shock when she saw the cigarettes that half filled the interior. Despite how extremely neatly they were rolled, there was no mistaking what they were. 'She gave you these as well?' she said, looking up at him.

He was grinning. 'Shall we have one? Now?'

Anna looked at them again. It wasn't that she'd never smoked marijuana, because she had, several times, it was just that she wasn't sure she wanted to now. 'Why did she give them to you?' she asked.

'Because . . .' His eyes darted to one side. 'Because she thought they would help me to relax.'

'Were you nervous then?'

'I always am, you know that,' he responded, with a laugh.

'Is that why you want to smoke one now?' she said, frowning.

He was looking uncomfortable again, which was making her more anxious than ever. 'When did she give them to you?' she asked.

'The other night, when I was over there. She was just being generous,' he told her, taking the box. 'If you don't want to share one, then I'll smoke it alone.'

'No, please don't,' she said.

His eyes came up, full of surprise, bordering on resentment. 'You're creating an issue,' he said accusingly.

'No.'

He stared down at her and she could sense the anguish that was making him defensive, so softening her tone she said, 'Why didn't you go to Ernesto's studio today? Isn't he doing the first portrait?'

Several seconds ticked by during which she could see him growing stiffer and more agitated. It was as though something was trying desperately to break out of him, but he just wouldn't let it. Finally he said, 'I didn't go, because I think her husband was going to be there, and I just wouldn't feel comfortable looking at another man's wife with no clothes on, while he was standing there.'

'Why would she have no clothes on?'

'Because that's the way Ernesto wants to do it.'

'But he's following your poems.'

'With his own interpretations. You're turning this into some kind of inquisition,' he snapped. 'What difference does it make whether her clothes are on or off?'

'To me none, but to you it obviously does.'

'Yes. While her husband's there.'

'What about when he's not there?'

His face was trembling and white. 'You're being disgusting, Anna,' he said through his teeth.

Startled by the word, she said, 'How am I being disgusting?'

'By accusing me of things I've never done.'

'What kind of things?' she cried. 'I haven't accused you of anything.'

'You think I've seen her naked.'

'I know you have. She appears so in the film. And on the stage.'

'But those are the only times I've seen her naked.'

She was about to ask why he was defending himself over something that shouldn't even be an issue, when she realized that it probably wasn't the best way to go. So, deciding to take another tack, she reached for his hands and pulled him back down on the sofa. 'Darling, you know how much I love you,' she said, gazing earnestly into his troubled eyes. 'You know that I trust you, implicitly, but we both know how confused and upset you can sometimes get over things that turn out to exist only in your head. So if there's anything you want to tell me, whether you think it's real or imagined, you know I'll understand.'

He looked so helpless now, and stripped of his manly pride, that she wanted to gather him up like a child and tell him it didn't matter. But she knew she couldn't do that, for he needed to articulate what was happening inside him or it would only grow and fester.

'I don't want to hurt you,' he said miserably. 'I never want to hurt you.'

Her heart groaned with despair, for she recognized the words and the tone immediately. 'Is this you talking?' she said. 'Those are lines from the script.'

'I know, but they still apply.'

'So why are you going to hurt me?'

'I just told you, I never want to. No one means as much to me as you. No one. That's why I never want to hurt you.'

'When you say it like that, it makes it seem as though it's a possibility,' she said, trying to ignore the stirrings of unease in her heart. 'Or even imminent.'

'Of course, it's always a possibility,' he snapped, 'because that's what we do to those we love – we hurt them.'

'You're starting to sound angry again. Why are you angry?'

His hands tightened painfully on hers as his head fell back. 'Because I don't want to hurt her,' he cried to the ceiling, 'but I know I'm going to. I'm compelled to.'

'Hurt who? Who are you talking about?'

He seemed confused by the question, then his eyes closed and a moment later his shoulders started to shake. It took her a moment to realize he was laughing. 'At last,' he declared joyously, 'I've got the scene right. I've been trying for days to hit the right note, to find the right words, and we're due to shoot it on Monday. Anna, my darling, my saviour, do you see what a difference it makes to have you here? Kiss me, and lie here in my arms where I can breathe you in like the true and sublime inspiration you are.'

'Robert, stop it,' she cried, laughing too as he tried to pull her down. 'You're quoting from the film again, and now I don't know whether we're supposed to be dealing with a crisis in confidence, or a lapse of fidelity.'

'Neither,' he assured her, burying his face in her neck, 'because nothing's ever a problem when you're here. Now let me ravage you, woman, while the children are out of the way and the urge is upon me.'

Stacey was draped across a white mattress in Ernesto's studio, a long, diaphanous shawl wound round her body like a loving pet python, and her magnificent hair spread out in glistening crinkles of amber. Later, Ernesto, who was hoisted with his easel and paints on a small platform above and adjacent, would create the strange, Gothic backdrop of beasts described in the poem, who were the temptress's victims and tormentors, but first he needed her here, as the centrepiece to the verse that was his inspiration.

The remains of the lunch Petey had brought in still cluttered the kitchenette, awaiting his return from the business he was conducting in various other parts of London. He'd taken Stacey's mobile, since she didn't really want to talk to anyone right now, not even dear Robert, for as deeply as she adored him, she simply wasn't in the mood for his passion today. Fortunately, she didn't have to feel too guilty about that, because Anna was back from Cornwall, so it wasn't as if he was alone. Her heart did rather go out to Anna, for as devoted as she undoubtedly was to her darling husband, it couldn't be easy living with the extraordinary ramblings of his writer's mind. Not that Stacey was sitting in any kind of moral judgement, for heaven knew she had enough sexual idiosyncrasies of her own, but Robert's, she could see from the very private poems he had begun sending her, had the potential to become more than a little bit disturbing. So no, let Anna resume responsibility for him while she, Stacey, concentrated on the rather frustrating dilemma she seemed to be facing regarding her own beloved spouse.

Where in the world, she wondered, as she stifled a yawn, was he now; and when might he be back? He'd left again yesterday, having spent less than twenty-four hours at home, and he hadn't called since. Nor was he answering his mobile, which wasn't so much unusual as irritating, because she felt rather in need of hearing his voice. However, the frown between her brows, which Ernesto kept complaining about, was easily erased by allowing her mind to drift to their dinner last night, when she'd been so naughty in the restaurant that he'd had to take her home before the main course arrived. The memory of what had followed caused her lips to curve in an indolently satisfied smile, while delicious *frissons* of lust buzzed like small shocks between her legs. The resulting glow in her expression certainly seemed to please Ernesto, though not nearly as much as the recollection pleased her.

She sighed again. There was so much about her husband that set him apart from other men: not just his looks, or his intellect, or his incomparable skill as a lover, but other qualities too, equally potent, though much harder to define. She wasn't even sure she wanted to, for sometimes putting things into words rendered them mundane, and mundane was a label she could never attach to him. No, her dilemma had nothing to do with the exceptional affinity they shared, both physically and mentally, for she never doubted for a moment how much she was loved, and knew he didn't either. It was how much of his life Franz Koehler and the Phraxos Group had started to take up in recent months that was causing her concern.

She didn't exactly mind the secrecy, for she understood, on the whole, why it was necessary, but she did object to the increased pressure he seemed to be under lately, and to the fact that it was creating the feeling that she had a much more formidable rival in Koehler and Phraxos than she'd ever really been aware of. So the question she was asking herself now was, what could she do to refocus his attention on her, and their life together, in a way that wouldn't jeopardize his privileged status as one of Koehler's trusted inner circle, but might at least make him re-evaluate his priorities and spend more time with her?

'Sweeties! I have returned!' Petey declared, sweeping in through the door like a diva. 'Ah, what a vision,' he swooned, standing so that he could get a view of both Stacey and Ernesto's evolving masterpiece.

Ernesto grunted through a brush that was clamped between his teeth, and pointed to the ornate wooden box that was just out of his reach.

'Oh, do let me,' Petey insisted, as a response to the order.

Smiling, Stacey said, 'Did everything go OK?'

'Perfectissimo,' Petey purred, taking a joint from the box and lighting it. 'Everyone is happy, and believe me, our good friends will be too, *"for they shall be greatly rewarded."'*

'Yes, but will I?' she murmured. Then before he could answer, 'Try my husband again, will you? I need to speak to him.'

'You sound desperate, ducky,' Ernesto commented, taking the joint from Petey and raising it to his lips.

Stacey slanted him a look. 'If you had such a man, so would you,' she told him.

Ernesto sucked in the substance, held it, then slowly let it go. 'If I had such a man,' he responded, 'I'd never allow him such a loose rein.'

Stacey's lips twitched with laughter. 'But you're such an ugly bastard, you couldn't afford to,' she told him.

Ernesto chuckled with delight. 'All the same, ducky,' he said, taking another puff, 'you're worried, I can tell. You don't know where he goes, or what he does when he's gone. So time to clip the wings, methinks? Or, like father, like son?'

Stacey reached out for the joint. 'Actually, Ernesto,' she said, 'I know a great deal more about where he goes, and what he does, than you might think, I just choose not to discuss it with the likes of you two gossiping queens.'

'Blast,' Petey muttered, clicking off the call. 'Misdialled.' Trying again, he waited for the ringing tone then passed the phone over.

Putting it to her ear, Stacey took a deep pull on the cigarette, and was about to respond to the hello at the other end when she suddenly recognized the voice. Casting a daggered look at Petey she said, 'Robert, darling, how are you? We're all here at the studio, so inspired by your mastery that I just had to call and tell you.'

'It's – it's going well?' Robert responded.

'Oh yes. Ernesto's performing such magic with his little brush, anyone would think it was a wand, and I am lying here, quite naked, thinking of you and the very naughty poem you gave me yesterday. It's helping so much.'

There was a long silence at the other end, before Robert said, 'You haven't shown it to anyone else?'

'Of course not. It's our little secret.'

'But Petey and Ernesto, aren't they there, listening to this?'

'Yes, but the only poems they're *seeing* are those from *The Geddons*. Everything else is just between us, the way we agreed. Is Anna there?'

'She's upstairs.'

'So you're alone at the moment?'

'Yes.'

'Then speak the poem aloud to me, and think of me, lying here, unrobed and undone by the beauteous rhythm of your words.'

Again he was silent, until the tightness of lust sounded in his voice as he said, 'Your husband, isn't he there?'

'Oh no, darling. I've no idea where he is.'

She looked up at Petey and Ernesto, but they were paying scant attention as they smoked their own joints and watched something on the TV.

'I was thinking,' Robert said. 'Maybe I should pop over, to see how it's all progressing.'

Knowing now why he hadn't come earlier, she said, softly, 'You'd be most welcome, you know that, but my husband could drop in at any minute, and I wouldn't want him to see the kind of effect you have on me.'

'No, no, of course not,' he said shakily. 'And I really shouldn't leave Anna on her own. Perhaps we could have . . . a few private moments in your dressing room on Monday?'

'Consider them yours,' she murmured, and clicked off the line.

'Bitch,' Petey muttered, throwing her a sideways look.

'You're the one who called him,' she responded, dialling her husband's number. 'And he loves it, so why shouldn't I do what makes him happy?'

'Ask Anna that question, see what she has to say.' Petey retorted, turning back to the TV.

Stacey poked out her tongue, then getting up

from the white mattress she trailed the long, chiffon shawl over to the kitchenette and closed the door behind her. 'Hello, my love,' she purred into her husband's message line, 'I have several things I need to discuss with you, but they can wait until you come back. I know you were stressed and worried before you left, even though you tried to hide it, so I hope everything's OK. Call me as soon as you can. I love you. Meantime, I hope you're in a comfortable place when you listen to this, because I'm naked right now, and very aroused, so I'm going to describe exactly what I wish you were doing to me, while I do as much of it as I can to myself.'

Chapter 11

It was just after eight in the evening. The sun was still high, though subdued by a gauzy layer of cloud, while the sound of the sea was a constant, low growl in the bowl of the bay. The boats were all in, winched up on to the beach, disturbed only by the gulls that pecked around the crab and lobster pots, and a dog whose owner was gamely throwing a ball into the slowly returning tide.

As they wandered down the coastal path, heading for the big night out at the pub, Rachel and Laurie were discussing when, and where, they might shoot Rachel's first interview for the programme. The idea of exposing herself publicly over something that was so intensely personal was making Rachel more uncomfortable than she was prepared to admit, in fact she really didn't want to do it at all, even though she knew if she really wanted to get to the truth, it had to be done.

As they talked, Laurie's mind was more focused on an email she'd just received from one of Elliot's researchers in London, telling her about a man's body that had been dragged out of the harbour at St Tropez a few days ago. There was one bullet wound to the head 'execution style', Liam had written, though he wasn't sure why Elliot had asked him to make her aware of this killing. Nor was she, yet; however, since the location was France, her first thought had been of Xavier Lachère, the Frenchman Katherine had spoken of to her friends. But after reading on she'd discovered that the victim had been identified as one Gustave Basim, a twenty-eight-year-old unemployed construction worker whose mother was Parisian, and father Algerian.

Naturally she'd sent an email to Elliot asking him exactly who this Gustave Basim was, and why she should be interested in his fate. As yet she hadn't had a reply.

'So how long do you think it'll take to shoot the first interview?' Rachel was asking, as Laurie held back for her to go ahead through a narrow part of the path.

'I'll set a day aside for it,' Laurie answered, 'but we won't do it until Dan gets back from holiday.'

'Dan being the cameraman?'

'And co-producer,' Laurie added. 'He's Rose's son, did you know that?'

Rachel nodded, but her mind hadn't really connected with the question, because she was watching Tom Drummond, one of the oldest and most respected of Killian's fishermen, who'd just come out of his cottage with Candy, his partly lame King Charles spaniel. Had he just deliberately snubbed them, or had he just not spotted them? Either way, he was a reminder of how jittery she was feeling about the kind of greeting she was going to get when she walked into the pub.

'Tell me again what Chris Gallagher said in his message,' she pressed Laurie, still watching Tom Drummond, as he marched on ahead.

Laurie laughed. 'You heard it,' she replied. 'Apparently everything's been taken care of and everyone's looking forward to seeing us. That was it.'

Rachel's expression showed her lack of trust, but before she could comment Beanie came scooting up behind them with Romie.

'Here I am,' she declared. 'Sorry to keep you.'

'There's no rush,' Rachel assured her, smiling fondly at the old lady's awkwardly backcombed hair and pink frosted lipstick. 'You look lovely,' she said, as Laurie stooped to fuss over Romie.

Beanie's eyes glowed. 'It's Saturday night,' she said. 'Got to make a bit of an effort.'

Laurie and Rachel's eyes instantly performed a droll appraisal of each other's Saturday night attire of old jeans and sweatshirts, with next to no make-up.

'Have you taken Laurie up to the other side yet?' Beanie asked, as they walked on.

'You mean to the Devil's Frying Pan?' Rachel asked. 'No, we'll probably walk over there tomorrow. Are you going to come?'

'Mmm, why not?' Beanie replied. 'Romie will too, won't you, cabbage? I'll make us all a picnic, why not?'

'You mentioned it before,' Laurie said, laughingly, 'so what *is* the Devil's Frying Pan?'

'It's a kind of collapsed cave,' Rachel explained.

'It's incredibly deep and dramatic. Well, you'll see when we go over there.'

'But why is it called the Devil's *Frying Pan*?'

'Oh, because the way the sea hisses and spits around the boulder in the middle of it is like an egg bubbling in fat,' Rachel answered.

By now they were passing the small terrace of bright white cottages with cornflower blue window frames that led down to the path, and the flutterings in Rachel's stomach were getting stronger, for the noise they could hear coming from the bar confirmed that the place was already crowded. She was so dreading a sudden silence at her entrance again that, were it not for the fact that she knew neither Laurie nor Beanie would allow it, she might actually have turned back.

However, as Beanie pushed the door open the noise instantly crescendoed, as though billowing an escape, or even reaching out to absorb them. The occasional strumming of a guitar was vaguely audible through the din, as well as something that sounded like maracas. The TV was on too, and Romie, thrilled to be out for the evening, bounded through the maze of legs to get to Dapper, who kept a ready stock of biscuits for his canine customers.

Beanie launched into the fray too, pressing her way to the bar, while Rachel and Laurie's eyes moved warily around the room, as they waited to be noticed. Then Nick, Beanie's nephew, shouted, 'Hey, Rachel, what are you and your friend having?'

'What? Who?' Pinkie Pinkerton boomed. As though his surprise was the cue for a stream of generosity to break its dam, they were suddenly inundated with offers of drinks.

'Mine's a white wine. Australian Chardonnay, if they've got it,' Laurie called out, giving Rachel a gentle shove to get her moving.

'Coming up,' Dapper assured her.

'What about you, Rachel?' Nick said, rudely brushing bodies aside to let her through.

'Uh, lemonade, thank you,' she said, still slightly stunned. Then trying harder, 'How's Jenny?'

'Me? I'm great,' Jenny cried, ducking out from behind a group of her neighbours. 'How are you?' and before Rachel could answer, the pretty, over-weight young woman with dark curly hair and vivid red cheeks, scooped her into an embrace. 'I'm so sorry about what happened,' she murmured in Rachel's ear. Rachel wasn't sure if she was referring to the recent hostility, or to Tim's death.

Rachel smiled, then laughed when several men in the far corner started to bay like hounds as Zac broke out a tune on the guitar. Chris Gallagher was over there too, though his back was turned as he talked to someone who was sitting down, while Jake Tucker rattled the maracas and performed a silly dance.

'I can hardly believe this,' she shouted into Laurie's ear, as someone passed her a lemonade.

'Me neither,' Laurie laughed. 'Have you seen Chris Gallagher? We need an explanation.'

'He's over there,' Rachel answered, turning to nod in his direction.

As Laurie looked she moved in closer to Rachel and said, 'On second thoughts, when a man looks like that, we need more than an explanation.'

Rachel bubbled with laugher. Jenny took her arm, shouting, 'There are some seats over next to the door. Mum's keeping them with Millie Phelps. We should have a pretty good view, because Zac's set himself up next to the fireplace. That's provided we can get this lot to settle down and *clear some space!*' she hollered. Laughing, she shouted in Rachel's ear again, 'Everybody's here. They must have come all the way from Helston. Penzance even. You know, he's getting a right reputation, our Zac?'

'Zac is Jenny's brother,' Rachel explained to Laurie. 'By the way, Jen, this is Laurie.'

Laurie smiled warmly as she said hello, and was pleased to see nothing but friendliness in Jenny's eyes too. It really was as though the past few days hadn't happened at all, for there wasn't even the slightest hint of embarrassment or wariness, or anything at all to suggest that she and Rachel had ever been anything but wholeheartedly welcome. So just what, she wondered, had Chris Gallagher done to change things so radically?

Rachel had just spotted Beanie wriggling her way in next to her reluctant beau, Vince Tucker, when a chorus of spontaneous singing erupted from the centre of the room. Soon everyone was joining in, for the song, 'White Rose', was well known to them all, and as Jenny steered a route through to the seats her mother was saving, she and Rachel began singing along too.

Not knowing the words, Laurie could only hum and listen and love the way hearts and souls seemed to pour into the lyrics, while the old stone walls and low wooden rafters resonated with the

264

velvety dark sounds of the rhythm. The final verses were barely over, before 'Robber's Retreat', a lively shanty, and the Killian anthem, was starting to bound about the room, getting feet stomping, and hands clapping, while Dapper, who was singing loudly too, pulled more pints, and his wife jigged to the beat as she and the barman cleared tables and took more orders.

Several more shanties followed, each louder than the last, until finally Pinkie Pinkerton got up to perform his party piece, which was such a deeply moving ballad about a young father who went out fishing one day and never came back, that it actually brought tears to Laurie's eyes – until she caught Chris Gallagher regarding her with a humorously cocked eyebrow. She pulled a face, then bent an ear towards Rachel who was saying, 'I think he quite likes you, and he seems to be on his own.'

Laurie's expression was comical as she slanted Rachel a look, then finishing her wine she demanded to know what everyone else was having, and got up to go to the bar.

As she weaved her way through, Rachel kept an eye on Chris Gallagher, feeling certain he'd watch Laurie, but his attention seemed focused on Zac now, who was getting ready to sing. Then she found herself blushing as his eyes suddenly caught her watching him.

Laughing at the droll expression he pulled, she turned aside to listen to Jenny and her mother discussing how many cigarettes they'd rolled that day.

'It saves the lads doing it when they gets out to

sea, in all that wind and weather,' Jenny explained, giving her a wink.

Rachel nodded understanding, and winked too, while raising her glass to Beanie, who was being purposefully shunned by Vince Tucker. Hearing someone call her name, she looked round to find Laurie signalling for help, but before she could get even halfway to the bar at least a dozen hands swooped in to provide assistance. Turning back, she found the way blocked by Chris Gallagher, who had just stood up to rest his foot on a stool, and a guitar on his knee.

'Sorry,' she gasped, almost colliding with him.

'No problem,' he answered, standing aside. 'Do you have a drink?'

'Oh yes, thanks. Laurie's just getting them. Are you about to sing?'

He nodded and grinned, and to her surprise she felt a genuine warmth in her smile of response.

'We've been wondering how you managed to sort everything out,' she said, leaning towards him and shouting to make herself heard.

He looked surprised, as if not quite sure what she meant, then his eyes showed humour as he registered. 'Oh you mean the Coventry thing,' he said.

'How did you do it? What did you say?'

His eyes were still full of laughter, but for a fleeting moment they seemed to penetrate hers in a way that she found almost disturbing. 'I gave them my word,' he said, 'that their secret would be safe with you.'

She frowned. 'What secret?'

His face lit up. 'You see, that's how safe it is, and

how easy it'll be for me to keep my word. So don't let me down, OK?'

Shaking her head and laughing, since now was hardly the time to go into it, she turned back to her seat, and was just sitting down, when Zac began calling for quiet.

'OK, we're going to perform a new song of mine now,' he announced, as everyone turned to listen. His youthfully handsome features and tousled curly hair appeared more romantic than ever in the candlelight that was flickering along with the dimmed overhead lights, and the sound of his voice, Rachel knew, was going to melt every female heart in the room, for the simple reason that it always did.

'He looks like Rufus Sewell, don't you think?' Laurie whispered, as he leaned over to talk to Chris Gallagher.

Rachel's eyes widened in surprise. 'Yes,' she said, wondering why she hadn't noticed it before. 'Younger, but yes he does.'

Laurie took a sip of her drink, then said, 'Did you ask Chris Gallagher how he got everyone over their problems?'

'I did, though I didn't exactly get an answer. I'll tell you later.'

Zac was talking again. 'Right, well, what's going to happen,' he said into the microphone, 'is Chris is going to sing, and me and Jake are going to be the backers.'

'No! We want you to sing!' his sister shouted.

'See! That's what I told him,' Chris cried, throwing out his hands.

'No, he does it better,' Zac insisted.

267

There were more cries of support and protest, until finally Zac just began strumming the opening bars, and kept going until Chris gave up and followed, at which point Jake started a gentle shake of the maracas. When everyone had settled down, the opening refrain really began, with a few seductive moments of golden-toned guitar, before Chris's voice came in as a low, almost baritone accompaniment, that gradually asserted itself in such a smooth and melodic way that Rachel could feel the air starting to slow in her lungs. Laurie's lips parted in surprise, as she too felt herself responding to the hypnotic cadence of the tone as it turned the beauty of Zac's lyrics into something truly magical.

The song was all about trying to make a woman understand that her heart was with the wrong man, and by the second time the chorus came round some were starting to join in.

'"Can't you see that it's over?"' they sang, '"He doesn't want you any more; and though I know how much you're hurting, I want you to know, that I'll never go, no, I'll never go. I'll be here for you always; I'll never cheat or lie; I'll only love you, my darling, so please don't keep telling me goodbye."'

At the end Chris's voice reached such a pitch of emotion that Laurie found herself wondering if, like her, he wasn't entirely unfamiliar with unrequited love.

For her part Rachel was more than ready for the song to end; it was simply too harrowing for her, in her present state, though she readily and warmly joined in with the applause and cheers, for there was no denying the song's beauty, or the singer's talent. And it seemed to know no end, because

Chris and Zac were soon singing more of Zac's compositions, livelier and much less tragic than the first, which then yielded to cover versions of old favourites by the Beatles, the Stones, the Back Street Boys, and even Madonna. Since most could sing along to those, the place was soon rocking, and it wasn't long before Nick pulled his wife, Jenny, to her feet to start the dancing.

Old Tom Drummond was Laurie's first partner, while Rachel was claimed by Jake, and Beanie gave up on the curmudgeonly Vince Tucker to go and jive with Pinkie. In the end, it wasn't clear who was dancing with whom, there were so many on their feet, and having got fed up with the way Pinkie was so cockily strutting his stuff with Beanie, Vince had now shuffled in front of her and was dodging about as though he were a goalie trying to stop her from scoring.

It wasn't far off midnight by the time the music finally ended, and those who were still up flopped breathlessly back in their seats. Then spotting the nearly full moon outside, Nick shouted an invitation to anyone who felt like taking a stroll on the beach.

'Well, that's romantic, innit?' Jenny remarked. 'Asking everyone else to come too.'

Nick looked chastened, until Chris Gallagher put an arm round his shoulders and said, 'Count me in. And these two,' he added, nodding towards Laurie and Rachel.

'No, Vince! I'm not going!' Beanie declared hotly. 'You'll only try getting saucy with me, and I'll have none of it!' Everyone burst out laughing at the look of utter bewilderment that crossed Vince Tucker's face, before, realizing what was happening, he coloured to the roots of his few strands of hair.

A few minutes later, Rachel and Laurie were following the others down past the old winch house and on to the pebble beach. The moon was thinly veiled by a cloud now, though its glossy white reflection shimmered across the waves and gave enough light to see the fishing boats, listing gently to one side as though resting, and the huge black outlines of the headlands that rose up on either side of the bay like outstretched arms.

They were a few yards from the shore when the others stopped next to Nick's boat, and began discussing some new equipment he'd just had installed. Neither Laurie nor Rachel was paying particular attention as they drowsily enjoyed the warm night air and listened to the muted sounds from the pub mingling with the swirling rush of the tide. Rachel was trying very hard not to think of how often she had done this with Tim, but as the persistent nostalgia swept over her, the need for him became so strong that she actually lifted a hand to touch him. Whether Chris Gallagher noticed she had no idea, she only knew that as he was standing the closest, it was his arm her hand found, before she gently pulled it away.

Jenny's eyes were gleaming in the moonlight as she said, 'This is the kind of night you could expect to see Todd's ghost.'

Laurie turned to look at her.

Jenny smiled. 'You've seen her, haven't you Rachel?' she said.

'We thought we did,' Rachel answered. 'About a year ago.'

To Laurie Jenny said, 'She walks out of the sea and up over the beach. Never hear the pebbles crunch. Just glides over 'em, silent as a cat. No idea who she is. Todd was the first one to see her, so that's why we calls her Todd's ghost.'

Laurie glanced at Rachel. 'It sounds as though there are a lot of ghosts around here,' she said.

Jenny chuckled.

Rachel shivered, then realizing how close she was standing to Chris, she moved away saying, 'Come on, let's go back. It's starting to get chilly.'

Linking Laurie's arm as they walked, Jenny said, 'We can tell you some stories if you want to hear them.'

'Do I?' Laurie asked Rachel.

Rachel smiled. 'They're worth it,' she answered.

Chris walked on ahead and opened the pub door.

'What's going on?' Jenny's mother wanted to know, as they all started to sit down.

'Nothing. Just thought we might catch sight of Todd's ghost,' Jenny answered. 'D'you hear that, Todd?' she shouted. 'No sign of your girlfriend tonight.'

Todd grunted and Jenny and her mother laughed. 'Frightened the bejesus out of him, the first time he saw her,' Jenny's mother explained. 'Didn't have another drink for a week.'

'Tell her about old Lorna, with the keys,' Jenny prompted. 'Or the horses we do hear galloping down from Roon Moor on Hallowe'en.'

Laughing at the look on Laurie's face, Rachel left them to it while she went off to the ladies. She'd heard all the stories before, so knew how wonderfully thrilling they were, though some, she suspected, were probably no more than tall tales for long winter nights. However, she'd never doubt the entirety of their veracity, for this was Cornwall after all.

Laurie was so engrossed in the stories that she wasn't sure what exactly finally drew her attention to where Rachel was standing, outside the ladies, she only knew that the tease of asking if she'd seen a ghost died on her lips as she realized the stricken look on Rachel's face wasn't a joke. She started to get up, but even before she could clamber free of the group around her, Beanie was at Rachel's side.

They were too far away, and Beanie spoke too quietly for Laurie to hear what she was saying, but she was already guiding Rachel to the door as Laurie reached them.

'Sssh, it's all right,' Laurie heard Beanie soothing. 'It's not what you think.'

'What is it? What's happened?' Laurie said anxiously.

Beanie smiled up at her as though to say, 'not now,' then held Rachel steady while Laurie opened the door.

As they stepped into the night Rachel turned to put her arms round Beanie's neck, and sobbed into her shoulder. 'Beanie, please don't let this be happening. Please, please, make it stop,' she begged.

Beanie held her close, while Laurie gently rubbed her back as if in some way that might help too. Then the door opened behind them and Chris Gallagher said,

'Can I do something?'

Both Beanie and Laurie looked at him, then back to Rachel, as she broke out of Beanie's embrace and started to walk on.

'She'll be fine,' Beanie assured him. 'We just need to get her home.'

By the time they reached the cottage Rachel was calmer, though still very pale, and didn't even try to object when Beanie insisted on seeing her into bed.

Laurie waited downstairs, not sure what to do, and still in the dark over what had happened. All kinds of things were going through her mind, but not until the following morning did she learn the real reason for the suddenness and depth of Rachel's distress. And that was when she finally understood, in a way that perhaps she hadn't before, just how very, very hard these next few weeks and months were going to be for the woman she already considered a friend.

It was two days later that a four-seater Rockwell swooped down towards a remote, private airstrip in the Western Sahara. As the pilot eased the throttle, readying to land, he glanced over at Rudy who was gazing out at the endless miles of rich, golden sand, undulating like a tide to the distant blue horizons. Behind them Franz Koehler was working on his laptop, apparently oblivious to the fact that they'd arrived, while far below a black limousine began moving out of the exclusive compound, ready to greet the new arrivals.

After lowering the flaps the pilot made a slow circle of the strip, checking for wind direction and any obstructions on the runway. There were none.

This would be easy: next to no turbulence, no awkward approaches, or air traffic controllers who hadn't mastered English. He'd landed in similar locations before, so knew what to expect, and using the throttle to smooth out the sudden lift that greeted him as he crossed the threshold, he took her down. The runway was one of the smoothest he'd experienced, though with temperatures reaching the low forties, he needed all its length.

A few minutes later he stepped down from the cockpit, wincing at the dry, fiery blast of heat that greeted him. He looked around. This place was like nowhere else on earth; an ungodly wilderness of sand and more sand, with the tantalizing promise of an exotic adventure seeming to exude from the golden domes and glossy white crenellations of the Topkapi-style palace nestled at the end of the runway.

Behind him Rudy jumped down on to the blistering tarmac, while Koehler continued his assessment of the markets. The journey had been long, and in spite of the dark glasses, Rudy's tiredness showed.

'Nice wheels,' Rudy commented, as the limousine glided towards them. 'I have a feeling Professor Bombola's new chum is going to be my kind of host. What do you say?'

What he really wanted to say he kept to himself as Koehler came down from the aircraft.

'A good flight,' Koehler commented. 'Should be a productive few days now.'

Without waiting for a response he started towards the limo, leaving the others to haul the luggage out of the plane. 'I'm guessing we're going to fly out of here with the promise of at least ten mill,' Rudy murmured.

'Depends who else is coming to the party,' the pilot responded. 'It could turn out to be twice that.'

'Then we'll be throwing a couple of parties of our own,' Rudy quipped, with a waggle of his eyebrows. 'Once we've got it safely into Dubai, of course.'

The mention of Dubai caused a muscle spasm near the pilot's left eye, a small, physical manifestation of just how big a deal the Dubai operation was going to be. However, several phases of the project still had to be completed before he started worrying about that, not least of all this one, whose purpose was to provide at least some of the funding required by the opposition forces in their exiled host's homeland.

'Are we expecting anyone else from the Group?' Rudy asked, as they started towards the limo.

'Two guys from Phraxos US, I believe, and three from HQ in Zurich.' Even as he answered Rudy's question, his thoughts were moving on, taking him in the direction of Paris, where another big meeting was planned three weeks from now, which in turn reminded him of the body that had been fished out of St Tropez harbour a week ago. His own Establishment sources had informed him that the British police had received an anonymous tip-off a few days ago, alerting them to the fact that the dead man could be connected to the murder of Tim Hendon. He'd immediately passed the information to Franz Koehler, but as yet he wasn't aware of Koehler taking any action. He almost certainly would though, because the

Hendon murder could, in the end, prove the David they all dreaded, for in spite of the fact that there were few mightier Goliaths than Phraxos, the murder of a prominent British politician and subsequent disappearance of Franz Koehler's girlfriend provided not one, but two, potentially fatal stones for the slingshot.

'Any news on how the search for Katherine's going?' he asked Rudy, just before they reached the car.

Rudy shook his head. 'Nothing doing. No sign,' he replied.

'Do you believe Koehler doesn't know where she is?'

Rudy's eyes flicked in his direction. 'The last I heard he's got a team of over a hundred out there looking for her, and the trails are running drier than a Sudanese well.'

'But do you think it's a sham?'

Rudy shrugged. 'Who knows? But what seems to be bugging him most right now, like he said on the way over, is whether Mrs Hendon will make the transfer without a fuss.'

His tone was impatient as he said, 'Why doesn't he just let it go? Four million's nothing to him.'

Rudy's incredulity showed. 'You're forgetting, Katherine knows all about it,' he reminded him, 'which suggests he really doesn't know where she is. And if he doesn't, and she decides to come out of her little hidey-hole, wherever that might be, to spill the beans, it's going to be a whole lot easier to discredit her if no trace of that money is ever found.' Handing the luggage to the chauffeur, he turned back and grinned. 'I'm just glad I'm not in your shoes, my friend,' he muttered, 'because if she don't pay up, it's going to be your job to make her, and getting heavy with ladies just isn't nice.'

Chapter 12

'So taking everything I've told you into consideration,' Laurie said, watching Elliot's hands as he uncorked an expensive Californian Voignier, 'what do you think Rachel should do about the money?'

'Well,' he answered, after tasting and approving the wine, 'if it were me, I'd do exactly what she's doing, and try to find out more by hanging on to it. But whether that's what *she* should do, as a woman, on her own . . .'

'You're being chauvinistic.'

'Realistic,' he corrected, filling their glasses. Then putting the bottle down he began to serve the food.

Letting the subject rest for a moment, she stood quietly watching him, noticing that tiredness was making his ill-matched features seem even heavier than normal, though despite the shadows under his deep, grey eyes and two-day stubble around his jaw, he was still, to her mind, the most attractive man alive. He was also, for all sorts of reasons, the most fascinating human being, as well as one of the most successful journalists of his time – and if it were possible to love someone more, she'd want none of it, because this was quite painful enough, thank you very much.

When they were both sitting down, he helped himself to a mouthful of the delicious sea bass in soy and ginger sauce, then after taking his time to savour the delicate flavours, he picked up his wine. 'OK, here's what I think she should do,' he said. 'She should hold off making this particular transfer, just to see what happens. I doubt anyone will get too heavy at the first refusal, and there's always a chance it might yield up at least some of the information she's looking for. But the minute any signs of ugliness start showing up, she should let it go faster than she can say her own name, because if Franz Koehler, or anyone from Phraxos, is behind this, she definitely won't want to be messing with them.'

Laurie nodded, for that was more or less what she and Rachel had agreed on before she'd left the cottage that morning, when Rachel had still been looking alarmingly pale after the threatened miscarriage last Saturday night. What a dreadful experience that had been for Rachel, even though the doctor had been quick to pronounce an all-clear. It had given Laurie an even greater insight into just how much this child meant to Rachel; not that she'd ever really been in any doubt before.

'By the way,' Elliot said, adding a twist of black pepper to his meal, 'you got my message about the chap they pulled out of the St Tropez harbour?'

'Yes, what about him?' she said. 'Who is he?'

'Good question. Apparently they're running a

match with the unidentified fibres and skin cells found in Katherine Sumner's flat.'

Laurie's surprise and intrigue showed. 'Why? What makes them think he was there?' she said.

'They had an anonymous tip-off.'

'How do you know?'

'It came our way when Max was talking to one of his contacts inside the Phraxos Group. I just made a couple of follow-up calls, and now you know as much as I do.'

Laurie became very still. 'So you are investigating Phraxos,' she stated.

He nodded. 'Or one aspect of it.'

Hardly able to contain her eagerness she said, 'Was Tim Hendon involved with them? Has his name come up at all?'

'No. I'd have told you if it had, but we haven't exactly been looking for it, so don't discount the possibility. It's more the American angle that we've been taking, because by comparison Phraxos investments in the UK are small. In the US they're enormous, and with US defence spending now at a record two hundred and forty-six billion, the Phraxos shareholders are getting very rich indeed.'

'And how many of its directors are inside the Pentagon?'

'None that we know of, but most of them have come from there, so they have all the right contacts.'

Laurie picked up her wine. 'Can I ask which aspect of Phraxos you're investigating?' she said.

His eyes met hers as he seemed to debate his answer. She knew it wasn't because he didn't trust her, he was just deciding how safe it would be for her to know. 'Arms to Africa. Sanctions-busting,' he said finally. 'It's a very lucrative part of the world as far as weapons are concerned, and conflicts aren't difficult to find, or even create.'

Her eyes opened wide. 'You believe they're actually creating conflicts?' she said, shocked, though she knew she probably shouldn't be.

'We're becoming increasingly convinced of it. It's a great way of guaranteeing a good customer base, to help along rebel causes, civil wars, political uprisings, military coups . . . There's even evidence to say that they help raise the finance to arm the warring factions, money that ultimately ends up in their pockets. If you like, I'll give you a copy of a report from the World Policy Institute, it'll confirm all your worst nightmares about how America supplies weapons and military training to just about every corrupt regime or rebel cause you can think of. And how a goodly portion of the humanitarian aid that goes to those countries, ends up back in the US – and Britain and France – to purchase arms.'

Knowing that this was Rachel's worst nightmare coming true, as it would be anyone's if they really paid attention to what was happening, Laurie said, 'It's inhuman. Insane.'

'It's trade. Big business,' he corrected. 'And since the end of the Cold War the military and arms industries have had to find other ways of justifying their existence and making their profits. Of course, they don't have too much of a problem now, with everything else that's going on, but then we could get into how all that really got started.'

Laurie considered the unthinkable meaning of his words, but then realizing they were moving

281

away from the real point of the discussion she said, 'Going back to the body they found in St Tropez – what was his name? – Gustave Basim? Do you think there's a chance that he and the Xavier Lachère Max mentioned in his email could be one and the same person?'

He looked doubtful. 'Given the dead man's age, and background, it doesn't seem likely,' he answered, taking another mouthful of food. 'Have you managed to find out anything at all about Lachère?' he asked, after he'd swallowed.

'Not a thing. We're all drawing blanks.' She looked down at her plate and wished she wasn't finding it so hard to eat, but with their own unresolved problems ebbing and flowing through all they were discussing, it was hard to summon an appetite. 'This Basim doesn't seem to fit the profile of Katherine's friends at all,' she said, remaining on the safer ground of other people's affairs. 'Or not what I've managed to find out about him.'

'Which leads you to think?' he prompted.

'That he could be a hired killer?'

He tilted his head to one side as he considered the possibility. 'Does he have any kind of record that might support that?'

'Not exactly, but he has been questioned about links with GIA, the Algerian Islamic Group.'

'So are you saying you think Katherine let him into the flat to do the deed, then when it was over they left together?'

She shrugged. 'Why not?'

He shrugged too. 'Certainly Koehler would consider someone like Basim to be as disposable as Kleenex,' he said, 'so, if you're right, maybe, as a precautionary measure, to stop the man blabbing should he ever feel the urge, Koehler arranged for him to be shot and flushed off into the harbour. After all, who would ever make a connection between the corpse of a Parisian low-life and a prominent British politician, or to a sophisticated American woman – or indeed to an exclusive organization like Phraxos? They probably never would have without the tip-off.'

'So who gave the tip-off? Katherine Sumner?'

'Why? If she was involved in the murder?'

Laurie shook her head, and they continued to eat in silence for a while, each running with their own thoughts, until Laurie said, 'Rachel's hoping that the evidence of someone else being in the flat will stretch to the semen on the sheet. I must admit, I was beginning to think it might too, but it doesn't seem very likely if Gustave Basim *does* turn out to be the mystery man, does it?'

Elliot shook his head, then after topping up their glasses, he said, 'Between you and me, my money's on Tim Hendon for that. Everything points to it, and I haven't heard anything yet that swivels the finger. When are the DNA results expected?'

'You know how long they take.'

He waited as the music changed, then, satisfied with the new track, said, 'Now I have a question for you.'

Instinctively she knew that it wasn't going to be the question she wanted to hear.

'How convinced are you that Rachel Hendon is totally genuine?' he said.

Swallowing her dismay, she said, 'Ninety-nine per cent.'

He smiled, for that was as certain as anyone in their field would ever be about anything.

Feeling herself respond to the smile in a way that could so easily make her forget that any problems existed between them, she got to her feet and began loading the empty plates on to a tray. Tonight really wasn't a good time to try opening a discussion on exactly where they were going with this relationship, so she'd just keep it bottled up, the way she usually did, and carry on pretending that everything was normal and fine.

After carrying the tray through to the kitchen, she dumped it on a draining board then put a hand to her head as she tried to calm down. She was angrier with herself than with him, for she always managed to find an excuse to avoid the issues – he was too tired, he'd had a long journey, they were both too busy, maybe it was all in her head anyway. But it wasn't all in her head, it was real, and she knew it, so she'd have to find the courage to bring it up sooner or later, because she just couldn't go on hoping that it would all somehow work itself out, when it simply couldn't. He didn't love her, at least not the way she loved him, and that was that. Oh, he cared for her deeply enough, and enjoyed her company every bit as much as she did his, particularly on a professional level, but in their hearts they both knew that on a personal level he was only with her out of guilt, because he still considered himself responsible for Lysette's suicide; so having deprived her of her twin sister, he couldn't bring himself to deprive her of their relationship too, when he knew how much it meant to her.

The very idea that pity should be his defining emotion was too humiliating for words, but she wasn't going to think about it any more tonight, when she had no intention of discussing it, and when the Hendon case needed her full attention, for she had to decide, before she spoke to Rachel tomorrow, how she was to break the news about Gustave Basim.

Picturing the way Rachel had looked when she'd left, so bewildered and afraid of losing her baby, she hardly wanted to call her at all, never mind burden her with anything more. But she had to, if for no other reason than to find out how she was now, and whether she'd changed her mind and decided to make the transfer. If she hadn't, then Laurie was toying with the idea of persuading her to confide in someone local, for she certainly needed some kind of back-up down there, especially if she decided to hang on to the money. To her mind Chris Gallagher seemed the obvious choice, for he was known by everyone, and was extremely popular too, but Laurie couldn't help feeling just a tinge of concern at the way he'd turned up in Rachel's life now, when there had surely been so many other opportunities for them to meet.

Starting as the telephone rang, she waited to see if Elliot would answer, then hearing his voice, she finished loading the dishwasher, turning her mind to the questions she was going to ask Robert Maxton when she met him tomorrow.

'That was Rose,' Elliot said, coming into the kitchen a few minutes later, carrying both glasses of wine. 'She was confirming lunch on Friday with you and your mother.'

'Actually, Mum's not coming,' she said, taking her glass. 'But she and Dad are going to be here on Thursday night. Can you make it for dinner?'

'I'll check my diary,' he answered. 'It's a busy week, I know that, so I would doubt it. In fact, I think I'm going to Stockholm on Thursday morning.'

She nodded, then smiling past her disappointment she took a sip of wine and tried to think of something to say. She wondered if he was trying to think of something too, and felt utterly wretched that they should have reached the point where all they had to talk about were the stories they worked on.

'Oh, by the way, I had a call from Murray today,' she said, referring to his office manager. 'It seems there's some office space going in your building that he thinks I should take a look at.'

He frowned as he said, 'When's Rose's lease up in Chelsea?'

'The end of this month, and since she's off to Jakarta next week, it's up to me to find somewhere soon. I had a look at the new building in Limehouse, just off Narrow Street, before I went to Cornwall. That was very promising.'

'Good location,' he commented. 'What was the rent?'

As she answered she could feel the frustration building up in her again, for she'd wanted him to show some enthusiasm for her moving the programme into the docklands building where he was based so that eventually, or even immediately, they might discuss joining forces, her and Rose running the TV side of things, him the newspapers, with a combined staff of researchers. But he obviously wasn't going to encourage that, for the only interest he'd shown was in Narrow Street, which he himself had put her on to. Yet more evidence that their minds weren't working in the same direction at all.

'So, what's happening in Stockholm?' she asked, as he went to rinse his empty glass under the tap. She couldn't have cared less what was happening in Stockholm: all she really wanted was for him to take her in his arms and tell her how much he'd missed her, and how he'd hardly been able to wait to hold her. But of course he didn't, because he never did. He just started to answer the question, then the phone interrupted him and he went back into the sitting room to answer it.

She was becoming so angry now that she actually wanted to hit him. They hadn't been together since she'd flown over to join him in the States, four weeks ago, at which point she hadn't seen him at all in over two months. To be fair, when she'd got there and suggested they snatch a few days in the Bahamas, he'd agreed right away, so in that instance, at least, she couldn't accuse him of putting his work first. Besides, she could be every bit as focused when she got her teeth into a story, so it wasn't the work she had a problem with. It was the fact that he hadn't suggested the Bahamas himself, or anywhere else, just like he hadn't attempted any more than a perfunctory kiss since she'd picked him up from the airport, and even now he didn't seem to consider any kind of personal contact or even words to be necessary. So what more evidence did she need that she wasn't anywhere close to the front of his mind, while he was always right there, at centre-stage in hers?

It was probably because she was getting herself so wound up that it took her a while to register the music that had started to drift from the speakers and fill the apartment. When she did it was as though every ounce of hostility was draining from her body, for the sheer emotion that this opera could stir in her left little room for anything else. How did he always manage to do this? To make her love him more, when she was trying so hard to love him less. For it was to *La Bohème* that they'd first made love, in a candlelit garden, at Max Erwin's impossibly romantic villa in western Mexico, just after they'd finished the Ashby story. And knowing he'd probably chosen it because he'd sensed her mood, and because this memory was so very special to them both, she could feel her throat tightening. She wanted nothing more now than to be in his arms, with his mouth and body pressed hard against hers, for it was only when they made love that the doubts and insecurities ceased to exist.

Looking up as he came into the kitchen, she smiled shakily at the desire clouding his eyes. Then going towards him she raised her mouth to his, knowing she shouldn't be this willing, but loving him as much as she did, all she could do was promise herself, yet again, that this really would be the last time.

Though Gloria Sullivan wasn't called to the film set until two, she'd made a point of arriving early in the hope of running into the journalist, Laurie Forbes, who she'd heard was meeting Robert

Maxton at noon. Knowing how unlikely it was that the unit would break on schedule, Gloria had surmised, correctly as it turned out, that Ms Forbes would be kept hanging around for a while, so Gloria was going to take the opportunity to talk to this famous reporter.

The shoot had now moved into one of the vast studios at Pinewood, on the outskirts of London, so it no longer had the warm, intimate feel that it had had when they'd been crammed into the theatre – at least that's how it seemed to Gloria. For certain others, that didn't appear to be the case at all. In fact, Stacey Greene and Robert Maxton were becoming so close these days that he'd actually had the nerve to tell Gloria that he *and Stacey* thought she was doing a marvellous job with her role. As if anyone gave a shit what Stacey Greene thought! Just who the hell did she think she was, linking her praise with the director's, as though he was her damned mouthpiece and she was just too high and mighty to speak to a lowly fellow actor in person. Ugh! Such arrogance made Gloria want to throw up. OK, Stacey had helped her in the beginning, but hey, Stacey had been getting the extra rehearsals too, so how about she woke up to the fact that it was a reciprocal thing that they'd both benefited from, not just little newcomer Gloria. Then of course the minute Stacey felt she didn't need any more private sessions, it had all been abandoned so fast it might have made Gloria's head spin, if she'd even seen it coming. As it was, she'd been expected to accept the snub as though she were some snivelling little sycophant, who should just be grateful she'd ever been noticed at all. And it hadn't helped, hearing one of the snidey make-up artists comment, 'Gloria Icarus flew too close to the sun.' As if Stacey Greene was the effing sun! Though the way the woman behaved, a person could be forgiven for thinking she was the whole frigging universe.

But Stacey Greene was like that, everyone said so. With her, you could be in favour one moment, out the next, never knowing what you'd done to earn her disapproval, nor would you ever, because to a person's face she was always as sugary dahling as ever, though, of course, without the flirtation and promise that had gone before. And that was exactly how it had happened with Gloria: one minute she was being lavished with coveted invitations – OK, one invitation – to the exclusive country home, the next she wasn't even welcome in the damned dressing room. Well, screw her, Miss Naked-Horseback-Rider with lesbian tendencies! Let her find out now what it was like to have people sniggering behind her back, the way they'd sniggered behind Gloria's after she'd made the grandiose mistake of boasting about her special relationship with Lady Muck. And that ridiculous acolyte who called himself a director could find out at the same time just what a pathetic joke he was making of himself, mooning about after her like a lovesick retard with respiratory problems, getting Ernesto Gomez to paint her portrait a dozen times over; writing her poems that he slipped to her when he thought no one was looking, and now, according to the grapevine, he was writing a new play, just for her. Poor Anna, was all Gloria could say, though frankly, if the man was going to behave like a prize perve with another woman, then she was probably better shot of him.

Though Laurie had been to plenty of TV studios before, this was her first visit to a sound-stage, and so far she was rather enjoying it, for someone had set her up with her own chair, and a monitor, and every now and again Robert Maxton himself was coming over to explain what was happening on the set. At the moment Stacey Greene was playing a scene with Bryn Walker that was impressing the heck out of Laurie, for the way it looked on the monitor was exactly as though it was taking place on a forested riverbank in the dead of night, rather than in a breeze-block studio just after midday. The reason they were doing it this way, Robert had explained, was not only because it saved the cost of a night shoot, but because of the special effects that were going to be edited in later.

Laurie hadn't pressed him on that, for she'd known she probably wouldn't understand it anyway, and besides she didn't want to ruin it for when she went to see the finished version in the cinema. It could be the kind of arty film Elliot would enjoy, so maybe, if she played her cards right, she'd be able to wangle them an invite to the première. She probably wouldn't still be with him by then but there was no reason for them not to remain friends, and anyway, after last night she was feeling slightly more confident that they might actually be able to work things out. Not that they'd discussed anything – heaven forfend that they should ever vocalize their feelings – but the fact that he'd seemed to recognize the need for some kind of romantic gesture was definitely a move in the right direction.

Smiling politely, as a petite, blonde woman with an attractive retroussé nose and large brown eyes pulled a chair up next to her, she turned her gaze back to the set where they were still blocking the same shot. She had to confess that she hadn't paid much attention for a while, for the haunting dialogue and creepy feel of the atmosphere had reminded her of the Cornish ghost stories she'd heard at the weekend, which in turn had made her think about Rachel, whom she'd spoken to just before coming here.

'First things first,' Rachel had declared, even before Laurie could ask how she was, 'the baby's OK. I saw the doctor yesterday and he's satisfied that everything's as it should be. So it was just a show. Now you want to know about the transfer. Did you mention it to Elliot, by the way?'

'Of course,' Laurie answered, and repeated what Elliot had said about holding out, but at the first sign of anything unpleasant, to give it straight back.

'I agree,' Rachel said. 'Under any other circumstances I'd probably hold out even longer, but I'm afraid the baby has to come first, and life is already stressful enough.'

It had been Laurie's intention, at that point, to bring up the possibility of confiding in Chris Gallagher, or at least someone other than Beanie – if nothing else it would be interesting to find out whether or not Rachel had any concerns about her new friend – but her second line had rung then, and since it was William Haynes from Special Ops, she'd cut Rachel short and taken the call.

'She's amazing, isn't she?'

Regaining a sense of where she was, Laurie focused on the set again, and since the young woman next to her could only be talking about Stacey Greene, she had no problem agreeing.

'She absolutely makes this movie,' the woman declared. 'And the play. Did you see the play?'

'I have to confess, I didn't,' Laurie answered.

'She was amazing in that too.' The woman was shaking her head in awe. Then suddenly she smiled, and turning to Laurie, stuck out her hand. 'Gloria Sullivan,' she said. 'I'm playing Alma, the wife, which probably doesn't mean anything if you don't know the story.'

'Laurie Forbes,' Laurie said, shaking hands.

Gloria's smile widened, then turning back to the set she continued to watch the blocking, until, apparently sunk again in admiration, she said, 'I wasn't in the play, so I had a lot of catching up to do when I joined. But Stacey's been so good to me, even to the point of giving up her own time to rehearse privately with me.'

Not sure what to say to that, Laurie merely smiled, and continued to watch what was happening on the set.

'Do you know her?' Gloria said. 'Have you met her before?'

'No.' Laurie wasn't about to confess that she'd barely even heard of her until today, because she knew that actors got touchy about such things.

'Well, I'm sure Robert will introduce you,' Gloria said. 'It is him you're here to see, isn't it?'

Laurie nodded.

'About all that terrible business with his brother-in-law, I suppose.' Gloria was still staring at the set, her expression set in tragedy.

Laurie was tensing slightly, for she was beginning to wonder if this woman had singled her out in the hope of getting some gossip. If so, then Ms Sullivan was going to be disappointed, for Laurie had no intention of discussing the Hendon case with anyone, least of all someone she didn't know.

Another minute or two passed, then Gloria said, 'I've been to the country house, actually.'

Not having the faintest idea what she was talking about now, nor really caring, Laurie said, 'How nice.'

Gloria sighed. 'It's to die for,' she said. 'You've never seen anything like it. And the lengths she goes to, just to keep everyone happy, including her husband, well . . .' Gloria was shaking her head, apparently too overwhelmed for words.

Realizing she must still be talking about Stacey Greene, Laurie made no response.

After a while, Gloria said, 'You know, I probably shouldn't say this, I mean, they keep it all very hush-hush . . . Well, they have to, but it came out while I was down there, well it couldn't *not* come out, because there's just no way she's earning enough to support all that. If she was in Hollywood, maybe, but she's not, so it has to be her husband who's got all the money, which means that there's a good chance he really is who they say he is.'

Laurie was happy to go for it. 'And who do they say he is?' she asked.

'Well, let's put it this way,' Gloria replied, 'her assistant, Petey . . . Yeah, that's right, she's got her own assistant! Can you believe that? No one else has, but he's not on the budget. Anna would never allow that. No, he's one of the expenses her husband covers. Anyway, Petey was the one who told me that her husband's as big as that Colombian chap, what's-his-name? He's dead now, but apparently he was one of the world's biggest, you know, in his time.'

'Pablo Escobar?' Laurie suggested, citing the only 'biggest' she'd heard of from that part of the world.

'That's him. Not that I think Stacey's husband's that big, but honestly, if you saw the way they live . . .'

Laurie slanted her a look. She surely wasn't serious, for Escobar was a notorious drug lord and murderer, and though Laurie knew nothing at all about either Stacey Greene or her husband, she was having a hard time seeing them as a couple of Escobar wannabes. Much more likely that Ms Sullivan was the victim of an elaborate wind-up, or she was attempting to use Laurie to settle some kind of grudge. Whichever, Laurie was no longer particularly interested, for she had too much else on her mind to concern herself with a stranger's petty peeves.

Several minutes ticked by as Gloria slouched more comfortably in her chair and made appreciative noises at what was happening on the set. Then finally she said, 'You know what's so wonderful about this shoot is the way everyone on it has turned into a kind of family. We all really support each other, and Robert, well, he's just the best director in the world. I've never worked with anyone who cares so much about the cast.' She leaned in closer and kept her voice low as she said, 'Of course, he cares a lot more about Stacey than the rest of us, but who can blame him for that? Apparently he's been writing her poems in private, which Petey, her assistant, says are absolutely pornographic. Personally, if it were me, I'd be offended, but Stacey's so tolerant, and kind . . .'

'OK, everyone, that's lunch,' someone suddenly shouted. 'Back at two-fifteen.'

Laurie got to her feet and smiled down at Gloria. 'It was very nice meeting you,' she said. 'Good luck with the film.'

As she walked away she could feel Gloria's eyes on her back like two hot rods, and wouldn't have minded knowing what was going through her malicious little mind now, or indeed what she was expecting to come of the information she'd just deliberately fed to a journalist. She'd probably be quite put out to discover that she'd talked to entirely the wrong person, for Laurie simply wasn't in the business of celebrity scandal, or of settling other people's scores.

'I'm sorry to have kept you waiting so long,' Robert said, coming to meet her and reaching for her hands. 'We're having a bit of a problem with this particular scene. But we're getting there. Are you hungry? We can go to the dining room, or maybe we should be more private. Of course, what am I thinking? Private. My office. I'll get someone to bring us a couple of sandwiches.'

'Actually, I'm fine, thanks,' Laurie responded, going on ahead as he indicated the way. 'But please, don't let me stop you.'

'I'll get something later,' he said. 'I'm sorry Anna's not here, she has a big meeting with the distributors today. But I think you're seeing her tomorrow, aren't you?'

Laurie was about to reply when someone came up behind them and began talking to Robert, keeping close behind as they wound their way through a labyrinth of corridors and stairwells. Finally Robert stopped at a plain white door with his name on, thanked the person who still didn't look as though he'd finished his diatribe, then winked at Laurie as though to say, 'time to make a getaway.'

A few minutes later they were sitting either side of his desk, in an office that was small and functional, though not particularly impressive for a man of his standing. 'So how was Rachel when you left?' he asked, reaching behind him to adjust the blinds so that the sun would no longer dazzle her. 'I don't mind telling you, Anna's quite worried. Well, we both are. This is a terrible time she's going through.'

Laurie nodded a sober agreement. 'She didn't sound too bad when I spoke to her earlier,' she said. 'Apparently everything's OK with the baby.'

'Yes, she called Anna before we left this morning. What a relief it was to hear that, but we're still going to try and get down there this weekend. Oh, excuse me,' he said as the phone on his desk started to ring.

As he answered, Laurie's eyes dropped to the wooden box he'd begun toying with, flicking the ornately carved lid up and down with his thumb. For some reason it looked familiar, though she couldn't think why. Then it came back to her: she'd spotted one like it in Killian, and almost had it snatched from her hand. Obviously, if that was where he'd got it, he hadn't been considered such an undesirable customer.

She forgot about it then as he laughed and her eyes rose to his face. Not for the first time since meeting him she found herself thinking how much more appealing, and somehow substantial, he seemed in person than he did in pictures, or on TV, where he looked rather bland and slight. Nor did he give the impression of someone who experienced the insecurity that Rachel had mentioned, for he looked perfectly relaxed now, and had seemed in total control of the shoot while she was watching. However, she knew very well how deceptive appearances could be. After all, who would know that she was experiencing her own personal dilemmas right now?

'Sorry,' he said, putting the phone down. 'Maybe we should have met at the end of the day, because it's probably going to be a bit like this. But you're here now – and by the way, thank you for taking this on, because the last thing Anna or I wanted was to see Rachel trying to do it herself.'

Laurie smiled. Her notebook was open, her pencil poised.

Robert was still talking. 'It would have probably come close to destroying her if she had,' he was saying, 'as if it's not that close already.' He gave a despairing shake of his head while gazing absently at the small wooden box. 'What the hell happened that morning, eh?' he said. 'What was the man doing in another woman's flat at such an ungodly hour?'

'So you don't believe they were having an affair?' Laurie said.

His eyes came up, showing surprise and a little offence. 'I know it looks that way,' he answered, 'but frankly I'd have staked my life on Tim's fidelity. They were very close. There was no pretence put on for the media. The man loved his wife.'

'But you hadn't seen much of them for a while,' Laurie reminded him.

'Actually, I saw more of them than Anna knew,' he confided. 'But even if I hadn't, if anything changed between them during the year she and Anna didn't speak, then it was simply that they got closer. Anna herself remarked on it, not long after she and Rachel made up their differences.'

'Did he ever talk to you about Katherine Sumner?' Laurie asked. 'In any context.'

His eyes narrowed as he thought. 'Not really,' he said finally. 'In fact, the only time I remember him mentioning her is when he called to ask if she could come to my fortieth birthday party. As it turned out, she was there longer than Tim and Rachel, because she got an earlier plane back from Scotland. That was only the second or third time I'd met her. The first time was at their house, the second was . . . Well, I think it was the party.'

Laurie's smile was bland. 'And obviously she hasn't been in touch with you since?'

'No. Well, she wouldn't. We didn't really know her.'

Laurie was about to move on to his interviews with the police when the door opened and Stacey Greene swept in, creating a small whirlwind of perfume, chiffon and deep throaty tones. 'Robert, darling, I was hoping to find you here . . . Oh gosh!' she gasped, seeing Laurie. 'I'm so sorry. I totally forgot you had a visitor. Please, excuse me. I didn't mean to interrupt.'

'No, no, it's quite all right,' Robert assured her, getting to his feet. 'Have you met Stacey Greene?' he said to Laurie. 'Stacey, this is Laurie Forbes.'

'How do you do?' Laurie said, standing up too. Though she was tall, Stacey had at least another two inches on her, and with all that flowing red hair and heady sensuousness she was a truly dazzling creature to behold. However, quite of their own accord, Laurie's heckles were definitely on the rise.

'It's a pleasure to meet you,' Stacey told her warmly, using both hands to shake. 'I've heard of you, of course. But please, don't let me interrupt any further.'

Laurie smiled politely and hoped her antipathy didn't show.

'Actually, I don't think it would be a problem if you stayed,' Robert said, reaching for Stacey's hand. 'Would it?' he asked Laurie.

Surprised that he'd want her to, and even more surprised that Stacey seemed willing, Laurie was about to protest, when recalling what Gloria Sullivan had told her, she felt mildly intrigued to see where this might go. Not that she wanted the scandal, but the timing of Stacey's entrance was . . . interesting, and for all she knew Stacey might have something worthwhile to contribute.

As Laurie and Robert sat down again, Stacey went to stand behind him, and placed an almost proprietary hand on his shoulder. Laurie couldn't be sure whether his act of covering the hand with his own was a conscious one or not. It could be just a showbizzy thing, because actors were always touching each other, though it had to be said, this little tableau was conveying an air of togetherness that she knew very well, were she his wife, she wouldn't appreciate at all.

'You're here to talk about that terrible tragedy, aren't you?' Stacey said, looking at her with such soulful eyes that Laurie could almost be convinced by their compassion. 'That poor woman. Robert's been so worried, haven't you, darling? It's been affecting his work, or so he thinks, but actually he copes much better than he gives himself credit for. It hasn't been easy for him, though.'

'But worse for Rachel,' Laurie couldn't help saying.

'Oh, of course. No one's ever doubting that. And I believe she's pregnant. How on earth does a woman deal with so much, I wonder.'

'Do you know Rachel?' Laurie asked.

'Not personally, no. But Robert's talked about her such a lot that I feel as though I do. I only wish there was something I could do to help.'

Feeling certain that Rachel would be glad there wasn't, Laurie looked at Robert as he said,

'Oh, but you do help.' He was pressing her hand to his cheek. Then he turned to look up at her with an expression of such naked adoration that Laurie actually felt herself cringe. 'You do,' he whispered to Stacey.

Stacey smiled down at him, then stooped to press her mouth to his forehead.

He whispered something that Laurie didn't catch, and Stacey smiled and kissed him again.

Feeling horribly like a voyeur, and resenting it, Laurie cleared her throat, but as they looked at her she suddenly realized that she couldn't continue. She was in no position to ask Stacey to go, and since she had at least a dozen other people to interview over the next few days, she saw no point in wasting her time here, watching this bizarre little performance that was making her skin crawl. So starting to pack away her notebook, she said to Robert, 'I think you're right, we should meet at the end of the day, when you're less . . . distracted.'

As she looked up again, Stacey smiled sweetly, so she did too.

'It was a pleasure meeting you,' she said, noting how Stacey had made no attempt to leave, the way most people would have after such a blatant hint.

'The feeling's mutual,' Stacey replied.

Wondering whether she meant the pleasure, or the dislike that she surely must have picked up on, Laurie felt herself flush, for she'd never been good at bitchiness. 'Thank you,' she said, holding a hand out to Robert. 'I'll probably be in touch again after I've spoken to Anna.' Had she put too much emphasis on his wife's name? She hoped so.

'Any time,' he told her, standing up to shake hands.

It took a moment or two after Laurie had gone for Stacey to regain her composure, for her heart had begun pounding with an unexpected rush of adrenalin when she'd realized that Laurie had taken such an instant dislike to her. It was so rare an occurrence that Stacey still couldn't quite make herself accept it, though she had to wonder why she cared, when Laurie Forbes meant absolutely nothing to her, wouldn't even have come into her life, had she not inadvertently walked in on this meeting.

Realizing Robert was watching her she turned to him and smiled. 'Are you all right?' she asked gently, smoothing a hand over his face.

'Of course,' he replied, taking the hand and kissing it.

'I would have left,' she said, 'but you seemed to need me to stay. What was she asking you?'

'Nothing, really. We'd barely got started. But you were right to think I needed you, because I always do.'

Laughing softly, she leaned forward to plant her mouth briefly on his. 'You are such a darling,' she told him.

His hands rose to her shoulders and gently massaged them. 'Did you read what I left for you this morning?' he murmured, his palms cupping the perfect bones as though they were breasts.

'Mm, yes, I did,' she said darkly. 'And you're a wicked boy, Robert Maxton. I hope you know that.'

'Wicked enough to be spanked?' he said, gazing hopefully into her eyes.

'Almost,' she promised.

His hands moved up to her neck, and began lovingly to stroke it. 'Do you feel me making love to you when you read the words?' he asked.

'I feel everything,' she assured him.

'And you're not offended?'

'How can I be, when you write it all so beautifully?'

303

'You don't find it obscene?'

She smiled. 'Is that how you want me to find it?'

'I want you to let me do all those things to you,' he said gruffly, tightening his grip on her throat.

Unfazed, she said, 'I know. But we agreed, didn't we, that fantasy only has power when it's not forced into reality. And do you really want to lose what we have?'

'Never.'

'Then let me stand here for you, my darling,' she murmured, paraphrasing the script, 'so that you can imagine me any way you like, in all the positions you describe, experiencing all the lust you pour so eloquently and erotically on to the page.'

As she stepped back, away from his hands, he watched her raise her dress to her waist, so that he could see her long, slender legs with their powdery smattering of freckles, her exquisitely flared hips and the neat, fiery bush of hair that protected her most precious place. His heart began to race as she sank back on to the desk and, lying across it, opened her legs wide. His penis was an engorged mass of urgency, bursting from his pants, so ready to make the plunge into her wet, golden abyss that he could already feel it, sliding in, so big and tight, and deep . . .

Then someone knocked at the door, and reality slipped cruelly back into focus.

'OK?' she whispered, taking his hand. 'Did it work?'

He nodded. 'Yes. Thank you.'

'Then maybe we should tell whoever it is to come in.' She smiled. 'And after, you can tell me what we just did.'

Chapter 13

Though Killian in the sunshine was one of the most enchanting places on earth, Killian under dark, turbulent skies, which seemed so low and dense they could be dipped into like clay, had a whole other kind of charm that Rachel often found even more stirring than the storm itself, when it came. For, under this great glowering expanse of grey, as the sea turned leaden and the craggy shores seemed to vibrate with the might of the thunder, it felt as though an ungodly power was trying to break though the earth's crust to meet a descending vengeance from the heavens above.

She knew that if Robert were with her now, gazing out of this small, bedroom window, he'd say, 'Such glorious majesty, and monstrously wicked beauty.' She'd always liked the description, for it captured both the visual and the visceral, while recognizing that there were forces beyond the eye, deeper than the rational mind, and even contrary to the forward journey of time. She adored the uniqueness of Cornwall, and its incredible wealth of superstition. Beanie had so many books and stories and memories that Rachel and Tim had never tired of hearing, or reading, losing themselves in swashbuckling adventure or heroic skulduggery. Yet the thrill of believing only ever seemed to happen when they were here, for once back in London it all felt so improbable and fanciful; they'd never minded that, because the magic belonged here, in this wickedly beautiful cove with its hidden secrets and chillingly restless past.

Starting as the phone bleated into the silence, she turned to pick it up from the bed behind her, where Beanie had left it, under an untidy pile of the papers they'd been sorting.

'Hello?' she said, stepping over the books and small boxes she'd turfed out of an old metal chest they'd dragged down from the attic.

At first no one answered, and her heart turned cold, for today was the deadline for the transfer. 'Beanie?' she said tentatively. 'Is that you?'

'No, it's me, Laurie. Sorry, I was just paying a cabbie. How are you?'

'OK,' Rachel answered, breathing again. 'A bit jittery, I suppose, but nothing I can't handle.'

'Are you keeping yourself busy?'

'After a fashion.' She glanced at the mess on the floor. 'Beanie and I have been going through Tim's grandfather's things, if you call that busy,' she said. 'Actually, there are some interesting letters here, from a family perspective, and so many photographs and books you wouldn't believe. But tell me what's happening your end. Did you see Haynes?'

'Yes, I've just come from there. Sorry about all

the noise. Can you hear me? I'm in the foyer of our apartment block, where they've got the floor up for some reason. I'll be indoors in a couple of minutes, so bear with me. Are Anna and Robert coming for the weekend?'

'Anna and the children,' Rachel corrected. 'Robert has to stay in London.'

There was a brief pause before Laurie said, 'Well as long as you're not on your own.'

'No, I won't be,' Rachel replied, and closing the bedroom door behind her she walked along the narrow, book-lined landing, ducked beneath the ladder that led up to the attic, then started down the stairs.

'Is Beanie there with you?' Laurie asked.

'No, she's popped up to the post office at Roon Moor. Why? Do I need her to be?'

'No, I was just wondering.'

'Then please don't keep me in suspense any longer,' Rachel responded, pushing open the door at the bottom of the stairs and stepping down into the sitting room. 'What did Haynes say?'

'Sorry. OK, I've got everything now, so let's start with Xavier Lachère. The answer to my question was yes, they have heard of him, but they're claiming to have no idea who he is. They're also adamant that every sighting of Katherine to date has taken them down a dead end, and I suppose we don't have any choice but to believe it. There was one in Madrid at the weekend that they got quite excited about, but it came to nothing.'

'Would they lie about Katherine?' Rachel asked. 'I mean, do you think they might know where she is, and this whole manhunt thing is just a massive front of some kind?' She was already shaking her head, for it defied logic.

'A front for whose benefit?' Laurie said. 'Who would they be hiding her from, except themselves? Though I have to say, I'm pretty damned certain that this entire investigation, as far as the rest of us are concerned, is running on parallel tracks to the truth. However, this time when I asked who had reported the murder there was no hedging or stalling, he told me right out that the call had been made *direct to Special Ops* at nine-fifteen in the morning, which, as we know, is about four hours after it happened. They haven't been able to trace where the call came from, it was too fast, and they don't know who it was either, except he did tell me it was a woman. Of course everyone's thinking Katherine Sumner, though your guess will be as good as anyone else's as to why it would be her.'

Rachel didn't feel quite steady, for the thought of Katherine alerting the police to a murder she herself had committed, or at least been involved in, was too disturbing to comprehend. 'Did this woman have an American accent?' she said, asking the obvious.

'Apparently they couldn't tell, but she could have been disguising.'

'So what did she say?'

'She told them there had been a shooting at the address we know is Katherine's, and that she believed someone important had been murdered.'

The blood was draining from Rachel's face.

Laurie took a breath. 'This next bit you need to brace yourself for,' she cautioned. 'Are you sitting down?'

Rachel sank on to a chair next to the table.

'I thought, instead of telling Haynes that I knew about Gustave Basim, I'd ask instead if any progress had been made in identifying the third set of prints at Katherine's flat, if there were any suspects or leads. He said there was nothing.'

Rachel hesitated. 'So he lied?' she said.

'I'm afraid so.'

Rachel's eyes moved to the window: the rain and wind was now lashing against it like an evil force trying to break its way in. It was frightening her, because it felt unreal and unstoppable, just like what she was hearing, for there was simply no knowing who Haynes and his team might be trying to protect, or exactly what they were being protected from. 'Why would they lie about that?' she said quietly.

'I don't know, but it could just be that they want to be sure there's a connection before they go public.'

Rachel nodded. It made sense, she supposed. Her eyes were focused on nothing, as her hand moved distractedly to the keyboard of her laptop. She hardly knew what she was thinking or feeling now, as she double-clicked to go on line. 'This search Franz Koehler's supposed to be conducting,' she said. 'If it's genuine . . . Does that mean this Gustave Basim character was supposed to have killed her too, and somehow she got away? But if that is the case, why doesn't she just go to the police?'

'Both very good questions,' Laurie responded.

'Has Elliot ever met Franz Koehler?'

'No,' Laurie answered. 'Not in person.'

'Does he think Phraxos might have infiltrated the British system more than we realize?'

'He hasn't found too much evidence of it yet,' Laurie replied. 'Just the expected type of share-holdings in companies like British Aerospace and GEC. Nothing untoward, but they're working on it.'

Rachel was thinking of all the people she knew in government, and those who advised them, the dozens upon dozens of grey suits who peopled the Janus Conventions, as Tim used to call them, the covert meetings that plotted the annihilation of their political enemies, controlled policies, buried or spun scandals, manipulated the law – there was no end to the iniquity or the power of those men. She'd put nothing past them.

'Have you managed to talk to Gordon or Dennis yet?' she asked. 'Tim's senior aides.'

'No, but I'm seeing Dennis tomorrow. I've also got a meeting with a professor from the London School of Economics, who's a bit of an expert on Phraxos and their style of investing. He's an American who's been over here for about ten years. George Monheit. Ever heard of him?'

Rachel thought. 'No, I don't think so,' she answered.

'Well, there's a good chance he could be quite helpful, so I'll let you know how it goes. Just give me a minute now while I run through my notes to see if there's anything I've missed.'

As Rachel waited she gazed blankly at the screen in front of her, barely registering the list of new emails as she tried not to think of how everything seemed to be closing in on her like an ugly, chanting crowd: Haynes, Koehler, Basim, Katherine, Dennis . . . She shifted restlessly, then focused on the messages to escape her thoughts. There were at least a dozen. One in particular caught her eye, at the same instant as it caused a horrible twist in her heart. Taking the cursor to it, she clicked it open. As she read it her eyes dilated with shock.

'Laurie, listen to this,' she said urgently. 'I've got an email here from the woman who manages the villa on Virgin Gorda – the one Tim and I were supposed to be staying at. She's saying she's sorry she hasn't been in touch before, but she hopes we enjoyed our stay, and that she's put the things we left behind in the mail so we should be receiving them soon.'

Laurie was stunned into silence.

'Lucy cancelled the holiday,' Rachel said, her heart pounding with unease. 'I remember her doing it.' Her voice turned shrill as she cried, 'Well, obviously we weren't there. How could we have been?'

'OK. Don't worry,' Laurie said quickly. 'It's probably just a mistake. Forward the email to me, and make sure the villa's address and phone numbers are there too, because its ownership has just gone to priority number one.'

As Rachel hit the send button she was praying with all her might that it didn't turn out to be Franz Koehler. 'It's on its way,' she said.

'Good. Are you all right?'

'Yes. Fine. Just a bit . . . shell-shocked.'

'When's Anna arriving?'

'She called from Truro about an hour ago, so any time now.'

'And how long's she staying?'

'Just until Sunday. The girls have to go to school on Monday.'

Which left Rachel alone on the day the transfer issue could turn crucial. 'Tell me,' Laurie said, 'have you thought about confiding in someone down there? I mean, someone who's got a bit more testosterone than Beanie.'

Rachel didn't answer straight away, because the truth was, she had considered it, several times, though she couldn't even begin to imagine why someone like Chris Gallagher would want to be burdened with the problems of a grieving widow whom he barely even knew. 'I could talk to Nick,' she said tentatively.

'I'll let you be the judge,' Laurie replied. 'Just make someone aware of what's happening, so that they can be on the lookout for any strangers who might start hanging around, or . . . Well, I don't want to spook you any further. You know what I'm saying.'

'Yes,' Rachel responded, wondering if Laurie was thinking about Chris Gallagher too, though he could hardly be termed a stranger when Beanie, and everyone else, knew him so well.

'OK, well I'd better crack on here,' Laurie said. 'I'll speak to you in the morning.'

After putting the phone down, Rachel got up to turn on the lights. The main thrust of the storm seemed to be dying now, but it was still dank and gloomy outside, and the air in the cottage felt chill. She stared at the wide inglenook hearth. It seemed disheartening to light a fire at the beginning of July, but the children would enjoy making toast in the flames, and there was something reassuring about a real fire flickering away in the background that might still the restlessness inside her.

With so much wood, stacked up as high as the cloam oven, it didn't take her long to fill the cast iron basket, and she was on the point of putting a light to the scrunched-up newspaper under the logs, when Beanie came bustling in the back door.

'Anna's just pulled up,' she called out. 'I'm putting the kettle on.'

Rachel grimaced at the surge of relief she felt, then reaching for the bellows to help things on their way, she said, 'I was thinking, Bean, should we invite Chris Gallagher over for dinner tomorrow night?'

Beanie came to stand in the archway, drying her hands on a tea towel. 'Oh, a fire, lovely,' she declared. 'Just the season for it.'

Rachel smiled. 'So what do you say?' she prompted.

'I'd say it's a lovely idea,' she replied, 'but I haven't seen him all week. I think he went over to Mousehole, someone said, then he was going to Falmouth to take his boat out. Or was he going to Fowey? Can't remember. But we can always try calling his mobile.' She beamed happily. 'If he can make it, I reckon he'd love to come.'

She'd barely finished speaking when the door burst open and everything seemed to happen at once: as the girls threw themselves at Rachel, the phone started to ring and the kettle to whistle.

'I'll get the kettle,' Anna shouted from the kitchen.

313

'I've got the phone,' Beanie shouted, from the table.

'And we've got Auntie Rachel,' Emily and Justine giggled, grabbing her round the waist.

Laughing, Rachel embraced them, while at the same time listening anxiously to Beanie as she took the call.

'All right. All right,' Beanie was saying. 'Yep. I heard. Oh, sorry, yes, it's brilliant. Well, you know I think that about everything you do. OK. She's here. I'll pass you over,' and handing the phone to Rachel, she said, 'It's our Nick.'

'Nick,' Rachel said, into the receiver. 'How are you?'

'Flush,' he answered. 'I just had a call from Chris's gallery over in Fowey, they've only gone and sold one of my paintings for nearly a thousand quid. So what do you think of that, then?'

'Nick, that's fantastic,' she cried. 'Congratulations. We always told you you were a genius.'

'Well, I don't know about that,' he said modestly, 'but I'm calling because we're going to have a bit of a celebration when Chris gets back on Sunday night. He's going to bring the loot with him, so we thought you and Bean might like to join in, if you're free.'

'Of course. Just tell us the time and the place and we'll be there.'

'We're still working that out. I'll talk to Jen and give you a call back.'

As she put the phone down Rachel was still smiling at Nick's news, and feeling suddenly less tense now that Anna was here.

'Auntie Rachel, I can feel your bump, it's getting

314

big,' Justine declared, running her little hands over Rachel's tummy. 'Does it kick yet?'

'No. Not yet,' Rachel said, smiling as she covered Justine's hands with her own.

'I can't wait for it to be born,' Emily announced. 'I hope it's a girl.'

'Me too,' Justine sighed.

'But what if it's a boy? Won't you want it then?' Rachel teased.

'Oh yes, yes,' they cried.

'OK you two, on the phone to Daddy and tell him we've arrived safely,' Anna instructed, coming in with a tray of tea and a bag of sugary doughnuts. 'Are you all right?' she said to Rachel. 'You look a bit flushed.'

Rachel frowned. 'Do I? It must be the fire. Or these two, getting me excited about the baby,' she added, ruffling their hair.

Anna spun them round by the tops of their heads and pointed them in the direction of the phone. 'Daddy first, then doughnuts,' she told them.

'Peppermint or camomile?' Beanie said to Rachel.

'Isn't there any more peach?'

'I'll go and check.'

'No, I'll go.'

'No, you just sit down there.'

Rachel looked at Anna as she dutifully did as she was told. A moment later her smile faded at the expression that came over Anna's face as Emily said crossly, 'He's not at home and his mobile's switched off. He said he'd keep it switched on.'

'Just call back and leave a message,' Anna said, pouring a slug of whisky into her tea. She looked strained and edgy, almost as though she wanted to grab the phone herself and scream into it.

Rachel didn't ask any questions, not while the girls were there. She'd bring it up later, when they were alone. In the meantime, she resolved to make this the last time she asked Anna to come here, until she was certain that whatever problems Anna was having with Robert were completely sorted, because she couldn't have her sister's loyalties split like this, nor could she bear the shattering of her nerves *every time the telephone rang*.

But it was only Nick again, telling her where they were all going to meet on Sunday night.

'I'm curious,' Stacey said to her husband, from where she was lounging on the sofa, wearing only a short satin nightie and a thin gold ankle chain, 'why would you say no, when we have a perfect relationship, more money than we could ever need, wonderful homes with more than enough room, and when you surely want someone to pass it all on to one day.'

In what he already knew to be a vain attempt to avoid the issue, he turned over a page of the paper and carried on reading.

Taking a half-smoked joint from an ashtray, she relit it and inhaled deeply. Her eyes were glittering and sphinx-like as she gazed up at the gently vaulted ceiling of the penthouse, while trailing a lazy arm along the floor. The rustic brick walls and huge funnel-shaped fireplace glowed rosily in the dying rays of sunset, while the large black leather sofas and scatter rugs and pillows cast long, shapeless shadows over the teak wood floor.

'Just tell me why you're so set against it,' she said after a while.

Still he didn't answer.

Taking another long pull on the cigarette, she held it for several seconds, then watched the small cloud of smoke curling around the dwindling strands of sunlight. 'So is this a no for all time, or just for now?' she ventured.

Finally he lowered the paper and looked across the room to where she was lying. 'Why do you want a child now?' he asked bluntly, raising a hand to refuse as she offered the joint.

Surprised by the question, she turned on her side to look at him. Then a playful smile started to shape her lips as she said, 'I want your baby, my darling, because I love you, and because I want us to make that ultimate commitment of bringing another human being into the world, that is a part of us both. A symbol of our love.'

His eyes remained on hers, seeming to assess how serious she was, then with a sardonic tilt of his eyebrows, he said, 'Which, loosely translated, means you want me to be at home more, and you're hoping this will make it happen.'

Stung that he had seen through her so easily, yet amused by it too, she said, 'Is there something wrong with wanting you to be at home more?'

'Not at all. But it's just not possible at the moment – and for the same reasons, nor is a child. But I do want one, very much, if that helps.'

She kept her eyes on his, watching his darkly handsome features as he stared back at her, then rolling on to her back she gazed up at the ceiling again and toyed with the idea of asking him, straight out, what had changed in his association with Franz Koehler that was making his absences so much more frequent, and often longer than they'd been before.

'What's happened to your painting?' he asked, breaking a ten-minute silence as he reached out to turn on the arced chrome lamp beside him. 'You don't seem to have done any lately.'

Deciding not to answer, she continued to gaze through the skylight, watching the stars emerge in the growing darkness.

'We had a studio put in here for you, as well as at the house,' he reminded her. 'Is there something wrong with them?'

'No,' she answered. 'Nothing. But while I'm engaged in this project with Ernesto and Robert . . . Well, my own efforts seem rather feeble and amateur by comparison.' She smiled drily. 'I've never considered myself a talent in the field,' she confessed, 'but I do love to dabble, and I do love you for indulging me.' She turned to face him. 'It doesn't make up for a child though, so I hope that's not what you're suggesting.'

'Not for a minute,' he replied. 'I just like to watch you work, whether you're painting, acting, or simply sitting at your desk answering correspondence and talking on the phone.'

She liked the answer because it confirmed he still found her interesting and beautiful, even though she knew it anyway. However, it didn't go nearly far enough, when what she really wanted was to be reassured that she, and their life together, meant more than his work with Franz Koehler.

As he got up to go and refresh his drink, he

looked at the table she'd had specially designed for him, and felt a rush of guilt at the way he was now going to use it to distract her. It hardly seemed fair to use her love of their sex life against her like this, when she was right to be concerned, because what he was undertaking for Koehler and Phraxos wasn't at all as straightforward as he'd led her to believe.

After fixing himself another drink he stood gazing at Ernesto's remarkable craftsmanship, the beautifully sculpted contours of her bottom and vulva, the exquisite curves of her thighs, the slender bones of her ankles and feet, the small mounds of her breasts beneath the table's flat-topped surface. What an extraordinary gift it was, and so like her to have thought of something so intimate yet brazen. Of course it aroused him to look at it, yet, in a way, it made him feel vaguely melancholy too. Deciding it would be a cheap and unworthy exploitation of her feelings to use it now as he'd intended, he turned and walked back to his chair. 'So how're the portraits coming along with Ernesto?' he asked chattily. 'Was Robert there today?'

The thought of Robert brought the silky smile back to her lips, and stretching one long leg straight up in the air, she smoothed a hand over the faintly freckled flesh of her thigh. 'Why ask about Robert?' she said. 'Are you concerned I might be having an affair with him?'

His eyebrows went up, as he swilled the Scotch round the ice in his glass then lifted it to take a sip, before saying, 'Are you?'

'Would you mind if I were?' she countered.

He continued to watch her, then said, 'If you're

waiting for the jealous husband to fly into a rage, it can be arranged.'

Her eyes darkened, and then she laughed.

He put his drink down and picked up another section of the paper. 'So, are you having an affair?' he asked, after a while.

Surprised, and pleased that he'd stayed on the subject, she considered the question for a moment, then said, 'Well, he doesn't touch me, exactly, and he knows how utterly devoted I am to you, but if one were to look at it from Anna's point of view I'd say *he* was having an affair.' She sighed pleasurably, and stroked a hand idly over one breast. 'And the answer is yes, he was at the studio all day today, just watching me, as Ernesto worked. You know, it's rather touching to have someone so besotted with you.'

A few minutes ticked by before he said, 'You don't think I'm that person?'

Satisfied that he was at least slightly irked, she sat up and removed her nightie. Lying down again, naked and semi-aroused, she said, 'This is how I was, all day. I don't know if he took his eyes off me once.' She smiled dreamily, and hummed for a while, then turning her head to look at him was pleased to see that she still had his full attention.

'Do you really have to go away again tomorrow? On a Sunday,' she said. 'You only got back yesterday.'

'It shouldn't be for long,' he assured her.

She looked doubtful about that, then her eyes drifted to nowhere as she said, 'Robert's wife is away at the moment. He should have gone with her, but he stayed in London, he said, to be near me.'

Both amused and riled by the barb, he retaliated by saying, 'Then maybe we should invite him over tonight.'

She shot him a look, then struggled to hide her smile, as she said, 'That would be cruel.'

'And cruel is something you're not.'

With slanted eyes she turned on to her side and felt the sharpness of desire sliding between her legs as she said, 'And what about you, *mon beau mari*? How cruel are you?'

His answer was to let his eyes roam her nudity while she watched him and felt the air charging with the tension of what was to come.

After a while he said, 'Have you got rid of all the boxes?'

'Oh yes. Did you think I wouldn't?'

'Not at all.' Then after a beat, 'I imagine you've made a lot of people very happy.'

'I certainly hope so. I'm expecting another shipment soon. Would you mind unzipping your trousers so that I can see if I'm turning you on.'

Lowering his fly he obligingly removed his almost fully erect penis.

Smiling, and inhaling deeply, she curled up like a cat to watch her prey.

For a long time they merely looked at each other, allowing the eroticism to dance through their minds and thicken the air, until finally, he crooked a finger to summon her over.

Her pulse quickened, for she knew what he wanted, and slipping on to her hands and knees she crawled over to his chair, and with no preamble at all, took him deep into her mouth.

321

His hand was in her hair, stroking her with his fingers as she performed pure magic with her lips and tongue, when to his intense annoyance, the mobile on the table beside them started to ring. Stretching out an arm he lifted it to one ear, while holding her head down to prevent her from stopping. But she had no intention of stopping, for she loved nothing better than when he treated her crudely like this, and only wished he'd do it more often.

As he listened to Rudy's voice his eyes were closed in an effort to help his concentration, though it was hard to think about Mrs Hendon and her four million dollars when his wife was launching such an assault on his senses. Then Rudy said something that made his eyes open. 'Run that by me again,' he said.

'They reckon they've traced this Xavier Lachère guy,' Rudy repeated.

Easing Stacey aside, he got to his feet and began striding across the room. 'Who is he?' he said.

'Franz didn't say, but he's convinced Lachère knows where Katherine is, which kind of confirms that he doesn't, don't you think?'

'So when you say they've traced him, does that mean they know *who* is he, or *where* he is?'

'Pass on both. I'm just telling you what Franz told me, but you've got other issues to deal with right now.'

As he disappeared into the bedroom Stacey got to her feet and sauntered over to the sideboard where she kept other methods of satisfaction, some of which he didn't entirely approve of. But since he'd left her so abruptly, and in such a state of arousal, what did he expect? And these special little panties with their joyful appendage would keep her going very nicely until he came back. So stepping into them, she pulled them up over her legs, inserted the most special part where it was intended to go, then pushed the little button at the base. It caused such a sudden and formidable onslaught of sensation that she actually moaned aloud, then found herself thinking of naughty Robert, and how it would blow his mind to see her like this. She wondered if he was parked in a street nearby, staring up at her apartment, the way he'd told her he had last night. She'd ask him on Monday, and if she found out he was, she might tell him what she'd been doing while he was gazing up at her windows, because, in fact, it was something she really ought to be punished for, when her husband was right there in the next room, with no idea that she was pleasuring herself to an orgasm while thinking of another man.

But the very instant the door opened, all thoughts of Robert fled, for there was no man on earth who meant more than the one coming towards her now, or ever would. He was, quite simply, the beginning, middle and end of her existence, and all the little games she played with anyone else were just that, games, to while away the time he wasn't here.

'I think this can go now, don't you?' he murmured, reaching a hand between her legs.

'Whatever you say,' she responded.

She stood still as he slid the panties down over her legs, then melted against him as he pulled her into his arms and kissed her deeply. She wanted to tell him then that she didn't care how insecure or vulnerable the Koehler connection made her feel, and that she didn't even care how often he had to go away, because none of it was ever going to make a difference to the way she felt about him. But he knew that already, and as his own clothes were coming off now, she really had no intention of discussing anything as mundane as the Phraxos Group, when it was already laying claim to enough of his life, so the hell was she going to let it spoil the rest of this rare, relaxing evening at home.

Chapter 14

The weekend's storms had passed, leaving the cove damp and glistening in the sunlight that was casting slick puddles of light on the rocks, and dancing like diamonds on the idly chopping sea. The gulls seemed restless and raucous, as they swooped around the cliffs and rooftops, while the warm, sluggish air was thick with the scent of wild garlic and wet grass. Everything was perfectly normal and benign, yet to Rachel there was an eeriness to the calm that was making her doubly glad that Chris and Nick were around, helping clear up after the torrential rain, for it was late on Monday morning, and the Swiss banks had already been open for several hours, so it must have been discovered by now that she had ignored the transfer instructions.

She still hadn't mentioned anything to either of them about the situation, mainly because she hadn't wanted to spoil the celebration last night, when Nick had treated them all to dinner at the Mullion Cove Hotel with his newfound wealth as an artist.

He'd been so thrilled by his success that it would have been unforgivably selfish to turn the evening into something about her. And later, when Chris – who she now knew had galleries in Mousehole, Fowey and London – had driven her and Beanie home, Beanie had taken the front seat, so she hadn't been about to spill it all out from behind him, and when they'd got back, she just hadn't felt right about inviting him in so late at night. Maybe if Beanie hadn't been so tipsy and eager to get to bed, she might have suggested they all have a nightcap, but she had vanished faster than her pixie friends, and because the mild, moonlit night had unsettled Rachel with its air of romance she had said goodnight perhaps more abruptly than she should have, and hurried into the cottage.

Once inside she'd felt foolish for rushing off so fast, especially when she hadn't even thanked him for walking them up the footpath. Though she didn't imagine he'd lose any sleep over it, it had bothered her enough to make her go back outside in the hope of finding him still close enough to call out to. But he was already as far as Tom Drummond's cottage, at the bottom of the path, so unwilling to make herself absurd by trying to attract his attention, she'd merely stood watching him walk down past the pub, then on to the upper part of the beach where he'd left his car.

'OK, I'm taking this down to the bins,' Nick announced, startling her from her thoughts. 'Then I'm going home for some dinner.'

Rachel's unease instantly welled up again. 'Are you coming back this afternoon?' she asked.

'No, I'm going to sea this afternoon,' he replied,

manhandling a large plastic dustbin through the gate. 'But everything's fixed here. Shed's as solid as a brick whatsit.'

She looked round. 'Where's Chris?' she asked, seeing only blue sky above the shed roof, which was where she'd last seen him.

'He just jumped over the wall to take Beanie's ladder back.' The bin was through the gate now, and he was starting off down the path. 'OK, see you!' he said.

'Nick! Wait!' she called after him.

Stopping, he turned round, but then someone shouted up from the cove and he laughingly waved his arms, shouting back that he was on his way.

Realizing she couldn't just blurt it out, as though it were some small favour she was asking, she gestured for him to go on, saying, 'It's all right. It's nothing. Is Chris coming back?'

'Dunno. Said he was going over to Penzance later, but whether he's already gone . . .'

Hoping he was still in with Beanie, Rachel put down the cutters and wire she was holding, and was just about to go and find out when the telephone shrilled from the sitting room.

'Oh God,' she groaned, pressing a hand to her mouth as her mind started to reel. But it wouldn't be them. They thought she was in London, and if they couldn't get hold of her there they'd contact Michael Jarrett, her lawyer. That was what she and Laurie and Michael had deduced on Saturday morning, during a conference call, so at worst it would only be Michael . . .

'Hello?' she said, praying it was going to be Laurie or Anna.

'Mrs Hendon?'

Immediately her insides froze, for the voice was both male and accented. So they did know where she was. The very thought made her almost dizzy with dread.

'Who's speaking, please?' she responded, tersely.

The reply was silky smooth. 'Mrs Hendon, we had hoped to receive a certain transfer of funds from you on Friday,' the voice said. 'Today is Monday, and it has not arrived. Please assure me that it is merely delayed and will be with us by the end of the day, tomorrow at the latest.'

'I'm afraid I can't do that,' she said, a quick anger holding her firm, despite the weakness in her legs. 'I don't know who you are, and until I do that money is going to stay where it is.'

'That would not be a wise course to take,' he told her calmly.

She was shaking, badly, but still managed to keep her voice steady, as she said, 'I hope that isn't a threat.'

'It is merely advice,' he corrected.

'Then let me advise you,' she responded, her face paling with outrage as much as fear, 'that until I know who you are, and how my husband managed to acquire so much money . . .'

'Mrs Hendon, you will please initiate the transfer by the end of the day today.'

Her hand was so tight on the phone she might crush it. Briefly she noticed Chris coming in through the gate. 'And if I don't?' she demanded.

There was a moment's pause before he said, 'They tell me that pregnant women should avoid causing themselves any unnecessary stress. So please, do as I ask, effect the transfer by the end of the day today,' and the line went dead.

She was trembling so hard now that it took two efforts to get the phone back on its base.

'Hi, I'm just –'

She almost screamed as she spun round.

'My God, are you all right?' Chris demanded. 'Has something happened?'

Rachel's hands went over her face as more fear broke through the dams in her heart. 'Yes, yes it has,' she gasped. 'Or no. Not yet, but . . .'

Coming into the room, he took her wrists and gently parted her hands.

She glanced up at him, then turned abruptly away.

'Rachel, what is it?' he urged, holding on to her.

Adrenalin was making her breath ragged, so it was hard to speak, then almost before she knew what was happening, he was drawing her into his arms and holding her in a way that felt so good there was nothing she could do to stop the tears.

'It's all right,' he soothed. 'Whatever it is, it's going to be all right.'

She stood against him, her face pressed into her hands, her body turning weak with the need to just carry on leaning, and feeling safe and protected and so, so thankful not to be alone at this moment.

But eventually she broke free, sniffing and drying the tears with the backs of her hands. 'Thank you,' she said, her voice still thick with emotion. 'I really needed that.' Then with a faint smile she added, 'I hope you don't mind.'

A glimmer of humour shone through the concern in his eyes. 'Not at all,' he assured her. 'But I do mind not knowing what upset you so much. Or maybe I shouldn't pry?'

'No, no, you should,' she told him. 'I want to tell you. I've been meaning to . . .' She looked around, distractedly. 'I just, I suppose . . . Oh God, I hardly know where to begin.'

'How about by sitting down?' he suggested, indicating one of the sofas.

She nodded. Another sob suddenly shuddered out of nowhere, which she tried to turn into a laugh. 'I'm sorry,' she said, 'I'll pull myself together in a minute.'

'Can I get you something? I know alcohol's out of the question, but . . .'

'You know I'm pregnant?' she said, shocked.

He seemed confused by her response. 'Am I not supposed to?'

'No. I mean, I just don't remember telling anyone, except Beanie, and she'd never . . .'

'It was Jake who told us,' he said, 'but I don't think he knew it was a secret.'

Her mind was casting about wildly, trying to think how Jake could know, until she remembered the day he'd been here, repairing the thatch. There was a good chance he'd overheard her and Beanie discussing it then.

'I'm sorry,' she said, dashing a hand through her already dishevelled hair. 'I'm just very edgy right now. There's such a lot going on, and . . .' Taking a deep breath, she pressed her fingers against her forehead as she tried to remember what they'd been saying before she'd fallen prey to paranoia. 'OK, I should sit down,' she said, starting towards the sofa. 'And no, I don't need anything, thank you.

Except your promise not to tell anyone what I'm about to tell you now.'

'Of course not,' he replied, going to sit in the armchair next to the hearth. 'But are you sure you don't want something? Tea. Juice. Valium?'

Smiling despite herself, she shook her head, then took a couple of deep breaths to set herself on the way, but it was still a struggle to get started as she kept going off on tangents and forgetting why, or leaping too far ahead then realizing she wasn't making much sense. However, at last she found her stride, and managed to relate more or less everything that had happened since the day Tim died, right up to the phone call he'd just walked in at the end of.

By the time she'd finished his handsome features were drawn in a deep scowl of concentration, until realizing she wasn't going to say any more, he glanced at her briefly, then scraped a hand over the stubble on his chin. 'Well, as far as the money is concerned,' he said, 'you seem to have two choices, either to tell the police of its existence, or to make the transfer now, before someone starts ratcheting up the intimidation levels.'

Jolted, though not entirely surprised by his answer, for no sane person would surely counsel anything else now, she said, 'But if I do give it back, how am I ever going to find out who's making the calls, or how Tim got the money?'

'You've just said you're pretty sure it's all linked to the Phraxos Group, and given what you know about how powerful they are, it doesn't seem a good idea to mess around with them. So if I were you, I'd just give it back and carry on the investigation without it. You know it was there, and though keeping it might make you feel as though you have an edge, it could be an edge you don't need.'

She was staring down at her hands as she considered his words. 'Maybe I should go to the police now,' she said, looking up at him.

'You could. So what's stopping you?'

She sighed. 'I just don't trust them to tell me the entire truth,' she answered.

'Why wouldn't they?'

'I don't know. Maybe because they can't, or because they're trying to protect someone, or because there's a lot more to the situation than we've managed to uncover.'

'In which case you could be jeopardizing their investigation.'

Her eyes flashed. 'I have a right to know what my husband was involved in,' she retorted. 'God knows I don't want to see his name dragged through the mud, but if he was paving the way for Phraxos to make inroads into the UK so that he, and probably dozens of others in equally privileged positions, could get rich from the misery and strife in Africa, or anywhere else, then he has no right to have his name protected, and the people who elected him have a right to be told.'

He sat quietly, appreciating the kind of integrity it took to put her duty as a citizen before the shame of having her husband hated and despised for such a heinous abuse of his power. Moreover, it would be hard for the public to accept that she, as his wife, hadn't been involved too, particularly when they were known to be so close, so the disgrace would be hers to bear, probably for the rest of her life. It made him wish that there was something he could say to convince her she was wrong, or even help her over the awfulness of being right, but there was really nothing.

'You mentioned once that you knew him,' she said after a while.

'We only met a couple of times, in the village,' he responded, 'though with politics being something of a hobby of mine, I knew a bit about him.'

She glanced at him with dark, troubled eyes. 'It really isn't looking good for him, is it?' she said.

No it wasn't, but rather than speculate on the abstract, he moved on to the immediate need for action, by saying, 'Why don't we just get rid of that money, then take it from there?'

She looked away, still unsure.

'What do we have to do to make the transfer?' he prompted.

'Call my lawyer, in London,' she answered.

When she made no attempt to go to the phone, he said, 'Don't see it as giving up, because really it's not. Once you've made the transfer, you'll have documentary evidence of it, should you need it later.'

'It won't prove anything, the accounts are only numbers.'

'Those numbers have names, and under certain circumstances the Swiss will release names.'

'How do you know?'

His eyes narrowed, humorously. 'Because I followed the Ashby scandal as it unfolded,' he answered. 'So ask Laurie, she'll tell you: information can be had from a Swiss bank when there is certain evidence of a crime.' He didn't add unless it was a government trying to cover it up, because he had no idea if that was the case. He wouldn't want to bet against the Phraxos capabilities either, but she really had to let go of that money.

She looked over at the phone, then finally got up from the sofa and went to pick it up. As she started to dial Jarrett's number, she suddenly clicked off again. 'You know, I don't want you to feel you're responsible for me now, or in anyway obliged to –'

'Keep dialling,' he interrupted. 'I'm going to get myself a beer, if there's one in the fridge.'

'I'm afraid there's not.'

'OK, Beanie will have one. I'll be right back.'

A few minutes later he returned with the top off a bottle of Sharps, and a quizzical look in his eyes.

'It's done,' she told him, still standing beside the phone.

He frowned.

'It only took a moment,' she assured him. 'I just had to tell Michael to go ahead and do it.'

'So how do you feel?'

She thought about it, then smiled shakily as she thought of how the caller had mentioned the baby. 'Actually, a bit as though a weight has been lifted,' she said. 'Which is good, because I'd expected to feel pathetic and wretched because I'd let Tim down in some way. Now how much sense does that make?'

His eyes stayed on hers, until feeling herself starting to colour, she walked over to the window and closed it.

'I should probably get in touch with Laurie,' she said, 'to let her know what's happened.'

'Are they going to call again, to check if you've made the transfer?'

'They didn't say.' She shivered, and felt unnerved by the prospect. 'I hate them knowing where I am,' she said. 'Do you think they'll come here?'

Knowing that she didn't have the first idea that 'they', in the shape of him, were already here, he kept his expression neutral as he said, 'What reason would they have, if they've got the money?'

Having no answer to that, she turned to stare out at the sky. Then with a sigh and a laugh, she said, 'What a ghastly time to be pregnant, eh? It's making me feel so damned helpless.' She waited for him to respond, but he didn't, so turning back she said, 'You know, normally I would never have handed this over to Laurie. Investigative journalism was what I did, before I married Tim, and I was good, even if I do say so myself. But now, half the time I'm even afraid to go on line in case I stumble into something . . . Well, like the villa, whatever that's about . . . But then the other half of the time, I can't stay off the damned computer. I become so consumed with it all, as though there's nothing else in the world but the Phraxos Group, and Franz Koehler, and Katherine Sumner.'

His smile was sardonic as he looked at her from under lowered lids. 'I think you're in need of some alternative excitement,' he said, 'something to take you out of yourself for a while. So what would you say to tea down at the most southerly point? Or a trip into Penzance?'

She was about to shake her head and say she couldn't, when she realized that actually, she could. 'OK,' she said, attempting a smile. 'When can we go?'

He looked at his watch. 'What about now? I need to make a trip into Penzance anyway, to calm down the bank manager, then maybe we can do something fantastically decadent like going to see a film, or buying you some baby books?' He peered down at her waist. 'Or maternity clothes,' he added, with a playful tilt of an eyebrow.

Mirroring his look, she said, 'Thank you for that. And yes, let's hit Penzance, and while we're there, perhaps you'll let me in on the great Killian secret that I'm supposed to be keeping.'

'You mean you haven't guessed it already?' he said, surprised.

'Probably. I'd just like to hear –' She stopped, abruptly, as the telephone rang. She looked at it, then back to him. 'It won't be them again,' she said, as though to reassure herself.

'Would you like me to answer?'

She nodded. 'Yes. Just in case. It might be good for them to hear a male voice.'

'Hello?' he said, lifting the receiver.

'Hello? Chris? Is that you?'

'Bean,' he declared, turning to waggle his eyebrows at Rachel.

'Ah-ha, it's you I'm after,' Beanie told him. 'Are you still going to Penzance?'

'I am. Do you need something?'

'I want to come along. I don't like taking the motorbike that far, and I need to change my library books.'

'Be my guest,' he told her. 'Rachel's coming too.'

'Is she? Wonderful. She needs to get out more.

Holler as you go by, I'll be ready when you are.'

Putting the phone down, he said jokingly to Rachel, 'Well, it seems we've got ourselves a chaperone.'

Immediately Rachel stiffened.

'Sorry,' he said, looking uncomfortable too. 'Bad choice of words. I meant, we've got company.'

Though she attempted a smile, she was already searching for an excuse not to go, until finally common sense prevailed, as she saw that it would be ridiculous not to, when she really didn't want to stay here alone. 'OK, I'll just call Laurie,' she said.

As she took the phone upstairs he finished the rest of his beer, then went to pop the bottle in the bin. Though still annoyed by his *faux pas*, he was thinking more about everything else she'd just told him, the most important aspects of which, for the moment, were that she'd had no contact with Katherine herself – which hadn't really been expected, but still had to be checked – and that the four million dollars was on its way back to Franz Koehler. He'd also learned how far Laurie Forbes had got in her investigation, which had turned out to be further than they realized, though no links had yet been established between Tim Hendon and Phraxos. The copy of *The Magus* that was lying on the table hadn't been a great surprise, for both Laurie and Rachel were obviously well-read women, so it wouldn't have taken much for them to make that connection. However, that in itself wasn't going to get them very far, other than to give a little insight into Franz Koehler's character. It was Elliot Russell's investigation which could prove the single most serious threat, to Phraxos and its investors.

His prime concern right now though, was for Rachel to continue feeling she could trust him, and so far, with the exception of the gaffe about a chaperone, which would repel any woman who was so recently bereaved and pregnant, they seemed to be off to a reasonably good start. Which meant that Franz Koehler's idea of capitalizing on the extreme good fortune of him having a home near Killian was already paying off, and in exactly the way Koehler had predicted, for being the smooth strategist he was, Koehler had timed his most recent phone call to coincide with Chris being there to catch the distress.

Laurie's face was colourless, and strained, as she stood in front of the door, looking back at Elliot. He too looked tense, as he stared hard into her eyes.

'I wish you wouldn't do this,' he said gruffly. 'I know we need to talk, but this isn't going to make it happen.'

'We've talked before,' she reminded him, 'and nothing ever changes. So I've decided to face it, even if you won't. There's no point to our relation-ship, and I can't go on unless there is one.'

'Isn't the point that we're together, that it works . . .'

'It works for you! Not for me. And the truth is it only works for you because it eases your conscience. You don't love me – no, *listen*,' she snapped as he started to interrupt. 'I know you're about to tell me you do, because you always say it when you're going to lose me. And the only reason you want to keep me is because you still haven't finished doing penance for my sister's death.'

'Oh, for God's sake,' he cried. 'It's you who can't get over it. You who feels guilty at being in this relationship, because you think you've stolen something of hers. But it was over between me and Lysette before she died . . .'

'The *night* she died,' Laurie corrected. 'You ended it that night.'

His eyes turned suddenly hard, and angry. 'So it's my fault?' he challenged.

'No, it's all our faults, including hers. You ended that relationship cruelly, and you know it. She was heartbroken. She really loved you, and because I did too I wouldn't listen when she called, needing to talk.'

'Just stop this,' he growled. 'We've been over it a thousand times, and you're still no closer to forgiving yourself, or me, or her, and it's damned well time you did.'

'No, it's time *you* did, because you're the one who's holding on to me out of fear that I'll do the same as she did. Well, I'm not Lysette. I'm not going to kill myself. I'm just going to get out of a relationship that only one of us really wants.'

'Since when did you start deciding what I do, or don't want?'

'It was you who made the decision on how this relationship was going to be, how it could work for you without interfering too much with your life, while what I want, or how it might work for me, doesn't even feature. You don't even think about it. *You don't even know that I'm here half the time,* unless we've got a story to discuss. No. I don't want to argue any more. I've made up my mind. I'm going now. I'll be staying at Rhona's if you need to get hold of me.'

As she picked up her bags he dashed a hand angrily through his hair. 'Laurie, listen,' he implored. 'If you won't stay for us, then stay because . . .'

'I don't want to discuss it any more,' she said.

'For God's sake, this is *not* a good time to go, and you know it,' he raged. 'The information I gave you today is going to put you in danger if you follow up on it, and I know you will. So please, at least stay until this is over. I'm going to help you, I've already told you that, and it'll be easier, safer, if you're here.'

Her face had turned paler than ever, for what he was saying was true, but they hadn't lived together during the Ashby case and she'd been in danger then and survived. And now she'd got this far, she couldn't allow herself to back down again.

'Thank you for your concern,' she said quietly, 'but I've told Rhona to expect me, and I don't want to keep her waiting.' Her eyes suddenly flashed as she belatedly realized how he hadn't used his heart to keep her, just his damnable chauvinism, and before she could stop herself, she spat, 'And I'm especially not going to stay in order to pander to your male ego.'

'God damn you!' he thundered. 'This isn't about ego, it's about you, and caring what happens to you . . .'

'But not about loving me, and that's what I want.'

'I do love you, for Christ's sake. I don't understand why you think I don't.'

'Because you never tell me!' she shouted. 'In the eighteen months we've been together you've only ever said it when you think I'm about to go, or because I almost got killed. The rest of the time we just have great sex and talk about work.'

He sighed in exasperation, started to turn away, then turned back again. 'Look, you know I'm not good at that kind of thing,' he said, 'but it doesn't mean I don't feel it.'

'No, Elliot, you don't have the same feelings for me as I have for you, because I really do love you, and frankly this is hurting me more than I can bear, but I'd rather live without you than be here as some kind of salve to your conscience.'

'Jesus Christ! What do I have to do to convince you?' he yelled. 'I love you, I want you here, and I know you wouldn't kill yourself if we finished. So what more can I say?'

'It's what you do that matters.'

'So what do I have to *do*?'

Her blue eyes were heavy with pain as she looked at him. Then shaking her head, she said, 'The fact that you need to ask that question proves how far apart we are.' Pulling the door open, she struggled with her heavy bags into the corridor, then closed the door quietly behind her.

As she walked to the lift, everything in her was straining to go back, almost as though she was still physically joined to something inside. She longed to hear the sound of the door opening, and him finally saying the words that would make it all right to give in, but each step was taking her further and further away, and the door simply stayed closed. It was hurting so much that the only way she could deal with it was to force herself to think solely of the practical movements of the next few minutes, and hours. There should be plenty of taxis downstairs; her mobile was charged so she could call Rachel on the way to Rhona's. The thought caused her heart to contract again, for she hardly wanted to think about how Rachel was going to take this latest news. Was she, Laurie, even in a good enough emotional state to deliver it right now?

Her throat was so tight and her eyes so full that it took a superhuman effort not to scream with anger and despair as she heaved her bag into the lift and pressed the button to go down. He really wasn't going to come after her; he'd know that at this point she'd still be outside, but he really was just letting her go, and though she'd more or less known he would, she so desperately hadn't wanted to be proved right. But she had, and knowing him as well as she did, she guessed that by now he'd already be back at his desk.

'Narrow Street, Limehouse,' she told the cabbie, throwing her holdall in the back. Climbing in after it, she fastened the seat belt and took out her phone. At least calling Rachel would stop her calling Elliot, or telling the driver to turn back.

'Rachel? Hi, it's me,' she said, when Rachel answered. 'Is everything all right your end?'

'It seems to be,' Rachel replied. 'I've been on the Internet this afternoon, getting more information on the African professor George Monheit at the LSE told you about. Patrice Bombola? Apparently he's Congolese by birth, but grew up mainly in Nigeria, went to the University of Benin there, then did his postgraduate work at the African Studies Centre at Boston University. He lectures all over the world now, on trade and finance in developing countries . . .'

'Rachel, there's something I need to tell you,' Laurie interrupted.

Rachel fell silent.

Laurie turned to gaze out at the grey slumbering walls of the Tower of London, and almost wished she could be one of the late, great, or even not so great, beheaded. 'Elliot gave me some information on Professor Bombola today,' she said. 'He's . . . There's a very good chance he's an integral part of a Phraxos special project that helps raise finance for rebel or guerrilla forces, mainly in Africa, who then use the money to buy their weapons from Phraxos-owned companies.' She took a breath. 'Tim had a meeting with him, at the Kensington Palace Hotel, about four weeks before he died.'

There was no response from the other end, but Laurie could easily picture Rachel there in the cottage, all alone, afraid and confused, and trying desperately to deal with the shock of this, her worst nightmare, coming true. The seconds ticked on, until at last her voice came down the line, sounding slightly firmer than Laurie might have expected, though nonetheless strained,

'How do you know Tim met him?' she asked.

Realizing she'd have to explain fully, Laurie said, 'When I saw George Monheit and he told me about Bombola, he said he'd met him personally, in London, about a month before the election, at the Kensington Palace Hotel. They've known each other for years, so it wasn't unusual for them to meet, and Monheit only brought his name up because he was someone he knew who had a personal relationship with Franz Koehler. I don't think he knows the exact nature of the relationship – Elliot only told me that later, when I mentioned Bombola to him. It was after I spoke to Elliot that I called the Kensington Palace. They wouldn't give me the information over the phone, so I went round there, earlier today, and by the time I left I knew that Patrice Bombola had stayed for two nights in mid-May, and that amongst his many visitors were Tim, Katherine Sumner *and* Franz Koehler.'

Rachel's intake of breath was barely audible, but Laurie heard it, and gave her a moment to recover before continuing.

'So essentially,' she said, 'what we appear to be looking at is not just a link to Phraxos, but to this highly secret special project they've got going, which is to supply arms for both sides of any given conflict, i.e. the US-backed regime, *and* the opposition forces. It doesn't get much more corrupt or lucrative than that.' She sat forward to direct the cabbie to Rhona's apartment block, which backed on to the river side of Narrow Street. 'And if we put this meeting together with the four million dollars,' she continued, knowing that Rachel would already be bitterly aware of what she was about to say, 'the most likely scenario we come up with is that the four million dollars was an incentive to direct at least some of the extremely lucrative orders from the British Defence Department to Phraxos-owned companies. It's easy enough to check, so I did, and there are three orders in the pipeline.'

Rachel's voice was still strained as she said,

'They would be legal, though. Unethical on Tim's part, obviously, but legal.'

'Of course. But the fact that Bombola was at that meeting . . .' Laurie didn't want to rub it in any more than that, so asking her to hang on while she paid the driver, she then picked up her bags and started into the building. 'OK, back with you,' she said.

'Has this person at the Kensington Palace spoken to the police?' Rachel asked.

'Yes,' Laurie confirmed. 'And wait for this, he was made to sign the Official Secrets Act and reminded he would be under penalty of prosecution if he spoke to the press, or anyone else about his interview.'

'Oh my God,' Rachel murmured. 'So how did you get him to talk?'

'He didn't tell me anything about the interview. I just asked the right questions about Bombola's guests during his stay, he'd either nod, or shake his head, and I swore I'd never reveal where I got my information.' Pushing open the door, she propped it open with one bag, then turned to haul the other inside. 'I'm really sorry about the way all this seems to be going,' she said when Rachel stayed silent. 'But I suppose what can be said for it is that we're making some headway. We've also got more confirmation that Haynes and his Special Ops team are not being very forthcoming with what they know.'

Rachel's voice sounded distant, and distracted as she simply said, 'No.'

'Is anyone there with you?' Laurie asked.

'No. Uh, Beanie and I are going to the Caves for dinner. Chris said he might join us.'

'Any more phone calls about the money?'

'No. They must have it by now.'

'OK. I'm sorry, but I have to go. There is one last thing, though. I heard today that we should be getting some news on the DNA by Friday at the latest.'

There was another long pause and once again Laurie could feel her own heart responding to what must be going on in Rachel's now. 'The stains on the sheet,' Rachel mumbled, sounding as though she was hardly connecting with the words. 'Frankly I could almost live without knowing any more about them.'

'I know,' Laurie said quietly. Then after promising she'd call again in the morning, she rang off and dropped the phone into her bag.

For a moment she stood staring back across the street to the neat terrace of town houses that made up Ropemaker's Fields. She was recalling Elliot's words as she'd left tonight, and felt a shudder of fear run through her, for the prospect of taking on a syndicate of arms dealers was so much more daunting than anything she'd ever done before that were it not for the loyalty she felt to Rachel, she might actually consider backing out.

imperfection?'

Chapter 15

Stacey's laughter rang out around the set as Bryn,
who was playing the husband and poet, minced
out from behind a camera, wearing one of her
dresses and an outrageous red wig.

Catching Robert's eye Bryn threw back his head
and trilled, 'Darling, am I looking beautiful for you
today?'

Though he could feel himself colouring, Robert
went gamely along with the tease, and recited the
next line of the script. 'Too ravishing for words,' he
declared, with a delivery that made it fortunate he
hadn't chosen acting as a career.

'Am I too capricious or gay?' Bryn sang, in a
ludicrous falsetto.

'You are simply perfection,' Robert responded.

Aghast, Bryn clapped his hands to his heavily
rouged cheeks. 'Simple? I?' he cried. 'How can you
say such a thing? I am the Venus of Arles.' And
dropping the front of the dress to bare his chest, he
threw out his right hand to show an apple. 'Do you
not understand my complexity, my likeness to

Aphrodite?' he demanded. Then with a mischievous twinkle, 'Or do you only see my little *tootie fruitie?*'

At that a roar of laughter went up, for the twist of the nipple was, without a doubt, a reference to the visibility of Stacey's, no matter what she was wearing.

Deciding not to let it go any further Robert clapped his hands, shouting, 'OK. That's a wrap. Rushes at . . . seven?' He looked to the first assistant, who gave the thumbs up, then watching Stacey wander off into the shadows with the ghastly Petey, he went to put an arm round Bryn's shoulders to walk him to the dressing rooms.

It was a transparent ruse to get him where he wanted to be, for though they discussed Bryn's role and performance the whole way, as soon as they reached Bryn's door, Robert said, 'It's working even better than I hoped, so keep it up,' and after playfully cuffing the wig from Bryn's head, he continued on to Stacey's small suite of rooms.

His mouth was dry, his body already trembling with excitement, for they were about to spend the next hour alone, before attending rushes. He just hoped she'd already got rid of Petey, as she'd promised when they'd spoken earlier to confirm this now regular end of the day tryst. All too often Petey hung around, brushing her hair or cleansing her face, while she read Robert's poems, casting him sultry, tantalizing smiles in the mirror. He wondered what she'd made of the one he'd slipped her earlier, which was longer and even more graphic than the others, and had been written only last night, while Anna was asleep.

The thought of Anna caused a brief hesitance in his step, for he'd noticed again this morning how tense she was looking. She'd been impatient with the girls too, and with him, and when she'd burned her hand on the kettle she'd sworn in a way she never did in front of the children. But though he knew he was the cause of her stress, and though he loved her with all his heart, he just couldn't turn back from this now. He was utterly compelled to go on, for it wasn't just a mad and dangerous game that was inspiring him to the greatest heights of creation, nor was it simply a slavish following of his own rampant bodily urges; it didn't even stop at a connoisseur's delight in the perfect female form, because it was all of those things – and more. So very much more that even he couldn't describe it, for nothing so consuming, or controlling, or so intrinsically powerful had ever happened to him in his life before.

By the time he reached Stacey's door a thin film of sweat had broken out on his face. To his dismay Petey answered his knock, but Stacey's smile as she greeted him all but dazzled the acolyte from Robert's tunnel vision.

'Darling,' she purred, turning from the brightly lit mirror and holding out her hands. 'Wasn't Bryn just too funny? And you, the way you played along,' she crossed a hand over her chest, 'you are my hero.'

'And you are my destruction,' he responded, on script.

Laughing, she got to her feet and planted a kiss full on his mouth. 'Now tell me, because I've been dying to know,' she said, waving him towards a red velvet chaise-longue, while she untied the belt of her robe. 'What did the producers think of the rough cut scenes they saw at lunchtime?'

Watching, tensely, breathlessly, as Petey peeled the robe from her shoulders and dropped it on a chair, he sat on the end of the chaise-longue, saying, 'Hardly any notes. They loved it.' He swallowed hard as she stretched out her arms while Petey sprayed her naked back and buttocks with a lemon scented cologne.

'Were they all there?' she asked, turning to face him.

'Yes,' he murmured, gazing rapturously at the flawless beauty of her skin, the small, upturned mounds of her breasts with their big, tightly puckered nipples; the golden triangle of hair nesting in a landscape of soft white flesh. And then there was the most thrilling part of all, her most intimate part, protruding from her lower lips like a small pink tongue.

'Even Anna?' she asked, rotating back towards Petey who was now holding up a dress to slide over her head.

'Yes,' he murmured again, and almost groaned as the dress fell like a curtain, cutting him off from a performance that was surely far from over. Then realizing she had spoken Anna's name, he lifted his eyes to look at her face.

'What did Anna say?' she asked, sitting down at the mirror to allow Petey to brush out her hair.

He cast his mind back, and realized that his wife had said very little. 'She thought your performance was outstanding,' he lied, and his eyes closed as Anna's pain seemed to move through his chest.

350

What was he doing? How could he have hurried away from the viewing like a frightened, anxious lover whose mistress might not wait? He had all but ignored her, not wanting to get into any kind of discussion about the film, because it was eating into precious time he might spend with Stacey – and because he knew that Anna would tell him what he already knew, that the film was starting to show signs of his distraction.

'Are you all right?' Stacey asked.

He met her gaze in the mirror. 'Yes,' he answered, but his voice was cracked with anguish.

Glancing up at Petey, she took the hairbrush and nodded for him to go. After the door had closed behind him, she went to join Robert on the chaise-longue, arranging herself so that she was propped up by cushions, with her feet crossed behind him, her thin, crêpe dress falling decorously around her knees.

Turning to face her he smoothed a hand along her bare freckled calf. 'You're a cruel and wanton witch,' he told her. 'To tease me the way you do heightens my pain and drives me mad with desire.'

'Of course,' she smiled. 'It's why I do it.'

He smiled too, and as her head fell back against the cushions, displaying her gracefully long neck, he lifted her feet on to his lap.

'Your latest poem tells me,' she said, 'that you must be glad I shared the experience of what I did with my husband last Saturday night.'

'Glad, because I know you were thinking of me,' he responded, gently massaging her toes. 'Otherwise tormented by jealousy.'

351

'You seemed to like the special panties,' she commented silkily.

'Of course, I want to see you in them.'

Opening her eyes to look at him, she said, 'You can *see* me any way you choose,' she reminded him.

His smile was small, and full of despair, as his hands circled slowly towards her ankles. 'Sometimes I feel that I never see anything but you,' he replied.

She murmured sleepily as his fingers moved round to stroke the backs of her knees. 'Tell me what we're doing in your mind right now,' she challenged softly.

Looking down at his hands as they tenderly massaged her flesh, he said, 'We're in the position you and your husband were on Saturday night. And your mouth is full of me.'

'Mmm,' she moaned, lifting her arms up over her head. 'But did you beat me first?'

'Of course. Just because he won't punish your wickedness, doesn't mean I won't.'

'And did I beat you?'

'Savagely.'

She sighed, ecstatically, as his hands travelled under the hem of her dress, up to her thighs. Then, as though not wanting to break the erotic tension of the tease, they stayed silent, as his fingers crept closer and closer to their goal.

'Very soon,' he said softly, as he lightly touched her pubic hair, 'this will be full of me.'

A small gasp escaped her lips as the sensation shot through her like an arrow.

'But you know that isn't allowed,' she reminded him.

'Can you resist it?' he challenged.

She didn't answer at first, so he dared to brush a finger over the moist flesh of her labia.

'You've already gone too far,' she warned, though she made no attempt to stop him.

After a while he said, 'I see your legs opening and feel myself sliding deep inside you.'

She moaned softly again, and her hips writhed a little, as though searching for the finger he'd removed. 'Are you going to carry out the promises in your new poem?' she asked huskily.

'I already am,' he told her, caressing her. 'Can't you feel the brutality; the merciless degradation and pain?'

She smiled and closed her eyes.

'How much of it can you stand?' he asked.

'All of it.'

'Can you see how huge you're making my cock?'

Her eyes remained closed as her tongue circled her lips. 'Mmm, yes, I see it,' she moaned.

'Is it too big for you?'

'Oh yes.'

'But you know you're going to get it.'

She nodded, and drew in a shuddering breath. 'You're going to rape me,' she said.

'That's right.'

He looked down at his hand again. Her knees were still together, but he could see how aroused she was by the circling motion of his fingers, and wondered how much further she would allow him to go.

Her eyes opened as he pressed two fingers in deeper, seeking to penetrate. 'You like being raped,' he told her.

She said nothing, only watched his face and let his fingers continue their quest. Then one of her feet fell to the floor, parting her legs, and as she sat up, playfully reminding him it was almost time for rushes, his fingers slipped all the way in.

Then she was on her feet, her dress round her knees, and her hand out to help him up.

'It will happen,' he told her gruffly.

Laughing softly, she cupped a hand over his erection, squeezed it hard, then sauntered to the door. 'Before I go, tell me you love me,' she said over her shoulder.

'I love you,' he replied.

'More than Anna?'

His eyes showed his pain as he said, 'More than anyone.'

'Are you my slave?'

'Always and for ever.'

Her eyes were smouldering as she looked at him.

'I will have you,' he said softly.

She only smiled, then after dropping her gaze to the thick bulge in his trousers, she pulled open the door, leaving him to use the en suite bathroom alone.

Rachel was standing in the middle of the front lawn, surrounded by boxes of old junk and papers that she'd carted down from upstairs. Since the sun had finally found its midsummer might, it had seemed a good idea to start sorting all this outside, but as she stared down at it, it felt like such a trivial, time-wasting pursuit when she so desperately wanted to get out there and do something to help Laurie that she couldn't even think why she was here. It was imperative now that they find Katherine, even before the police, should such a miracle prove possible, but there were just no leads at all. And with the investigation moving on to such dangerous ground, she really had no other choice but to suppress this almost overwhelming urge to act, and put the baby first.

Sighing irritably she sank down on the blanket, not sure whether she liked the way her waistline was expanding so rapidly, for her belly was bulging out between the bottom of her T-shirt and the elastic waistband of her Capri pants. Still, at least it had started to turn brown, thanks to the last few days of hot weather, and in truth, despite her irascible mood, there was almost nothing she longed for more now than to feel the baby starting to move. It would be like a single ray of hope to carry her through this nightmare she was amazingly calling a life!

Digging into the nearest box, she was about to pull out a handful of papers when the sound of someone singing made her look up. At first she couldn't quite make out where it was coming from and assumed it was a radio, until laughter began bubbling up inside her as she spotted Chris Gallagher, strolling up the footpath with his guitar, serenading anyone who cared to listen. Though she didn't recognize the tune, as he drew closer she realized the words were familiar, and by the time he reached the gate, she was joining in with the final chorus.

'*So watch the wall my darling, watch the wall my darling, oh watch the wall my darling, while the Gentlemen go by.*'

He finished with a flourishing stanza of chords, and she clapped and laughed as he bowed his thanks.

'Rudyard Kipling's "A Smuggler's Song",' she declared, as he came to join her. 'Did you set it to music?'

His expression crooked with irony. 'I confess that was Zac's doing. Did you like it?'

'It's wonderful. I've never heard him sing it.'

'I'm sure you will.' Resting the guitar against one of the boxes, he dropped down on to the blanket and sat cross-legged facing her. 'So, are we playing jumble sales, or is this your normal diet for an afternoon read?' he said, peering into the closest box.

She looked at it in despair. 'I'm almost tempted just to throw it all away,' she confessed. 'It's mainly old bills, or letters from the council . . .' She let a pile of it cascade from her hands. 'I suppose it would be disrespectful, though, not to go through it completely.'

Plucking a long blade of grass from a clump that was sprouting nearby, he popped it into his mouth and lay down to rest on one elbow. 'So how long did you sit up searching the Net last night?' he asked.

She grimaced as her anxiety returned. Then narrowing her eyes, she said, 'I'm not sure I like how well you seem to know me.'

He laughed, and threw away the grass. 'I was trying to call you for a couple of hours and couldn't get through,' he explained.

'Ah, that's because I was talking to my sister. The fax and computer are on another line. But you're right, I did spend a long time on line last night, knocking around what you might call some of the roughest neighbourhoods on the Net, and managing to scare myself half to death into the bargain.'

'Let me guess, guerrilla and terrorist groups?' he said.

She nodded.

'So are you any wiser about anything now?'

Sighing, she shook her head. 'No, and I don't suppose I really expected to be, so you have to wonder why I put myself through it. After all, these sanctions-busting shipments are hardly going to be recorded on someone's website, are they?'

'I wouldn't imagine so,' he responded. 'What about the professor? Any more on him?'

'Patrice Bombola? Yes, actually, there is. Laurie informs me that his assets, which turn out to be quite considerable for a mere professor, were frozen by the US Government until January this year, at which point they were promptly unfrozen.'

'Oh,' he commented.

'Oh indeed, because when put together with his Phraxos connections, you have to ask, how come he got unfrozen so fast?'

'And the answer is?'

'Wouldn't we like to know.' As she spoke, her eyes were drifting off to the middle distance where a flock of gulls was flying harum-scarum over the cove, and a couple of fishermen were puttering out around the far headland in their boat, though she wasn't registering much of anything beyond her own thoughts at that moment. Then quite suddenly she said, 'The transfer's obviously arrived by now. I wonder if I'll hear anything about it again.'

'You still haven't mentioned it to . . . What was his name? Haynes?'

She shook her head. 'I haven't spoken to him in over a week. Laurie saw him again yesterday though, after the *Guardian* broke the story about Gustave Basim and the possible connection to Tim. She leaked it, by the way. This time Haynes didn't even try to deny it – he couldn't really, could he, after the French police confirmed they'd been contacted about the body. So now we know for certain that Gustave Basim was the third person in the flat.' Her heart sank then, as she remembered that the DNA results from the sheet were due any time now. 'Still no leads on Katherine,' she continued, wanting to get herself past it. 'Or on this Xavier Lachère. In fact, it's almost as though everything's come to a grinding halt on that front, and considering where it's probably all heading, to my husband being the kind of human being I despise, I can't really say I'm sorry.' She turned back to look at him, slightly embarrassed by her note of self-pity, and seeing how earnestly he was scowling, as though trying to puzzle out how he could help, she found herself saying, 'OK, that's enough about me. Let's talk about you for a change.'

His eyebrows rose in surprise.

'Beanie tells me you're a very important art dealer with galleries in Mousehole, Fowey, and London.'

'Beanie exaggerates,' he responded, his eyes twinkling.

'So you don't have three galleries?'

'Yes, I do, but I'm definitely not very important.'

She laughed. 'Beanie also tells me that she was madly in love with your father, and would have left home for him if she hadn't been madly in love with her own husband at the time.'

It was his turn to laugh. 'My father would have been a lucky man to get Beanie,' he declared. 'Or so my mother used to tell him. Did Beanie also happen to mention how she pops into the church at Roon Moor to put flowers on his grave, every month?'

Rachel smiled past the guilt she felt at not having visited Tim's grave at all since his death. 'No, she didn't,' she said.

'My mother's too, actually,' he added. 'They all knew each other for a long time. Even when we were living in London and didn't come down here much, they still kept in touch. Beanie used to take care of the house then, but she hardly comes up there now. Maybe it brings back too many memories.'

'Where exactly is the house?' Rachel asked.

'Just off the road to Kynance. Not far.'

He gave her a wink then, and rolled on to his back to stare up at the sky.

As she looked at him she could feel sadness welling up inside her. Even this small, merely polite interest in another man was making her feel horribly disloyal to Tim. 'OK. The Killian secret,' she said, changing the subject again. 'You keep avoiding it, but this time I'm not letting you go until you've confessed all.'

His expression immediately altered as a droll light came into his eyes. 'Don't I get some kind of bribe?' he protested, turning his head to look at her.

'Such as?'

'A cup of coffee. A dance at the Roon Moor village hop. A promise that you'll come sailing in my boat?'

'All three, but the secret has to come first.'

He laughed, and turned his eyes back to the sky. 'All right, let me see,' he began, putting his hands behind his head. Then glancing at her again, 'Are you sure you don't know what it is?'

'Well, I could make an educated guess,' she responded.

'Then you'd be absolutely right,' he told her. 'So that's that. What shall we talk about next?'

Laughing, she said, 'Oh no, you don't get away with it that easily.'

Pulling a face, he said, 'All right. So what have you guessed?'

'Smuggling?' she ventured.

Faking amazement he cried, 'What on earth makes you say that?'

Unable to stop herself laughing again, she said, 'This is Cornwall. Old traditions die hard.'

After a moment he turned his eyes back to the sky. 'Do you actually want to know any more than that?' he asked. 'Because if you do, it'll make you an accomplice – and I think you've probably got enough on your plate.'

The reminder caused her heart to sink, for it seemed there really was no getting away from her problems. 'You're right,' she replied dismally. 'I don't need to know.' After a moment's reflection that left her feeling more isolated than ever, she said, almost jealously, 'How involved are *you* in it?'

'Me? Not at all,' he replied. 'I know it's

happening, and how they're doing it, but as for a hands-on – I don't need the trouble either.'

Several seconds ticked by, then suddenly aware she'd been looking at him for too long, she dug into a box and pulled out a sheaf of yellowing papers. 'My goodness,' she murmured, after she'd been reading for a few moments, 'this looks like a book of some kind. Or a diary. But no, there aren't any dates.' She passed a handful over for him to read too.

'Ghosts, witches, goblins,' she said, starting to smile. 'They must be some of the stories Beanie tells. Who wrote them down, I wonder? Oh, this is wonderful. I keep asking Beanie to do it, but she claims not to have the time. By the way, is she a part of the smuggling?'

'Not as far as I know, but she'll be aware it's happening, I'm sure.'

'And Nick?'

'Of course. And Zac and Todd and Pinkie. They all are.'

'What about their wives?'

He laughed. 'I'm pretty certain it was one of the wives, or a sister, who came up with the idea in the first place,' he answered. 'But I won't name any names, because I don't know for sure.'

Rachel let her head fall back and inhaled the pungent scent of roses mingled with salt and fish. This was just the strangest time, making her feel as though she'd somehow got caught up in scenarios that really had nothing to do with her at all, and in many ways they didn't, either here in Cornwall, or in the distant African lands she'd never even seen. Yet she could no more divorce herself from it than she could from the man who'd brought it all into her life.

'Do you know what I'd like to do now?' she suddenly declared. 'I'd like to go somewhere for a genuine Cornish tea.'

His eyebrows made a comical arch. 'Well, considering where we are, that could be easier to arrange than a genuine Chinese tea,' he said drily, handing back the story pages. 'And as I recall, we still owe the Most Southerly Point a visit, so, shall we walk?'

She took a moment to think. 'We could, and if we don't want to walk back, I can always get Beanie to come and fetch us.'

'Will we fit in Romie's trailer?' he asked, puzzling it out.

The very image made her laugh, but then the phone rang and her laughter instantly died.

'Shall I get it?' he offered.

She nodded, and stayed where she was, not proud of her cowardliness, but willing to let it rule this time, for light-hearted moments were so rare these days that she wanted to hold on to this one for at least a few moments more.

'Got a registered one here,' a voice called out from the gate.

Starting, she turned round. 'Oh Reg, I didn't see you coming,' she said, getting up. 'How are you?'

"Ot,' he grumbled, wiping a limp hanky round his neck. 'Got to sign for it,' he told her, holding up the medium-sized package.

As she walked over to the gate she could hear Chris's voice inside, though was unable to make out what he was saying. 'Thanks,' she mumbled as

Reg passed her a dog-eared book and pen.

'Just put your moniker there,' he said pointing.

She blinked and looked down. Then after quickly scrawling her name in the right box, she took the package and looked to see who it might be from. It was Lucy's handwriting, so presuming it must be the mail, from London, she absently tore the top of the envelope open, while still glancing at the house, wondering who was on the phone.

'Nice stamps. Haven't seen them before,' Reg commented, as she pulled an envelope out of the package.

'It's Laurie,' Chris finally called out.

Rachel turned back to Reg. 'Thanks,' she said, and clutching the package to her chest she ran inside to take the call.

When she reached the kitchen Chris was already coming out again.

'Is everything all right?' she asked anxiously. 'What did she say?'

'She's about to tell you herself,' he responded, gesturing for her to go on into the sitting room.

A moment later she was holding the phone to her ear, while putting the package on the table next to it. Her heart was thumping unnaturally, as it always did when she spoke to Laurie now. 'Hi. How are you?' she said, infusing as much warmth as she could into her voice, as if it could turn Laurie's bad news into good.

'Fine,' Laurie answered. 'Chris tells me you're having lovely weather down there.'

'Yes, we are.' She glanced down at the package, and was about to look away again when she noticed the stamps Reg had mentioned. 'Oh God,' she said, feeling a twist in her heart. 'The package has just turned up from the Virgin Islands.'

'Well there's a coincidence,' Laurie responded, 'because I've got good news on the villa front. It belongs to an American woman by the name of Bettina Margolis, who owns two other villas in the same bay, and her own line of cosmetics in Texas. Franz Koehler's villa is about five or six miles away, in a place called Mahoe Bay, so it's definitely not the same one.'

Rachel's relief was so immense she felt herself turn weak.

'Are you still there?' Laurie asked.

'Yes, I'm just trying to get over the shock of some good news,' Rachel answered.

The smile was audible in Laurie's voice as she said, 'I thought you'd be pleased. But hold on, because it doesn't stop there. Katherine's ex-senator friend, Patrick J. Landen, has, would you believe, suddenly started taking my calls. I spoke to him this morning, in person, when he informed me that if I care to get myself over to Washington, the week after next, he'll be happy to see me.'

Rachel blinked a couple of times. 'I'm amazed,' she said bluntly.

'You and me both, but as we know, it can happen like that. One day they give you nothing, the next they're asking if the world's enough.'

'Of course, he might be about to spin you a pack of lies,' Rachel commented sceptically.

'Of course. But that's no reason not to go, because there's always the chance he'll tell us something that could lead us to Katherine. He might also be able to shed some light on the elusive Professor

Bombola, who, I'm told, is in Paris at the moment, so I'm trying to get through to his hotel. If I can persuade him to see me I'll go right away. Or, at the very least, I'll try asking him on the phone about his meeting with Tim at the Kensington Palace.'

Feeling restless and frustrated again at being so far away, Rachel said, 'Maybe I should come back to London. I can be more help to you there.'

'I promise you, I have plenty of help,' Laurie responded, 'and all you'd be doing is feeding me the numbers of your contacts when I need them, and you can do that from where you are. Anyway, there's more news, and I'm afraid this is where it starts to go a bit downhill.'

Immediately Rachel tensed, and for a brief instant she almost put the phone down rather than hear what was coming next.

'The results are back,' Laurie said. 'From the sheet.'

Rachel's head started to spin: the very fact that Laurie had prefaced it the way she had, told her all she didn't want to know. 'It was his,' she murmured, feeling the final, tiny shred of hope shrivel and die.

'I'm sorry,' Laurie responded. 'I prayed it wasn't going to turn out that way . . .'

Rachel started to speak, but her chest was too tight. She tried to breathe, but seemed unable to get any air, then she began to shake as though her entire body was in some kind of seizure. 'I can't stand any more,' she cried helplessly. 'It's got to stop! Please! It has to stop!' She dropped the phone and pressed her hands to her face. 'It has to stop,' she sobbed.

'It's all right. It's all right. Take it easy,' Chris said, holding her as if to keep her together.

'I'm OK,' she gasped. 'I'm fine. I'll be fine.' She was looking wildly around the room, not sure what she wanted to do, or say, where to go, how to get there . . .

'Just take it steady,' he cautioned, still holding on to her.

Cruel images were flashing through her mind of Tim and Katherine making love, of them laughing together, whispering, shutting her out . . . Oh God, how could he have done this. *How could he?* She'd tried to believe in him and he'd betrayed her. All this time . . . What a fool she'd made of herself. It had all been a lie. Everything. His love, his loyalty, his politics, his integrity . . . How she hated and despised him now. How she wished she could erase him from her life and stop feeling this endless pain.

'Rachel?' Chris said softly.

She turned to look up into his face, then suddenly her arms went round him and she was pulling his mouth down to hers.

His lips were firm, yet tender, holding to her own as his fingers splayed over her throat. She pushed her tongue deep into his mouth, then began fumbling frantically with his shirt.

Catching her hands between his, he pulled gently away, and looked down at her grief-stricken face.

'Oh God, I'm sorry,' she sobbed, wrenching herself free. 'I'm so sorry. I don't know why I did that.' Shame was almost choking her. 'I have to go . . .'

'No,' he cried, grabbing her before she could run from the room. 'It's all right. Laurie told me . . .'

'What did she tell you? That my husband was a lying, cheating bastard . . .'

'She told me about the results,' he cut in, 'because she was afraid you wouldn't, and she thought you'd need someone with you when you found out.'

Her eyes were darting around the room again. 'She was probably right,' she said, distractedly, 'but I don't expect she thought I'd try and seduce you. Oh God, I can't believe I did that. I'm sorry. I'm just so sorry.'

'Don't be,' he said gently.

She turned away, still shaken by how determined she'd been to get him to make love to her. Even now she wasn't entirely sure she'd stopped wanting it, if only to blot out the terrible hurt of being so wrong about someone she loved so much.

'Would you like me to leave now?' he offered.

No, she wouldn't. 'Yes, I think so,' she said. 'I'm sorry, I just . . .' She turned to look at him, and her heart seemed to crumble at the concern in his sombre dark eyes. Somehow she managed to smile as she said, 'If I promise not to take it any further will you hold me?'

Bringing her to him, he folded her deeply into his arms and pressed his mouth to her hair. She held him too, her face hidden in his shoulder, her body feeling swamped and comforted and totally protected by his. She wasn't going to think any further than this, because it didn't matter that he wasn't Tim, or that she might feel ashamed again when he finally let go. All she was going to do was stand here and pretend, just for a moment, that everything in her life was good and safe and true, and not crashing down around her like an avalanche that just didn't know when to stop.

'Thank you,' she said, finally stepping back. Then with an awkward laugh, 'It's the second time you've been there when I needed that.' Then her eyes closed as the truth of Tim's betrayal swept over her again.

'It was probably just a one-off thing,' he said, as though reading her mind. 'A post-election high . . .'

'Please, don't defend him,' she interrupted. 'I don't think I can take it right now.' Already she could feel the hurt turning to anger, which was a better place to be than this awful lonely despair and foolish delusion, and her voice was edged in bitterness as she said, 'To think of all I've been going through, everything Laurie's doing . . . My stupid, pathetic belief that I could clear his name, when all the evidence . . . What's the matter with me? Why can't I accept what's staring me in the face? Oh, no, not my husband. He couldn't possibly be involved with a company like Phraxos. Nor could he *possibly* be unfaithful. The stain must belong to somebody else. He'd never do anything like that. We were too close . . .'

'If you don't stop giving yourself a hard time we might have to go back to the seduction scene,' he warned.

Not quite able to laugh, she shook her head and turned to where the phone was still lying on the floor. Picking it up, she put it back on the base, then spotting the package from the Virgin Islands, she took a deep, shuddering breath and picked it up.

How trivial and long ago the good news about the villa seemed now.

Imagining the worst she was facing with this was the post office queue to send whatever was inside back again, she tore open the envelope and drew out a neatly folded single white sheet, and another sealed brown envelope. Casting a quick eye over the covering letter from Mrs Willard, the villa's manager, to Mrs Hendon apologizing for not returning her things earlier, she opened the other envelope and pulled out its contents.

Frowning, she turned the passport and driver's licence over in her hand. 'Whose is it?' she said. Then she registered the name on the licence. 'It can't be,' she murmured, a strange buzzing starting in her ears as she glanced up at Chris.

He looked down at it, then his eyes came up to hers, equally shocked. 'It's yours,' he said.

She was shaking her head. 'But I wasn't there,' she cried.

Taking the passport he flipped open the back page. 'This is yours too,' he said, turning it so she could see.

'But it can't be, my passport's here in . . . Oh my God! Oh Jesus Christ!' The world was starting to spin very fast now. 'The picture,' she said. 'That's not me.'

He looked at her incredulously, then snatched it back again.

His eyes returned to hers, for there was no doubt that despite the dark hair, and printed name, the woman in the picture was very definitely not Rachel Hendon.

Rachel clasped a hand to her head, still unable to

believe it. 'You recognize her, don't you?' she said. 'You've seen her on the news. You know who that is?'

He nodded. Yes, he knew who it was. How could he not, when it was the woman they all so urgently wanted to find.

Chapter 16

Laurie was sitting at a trestle table in the middle of
removal chaos. She was in the new office that she,
in Rose's absence, had rented for the programme.
Her laptop was open, her mobile phone tucked into
her neck as she typed in the information she was
receiving from an AP correspondent, stationed in
Paris. Each time she spoke her voice echoed up into
the domed ceiling and around the fan-shaped room
with its two red brick walls forming a V behind her,
and one wide arced wall full of windows that
looked out on to Narrow Street beyond. A mere
three-minute walk from Rhona's flat, the office
could hardly be more conveniently located,
especially as it was a stone's throw from a DLR
station, and it wouldn't be hard to get to and from
Elliot's apartment either – though that was
irrelevant now she no longer lived there, so she'd
just drop it from the equation.

Right now she was so involved in trying to get
more information on Professor Bombola while co-
ordinating everything else that was coming in that

the subject of Elliot wasn't causing quite so much distraction as it normally did. The fact that it would come back later, with a vengeance, was something she'd have to deal with then.

'OK, yes, I've got that,' she said, glancing up as Rose's son, Dan, who was one of the programme's co-producers as well as chief cameraman, struggled in with a huge box of files and tapes. 'Can you email me a list of the addresses?' She typed, listened, typed again, then said, 'Brilliant. I really owe you for this. If you hear any more, you've got my number,' and ringing off, she jumped up just in time to catch a stack of cartridges that was about to cascade from Dan's box.

'Just as I thought, the Associated Press has been tracking our professor for a while,' she told him. 'He's got some very interesting friends of the presidential or fabulously rich kind, and they meet in some very way out places. What time are the removal men coming back? We need proper desks, and decent chairs to sit on.'

'They're on their way, should be here in about half an hour,' he told her, fanning his lightly bearded face with a rag as he headed back out to his car. 'When's Gino starting?'

'The week after next,' she called after him, then snatched up her mobile as it rang, daring to hope it might be the good professor himself, or someone affiliated, with a positive response to her request for an interview. 'Hello, Laurie Forbes.'

'Hi, it's me,' Elliot said.

Her heart turned over. 'Hi,' she responded.

'We need to talk.'

Though she'd have liked to think he was

referring to their personal situation, she just knew he wasn't, so disabusing herself of the hope, she said, 'What's up?'

'In person,' he responded. 'Where are you now?'

'At the new office, in Limehouse. Why don't you come and see it?'

'I should be there in ten minutes. In the meantime, do me a favour, don't make or receive any more calls.'

Her head drew back in surprise, but in his usual fashion he'd already clicked off the line, leaving her annoyed that he'd just assumed she'd do as he said. 'Elliot's gracing us with a visit,' she told Dan, as he struggled in with a stack of shelves and a toolbox. 'We're not supposed to answer the phones until he gets here.'

Dan's bushy black eyebrows arched with intrigue. 'Did he say why?' he asked.

'You know Elliot,' she responded drily. 'Why explain anything if he can get away with a simple command?' Then starting out to Dan's car to help carry in more boxes, she said, 'Did you make any progress booking our flights to Washington?'

'Oh, yes,' he answered. 'We've clocked up enough air miles between us to do this one for free. The accountants will like that. We go next Tuesday, and Mr Landen's secretary assures me he'll be available for a whole hour on Wednesday morning at eleven.'

'So magnanimous!' she said. Then setting down the stand for a water-cooler she helped him put the tank on top, and filled a small paper cup. 'You know, regardless of whether or not we get hold of Bombola,' she said, 'I still think we should go to Paris later today.'

Finishing his own drink Dan tossed the cup into a black plastic sack. 'Sure,' he said. 'At the very least we might be able to grab a couple of shots of him coming or going from his hotel.'

'Exactly. The mysterious Nigerian professor whose assets were frozen by the dead-or-alive guy until January of this year, when suddenly, boing, they're released again. Add that to his shares in the Phraxos Group, and his meeting at the Kensington Palace Hotel with Tim Hendon, a month before Tim Hendon was murdered . . . Sprinkle in Katherine Sumner's presence at that meeting, her known romance with Franz Koehler, and now also with Tim Hendon . . . And what have we got? OK, nothing that adds up to more than a bag of juicy maybes, but it does comprise the kind of speculation that you and I know very well is going to open a few more doors than are opening right now, if only to throw out some hefty denials – and oh, how incriminating those denials can be!'

Dan was chuckling. 'What about this passport thing?' he asked, starting back out to the car. 'Any more there?'

'Yes, there is. I spoke to the villa manager last night. Apparently Katherine – or Mrs Hendon, as she called her – *and her husband* turned up a few days later than their original booking, and stayed the rest of the three weeks. An ingenious move, really, to pose as Mr and Mrs Hendon, whose booking had been made long before the killing and whose name isn't so uncommon, so, if you're the villa manager, you probably don't give any more than a passing thought to the scandal going on in Britain. Obviously they can't be the same Mr and

Mrs Hendon, because there's not much chance of a dead man and his wife turning up for their Caribbean holiday, is there? So now what we need to know is, *who* was playing Mr Hendon? Xavier Lachère?'

'Did the villa manager say what he looked like?' Dan asked, lugging another heavy box back in through the door.

'"Nice looking man. Very quiet."' Laurie quoted, going after him. 'That was about all I could get from her without alerting her to the fact that something was wrong, but I'll call again later and give it another go. We should go straight after, though, get some interviews with the locals who might have seen Katherine and the mystery man, and some footage of the villa. We might even track someone down who knows where they went afterwards – unless they're still there, on another island, or in another villa. I need to contact a local hack to start asking questions, especially round Mahoe Bay where Franz Koehler's place is.'

'Well, if you ask me,' Dan said, going to help himself to more water, 'she's in some exclusive Swiss clinic, recovering from a serious remodelling of the face and reading up on her new life history, all paid for by Herr Koehler himself, while little friend Lachère gets a nice fat reward for minding her and keeping the big bad policemen away.'

'There are two problems with that,' she responded. 'First that Koehler's looking for her himself – that's if his press statement's to be believed, of course. And second, why go to the Virgin Islands first, and not straight to the Swiss clinic?'

'They have clinics in the BVIs, don't they?'

She nodded. 'Of course. So OK, maybe you're right, she went straight to the Caribbean, had plastic surgery, then convalesced at a villa she knew would be free.'

'What about Koehler, are they still questioning him?'

'I don't know what the game is with him,' she replied. 'When you get to that level, none of the normal rules seem to apply. However, Haynes admitted the other day that he believes Koehler really doesn't know where she is.'

Dan frowned, then shook his head. 'Not buying it,' he responded. 'Of course he's going to tell the police he doesn't know where she is, he's hardly going to admit he's got her propping up a bridge in Sydney, or morphing into a Pamela Anderson lookalike at some la-di-da spa in the Bahamas, is he?'

'No. But look at it this way. Gustave Basim, the third person in the flat, obviously knew what happened that morning, and now he's no longer with us. Katherine also knows what happened, and she's vanished. The general consensus seems to be that she's still alive, so is she afraid of going the same way as Gustave Basim? She clearly took part in the killing, either as an accomplice, or as the killer herself, so she can't go to the police for protection, and though Koehler might have been involved in helping her get away from the scene, since he was in London at that time and left his hotel at an hour that coincided rather neatly with her need for a ride, she's since realized what a vulnerable position she's in, so is now on the run from just about everyone.'

Dan looked thoughtful, then swung round as a voice behind him said, 'Hi! Anyone home?'

'Gino!' Laurie cried, jumping up to embrace the old friend she'd just enticed from newspapers into TV. 'What a lovely surprise. We weren't expecting you for a fortnight.'

'I know,' he said, hugging her warmly, 'but I've got a day off, and I thought you might need a hand with the move. Hi, Dan. How's it going?'

Dan gave him a thumbs up as he filled another cup from the cooler, then indicating the car he said, 'There are more boxes out there, or you can start putting up some shelves.'

'OK, in at the deep end,' Gino responded, rubbing his hands together. Noticing a black Porsche pulling up outside, he looked curiously at Laurie. 'Is that Elliot?' he said.

Glad no one knew how nervous she felt, she nodded.

His brown eyes widened. 'So have you two . . . ?'

'No,' she interrupted, wishing she knew how to put her feelings aside. Hoping that it might in some way distract her, she went to tug the drill out from under the shelves. 'How shall we go to Paris?' she said to Dan, while handing the drill to Gino. 'Train or plane?'

'Probably train,' Dan answered, glancing at his watch. 'We could leave Gino in charge here and start making a move, if you're willing,' he said to Gino.

'No problem,' he responded. 'I've got to be back at the office tomorrow, though.'

Dan nodded, then turned to high-five Elliot as he

came in the door. 'How are you, my friend?' he said. 'It's good to see you.'

'You too,' Elliot responded, his tall, muscular physique filling the doorway.

'How's tricks?' Gino said, giving him a wave.

Elliot smiled, but his eyes were already moving to Laurie, his permanently austere expression masking anything he might be feeling inside, so whether he was finding this difficult, as it was the first time they'd seen each other since she'd left, she had absolutely no idea.

'So, what do you think of our new office?' she said, waving an arm.

'Very nice,' he replied.

There was a moment's awkwardness, then she said, 'Right, we need to talk. Here? Or shall we go over to Rhona's flat? She's at work.'

'No,' he answered. 'Gino and Dan need to hear this too.'

Both Gino and Dan glanced at Laurie, then back to Elliot, as he said, 'I know you've been trying to get hold of Patrice Bombola and I want you to stop.'

'What?' she cried. 'But you know very well he's one of our prime –'

Elliot cut across her. 'I warned you the other night that he could be a dangerous man to approach,' he said. 'That hasn't changed, if anything it's become worse, so I'd rather you let me approach him first.'

'And how are you going to do that?' she responded, testily.

'I'm going to Paris, tomorrow. There's a chance one of his people will get me in to see him, not as a journalist, as a scientist. If it happens, then I could be in a position to learn a lot more than either of us would trying to go in as ourselves.'

Laurie's eyes had become large and forbidding. He was going undercover and she hated it when he did that, for the risks were always too high. 'I want to go with you,' she said shortly.

'You know you can't,' he replied.

Since she'd only make herself ridiculous if she argued, she said, 'Then, at the very least, we need you on camera talking about this, I mean, if we don't end up getting him ourselves.'

Though he didn't answer, she could see the refusal in his eyes.

'If we don't manage to find out *why* Tim Hendon was killed,' she said sharply, 'then we'll need people like you to talk about what *might* have happened.'

'But he and Katherine Sumner were lovers,' he reminded her. 'The public knows that now, so is your programme going to look like a grieving widow concocting some incredible high-level corruption scandal, because she can't accept her husband was unfaithful?'

Laurie's mouth fell open, though of course he was right, it could all too easily be made to look like that. She glanced down at her computer screen, then back to him. 'That's all the more reason why we need you on camera, talking about this,' she said. 'People know your name; they respect what you say, so if you present this case, with me, it'll have some credibility. No, you've got to do it, Elliot,' she cried, as he started to resist, 'because I'm just not prepared to let Rachel Hendon suffer the humiliation of people thinking all the fuss was because she just couldn't let go – especially when I *know* there's more to it, and so do you. So if need be, I want your word that you'll back me up.'

His eyes moved to Gino and Dan, who, unlike him, showed how uncomfortable they were with the challenge. However, their silence spoke their solidarity with Laurie, so all he could say was, 'Give me a couple of weeks. Let me see where this goes with Bombola, then maybe Max and I will be in a better position to see whether our own theories really are bearing up.'

'OK. But if you're not going to co-operate with us, I'm going to want to know why.'

His only answer was to match the harshness of her stare. Then quite unexpectedly he said, 'There's a chance Franz Koehler will be there too. In Paris.'

Though her gaze didn't waver, her personal feelings were once again ambushing her professional self, for if Franz Koehler was going to be there, in person, she felt an extremely long way from good about Elliot being there too, posing as somebody else. On the other hand, she desperately wanted to meet Franz Koehler herself.

Dan said, 'Can I answer that phone now? It's driving me mad.'

As Elliot glanced at him, Laurie said, 'I hope you're not going to warn me off Patrick Landen too.'

'Not at all,' Elliot replied. Then, clearly realizing how annoyed she was at having to give up on Bombola, he said, 'Look, you know you can trust me, and I'll do whatever I can to get you some answers – but this just isn't as simple as one man's murder.'

Since she had no argument to that, she said, scathingly, 'Next you'll be reminding me that no one is all good, or all bad.'

At that a flicker of humour showed in his eyes, which momentarily reflected in hers, for it was a cliché they often teased each other with, then finally swallowing her pride, she said, 'So when will you know if it's all going to happen?'

'By the end of the day.'

'Isn't someone likely to recognize you?' Dan said.

'On the whole, my face isn't known,' Elliot responded, 'only my name, so obviously I'll be using a false one.' Glancing at his watch, he said to Laurie, 'I have to go. Will you come out to the car for a moment?'

Sensing it was going to turn personal now, her heart skipped several beats as she followed him outside. When he reached the car, he turned to face her. 'I'm sorry if I seem to be interfering,' he said. 'And I'm sorry that I can't be more explicit.'

She shrugged. 'That's OK. I know you would be, if you could.'

He kept his eyes on her face, even though she'd looked away. 'So how are you?' he asked.

'Fine. Thanks,' she answered.

He waited.

At last she met his eyes, then wanted to scream: no one she knew could mask their feelings the way he could. 'OK, so now we've got that settled,' she said. 'I'm fine and I also have work to do.' She started to turn away.

'Laurie. Stop.'

Wishing she could refuse, she looked at him

again, and said, 'Why? You've got nothing to say. You're not prepared to change anything . . .'

'What do you want me to change?' he demanded.

'You. Us. I want to know how much you care . . .'

'I've tried telling you, but apparently my word's not enough . . .'

'No, it isn't!' she snapped.

His eyes were suddenly impatient. 'So you're not coming back?' he said tersely.

'What's the point?'

He looked at her, harshly.

'No. I'm not coming back,' she said, ignoring the way her heart was crying out for him to persuade her, to say the words that would convince her that he really did care. And maybe he would, because surely by now he must be missing her as much as she was missing him.

'Then does this mean we're free to see other people?' he said shortly.

Her mouth almost fell open as his words hit her like a physical blow. Not for a single instant had she expected them, nor had she even imagined there might be someone else in his life – and now suddenly this was so frighteningly reminiscent of how he'd broken up with her sister, telling her that there was another woman in order to get her out of his life completely, that the shock of history repeating itself was making it hard to breathe, never mind think.

In the end, letting pride speak for her, she said, 'Yes, that's exactly what it means. Now, if you'll excuse me,' and before he could stop her again, she stalked back into the office, knowing she'd handled it badly, but Jesus Christ, how did anyone handle someone like Elliot Russell?

For the next half an hour she struggled to immerse herself in other things and forget the awful scene outside, the dread of him going undercover, the anger that he didn't seem to be missing her, and jealousy that there was already someone else . . . But it just kept going round and round in her head, an endless cycle of self-torment and worry, until she finally heard Gino say, 'Laurie, are you listening to me?'

Collecting herself, she looked up to where he was, at the top of a ladder. 'Sorry, I was miles away,' she said. 'What were you saying?'

'I was telling you about the actress Stacey Greene's husband,' he said. 'Didn't you want some background on him?'

Frowning, since she'd all but forgotten why, she said, 'Yes, but I thought I asked Liam from Elliot's office.'

'You did. I saw him earlier, so I'm passing the information on.'

'So, does Pablo Escobar need to fear for his reputation?' she asked, attempting some humour, as she clicked to go on line.

'Escobar?' Gino said, confused. 'What's he got to do with it? Anyway, he's dead, isn't he?'

'Very,' she confirmed, not especially interested in this now. 'So what did Liam tell you?' she said, opening up an email from Rachel.

'Just that he's some kind of mega rich art dealer, with some mega rich clients.'

She nodded, absently. There was no particular surprise in that, for even without Gloria Sullivan's sugar-coated envy, she wouldn't have imagined Stacey Greene married to anyone uncultured, or unmoneyed. She probably wouldn't have imagined her having an affair with Robert Maxton either, but after the embarrassing episode in his office, combined with the interview she'd managed to prise out of him yesterday, and then with Anna, later in the day, there was obviously some considerable strain in the marriage. As she thought of it, Laurie couldn't help but feel sad for Anna. This must be a very difficult time for her, trying to cope with the demands of two small children, her role as a producer, a husband who was besotted by another woman, and a sister who was pregnant, recently widowed and hell bent on finding out what had really led to her husband's death. It was no wonder she'd appeared so uptight and distracted when they'd talked. Who wouldn't when they were going through so much?

Sighing, she carried on reading the email. She hadn't bothered to type up the notes she'd taken during Anna's and Robert's interviews yet, since they'd told her nothing she didn't already know, other than the fact that they were both so completely wrapped up in the film, and their own lives, that they hadn't even really connected with the fact that the people Rachel was so determined to expose would almost certainly rather see her dead than ever allow that to happen. But what was the point in alerting them, when the reality was that she, Laurie, was probably much more in the firing line than Rachel – and before her were Elliot, and his partner, Max.

*

Anna's face was pale with shock as she stared down at the pages her husband had written. Were she not reading this for herself, she'd never have believed him capable of such imaginings, and maybe she couldn't anyway, despite the fact that it was written in his hand.

Feeling weak and faintly nauseous, she sat down at his desk. There was no doubt in her mind that this was a depraved and diabolical version of *The Geddons* that featured only the poet and the mistress, and the poem she'd found earlier, tucked into the pocket of a sports coat, was obviously part of the same piece. It was finding the poem that had led her to search his desk, something she'd never done before, and bitterly regretted doing now, for she just didn't want to know that her husband was capable of anything like this.

She looked down at the pages again, and started to shake. Any other woman would be as disgusted, even as frightened, as she was by this, but Stacey Greene, for whom it was presumably intended, just wasn't like other women. She wondered if Stacey might even be encouraging it. If she was, and these scenes were anything to go by, then Anna had to believe there was no actual physical affair, for it only told of the woman enjoying the spectacle of the fantasy, while sometimes permitting the brief touch of her private parts, or a lingering kiss on the mouth. If that were the case, and in her heart she very much feared that it was, then he had fallen prey, not just to his own sexual urges, but to the most narcissistic and exploitative tease she'd ever known.

Unable to read any more, she screwed the pages

into a ball and clutched them to her chest. In her mind's eye she could see him gazing adoringly, slavishly, at Stacey's naked body, as she posed for Ernesto's portraits. She could see him on the set, struggling to focus on the proceedings, instead of just Stacey; sloping down corridors after her at the end of the day; submitting himself to her every whim, hanging on to her every word. She knew the scenarios, because many of them were there in the script, and her heart ached with jealousy that he could want another woman so uncontrollably that nothing else, not even his own wife or children, seemed to matter any more.

Tears filled her eyes, as she stared blindly at the walls of his study. She must fight this, there was no question about that, but her instincts were to handle it like the wife in the film, and that would be a disastrous route to take. She had to think of something though, because there was just no way in the world that she was going to allow everything she'd worked for, everything she held precious, to be destroyed by this crazy obsession, this abominable shadow plot that he was contriving for Stacey. She had to find a way of making him understand that to Stacey he was no more than a besotted fool, someone she could tease and torment with the fantasies he fed her, because it was all a game to her that fed her vanity and increased her female power.

'What are you doing?'

Anna started.

He was standing at the door staring at her with cold, accusing eyes.

She stared back. Her face was stricken, and

blotched with tears, her heart loaded with guilt at being found snooping. 'I should be asking you that question,' she said quietly.

'That script isn't for public consumption,' he told her. His tone was as chilling as his expression.

The "public" hurt, a lot, but moving past it, she said, 'This script should be destroyed.'

'That decision isn't yours to make.'

'Then whose? Yours? Or Stacey's?'

His face blanched and for a moment he seemed about to shout, or maybe storm off. Then his eyes were glinting like steel. 'She understands it in a way I knew you wouldn't,' he snarled.

Anna's heart twisted, for now there could be no doubt that Stacey was a party to this. 'What is there to understand, but the delusional imaginings of a middle-aged man?' she said.

'Are you going to call me disgusting now?' he challenged.

'I don't have to, you already know it.'

'Then why not add debauched, depraved, sick in the head?'

She only looked at him.

'That's what you think, isn't it?' he demanded, his mouth starting to tremble.

'I'm not playing the game,' she replied. 'I'm not one of your characters, and I won't stick to the script.'

His eyes flickered to one side, and her heart ached, for she could sense the loneliness and confusion even though there were no visible signs of it. 'I love you,' she said, shakily, 'and whatever you've done, you know I'll forgive you, but you have to stop this before it goes any further.'

His eyes were glassy as he stared back at her.

'Robert, if she has any poems, if she has anything written by you that . . . You have to get them back. Not only for your own sake, you have to do it for me, and the girls.'

'They're hers,' he said shortly. 'I wrote them for her, and now they belong to her.'

Anna's eyes closed as a wave of fear stole through her. But she wasn't going to let this happen. Somehow she was going to put a stop to it, because she just couldn't bear to think of how destructive the disgrace would be to him, more than anyone else, should those poems ever fall into the wrong hands.

She spoke in a sharp yet quiet voice as she said, 'I want you to let me finish directing the film.'

He frowned in confusion. 'You think I'd walk out on my own project when it's only half finished?' he said, more surprised than indignant.

'Darling, you have to,' she told him. 'You can't keep seeing her, it's only going to make things worse.' Hearing herself quote almost directly from the script, her mind shied away in alarm. It was almost as though he'd foreseen all this in some mad, graphic dream, and now, like brainwashed puppets, they just kept returning to the lines he had given them.

'You're not going to stop me seeing her,' he said, firmly, but she could hear the turbulence behind the words, telling her that if she fought he might, ultimately, back down. But she wasn't going to create a scene with the children upstairs, at least not tonight.

'Are you in love with her?' she asked, her voice faltering slightly.

His answer came with no hesitation. 'I love you,' he told her.

'Then where is this going to end?'

He took a breath that shuddered deeply in his chest, then looking at her with as much sadness as resolve he said, 'I have to have her.'

Anna's eyes were shining with tears as she said, 'The sexual acts you're describing . . . Is that what you really want to do?'

He didn't answer, nor did he meet her eyes.

'If it is, then can't you do them with me?'

'Would you want to?'

'No. But I don't want you to do them with her either.'

'I don't do them with her. They're only fiction.'

'But you're trying to make them real.'

His shoulders were unsteady, as his hands clenched and loosened at his sides. 'Anna, please, try to understand,' he said, his voice starting to break.

'I do,' she answered. 'If I didn't, do you think I'd be sitting here, talking to you like this? Do you think I could read what you've written and still want to be in the same room as you?'

He only looked at her, seeming lost, yet defiant; angry, yet afraid.

Getting up she went to put her arms around him. 'Together we can get through this,' she told him gently. 'You just have to let me take over from here, because if you don't . . .'

'I'm the director!' he snapped. 'I'm not walking out on my own film.'

'And that's all it is, a film,' she responded. 'I'm talking about us, our marriage, our life together.'

His eyes met hers, and her heart grew heavy with dread, for she could see that she was failing to reach him. 'I love you, Anna,' he said softly. 'I love you with all my heart, and I really don't want to hurt you, but I'm not going to let you direct this film.'

'Then I shall come to the set, every day.'

'You can come, but you can't interfere.'

'I don't want to. I just want you to know I'm there.'

He lifted a hand to touch her face. 'You're my strength,' he said tenderly. 'And she's my weakness.'

The next line of the script was the wife's, 'So use me to overcome her', but she wasn't going to say that. She was only going to hold him, and love him, and use the entire might of her will to bring them through this in a way, please God, that would avoid anything like the tragic denouement of the film.

Chapter 17

A dense, early morning dew covered the airfield as Chris Gallagher and an aircraft mechanic walked towards one of the hangars that was framed in the hazy orange glow of sunrise. The building's shadow spilled out over the tarmac and quickly absorbed theirs as they disappeared inside. Rudy was striding along a short distance behind, talking rapidly to the person at the other end of the phone.

'How many passengers today?' the mechanic asked, as they approached the twin-engine plane.

'Two,' Chris answered. 'The other'll be along shortly. Could you take a look at the transponder, air traffic queried it when I brought her in yesterday, it seemed to be giving a false reading.'

'No problem,' the mechanic responded.

As they reached the plane he slapped the mechanic on the shoulder, then turned to Rudy, who was just ending his call. 'So?' he said.

'Bombola's already in Paris. Franz is arriving later today.'

'What about the Dubai operation?'

'Everything's on schedule. There're people out there already paving the way.'

Chris nodded, thoughtfully. Then changing the subject he said, 'Did Franz say how the search in the Virgin Islands was going?'

'No sign of her, apparently, but they're not finished yet.'

'So I guess we have to assume that he really doesn't know where she is,' Chris said.

'It sure doesn't look like it.'

'Then what's the story behind what happened to Hendon?' Chris wondered. 'Why would she be hiding from Franz when he set her up for it?'

Rudy shrugged. 'She knows everything, and you know how much Franz hates that. It makes him vulnerable. He's pretty ticked off over this Lachère character too. They thought he was someone she went to college with, but it turned out they were wrong.'

Chris's eyebrows arched. 'I take it he's the man who was with her in the Caribbean,' he said.

'Not confirmed, but everyone's assuming so.'

Chris's expression revealed nothing as glancing at his watch he said, 'OK. We're in good time. I need to make a call.'

Misty bands of sunlight were beginning to seep into the hangar's dark hollow as he walked back towards the open air, punching in Stacey's mobile number. After three rings Petey answered.

'Is she there?' Chris said.

'You're in luck, she's just about to go on set. I'll pass you over.'

A moment later Stacey's voice came softly down

the line. 'Hello, darling,' she said. 'Thanks for calling me back.'

'You must have had an early start this morning,' he said, 'it's only just after six.'

'I did,' she confirmed, then yawned, as though to prove it. 'Sorry,' she laughed.

'Are you all right? You sounded upset in your message.'

'No, I'm OK. I just wanted to talk to you. I haven't heard from you much this last week or so.'

'I'm sorry. Things have been hectic.'

'So where are you? Or shouldn't I ask?'

'I'm in England, but about to leave.'

'I spoke to Elwyn and Felicity. They said you'd been in Cornwall.'

'Yes. For a while.'

Though there was no rebuke, he knew she was hurt that he hadn't told her, but if he had he knew she'd have tried to rearrange her schedule to get down there too, and though it might have looked as if he was taking some time out that he could easily have spent with his wife, it definitely hadn't been the case.

'When will you be back from wherever you're going now?' she asked.

'I'm not sure. It could be a couple of days, or a couple of weeks.'

In the background he heard someone speak to her, then to him she said, 'Can you hang on? Don't go, will you?'

'No,' he responded.

As he waited he struggled with his conscience, for she was clearly feeling insecure and in need of reassurance, which was rare for her. Still, he could

393

hardly blame her when this added role he was playing for Franz Koehler was forcing him to spend so much time away from her now.

'Darling, are you there?' she said, coming back on the line.

'Yes, I'm here.'

'I'm alone now, so I can speak. I just want to know if you're avoiding me because of the baby thing.'

His eyes closed, as much in exasperation as in guilt, for this was hardly the time to discuss it.

'It is about that, isn't it?' she prompted.

'Listen, I'll call you tonight,' he said. 'We can talk then.'

'OK.' Then after a pause, 'You know, there's nothing between Robert Maxton and me, just in case that's what's bothering you. It's all just a silly game.'

'I know,' he told her.

She hesitated, then with a smile in her voice she said, 'Tell me you love me.'

'You know I do,' he responded.

'Say it.'

'I love you, and I miss you, and I'll come home as soon as I can.'

'I love you too,' she purred.

After ringing off he turned back into the hangar to find Rudy coming towards him.

'OK, our guest is about to arrive,' Rudy announced, with jaunty eyebrows, 'and is very much looking forward to meeting Professor Bombola and Herr Koehler, I'm told.'

Chris's smile was thin. 'I'm sure the pleasure will be all his,' he commented, walking on towards the

Rockwell. He was about to call out to the mechanic when his personal mobile rang again. Assuming it was Stacey calling back, he lifted the phone to his ear. 'Hello?' he said softly.

For a moment there was only the background sound of a station, or a busy street, then a female voice said, 'Chris? Is that you?'

He hesitated, recognizing the voice immediately, though he was slightly thrown that she had called him now, so early in the morning – and when it was Stacey's voice he'd been expecting to hear. 'Yes, it's me,' he responded, turning aside from Rudy. 'How are you?'

'Fine,' Rachel answered. 'I hope you don't mind me calling, it's just . . . Sorry, can you hear me, it's a bit noisy here.'

'Yes, I can hear you. Where are you?'

'At Heathrow.' She laughed. 'You're going to think I'm crazy, I know, and I probably am, but I've been in touch with the woman who manages the villa on Virgin Gorda, and it's free for the next week, so I'm going over there to find out what I can about Katherine. Mrs Willard doesn't think she's on the island any more, but –'

'Hang on, hang on,' he cut in. 'I thought Laurie was investigating this?'

'She is, but she's going to Washington on Tuesday, and I just feel that we should be on this now. I was going to ask Anna to come, but she's too busy with the film . . .'

'But you're not allowed to fly.'

'I'm not that far gone yet,' she assured him. Then with a laugh, 'though I'm starting to look it.'

He was silent, wondering how the hell he was

going to talk her out of this. In the end all he managed was, 'You can't go alone.'

'I could,' she retorted, 'but I was kind of hoping . . . Well, I mean, if you're free . . . I know you're probably not, and why would you want to . . .'

He was quietly reeling. If the timing could be worse for this, he'd like to know how. Turning to Rudy he opened his eyes wide, to show alarm. 'Rachel, I don't think this is a good idea,' he told her bluntly. 'It's where you were going with Tim. Have you thought about how painful that's going to be?'

'Yes, but I can handle it, and honestly, I have to do something. I can't just sit down there in Killian twiddling my thumbs and reading old letters, and please don't tell me I'm hormonal and incapable of thinking rationally, because though it might be true, it's patronizing, and it isn't going to change my mind. We know Katherine was on Virgin Gorda, we know which name she was using, we've even got a photo from the passport, so it makes sense to go and find out what we can. Or what *I* can, if you don't want to come. Sorry, I'm sure I'm asking too much.'

Everything they had set up for the next three weeks was flashing through his mind. Though he only had parts of the picture, he knew very well that dozens of people were already preparing to receive and dispatch, then communicate and disappear. And his own role was to be key since he was due to receive a new shipment of cash at a Dubai airfield twenty-one days from now. The logistics of that were still being worked on, though not by him. The information he needed would come via a hotmail, or mobile phone, some time in the next week . . . So his actual presence this side of the Atlantic wasn't really vital until a couple of days before the operation – and if Rachel was going looking for Katherine Sumner then someone had to go with her, and that someone absolutely should be him.

'Are you still there?' she asked. 'Have I shocked you?'

'No. I was just thinking. You say you're at Heathrow?' He was looking at his watch. 'Jesus, what time did you leave this morning?'

'I caught the train up last night and stayed at a hotel. I've been trying to call you, but I've only just got through. Hang on, I need to put some more money in.' A beat later she said, 'I'm meeting Laurie's partner, Danny, in a minute. He's bringing a camera and some stock so I can get some footage for the programme.'

'So Laurie knows about this?'

'Yes, and she doesn't approve either, but I'm booked on a flight now . . .'

'At what time?'

'Ten o'clock. Where are you? Are you still in London?'

'Sort of.' His eyes were back on Rudy. 'OK. Count me in,' he said. 'Book me a seat on the same flight. I'll get there as soon as I can.'

Without waiting for her thanks he rang off, and started towards the Rockwell. 'Rachel Hendon's taking herself on a trip to the Caribbean to look for Katherine Sumner,' he told Rudy as he fell in beside him.

Rudy's eyebrows reached for his hairline. 'Holy shit!' he murmured. 'So what are you going to do?'

'Go with her. What else can I do?'

'Are you crazy, man? You can't do that.'

Ignoring him, Chris ducked under a wing of the aircraft to go and talk to the mechanic. A moment later he was back. 'We need to know what she knows, agreed?' he said.

'Sure, and I understand why someone has to go with her,' Rudy said. 'But not you. Not now.'

'Then who would you suggest?' Chris countered. 'Who do you know that she'd allow to go with her, that's of any use to us?'

'We can get someone who's already over there to watch her,' Rudy replied. 'She doesn't have to know they're there.'

Chris picked up the luggage he'd dumped next to the plane and swung a holdall over his shoulder. 'And how much of what she finds out do you suppose she's going to tell this person watching her?' he said, and started out of the hangar.

Rudy went after him. 'She's not going to find out any more than Franz's detectives,' he protested.

'Can you guarantee that?'

Rudy's expression was bleak. 'You're needed here, man,' he said.

'Look,' Chris responded, 'everything for the next couple of weeks is going to happen by phone or email, and the last I heard, the Virgin Islands has both. So here, there, what difference does it make? And if Katherine Sumner happens to still be around over there, knowing all there is to know about the Special Project, the last thing Franz is going to want is her getting together with Rachel Hendon, right?'

Finally Rudy said, 'OK, but even if you do

manage to square this with Franz, and I can see why it has to be you, what about her?'

Chris threw him a quick glance. 'What about her?' he said.

'Well this isn't just any dumb broad you're talking about here,' Rudy reminded him. 'So don't you think she's going to find it just a little bit strange that you can drop everything at a moment's notice to go out there with her?'

'I've got clients out there.'

'*Clients*? What kind of clients?'

Chris's expression was tight. 'I've got another life,' he reminded him.

They'd reached Chris's car by now, and as he threw his bags in on top of a guitar case, a black Porsche pulled up next to them.

Rudy turned round. 'Looks like our paying passenger's just arrived,' he murmured disapprovingly.

As Elliot Russell got out of the car Rudy walked round to greet him.

'One way to Orly,' Elliot said, using the code he'd been given.

Rudy shook his hand, while glancing over at Chris as he got into the driver's seat of his car. 'Slight change of plan,' Rudy informed Elliot. 'It's going to be just the two of us flying today. I'm your pilot.'

Elliot glanced at Chris too, then reached back inside the car for his luggage.

'Only final transactions are being conducted today and tomorrow,' Rudy told him. 'New initiatives will be on the agenda for the two days following, so I hope you're prepared for a wait.'

'I have as long as it takes,' Elliot replied, taking a mobile phone from his pocket as it rang.

Chris was watching him closely, his dark eyes glinting suspiciously. He was sure he knew that face, but couldn't seem to place it.

Rudy came back to the car, and stooped down to the driver's window.

'What's his name again?' Chris said.

'Hastings. Mark Hastings.'

Chris looked at Elliot. The name wasn't familiar.

Rudy said, 'Make Franz your number one call. I don't want him on my phone before he knows what's happening.'

Chris nodded, and started the engine. 'I'll keep in touch,' he said.

'You better.'

Laurie's face was taut with concentration as she typed rapidly into her computer, setting out a provisional running order for the programme, based on what they'd learned so far. Though the potential magnitude of it was certainly not lost on her, the very real apprehension of where it might lead them was, for the moment, comfortably at bay as she went through this routine discipline of planning.

Her notes, reference books, printouts and audio tapes had all but taken over Rhona's dining table, which was in the corner of the L that connected the small, but artfully Moorish, kitchen and rather harem-style sitting room. Behind her the evening sunlight was starting to dwindle over the river, while a gentle, cooling breeze drifted in through the open window.

'There you go,' Rhona said, plonking down a tall,

frosted glass full of rum punch. 'Probably not as good as you make it, but I don't expect any complaints.'

'Thanks,' Laurie mumbled, barely looking up.

Neither surprised, nor offended, Rhona sauntered on into the sitting room, pausing a moment to glance in the mirror, where her reflection showed a woman whose features were too large and irregular to make her a conventional beauty, but whose brazenly voluptuous figure and wickedly suggestive eyes made it certain that she'd never be short of admirers. However, as far as lovers went, she'd lately been restricting herself to just the one who'd bought her this lovely river-view apartment, which was his home too during his occasional visits to London.

Moving on to where she'd left the page proofs of a new book that she, as a publisher's publicist, would soon be promoting, she put her drink on a small, Indian table, and sank into the pile of sumptuous cushions beside it. She was just getting engrossed in the book again when Laurie suddenly said,

'You know, this is one of those situations where the answer could be a million miles away, unless you just happen to walk round the right corner and bump smack right into it.'

Rhona's eyes remained on the page. 'Are we still talking about Elliot, or have we moved on?' she asked.

At the mention of Elliot's name Laurie's heart turned over. 'Elliot?' she said, frowning. 'I'm talking about the story I'm working on for the programme.'

'Oh, right.'

'Why did you think I meant Elliot?'

'I can't imagine,' Rhona responded wryly.

At that Laurie rolled her eyes and picked up her drink. 'Sorry if I'm boring you,' she said, taking a sip while pulling her notebook out from under a sheaf of papers.

'You're not. I'm just trying to keep up, that's all. Because one minute we're discussing Elliot, the next Rachel Hendon, the next some wicked professor and his Swiss friend, and now, hello programme.'

Laurie laughed. 'Actually, they're all one and the same thing,' she said, 'though Elliot's more of an overlap.' Resting her chin on one hand she began another multi-front assault on the various developments in the Hendon case, until a few minutes later she was back to Elliot as she said, 'Do you think he *is* seeing someone else?'

Rhona's sleepy dark eyes gave a flicker of amusement. 'Darling, why not apply that marvellous brain of yours to a problem that really needs solving,' she said, 'instead of allowing it to plague you with issues that don't exist?'

Laurie smiled. 'So you don't think he is,' she said.

'No. And nor do you. In fact, I still don't know why you're here, because it seems pretty obvious to me that he loves you, even if he does have a hard time saying it, so you're either just being obtuse, or you've got some other agenda going that you're not admitting to.'

At that a faint heat coloured Laurie's cheeks, but thankfully Rhona's eyes were still on the book, so abruptly changing the subject she said, 'You know,

I'm still not sure what to think about Rachel Hendon going off to the Caribbean like that.'

Rhona turned over a page. 'What's to think when she's got a gorgeous man in tow?' she responded.

Laurie sighed. 'This is the first time she's gone so long without checking to find out what progress I'm making,' she said. 'What's more, I wouldn't mind knowing how *she's* getting on, because it's been over twenty-four hours since she took off with a mission, a camera, and said handsome man, so surely to God she must have something to report by now.'

Rhona's voice was steeped in irony as she said, 'Well, surely that tells you all you need to know.'

Laurie looked at her.

'Paradise, camera, gorgeous man,' Rhona said, incredulously. 'It doesn't take that vivid an imagination – or does it?'

'You've just got a one-track mind,' Laurie told her. 'And her husband's hardly been dead for two months, so I don't think it's very likely she'll be getting involved with anyone else just yet. No, what I'm more concerned about is what she'll do if Katherine does turn out to still be on the island. Or, maybe more importantly, what Katherine, or someone else, might do to her.'

'Well, this Chris guy sounds quite capable of taking care of her,' Rhona commented.

Laurie stirred her drink with a straw. A few seconds passed, then she said, 'I was thinking about calling her sister if I don't hear by tomorrow.'

'And what's her sister going to do?'

Laurie frowned. That was a good question. What *was* Anna going to do, not so much about Rachel, as

Robert, or the film, or whatever was stressing Anna so much that she'd actually put the phone down on Laurie earlier. She'd called back to apologize, but she'd still sounded frazzled, and Laurie could only imagine that things were going from bad to worse on the husband/actress front.

'You know,' Rhona said, still half reading her book, 'people can be in a weird place in their heads during grief, so give Rachel a break, and let her do this her way. And what's more, if a rebound situation does develop, what's to say that a Caribbean island and a few nights of rampant sex won't do her the power of good.'

Picking up a pen Laurie threw it at her, for Rhona's sexual appetite was no secret amongst her friends, nor was her belief in its healing powers, which, it had to be said, had never seemed to fail for Rhona. However, the two personalities were so entirely different that Laurie found it hard to imagine Rachel going for the same kind of wonder cure, especially while pregnant – or maybe she was just attributing her own feelings to Rachel, because the very idea of sleeping with anyone but Elliot turned her cold inside and out.

However, she wasn't going to think about that, so returning to the programme's opening sequence, she began jotting down the kind of library footage they were going to need of Tim Hendon – at work with his colleagues, relaxing with his family, debating in the House, campaigning for the election, celebrating the victory with his wife – and Katherine Sumner, of course, though Rachel probably wasn't going to like that much – then the horrible, and unexpected, transition to this very vital man's very public funeral. When she got back from Washington she'd put several days aside to go through as much news coverage as she could find of all this, and on the many public statements he'd made regarding world events, particularly in Africa . . . There was even a chance that in there somewhere would be the keys to a few of the right doors.

A few minutes later she was staring at her mobile phone, willing it to ring.

Noticing, Rhona said, 'Does he know you're going to Washington tomorrow?'

Laurie nodded. 'Unless he's forgotten, but that would be unlike him.'

Rhona rearranged the pages on her lap to settle in more comfortably. Then fixing Laurie with frankly probing eyes, she said, 'Tell me, what exactly do you want from Elliot, because I don't mind admitting I'm as baffled as he is over why you've left him.'

Again Laurie's cheeks reddened. She'd rather not confess the truth, even to Rhona.

'If you're still having problems over Lysette . . .' Rhona began.

'No, we're not. Well, we are, but I know we could get past them if he'd just . . .' She broke off, not wanting to continue.

'He'd just what? You can tell me, surely.'

Keeping her eyes lowered, Laurie shrugged. 'Give more, I suppose,' she said.

'Ah, you mean like diamonds?' Rhona said, waggling her eyebrows. 'Now you're talking my language.'

Laurie's eyes came up. 'No, it's not about

material things,' she said, her sense of humour for once failing her. 'They're not important . . .'

'Oh, but they most certainly are,' Rhona protested. 'Where on earth would a girl be without them? I mean, look at me. This flat, my car, all the jewels and furs . . .'

Rolling her eyes, Laurie said, 'You're not at all as mercenary as you make out, so don't think I'm fooled.'

'Oh dear,' Rhona sighed, 'she really doesn't know me at all. But regrettably this isn't about me, so we'll save that for another time and return to you, and,' she said, drawing out the word, 'the fact that I think I've just rather brilliantly hit the nail on the head, haven't I?'

Laurie frowned, but couldn't quite meet her eyes. 'What do you mean?' she said innocently.

'Diamonds, darling,' Rhona trilled. 'Or most particularly one single diamond, preferably oval, or maybe round, but no less than three carats and no smaller than a sixpence, on the third finger of your left hand, where, I might add, it would look absolutely stunning. So, I think that's what we're talking about here, isn't it? Yes, I can see that it is. So you, my darling, independent, career-driven, stand-on-her-own-two-feet, celebrated-investigative-reporter, are just an old-fashioned girl at heart, because what you really want is Elliot Russell to make an old-fashioned proposal of marriage.'

'And if you ever tell him that, I'll kill you,' Laurie vowed. 'In fact, I even want to kill myself for being so . . . disgustingly conventional and embarrassingly . . . Oh God! I can't believe I'm doing this, or that it should matter so much, but it damned well *does*!'

'Darling, even Gloria Steinem's done it, so give yourself a break. And while you're at it give Elliot one too, and tell him.'

'No! Never. I don't want him asking me to marry him because I *told* him to. He's got to want to do it, and if he cared about me the way I do about him, he wouldn't need any prompting. It would just happen. But it doesn't even cross his mind. He thinks we're fine the way we are. It works for him, but he never even stops to wonder if it works for me. I've become a habit, and I deeply resent that.'

'You don't think a wife might turn into a bit of a habit after a while?' Rhona tentatively suggested.

'That's not the point. The point is, I want to know that he loves me enough to make that commitment, but he obviously doesn't, or he'd have done it by now.'

'I don't think that quite follows, but I can see we're not really worrying too much about that,' Rhona responded.

'Well it all seems perfectly logical to me,' Laurie retorted.

'Oh, I'm sure, but it obviously doesn't to him, and I'm afraid, my darling, if you want your own way over this, then you're at least going to have to give him a hint.'

Laurie's face showed her disgust. 'What, you mean wheedle it out of him?' she snorted.

Rhona laughed. 'No, I don't believe that's what I meant,' she responded. 'But if you don't want to give a hint, why don't you go right out there on an emancipated limb and just ask *him* to marry *you*?'

Laurie looked at her, aghast. 'Absolutely no way!' she cried. 'I want to be asked.'

'On bended knee?'

'Preferably. Yes, all right, you can laugh. But that's what I want – him asking my dad, and . . . Oh stop it, will you? It's not funny. In fact, it's very serious to me. But anyway, it's never going to happen because he's actually anti-marriage. He just doesn't believe in it, either as a concept or an institution.'

'So you *have* discussed it?'

'No. I just know that's how he feels.'

'Well his first marriage wasn't such a disaster,' Rhona pointed out. 'In fact they're still friends, so I don't know why you think he's so against the idea.'

Laurie's eyes were sparking. 'Even so, there's still just absolutely no way that I am going to ask him to marry me,' she declared, 'not when I know already that he'll turn me down.' Shuddering as a bolt of nerves shot through her at the very idea, she said, 'Now, I'm sorry, but I need to get on with this before I go back to the office to see Dan.'

Still smiling, Rhona obediently returned to her book, then a moment or two later she remarked, half seriously, 'You know, I'm surprised you feel that way about marriage, when just about everyone around you, right now, is having such a rough experience of it.'

Laurie looked up.

'Well, there's Rachel Hendon and what she's going through thanks to her husband. Then there's her sister whose other half, according to you, seems besotted with some actress. Then there're your own parents who've decided to explore wife-swapping parties . . .'

'Don't, don't,' Laurie shuddered, covering her ears.

Laughing, Rhona said, 'It just doesn't seem that *anyone's* sticking to the rules, so a fat lot of good those vows have done them. Whereas you and Elliot have never slept with anyone else in the entire eighteen months you've been together. Nor do you want to.'

'No, we're only presuming that about Elliot,' Laurie responded. 'And since it took him all of a week to ask if we were now free to see other people I would say the presumption is wrong.'

'It could have been his ham-fisted way of trying to find out if you were seeing someone else,' Rhona suggested.

Laurie took a moment to think about that, then finding she quite liked the idea, she decided to leave it exactly as it was, rather than risk diminishing it with analysis. So changing the subject slightly, she said, 'I wonder how he's getting on in Paris? I wish he'd call and let me know. We don't normally go this long without speaking, so it's starting to bother me. Even after I left we were on the phone to each other again the very next day, and every day after that.'

'Then why not call him?' Rhona suggested.

'I've tried. His phone's turned off. And Max hasn't heard anything either. That's what's really bugging me, that Max hasn't heard.'

'Where's he staying? Can't you leave a message at the hotel?'

'I have. So at least I know he's still there, or

presumably they wouldn't have taken the message.'

'This is hardly the first time he's gone a few days without calling,' Rhona reminded her. 'So stop worrying, will you? I know it's in the air these days, and most of us are doing it anyway, but you're starting to give me sleepless nights lately.'

Sighing, Laurie looked back down at the screen, where the name Hendon was standing out large amongst all the others. It was true, it wasn't so unusual for Elliot to go a few days without getting in touch, but it was for Rachel, so just what on earth was going on over there on Virgin Gorda?

Chapter 18

'OK,' Rachel said, coming out from behind the camera. 'We're all set. So all you have to do is answer the same questions I asked earlier, when Chris was here, but this time we're going to record your answers.'

Mrs Willard, the villa's manager, beamed into the lens.

Rachel was too edgy to laugh, and only just managed to stop herself delivering a sharp reminder to ignore the camera. She pulled a chair up alongside the tripod, then peering into the viewfinder again, to check that the pristine blue sea and a clutch of bright pink oleanders was caught in the frame around Mrs Willard's milky brown face, she said, 'We'll start with the woman you were calling Mrs Hendon. Can you tell me again about the booking she made?'

Mrs Willard delivered another cheesy grin to the camera, and kept her eyes fixed right on it, as she said, 'Well, you see, the booking was cancelled, just a few days before Mr and Mrs Hendon due to come. Then they contact me again and say there was a mistake, they not mean to cancel, so everything all right, they coming again now, but six days later. They pay for the whole time though.'

'How did they contact you?' Rachel asked.

'By the email.'

'And how did they arrive?'

'They come in by plane, down at the Virgin Gorda airport.'

'Was that a private plane?' Rachel prompted.

Mrs Willard nodded. 'It come in from San Juan.'

Rachel handed her a photograph of Katherine. 'Is this the woman who was calling herself Mrs Hendon?' she said.

Mrs Willard looked at it. 'Yes, that her.'

Rachel had just drawn breath for the next question when a sharp gust of wind suddenly blew in, rocking the camera. At the same time, Mrs Willard spotted something behind it and waved.

Rachel glanced over her shoulder, wondering if Chris had returned sooner than expected, but it was the villa's gardener, hauling his equipment up the steps to the patio. She turned back to Mrs Willard and waited for her to refocus her attention.

'Tell us about Mr Hendon,' Rachel said. 'What did he look like?'

Mrs Willard immediately started grinning again. 'What he look like?' she said. 'Yes. He very nice man. I think, when they come, that he her father, or her uncle. But they Mr and Mrs, so I know he her husband. He very dark. I think maybe he Indian. Nice looking man, with moustache. But like I told the other people that come here, he don't speak very much. Not to me, or my daughter. She the

412

maid here. He keep himself to himself. And he sleep in separate room.'

'The other people that came,' Rachel said. 'Who were they?'

'They the police,' she answered.

'When were they here? How long ago?' Rachel asked.

'First time they come, about five days ago, and second time was yesterday.'

It was that piece of information that was interesting Rachel more than anything else, for she had no way of knowing, yet, whether it really had been the police, or if it was Franz Koehler's private investigators masquerading as the police. Considering the two trips, there was a good chance that both parties had got here before her, and she was curious, even anxious, to know what, or who, had tipped them off to Katherine's stay, when she'd assumed that only she knew.

'What kind of questions did the police ask you?' she said to Mrs Willard.

'The same as you,' she answered, her thick, woolly hair being buffeted by the strengthening breeze. 'They want to know how Mr and Mrs Hendon come here, how long they stay. What he look like. If I hear them using other names . . .'

'Did you?' Rachel jumped in.

'No. I don't really see them much, so I don't hear them talking.'

'What else did they ask?'

'They want to know how Mr and Mrs Hendon leave the island.'

'What did you tell them?'

'I tell them I don't know. I not even know they

gone till my daughter come up to villa to clean and find it empty.'

'Was that when –' She broke off as the gardener abruptly started up his strimmer.

She was about to go and stop him, when she decided that, in fact, she really had all she needed from Mrs Willard now, and since another storm seemed imminent anyway, this would probably be a good time to wrap.

A few hours later she was sitting cross-legged on the bed, the interview all but forgotten, as she read over what she'd written in her journal during the past three days. Through the open french windows the sky was by now a wildly billowing mass of grey and blue, while the wind scudded sharply across the churning Caribbean waves, and up over the hillside to shimmy her curtains and join the overhead fan in dispersing the cloying humidity in the room. The camera and tripod was beside her on the floor, along with the cassette of Mrs Willard's interview, and the one other tape she'd managed to fill, mainly with shots of people shaking their heads and shrugging, or pointing her on down the beach to another café, or along the road to another shop, where someone else might be able to help. No one had yet, except Mrs Willard, and the little she'd told them hadn't really got them any further.

But what had she expected? To be told that Katherine was still hiding out somewhere on the island? That she'd revealed her plans to some barman or waitress? That someone would recognize the picture and say, 'Hey, she's the one who chartered a plane to St Thomas, or a private speedboat to Tortola? Whatever she'd expected, or merely hoped for, it certainly hadn't materialized, and she could only wonder if the police, or Franz Koehler's people, had met with the same frustration.

Looking up from her journal, she gazed around the master suite of the luxury villa, with its tastefully simple décor and spectacular sea view, and felt such a painful and conflicting mix of emotions that it was hard to separate one from another. The sharpest and most hurtful of all was the constant longing she felt for Tim, and the happiness they should have shared here, in this very room, where she'd planned to tell him about the baby. In her mind's eye she could see him, even now, shouting with joy, and scooping her into his arms. She pictured them holding each other tight, laughing and kissing; then walking hand in hand on the beach, swimming naked in the pool, making love on this bed. It was so easy to capture the happiness they'd have known as they celebrated each other, their love and delight in having conceived a child. But an unbearable grief soon swallowed the imagined joy, turning it into a seemingly endless pain, for added to all the terrible doubt now was the fact that he really had made love to another woman, and that he'd obviously had secrets with that woman that he'd never shared with her.

'Just thank God,' she'd written in her journal, 'that no one can see what I'm feeling inside, because I'd almost rather die than have anyone know just how wretched and broken apart I am by all this.' But she was angry and vengeful too. Her mind was swollen with hatred for the woman who had dared to trespass on her marriage; who had known more about Tim than she had, who had presumably been with him when he was shot to death, who might even have pulled the trigger herself. And then had come the final, insufferable insult of hiding out here, taking refuge in Rachel's identity. It was as though all her memories and dreams had been torn from a precious place in her heart and trampled to dust by the callous and cunning use of a location that should have been so private that no decent person would have even considered it. It was a kick in the face of her grief that hurt and enraged her maybe even more than Tim's betrayal.

Catching her breath, she pressed a hand hard to her head. Chris was right, being here was proving even more difficult than she'd expected, but it was OK, she'd get through it. Having the camera and feeling productive helped; so did Chris's unfailing support. As she'd written in her journal, she wouldn't want to be here without him, but nor did she want him to come too close. As though sensing that, he was keeping a respectful distance, by taking a room at the other side of the pool, in a quaint pavilion that wasn't even connected to the main house, and by never pressing her to discuss anything personal. It was as though they were on a joint project, producer and researcher, and while he went out around the island, and over to the main island of Tortola, to see what he could find out, and conduct some business of his own, she would either plan what they were going to do next, or go with him to shoot what so far had only been negative leads.

Looking down at her journal again she began reading through the entry she'd made a few minutes ago. It had been an attempt to express, or perhaps unravel, the disturbing emotions she was experiencing about Chris himself, that ranged from guilt at being here with him, and awkwardness at their close proximity, right through to affection for his friendship, and even a sometimes quite strong sexual desire – which took her full circle right back to guilt for even thinking of another man that way. 'Though I long to be alone here,' she'd written, 'to share my grief with no one, the minute Chris leaves I feel empty and want him to come back. I don't tell him that, of course. I can't. I would either become a liability, or he might think it means more than it does. I am in such a dilemma, about him, and so many other things. I long to go home, yet I can't even bring myself to call anyone there. It's as if I'm afraid, though I'm not entirely sure what of, except where all this might end, of course. If Chris weren't so attractive would I be having these same concerns about the inappropriateness of being here with him, such a recent widow, and pregnant too? Earlier, when he came back from Tortola, and I was down at the quay, waiting to meet him, I so very much wanted to hug him and thank him for coming. Of course, I didn't. It's such a delicate and difficult situation we find ourselves in, with us both seeming to go out of our way to make sure we never touch.'

As she finished reading she heard the Jeep pulling up outside, and felt a glow of pleasure coast through her heart. Putting aside her journal, she got up to go and meet him.

'Hi,' she said, watching him come up the steps on to the patio where the glistening blue pool gave the illusion of falling over the hillside into the sea. 'How did it go?'

His dark, often inscrutable, eyes were alive with mischief, as he produced a six-pack of beer and carton of mango juice from behind his back. 'Time to celebrate,' he declared, heading for the kitchen. 'I've just found someone who not only saw her, but actually told me her name before I could tell him.'

'No!' she cried, following him. 'But that's fantastic. I was almost starting to lose hope. Was it my name or hers?'

'Yours, I'm afraid,' he confessed, setting the drinks down on a slate counter top and reaching into a cupboard for two glasses. 'But this guy recognized the photograph instantly, the passport one of her with dark hair, rather than the blonde one.'

'Did he mention anything about a man?'

He shook his head. 'He didn't tell me much more than that. We were down at the jetty and he was just getting on to the ferry over to Bitter End, so I had to leave it there, but he said if we can get ourselves over to his part of the island he'll be happy to divulge all he knows.'

'Will he do it to camera?'

'Didn't get the chance to ask, but he didn't seem the type to have a problem with it.'

Her spirits were lifting by the second. 'So who is he? What does he do?'

'Actually, he's a dive master for some scuba outfit over at the Yacht Club,' he replied, shaking up the juice carton before tearing it open. 'Business has been slow, thanks to the weather, so he's been back in Finland for the past few weeks, which is why we haven't run into him before, which presumably means that the police haven't either. So, Watson, we could be getting ourselves an exclusive.' He filled a glass to the top. 'Here you go, mango juice, straight up,' he said. 'I tried to find fresh, but no luck.'

'Thanks, Holmes,' she smiled, taking the drink. After waiting for him to flip open a beer she touched her glass to the can. 'Congratulations,' she said. 'A break-through at last.'

He grimaced. 'A possible one,' he corrected. 'After all, we don't know what he's going to tell us yet. But at least someone other than Mrs Willard has actually seen her.' Then nodding towards the outside: 'Shall we go and watch the sun set? I'm told it's pretty impressive in these parts, when it manages to get through the clouds.'

Though the wind had dropped slightly, before joining him she went to get a shawl to wrap round her shoulders. Then on impulse she smoothed a transparent gloss over her lips. It would help against the wind, and it made her feel good to see how attractively it accentuated the tan she'd been building up, first in Cornwall and now here, during the infrequent, but blazingly hot spells that broke through the clouds. Looking down at the growing swell of her belly, she felt her heart melt, for earlier that day, for the first time, she'd actually felt the baby stirring. It had made her so happy, and sad, that she'd cried and laughed, and picked up the phone to call Anna. But she'd only got the machine, so she'd hung up, wanting to tell her the news in person.

When she wandered back outside she found Chris sitting at the long, teak wood table, legs stretched lazily out in front of him as he gazed out across the bay to where the grey and orange smudged sky was beginning to shroud the horizon. As she pulled up a chair he hardly seemed to notice, so she sat quietly watching the sunset too, and wondered what he was thinking that had caused such a deep frown line to appear between his eyes. She knew if she asked he'd insist it was nothing, but from the number of phone calls he'd been making and receiving since they'd got here, she couldn't be in much doubt that it was far from convenient for him to be away from his business now. It made her feel selfish and guilty that she hadn't insisted he put himself first and leave, but for the moment she couldn't quite bring herself to.

Taking a sip of her drink she allowed her eyes to drift down from the sky to the lolling peaks of the waves that were riding in to shore like small white boats. She was thinking about Katherine now and how she'd arrived on the island, by private plane from San Juan, all those weeks ago. From the small airfield she and her companion had taken a taxi to Speedy's, the car rental place in Spanish Town, which was how they knew they'd been here almost since Tim was murdered. But where had she been during those first crucial days, and where was she now? Indeed, *who* was she now, considering she no longer had a passport or licence in Rachel's name? How had she got those documents? Who had forged them, and how long had she had them? She'd presumably used them to get herself into the Virgin Islands, though obviously not out again.

What state of mind had she been in whilst here? Who had she been in touch with, and how? The villa's phone records told them only that the phone hadn't been used at all.

Though the light had faded almost completely now, the air remained sticky and warm, so she unwound the shawl and draped it over a chair. Then feeling Chris's eyes on her she turned back to him and smiled.

'Are you OK?' he asked.

'Yes, I'm fine,' she answered, 'but I don't think you are.'

His eyebrows immediately went up. 'What makes you say that?' he enquired.

With a self-deprecating laugh, she said, 'I'm actually still a bit dazed by my own audacity in asking you to come here, but I wish you'd have said no, because it's obviously caused you a problem, taking off at such short notice.'

His eyes were steeped in irony as he said, 'I confess, your timing could have been better.'

'Then please, feel free to go,' she replied, knowing she'd hate it if he did.

'I do,' he told her. 'But I'm choosing to stay.'

Her eyes remained on his as a faint colour stained her cheeks. 'Thank you,' she said quietly.

He was still watching her, seeming to take in every contour of her face, until finally he said, 'Can I talk you into coming out for dinner tonight?'

Feeling her heart respond, as much to his tone as to the idea, she said, 'Yes, why not? It gets a bit dull sitting around here on my own.' Then after a beat, 'Sorry I haven't been much company before. I just haven't really felt like eating.'

He glanced down at the mound of her tummy. 'Then I expect that little fellow's pretty hungry by now.'

'I think you could be right. He gave me a bit of a kick today, probably to let me know.'

'You know it's a boy?' he said.

She shook her head. 'It could be a girl. Whichever, we're both famished and ready to go wherever and whenever you like.'

'Fifteen minutes to shower and shave?' he said, scraping a hand over his jaw.

'Then I'll go and give my sister a call,' she said. 'She's probably wondering what on earth's happened to me by now.'

'You still haven't spoken to her?' he said, surprised.

'I know I should have, but . . .' She shrugged. 'Do you think midnight's too late to call? Yes, it is. I'll wait till tomorrow. I should call Laurie at the same time, let her know how it's going.'

A few minutes later she could hear the pounding jets of his shower, coming from behind the frosted windows at the corner of the pavilion, and not for the first time she found herself picturing him naked. His firm, masculine physique made it all too easy to imagine making love with him, even though it filled her with guilt every time she did. She recalled the way she'd kissed him the day she'd found out about Tim and Katherine. Though those moments were blurred in her mind now, she was certain he'd kissed her back before stopping her attempt to undress him. She still felt horribly embarrassed about that, and profoundly grateful that he'd never brought it up again, but she couldn't help wondering if the same good manners would make him turn her down again, were she to walk in there now and step into the shower with him. Not that she had any serious intention of doing so, but it was a pleasing fantasy to spend a few minutes mulling over as she waited.

After a while the shower went off, and for a moment she thought he was playing the guitar he'd brought with him, until she realized it was the radio she could hear. And beyond that, she was certain, was the sound of his voice, presumably talking to someone on the phone again. She wondered who it might be, considering the time difference between here and Europe, but maybe it was someone local.

'OK!' he declared a few minutes later, finding her in the kitchen, rinsing her glass. 'Let's hit the town. Oh hell! Who's that now?' he groaned, as his mobile started to ring.

Taking it out of his pocket, he turned towards the pool and while talking, walked on back to his room. Just before going inside he suddenly cried, 'Rudy, my man, you're a genius. Tell them from me, everything will be standing by.'

'Sounds like you've just had some good news,' she commented, as he joined her at the top of the steps leading down to the Jeep.

Grinning he said, 'You could say that. And one of these days I might just tell you what it was.'

Her eyebrows rose. 'You mean you're keeping secrets from me, when you know my life inside out? Definitely not fair.'

'Then to make up for it, I pay for dinner,' he said, opening the car door for her.

'Which will only buy you time, not dispensation,' she warned.

After she was settled in her seat, with the safety belt strapped round her, he rested a hand on the side of the windscreen and looked at her through the open window. 'Am I allowed to give you a compliment?' he enquired.

Despite the instant reaction of her body, she shook her head. 'Definitely not,' she told him. 'It might go to my head, and failing to seduce you once was quite enough, thank you.'

His surprise was as great as her own, as he stared, laughingly, into her face, while clearly trying to gauge just how serious she was.

'You know, I can't believe I just said that,' she declared, looking straight ahead and trying not to laugh too. 'Please just get in the car and try to pretend it didn't happen.'

Chuckling, he walked round and got in the driver's side. 'It was going to be a good compliment,' he told her, 'but I don't think it was that good.'

Spluttering with laughter, she said, 'You're supposed to be pretending it didn't happen.'

'Oh right, yes,' he responded. Then cocking an eyebrow, he glanced over at her again and there was nothing she could do but cover her face and carry on laughing.

The air was thick with the choking cumuli of cigarette smoke; pungent with the fumes of the previous night's whisky. No windows were allowed to be opened, every movement was monitored by security cameras and guards. Not even the hotel's catering staff was allowed into the claustrophobic second floor conference room.

After three days of attending sessions in this highly noxious setting Elliot was feeling a lot more than nauseous, though it wasn't so much the air that was affecting him as the mind-numbing reality of what he'd been hearing – and was continuing to hear, as this bizarre, terrifying summit unfolded.

Around the table at that moment were fourteen men, including him. Their nationalities were as diverse as their religions and political persuasions; their dress as eclectic as the many regions of the world from which they came. Most spoke English; those who didn't brought their own translators. Occasionally a woman joined them, like the Iranian biochemist who'd just left, and the nuclear physicist from a former Soviet Republic who'd made several appearances, all of which had instilled more horror in Elliot than anything else he had heard.

The name of Phraxos had not yet been mentioned, nor did he imagine it would be, for this could never be considered part of any legitimate company's portfolio, and surely no documentary evidence existed anywhere to connect this Plutonian convention to the parent organization. In fact, it was so much worse than anything he or Max had imagined, that it was almost impossible to link it to the highly respectable outward image of the Group, with its glossy high-rise office blocks, dark-suited executives and legitimate corporate powers. It truly was the cancer within, the dark side of humanity, the ugly face of greed gone mad.

His own contribution to this hellish marketplace

was to present his 'client's' willingness to supply certain pathogens, and the follow-up education in their weaponization. This he did three or four times a day, as the interested buyers changed and potential new customers, mainly from Africa, were brought in. The five-page document he read from, after handing copies around the table, had been meticulously prepared by an elite team of micro-biologists, and various other scientists affiliated to the British Special Investigation Service, all of whom remained faceless and nameless to him, though he'd been assured that a laboratory had long ago been established to satisfy any number of orders, or customer visits, as well as the inevitable background checks. And those checks had certainly happened, for though representatives from 'his laboratory' had attended these meetings before, as a newcomer he'd been questioned intensely, and repeatedly, almost since arriving. So far it seemed his pseudo-identity, which had a background so full of detail he could only thank God he'd had more than three months to digest and prepare, was holding up, but he was all too aware of how easily, and catastrophically, it could all fall apart.

Though it wasn't possible to know the motives of everyone who spoke, whether selling their talents or product or buying for non-governmental sources, it was clear that they ranged from simple financial greed to political or religious ideology, to sheer fanaticism and hatred. Listening to them wasn't too unlike listening to a rehearsal for the end of the world. In fact there were moments when it moved so far beyond the limits of normal comprehension that he could hardly credit it with reality.

Franz Koehler was at the head of the table now, shirt sleeves rolled back, elbows resting on the blotter in front of him, bunched hands supporting the wide, brutal jaw that did little to detract from the strikingly handsome features of his Germanic face. His height, much like his presence, was imposing, his words, though few, were spoken in English, in educated, though slightly accented tones, while his chillingly pale eyes seemed to drill an unnerving intensity into anyone who fell into their path. There had been some talk yesterday, which had particularly interested Elliot, of the transportation of large cash sums to key locations, presumably to avoid the paper trail, though where those locations were, and what happened to the cash then, he still didn't know.

Glancing up as the door opened, he saw Rudy, the man who'd flown him here, go up to Koehler and speak quietly in his ear. Koehler nodded, then murmured something to Professor Bombola, who was seated next to him, before returning his piercing eyes to the current speaker – a small arms manufacturer from South Dakota. Since the man, for the most part, was repeating the kind of sales pitch that had more or less dominated the proceedings, Elliot waited only a few minutes to see who was interested in his product, then quietly got to his feet and left the room.

Minutes later he was on a busy Paris street, taking in air that seemed to be from a whole other world. Not for the first time in the past few days, he felt almost dizzied by the reality of what was

427

happening here, at the very heart of a civilized city. It bespoke such contempt for decent values, not to mention human life, that were it not so sick, it could almost be considered spectacular in its audacity. More disorienting still was the fact that such an operation even existed, never mind on such a scale. Just thank God it had been infiltrated by the intelligence organizations, though to what extent he had not been told, for his SIS contact, who had so painstakingly prepared him for this mission, hadn't seen fit to inform him. Whether he would ever be able to report his findings he had no idea, for that decision would be taken by a far higher authority in the SIS than he was dealing with personally, and depended totally on the outcome of this extremely intense operation, which was as much about following the munitions as it was about tracking the money. At what point he might be given clearance to print, he had no idea, but he was already aware that no agents' names could be used, which was only to be expected, and he'd also been advised to keep his own off the series of articles too, in order to lessen the risk of Franz Koehler's people, or any of the other guilty parties, coming after him should they escape the trap.

With that sobering prospect hanging over him, he strode briskly on along the Boulevard Saint-Germain towards the heavily guarded Musée d'Orsay. The walk back to his hotel took a little over thirty minutes. By the time he got there the early evening rush hour was under way, clogging up the streets either side of the Seine and the bridges that spanned it. When he reached his expensive, though unostentatious, room on the fourth floor he went to stand at the window, gazing down upon the historical and architectural splendour of this most romantic of cities. What would they all do, he wondered, watching the people, were they to be told that right now, at the heart of their beloved capital, a small, select group of men, operating under the guise of an international scientific research group, was involved in negotiations that would ultimately send thousands, if not millions of innocent people to their deaths, just so that one huge private equity firm could continue paying out big fat dividends to its investors?

Turning back towards the king-sized bed where he'd dropped his briefcase and jacket, he saw the message light flashing on his phone. Since arriving he'd ignored it, not wanting, or even trusting, to have contact with anyone outside the peccant circle he was now a part of. Everything felt like a risk, from a mere walk in the street, to the private meetings he attended to discuss an interested customer's specific needs. He'd been repeatedly warned before coming here how precarious, and life-threatening, this mission would be, and to be aware that issues he wasn't prepared for would be sure to arise. For those he'd just have to think on his feet, and already he'd had to do plenty of that. He wondered how much more his nerves could take, though outwardly he appeared as calm and assured as any of them. However, that was no green light for complacency, and certainly he must not make the mistake of believing that Koehler's agreement to let him attend the summit, or the interest in Mark Hastings's 'company', was in any way a statement of trust. It was merely a beginning, the opening gambit of the most dangerous assignment he'd ever undertaken in his life, or probably ever would.

Pulling a hand over his tired face, he was just crossing to the bathroom when he spotted a small card on the floor, next to the nightstand. Assuming it had been dropped by one of the maids, he stooped to pick it up, and gave a sigh of irritation when he saw it was a calling card for 'Chantelle' an anything-goes masseuse. Tossing it in the bin, he continued on to the bathroom, and was about to start the shower when he made a sudden U-turn back and snatched up the card. Sure enough, on the flip side was a handwritten number. It was a code he and Max had dreamed up, months ago now, should they ever need to make contact in difficult situations.

Moments later he was knocking on room 448, only three along from his own. There was no sign of anyone as the door opened, not even of Max himself.

Amused, Elliot stepped inside, saying 'Chantelle. It's been a long time.' Then as Max quickly closed the door, 'You've grown hairy.'

'Funny,' Max grunted, his closely cropped beard framing a thin, down-turned mouth, that soon revealed a healthy white grin as he clapped Elliot hard on the shoulder. His eyes were lichen green, his hair a wiry mass of silver, and his handshake as firm as any Elliot had known. 'I got nervous when I didn't hear anything,' he explained. 'Then Laurie told me you hadn't been in touch with her either, so I took it upon myself to saddle up for the rescue. So what gives, my friend?'

430

Going straight for the minibar, Elliot took out four miniatures of Scotch and two glasses. 'It's a lot worse than we thought,' he stated, unscrewing the caps.

Max's face was immediately serious. 'Tell me you're not talking nuclear,' he said, watching Elliot empty two bottles into one glass.

'Not yet,' Elliot responded, passing him a drink. 'But don't rule it out.' He swilled his Scotch round the glass then downed half of it in one go. 'The rest of the world might like to think of Africa as a bunch of warring savages,' he said, 'but with these brains behind them I'm telling you, they're anything but. So if they get the funding, and from what I've been hearing they could, they're certainly not going to have any problem getting the experts.'

Max's eyes remained on Elliot's as he drank again. 'So what was on the agenda?' he said, going to sit at a desk next to the TV.

'What we expected. A lot of traditional weaponry, handguns, rifles, grenades, but the chemical and biological variety were mentioned fairly often too.' Then throwing back the remainder of his drink, he reached into the Frigo for two more bottles.

'So what's the brief?' Max asked. 'Are they going for exposure, or close-down? Where do they go with this?'

'You mean the SIS? I'm not sure. No one's mentioned the endgame to me, but it's probably up to the Americans. Their intelligence units have been monitoring the project virtually since its inception, I'm told, but I think that's all they do, because Phraxos is so deep inside the current administration that no one's going to rock the boat.

They just want to keep tabs on what Koehler is up to.'

'Oh shit,' Max murmured.

'I don't know if the Brits are any better,' Elliot said. 'They're not as riddled with Phraxos money, but they know what's going on and so far they're doing nothing about it. They're even supplying some of the product themselves, like the stuff I've been peddling – though that won't get under way for at least a year, I'm told. And believe me when I tell you it really does get shipped, because it's the only way they can follow the trail right to the bitter end and find out who the middle men, like Bombola, are representing.' He shook his head and stared down at his drink. 'It's one hell of a fucking gamble,' he muttered. 'I guess we just have to trust that they know what they're doing.' Then swallowing more whisky, he went to sit on the end of the bed.

'So when do you get out of here?' Max asked.

Elliot's eyes came up. 'Tomorrow. I'm taking the train back. Rudy, my personal pilot, has apparently got other commitments.' Again he shook his head. 'I assumed he was on our side,' he said, 'but now I'm guessing I got thrown straight in at the bad guy deep end, because he's obviously one of Koehler's inner circle.'

'So what do the good guys want in return for this little world exclusive?' Max asked drily.

Elliot drank some more. 'Whatever information I manage to acquire, naturally,' he answered. 'And a promise not to go public until they give the go-ahead.'

'Which might never happen.'

'Which might never happen. But just in case it

does, I was in there, witnessing first hand what goes on, which some might call a privilege, though I'm not sure that's the label I'd give it right now. Anyway, they want it told from another perspective, not just their own, and obviously none of their names ever get mentioned.'

Max's smile was grim. 'Sounds like they got themselves a pretty good deal,' he commented wryly. 'So tell me about Koehler. I take it he was there.'

'Oh, he was there all right, and he's got to be operating some kind of network of his own, answering directly to him, that does the basic organizing, recruiting, money laundering, etc. They'd be like the set of actors in *The Magus*, who Maurice Conchis hired so he could play God with everyone's minds . . . But this version definitely doesn't restrict itself to a Greek island. This has got the entire African continent as its stage.' He paused for a moment, then said, 'Shit, it's like they're waging their own personal war against the whole of civilization, and all just to make money.' He went on, incredulously, 'I can get religion, or revenge, or even self-glorification and power, but *money*! Don't they get it, we've already had the Islamic world erupting like the first act of Armageddon around our ears, so if they go on arming the world like this there won't be anywhere left to spend their fucking spoils!'

They both sat quietly with that, until finally Elliot finished his drink and said, 'You've spoken to Laurie?'

'She's in Washington. Left today.'

Elliot suddenly looked tired. 'You've got to get in

touch with her,' he said. 'I can't yet, my mobile's only local, but you've got to tell her again to keep away from Bombola. It might not be a bad idea for her to forget she's ever heard of him, though I know she won't.'

'So how do I persuade her?'

'With the truth. I don't know where the intelligence agencies are at with him, but obviously if they wanted his name out there, they'd have let it go at the time of Hendon's murder.'

'Did you manage to ask Bombola anything about the meeting with Hendon?'

Elliot's expression was sardonic. 'Believe me, to bring that up would have been like signing my own death warrant,' he responded. 'I had no good reason for asking, and how would I explain even knowing it had happened?'

'How do you know?'

'Laurie found out from a receptionist at the Kensington Palace. But I've since had it confirmed by my SIS insider. Don't ask me if they know what it was about, because if they do, they're not saying. One person who does know, of course, is Katherine Sumner, because she was there.'

'Any mention of her in the last three days?'

'Nothing.'

Max fell silent again, drinking slowly as he assimilated everything Elliot had just told him. Even being as involved in this as he was, much like Elliot, he couldn't always suppress the feeling of unreality that seemed to shroud it, for it was hard to get to grips with the fact that Western greed was playing such an iniquitous and effective role in its own ultimate destruction.

Chapter 19

'Laurie! It's Rachel. Where are you?'

'Where am *I*?' Laurie cried into the phone. 'Where are *you*?'

Rachel laughed. 'Sorry I haven't been in touch,' she said. 'I got your text messages, but actually, you haven't been that easy to get hold of.'

'I was in transit,' Laurie reminded her. 'We're in Washington now, just about to interview Landen the ex-lover at our hotel.' To Danny, who was coming in the door with camera and tripod: 'Put it over there, next to the chair facing the window, and try to get some background of the Pentagon, if you can.' Then to Rachel again, 'How's it going down there? Have you found anything yet?'

'I've just sent you an email, bringing you up to date,' Rachel answered, 'but if you're asking have we actually found Katherine, the answer's no.'

'Pity. What else? Give me the highlights.'

'OK. The police, or someone, have already been here, asking around. Did you mention anything to Elliot, or anyone else, about Katherine being at the villa, because I thought we were the only ones who knew.'

'To Elliot I did, yes.'

'Do you think he'd have told anyone?'

'I doubt it. I'll check when I speak to him. What about Chris, did he tell anyone?'

'He says no, so I don't know how the police found out, unless they're intercepting my emails, or listening in to my phone calls.'

'Elliot's got a great person, Sam deBugger, who can check that out for you,' Laurie told her. 'So what about the bogus Mr Hendon, anything on him?'

'Mrs Willard says he's an older man, and we know Katherine goes for them, because of Patrick Landen and Franz Koehler. A father figure type, though in this instance they apparently didn't sleep in the same room, so we have to deduce no romance. Which was when I got to wondering if this Xavier Lachère, presuming that's who it is, might, in some way, be connected to her father. Mrs Willard says he was very dark, she thought Indian looking, but that could work for Iranian. Long shot, I know, but what do you think?'

'I'll get Gino, or someone at Elliot's office, to carry out an in-depth on her father's time in Iran,' Laurie responded. 'There was no official inquiry into his murder, as we know, so it won't be easy. Anything else?'

'It's all in the email. Now tell me, have you actually met Patrick Landen yet?'

'No, but I spoke to him on the phone last night. As usual he sounded quite charming, in that all-American, I'm-Mr-Powerful way. Very patient, eager to explain every point he's making, in case he's speaking to an idiot –'

'Which is another way of slowing things up to avoid making a mistake,' Rachel interrupted.

'Precisely. Oh. Hang on. There's someone at the door.' Pulling it open, Laurie waved in a waiter and pointed to a desk for his coffee tray, then watching to make sure he didn't trip over any cables she said to Rachel, 'Back with you. Where were we? Oh yes. He wanted a list of questions in advance, not surprisingly, so I faxed them over, with the exception of the few I intend to left-side him with. Even if he doesn't answer them, his reaction could speak volumes. What on earth's going on down there. It sounds like you're having a party.'

Rachel laughed. 'Hardly that,' she responded. 'I've just walked from my bedroom across to the main house, so what you can hear is the radio in the kitchen combined with a gale force wind that howls like a chorus of spooks all day and all night. The weather's horrible. It's barely stopped raining since we got here. And when I say raining, I mean *raining*.'

Laurie was stooping to look through the viewfinder. 'Great,' she said to Dan, satisfied with the angle. 'Final adjustments when he gets here. Meantime, we should get some close-ups of the Pentagon.'

'What time's he arriving?' Rachel asked.

'Actually, any minute. We've got four other interviews whilst here, all egghead types who should add some interesting perspectives on defence industries, Phraxos, arms sales policies, etc, plus as much as we can get about Katherine.

Have you managed to shoot anything your end yet?'

'Just an interview with Mrs Willard, and some general shots of the island. We're seeing someone later though who we're quite hopeful about.'

Hearing the 'we' Laurie was tempted to get into more detail about how it was going with Chris, but now just wasn't the time, so letting it pass she said, 'Do you want to do a quick run through the questions for Landen? You might come up with something I haven't thought of.'

'Good idea,' Rachel responded. 'Shoot.'

As Laurie began listing them off she could still hear the angry rush of a storm in the background, together with the occasional sound of a male voice, though whether it was the radio, or Chris Gallagher, she had no idea. Certainly Rachel didn't speak to anyone, except her, so she had to assume it was the radio, until Rachel suddenly laughed in a wrong place, then apologized and told her to continue.

Laurie glanced at her watch. She'd have to wrap this call up now, since Landen was due in less than five minutes, and she'd received a message from Max telling her to call *before* she did the interview, which she'd been about to do when Rachel had rung.

'What about Professor Bombola?' Rachel was saying. 'Are you going to ask about him?'

'Definitely,' Laurie assured her. 'But listen, I have to go, he'll be here any second. I'll call when it's over. No, hang on, you'd better give me another number besides your mobile.' As she grabbed for a pen, she said, 'By the way, have you been in touch with Anna? I had a message from her yesterday wanting to know if I'd heard from you.'

'I spoke to her about ten minutes ago,' Rachel replied.

'Good. OK, number.' She'd just finished jotting it down when the hotel phone rang. 'That'll be him,' she said to Rachel, and clicking off the line she snatched up the other receiver.

'Miss Forbes?' an American male voice said. 'Mr Landen's arrived. We're on our way up.'

Deciding that the call to Max would just have to wait, she quickly went over a few last-minute details with Dan, then stepped out into the corridor to greet the ex-Senator. A first glance both ways showed only a housekeeping trolley, but then the ding of the lift arriving, followed by the muted swish of the doors, preceded two grey-suited men emerging into the corridor.

Recognizing Landen immediately she started forward, hand outstretched. 'Mr Landen, it's a pleasure to meet you,' she told him, smiling warmly, though thinking what a prat he looked with his dyed and woven rust coloured hair. There was also a good chance that his smooth, tanned features owed as much to a surgeon and a heat lamp as they did to genetics, but the patronizing friendliness in his eyes seemed genuine enough.

'Miss Forbes,' he responded, in avuncular tones. 'I hope it wasn't inconvenient for you, coming all this way, but my schedule doesn't see me in London again until late next month.'

'Really, it's no problem,' she assured him, glancing politely at the aide who was at least a foot taller than his boss and so thin he might snap.

'I've ordered coffee, if you haven't already had any,' she said, waving them towards the room. 'I hope you got the fax outlining my questions.'

'I've been through it,' Landen assured her, almost swaggering in through the door. 'There don't seem to be any problems.'

'Good,' she replied, then almost laughed at the way Dan's head kept going back and back as he looked up at the aide.

A few minutes later, having performed the necessary introductions, she gently steered Landen and his coffee towards the chair she'd set up for the interview, then stepped back towards her own. The camera was next to her, presumably loaded and focused, and while Dan pinned on the mikes, they chatted generally about the weather, and Washington sights and Landen's relief to get out of the office for an hour.

She smiled sweetly and said, 'So, are you ready to begin?'

'Certainly,' he responded, tugging down his shirt cuffs, then linking his elegant fingers together in front of him.

'OK.' she said, giving Dan the nod. 'Let's start with Katherine.' She waited a moment for the camera to get to speed, then said, 'I believe you first met Katherine when she was still at university.'

'That's right,' he responded, with the kind of aplomb that was going to make taking him apart an absolute pleasure. 'I was giving a talk at Stanford, and she sought me out after to ask if I'd give an interview for the college magazine.'

'You'd never met before that?' she said.

'No. That was the first time.'

'So you didn't know her father?'

There was a beat before he said, 'Her father died back in the seventies, it was the late eighties when Katherine and I met.'

Which didn't answer the question at all. 'Did you know who her father was, what had happened to him?' she asked.

'When she told me, I did,' he replied.

Deciding it might be a good idea to have him articulate exactly what Katherine had told him, she talked him through it, then, having heard nothing that contradicted what she already knew, she struck out in the direction of the affair, which he presumably had no objection to, since she'd put it in her fax. 'So during the personal relationship that developed between you and Katherine, after that meeting at Stanford,' she said, 'were her politics always the same as yours – and her father's?'

'Yes, they were, but they changed some years later, when she joined the Democratic Party.'

'Do you know why she changed?'

'I'm afraid not. After our relationship ended I didn't see her again for probably ten years, when she called me up one day, out of the blue, and asked if I'd like to have lunch.'

'At which time you were still a United States senator?'

'That's right.'

She wanted to say *and still married*, but decided not to, because she already knew the answer, and didn't feel there was anything to be gained from the dig. However, she did want to get to one of the major points of the interview, so with no more preamble she said, 'Was it around that time that Katherine introduced you to Franz Koehler?'

'Not at that lunch, but later, yes, she did.'

Good, he hadn't denied it, though she hadn't really expected him to. 'And some time after that you were invited to join the board of the Phraxos Group?' she said.

'Probably six months after.'

Since there might be some value in having the Phraxos Group explained by him, on camera, she asked him to do so, getting him to finish on a statement that confirmed the US Defense Department as Phraxos's biggest client. She could see he didn't much appreciate the way he'd been manipulated into that, but tough.

'How long after you joined the Phraxos Group did you resign from the Senate?' she asked.

His eyes gave a flash of annoyance, for the question hadn't been on the list. 'A few months,' he answered.

'Because of a conflict of interests?'

'Yes, and because my wife was ill, so I wanted to spend more time with her.'

'I'm sorry,' Laurie dutifully responded, noting the way he'd used his wife's death to detract attention from the conflict of interests. 'So you gave up your position in the House, took a very senior role behind the scenes at the Pentagon, which included membership of a Strategic Arms Committee, and joined the board of a major international investment company, specializing in defence industries, in order to spend more time with your wife?' She smiled pleasantly.

He didn't answer, but he didn't have to, his expression said it all.

'Does your position at the Pentagon involve you in budgetary decisions?' she asked bluntly.

'Yes, it does.' His collar was starting to look a little tight.

'And those budgetary decisions – or increases, we should probably call them, considering the size of the US defence budget now – frequently result in some multimillion-dollar orders for Phraxos-owned or affiliated companies? Yes?'

His discomfort was clearly growing. 'Yes,' he said shortly.

'So was that why you eventually resigned from the Phraxos board too? Because of another conflict of interests?'

His eyes were piercing right through hers.

She waited.

'I resigned because my duties at the Pentagon are such that I no longer had the time to do both,' he said.

She nodded. 'But you're still a shareholder in the Group,' she continued, 'so you personally are still reaping considerable financial rewards from the increases in defence spending that you, personally, are involved in deciding?' Then she added, 'Albeit indirectly.' The crafty placing of those final two words had given her point a much stronger impact, and she could see, from his expression, that it had not passed him by.

Again he didn't answer, but again he didn't have to.

'Do you know, in dollar terms, what America's arms exports have been to African nations since the end of the Cold War?' she said.

'Approximately one hundred million,' he answered.

She knew where he'd got his figures, and almost wanted to cheer, for she'd got hers from non-governmental sources, such as the World Policy Institute, and they showed an amount so far in excess of the one he'd quoted that when she came to put the programme together this was going to demonstrate perfectly what a slippery character he was. She then got him to talk about refugee crises, famine, human rights abuses and the US role in the Rwandan genocide – all subjects that she would later visualize with library footage, and some rather different statistics, that would show the abject misery and insufferable loss of life that the constant flow of arms to Africa caused its people, and how at least one Pentagon official, though fully aware of the African plight, was quite content to go on making literally pots of money off the back of it.

However, for now his self-interest, and the Phraxos Group's high-level Government con-nections, had been sufficiently dealt with, so she promptly changed the subject. 'Going back to Katherine – have you seen or heard from her since Tim Hendon's murder?' she said.

Shifting slightly, he said, 'No. Not at all.'

'So you don't have any idea where she might be, or who she might be with?'

'None whatsoever.'

'When was the last time you saw her?'

'About six or seven months ago.'

'Before she went to England.'

He nodded. 'I had dinner with her and Franz Koehler, at a restaurant here in Washington.'

'Was it business, or pleasure?'

'Both.'

'Was Tim Hendon's name mentioned at all?'

'No.'

As if he was going to admit it.

'I don't believe,' he added, 'that she'd been asked to run his campaign at that point.'

'Did you talk to her at all after she had been asked?'

'No.'

'Did you know about her plans to go to Europe, other than to run the campaign?'

'She mentioned them, yes. She and Franz had been seeing each other for some time by then, so it wasn't any surprise.'

'Is that what she said to you, that she was going to Europe to be with Franz Koehler?' Laurie said, wondering if he knew that wasn't the story either Katherine or any of her friends had told. In fact, just about everyone else who'd been spoken to had believed the relationship to be over.

'Yes,' he answered, though she could see that he wasn't sure why she was asking, or if he was giving the right answer.

'Do you think she's still alive?' she asked.

His colour was deepening. 'I don't know. I certainly hope so.'

She nodded. 'Would you consider Katherine Sumner to be a patriotic American?'

Sooner or later he was going to object to all these questions that hadn't appeared on the list, but for the moment he either seemed to have forgotten that he could, or was more nervous of how it would

445

look if he did. 'That's a surprising question,' he remarked. 'But yes, I suppose I would.'

'So you wouldn't imagine her to be involved in any kind of business that could be termed anti-American?'

She could see he really didn't want to answer that, so she decided to help him a little by adding, 'Might she have been involved in, say, certain arms transactions that might end up in the wrong hands?'

To her surprise, and dismay, he breezed right over that one, by saying, 'As far as I'm aware she wasn't involved in any arms transactions at all, never mind any that could, as you say, end up in the wrong hands.'

'But couldn't her relationship with Franz Koehler be seen as an involvement in arms transactions?'

'Her relationship with Franz was entirely personal, and Phraxos is a private equity firm, not an arms dealer.'

Pull the other one, she thought wryly, it shoots bullets! Still, she'd deal with that little spin in the edit, rather than now, for she was realistic enough to accept that there was no way she'd get him to admit to a Special Project of arming the other side, either on or off camera. 'Is there a chance that her personal relationship with Franz Koehler might have helped facilitate a grudge she'd been nurturing for years, against the US Government?' she said.

He frowned, but she knew very well that he was aware of her meaning. Nevertheless, for the viewers' sake, it needed to be spelled out.

'There was never an official inquiry into her father's murder, was there?' she said. 'Though he was a long-serving member of the American Bureau of Intelligence and Research, and a loyal supporter of the Republican Party, it was never satisfactorily explained who was behind the assassination attempt on Prime Minister Hoveyda, in Iran back in '77, which resulted in John Sumner's death. Later, very probably as a direct result of the stress of her husband's murder, and failed support of the Government he had served, Mrs Sumner turned to alcohol, and now has Alzheimer's, while her son, Katherine's brother, ended up committing suicide. It possibly doesn't leave a lot of room for patriotism when you've seen your family decimated like that, does it?' she concluded. 'Or betrayed, is perhaps how she sees it.'

'What is your question?' he responded stiffly.

'My question is, in the light of what's happened to her family, might Katherine be waging some kind of personal vendetta against those who were involved in the cover-up of her father's murder? And if she is, wouldn't aiding the supply of arms and munitions from US manufacturers to the wrong hands be an extremely effective way of discrediting those people? By "those people" I, of course, mean the US Government.'

'I'm afraid you'd have to ask Katherine herself,' he said, actually running a finger under his collar.

She smiled, then abruptly changed the subject again. 'Did you ever meet Tim Hendon?' she asked.

Taking no more than a second to adjust, he said, 'No.'

'Speak to him on the phone, via email, or fax?'

'No.'

'What's his involvement with Phraxos?'

'I'm not aware that he had one.'

'Do you know anything about four million dollars in a Swiss bank account?' she said, hoping Rachel would forgive her – but by the time this was transmitted she'd probably be ready for it to be made public.

'No,' he answered. But he did, she could tell.

'Do you know an African professor by the name of Patrice Bombola?' she said.

From the look on his face she half expected his next words to be a refusal to answer the unscripted question, but to her surprise, he said, 'Dr Bombola is an eminent scholar; a leading expert in his field.'

'What's his relationship to Katherine?'

Without missing a beat he said, 'I wasn't aware he had one.'

'What about his association with the Phraxos Group? Are you aware of that?'

'The Group is a global concern, and Dr Bombola's expertise has, I'm sure, been called upon to help guide certain business transactions on many occasions.'

A very smart way of putting it, Laurie commented to herself, then said, 'Would those include arms transactions?'

'I would imagine so, given the nature of Phraxos.'

'Does that give you any cause for alarm?'

'I don't know what you're implying,' he said, 'but I do know that Professor Bombola is highly respected the world over.'

'So respected that the US Government froze his

assets until January of this year?' she responded, almost wanting to embrace him for walking straight into it.

He glanced at his aide, then put a hand out to block his face from the camera. 'Please turn it off,' he said to Dan.

Laurie turned to give Dan the nod.

'I came here,' Landen said, struggling to hold on to what was left of his composure, 'on the understanding that we would discuss the questions outlined in your fax. I did not expect you to dishonour the agreement, the way you repeatedly have, yet still I have attempted to be as straightforward and helpful as I can. Now, I'm afraid, unless you return to your own scripted interview, I will be forced to draw the interview to a close.'

'I'm very sorry,' she said earnestly. 'It wasn't my intention to offend you, but perhaps you can tell me, off the record, why you're behaving so sensitively about Dr Bombola.'

His colour was still high, and by the look of it her request hadn't helped. 'I know how very aware you and people in your profession are,' he countered tersely, 'of the very different climate we now find ourselves in, so you will understand that there are occasions when it simply isn't possible to tell you all you'd like to know.'

At last, the catch-all curtain of national security that came down every time a politician found himself in a hole. She'd been waiting for it, knowing it would come sooner or later. How interesting that it should descend over Bombola. 'Please be assured,' she told him, 'that we're not about putting lives in jeopardy, if that's what you're suggesting. To the contrary, we're trying to find out why Tim Hendon is dead, and very possibly at the hands of Katherine Sumner.' She wanted to add, or perhaps someone affiliated to the Phraxos Group, but she could find herself in legal hot water if she did, so instead she said, 'We've already outlined Katherine Sumner's possible grievances towards the party that let her father down, and how she and the Phraxos Group have mutually exploited those grievances, by using her extremely high-level government connections, particularly in the Defense Department . . .' She could have said ex-lovers, but high-level government connections seemed more polite. 'So what I'm trying to establish now,' she continued, 'is how Dr Bombola, who met with Tim Hendon, Katherine Sumner and Franz Koehler only weeks before Tim Hendon was murdered, fits into this picture.'

Though he was clearly perspiring, and moving towards the edge of his seat, as though making ready to go, his reply was delivered in quite firm tones. 'I understand your frustration in trying to get to the truth,' he said, 'and in many respects I share it, though perhaps for different reasons. This really isn't the same world as we once inhabited, and to be frank with you, I'm very much afraid that Katherine was standing on the wrong side of the line when those airplanes hit, and now she can't get back again. If she's trying we need to give her the chance, because she could be holding a whole wealth of information that we'd very much like to have.'

Brilliant! she was thinking. A truly brilliant stroke that could almost, but not quite, have her convinced, because though she didn't doubt for a single minute that Katherine had a whole wealth of information, nor did she doubt for a single minute that they knew exactly what that information was, and were now doing their damnedest to make sure it never got out. So Katherine's position on the line of good citizenry the day disaster struck was, to them, irrelevant. In fact, she could see much more clearly now why Franz Koehler and certain members of his board were so keen to find Katherine before the police did, because once she was arrested, and in court for the murder of Tim Hendon, there was just no knowing how garrulous she might become regarding the various names and practices of her old pals at Phraxos, so many of whom were, one way or another, tied up in the higher echelons of this particular Western government, and probably a few others too.

'So,' she said to Dan, after Landen and his aide had left, 'we still might not be any closer to knowing why Tim Hendon was killed, but we do know that Katherine has very good reason to be fleeing from the good guys and the bad guys, because there's not much to distinguish between the two, is there?'

Dan was pouring himself another coffee. 'I've got to tell you,' he said, stirring in a dash of cream, 'you just get better. The way you handed him the rope and got him to hang himself, it was so sweet, I'm still dizzy from the rush . . . And he came in here thinking he was going to have you for breakfast. It was written all over him.'

Laurie laughed. 'I have to admit, I did enjoy the experience,' she said, reaching for her mobile to see if anyone had called while it was turned off. Seeing no one had, but remembering Max's message, she began dialling his number, feeling slightly sheepish now about having to admit that she'd gone ahead with the interview before calling. But it had been such a great interview . . .

'You should have seen him squirm,' she told Max. 'It was a treat. And he got in such a sweat when I mentioned Bombola . . .'

'Oh shit,' Max muttered.

Laurie glanced at Dan. 'What?' she said, her smile starting to drain.

'That was why I wanted to speak to you first. Elliot didn't want you to bring up Bombola.' Then after a pause, 'It's bad, Laurie. I mean really bad. We're going to put it all together, what you've got there, what we've got here, but I don't mind telling you, they're going to do everything they possibly can to stop that from happening – and now we've got to ask ourselves, is that why Tim Hendon's dead, because he was threatening to expose them?'

Laurie's heartbeat was a dull thud in her chest. 'What about the four million?' she said.

'I don't have an answer for that, and he was sleeping with Katherine, so I'm not trying to paint the guy white. I'm just saying, if someone like him can end up the way he has, then so can anyone.'

Completely sober now, Laurie said, 'Where's Elliot? Have you see him?'

'Yeah. He should be leaving Paris in a couple of hours. When are you back?'

'In London? The day after tomorrow. Is that where you are now?'

'I will be in about half an hour.'

'Good. I want you to see this interview. And I need someone to check on Katherine Sumner's father, and why there wasn't an inquiry into his death.'

'OK. I'll get on to it.' Then he added, 'Just be careful who you talk to over there, and especially who you trust, because if Koehler is styling himself on this Maurice Conchis character from *The Magus*, then he's got some of the smoothest operators working for him that any of us have probably ever come across, and from what I remember of it, they're so damned convincing you could find yourself going so far as falling hook, line and sinker for one of them and only find out when it's too late that you've been conned.'

Chapter 20

'There you go, one Virgin Mary,' the barman announced, setting a tumbler full of iced tomato juice on the low-level table in front of Rachel. 'And one Planter's punch,' he added, putting another glass, topped off with nutmeg, in front of Chris.

Chris waited for him to clear, then picked up his drink to salute the other two men who'd joined them under the flamboyant tree, which formed a huge feathery green umbrella outside the bar at the Bitter End Yacht Club. 'Scott, Fenn,' he said, clinking his glass against their beer bottles.

'To Scott and Fenn,' Rachel echoed, following suit.

'And to finding . . . what did you say her name was?' Scott asked, in an unmistakably Australian drawl.

'Katherine Sumner,' Rachel provided.

As they drank, Rachel regarded their sun-weathered faces, Fenn's much older and lived in than Scott's, whose was smoothly chiselled and extremely good looking, though both men seemed

454

to share an enviable *laissez-faire* attitude that no doubt came from living a much more natural kind of existence than urban pressures allowed. The temporary break in the storm must have helped too, for even she was feeling more relaxed now that they were no longer being battered by gale force winds, and blasted out of their wits by clashing explosions of thunder. The strain in Chris's eyes had lessened since this morning, though she suspected that had much more to do with the lengthy call he'd taken from someone in Europe, than with a change in the weather. In fact the call had gone on for so long that the battery on his mobile had run down, making it necessary to ring back on the house phone – and by the time he'd come to find her the tension he'd been struggling to hide these past few days had already noticeably eased.

'Aaah,' he sighed ecstatically, as the rum punch hit the right spot. 'Nectar.' He offered the glass to Rachel. 'Do you want to try?'

Taking it, she helped herself to a generous sip, then instantly regretted it, for one simply wasn't enough. She looked at it longingly, painfully even, then groaned and laughed as the baby delivered a hearty kick, as though to remind her that he, or she, was far too young for such indulgences. So handing it back she started to get the video camera out of its case, while Chris turned to Fenn saying,

'Thanks to you, my friend, I believe we're at least one step closer to finding Miss Sumner than we were half an hour ago.'

Fenn's leathery brown skin folded over his eyes as he frowned, though whether he was shy of the camera that was now being directed at him, or embarrassed by the praise, wasn't too clear. 'Europe's a big place,' he said gruffly. 'I only know I flew her to St Thomas, where she got a flight to Madrid. And that was weeks ago. She could be anywhere by now.'

'But the name she used was Sandra Grayson?' Rachel said, checking the camera's visual display to make sure he was framed right.

He nodded.

'What about the man she was with?' she asked. 'Did you get his name?'

'I didn't see him,' he replied. 'He didn't come on the flight. It was only Scott here who saw him.'

Rachel turned the camera to Scott, then handed it to Chris, since he was in a better position to get a good angle.

'He was with her when she came asking about going on a night dive,' Scott said. 'He was a quiet bloke, older, didn't say much. I kind of got the impression that anything she wanted was OK by him.'

'Did you take them on the dive?' Rachel asked.

He shook his head. 'It turned out that it wasn't your regular night dive she was after,' he answered. 'What she wanted was a cover for getting out to sea, where she was arranging for another boat to meet them, to take them on to St Thomas. If anyone asked, when I got back, I was supposed to say I'd dropped them at the Baths, at the far end of the island.'

'So what happened?' Rachel said.

He shrugged. 'Nothing. I agreed to do it – she was paying well, let me tell you, but when the time came she just didn't turn up. Then I got talking to Fenn, here, a few days later, and he told me how she'd paid him to fly her to St Thomas. She was using another name by then, but we kind of worked out it was the same woman, which was why I asked him to come and meet you this afternoon.'

Rachel glanced at Chris, who was still watching the visual display as he said, 'What about the man's name? Did you catch it?'

Scott pulled a face as he thought. 'It was unusual,' he replied. 'Zac? Zachary?' He shrugged. 'Something like that, but not that.'

'What about Xavier?' Rachel said. 'Could that have –'

'That was it!' he cut in. 'I'm sure that's what she called him. Bit of a blinder, eh?'

Rachel couldn't help smiling, and was about to continue when Chris's mobile started to ring.

'Sorry,' he grimaced, and passing her the camera, he took the phone from his shirt pocket and trotted down the steps towards the harbour edge, where rows of colourful surfboards stood to attention like sentries and the club's single-mast sailboats were floating at anchor just offshore.

Carrying on with the interview, Rachel took them back over Katherine's request for a night dive, then the approach she had made to Fenn, for an eight hundred dollar flight in his Piper Aztec to St Thomas's international airport. Later she'd get some shots of the aircraft itself, hopefully taking off from Virgin Gorda, as well as some footage of the dive-boat that ended up not being used. Meanwhile, she got Scott to hold the photograph of

Katherine, then to look to camera as he nodded, saying that he'd seen her.

'Great!' she declared, when he'd finished. Then with a big smile, 'I can't tell you what a relief it is to hear all this. I was beginning to think the woman had some kind of invisible powers.'

Scott cocked an eyebrow, and reached for his beer. 'So, who is she?' he said, taking a sip. 'Why are you guys looking for her?'

Though Rachel's expression didn't change, the professional objectivity that had kept her aloof from her personal feelings immediately dissolved. 'Chris didn't tell you?' she said. 'You don't recognize her from the news?'

Scott looked at Fenn, and both shook their heads. 'We tend to switch off when the news comes on,' Scott confessed. 'Too bloody depressing.'

She nodded agreement. Then forcing another smile she said, 'I'll tell you what, if you're going to join us for dinner, over at Saba Rock, I'll let Chris fill you in, if that's OK?'

Scott glanced at Fenn. 'Fine by me,' he said.

'Me too,' Fenn replied, looking round at the sound of a motor launch that was scudding across the waves towards the jetty in front of them.

Rachel turned too, and saw that it was the same boat that had brought her and Chris across the bay half an hour ago, from the tiny dock at Gun Creek. Though it was only a five or six minute journey, from where they were sitting the creek was no more than a speck at the bottom of the big, rolling green hills that flanked it like giant paws. On top of one, at the very end of the peninsula, she could see the white pointed rooftops of their villa, and above that a menacing grey mass of cloud that was starting to form like a Thoric netherworld. So it seemed the forecast was right: the storm would return some time later tonight. In the meantime, the calmly glittering blue sea could hardly appear more idyllic.

By the time Chris finally came back Scott and Fenn were on their third beers, and umpteenth island story, while Rachel, awash in Virgin Marys, was quietly fearing that the call might have upset whatever the morning's good news had been. But to her relief, though the battery on his mobile had given up the ghost again, he appeared every bit as relaxed as he'd been half an hour ago, and more than ready to take off to Saba Rock, the restaurant that was its own small island, in the middle of the bay, where the catchy sound of a steel band was already beginning to liven up the evening.

For Rachel, as the boat carried them closer to the twangy rhythm and the smell of barbecuing fish, it was as though the real magic of the Caribbean was at last starting to work its charms. She could see it in Chris's eyes too, which didn't surprise her, for one thing she knew absolutely about him was his love of music. And of art, for he'd been entertaining her with many wonderful stories about Picasso, Diego Rivera, Modigliani, and others whose names she wished she could remember, because it was like stepping into a whole new world of intrigue and romance, that was so far from the darkness and complications of her own that she almost wished she could just close the door behind her and never go back. He also loved to fly, she'd just discovered, because he was discussing it now, with Fenn, as they sped across the waves. He even owned a small plane, it seemed, though maybe that shouldn't be so surprising, for these past few days had left her in little doubt that there was a great deal more to this man than good looks, a cultured mind and a very wicked sense of humour. But as fascinated and charmed as she was by him, she'd been careful to keep her barriers up, for she was afraid of the closeness it might create if she got to know him too well. Yet, thinking about that now, especially in the light of how supportive and generous he'd been, she could see that such caution wasn't only absurd, but mean-spirited, which was why, as they stepped off the boat at Saba Rock, she made a firm decision to stop resisting their friendship. After all, whether she liked it or not, being with him was one of the few things right now that made her feel even close to happy.

The large, crescent-shaped restaurant, with its highly varnished tables and hanging baskets of luscious green plants, was already half full as they were shown to a waterfront table with a view across the waves to the elaborate Creole-style yacht club that was glistening like a Mississippi steamboat in the reddening twilight, and out across the wide blue bay where pristine white yachts were gliding like swans through the waves. Though no one was dancing yet, plenty of feet were tapping and Rachel could see that Chris was only minutes away from getting them all going. However, there was the serious business of cocktails to be dealt with first, and the bushwhacker that Scott and Fenn insisted she had to try.

'I can't possibly,' she laughed, clasping a hand

over the growing mound of her tummy. 'Not with all that alcohol.'

'Ah, but I have a hot line to that little fellow down there,' Chris informed her, 'and he tells me he wants to have some fun.'

'It's a she,' she protested, 'and she only drinks wine in very small and diluted amounts.'

Scott turned to the waiter. 'Bring us a bush-whacker for the boy, and a glass of champagne for the girl,' he demanded.

Rachel glared at him helplessly, then turned as Chris pointed out the sudden eruption of an air battle between one of the peculiarly prehistoric looking frigate birds that glided like an ugly military jet around the skies of the bay, and a young brown booby that was trying desperately to hold on to a fish. The frigate bird soon won, and swept off towards the setting sun to a chorus of boos from the restaurant, that turned to cheers for the booby as it began the search for supper all over again.

'OK, food for us now,' Chris declared, returning to the menus.

'Mahi Mahi in Cajun spice and wine-lemon sauce,' Rachel responded, starting them off.

'Jalapeño poppers and chips for me,' Scott said, rubbing his hands together.

'I'll go with the popcorn shrimp and chips,' Fenn added.

'And I'll have the Ahi tuna with wasabi-soy sauce,' Chris finished, passing his menu back to the waiter, then taking hold of Rachel's hand he promptly spun her out into the aisle.

'This is one of my all-time favourites,' he told

461

her, jigging about and shouting to make himself heard over the jaunty beat.

Guessing he'd probably never even heard it before, she treated him to a sceptical look and tried to follow his rhythm, but the way he was flapping his elbows and stamping his feet, was just too hilarious for her to do much more than laugh, until suddenly he swooped her off into his own version of the tango.

Within minutes the other diners were up, including Scott and Fenn, bobbing and rocking, twisting, jiving, throwing their arms in the air and in some cases, attempting to sing along. A couple of blondes in microscopic shorts and tight Lycra crop tops made a beeline for Scott and Fenn, treating them to outrageously suggestive hip wiggles and hair tumbles, while the two men responded with gusto. Noticing, Chris waggled his eyebrows at Rachel, making her grin, though she couldn't help wondering if he wouldn't prefer to be partnering a girl with a flat stomach, large breasts and free love written all over her. Suddenly feeling certain that he would, she beckoned one of the blondes over, then stepped deftly aside as the tanned beauty shimmied up to him, big brown nipples all but visible through her skimpy top, and wicked blue eyes giving as blatant a come-on as Rachel had ever seen.

Returning to the table she found the champagne and bushwhacker waiting, though what she needed right then was water. By the time the waiter brought it she had her breath back, and was watching the blonde's stunningly unsubtle seduction technique, which amounted to clamping Chris's hips hard to her own as she gyrated like a stripper, and arching her back away to make sure he couldn't miss her gigantic breasts. For his part Chris seemed to be lapping it up, and put on a playful show of aggression when Scott suddenly wrenched her away. However, he'd no sooner started dancing with a middle-aged woman with carroty red hair and braces, than the blonde was back, clinging on to his waist as though the other woman simply didn't exist.

As she watched, Rachel could feel the warmth in her smile starting to fade. She tried to bring it back, but, to her dismay, her mood was on a downward spiral, heading back to the grief it could never escape for long. Then she began to feel the oddness of being here with so many strangers and the guilt of disconnecting from the painful reality of her life, as though she were in some way neglecting Tim. Turning to gaze out at the darkening red night, where the first stirrings of the next storm were now starting to blow, she tried to will herself away from the encroaching sense of loneliness, but it seemed as determined and irreversible as the wind, sweeping around her like a shroud, as though to close her off from the laughter and light-heartedness behind her and lock her back into the awful prison of despair.

As her eyes pricked with tears, she quickly grabbed the champagne and took a sip. Self-pity had no place here, when everyone was having so much fun and when it was no one's fault but Tim's that he had deceived her, then been killed in such a horrible way. Why should they have to put up with her misery, when they'd played no part in the lies and cheating that had deprived her of her husband, and their baby of its father? They didn't want to know how hard she was finding it even to think about a future that couldn't now be with him, but might instead be cruelly blighted by the scandal of his death. Nor would they even care that thanks to a monstrously cruel twist of fate, she was here searching for the woman he'd not only deceived her with, but who had taken his life.

Feeling more anger and emotion well up inside her, she took another sip of champagne, then turned her face back into the cooling wind. Behind her the music changed, and a raucous whoop of laughter was followed by resounding applause. She felt such a longing to go back and join them, to be able to pretend that there was no pain in her life, or fear in her heart, that she just didn't understand why she couldn't. Surely she was strong enough to hold on to these few minutes of happiness without letting the inner demons chase it away like this? She wished she could be more like Chris, able to throw herself into the moment and enjoy it no matter what was going on inside. She'd heard him on the phone often enough, sounding angry and frustrated, then seen the way he could so easily let it go once the call was over. So why didn't she at least try? Why not just go back out there and dance? It didn't even have to be with him, it could be with Scott or Fenn, or someone she'd didn't know. It didn't matter, just as long as she tried.

Forcing herself to turn round she looked for Chris in the crowd then felt her heart flood with affection as she spotted the devilish expression on his face. He wasn't looking in her direction, so she was able to watch him for a while, still enjoying the lascivious attentions of the blonde, who was now rubbing her bottom up against him, while clasping his hands around her bare midriff. Rachel knew she was in no position to feel jealous, especially when she already had enough confusing emotions to deal with, but she was, because it felt ridiculously as though the blonde was coming between them.

Refusing to go on with that kind of foolishness, she took another large mouthful of champagne, and was about to get up to make her bid for survival when the food started to arrive and everyone returned to the table – including the blondes, who Scott pulled up extra chairs for and introduced as Sherry and Tanya.

It was Tanya who all but sat on Chris's lap, and Tanya who started to share his meal. It was also Tanya who ordered the next round of drinks, managing to forget one for Rachel, and Tanya who suggested that since the storm was getting worse they should all stay in the rooms upstairs, because the restaurant was also a hotel.

'In fact,' Sherry giggled, 'I think we should book the rooms now, then throw in the keys to decide who shares with who.'

'No way!' Tanya cried, putting an arm round Chris's shoulders. 'I've got mine right here, and I'm not giving him up.'

'How about we all shack up together?' Scott suggested, beer sloshing from his glass as he banged it against Sherry's. 'It'd save on the cost of the rooms, and think what we could get up to.'

Chris was about to speak, when Scott suddenly burst in over him. 'Hey, hey,' he cried excitedly.

'Chris here's got one of those digital camera jobs, haven't you, mate?' He gave Fenn a bawdy nudge as he winked at Tanya. 'You girls could put on a show and we'll turn you into movie stars,' he guffawed.

'What about the blow?' Sherry demanded, sucking rum punch up through a straw. 'You said you had some.'

'Fenn!' Scott barked. 'You got it.'

'Sure,' Fenn replied, from the corner of his mouth. 'But not right here, mate. Upstairs, when we go.'

'Let's get someone over here to sort out the rooms,' Scott declared, swaying in his chair as he turned to beckon a waiter.

Since they were all being so loud Rachel was sure no one noticed when she called another waiter to ask about getting back to the mainland.

'No problem,' he told her, quietly, 'the boat will take you when you're ready.'

'Maybe I should go now, before the storm gets any worse,' she said, trying not to sound too eager.

He looked out at the pitch-black bay, where small pinpricks of light scattered in the distance marked the dock of Gun Creek. 'Maybe,' he agreed. 'But I think nothing going to get too bad for a while yet.'

As she left she turned back to her food, knowing that all she wanted now was to get away, especially as all the vulgar innuendoes and furtive groping of hands was obviously only going to get worse. Then suddenly aware that there was nothing to stop her except her own innate sense of politeness which was clearly totally out of place here, she put her knife and fork down and excused herself to anyone who was listening, though no one seemed to be. As she walked away she heard Tanya telling everyone about the four kilos of cocaine that had washed up on the shore of Prickly Pear island a month ago, which had led to a week-long party during which she, personally, had water-skied naked off the back of a chopper.

In the ladies' room, in front of the mirror, Rachel rotated her neck to relieve some of the tension, then tilted her head back and took a deep, shuddering breath. She'd just give herself a few minutes then, without making a fuss, she'd ask the boatman to ferry her back to Gun Creek. From there she'd take a taxi up the hill to the villa, since Chris had the car keys, and she didn't want to tell him she was leaving in case he felt obliged to come with her. Besides, he'd need transport in the morning if he decided to stay the night here, or if he got back after nine, when there were no more taxis at the Creek.

As she left the ladies she could hear the boisterous banter still erupting and fizzing like fireworks around their table, though she couldn't quite see them now. She could see the rain though: it was starting to come down in torrents, bouncing off the deck of the restaurant and drumming the overhead canopy as loudly as if it were hail.

'You OK, ma'am?' a waiter said, as he passed.

'Yes. Thank you. Actually, I was looking for the captain of the boat.'

'He over there, at the bar,' the waiter told her, pointing to a group of men watching some kind of ball game on a suspended TV set.

'As a matter of fact, he's already on the boat,' a voice said behind her.

Rachel spun round.

Chris smiled.

She took a breath, then couldn't help smiling too. 'I'm sorry, I hope you don't mind,' she said. 'I sort of lost the mood.'

'It's OK,' he assured her. Then, glancing out at the rain, 'We should go now, while we still can.'

She frowned. 'Oh, but no,' she protested. 'You don't have to come. You're having a good time . . .'

His eyebrows rose with mock eagerness. 'You mean I can stay?'

She met his eyes, then her own narrowed as she realized he was teasing.

'I just went with the flow,' he told her, taking her arm and steering her out towards the jetty where the boat was waiting.

Casting him a wry look, and having to shout now that they were out in the wind, she said, 'Oh, so that's her name, Flo?' Hearing him laugh she took the hand he was offering and stepped over the side of the boat, ducking into the covered front seats where the captain was checking the radio.

'Have you got the camera?' Chris called from the dock.

'Oh God, no! Oh hell, how could I have forgotten?'

'Stay where you are,' he said as she started to get up, and turning back he almost collided with Scott who'd come after them with the small leather case.

'Here,' he shouted, handing it over. 'And you left too much money, mate.'

'It's OK, we owe you,' Chris shouted back,

468

passing the camera on to Rachel. Then signalling the skipper to start the engines, he helped one of the waiters with the ropes before leaping on board.

'Are you all right?' he said, sliding in next to Rachel. 'Not cold?'

'No. Not at all,' she answered, falling against him as the boat abruptly circled away from the dock. 'Are we going to get back in one piece?'

'Sure,' he laughed, straightening her up. 'Could be a bit bumpy though, so hold on tight.'

Almost immediately the boat began a reckless challenge to the elements as it dipped, bucked, rolled and tilted so sharply in the violent gusts that assailed it that Rachel's mounting fear was only matched by Chris's apparent exhilaration.

'Come here,' he yelled, as she was suddenly thrown up against the side.

Feeling the strength of his arms pulling her to him, she gripped hard on the seat back in front and turned her face into his chest. Overhead the thunder rumbled and crashed through the skies, while daggers of lightning lit up the night as though flashing the hidden secrets of darkness.

'Almost there,' he told her, a few minutes later.

She started to look up, then quickly ducked again as his embrace tightened and a second afterwards the boat reared up like a horse, before smashing down with a sickening thud. There were at least a half dozen more rears and thuds like it, until the boat was virtually standing on its stern, where it hovered for an impossible moment, then slammed so hard into the waves that she screamed.

'Is no problem,' the skipper shouted. 'We there. See, there the dock.'

Letting her go, Chris jumped up on to the side of the boat to begin throwing the fenders overboard. Then turning a dangerous loss of balance into a spring on to the jetty, he grabbed a rope and began winding it tightly round one of the cleats. The skipper, being no novice at docking in a storm, revved and slowed the engines as he sidled the boat in, while Chris snatched another rope, coiled it around another cleat, then used all his might to heave the boat up against the dock.

'Take it steady,' he yelled to Rachel, as she started to climb out. 'Here, grab my hand.'

'I'm OK,' she shouted, holding on to him as she stepped quickly on to the jetty. The captain was right behind her, hands out ready in case she staggered.

'Are you going back?' Chris cried, hardly able to stand still in the raging wind.

The captain grinned. 'Not tonight,' he answered, checking the rope knots. 'I stay here with the woman.' Then to Rachel, 'You need get that baby home. No weather for a baby.'

Wrapping an arm round her shoulders, Chris ran her along the jetty to where the car was parked, just below the Last Stop bar, which was no longer visible through the misty grey thickness of rain. They were almost there when the wind suddenly gusted them back, spinning them round into the bus stop, then hurling them forward again.

'Up you go,' Chris shouted, managing to wrench the car door open.

Rachel clambered in, grabbing the seat back to haul herself clear of the door. It slammed behind her, then a moment later Chris was climbing in the driver's side.

'Holy shit!' he laughed, dripping wet and unable to see a thing through the windscreen. 'Are you OK?'

'I'm fine,' she answered, still trying to catch her breath. Then laughing too, she said, 'Are we going to get up the hill, or shall we join the captain and his woman?'

'Trust me,' he declared, rashly, and inserting the key he started the engine.

The journey was nothing short of perilous, as the wind thrust its might into the car as though to force it from the road and over the cliffs into the sea. They took each bend cautiously, bracing themselves for the worst each time the gale caught them, then leaning steeply to the right to counterbalance the dangerous tilts on to two wheels. Their bodies became hard with tension as they used as much willpower as fuel to force the Jeep up the twisting, potholed surface of the hill. Finally they reached the church, which was no more than a white blur in the fog, where they turned right at a tile-roofed bus stop, and began heading along the road towards the villa.

Being on a flatter surface helped them to relax a little, though when Rachel glanced at Chris she could see the strain in his face, as he held firmly to the wheel and brought them safely out of a skid.

'You know, someone told me earlier that this was the most rain they've had at this time of year in two decades,' he remarked, coming to a complete stop before taking the wheels slowly over a banana-thin speed bump.

Rachel's voice was ironic, as she said, 'Don't you find it amazing how you always manage to hit a worst record?'

He laughed, then let the car roll into a dip, before accelerating out again.

A minute or two later they passed the school where earlier they'd spotted goats and chickens roaming the yard with crisply uniformed children. Now the single-storey classrooms seemed to hover like an apparition in the low cloud and rain. Further along the road the charred remnant of an aircraft engine had rolled from the bank on to the tarmac. Chris steered the car round it, edging frighteningly close to a ditch, then drove on to the junction that finally turned them towards the villa.

When at last they reached the top of the drive, he turned off the engine and let his breath go in a loud, drawn-out sigh of relief. Turning to Rachel he said. 'Told you to trust me.'

'But I never doubted you,' she assured him.

Cocking an eyebrow he said, 'There's an umbrella in the back. Stay where you are, I'll get it and come round for you.'

'Are you mad?' she laughed. 'I'm already soaked to the skin. What good's an umbrella going to do now?'

But he was already out of the car, slamming the door behind him and opening the tailgate.

'You should have stayed at Saba Rock,' she told him, as he held the umbrella over them while ushering her up the steps to the villa compound.

'You wanted to do that drive alone?' he challenged.

'No, but you were having fun.'

472

'We've already dealt with that,' he responded, pushing her towards the porch outside the master suite.

'Oh my God!' she gasped, leaping back into him.

'What? What is it?'

'A crab. It's *huge*.'

Stepping around her he looked down at the frightened eyes of a big yellow ghost crab whose arched legs were quivering like a dancer's who didn't know the next move. 'Poor chap,' he said, stooping towards it. 'Her name's Rachel, but she won't hurt you, so you're free to go.'

Shoving him forward, she was about to grab the umbrella when the outdoor lights started to flicker.

'Oh no,' she murmured, holding her breath as she looked at them.

A few seconds passed. Nothing happened, then, with the suddenness of a flick, they went out, plunging the night into absolute darkness.

'Oh hell,' she muttered, unable to see even the white wall that a moment ago was in front of her.

'Got any coins?' he asked.

'You're so funny,' she responded.

Laughing, he took her by the shoulders and eased her into the porch. 'Wait there,' he told her, 'I'll go and find a torch.'

'There were three, in a drawer next to the fridge,' she called after him. 'But I don't know if they have batteries.'

As she waited she decided to use her keys to prod around for the lock. It took several attempts, but finally she made the right connection and was able to let herself into the room. She still couldn't see, but the lightning flashed some assistance as she moved gingerly towards the bed, then groped her way along it to the nightstand. As she pulled a drawer open her copy of *The Magus* fell, making her wince as it hit the tender bones on the top of her foot. Then the baby suddenly made some vigorous movements, probably because it had just got the champagne. Smiling at the wonderful sense of connection it gave her, she reached into the drawer and began fumbling around for the candles she was sure she'd spotted just after arriving.

'Are you in there?' Chris said, from the door, painting the room with a torch beam.

'Over here,' she replied, turning towards the moving wand of light. 'So they work. Great.'

'Only one, I'm afraid,' he said. 'But I found a full box of candles, about a dozen books of matches and an electronic lighter.'

'There are more candles here,' she said, pulling them out of the drawer. 'We just need saucers, or something to stand them in.'

He looked at her.

She looked back. 'There're plenty in the kitchen,' she told him.

'Heavens, why didn't I think of that?' he cried, hitting his head, and swivelling on his heel he took off back through the horizontal rain to the kitchen.

A few minutes later they had managed to turn her room into a cocoon of treacly soft candlelight that seemed so impervious to the roaring storm outside that the sound of it, mewling its eerie cry around the balcony and howling angrily against the shutters, was like an effects track that belonged to another scene.

'You should dry yourself,' he told her, as she

474

turned round from lighting the last candle.

She blew out the match, then put it in the saucer. The air smelt of sulphur from the matches, and damp from their rain-soaked clothes. 'So should you,' she replied.

As they looked at each other in the shadowy darkness she could feel the air starting to lock in her chest and knew that more than anything right now she wanted to step into a shower with him. Would he be shocked if she suggested it? She wouldn't, of course, but the thought stayed with her, spreading a gently insistent desire all the way through her.

'I'll get some towels,' he said.

As he went into the bathroom, lighting the way with a torch, she began reasoning firmly with herself, telling herself that he wouldn't want to make love to a pregnant woman, that he'd already rejected her once, and that it was just a pathetic need to be held that she was feeling, nothing more. But the desire for the kind of physical closeness she hadn't had in so long was just getting stronger.

When he came back he put the torch on the bed, then covering his hands with a towel he lifted them to her face and began gently to dab her dry.

She looked up at him, and felt her mouth tremble as she attempted to smile.

His eyes remained on hers as he moved the towel to her neck, and over her hair. Then drawing one hand free, he put his fingers under her chin and tilted her head back. For a long, breathless moment he merely gazed down at her, then very slowly, he lowered his mouth to hers.

It was as though her heart was afraid to carry on beating as her eyes flickered closed and her lips parted to receive his. The kiss was sublime in every way, for the feel of him was as beautiful as the taste and as evocative as the smell.

'You should take those wet clothes off,' he murmured.

'So should you,' she said.

He looked deeply into her eyes, then, unable to stop himself, he kissed her again.

She lifted her hands to his, and felt him enfold them and bring them to his chest. She longed for him to put his arms around her, but as she leaned in closer to his body, he gently drew back from the kiss. 'We can't do this,' he said softly.

Confused, and embarrassed, she said, 'I'm sorry, I . . .'

'No, don't be sorry. It's not you, it's me.'

She looked up at him, but he wouldn't meet her eyes.

'There was a time,' he said, sounding almost bitter, 'when I considered myself an honourable man, so maybe I should be thanking you for giving me the chance to be one again.'

She continued to look at him, wondering if this was some oblique reference to the baby. 'I don't understand,' she said. 'What . . .?'

'I know you don't,' he said gently. 'I thought you did, but . . .' He stopped as his eyes closed. Then looking at her again, he said, 'We can't do this, Rachel, not because I don't want to, but because I'm married.'

Everything in her suddenly stopped; suddenly reeled back from the word whose meaning she understood perfectly, but couldn't accept. She'd come to trust him, confide in him . . . How could he not have told her this? How could he even be here, if he had a wife? So maybe she hadn't heard right. Maybe he'd said something else . . .

'I'm sorry,' he said.

She took a step back. 'But where is she?' she said, still unwilling to believe it. 'I've never seen her. I've never even heard you talk about her.' *Did that mean he was lying? Oh God, please let him be lying.*

He dashed a hand through his hair. 'My wife is Stacey Greene, the actress,' he said. 'Your sister knows her . . .'

She looked at him, blankly, then as the words registered a wave of horror swept over her. 'Oh my God, no!' she cried, covering her ears. 'No! No! This is horrible. It's just too horrible.'

'Rachel, listen . . .'

'No, don't touch me!' she shrieked, snatching her hands away. 'I don't know what this is about, what you're trying to do to my family, but whatever it is, it's *sick*!'

'I'm not doing anything to your family,' he told her fiercely. 'For God's sake, I could have taken advantage of you just now, I could have waited until the morning to tell you, or not told you at all . . .'

'You could have told me a long time ago,' she yelled. Then looking wildly round the room, 'You've lied to me in the very worst way you ever could,' she said incredulously. 'You have to know, after my husband . . .' She shook her head angrily. 'No! No. Just go!' she said. 'I don't want to discuss it. I just want you to go.'

'That's not going to solve anything,' he protested. 'We need to talk.'

'What about? How you've deceived me?' she said shrilly. 'I don't need to talk about that. I don't need to *talk about anything with you!*'

As she spun away he pulled her back. 'OK, I should have told you before,' he cried, 'right at the start, when we first met, but I swear I never expected . . . I had no idea this was going to happen, that we . . . you and I . . .'

'What are you talking about?' she almost screamed. 'There's no we! No you and I! There's only your lies, and some sick game your wife is playing with my sister's husband. So just who the hell are you, you people, who think you can come into our lives, causing us all this pain? Don't you think we've got enough already?'

'Rachel, stop it! There's no collusion between Stacey and me, no plan to hurt you, or anyone else. *No, listen.* I know Stacey's leading your brother-in-law on, and I know what she can be like when she does that, but I swear to God, it's got nothing to do with me, or you, or why I'm here.'

'Then why *are* you here?' she demanded, her eyes glittering with pain.

'I came because you needed me to, and because I didn't want you to have to do this alone,' he said, looking right into her eyes.

She was staring at him hard, wanting so desperately to believe him, but even if she did, what difference would it make? He was married, he'd held back that vital truth, and she was so hurt by it that she just couldn't get past it. 'I trusted you, and you deceived me,' she said brokenly. 'It wasn't enough that my husband did it, now you've had to do it too.'

'I swear, it's not like that.'

'No! It's exactly like that,' she said. 'You're married and you didn't tell me. In anyone's book that's deceit, and now I look at you, I see a stranger. You're someone I don't know any more.'

'I understand why you think that,' he said, 'but if you'll let me explain . . .'

She was shaking her head. 'With more lies? No, I don't want to hear what you have to say. I just want you to go. Go home to your wife, Chris, because if Tim had done that when he should have, he'd be alive today,' and picking up a towel she walked off to the bathroom.

'Rachel,' he said, before she could close the door.

She stopped, but didn't look up.

'I have to leave in the morning,' he said. 'I don't know whether you want to come with me, or if there are still things you need to do here . . .'

'Don't worry about me,' she said. 'I'll sort out my own flight.'

'Please, I don't want us to say goodbye like this.'

Closing the door quietly, she rested a cheek against it, then stood in the darkness waiting for the sound of the other door opening and closing, and his footsteps retreating in the storm. When it finally came she just carried on standing where she was, unable to move, because this was hurting so very much more than it should that she was afraid, if she did, she might just fall apart. Later, perhaps, she would be able to think more clearly, and make some sense of it all, maybe she'd even let him explain, but right now it all felt so ugly and wrong, and she was so full of pain and loneliness that she just didn't want to deal with anything else that would hurt her. Nor could she bear to think about how much she was going to miss him, because despite his wife, and the lies, she still desperately didn't want to lose him. A part of her even wanted to go after him now to tell him how much he'd come to mean to her, and how afraid she was of losing someone else she'd put her trust in. But she'd never do that, because she could no more forgive the deceit than she could understand why no one else had ever told her he was married either. She would find out, of course, but not now, not tonight, because tonight she was just going to think about herself, and the baby, and try to forget that he, or Tim, or Katherine Sumner, or even Laurie Forbes, had ever come into her life.

Chapter 21

Katherine had arrived in Venice two days ago, alone and still very afraid, as she'd checked into a small *pensione* near the Accademia, which was where she was now, in a third floor room with its restricted view of the Giudecca canal and faded old frescos. It was strange, she was thinking, to see Venice as another person, it made her feel as though her perspectives and responses should in some way alter along with her name, and maybe they had, for nothing was the same now. Everything had changed, even her.

As Sandra Grayson from Eugene, Oregon, she was a middle-aged, dark-haired single from a north-western state, on a two-week tour of Italy. She was intending to stay here, in Venice, for only a few days, as this was not a safe house organized by Xavier, it was merely a stop along the way, until he could arrange somewhere else for her to go, someone else for her to be. Were it not for his connections throughout much of Europe and North Africa, she knew it was unlikely she'd still have her freedom, if this existence could even be termed freedom, but at least, for what it was worth now, she still had her life. However, the pressure this was starting to put on Xavier was becoming so great that she had determined to find a way of releasing him soon. He'd fight it, of course, for they both knew how impossible it would be for her to survive without his protection, and that of his many friends, but Franz's people were closing in, and sooner or later they were going to work out who Xavier was. Then it would only be a matter of time before they captured him and forced him to lead them to her.

Afraid that he'd rather give up his own life than betray her, she'd begun taking steps now to avoid having the death of someone else she cared about on her conscience. These last few months as a fugitive had given her more than enough time to think and evaluate, so that she finally understood and accepted the only road that was now left open to her. It was not going to be an easy one to take, for there were no guarantees she would make it to the end, and even if she did, there was only the certainty of a life in prison to look forward to. But she'd made up her mind to do it now, and though she was going to be dependent on Xavier to help her initially, there would come a time when she'd have to act without him, and she still hadn't yet worked out how she could do that, because she just couldn't imagine why Rachel Hendon would agree to see her alone, without alerting the police, or a relative, or one of her old colleagues from the press.

Clutching her guidebook and camera, she stepped out of the shadowy doorway of her hotel into a thin, shady lane, and walked towards the small piazza at the end, where a couple of artists had set up their easels in front of a church, and the sound of an English rock band thrummed from an empty café. The first time she'd come to Venice was as a child, with her father: when she was eight years old. Though she had little memory of it now, just being here, walking around the ancient streets and crossing the narrow, meandering canals, made her think of him, and long for the time when he'd been there to turn all her problems into solutions. Franz used to remind her a lot of her father: tall, strong, permanently glowering disapproval, yet revealing secret chinks in his armour that always allowed her through to his heart. Her mother had been so bad at finding those chinks, but she'd loved her irascible husband anyway, despite his constant criticism of her appearance and contempt for her tears. He was gruff, authoritarian, but he'd loved his wife, and his children, and they'd always known that. Katherine had never shown the kind of weakness her mother had, not with her father, or with Franz: she'd stood up to them, argued back, which was why her father had always loved her best. But it was her mother and brother who had been destroyed by his death, not her, and she'd considered it her place to avenge them.

How idealistic and naive she'd once been. She could almost hear Franz saying it now, indeed she almost wanted to hear it, for she'd been alone for so long she needed to hear a familiar voice, see a smile she knew, feel a tenderness that was returned. Where was Franz at this moment, she wondered? What was he thinking? Did he despise her, want to crush the life from her, or was there a part of him that was enjoying the game? Of course he would be, because to him this was an exhilarating battle of wits, a series of conjuring tricks, a night of nihilistic illusions that, just like his role model Maurice Conchis, only he understood. But she knew enough to understand that he'd catch up with her in the end, and time was already running out more quickly than she'd expected. She just hoped that Xavier managed to get here soon, with more papers, another identity to help Sandra Grayson to disappear into the ether, like the many ghosts of this historic city, though for her there would be no nocturnal returns. What was Xavier going to say, she wondered, when she told him what she intended to do next? He would resist, there was no doubt about that, but she felt sure he could be persuaded to understand, and might even then insist that he talk to Rachel Hendon himself. But she wouldn't allow him to do that. For his own sake his role would have to end as soon as she'd worked out how to turn herself from the hunted into the hunter.

After wandering around for an hour or more, she inevitably found herself strolling through the sprawling cafés and hungry pigeons of St Mark's Square, heading towards the magnificent basilica. The midsummer heat was intense, the crowds sluggish and sweaty, a swirling, tired mass of jabbering humanity. She glanced at their maps and bird food and envied the safe, uncomplicated corners of the world they could return to, or hide away in, should they ever need to. Rachel Hendon had her haven, in a remote Cornish village where roses grew over the front of her cottage, and the sea swelled like a blessing around the rocks of the cove. Apparently she wasn't there now, because she was in the Caribbean, trying to find the woman who'd seduced, then murdered her husband before disappearing with her own identity. Was that what Rachel believed, she wondered – that Katherine had pulled the trigger? Or did she know about Gustave Basim by now?

After joining the line for the basilica, she turned to look back past the Doge's Palace to the rows of black gondolas that were bobbing like horses on the water's edge, while the gondoliers, in their striped T-shirts and berets, sang a welcome for tourists. She inched forward with the line, gazing up at the distant bell-tower of the campanile, where sightseers were drinking in the views. Then quite suddenly not wanting to wait any more, she started down towards the Grand Canal, and cut along to an arced bridge that crossed over to the white, light and airy palazzo, which had once been the home of the late Peggy Guggenheim. As much as she appreciated the towering, tempestuous masterpieces of the Renaissance and Rococo periods, and the Gothic magnificence of the churches and museums, stepping into the glossy, sun-drenched rooms of this modernist's home was like stepping out of a labyrinthine underworld into the bright, flowering meadow of a nursery rhyme.

There were unusually few people around as she wandered from one room to the next, losing herself in the Mondrians, Kandinskys and Picassos, and then allowing herself a wry glance at the infamous *Angelo della Città*. Amongst the photographs of the palazzo when the high-spirited Peggy had lived there, was one of Peggy herself reclining on the bed with her Lhasa terriers, against the famous Calder bedhead. Katherine lingered for a while, contemplating the extraordinary life this rogue Guggenheim had led. All those artists. All that money, and all the many adventures. Like Peggy, she too was an American in Europe, but apart from that she wasn't like Peggy at all.

A few minutes later she moved on to admire the works of Max Ernst, Peggy's second husband, and then Joan Miró's *Interno Olandese II* which she'd had a copy of in her Washington apartment. Strangely, she was starting to feel sadder, and lonelier now than she had at almost any other time in these long, harrowing weeks since Tim Hendon's death. She found herself almost buckling inside, as she wished there were some way she could reach out to this other American woman, as though she were someone she could talk to and confide in. She wondered if it was just their shared nationality that was making her feel she had found an ally. Or was something on a deeper, more spiritual level touching her now?

Absorbed in her study of the art and thoughts of Peggy, she didn't notice the man who was regarding the Malevich at the other end of the room, nor was she aware of him following her into the hallway a few minutes later, where yet more abstract and Cubist masterpieces led towards a staircase at the end. In fact, in the moment that she came slowly to a halt, with her head cocked quizzically to one side, her mind was moving in such a very different direction to Franz Koehler and this desperate run for her life, that it simply didn't occur to her even to consider that she'd already been found.

Anna was in the car driving back through Central London. It was just after six, so she was in plenty of time to make the girls' music recital by seven. Still the traffic was stressing her, and the constant bad news on the radio was making it worse. Punching the button to find a soothing, classical station, she suddenly had to brake hard to pull up in time for a red light. Someone behind leaned angrily on his horn. She didn't know if it was directed at her, and didn't care. He wasn't a part of her life, nor would she let him be.

Drumming her fingers against the wheel as she waited, she cast a nervous glance towards the mobile phone on the seat beside her. But it was OK. The battery was charged, anyone could reach her, at any time, including Robert, as soon as he'd wrapped. That would happen at six-thirty, so she should hear from him by quarter to seven at the latest. He'd promised, and since she'd decided not to doubt him, she knew the call would come. By then he should be on his way to the recital himself, to slip in quietly as soon as he could get there. He wouldn't let the girls down, not his precious girls. Daddy being there was going to mean much more than reliable old Mummy, but she didn't mind about that, it was simply the role of a mother, especially in their house, to take second place to their busy and famous father.

Accelerating too fast away from the lights, she sped on towards Primrose Hill, cutting in front of a taxi that was dawdling out of a turning, then swerving dangerously to avoid a cyclist she hadn't seen. She knew she should slow down, and she was trying, but her adrenalin was up, making everything feel urgent and needful, even though there was nothing to worry about; nothing at all. Robert had shown no sign of seizing this chance to be with Stacey – though she knew full well that he still wrote her poems and even sometimes masturbated to release the prurient might of his passion. But ever since Anna's presence had been a constant on the set he had been more focused on the film, and less driven to push beyond the limits of normal behaviour. She was his rock, his reason; she inspired him just by being there, and strengthened him just by caring. No matter that it ripped her heart apart with jealousy that his thoughts were so often dominated by another woman, just as long as she was there, holding him together in a way that no one else could see, the filming would continue to the end, when cast and crew would go their separate ways. Then life could return to how it always was, with everyone having come through it safely and intact.

Sobbing a laugh at the total absurdity of her belief, she snapped on the wipers to clear the drizzle that had started. There was just no way this was going to end when the shooting did, it wouldn't even end when his obsession with Stacey transferred itself to somebody else, which it would, because she knew that from past experience. It would only end when she made herself accept that this time it was different, it was deeper and more tormented, and though she could, and often did blame Stacey for that, in her heart she knew that the blame was entirely hers. Because it was she who was destroying him, with her love and protection, and with her fear of taking him down a road that they could never come back from. With the strength of her will she'd tried to keep both the world and his demons at bay, thinking she could combat them alone, and keep him safely at the heart of his family. But despite his outward show of normality and intelligent rationale, there was a tragically delusional part of his mind that was spreading like a cancer to the rest of it, so that she knew it was only a matter of time now before people began to notice, if they hadn't already, and then rumours would start, gossip would follow, and before they knew where they were, everything about him, truth and lies, would be emblazoned in the press – and though she might be able to bear that for herself, she didn't even want to think about how devastating the downfall would be for him, or heartbreaking and life-scarring for the girls.

It was a little after six-thirty when she pulled into the drive of their home and dashed upstairs to get Justine's Pooh Bear. The bedraggled one-eared comfort had been a permanent fixture in Justine's life since she was born, going to bed with her every night, and drying her tears whenever she was sad or upset. Lately though, at least in public, he had graduated to good luck charm, which was why he had to be at the recital tonight.

Finding him balancing on his head in a basket of Lego, she tucked him under her arm, then ran back down the stairs. She was about to go out again when she noticed the light flashing on the answerphone, and hoping it might be a message from Rachel she quickly hit playback. But it was only another parent confirming they'd be car-pooling tomorrow. Scribbling the message for Cecily to find when she came home later, she ran back to the car, and in her haste, reversing out of the drive, managed to bang the front wing against the gatepost.

Swearing through the tears, she threw the car into first, stalled, then after several fast pants of breath, she got the engine going again and started back on her journey to the school. She wasn't coping as well as she should, she knew that, but she'd get some Valium, or something, from the doctor, just as soon as she had time to go. Or maybe Rachel still had some, left over from the shock of Tim's death. She must remember to ask when Rachel next called, which she hoped would be tonight, to tell her she was on her way back. She hated even to think of her sister being so far away, putting herself through untold hell trying to find the damned woman that Anna just hoped was dead. Fixating like this wasn't doing Rachel, or the baby, any good, so as far as Anna was concerned she should just come home now. In fact, she should move back to London, where she, Anna, could keep a closer eye on her, because she was too cut off down there in Cornwall, and Anna needed to know, on a daily basis, that she was managing to cope, and if she wasn't, that she could get to her quickly.

By the time she reached the church hall the lump in her throat was so big it felt like a football. As she made her way to her seat, smiling politely to the other parents, and clutching hard to the mobile, she felt she was either walking through some refined form of hell, or that she might burst from the sheer volume of her frustration and sadness. It was three minutes to seven, and still he hadn't called. He'd promised, damn him. He'd promised them all, and now he was going to let them down. What a fool she was to have trusted him. She should have known better, should have stayed till they'd wrapped, then crept into the recital late with him. Now, God only knew what he might do with Stacey, or what kind of pieces she might have to pick up after.

Some friends had saved seats for her and Robert in the fifth row: everyone knew he was coming. She sat in one, then tried to make small talk with a woman whose name she'd known for years and had now forgotten. The drone of voices, mixed with the sound of the musicians warming up, echoed round the hall, rising to the rafters and seeming to coast down the windows with the rain. She pictured Emily with her little violin, and Justine with her beribboned tambourine. They were so excited, so proud, and anxious that Daddy would be too. And Mummy, of course.

The woman next to her was talking again. 'Anna? Is that your phone?'

Anna stared down at it, then quickly pressing the keypad she tried to hunker down as she put it to her ear.

'I'm on my way,' he said, and the line went dead.

Almost laughing and sobbing with relief, she powered the phone down, then sat up straight, hugging Pooh to her chin, just in case Justine was able to see when the curtain went up. Dear Pooh, he was everyone's good luck charm.

When he'd called he'd meant it, he was on his way. In fact right up to the turn-off to Chelsea Harbour, he'd been on his way, and even now, as he rode the lift up to Stacey's apartment, Robert fully intended to make it to the recital. Just as long as he managed to slip into the back row before the lights went up, Anna would think he'd been there throughout – or at least for most of the show.

The cheating made him feel sick; the lies and deceit crawled over his conscience like lice. He loathed and despised himself, but not enough to change the direction of his footsteps as he exited the lift on the penthouse floor and walked along the corridor towards Stacey's front door. Then, as he turned a corner he felt his conscience shed like a skin, leaving him free to put a spring in his step and the roguish light of a lovable rake in his eyes.

'Is your husband at home?' he'd asked on the phone, when he'd called from the car.

'No. He left again, an hour ago,' she'd answered.

It was a sign. They were both free.

'Can you come over?' she'd purred. 'I've missed you.'

They were the words he wanted to hear. 'I can only stay a few minutes,' he'd warned.

She chuckled softly, 'When you know what you want, that's all it takes,' she'd replied.

The lubricious burnishing of her words sent a sharp burst of lust shooting through his cock. Yes, they knew what they wanted, for his poems of the

492

past two weeks had asked the questions, while her eyes had spoken the answers.

He pressed the doorbell then turned to stare along the plushly carpeted hallway where black-and-white photographs hung, tops out from the walls, their shadows dropping in long, thin triangles towards the floor. He saw nothing, and felt only the monumental ache in his groin. She'd asked him to come; she'd missed him.

'Darling,' she murmured.

He turned to look at her, fear and adrenalin pulsing through his veins. She knew and under-stood what would happen now, yet she was smiling, amorously, invitingly, while the curling tendrils of her cigarette smoke wafted between them like a perfumed potion. Her dress was the same kind she always wore, long, loose and some-how managing to reveal more than it concealed. She'd been wearing it when she'd left the set earlier, after the trauma of the film's climactic scene. She'd come to say goodbye because her wrap had been earlier than everyone else's. He'd thought then that she was rushing home to be with her husband, but even if that were true, he wasn't here now, and that was really all that mattered.

'Are you going to come in?' she said, tilting her head to one side.

He looked at her, seeing lewd, graphic visions of what she and her husband had probably been doing until he'd left 'an hour ago'.

Laughing she turned back inside, leaving the door open for him to follow. He stepped over the threshold, watching her retreating back. She was naked now, except for a narrow black thong and high-heeled shoes. The thong, he knew, was the outer layer of her special panties; he was certain he could hear the muted whirr of its inner vibrations.

He closed the door, his erection harder than rock. He considered unzipping it so that she could see the might of his desire, but decided not yet.

She was at the mirrored bar, putting ice into two glasses. The evening sunlight streamed in like mist, turning her dress into a translucent veil. She glanced over her shoulder and for a brief moment the dress vanished again. 'How would you like it?' she asked.

'Just a dash of water,' he replied.

If she turned round now would she be naked or dressed? Which way did he want her? The choice was his, for lately he'd learned to switch the images, like a slide show, inside his head.

'Help yourself,' she said, waving a hand to the open box of cigarettes at the end of the bar.

A brief recollection of where he should be, and why, suddenly halted him, but it passed, leaving only the dryness of guilt in his throat. He took the glass she was offering, sipped the whisky, and felt the burn on his throat like ice on a fire.

She smiled and indicated the cigarettes again. This time he took one, lit it, and inhaled so deeply that his senses began to swirl.

She sipped her drink, keeping her cerulean eyes on his. 'So, it's almost over,' she said.

He was inhaling again, holding the smoke in his lungs and feeling the largeness of his penis growing and growing. Would he bend her over the bar? Lie her across the table? Thrust her up against a wall? How was he going to penetrate her with this giant erection?

By the time he exhaled, her words had reached him, and he understood that she was talking about the film.

'Are you happy?' she asked. 'Has it lived up to your expectations?'

'In many ways it's surpassed them,' he replied.

She was regarding him intently, quizzically. 'And Ernesto's paintings? Have you seen them lately?'

He shook his head. 'But I know they'll be superior to my imaginings – and to my poems.'

Her laughter made him think of velvet. 'You underestimate yourself,' she told him, turning to walk to the sofa. 'Your poems have been the source of sublime inspiration, and not only to Ernesto.'

Before she sat down he let her dress fall away, so that once again she wore only the thong, as she had that night with her husband, before he'd made her remove it. 'The poems I give to Ernesto are quite different to those I write for you,' he reminded her, gazing at the small, upturned breasts that were peeking through the fiery tresses of her hair.

Leaning back she crossed one long leg over the other and watched him go to sit in an armchair opposite. 'Those you write for me are our secret,' she promised. 'No one knows about them. Just us.'

His eyes swept up over her body, clothing it again. 'You're sure they don't offend you?'

Her eyebrows made a gentle arch. 'They excite me,' she replied.

Several minutes ticked by as they drank and smoked, and felt the eclipsing patterns of their characters – poet and mistress, actress and director, man and woman – take a steal on their senses.

'Tomorrow and the next day your wife will begin to destroy me,' she said hoarsely.

Feeling his mind being sucked into the dimly lit scenarios of the film, he watched her fingers idling around her nipples, while somewhere, at a distance, a woman began to scream. 'Have you enjoyed playing the part for camera, as much as on stage?' he asked.

She turned her eyes to her drink as she considered the question. 'It's been different,' she answered. 'I feel much closer to the character now.'

'Maybe because you've had more time to become her,' he suggested.

She nodded agreement. 'I don't want to let her go,' she whispered. Then looking up at him, she said, 'Does Alma Geddon have to win? Can't the fantasy become our reality?'

His throat was suddenly dry again, and so tight he found it hard to speak. 'Why do you think I'm here?' he said.

A look of surprise lit her eyes, followed by a sigh of pleasure. 'You always seem to know what I want,' she murmured, kicking off her shoes.

His penis was an outrageous tumescent mass, pressing his clothes for freedom, knowing its goal and wanting only to be there now. 'I think I read you correctly,' he said, his hands quivering as he began loosening his belt.

'Oh, I think you do,' she agreed.

He was on his feet. His penis was free, bobbing from his trousers and straining towards her. She looked at it, then up at him, a hint of nervousness

496

behind her surprise. Reaching for her, he clutched the neck of the dress that had returned and hauled her to her feet. She gasped with shock, as he ripped the dress apart.

'Robert! What are you . . . ?'

She was struggling to break free, but not so hard that he could mistake her protest for real intent. She wore only the thong now, and as he thrust her down on the sofa her legs came apart, so that he could see the dildo vibrating inside her. Quickly he tore the thong aside, then grabbing the dildo he began ramming it in and out of her, so hard that he could no longer tell whether her writhings were of pleasure or pain. But she wouldn't care, they were both the same to her, so he carried on plunging it home, knowing that her efforts to push him away, and her screams for him to stop, were no more than an act, and that if he obeyed he'd disappoint her gravely, right at the height of her frenzy. Yet she didn't want this thing to bring her to climax, she wanted him, and the Priapic monster that was pounding between his legs.

The dildo clattered to the floor, as twisting her over, he shoved her to her knees and wrenched both her arms behind her back. With her wrists bound in a vicelike grip, he heard her laughter, and tauntings for him to be as rough as he dared. He positioned himself behind her, then finding his way in he slammed home with all his might. The volume of her scream got him riding like a madman, clutching her hips and grunting like an animal as her choking pleas for mercy fired his blood to the point of explosion.

'Stop! Please, stop!' she cried.

He let go of her hands, yet she did nothing to throw him off, only supported her shoulders, so that she was on all fours now, legs wide apart, bottom tilted up. She wanted him to carry on. And why else was a cane being thrust into his hand, but for him to use? He brought it down sharply, cruelly, beating her back and buttocks, her shoulders and arms. Then bunching her hair like reins he yanked her head back so that she rose up on her knees, baring her breasts and thighs for the blows.

Was he still doing as she wanted? Was it too much? She rolled sideways, parting their bodies. His erection loomed between them, huge and red and hungry for more. He looked down at her, breathless and dazed. Her eyes met his in a blurred, moaning moment of calm. Then spinning her on to her back, he thrust her legs apart and plunged into her again. Her face was beneath him, pale and frightened and tear-stained. Her legs were round his waist, urging him to go faster, harder and deeper. He kissed her mouth, while squeezing her breasts hard. She was crying, sobbing, begging him to stop. The sounds in his ears were like a storm receding and gusting. Grabbing her arms he pinned them to the floor as he pushed, and shoved and hammered himself into her, an Olympian journey towards a powerful, maniacal conclusion.

Then suddenly he was there, gushing, floundering, spluttering and quivering in the might of a climax that was worse than madness, carrying him as though he were a missile, to the very heart of his foe, smashing apart all resistance, only to dispense him in a place of frightening familiarity, where misery and fear were mingling with the bewildering horror and comfort of finding himself at home, in his own study, hunched over his desk with tears streaming down his face and semen spilling relentlessly into his pants.

'Robert? Oh my God, Robert.'

It was Anna, coming into the room, putting her arms around him, cradling his head and soothing his pain.

'Sssh,' she whispered softly. 'Sssh, it's all right. Everything's all right.'

'Yes. Everything's fine,' he gasped, trying to laugh and brush the tears away.

'Daddy? Oh Daddy, please don't cry.' It was Justine's frightened, quavery voice. 'We don't mind that you didn't come to the concert. Honestly. Please don't cry.'

'Daddy. Stop! *Stop!*' It was Emily, angry, yet trying to put her arms round him too. 'Mummy, make him stop,' she demanded.

Anna's arms were holding him together: if she let go, everything would collapse.

'Go upstairs,' Anna whispered to the girls. 'It'll be all right, I promise. I'll be up in a minute.'

The tiny, hesitant footsteps of his daughters moved from the room, as his wife's arms tightened around him. The smell of her was moving deeply to the core of him, trying to infuse him with her strength and soothe him with her calm. Yet he could feel her shaking too, worrying, fearing what had happened, what had brought him to this.

'Robert, why are you crying?' she said, lifting his face between her hands. 'Oh, God look at you. Please tell me what happened.'

'Nothing happened,' he said. 'Nothing.'

'Robert, please,' she implored. 'I have to know. Did you go there? Have you seen her?'

His head fell forward into her chest as his arms clutched her waist.

'Oh my God, Robert, please tell me you didn't do any of those horrible things.' She knelt down in front of him and clasped his face in her hands again. 'You have to tell me,' she said firmly. 'I can't make it all right, unless I know what you've done.'

He tried to speak again, then shook his head.

'Was it the scene we shot today? Is that what's done this?'

He nodded.

'So you haven't been to Stacey's this evening?'

'No, only . . .' He put a hand to his head. 'Here.'

'But only there, in your head,' she insisted, praying to God it was. But no, he wasn't that crazy. If he'd been at Stacey's, he'd know. 'You were deeply affected by the scene we shot today,' she told him. 'We all were. It was very powerful.'

He nodded, jerkily. 'Very powerful,' he agreed. 'I wanted to do all those things to her myself. I hate her, and yet I can't stop thinking about her.'

Her eyes closed as the pain of his obsession locked around her heart. Then reaching for the phone she dialled Stacey's number. She had to be sure.

After the third ring a male voice answered. Suddenly afraid it was the police, she almost rang off, then remembering Stacey's husband had just returned to London she said,

'Hello. It's Anna Maxton. I hope I'm not interrupting.'

'No, not at all. How are you, Anna?'

Yes, it was him. She'd only spoken to him a couple of times, but she was sure it was his voice. 'Fine. Yes. Fine,' she answered, so much relief flooding her that she almost laughed. 'Is Stacey there? Can I speak to her?'

'Of course. I'll put her on.'

Anna's heart was in her throat. But it was going to be all right. Stacey was there, her husband was too, so it really was going to be all right.

'Anna?' Stacey's voice came quizzically down the line. 'How was the recital?'

Anna's breath was short, but she could make herself sound calm. 'Good. Yes, it was very good,' she said. 'Thank you.'

'I'm glad. Did Robert make it in time?'

Anna's grip tightened on his hand. 'Um, no. Not quite,' she answered.

'Oh, what a shame. I know he was looking forward to it. I hope the girls weren't too disappointed.'

'A little, but he'll make it up to them.'

There was a short silence, then Anna realized that Stacey would be wondering why she'd called.

'Everything's all right, is it?' Stacey said. 'Only we've got a few friends here, and we're just on our way out for dinner.'

'Oh, yes, everything's fine. Sorry, I shouldn't keep you,' Anna said hastily. Then quickly added, 'How long is Chris staying? Is he home for a while?'

'Only until tomorrow,' Stacey answered with an exasperated sigh. 'So I want to make the most of him.' She paused then said, 'Dare I ask if Robert's happy with the scene we shot today? I know that's very actressy, but . . .'

501

'I'm sorry, that was why I was calling,' Anna jumped in. 'To say how thrilled we both are with the way it went today. It was very chilling, and moving. I can't wait to see the rushes.'

There was a smile in Stacey's voice as she said, 'I'm glad it worked. I don't mind admitting I was anxious about doing it, especially as I've never done a rape scene before. Frankly, I'm glad it's over.'

'I'm sure,' Anna responded. 'But you were very convincing.'

'Thank you.'

For several seconds after she rang off Anna remained where she was, the phone still in her hand. Then pressing it back on the hook she looked down at Robert. He was watching her, like a child waiting to be told what to do. Her heart ached with pity and love, as stooping over him she kissed the top of his head.

'I'm sorry I doubted you,' she whispered.

'No, you were right to,' he answered.

Realizing that some part of him had needed the reassurance too, she tightened her embrace and tried hard not to cry. He was really only slightly delusional, not a raving lunatic, or a dangerous psychopath. She could keep him safe from his confusions.

Attempting a smile, he said, ' "I shall die trying to pluck the moon out of a pond." '

She smiled too, for it wasn't the first time he'd likened himself to André Malraux's Baron de Clapique, though she might have preferred a less esoteric character. 'Come on,' she said, taking his hand. 'Let's go and get you out of those clothes.

502

Then we'll tuck the girls in and have something to eat. Are you hungry?'

He nodded. 'Yes, a little.'

They walked up the stairs arms around each other, her head resting on his shoulder. 'If I asked you to, would you agree to talk to someone – someone who might be able to help you straighten things out a little?' she said.

At the top of the stairs he turned her to face him and gazed tenderly into her eyes. 'I never want to hurt anyone, yet you, whom I love above all others, I keep hurting you.'

'That's a line from the script,' she admonished gently.

'But it was written by me, and it's the truth.'

She merely carried on looking into his face, her heart heavy with the very real weight of her love.

'Yes, I'll talk to someone,' he said quietly, 'but only if you'll come with me.'

She smiled and touched her lips gently to his. 'Of course,' she told him. 'I'll always be there for you. Always. You know that.'

He pulled her into an embrace and held her tight. If there were any fairness in the world, then if only for Anna's sake, his mind would now be wiped free of Stacey, never to be troubled again by the obsessive madness of wanting her. But there was no fairness, because the libidinous demons were already taunting him again, daring him to make love to his wife now, while reliving everything he'd done earlier with Stacey.

Rachel was just about to start locking up the villa when the telephone in the kitchen rang. Leaving the keys in the door, she dashed back across the room and snatched up the receiver.

'Hello?'

'Mrs Hendon?'

Her heart gave a jolt. But it was probably just the taxi company calling to say the driver was late. 'Yes,' she said. 'Who is this?'

'I am glad to catch you before you leave,' the familiar accented voice told her.

Oh dear God. This was the first time she'd heard from him since she'd given back the money, and for him to call now, at this villa, after she'd been left alone for two days with the very worst kind of suspicions building in her mind . . . Her eyes darted frantically around the room. It was ludicrous to think he was hiding in the shadows, but it almost felt as though he were. 'What do you want?' she snapped, fear tightening her voice.

'Just for you please to listen to what I say,' he answered politely. 'Your search for Katherine Sumner will not serve the purpose you are hoping for. You believe she will tell you what happened to your husband, why he was murdered, but she will not. She will only put you in the gravest danger if you approach her, and as an expectant mother I do not believe that is a position you wish to be in.'

Rachel's blood turned cold at the mention of the baby, but before she could speak a word of response he was speaking again.

'I should also warn you,' he continued, 'that there is a chance she will initiate some kind of contact with you. In this unlikely, though possible event, I urge you, Mrs Hendon, do not be taken in. No matter what she says she only means you harm,

504

so please, resist any invitations she might make for you to meet, and deny her all access to your home.'

Despite the turmoil in her mind, Rachel's anger was audible as she said, 'I don't know what you're basing any of these assumptions on, but if you know where Katherine Sumner is . . . Or if you know why my husband was murdered . . .' She spun round at the sound of a car pulling into the drive. *Please God let it be the taxi.*

'My advice to you, Mrs Hendon,' he said, 'is to forget what happened, put it behind you and go on with your life. It will be safer, for you and your child.'

'No! Don't hang up,' she cried as the line went dead. *'Don't hang up!'* But it was too late, he'd gone, leaving her anguish echoing around the doleful silence of the room. She almost screamed as a voice behind her said,

'Miss?'

She swung round to find a man looming darkly in the bright sunlight of the doorway.

'Taxi?' he said. 'Go to ferry at Government Dock?'

'Yes. Yes,' she gasped, pushing a hand through her hair. 'Sorry, I'll be right there.'

'I take bag down,' he said, and squealed round on his rubber soles to pick up her camera case and holdall.

For several moments she stood staring at the phone, still so thrown by the call that she was unsure what to do, or even to think. Then snatching it up she quickly dialled Laurie's number.

'Hi. I thought you'd have left by now,' Laurie said.

'I'm just about to. But you need to hear this.' Quickly she related what the caller had said. 'What really threw me,' she added, 'was that he seemed to think Katherine might get in touch.'

'I'm more curious to know why she'd mean you any harm,' Laurie responded, 'unless he's just saying that to frighten us off.'

'Whichever, he obviously knew where to find me, so does that mean the people who were here looking for Katherine before us *did* belong to him?'

'It certainly adds more weight, but without knowing for certain who the phone call came from . . .'

'Did you ask Elliot if he'd mentioned the passport and driving licence to anyone?' Rachel interrupted.

'No. Not yet. He's been held up in Paris, but Max didn't know about it, and if he didn't tell Max, I can't imagine who else he'd tell.'

Rachel's eyes darted back to the door. 'Then there is only one other person,' she murmured.

It was a moment or two before Laurie said, 'Have you heard from him since he left?'

'No,' Rachel answered. 'I'm not sure whether I expected to.' She laughed drily and didn't go any further.

'After your call,' Laurie said, 'I got Gino to do a bit of digging around. Apparently, about three years ago a London art dealer by the name of Chris Gallagher sold a Modigliani nude to the chairman of the Phraxos Group, Franz Koehler.'

Rachel's heart felt as though it were being torn in two. Images from the past two months began flashing through her mind, a bewildering circus of

506

kindness, laughter, music, a kiss, but those sudden disappearances, all the phone calls, the questions . . . 'And since then?' she said.

'Nothing else, so far.'

'So it could just be a coincidence?'

Laurie was silent.

'No, of course it isn't,' Rachel said flatly. Then after pressing a hand hard to her head, as though to still the chaos, 'So where do we go from here?'

'Well, first you'd better get yourself back to England . . . When's your flight?'

Rachel looked at her watch. 'At four. It's eleven now, and I have to get the ferry, so I should go.'

'OK. We'll talk more when you're home. Will you be going straight to Cornwall, or staying in London?'

'London, I think. At least at first. I'm concerned about Anna, and I don't much fancy the idea of running into Chris in Cornwall.'

'Have you told Anna anything about this?'

'No. She'd probably find a way of blaming herself, and she's got enough on her plate.'

'Do you think she knows him?'

'I've no idea. I've never mentioned him to her, I didn't want her jumping to the wrong conclusions.' Her laugh was brittle and derisory. 'This'll teach me to stop my sister from worrying about me.'

'I wouldn't mind hearing what Beanie has to say about it,' Laurie commented. 'Why did she never mention it, I wonder? I take it you had no idea Stacey Greene was a neighbour?'

'No. I've never seen her in the village, nor heard anyone talk about her. I wouldn't even know who she was if it weren't for Robert and Anna.'

'Yet everyone's so friendly to Chris,' Laurie said curiously. 'Which is about the only good thing he's got going for him at the moment, but as Elliot's too fond of reminding me, very few people are all good, or all bad, and we know for certain that Chris Gallagher's got several more dimensions to him than first appearances might suggest.'

Rachel said, 'I have to go. I just want to get out of here now. Why don't you try calling Chris to see what he has to say?'

'OK. I will. Have a good journey. I'll call you in the middle of the day, tomorrow.'

After putting the phone down Rachel locked the kitchen door then tucked the keys under a dustbin, as she'd been told to, and ran down the steps to the taxi. In her hand was a half-read copy of *The Magus*, which she intended to finish on the plane, but for the moment her mind was so full of Chris, and the appalling fact that he'd never once mentioned selling a painting to Franz Koehler, that she just couldn't think about anything else. Obviously it was no coincidence, any more than his failure to tell her was a momentary lapse of memory. Which could only mean that everything, from the day he'd turned up at the cottage to offer his condolences, to the night here, on Virgin Gorda, when they'd come so close to making love, had been based on a deceit far, far worse than she'd even begun to imagine.

Her eyes were turned to the window, but seeing nothing of the pristine blue spread of the sea as she wondered where he was now. She hadn't called him since he left, and he hadn't called her either. It was galling and disheartening to know how much she'd wanted him to, even though she'd known,

508

even before speaking to Laurie, that she could never trust him again, never confide in him the way she had, or even laugh with him any more. Nothing could be the same again now, so it was just foolish to think it could. She couldn't even be sure how much truth he'd told her about Katherine, for if he knew Franz Koehler, there was a strong possibility that he knew Katherine too. He could even be fully informed of the nature of Tim's connection to the Phraxos Group, so the reason he'd befriended her was to make sure that she never was. It made her head throb to think he'd been holding such crucial details back from her, but since he'd failed to mention Stacey Greene, or the Modigliani painting, she'd have to be some kind of idiot if she was prepared to believe that was all he was hiding.

So what should she do from here?

Looking down at the book in her hand she felt daunted and afraid of the fictional character whose supernatural and scientific experiments with the minds of his chosen players were starting to appear as some kind of model for a much more diabolical exploitation of wealth and power, an even greater abuse of human suffering and greed. And now almost as bad as fearing that Tim had been a part of that, was knowing that Chris was.

Chapter 22

Chris's face showed signs of his tiredness as he and Rudy were admitted into the private study of Franz Koehler's palatial lakeside home. The man himself was seated at his large, mahogany desk and didn't immediately look up when the butler announced his visitors by name. The early evening sunlight, streaming across Lake Zurich, and in through the wall of windows that overlooked the spectacular view, pooled on the Persian rugs and redwood floor. The air was stuffy and smelt of beeswax and the hundreds of leather-bound volumes that crowded the other three walls, except where the prized Bonnards hung in specially designed and appropriately lit niches.

'Thank you for being prompt, gentlemen,' he said finally, putting down his pen and getting to his feet as the butler discreetly left the room.

He came round the desk to greet them. He shook Rudy's hand first, then turned to Chris, regarding him carefully.

Chris met the scrutiny unflinchingly.

'I am glad to see you,' Koehler told him, in his softly spoken, accented English. 'I had intended this meeting to happen immediately on your return from the Caribbean, but I'm afraid other events rather overtook me, and it turned out not to be possible. However, as it allowed you some time with your lovely wife I don't imagine you're too angry with me.'

'Not at all,' Chris responded.

'You'll both take Scotch, gentlemen?' he said, walking to the bar and removing the stopper from a Baccarat decanter.

As Rudy accepted for them, Chris slid his hands into his pockets and walked over to the fireplace, staring up at the straining, taut figure of an extremely expensive nude whose sexually expressive pose and anguished features quite effectively revealed the artist's lifelong love-hate relationship with women. It was the Modigliani that had first brought him into contact with Franz Koehler, an event whose every detail was imprinted indelibly on his mind, from the initial approach of the seller, to the official unveiling right here in this room. By then his life had already begun its unexpected journey, but even so, he could never have imagined just how deeply involved he would become, or how dramatically his own role would alter. So dramatically in fact, that in many ways he'd almost lost touch with the man he'd once been, which, were he to admit as much to Koehler, would please the older man a great deal, since it was his purpose, his own personal challenge in life, to discover the strengths and weaknesses of a man's morals, by offering him riches and adventures beyond his wildest dreams, in exchange for what sometimes felt like yet another part of the soul.

'I hear your wife is posing for Ernesto Gomez,' Koehler remarked, bringing him a Scotch and gazing up at the Modigliani too.

Chris took the glass. 'She is,' he confirmed. 'It's a series to accompany a set of poems by Robert Maxton.'

'Interesting,' Koehler commented. 'Can I request a first look, when they're finished?'

'I'm sure it can be arranged,' Chris responded.

Koehler smiled, then took a sip of his drink. 'So, how was Mrs Hendon when you left her?' he asked, going to sit on one of the bulky leather sofas that flanked the hearth. 'Incidentally, you did the right thing going over there. Lucky she called before she left, mm?'

Chris nodded, and raised his glass to take a sip.

'So, we now know that her efforts yielded more than ours,' Koehler continued, 'only insofar as Katherine flew from the Caribbean to Madrid. But of course, we already knew she'd been in Madrid. And from there she went to a small village in the south-west of France. After that she disappeared for a while, but I'm happy to report that she recently resurfaced in Venice, attempting to blend with the tourists. It's rather unfortunate that we didn't manage to apprehend her then, but a chase through the streets of the city, which was what almost ensued, would have created a lot of unnecessary attention. However, it is now only a matter of time.'

Though Koehler appeared as unruffled as he sounded, as the head of one of the world's most powerful organizations, Chris knew he wouldn't be enjoying the experience of being outwitted by a mere woman, particularly one who should, by all calculations, be unable to make a single move without him either knowing about it, or even sanctioning it. Indeed, it was probably only the fact that the police had failed to find her too, that made this outrageous anomaly in his otherwise immaculately controlled existence slightly easier to take.

'Mm, by the way,' Koehler continued, after swallowing a mouthful of Scotch, 'I should tell you, if Mrs Hendon hasn't already, that I've had a small chat with her.'

Chris's eyes widened slightly.

'I wanted to make her aware of how dangerous it would be for her to continue her search for Katherine,' Koehler informed him. 'So far you have been very successful in learning all that she knows, and indeed in persuading her to return the money without alerting the police to its existence, but there's no knowing what she, and this journalist, might turn up, and in the event of you not being there, we can't rely on her to tell you.' He looked hard at Chris, then abruptly said, 'Speaking of journalists, I believe Rudy has informed you that the individual who was introduced to us as Mark Hastings has turned out to be a British reporter by the name of Elliot Russell. Fortunately, our friend, Dr Bombola, has taken care of things, and we are now conducting an investigation into how he managed to infiltrate so far before his true identity was brought to our attention. You will be interviewed following this meeting.'

Since it was routine for the entire inner circle to

be questioned after any breach of security, Chris merely nodded and drank some more.

Koehler seemed about to move on when Rudy said, 'Do we know if the police are looking for this reporter yet?'

'Apparently not,' Koehler answered, 'which is the advantage, or disadvantage, depending on which way you look at it, of undercover operations. Your disappearance can be somewhat old, and your trail therefore cold, by the time it's realized that something has gone wrong. However, we must assume that the police will, at some point, be alerted, which is why we are organizing a clean-up of Mr Russell's office and apartment.'

'Is it known whether or not he got any information out before you learned who he was?' Chris asked.

'There don't appear to have been any leaks, but of course we are monitoring the situation closely. Something of interest that has transpired is that his girlfriend is the reporter who's working with Mrs Hendon. Did you know that?'

'Once you told me his name, yes,' Chris answered.

Koehler was thoughtful for a moment. 'Mm,' he said finally. 'This search for Katherine is becoming extremely inconvenient, and costly in more ways than one, so it must be ended as quickly and satisfactorily as possible.' Then directly to Chris, 'When you have completed the Dubai operation, I want you to return to England and watch Mrs Hendon very closely. Under no circumstances is she to be allowed to meet with Katherine – and I am now increasingly of the opinion that that has become one of Katherine's intentions. It makes sense for only one reason, and that reason must not be revealed to anyone, least of all to Mrs Hendon. So, I hope you understand me, Chris, when I say that there can be no meeting.'

Chris was staring down at his glass, wondering, ironically, exactly when the title of hired assassin had been added to his job description, but since there was no precise definition of any of the inner circle's roles, it was only an idle muse.

Koehler was watching him. 'Speak your mind,' he said sharply.

Chris looked up. 'I was just thinking,' he said, 'that accidents are extremely easy to arrange in that part of the world. The terrain is rough and the sea notoriously unpredictable.'

Koehler nodded curtly. 'Maybe that could be pointed out to Elliot Russell's girlfriend too,' he said, impatiently.

Chris raised his glass in acknowledgement, then downed the rest of his drink.

'So,' Koehler said, 'we will now go through the details of your upcoming operation in Dubai. Rudy assures me everything is in order, but as we don't want a repeat of the débâcle we had at the airfield in Zurich, we will go over it again so that I can be certain you have been fully brought up to date with the changes that occurred during your absence. After we have finished, I must attend a shareholders' meeting in Rome, which I hope you will fly me to.'

Katherine was standing at the tall, balconied window of a three star hotel gazing down at the

515

Ticino river, where swans were gliding about in the untroubled flow, and small children were throwing in bread. She was in Sesto Calende, a small, picturesque town some fifty miles north-west of Milan, and no more than two from the southern shore of Lake Maggiore. It was no small miracle that she'd made it here, after managing to escape Venice complete with laptop, money and the few other essentials she carried, without being followed. Had it not been for the Guggenheim curator warning her to be careful of the pickpocket who appeared to be stalking her, she'd never have known he was there – until it was too late. But she might not be so lucky next time, which was why she hadn't risked leaving this hotel at all in the last three days, except once, to go to the bank to change more dollars into euro.

She was in a corner room on the third floor, whose other window overlooked a small piazza, which yesterday had been transformed into a bustling market offering everything from fruit and veg, to salamis and cheeses, to lace and cast iron kitchenware. Still she hadn't ventured down, for she'd become much more fearful of crowds since the narrow escape in Venice, and besides, what would she do with anything she bought? She had no room in her life now for bric-à-brac, no room for anything except this frantic bid for survival – and time, so much time to think the kind of thoughts that were becoming increasingly desperate and destructive.

The only coded message she'd received from Xavier since leaving Venice had been to reassure her he was still alive and in England. She'd sent him a message, telling him about the flash of inspiration she'd had at the Guggenheim, but whether he'd picked it up yet, she still didn't know. Maybe he was thinking it over, but even if he was, she knew he'd consider it too risky, which it was, to the point of utter madness, because she didn't actually know the woman she'd told him about, so she had absolutely no idea whether or not she could trust her, never mind if she would be willing to help. All she had to go on was her instincts, which, in themselves, were based on no more than one brief meeting, when the two of them had hit it off well enough for her to be invited for a weekend at the woman's country home. But the woman, whose name still eluded her, had had a certain quality about her that made Katherine feel that it could be OK to trust her, and when coupled with the fact that they'd met at a party for Rachel Hendon's brother-in-law, it was almost enough to persuade her that the stars, for once, had been working in her favour. This was the closest link to Rachel, outside of the British Government, that she'd been able to come up with so far, plus she was sure she remembered the woman saying that her country home was in Cornwall, and as big a place as Cornwall might be, anywhere in the county was going to be a hell of a lot closer to Rachel than where she was now. However, she needed Xavier to find the woman's name, then initiate the contact, and she knew very well that the chances of persuading him weren't much better than persuading Franz to give up his search.

Turning away from the window she stared down at the jazzy orange and blue covers on the skinnymattressed beds, then going between them she lifted the lamp and phone off the nightstand, unplugged them, and connected her computer. Minutes later, after checking her email for the third time that day, she came off line, having received no new messages. So the wait, the fear and the excruciating loneliness continued.

'I know what you're thinking,' Laurie said, looking into Rachel's anguished face, 'and I agree, it's painting as strange a picture as any Modigliani masterpiece, when we consider the timing of his entry into your life, how ready he's been to lend support since, the way he dropped everything at a moment's notice to fly to the Caribbean, the fact that someone else had been on the island asking questions before you arrived, when he was the only one, apart from us two and Elliot, who knew about the passport and driving licence . . .'

'Plus all the phone calls while we were there, his very abrupt departure, his failure to contact either of us since,' Rachel added sharply.

Laurie agreed. 'Plus all that . . . Like I said, it doesn't look good. However, there's a chance we could be viewing it all from the wrong angle. No, I'm serious,' she said, at Rachel's look of incredulity. 'Since I told you about the Modigliani, we've found out something else that *could* throw a whole other light on his relationship with Franz Koehler.'

Wishing she weren't quite so eager to hear anything that would throw another light on anything to do with Chris Gallagher, Rachel merely waited for her to continue.

'It turns out,' Laurie said, keeping her fingers crossed she wasn't holding out too much false hope here, 'that his father worked for the intelligence services in Borneo and Yemen, back in the fifties.'

Rachel's expression showed no signs of thawing. 'Is that it?' she said.

'Not quite,' Laurie replied. 'There's also the fact that Chris went to Cambridge, and as we all know that particular university is a fertile recruiting ground for the clandestine agencies.'

'So what you're saying,' Rachel responded, 'is that because he went to Cambridge, and because his father was working for British intelligence some forty-odd years ago, that he could be now?'

Laurie pulled a face. 'OK, I know it's a stretch,' she said, 'but when I talked it over with Max he actually didn't have too much of a problem with it. Apparently the intelligence services do know about the Phraxos special project, and there's no limit to who they'll use as contacts or informants or whatever they want to call them.'

Rachel's eyes moved to the small patio garden that Lucy had been taking care of since she'd departed for Cornwall. It felt like such a long time since she'd last been here, and so much had happened – it was like a different place, somehow remote and alien. She didn't really want to stay any longer, so she was going to spend the next couple of nights at Anna's, before going back down to Killian – and now, after hearing this, the prospect of bumping into him wasn't, in truth, quite so daunting.

'Have you managed to get through to him at all?' she asked, turning back to Laurie.

She shook her head. 'Phone's permanently off. I called his gallery in Bond Street. Seems he's out of the country, and they're not sure when he's due back.'

'Have you been to see the gallery?'

'Yes. It's just like any other in Mayfair. Small, with an air of stuffy exclusivity and a challenging display of modern art.'

Rachel's smile was weak. 'So we know what's in the shop front, it's what's being dealt under the counter that's the mystery.'

'A case of the silk stocking and the dagger,' Laurie responded wryly. 'Or the butterfly and the gun.' She glanced at her watch. 'I'm sorry, but I have to go. I'm meeting Max. I just wanted to come and say hello in person, and give you the good news . . . well, news anyway.'

Rachel got to her feet. 'I'm glad you did,' she said. 'If nothing else it's a mitigating circumstance, and since I'm still having such a hard time seeing him as the kind of monster it would take to have worked his way into my life the way he did . . . However, the fact still remains that he never told me he was married, and when he knew what a major issue that would be for me . . .' She was shaking her head. 'I still don't feel inclined to trust him.'

Realizing how hurt and shaken Rachel was by the duplicity, Laurie gave her a hug. 'If you ask me, he'd help his case a bit more if he were in touch,' she murmured. Then pulling back, 'Have you talked to Anna about any of it yet?'

'No, I just can't bring myself to, because that whole scene, Stacey and Robert, Chris and me . . .

It's still giving me the creeps . . . Just thank God I didn't sleep with him, because I came so damned close.'

Though Laurie knew, because Rachel had already told her, that Chris was the one who'd stopped it, she made no mention of it as she led the way through the kitchen to the front door. 'I'm going to be very interested to hear what Beanie says when you see her on Friday,' she said, turning back. 'You're still going, are you?'

Rachel nodded. 'It's the end of shoot party that night, and I really don't want to hang around for it, because, to quote Anna, "Stacey's husband is going to be there, thank God." So if he isn't in the country now, he's obviously expected by the end of the week.' She looked at Laurie, then put her hands over her face and gave a long, low growl of frustration. 'Why does this have to be happening?' she said. 'Why can't he just be who I thought he was?'

'It's rather a shame we can't ask Haynes about him,' Laurie commented.

Rachel scoffed. 'The chances of getting a straight answer there are about as good as getting one from this Conchis character, who by the way, is turning out to be as scary as hell.'

'Have you finished it yet?'

'No.'

'Me neither. Anyway, I'm presuming we've decided to give Chris the benefit of the doubt for the moment, by *not* going to Haynes.'

Rachel shrugged. 'I'll be guided by you, because personally, I seem to be messing up all over with who I decide to trust.'

Laurie smiled. 'I'll see you tomorrow,' she said, giving her another hug. 'You're coming to view the Landen interview, yes?'

'Yes. I wouldn't mind talking to Gino too, if he's free. Better still, I wouldn't mind talking to Chris. Or Katherine. Or Franz Koehler.' She laughed and raged. 'Please God, someone speak to us, before we go out of our minds.'

With those words still echoing in her ears Laurie ran down the street to the nearest station, and less than an hour later she was at Max's hotel, pacing up and down, as they both worked the phones, trying to find someone, anyone, who might have seen or heard from Elliot in the past six days.

Chapter 23

The following night Laurie was at Elliot's apartment, wandering aimlessly around and trying hard to keep herself focused as she spoke to Rachel on the phone. They'd spent the best part of the day piecing the Landen interview together with everything else they'd learned about Katherine, and Phraxos, though as yet they couldn't include anything Max had been able to tell them about Elliot's meeting in Paris. Since that was such a truly horrifying scenario – and one that was almost impossible for Laurie to think about in the light of Elliot's failure to return – she preferred, at least when talking to Rachel, to concentrate on other aspects of Phraxos, or the murder, or even what Chris's role might be.

Right now they were talking about the anonymous phone call Rachel had received before leaving the villa. From there they moved on to Patrick Landen, and all the time she kept glancing at the door, still daring to hope that it would open at any minute and Elliot would walk in, larger than life, and twice as ignorant of what she wanted from him. And who cared about that now, just as long as he came back.

'So the Landen interview,' Rachel was saying, sounding very like the producer she'd once been, 'when taken as a whole doesn't really tell us as much about Phraxos as it does about Katherine, and her motives for getting involved in the company. Her father is let down, possibly even sacrificed, by his own government, her family goes to pieces as a result, and she wants revenge. She's an intelligent woman, so she knows how to wrap it all up by making a public stand of opposing politics, to the point of becoming a campaign manager, then she gets herself involved with Franz Koehler, and Phraxos, and who does she invite to the party? Not the Democrats, who'd probably love nothing more than all that lovely loot, but the Republicans – i.e. those who refused an inquiry into her father's murder. The Phraxos money could be extremely effective in getting them back into power, which it did, so basically she was setting them up, and no one can deny they're a sitting target now, because their affiliation to Phraxos is crawling all over the Pentagon like a virus.'

'The last headcount gave us forty-three known investors,' Laurie said, 'though there are obviously more. However, the point is, we only care about America insofar as it affects Britain. So we need to know how deeply Phraxos has penetrated our own government, and what part Katherine Sumner played in it. We know about Tim, but there have to be others, though considering our failure to come up with anyone yet, there's a good chance that the penetration hadn't quite got going.'

'But the intelligence services are on it,' Rachel pointed out.

'True,' Laurie replied, sitting down on the edge of a sofa and holding herself tight. *Where was he? Where the hell was he? Please God, let him get in touch tonight.*

'So what we really need to know is *who* in Britain actually ordered the intelligence operation? And if you say the Government, you're not the journalist I think you are.'

'No, I know it doesn't have to be the PM, or someone at that supremely high a level,' Laurie replied. 'Basically, in this case, I'd say it depends on who the Metropolitan Police's head honcho is best mates with, because the intelligence services are conducting investigations into potential high office scandals all the time, and no prime minister is exempt – unless he happens to be the best mate who ordered it, I suppose.'

'So who is Mr Met best mates with?' Rachel wondered. 'The reigning PM, who is giving me a very public wide berth? Someone a little lower down the ranks with leadership ambitions? An Opposition member?'

'We obviously need to find out,' Laurie responded, not adding, *if Elliot were here he'd probably know already.*

'OK. So, going back to Katherine,' Rachel said, 'it's a pity that no one by the name of Xavier Lachère was at the scene of her father's murder, or holding a prominent position in Iran at that time, but I still think it's a lead worth pursuing.'

'We are,' Laurie assured her, then suddenly spun round, her heart in her throat, as someone approached the front door. A flyer was pushed underneath and her eyes closed as anger and disappointment extinguished the brief onrush of hope. Wiping a hand over her face, she took a breath to continue, then realizing she'd lost the thread, she said, 'Sorry, I'm a bit on edge. I keep hoping Elliot will walk in the door.'

'Is that where you are now? At the flat?' Rachel said.

'Yes. I don't know why, but it makes me feel better to be here. Oh! Hang on, someone's trying to get through.' Quickly she switched lines. 'Hello?' she said, daring to hope.

'It's Max. Where are you?'

'At Elliot's. Any news?'

'No. I was just checking to see if you had any.'

Laurie's heart tightened with even more dread. 'No. Nothing,' she said. 'I'm on the other line, can I call you back?'

'Sure. You know the number.'

Clicking back to Rachel, she said, 'Sorry. That was Max.'

'Anything?'

'No.'

'Is Max still in London?'

'Yep. His wife turned up yesterday too. They're staying here until we get some news on Elliot. We're going to the police if we don't hear anything by the morning.'

'Sounds wise,' Rachel answered. 'If nothing else it'll get the press on the case, and we're notoriously good at taking care of our own.'

Hating even the idea that it would be necessary, Laurie wandered into the dining room where the desktop computer she and Elliot often shared was set up on the table. She pushed the power button, wanting, needing, to bring it to life.

'Why don't you come and join us for dinner?' Rachel said. 'Anna and Robert are on their way home. We're having pizzas delivered.'

Laurie's smile was faint. 'Thanks, but I couldn't eat a thing,' she answered.

'Then would you like me to come and keep you company?'

'No. It's OK. But thanks for the offer. I'll keep myself busy with some work.'

Rachel's voice was curious as she said, 'I wonder if Chris knows anything about Elliot.'

'It's crossed my mind, more than once,' Laurie confessed. 'Anyway, I take it all the noise is Robert and Anna getting home, so I'd better let you go. We'll keep in touch by phone and email, and maybe I'll try to get down to Killian by the end of next week.'

'Let me know if you hear anything, won't you?'

'Of course,' Laurie promised, and quickly ending the call she put a hand to her mouth, to block the wretched fear that was making her want to cry and sob and do any kind of deal it took with God, or the devil, to bring him home now.

Taking a deep breath, she dashed a hand through her hair and reminded herself firmly that she wasn't going to fall apart over this. She was just going to keep calm and carry on, the way Rachel was somehow managing to do, though God only knew how, considering everything she was dealing with. She just wished she didn't feel so responsible, but how could she not when Elliot had vanished almost immediately after she'd interviewed Landen? He'd tried to get word to her, to warn her not to mention Bombola, but she hadn't heeded Max's urgent request that she call first, and now Elliot was paying the price.

Leaving the phone next to the computer, she went back to the kitchen and filled the kettle. *By the time this has boiled he'll either have rung, or walked in the door*, she told herself. Then feeling foolish and afraid, she put her hands to her head and cried, 'Oh God, Elliot, where are you? Why don't you call?'

Her despair fell into the growing darkness of the room as the sun sank behind a far horizon, and lights around the city started to come on. Staring down at them from her twentieth-floor window, she could feel her anguish and impotence growing – nightfall was a symbol of another day passing.

Turning away she walked into the bedroom where his clothes were still hanging in the wardrobes, next to those she'd left behind. The bed was covered by the huge, maroon coloured quilt that he'd always preferred, rather than one of the lighter colours she'd insisted on. It hurt to know that he'd made the change; he obviously hadn't felt the need to keep something of her present. The big mass of pillows had gone too, which shouldn't be a surprise, because he'd always complained about how they got in the way. Had he been as glad to get rid of her, she wondered? Maybe not, because the photographs were still on the dressing table: the two of them laughing at the celebration of her parents' fortieth anniversary, and another gazing into each other's eyes during what should have been a private moment in the South of France, but had been captured by the friends they'd been holidaying with. Her heart suddenly filled up with so much longing that she could hardly bear it. She banged her fists against the wall, then buried her face in her hands. No one, but no one, had heard from him – not an email, or a phone call, or even a coded message to Max.

Remembering Max, she went back into the dining room and picked up the phone. Then turning on a lamp in the sitting room, she curled into the chair beneath it and dialled Max's number.

'Hi, it's me,' she said, when he answered. 'Where are you?'

'Having dinner at Pont de la Tour. Why don't you come and join us?'

'No, but thanks for asking.'

'Ellie's saying hi.'

'Hi, Ellie,' she said, momentarily wanting to be there, rather than here, all alone. It would only take a few minutes in a cab, but then the will subsided and she said, 'So who have you spoken to today?'

'Enough people to have learned that Patrice Bombola is apparently at home with his family in Brussels, and that Franz Koehler left Zurich yesterday for Rome.'

'No sign of Elliot?' she said dully.

'Not yet.'

Glancing up at the sound of someone leaving the flat opposite, she said, 'I know you two were planning to go undercover in Angola, and I'd have been dead set against it, but frankly, I wish you were there now. At least I'd have *some* idea where he was.'

'From what I've been hearing Dubai's the place to be,' Max responded. 'Apparently something big's about to go down over there.'

'Any idea what it's about?'

'Considering the terrain I'd say money. I might take a trip over there, see what I can find out.'

Not interested enough to ask any more, she said, 'I spoke to Murray at Elliot's office today. He told me you went over there.'

'Did he also tell you that we decided to leave Elliot's Porsche at the Brize Norton airfield?'

'Yep,' she answered. 'The police will need to check it out, once we've told them.'

'That's right. The plane he flew out in, by the way, is registered to a Dutch manufacturing company. The pilot was someone by the name of Rudy Forester. We don't have much on him at this stage, but Elliot's team is working on it. Could be a false name.'

Not knowing what to say she remained silent.

'What time do you want to meet up tomorrow to go to the police?' he asked.

Though everything inside her was rebelling against it, she said, 'Ten?'

'OK. I'll come by and pick you up in a taxi.'

'I'll be at the office,' she said, looking up at what sounded like a key going into the door. Her heart started to race, for she suddenly realized what it meant. 'Max,' she cried. 'Oh my God, Max, he's here.'

'*What?*'

'There's someone coming in.' She was about to

run to the door, when a sixth sense, and Max's voice, stopped her.

'If it's him, why hasn't he called us?' he said darkly. 'Has anyone else got a key?'

'Not that I know of.' She was reeling towards panic now, for someone was definitely trying the lock. But it wasn't a key she was hearing. 'Oh Christ, Max,' she murmured, 'someone's forcing the lock and I'm *in here*.'

'Waiter! Waiter!' she heard him cry. 'Is there another way out?' he said to Laurie.

Her eyes fixed on the door, she began edging round the chair, towards the kitchen. 'Oh my God, Max, who is it?'

'I don't know, but you've got to get out of there.'

'It's the only door.'

'Fuck! Listen, I'm going to call the police . . .'

'No. Don't ring off,' she said, gripping the phone as though it were a lifeline.

'It's OK, Ellie's going to do it,' he said. 'Just find somewhere to hide. I'll be there as fast as –'

'Max! They're about to get in.'

'Just hide!' he shouted.

Galvanized by the words she spun round into the kitchen, ran through and along the short hall to the bedroom. At the door she looked wildly around, then quickly sliding open one side of the closet, she climbed on to a small chest of drawers and squeezed herself into a corner behind Elliot's suits.

'Are you OK? What's happening?' Max said, sounding as though he was running.

'I'm in the closet,' she answered, her heart thumping so hard it was like a bomb in her chest.

'Stay put. Don't talk unless you have to.'

For a long moment all she could hear were the muffled sounds of Max talking to Ellie, while trying to flag down a taxi. Moving the phone from her ear, she became aware of male voices inside the flat. 'Oh my God, Max, they're in,' she whispered in terror. 'You've got to get –' She broke off, as the heavy thuds of furniture overturning and glass breaking jarred her nerves like physical blows. Then suddenly there was silence again.

She didn't dare to speak as she peered out at the bedroom. It was in darkness, but she could see light from the sitting room spilling into the kitchen. More terrified than she'd ever been in her life, she reached for the closet door to slide it closed. It moved only a few inches, then jammed. *Oh no! God, no.* She jumped as a resounding crash came from the dining room.

Quickly drawing back she sat huddled in the darkness, fear drumming so hard in her ears she could barely hear. After a while she picked up the murmur of voices again, along with more furniture being moved, then a phone ringing. It stopped abruptly, and one of them spoke into it. It wasn't a language she knew. More fear erupted inside her heart. She was finding it hard to breathe now, but as the intruder carried on talking, and more things were beaten and smashed, she made another attempt to close the closet door, forcing and willing it to move. This time it slid all the way.

'They're smashing the place apart,' she said shakily to Max. 'Where are you?'

'Just getting into a taxi,' he answered. 'The police are on their way. Hold on. We'll get there.'

Hunched in tightly to the wall, she pressed the phone hard to her ear, while her other hand curled around a sleeve of Elliot's jacket. She could hear them still moving about, turning cabinets over and ripping curtains from rails. It hardly seemed real, yet it was more real than anything she'd ever known. Her mind pitched and swayed in the darkness, while her heart raced like thundering hooves. *Oh God, Elliot, please come back now,* she silently pleaded. *Please, please, wherever you are, come home now.*

Suddenly she realized the voices were closer. She thought they were in the kitchen, but no, they were coming into the bedroom. She stopped breathing, her body so tense it might break. She could hear them talking. Then she tensed even harder as something crashed to the floor. Drawers were dragged out and the bed was shoved aside. Lamps and mirrors smashed, fabric was torn. It could only be a matter of seconds before they opened the closet. Her eyes were closed tighter than her fists. Then the door at the other end slid open.

She was paralysed with fear. A torch beam was sliding over the shoes and clothes; hangers scraped the pole as they were swept aside. She couldn't escape this. There was just no way. Her head was spinning, her heart was on fire. The search at the other end continued, until suddenly the door next to her was wrestled brutally open.

'Turn the phone so I can hear what they're saying,' Max whispered in her ear.

But she couldn't move. The torch beam was on her. She hunched into the wall. She could hear him breathing. His hand knocked her as he moved the suits. He began emptying the drawers she was sitting on. Her mind was buzzing, her body rigid. He began tugging the chest, trying to turn it over. The suits parted again and she almost screamed as his hand found her leg. He paused for a moment, then began groping down towards her ankle. She didn't dare move. Then his fingers closed in a vicelike grip, and as he wrenched her from the closet, the chest fell with her, so that her back slammed into it and her head smashed against the wall.

Through a daze of terror and pain she heard a curse, then he grabbed her again and dragged her to the middle of the floor. The room flooded with light as the other man hit the switch. Two men were staring down at her through the slits of their knitted masks.

'No,' she whimpered. 'Please . . .'

But already she was being grasped by the throat and thrown against the foot of the bed. Then they were both slamming their feet into her, kicking her so hard that she could only grunt with the pain.

'Please, stop,' she somehow managed to choke. 'Just take what you want . . .' she cried out as she was grabbed by the hair. Her legs were lifted and they dumped her on the bed. A fist banged into her face, then another into her chest. Someone was sitting on her legs, pinning her down. She felt a fumbling at her waist. She tried to protect herself, but her hands were grabbed, then one of the men wrenched her finger back and broke it.

She screamed with pain, then sobbed and gasped as they laughed. Their hands were all over her, grabbing her shoulders and breasts, her waist, thighs, buttocks. Certain they were going to rape her she kept her eyes closed, as panic and fear over-powered her. *Please God let it be over soon,* she cried. *Please don't let them kill me.*

Suddenly everything changed. She could hardly make herself think as she tried to register what was happening. She opened her eyes. She was blinded by tears, half unconscious with pain. Someone was shouting, screaming at the top of his voice,

'Get away from her! Get away now! *Drop the torch!*'

The torch thudded to the floor, as both men lifted their hands.

Max came into the room, clutching a gun in both hands, aiming it straight at them. 'Who the fuck are you?' he shouted. '*Who the fuck are you?*'

Neither of them answered as they started backing away.

'*Take the masks off!*'

Suddenly one man dived at Max's feet and knocked him to the ground. Max quickly rolled over, but he'd lost the gun. Frantically he looked round, then grabbed a foot as one of them leapt over him. His grip wasn't good enough. The man staggered, then the other was jumping to his feet, and by the time Max was up too, they were dashing out the front door.

Max went after them, leaving Laurie alone. She rolled on to her side, then forced herself to sit up, holding her injured hand, and moaning with the pain that throbbed all over her. She stayed on the edge of the bed, staring down at the gun. She could hear someone sobbing, and dully realized it was her. Then Max was back.

'The police are on their way up,' he said, stuffing the gun into the back of his jeans. 'I don't want them to find this. Are you OK?' He was kneeling in front of her now, brushing the hair from her face.

Her lips were swollen and bleeding, making it hard to speak. 'My hand,' she said. Then, 'Did they get away?'

'I don't know how many cops are down there. With any luck they'll run straight into them.'

She looked at his face, still red from the adrenalin rush, and damp with sweat.

'Just thank God you're OK,' he said, pulling her against him.

She leaned into his shoulder and closed her eyes. She had never felt so afraid, or vulnerable, or unable to cope in her life. 'I want Elliot,' she said brokenly.

'I know,' he answered. 'I know.' Then at the sound of the police entering the apartment, he said, 'I guess now would be a good time to report him missing.'

'Hello?' Katherine said, hunching into the roadside phone booth, with a finger pressed to her other ear to block the sound of the traffic. 'Elke. It's Katherine. I need to talk to Franz.'

There was a moment's stunned silence, before Franz Koehler's PA said, 'I'm afraid he's not here, but if you can give me a number . . .'

'Where is he?' Katherine broke in.

Elke told her, and Katherine hung up.

Half an hour later she was moving through the crowds on the Stresa landing stage, on the south-western shore of Lake Maggiore. When she reached the end she stood gazing out at the glistening blue beauty of the lake and lush green mountains beyond. After a while the noise and people around her seemed to melt away, and not for the first time, when confronted by one of nature's more dramatic displays, she began experiencing a sobering sense of her own smallness and impermanence, and wondering why anyone, including her, could even think they mattered. So maybe she should stop now, and just accept that she was going to die in the end anyway, and that, in fact, it would make no earthly difference. All this would carry on regardless, it was nature, it wasn't dependent on man. Not even Franz could control it.

By now he would know she'd called, and would be intrigued by the new twist in what he no doubt viewed as a game, and already trying to calculate her next moves. But until she heard from Xavier there could be none. So the phone call was no more than the opening gambit of a strategy that was probably already doomed to fail.

With untold sadness spilling from her heart, she turned to look back along the short pier to where the splendid five star hotels were lined up across the street, like silly vain women whose beauty would fade, and in some cases it had already started. One of them, she'd learned from the guidebook, was the hotel that Hemingway had written about in *A Farewell to Arms*. Like Fowles, Hemingway was an author Franz greatly admired, though his true fascination, as the name of his company bore out, was with *The Magus*. However, it wasn't so much his taste in literature that she was thinking about now, as she watched a small stream of tourists disembarking a pleasure boat, as his home at the other end of this lake, in Locarno.

Allowing her eyes to travel northwards again, across the shimmering blue miles that seemed to go on for ever, she wondered if she might be seeing as far as the place where the waters merged from one country into another, and the Italian Alps became Swiss, but even if she were, Locarno was still a very long way away. Not so far, though, as Xavier, nor so unfamiliar as this wretchedness that was devaluing her existence to the point where it was hard to care about anything any more. So maybe she should just make the decision now, that if she didn't hear from Xavier by tomorrow, then it really would be time to stop running. She could throw fate to the wind, send an email to Rachel Hendon and be damned if it got there, and damned if it didn't.

But then she returned to her small hotel, connected her computer to the Net, and there, at last, was the long-awaited message from Xavier telling her that he was going to support her, even against his better judgement, for he'd always insisted that she needed to allow at least six months, if not an entire year, to elapse before even attempting to contact Rachel Hendon. It was barely three months now, but she just couldn't go on like this. The fear, the loneliness and despair were too overwhelming.

So Franz, she was thinking to herself as she closed down her computer, you're going to be seeing me a lot sooner than you might think. And so, Rachel Hendon, are you.

Chapter 24

Beanie was waiting at Redruth station when Rachel's train pulled in, her dear, weathered face beaming with joy as she watched Rachel step down on to the platform.

'Look at you! Just look at you,' she cried, enveloping Rachel's expanding waistline. 'The baby's grown so big. It's going to be a giant.'

Laughing, Rachel hugged her back, then between them they wrestled her suitcase and computer out to the trusty old Fiesta.

'Everyone's looking forward to seeing you,' Beanie declared, as they lurched out of the car park into the hare-brained one-way system. 'Jenny and I cleaned up the house a bit, and got you some shopping. Just something to tide you over till you can get to Tesco. Or we can stop on the way back, we're going past.'

'I'll leave it until tomorrow,' Rachel said, wincing as Beanie crunched the gears from second into third, then blithely ignored a No Entry sign. 'Good short cut this,' she informed Rachel, giving an indignant horn-blower a friendly wave.

Hanging on to the seat edge, Rachel pressed her feet hard to the floor. 'I suppose I should just be thankful you didn't bring the motorbike,' she said, as they clumsily merged back to relative safety.

Beanie grinned. 'So, how was your trip?' she said, casting her a quick glance. 'Got yourself a lovely tan, I see. But you had one before you went.'

Rachel started to answer, then was reminded that Beanie didn't always pause for breath.

'We've had some lovely weather while you were gone,' she was saying. 'Like it is now. Sunny, but not too hot. Not as many tourists as we'd like, though. Oops! Didn't see that,' she cried, as they bounced up over a jutting piece of kerb. 'Don't think it was there the last time I came up here.'

Since Beanie, by some mysterious Cornish fluke, had never had a single accident in her entire driving career, Rachel decided just to go with it, and tried to relax as she rattled merrily on about the excitement that had broken out at the end of last week when someone had reported seeing a chough over near Bodmin.

'That's the Cornish bird,' she explained proudly. 'No one's seen one for years, and they say that's why our prosperity's gone down the drain. The chough took it with it, wherever it went. So now it's back, we should be having some good times. And the Goonhilly Earth Station's doing really well. So's that Eden Project, so hooray for the chough is what we say.'

Rachel smiled and wanted to squeeze her. It was so good being back, truly like coming home, seeing all the familiar flowers and bushes; the old thatched pubs on the roadside and the madly spinning windmills on the horizon. Best of all was the sheer whimsical delight of listening to Beanie's cock-eyed, yet weirdly prophetic, superstitions. In fact it was all so heart-warming that it was no hardship at all to stick to her decision not to broach the subject of Chris until they got home. Besides, getting Beanie into any more of an excited, or even distracted state, while at the wheel of a car, would definitely not be wise.

However, they were just chugging over Nine Maidens Downs – so named for the virgins who'd been turned to stone by witches – when Beanie slanted a glance from the corner of her eye and said,

'So Chris went with you, I hear.'

Rachel turned to look at her. 'How do you know that?' she asked incredulously.

'Oh, you know what villages are like,' Beanie said fussily. 'Can't keep nothing a secret. Not that I'm saying I disapprove of the two of you going off like that, but it was a bit of shock, I don't mind telling you, with him being married, and you being . . . well, you know.'

Rachel's eyebrows were up. 'But not as big a shock as I got when I found out he was married,' she declared. 'Why have you never mentioned it before?'

Beanie appeared confused and surprised. 'Well, I presumed you knew,' she said.

'Then you presumed wrong.'

They drove on in silence for a while, then Rachel said, 'So if everyone knows he was in the Caribbean with me, can I assume his wife does too?'

Beanie's eyes stayed resolutely on the road. 'Don't know about that,' she answered shortly.

'OK, then how does everyone know?'

'Well our Nick told me, and I 'spect he got it from Elwyn, who takes care of Chris's house.'

Not quite sure what to make of that, Rachel said, 'So do you know his wife?'

'Not personally.'

Rachel was still regarding her closely.

Beanie sniffed.

Rachel waited, then quickly grabbed the edge of her seat as Beanie's foot went down and they picked up speed. 'OK, OK, let's leave it until we get home,' she said, as they flew over the brink of a hill.

Beanie slowed down.

A minute or two passed, then not quite able to let it go yet, Rachel chanced it again, 'Just tell me this,' she said. 'How come no one ever talks about his wife?'

Again Beanie looked surprised. 'Well, they wouldn't, not to you,' she retorted.

Rachel frowned. 'What's that supposed to mean?' she said.

Beanie blinked. Then quite suddenly her hands tightened on the wheel. 'Worst thing he ever did, marrying that woman,' she snarled. 'She's all wrong for him. His mother would never have liked her. He should just get out of it.'

'OK! OK!' Rachel cried, jamming a foot to the floor as they careered round a bend on two wheels. 'I can see you feel strongly about it, but let's not kill ourselves over it, eh?'

Beanie's lower lip jutted forward as she eased off the accelerator and carefully negotiated the roundabout at Helston. 'I thought Chris told you what's been going on in the cove,' she said after a while. 'We all thought you knew.'

'Well I obviously don't, so maybe you'd like to enlighten me,' Rachel said. 'Have you seen him, by the way?'

'No. Not since before you went.'

Rachel said, 'So what's been going on in the cove? Actually, no, let's wait till we get home,' she quickly added, as Beanie started speeding up again.

Half an hour later the car had been gratefully abandoned and Beanie was putting on the kettle while Rachel went round opening the windows. The breeze was warm, yet fresh, the scent of the sea and cry of the gulls such a soothing, welcoming tonic that it was tempting to pretend that she was no longer interested in what Beanie had to say about Chris Gallagher and his wife; but that would be a lie, so following Beanie outside with a biscuit barrel she said, 'OK, the cove and what's been happening. I'm all ears.'

Beanie put the tray on the table, then lifted the pot to pour. 'She's got them all into smuggling,' she stated, through tight lips. 'And they're just too stupid, or greedy or . . .' Breaking off she handed a cup to Rachel, then filled one for herself and sat down.

'They needs the money,' she said, less feistily. 'Fishing's no income now. Monkfish, spider crabs, it was all junk a few years ago, and now they're delicacies. But how long's that going to last, eh? These seas is over-fished and our boys have been saying that for ten years and more. But no one ever listened, did they? They didn't care, and now look what's happened. No one can make a decent living any more. They're up against all those super-crabbers from Europe and –'

'Beanie,' Rachel interrupted. 'I know the problems, and if you're using them to justify the smuggling of . . . Is it drugs?'

'Not me, I'm not justifying it. I'm just saying, that's all. They've been struggling for too long, our boys, and I'll give her this, she's made it possible for the young 'uns to start buying back the homes that have always been in their families. But this in't no way to do it, I know that. "Oh Bean," they keeps telling me, "it's only marry-jewana," but that's not the point, is it? It's illegal, and they're going to wind up in trouble. And then where will they be? She won't care. She'll just be out to save herself. But she's the one behind it all. She's the one who gets all the fancy boxes made by Alice Phelps and her sister over in Kynance. Regular little industry they got going over there now. And the women here, they rolls the cigarettes – joints they calls them, well, I expect you know that – they rolls 'em up all expert like, then puts them in the boxes. All done. Nice and tidy, and then they gets taken up to London for her to do whatever she does with them.'

Rachel was staring at her in amazement, for though she was fully aware that there were plenty of smuggling rackets going on all along the south coast, this one, for sheer inventiveness and designer-style convenience, was in a league of its own. 'So where does Chris fit into it?' she said, remembering how he'd managed to only half explain when she'd first asked him.

'Well, he knows about it, of course, and I know he don't like it much more than I do, because he said so, but it's his wife, innit? And she's got a mind of her own that one, that's for sure, so he just turns a blind eye.'

Since that was more or less what he'd told her, Rachel said, 'So where does it all come from?'

'The marry-jewana? Don't ask me. All I know is it gets dropped off in the crab pots and when the boys goes out for the catch they brings it in.'

'But someone's got to be putting it in the crab pots.'

Beanie shrugged. 'I expect that's something she sorts out, or one of her friends in London. They always know lots of people, don't they, actors, 'specially the kind that's into this sort of thing.'

Rachel was still thoughtful. 'So the reason no one ever talks about her, at least not to me,' she said, putting it together herself, 'is because Chris told them not to?'

'I don't think he told anyone that they wasn't to mention her in particular,' Beanie responded, 'just the smuggling, was what he said. He didn't want you to get involved in it, because it would make you . . . you know, one of those after the fact things . . .'

'An accessory?'

'That's it. So I s'pose no one ever mentioned her in case the subject got on to the smuggling. Anyway, she don't like them talking about her to anyone, so it's not just you, because in general they're as tight as a hog's bottom about it all. Well, they have to be, don't they? And anything she says goes, because she's the great provider. They all

545

worships her, but from afar, because she definitely never comes down here. Nick says she don't like the sea much, which just goes to show how wrong she is for Chris, because it's in his blood. His family's from around here.'

'Yes, tell me about them,' Rachel said. 'What did his father do again? I can't remember if you ever told me.'

'Oh, he was in stockbroking,' Beanie answered. 'Or something like that. He made a lot of money, anyway. And he was one of the top advisers to the Treasury, or something to do with the Government, for years. He knew a lot of important people. They used to come down here, in the summers, some of them. Molly, that's Chris's mother, me and her used to get down to some baking then. You should have seen us. And there was always something going on up at their house. They'd set up a gymkhana for the kids, or a donkey derby. Coconut shies, duck races over in the Helford river. There was parties and balls, all kinds of things. She loved to entertain, did Molly, and I loved to help her. Always music in the house – that's where Chris gets it from. He's really like his mother in that way, loves all those arty, cultural things.' She brooded quietly for a moment. 'Things is a bit different now, though,' she said. 'None of us ever gets invited up there now, or not very often. I don't go. Don't want to see what she might have done to Molly's house.'

Realizing it was highly unlikely that Beanie would know anything about any furtive activities of either the father or son, Rachel let the subject go, then a few minutes later said, 'I now understand why everyone was so nervous when I came here after Tim died. They thought the place was going to be inundated by reporters, and that was the last thing they needed. So they cold-shouldered me to try and make me leave.'

'Silly buggers,' Beanie grunted. 'Mind you, it didn't half put the wind up them when Laurie turned up. They really didn't want her around.'

Rachel's eyes showed her amusement as she recalled how Laurie had almost had her hand snapped off when she'd admired one of Alice's boxes in the village.

'It was Chris who sorted 'em all out in the end,' Beanie went on. 'Like I said, he told 'em you knew all about it, and that you was OK about keeping mum, just as long as no one tried to get you involved. So as long as they never mentioned it to you, you'd never mention it to them.'

'Ingenious,' Rachel remarked.

From Beanie's expression she obviously thought so too, though she clearly considered anything Chris Gallagher did was worthy of a halo. Which could just go to show what a gifted confidence trickster, or frightening split personality, he was!

'Anyway, you better keep all this under your hat,' Beanie said. 'Nick and Todd and Pinkie and everyone, they'll feel more comfortable if you don't ever mention it, you know, the way Chris said.'

'My lips are sealed,' Rachel promised. 'But you know it's bound to come out in the end, don't you?'

'That's what I keeps telling them,' Beanie cried. 'But they don't listen. They're getting their cars and their houses and holidays abroad, and that's all they cares about. Not that I blame 'em, I just don't want to see 'em all end up in clink.' She nodded towards the house. 'The phone's ringing.'

Rachel started, then got awkwardly to her feet, feeling weighted by the baby. 'It's probably Anna,' she said, looking at her watch as she started inside. 'Though it's a bit early. They should still be shooting. Maybe it's Laurie,' and she sprinted as best she could across the kitchen into the sitting room. 'Hello?' she said, rubbing a hand over her belly.

'Rachel? It's Max Erwin.'

'Oh, hello Max,' she said, surprised to hear him, for they'd never spoken before. 'If you're looking for Laurie . . .'

'No. I've been trying to get hold of you. There was a break-in at Elliot's apartment last night . . .'

'Oh my God!' Rachel cried. 'Was Laurie there? That's why you're calling.'

'No, no, Laurie's OK. They roughed her up a bit, and she's still pretty shaken up . . .'

'Where is she? Can I speak to her?'

'She's sleeping right now. They gave her something at the hospital. We're at her friend Rhona's place. If you call in a couple of hours she'll probably be awake. But she wanted me to let you know what had happened, because we don't know who they were, or what it was about. All we know is that the computer was at the front door, ready to go. They didn't get the chance to take it, but as it's a computer that both Elliot and Laurie use . . .'

Rachel already understood what he was saying. 'They could as easily have been after Laurie's work as Elliot's,' she said.

'Exactly. It's more likely to be Elliot's, because

Laurie hasn't used that computer since she moved out, but we can't be sure.'

'Have you got the police involved?'

'Sure. Laurie'll give you the whole story when you speak to her. She just wanted me to tell you so you could be on the alert. I don't think anything's likely to happen, but you could do worse than speak to the local cops down there.'

Rachel's mind flashed to the conversation she'd just had with Beanie. No, she didn't think she could call the police. 'OK,' she said. 'Thanks for letting me know. Is there any news on Elliot?'

'No,' he answered.

After ringing off she wandered back out to the garden, where Beanie was pouring more tea. It was disturbing to know that until a week ago she wouldn't have thought twice about calling Chris after receiving a phone call like that. Now, she could only stand here staring at the cliffs of the opposite headland, and the wash of the waves as they were sucked into the darkened mouths of the caves, and wonder just what the hell his role really was in all this. Surely to God someone who was held in such high esteem, and affection, by all his neighbours couldn't be the willing tool of a Machiavellian megalomaniac like Franz Koehler; couldn't be in any way involved in the corrupting influences of Phraxos, much less in the insidious marketplace Max had described to Laurie. How could the man who danced like a fool to a steel band, then kissed her as he had during a storm, know what Tim's involvement was in Phraxos yet keep it to himself and watch her suffer? How could he wander up the footpath like a minstrel, make her laugh and feel secure enough to confide in him, and then a few minutes later be on the phone to Franz Koehler telling him what he'd managed to get out of her? Was he really capable of doing something like that, of using his looks and charm to exploit her when he had to know that she was in the most vulnerable state of her life?

It seemed inconceivable, beyond credibility, until she asked herself the questions: where was he now, and why was he staying away? Had he deliberately not told her about his wife, knowing that it would be much easier to get her to trust him if she thought he was only concerned about her? Certainly if she'd known who he was married to she'd never have allowed him so close, and maybe he knew that. So had he been using a very subtle seduction technique to win her trust that had almost got out of hand in the Caribbean?

She shivered. Nothing had changed from a few minutes ago, the sun was still shining, the air was still warm, yet it was unnerving the way this place could present two such different faces in less than a heartbeat – one so serene and welcoming, the other so spookily malign. It made her think of the two theatre masks, with a frown and a smile, and then of Stacey, whose frown, she'd just learned, was exploitation, which was countered by a smile of benevolence. And what about Stacey's husband? What were his two masks? She certainly knew one, and had, unquestionably, been as drawn in by its warmth as everyone else. But there was obviously a dark side too, that, at best, could be a son following in his father's footsteps, in which case the lies and duplicity would, ultimately, be acceptable. But at worst . . . At worst it was just unthinkable.

Stacey's eyes were aglow with pleasure as Petey struggled a huge, cardboard box in through the door. 'Darling, you should have got the porter to help you,' she chided. 'It's far too heavy for you to manage alone.'

'He's obviously auditioning for David Copperfield,' Petey puffed as he headed into the sitting room. 'I mean the magician, not the orphan. There,' he declared, depositing the box in the middle of the floor. 'Approximately five-zero thousand pounds, or it will be once converted.'

Stacey's smile widened, as peeling back one of the flaps she reached inside to lift out a neat, book-size parcel, which she carefully unwrapped. 'Beautiful,' she sighed, admiring the intricate, hand-tooled carvings that covered the teak box. 'Such skill our friends in the south-west have.' Lifting the lid she took a quick peek at the precious inner cargo. 'Mm,' she murmured, inhaling the heady aroma that drifted out like an invisible genie. 'I can feel myself relaxing already.'

Petey took the box from her, re-wrapped it and slipped it back in with the others. 'Not for you, sweetie,' he told her.

Pouting childishly, she picked up the glass of wine she'd been drinking before he'd arrived. On the table next to it was a newspaper whose front page was completely taken up with the story of the missing journalist, Elliot Russell. She hadn't read it yet, though Chris had told her on the phone, earlier, that there were references in it to Franz

Koehler. Right now she was much more interested in this new delivery. 'I take it there were no complications?' she said.

Petey shook his head, while using a hanky to wipe the sweat from his neck. 'Did you miss me today?' he said, heading off to the kitchen to get some water.

'Do you need to ask?' she responded, tucking her legs under her as she settled into a corner of the sofa. 'I hate being on set without you, you know that. And no one ever does my hair the way you do.'

He reappeared in the doorway. 'You're such a liar,' he told her.

Laughing, she picked up the scenes she was memorizing for the last day of shoot. 'So how were Elwyn and Felicity?' she asked, scanning the page for where she'd left off.

His eyes darted in her direction, but she was still studying the script. 'Fine,' he answered, and flopped down in the armchair Chris normally used. 'So where's the end of shoot party?' he asked, plonking his feet on the coffee table. 'Has anyone decided yet?'

'As a matter of fact, they have. It's at No. 1 Aldwych.'

'Very stylish,' he commented. 'Do we all get rooms for the night?'

Her eyebrows rose with humour. 'I don't think so,' she answered. 'But I've booked one anyway, which you can use, my darling, if my adorable husband doesn't make it back in time.'

'Which of course he won't,' he said cattily.

Stacey looked up, her eyes beaming a warning,

but her tone was smooth as she said, 'This time he's promised he will, and he owes me after taking off to the Caribbean without me.'

Petey sat quietly for a while, watching her as she carried on reading, then sitting forward he gulped down the rest of her wine.

'There's more in the fridge,' she told him, turning over a page.

Getting up he went to fill two glasses, then brought them back into the room.

'So,' she said, taking a sip. 'Shouldn't you be calling our clients instead of impersonating a teenager with restless hormones? The list is there, on the table. They'll be eager to know their orders have arrived.'

Returning to the kitchen, he retrieved her mobile from its charger then went back to begin his duties. 'Oh, by the way,' he said, starting to punch in the first number. 'There was a message from your agent. Someone wants to get in touch with you.'

'Really?' she said, only half listening. 'Who?'

'Can't remember,' he replied, 'but I think I've got it here,' and cutting off the call he dug into his back pocket. 'Someone by the name of Lee Krasner,' he read, from the torn-off flap of an envelope. 'Apparently you met at a party and told him to call.' He tossed the piece of paper over his shoulder. 'Amazing how they actually believe your crap,' he spat disgustedly, and resumed dialling.

Not until he'd finished the third call did Stacey say, 'Surely you've heard the name Lee Krasner before.'

His eyes widened in exaggerated interest. 'Well, if you're talking about Lee Krasner the artist wife of

Jackson Pollock, then of course I know who *she* is,' he responded. 'But old and weird as you are, sweetie, I don't think you can have met *her* at a party when she's been dead for twenty years.'

Stacey laughed, and turned over another page. 'Did she leave a number?' she asked casually.

Petey leaned over the arm of the chair to pick up the message. 'It looks like a mobile,' he said.

'Give it a try.'

Obediently he started punching in the number. 'What am I supposed to say?' he asked, putting the phone to his ear.

'Start with hello.'

Casting her a withering look, he leaned back in the chair and waited. After fifteen rings he was automatically disconnected. 'Someone else doing Copperfield auditions,' he remarked, pressing the end button.

Stacey was quiet as she thought. 'Call my agent,' she said, after a while, 'find out if this Lee Krasner said anything else.'

A few minutes later he snapped off the line. 'In this case, Lee Krasner is a male,' he said. 'And he just left a number for you to call.'

Confused, Stacey shook her head. 'Then we'll try again tomorrow,' she said. 'Now, I need to concentrate, and you need to finish those calls.'

It was over an hour later when Petey finally put the phone down and wandered into the bathroom, where Stacey was soaking in the bath. 'All done,' he declared, perching on the edge and scooping up a handful of bubbles. 'We should have the full amount by the end of next week.'

She inhaled dreamily, and closed her eyes. 'Then

I should be able to take it it down to Cornwall myself,' she said. 'Unless Chris wants to go down any earlier. In which case, you can hang on here and bring it when you're ready.'

Petey's eyes dropped to where he was trailing a hand through the water. He didn't much want to get into a conversation about Cornwall, not after what Elwyn had told him today, so changing the subject he said, 'Do you think Anna Maxton's going to carry on babysitting her husband all the way through the edit?'

'I imagine so,' she responded, reaching an arm up high and watching the bubbles descend. 'Which reminds me, did you put one of the boxes aside for Robert? I want to give it to him as an end of shoot gift tomorrow night.'

'He's already got one.'

'He can have another, can't he?'

Petey shrugged. Then picking up the bath foam he unscrewed the cap and poured in more of the thick, perfumed liquid.

'I'm starting to get the impression that something's bothering you,' she remarked, as he put the bubble bath back, and picked up an emery board.

'Just tired,' he said. 'It's a long drive to Cornwall and back in a day.'

'Of course, poor darling,' she said sympathetically. 'And I don't expect you've eaten either, have you? How selfish of me. I'll make you something, *tout de suite*. Hand me a towel, then go and make yourself comfy in the sitting room.'

As she stepped out of the water, he wrapped her in a large, fluffy towel then started to leave.

'By the way, did Elwyn and Felicity have any news?' she asked.

'What sort of news?' he responded, stiffening. She never asked that.

She shrugged. 'Any sort? How are things going down there?'

'Fine, as far as I could tell. They wanted to know when they might expect you.'

'Soon. Very soon,' she said. 'I miss it, and Chris and I need to get away together for a while.' Letting the towel pool at her feet, she released her hair from its shower cap and picked up a brush. 'I wonder if Robert and Anna would like to come for a weekend?' she said, gazing critically at her reflection.

Petey looked at her in amazement. 'Sweetie, the woman's doing her utmost to keep him away from you,' he reminded her, 'and with those poems he writes you I'd have thought you'd be glad to be rid of him. The man's a psycho . . .'

'Stop, stop,' she interrupted. 'If you start saying those things, then so will other people, and it's not true. He's just highly . . . creative.'

Petey rolled his eyes. 'He's a pervert, and you know it,' he declared.

She started to protest again but he cut her off,

'The only reason Anna's there every day is because she's terrified to let him out of her sight,' he cried. 'She knows you're fucking with his mind . . .'

Stacey laughed.

'Sure, it might seem funny now,' he said, 'but you must know the way they're all gossiping, and if any of this gets into the press, which it will, because dear Gloria will make sure it does, then that's all we're going to need, isn't it, a bunch of reporters digging for dirt and finding fifty grand's worth of bloody pot.'

Stacey's expression was still full of humour. 'You worry too much,' she told him, slipping into Chris's bathrobe and belting it.

'Well, *yes*, because it just so happens I enjoy my freedom,' he responded.

'Mm, it smells of him,' she said, pressing the lapels against her cheeks.

'And what about the art show?' Petey continued. 'If anything gets out about the pervy poems that have been running in tandem with the others, and you're there, displayed in all your glory, you're going to end up looking like some kind of porn queen.'

'When Ernesto Gomez has done the portraits?' she said. 'I don't think so. Anyway, what do you want me to do? I can't help it if Robert's got a crush on me.'

'The man's a mental case,' Petey cried. 'I'm telling you, he's a psycho.'

'No! He's a sweet, kind, gentle man with an overactive imagination.'

'And a rampant libido. Not to mention a neurotic wife who's –'

'Petey, just stop this, will you?' she demanded. 'I understand why you're worried, but I won't put up with you encouraging or repeating the gossip that's going around the set. So, let's drop the subject, and go and get you something to eat.'

As she stalked out of the bathroom Petey yanked the plug from the bath, then stooped to pick up the towel she'd discarded. He was shaking with frustration, because it wasn't just her neck on the line here, it was his too. And she certainly wouldn't be jumping so fast to Anna Maxton's defence if she knew that Anna Maxton's sister had been cavorting in the Caribbean with her beloved husband, at least according to the gossip in Killian. Oh no, she'd be going bloody ballistic if she knew about that, which was why he was finding it so difficult to summon the guts to tell her, because everyone knew what happened to the messenger, and in this case the chances of the punishment being anywhere near as simple, or quick, as being shot, were about as good as the chances of Gloria Sullivan keeping her trap shut about Robert once the shoot was over. And that was all they needed, one nosy-face reporter digging a bit deeper than the others, and the whole bloody lot of them were going to find themselves spending the next few years on the wrong side of prison bars. So, like it or not, he was going to have to tell her about the gossip, so she could start the damage control now, before it was too damned late.

'Hello Franz,' Katherine said into her mobile.

'Hello,' he responded. He sounded calm, faintly amused. 'How are you?'

She could feel the breeze on her face, and the restful beauty of the lake and mountains like a calming force carrying her forward. 'Ready to end the game,' she said.

'I'm glad to hear it. Where are you?'

'Where I am now isn't important,' she replied, gazing across the water to the glinting buildings of Locarno as they came into view. Maybe he could hear the sound of the boat. Would it matter? She thought not. 'I want to meet you,' she said. 'I'm alone. Do you have the courage to come the same way?'

Again he sounded amused. 'If I said yes, would you trust me?'

'Do you trust me?'

This time he laughed. 'Where? When?' he asked.

She told him, and then rang off. A few minutes later, before the boat reached the shore, she allowed the phone to slip from her hand into the water.

Xavier might be waiting in the hotel they'd chosen, up in the old town. If not there should be a message, telling her whether or not the actress she'd met at Robert Maxton's had connected with the name Lee Krasner. It was obscure, but not so obscure as to be unfathomable. It was also one hell of a gamble, considering how little she knew about the woman, but it was that link to Rachel Hendon, through her brother-in-law, and the propitious directing of her footsteps to the Guggenheim Museum in Venice, where she'd remembered the woman, that was encouraging her to go on. And so far there was no reason to feel concerned, for Stacey Greene had no idea who had made the 'Lee Krasner' call, except that it was a man, nor did she have anything to connect it to the missing Katherine Sumner. So the opening moves of her strategy were barely under way, a mere dice roll at the beginning of a game that had no real rules to follow, and odds that were stacked so heavily against her that she stood very little chance of staying the course. Knowing Franz, he would already be several moves ahead, because he always was, and he never lost. But she was now going to spend the next two days psyching herself up to get them, at the very least, on to a level field, and at the very best, on to the kind of footing that would allow her a clear and steady aim straight at Rachel Hendon.

Chapter 25

'Yes! Oh, God yes!' Stacey gasped, clutching a pillow to her chest as Chris rammed into her from behind. 'Harder. *Do it harder,*' she cried.

The veins in his neck were bulging, his muscles were on fire. He was giving it everything he had, all the rage and frustration, the resentment, disgust, the whole damned farce of his life. But Stacey never liked it better than when it was like this, so why not just let her have it? It wasn't going to change anything, it could even make things worse if she ended up pregnant, but right now he was beyond caring.

Feeling himself starting to come, he grabbed her hips and rode them both to the brink. Then somehow managing to hold himself back as she went over the edge, he ended it sharply.

She moaned and whimpered, pushing her face into the pillow and collapsing on to her side. Still kneeling over her he wondered if she realized he'd withdrawn prematurely. He hated to do it, because he desperately needed the release, but in the end he hadn't been prepared to take the risk. A baby was the last thing they needed right now. OK, she could still get pregnant, even without a full climax, but what was he supposed to do, stop having sex with her at all?

Moving off the bed he walked into the bathroom and turned on the shower. A moment later she was behind him, wrapping her arms round his waist.

'Thanks for coming back in time,' she murmured in his ear.

Stepping into the water he reached for the soap. He could do without this party tonight, but since he didn't want to deal with the scene if he backed out, he would suffer it.

'Allow me,' she said, taking the soap.

Letting it go he turned to face her. He was still hard, and knew that if he sat back on the granite steam block, she'd finish him with her mouth.

It took only a few minutes, then they both showered, kissing and stroking each other, until finally she reached for a towel and went to stand in front of a mirror.

As she began to brush out her hair, it was his reflection she was watching, rather than her own. He seemed more relaxed now, she thought, but still not fully at ease, and though she was nervous about what might be distracting him, she wasn't going to pry. He'd just returned from an intense few days with Franz Koehler, which apparently hadn't gone well, so it was highly unlikely that his bad temper was linked to a guilty conscience, considering the rumours in Killian, so it wasn't going to help to bring them up. She seriously doubted there was any truth to them anyway, so she wasn't going to make the mistake of turning a rumour into a drama. As a neighbour, and being the kind of man he was, it stood to reason he would offer his condolences for the loss of Rachel's husband, and probably try to give some moral support as well. So that easily explained them spending 'quite a lot of time' together, and as for them being in the Caribbean for ten days, well unless someone could prove that they'd actually been there together, she was just going to assume it was a coincidence that malicious gossip had exaggerated into something more pleasing to their warped little minds.

Watching him shave, she felt unease eroding her resolve to stay calm. Those rumours might be a lot easier to dismiss if she hadn't sensed a change in their relationship these last few weeks, so trying to remain convinced that there was nothing to them was proving a lot harder than it should.

'If you'd rather not go tonight,' she said, watching him rinse the soap from his face.

He glanced up at her.

'We could stay at home, just the two of us,' she said, her eyes narrowing seductively. 'We don't spend enough time together and I miss you when you're away.'

'They're expecting you,' he reminded her. 'You're the star.'

'One of them,' she corrected.

Dropping the towel, he reached for his robe. 'How are the portraits coming along?' he asked.

'Almost finished,' she answered, forcing a smile over the deliberate change of subject. Why the hell didn't she know how to play this? She was normally so together where he was concerned, confident and sure of his feelings, but this gossip, his mood, it was unnerving her badly. 'I've just got a few more sessions,' she went on, wrapping her hair in a towel. 'I should be free by the end of the week, then I thought we could go down to the house. If you're going to be free too.'

When he didn't answer she turned to look at him.

'I don't know yet,' he responded, and was about to walk into the bedroom, when seeming to sense her confusion he sighed and came to put his arms around her. 'I'm sorry,' he said, kissing her head. 'I've got a lot on my mind right now. Things are getting complicated . . .'

'It's OK, you don't have to explain,' she said softly. 'Just as long as everything's all right between us.'

'Of course it is,' he said.

He kissed her neck, and then her lips, and she found it unsettling to realize that the games they sometimes played, of indifference and even cruelty, could make her feel more secure than this tenderness. With most couples it was the other way round, but they'd never been like most couples. They had something different, unique. She'd always loved the air of mystery and intrigue he presented, and the sense of danger that maybe she'd invented, but maybe not. It didn't matter, because it had added an edge to their marriage that had kept everything fresh and exciting and gloriously unpredictable. They'd never find that with anyone else, so no matter what the truth of these rumours, she just couldn't believe that he, whether playing Mr Jekyll or Mr Hyde, would be any more willing to let it go than she was.

Leaving her to dry her hair, he went into the dressing room to sort out his attire for the evening. It wasn't black tie, but if the long, silver gown hanging outside her closet was anything to go by, he guessed he'd have to make some sort of effort. The Versace suit would probably do it, she'd always preferred it to the others, so at least that was something he could get right. As far as everything else went he was screwing up big time, and he knew it. Regrettably not only with her, for just about every other aspect of his life felt as though it was sliding out of control too.

Starting to pull back a closet door he suddenly pushed a fist silently against it. Why the hell was nothing ever simple? The Dubai operation should have been a walkover, everything should be moving on to the next phase now, but he'd just heard from Rudy that there was a chance they were going to be called back. He'd know some time in the next few days, but in the meantime he should carry on as planned. Well wasn't that just dandy? Here he was with a wife whose insecurity was driving him crazy, a widow who was in danger of being confronted by her dead husband's mistress, and a vanished reporter who had every colleague this side of a print run chasing him down. So exactly what was planned about any of this, he wanted to know? Just how was he supposed to sort any of it out if he had to to take off again in the middle of it all, like the idiot who yelled fire then abandoned the chaos. And talk about the gang who couldn't shoot straight, because that was how they were all starting to look. It just wasn't credible that no one had found Katherine Sumner yet, and the fact that she was now throwing in a few moves of her own was just plain crazy. Of course the race was on for who got to her first, the Franz Koehler A team, or the police, and he knew where his money was, but for now he was just to *carry on as planned*.

A few hours later, after forcing himself to detach from at least some of the stress, he was at the end of shoot party, and even managing to relax and enjoy it, mainly thanks to the salsa band the film's publicist had booked for the evening. The wine helped too, and he was glad to be spending some time with Anna and Robert Maxton, who he felt he knew a lot better than he actually did. It was amazing how the four of them could sit there over dinner, chatting and laughing, as though there were nothing unusual going on in their relationships, no unspoken text behind the words they uttered, no anxiety on Anna's part, or guilt on his. He was longing to ask her about Rachel, to find out if she knew anything of what had happened in the Caribbean, but he guessed that if she did her manner towards him would be rather colder than it was. If anything she seemed relieved he was there, so for her sake he felt glad that he was. He watched Robert talking to Stacey, and felt sorry for the way she led him on, then relieved when she got up to do the rounds of the other tables, excelling in her usual fashion at making the lamest jokester feel like a stand-up comic, and the plainest woman glow like a débutante. Social skills were second nature to her, so he didn't imagine for one minute that anyone

566

but him was managing to detect the edginess that she was so expertly hiding.

But Petey could see it – from across the room where he was seated at a table with a handful of dressers, his beady eyes were moving between Stacey and her husband, sensing the strain and trying to gauge whether the initial rounds had been fired over the Killian rumours. When he'd driven her back into London earlier, after tactfully waiting until she'd shot her last scene before breaking the news, she'd been adamant that she wasn't going to bring it up, that she wasn't even going to entertain the idea that he'd been unfaithful, because she just knew he hadn't. For a woman with an ego the size of Stacey's that might be easier to believe than for some, and bully for her that she was managing to stay so calm, but she definitely had some high-charged jitters going on in the heart department, he could tell, despite the I'm-so-blessed-and-happy show – and the way Chris was watching her suggested that he wasn't entirely relaxed either. So, Petey was musing anxiously, unless it turned out that there really was nothing to worry about, they could be building up for a bit of an explosion some time soon, and he wasn't at all sure he wanted to hang around for it. There was just too much risk of the little boxes getting dragged into the action.

'Chris, how about a dance?' Anna said, putting her wine glass down for Robert to refill.

His eyes filled with surprise and pleasure. 'I'd love to,' he responded, and getting to his feet, he swept her out on to the floor where several of the cast and crew were wiggling and writhing in their attempts at salsa.

Once again it was right on the tip of his tongue to ask about Rachel, but instead he said, 'So how did it all go with the film in the end? Is everyone happy?'

'Yes, I think so,' she answered, trying not to tread on his toes. 'We start editing in earnest a week from Monday.'

As she spoke she was glancing over to where Robert was chatting with Bryn Walker and his boyfriend, who'd come to sit at their table. He seemed to be having a good time, and had handled sitting at a table with Stacey and her husband much better than she'd dared hope. He'd even eaten a full meal, which was more than she'd managed, so maybe she should have been the one to take Valium before coming, instead of just giving it to him.

'I hear Ernesto's portraits are almost finished,' Chris said. 'Have you seen them yet?'

'A couple, yes,' she answered. 'They're Ernesto at his best. Did Stacey ask you about putting on the exhibition?'

'Yes, she did, and I'm happy to take a look,' he responded.

Surprised that he hadn't leapt at an opportunity most dealers, without even viewing the product, would shoot real bullets for, she followed the direction of his eyes to where Stacey was now sitting with some of the crew, apparently enjoying their attention as much as their stories. *That dress,* she thought dismally, *is one of the most exquisite I've ever seen.* With its figure-hugging sweep to the floor, tight-fitting sleeves and drop-back right down to the very top of her bottom, Stacey could hardly look more elegant, or desirable. Whereas she, Anna, felt faintly ridiculous, and dowdy, in an ankle-length black dress that was cut too low at the front, and barely fitted her now she'd lost so much weight. If there had been time she'd have bought something new for the occasion, but there hadn't, and before they'd come out Robert had insisted she'd never looked lovelier. What was he thinking now he'd seen her next to Stacey?

'So,' she said, turning back to Chris as Stacey cast a crafty look in their direction, 'how long are you going to be in London?'

'Actually, I'm going down to Cornwall tomorrow,' he answered.

Anna's heart soared. With any luck, he'd take his wife with him.

'I've met your sister a few times lately,' he said, chattily. 'I don't expect she's mentioned it, though.'

'No, she hasn't,' Anna responded, surprised. 'Is your house near hers, then?'

'Not far. On the road to Kynance.'

'Really? For some reason I'd always imagined it to be on the north coast somewhere,' she said, not too sure how she felt about Stacey Greene being such a near neighbour of Rachel's. It could put a whole different complexion on future visits, which was horrible when they'd always loved going to stay in Cornwall.

'I hadn't realized her cottage was right in Killian,' Chris was saying.

'Oh, yes, up on the headland,' she responded. 'It's been in her husband's family for years.'

'So she mentioned.'

He was smiling, and she couldn't help thinking

569

how incredibly good-looking he was. It was the very first thing anyone ever noticed about him, and it was hard to stop noticing when his looks, in a male sense, even rivalled his wife's. Though his character, she felt, was quite different, but since this was only the second or third time she'd ever met him, she was in no real position to judge. Maybe she'd ask Rachel . . .

'Oh,' she laughed as the music changed and he twirled her round. 'I'm not as good at this as you are,' she said, trying to pick up the rhythm.

'Nonsense. You're better than Selina Cordova.'

'Who?'

'It's a name I just made up.'

Laughing, she looked round to see if Robert was dancing now, but he was still talking to Bryn, which might have pleased her had Stacey not returned to the table and draped an arm round his shoulders. Even from where she was dancing she could see the flush of his pleasure, and confusion, and though she knew it was unlikely he'd do anything to disgrace himself, or her, in public, she felt miserable and afraid, for having a rival as beautiful as Stacey wasn't easy, no matter how often he insisted he loved her.

'Do you have any plans to visit Cornwall yourself any time soon?' Chris asked, as she turned back.

'I'd like to,' she said. 'But it's difficult, with the children being back at school, and with the post-production schedule we've got.' She laughed a little too brightly. 'The shoot might be over, but now the hard work begins.' And she wasn't kidding, because they were about to embark on endless weeks of viewing almost nothing but Stacey Greene in various states of undress.

He was on the point of responding when Stacey brushed past with one of the camera crew. 'Hello, darling,' she murmured, flicking a quick glance at Anna.

Chris's eyes followed her, then narrowed as she began shimmying round her partner.

Loving the feel of him watching her, and wanting to remind him just how sexy she was, Stacey put all the tease and seduction she could muster into the dance. She was sure it was something he would appreciate, since music and dance were two great loves of his, and they certainly performed both beautifully together. In fact, she was considering asking him to sing a duet with her later, she just hadn't decided on the song yet, but it would be something soulful and romantic, a Roberta Flack sort of antidote to tongue-wagging syndrome.

'Is this a gentleman's excuse-me?'

Smiling, she turned to put her hands on Robert's shoulders to show that she was dancing with him now. 'You never need an excuse,' she purred. 'I'm always yours for the taking.'

'Oh how I wish that were true,' he murmured, clicking his fingers and moving around her. 'But you are everything in my dreams, the fulfilment of desire, the apotheosis of earthly woman. I'm going to miss you.'

She turned to press her back up against him, and swayed from side to side. 'There are still the portraits to finish,' she reminded him.

'I know, witch,' he growled in her ear as her

571

buttocks brushed against him. 'I shall plunge my desire into the –'

'Sssh, darling, someone will hear,' she chided, cutting him off. 'And Anna's watching.'

Taking a step back he said, 'She knows how I feel about you. She understands that I'll leave her as soon as you say the word.'

'Oh, but you don't mean that,' she countered mischievously, closing the distance again.

'Oh but I do.'

'But what about my husband? I love him.'

'You love me.'

'Of course.'

'Then say the word.'

'Leave her,' she challenged, throwing an arm skywards and twirling to press her buttocks in tight to his erection. 'Leave her and come to me.'

His voice was shaky as he said, 'If you meant that, it would cast me into an ecstasy of hell.'

Laughing, she was about to respond when she caught the look Chris was giving her. Anna was watching them too, and suddenly realizing that too much alcohol, combined with the headiness of so many emotions, was making her go too far, she took Robert's hands and spun round to dance in front of him.

'You do know this is just a game, darling, don't you?' she said.

'Of course,' he responded, making a playful snap at her neck. 'But I'm playing to win.'

She grinned, then glanced over at Chris and Anna again, but they were no longer watching.

'Uh, Rachel? Yes, she's fine,' Anna said, answering Chris's question. 'Well, not fine, actually, but you know. Coping. At least I think she is. It's hard to tell.' She willed herself not to look at Robert and Stacey again, but it was almost impossible not to, when all she wanted was to stand and glare until Stacey got the message and left him alone. 'She can put on a convincing front when she wants to, and I've been so busy lately. What did you think, when you last saw her? Does she seem OK to you?'

'Like you said, it's hard to tell,' he answered. 'But her husband's death has obviously been a terrible blow.'

Anna's heart contracted with guilt, for she really hadn't given Rachel enough attention lately, and Rachel didn't have anyone else. 'Yes, it was,' she said, thinking how she would feel if she lost Robert, 'and for him to have died that way . . . I just wish the investigation could be over, that they could find that blasted woman, so Rachel could get on with her life.'

'Yes, that would be a good thing,' he agreed, showing nothing of the anger he was feeling. Stacey was still flirting outrageously with Robert, and he knew very well she was doing it to try and make him jealous, but couldn't she see what it was doing to Anna, for God's sake? Why did she have to be so dammed selfish?

Anna looked around and saw Gloria Sullivan watching, clocking, and no doubt longing for something outrageous to happen. Probably one of her tabloid friends was already hanging around outside, just in case. After all, the shoot was over now, she wouldn't have to face anyone tomorrow. But Gloria wasn't the only one waiting for something to blow, because everyone seemed to be watching, expecting, hoping, as though the four of them, Stacey and Robert, her and Chris, were some kind of bill-topping circus act.

Stacey's smile was starting to fade. Chris had been dancing with Anna for a long time now, and she was afraid of what they might be discussing.

Robert moved in behind her. 'Did you fuck him before you came here tonight?' he growled in her ear.

Stacey smiled reflexively, but was only half listening. 'Of course,' she responded. 'Look at him – wouldn't you?'

'Tell me what you did. How you did it.'

'I was on my knees . . . Isn't that how you want me?'

'You know it is. And begging.'

'Oh, I begged.'

'Did he hurt you?'

'Yes, he hurt me.'

Anna looked over, and Stacey spun round.

'I'm sorry,' Anna said, turning back to Chris and trying not to show how upset she was by the look on Robert's face, 'what were we saying?'

'You were telling me about the investigation your sister's involved in. With a reporter.'

'Oh yes, Laurie. Apparently her flat was broken into the night before last. They beat her up and destroyed everything. Rachel's really worried now. She's in that cottage all alone, and since they don't know what the break-in was about, or who it was . . . Actually,' she said, looking up at him, 'if you're going down there, could you pop in to make sure she's all right?'

'Of course,' he promised. Then glancing at his watch, 'I'm sorry, I've just noticed the time, and there's a call I have to make. Let me take you back to the table . . .'

Stacey watched as he walked Anna back to her chair then turned towards the door. Surely he was only going to the bathroom. Or maybe to use the phone. He had his mobile with him, but it was too loud in here . . . Then suddenly convinced he was going to call Rachel Hendon, she made to go after him, but was grabbed round the waist by Robert.

'. . . present the glorious orb of your anus, and let me wave the wand of my soul . . .' he intoned in her ear.

'Stop it!' she snapped

'Ah-ha,' Robert cried. 'I know your protests are but a pretence; and that your dreams lie true . . .'

Stacey's hand suddenly rang across his cheek.

He blinked.

'Let go of me, you dirty little pervert!' she hissed.

Anna rushed forward.

The music stopped.

Robert's shoulders were hunched. 'I thought you wanted . . .' he began feebly.

'You thought! You thought!' she sneered. 'You're disgusting in your thoughts. Just get away from me.'

'Darling, come on,' Anna murmured, catching hold of him.

'Get him out of here,' Stacey snarled. 'He's sick. Get him some help.'

Anna glared at her, wanting to kill her, but she didn't dare to let go in front of the crowd.

'I don't want him around me ever again, do you

hear that?' Stacey shouted after them. 'You should keep him locked up, and while you're at it, keep that sister of yours locked up too, or –' She gasped as Chris suddenly grabbed her arm and dragged her away.

'Let me go!' she hissed, trying to break his grip as he forced her across the room. 'Just let me go.'

Ignoring her, he walked on, pushing her ahead of him until they were outside on the street. Then abruptly letting her go, he spun her to face him. 'If you want to come home with me tonight,' he raged, his eyes blazing with fury, 'then you're going to swear, right now, that you'll never see that man again.'

Astonished, and not a little pleased, she said, 'But darling, I had no idea you could be so jealous.'

'If that's what you want to tell yourself, then be my guest,' he snarled, 'but I want that promise, *now!*'

'Then you shall have it, but he *is* the director, and with post-synching and effects and everything, I'm not sure I can avoid . . .'

His head snapped up as a flash of light exploded around them. Spotting the photographer, lurking just past the taxi rank, he quickly turned and started towards the end of the street.

Going after him, she said, 'I need to get my shawl, my bag . . .'

He kept on walking, heading into the Victorian labyrinth of Covent Garden where he'd left the car. When they reached it he opened the door for her to get in, then drove them home in silence.

By the time they got inside he'd hardly cooled off at all, for everything, just everything, was getting out of hand, and now their goddamned picture was going to be emblazoned all over some tabloid in the morning. Just what he needed. And he still needed to find out more about Laurie, because as far as he was aware no one was supposed to have been at that flat, so what the hell had gone wrong?

Slamming the door behind him, he tore off his jacket and threw it down on a chair.

'Mmm,' Stacey murmured, sauntering in after him, 'you know how I love it . . .'

'This isn't a game, Stacey,' he snapped, putting out a hand to stop her.

She froze, and watched him walk to the bar. There was no pretence in this, she could see that. He was truly angry and the tone of his voice had sent a shudder of fear right through her heart. She stayed where she was, not knowing what to do, or say. She thought about removing her dress, since it had always worked in the past, yet this time she sensed it would be wrong.

'Do you want something?' he said, filling a glass for himself.

'Yes, the truth,' she answered, feeling her mind starting to buzz.

He turned to face her. His eyes were colder than she'd ever seen them. 'What are you talking about?' he said.

She didn't want to go on, but her finger was on destruct now. 'Rachel Hendon,' she said.

He was about to drink, but his hand stopped in mid-air. 'What have you heard?' he asked.

Her face turned white, her hands clenched tightly at her sides. Not, what are you talking

577

about? Or, who? But, what have you heard? 'That you've been seeing a lot of her,' she said shakily. 'And that she was in the Caribbean at the same time as you.'

He took a large mouthful of whisky.

'Aren't you going to deny it?' she cried.

He shook his head.

'So it's true?'

'Yes, it's true.'

The words tore through her, but rage suddenly burst past the pain. 'How can you just stand there and admit it?' she shouted. 'Don't you care what it's doing to me? You're my husband, for God's sake. I love you . . .'

'Did you care what you were doing to Anna Maxton?'

'That's got nothing to do with this. I'm not having an affair with Robert.'

'And I'm not having one with Rachel.'

'Then why are you rushing off to Cornwall tomorrow, when you haven't even been back a day? You can't wait to see her, can you? You took her to the Caribbean and now you're going to move her into my house . . .'

'Actually, it's mine,' he corrected, brutally, 'but as you're wrong about me moving her in . . .'

'Don't lie to me!' she shouted. 'You're *lying*,' and picking up a vase she hurled it across the room.

It hit the bar, a few feet from where he was standing, but an ashtray came flying after it that only just missed.

'Stacey, stop this!' he ordered.

'No. You stop!' she yelled, throwing a cushion, then a photograph, then a handful of books. 'You're not going down there, do you hear me! I'm not going to let you.'

Managing to grab her before she threw an expensive bronze, he held her in a powerful grip and spoke harshly into her face, 'Listen to me,' he said, furiously, 'there's nothing between me and Rachel Hendon. I love you. You're my wife.'

'Then what was the Caribbean all about?' she spat. 'What was she doing there, when you didn't even offer to take me?'

'I didn't take her either. She was going, so I went with her –'

'Bastard!' she screamed, trying to break free. 'You're a bastard and a liar and if you ever see her again I swear I'll kill you both.'

'Stacey, for God's sake, her husband's hardly cold in his grave,' he shouted. 'Do you seriously think she –'

'I don't care about her! It's *you*. You'd rather have her than me, even though she's pregnant with another man's child. What's the matter with you? Why won't you have a child with me? I'm your . . .'

'It's not about a child,' he shouted back.

'Then what? What can she give you that I can't?'

His eyes were gleaming with rage, his mouth tight with frustration. He was hating every minute of this, but just couldn't make himself back down. Then abruptly he let her go and turned to the bar.

Shaken by his failure to respond, she stood watching him. Then as realization dawned she said, 'Oh my God, you really do care for her, don't you? This is serious for you.' Her hands went to her head. 'Oh my God! Oh my God!' she groaned. 'This can't be happening. I won't let it. Chris, tell me this isn't happening . . .'

'It's not what you think,' he responded.

Her eyes were desperate, her heart churning like crazy. 'Because she doesn't want it,' she said, more understanding dawning. 'She's still not over her husband, but you're prepared to . . . what? Wait?'

'I told you, it's not what you think.'

'Then what is it? Tell me, Chris, or so help me God . . .'

'Don't threaten me, or her!' he growled. 'She's in enough danger . . .'

She blinked in astonishment. 'What?' she hissed. 'What the hell are you talking about?'

His eyes were like glass, hard and dangerously edged.

She stared back, challenging him to go further, but in the end he backed off. 'Just forget it,' he said, turning away. 'Forget it.'

Picking up a lamp, she landed it on his back. 'No I won't just forget it!' she yelled. 'I want to know what's happening between you and that woman.'

Reeling round, he grabbed her again, 'Have you forgotten who her husband was?' he shouted. 'Have you forgotten what happened to him?'

'What the hell's it got to do with you?'

'Everything! Goddamnit, Stacey, don't you listen to anything I tell you? Don't you ever read anything but trash papers? Franz Koehler is involved in her husband's murder! That in itself implicates me, and if Katherine Sumner . . .' He stopped.

'*No!* Don't you dare walk away now,' she

snapped, grabbing him. 'You owe me the truth, and damn you, you're –'

'If Rachel Hendon and Katherine Sumner ever meet,' he snarled, twisting his hand from her grip, 'then God help Rachel Hendon. In fact, God help us all.' His eyes were boring into her like lasers, his lips were completely white, then moving her aside, he went back to get his drink.

She looked after him, rubbing her wrist where he'd crushed it, and panting for breath. She had no idea where the truth was in any of this, or how dangerous it might be, to his very lucrative association with Franz Koehler, his well-being, or even his freedom, but what she did know, with every female instinct in her body, was that he'd fallen for Rachel Hendon. So it was best for Rachel Hendon to know *now* that she had a fight on her hands that she was never going to win.

It was ironic, Laurie was thinking, or perhaps the word was galling, to find that Elliot had been knocked off one of the front pages by a domestic spat between, of all people, Chris Gallagher and his spoiled brat wife. But at least it proved Chris Gallagher was in the country now, even if he still wasn't returning her calls – and she'd been trying ever since she'd got the papers that morning. She just hoped the police were having more luck, because she hadn't hesitated in giving them his name, even though she still didn't know if his connection to Franz Koehler went beyond a three-year-old sale of a Modigliani. But she didn't care; she was prepared to grasp at anything that might help them to find Elliot.

It was now early on Saturday afternoon, and despite how much it still hurt to move, and even speak her lips were so swollen, she'd come into the office to see if work might help her escape the horrors of her mind. However, operating the computer was frustrating to the extreme, with two fingers of her right hand splinted together, and it was almost impossible to think about anything but the lengthy and detailed session she'd been through at Scotland Yard that morning. Not for the first time, they'd made her go over and over everything that had happened, what she knew about Elliot's 'self-appointed assignment' as they were calling it, and everything she was working on herself. It was amazing, she thought bitterly, just how expert they were at extracting information without giving anything away. But she wasn't stupid, she knew the men questioning her were from Special Ops, even though there had been no sign of Haynes – some of them were probably even attached to the more clandestine agencies, for the simple reason that the nature of Elliot's story demanded it.

So, just how much they already knew, or how thorough the search for Elliot actually was, were details known only to them, but one thing she had managed to pick up was their suspicion that it was already too late. Max had got the same feeling, during his own interrogations, and though he wasn't coming right out and saying so, she knew that he was close to agreeing. But she just wasn't prepared to accept that, even though she knew they had people on the inside of Franz Koehler's network, who were presumably feeding back more

582

information than was being passed on to her. But surely to God if they knew he was already dead they wouldn't keep it to themselves, so that at least provided some room for hope. She still hadn't yet been able to discover the outcome of Franz Koehler's own interview with the police. However, she did know that the French authorities were claiming he was no longer in their country, and so far no one had offered even a suggestion as to where else he might be.

Lifting her head and reaching for a tissue to dry her badly bruised eyes, she turned back to the picture of Chris Gallagher in the paper. Had Rachel seen it yet, she wondered? If she had, what was she making of the claim that the Gallagher/Greene marriage was on the rocks? It would surely have had an effect, though the fact that her own sister and brother-in-law's marriage was so threatened by it would presumably far outweigh her personal feelings.

Reaching for the phone, she dialled Rachel's number in Killian, ever hopeful that she might have heard from the errant husband.

'You didn't get my message?' Rachel replied. 'I called a couple of hours ago to let you know he was on his way to Cornwall. He rang to ask if we could meet when he gets here.'

Adrenalin stirred in Laurie's heart. 'Did he say anything else?' she asked.

'Just that he was in the car, on his way out of London. He sounded, well, let's say, not his usual self. More aloof. Strained. But he could have taken a lead from me, because I wasn't exactly friendly. I didn't invite him to come here, it just doesn't feel right for him to be in Tim's house, considering the kind of question marks we've got hanging over him.'

'Did you mention any of it?'

'He didn't give me the chance. He just asked if we could meet, so we set a time and place, then he rang off. I've tried calling him since, but his mobile's turned off.'

Laurie looked down at his picture in the paper again. 'I don't suppose he has the first idea that we know about his connection to Franz Koehler,' she said. 'I imagine he thinks he's coming to explain why he never told you he was married . . . Have you seen today's paper, by the way?'

'Yes, I have,' Rachel answered grimly. 'Anna's taking it quite badly. She's terrified there might be some truth to the marriage being in trouble, even though she's adamant there isn't actually an affair between Stacey and Robert.'

Though it had certainly looked like one to her, when she'd seen them together, Laurie merely said, 'Let's hope she's right. What actually happened last night, did she say?'

'Apparently Stacey turned on Robert, started screaming at him in the middle of the party, then Chris dragged her out. It was pretty unpleasant by the sound of it, Robert was really shaken up. They've got a horde of reporters camped out on their doorstep now, trying to get comments or shots of them at the window. They're virtual prisoners, she said. And it seems I'm lucky my name hasn't been mentioned, because Stacey yelled something about keeping both me and Robert locked up, which I imagine answers whether or not she knows Chris and I were in the Caribbean together.'

Laurie shivered. 'The woman's got bad news written all over her,' she remarked. 'I felt it the first time we met. You have to wonder why Chris can't see it, unless it's written all over him too, and we're only just noticing.'

Rachel sighed. 'I wish to God I knew what to think about him,' she said. 'I still feel angry about the lies – or omissions, I suppose is what they are. He never mentioned he was married, never told us about the painting he sold to Franz Koehler, so what else hasn't he told us? That he's following in his father's footsteps, and using his art dealership as a means of getting close to Koehler? But if that is the case, why only the one sale? You'd think there would be more, wouldn't you?'

'There might be, and we just haven't dug them out yet,' Laurie answered. 'I don't imagine they'd all be as high profile as a Modigliani. Elliot's team have been working on it, but they have to make their own boss the priority at the moment. They're spread out all over the place, from Paris, to Liberia, to Cape Town, one of them's even on the Greek island of Spetses, which, as you know, was renamed Phraxos in *The Magus*.'

'But as we also know, a Greek island isn't big enough for Herr Koehler,' Rachel remarked. 'However, if anyone can get through this, Elliot can. So don't give up hope. And there's a chance, if Chris is involved in some way, that we might have some more news by this evening.'

'God, I hope so,' Laurie responded. 'Do your best – and good luck.'

Chapter 26

Two hours later Rachel was sitting on a lush, grassy bank that sloped down to the sheer cliff edge, where a vertical drop plunged two hundred feet to the rocks below, creating the chasm known locally as the Devil's Frying Pan. The open fissure had once been a cave, but the roof had long since collapsed, leaving only the ragged arch of the entrance bridging the hollow, and a huge, domed boulder at the heart that, on stormy days, when the sea crashed and boiled around it, looked like an egg frying in a pan. Even on mild days it was a dramatic and noisy display, for the waves were always big around this side of the headland, and the jagged, slime-covered rocks never appeared anything but treacherous, or deadly should anyone be unlucky enough to fall.

Since Chris's call, early that morning, she'd run up and down the entire gamut of emotions, as she tried to work out how she was going to handle this. She hadn't confessed to Laurie what a difficult time she was having with perspective, though Laurie had probably guessed it anyway, for one minute she was thinking of him as the man she'd become so very fond of, who couldn't possibly mean her any kind of harm, and the next she felt so hostile and angry, she almost didn't care if he was just being his father's son. The fact was he'd never told her things that were vital to her perceptions of him, and she just didn't see how they could get past that, until she remembered that he might not have had any choice, he simply wouldn't have been able to tell her anything that might expose his covert role, if such a role existed.

Round and round, back and forth, and still she was no closer to knowing how she felt about anything, apart from how glad she was that she'd chosen to meet here, for the day was so glorious, and the meadow all around so full of butterflies and flowers, that it was hard to feel oppressed by the weight of her anxieties, or even too apprehensive about how much more muddied the waters were by her personal feelings.

As her heart stirred with nervousness, she leaned back on her hands to feel the breeze on her face. The gulls were screeching and flocking round the cliffs as she gazed far out to sea, where the tiny specks of fishing boats were only just visible, and a larger vessel was passing slowly across the horizon. It occurred to her that a marijuana drop had just been made, though she knew it was unlikely, for the fishermen would hardly be out there at the same time as the suppliers, that would be far too much of a risk. Nevertheless, sitting here, high up on this remote part of the coastline, with the wind carrying the scent of mustard grass and hot 'n' tot through the air, it wasn't hard to imagine just how simple an operation it was for the locals to bring in their cargo. Stacey really had known what she was doing, for they were such regulars out there on the seas that even in these different, more security conscious times, the customs cutters rarely ever bothered the fishermen they knew, and it wouldn't even surprise her to learn that the contraband was brought right into Killian Cove, rather than to a more secluded, and uninhabited part of the coast.

Sighing, and trying once again to marshal her thoughts, she was just wondering whose boat was being followed by the cluster of birds when she heard a dog barking and turned to see Romie barrelling eagerly towards her. Laughing, and catching her in an embrace as she flung her fat body into her lap, she looked up again, expecting to see Beanie clambering over the stile. Her heart gave a lurch when she saw it was Chris.

Just as she'd feared, as she watched him walking towards her, she was aware of how deeply affected she was by him. It was threatening to make it almost impossible to be objective, or even altogether rational, for watching him now she was only able to see him as the man who sang and teased and told wonderful stories – and who'd made her feel almost glad to be alive at a time when she'd actually wanted to die. How could all that be just an act?

'Hi,' he said, when he was close enough to be heard. 'I saw Beanie in the village. She sent this, in case you were getting cold.'

She took the shawl, and wished she could get up, for she felt disadvantaged down on the ground, but since getting up was an undignified manoeuvre these days, she bore it out where she was. 'Thanks,' she said, putting an arm round Romie as she snuggled up next to her.

'It's a lovely day,' he said, turning to gaze out at the view.

She looked up at him, standing tall and slightly dishevelled in the breeze, and thought there was something different about him. Then she realized that his natural, easygoing manner had been replaced by a kind of distance, or anxiety, and she wondered if he was thinking about the fight with his wife last night, or her, or something much darker.

He looked down at her, and his deep, almost soulful eyes seemed to look right into hers. 'How are you?' he said.

She nodded. 'Fine.'

He was still searching her face, as though to make sure. 'I'm sorry about what happened . . . I should have called sooner, it just . . . It was difficult.'

She looked away, and he dropped down beside her, snapping off a blade of grass.

'I probably owe you more explanations than I know,' he said, resting his elbows on his knees, 'and frankly I'm not sure where to start, but the fact I didn't tell you I was married –'

'Actually,' she interrupted, 'I'd rather we started with a phone call I received, at the villa, after you left. It was another of the anonymous variety, this time warning me to stay away from Katherine Sumner. Laurie and I have been trying to work out how the caller knew where to find me.'

The accusation was clear in her tone, and a long, almost painful silence ensued, as his eyes remained focused out to sea.

'Did you tell anyone?' she prompted, unease stirring hard in her heart, for his silence was obviously answer enough, and for one awful moment she just wanted to cover her ears rather than have to face where this was going.

After a beat he threw down the blade of grass then picked another. 'It was Franz Koehler who made the call,' he stated flatly.

Her heart jerked a response, though the only real surprise was learning that it was Franz Koehler himself – and hearing him announce it like that almost made her feel sick. For a second or two she could only stare blankly down at the grass, while the dreadful reality of more betrayal and lies began to engulf her like a tide. 'How do you know that?' she finally asked, her voice slightly hoarse.

'Because he told me.'

She took a breath. 'You have to explain this,' she said, putting a hand to her head. 'How do you . . .' She cleared her throat. 'How do you know him? And why have you never told me before?'

His tone remained neutral as he said, 'I acquired a valuable painting for him, several years ago. It was a Modigliani nude, though that's only relevant insofar as a Modigliani painting features in *The Magus*. What's more relevant, is the fact that it was the start of what's been a three and a half year association between us, the last eight to ten months of which have become increasingly . . .' He stopped and snapped off another blade of grass. 'Increasingly demanding,' he ended.

'In what way?'

'In a way I can't go into,' he replied.

'Can't or won't?'

'Both.' He inhaled deeply, then still not looking at her, he said, 'Please, just take his advice and stop looking for Katherine. Let him and the police do it, and if she does approach you, don't, for God's sake, do anything without at least calling me first.'

Her eyes stayed on his profile. 'Why should I call you when I don't even know who you are?' she responded.

He glanced at her, then away again. 'You've probably drawn some conclusions,' he replied.

'Aren't you interested to know what they are?'

'I think I can guess.'

Struggling to hold on to her impatience she said, 'OK, if you won't address that, then at least tell me why I shouldn't see Katherine. Do I have something to fear from her?'

'Yes, you probably do.'

She waited for him to expand, but he didn't. 'Oh, no,' she said harshly. 'I won't let you get away with this. You have to tell me –'

'Please. Just trust me . . .' he broke in.

'And why should I trust you when you've lied to me from the start?' she threw back acidly.

'Then trust your instincts. Are they telling you you should see her?'

She was about to answer when she felt suddenly unsure. 'You're making it impossible for me to know,' she cried, 'so why don't you explain why I should be afraid of her, when any sane person would think she had more to fear from me.'

He nodded, as though agreeing with her. 'It

could be a Koehler feint to stop you from seeing her,' he said, 'or it could be serious. I'm afraid I don't know.'

'*So why don't you ask him?*'

'It's not as simple as that.'

More anger flashed in her eyes, but forcing herself to try and stay calm, she said, 'Then let's go back to who you really are, and what the *hell you're doing in my life.*'

He lowered his head, letting his breath go slowly, almost cautiously.

'I want to know,' she said through her teeth. 'And for God's sake, don't lie.'

'I'm here, because it makes more sense for me to be than anyone else,' he finally answered. 'We're neighbours, I've met your sister a couple of times, your husband too . . .'

'But you're here at Franz Koehler's behest,' she broke in bluntly.

It took a while, but eventually he nodded.

Her heart turned over. That wasn't the answer she'd hoped for and now she felt right back at square one. 'To keep me away from Katherine Sumner?' she said.

Again he nodded.

Adrenalin was pounding through her veins now, almost making her dizzy. 'And to persuade me to give back four million dollars?'

This time he didn't respond.

'So what was the money for?' she challenged, shaking with outrage. 'If you know, then I have a right to know too.'

He was shaking his head. 'Obviously it was some kind of pay-off,' he said. 'But Franz Koehler has never confided the details to me. I'm sure Katherine Sumner knows them,' he looked at her, 'which would be at least one of the reasons he doesn't want you to meet her.'

'And what would the others be?'

'I don't think he much wants your blood on his hands,' he answered frankly. 'But I'm afraid he might feel he has no choice if Katherine manages to tell you what she knows.'

Her breath felt suddenly short and ragged and she looked away, giving herself a moment to assimilate that. 'And all this,' she said bitterly, 'so a few very rich men can get even richer.'

He didn't answer.

'Do you have shares in Phraxos?'

He nodded.

She was about to ask what kind of role he played in the hellacious trading Elliot had witnessed, when suddenly she wasn't sure it would be wise to let on that she knew so much. 'Did you know Elliot Russell's apartment was broken into?' she challenged. 'And that Laurie was there?'

'Anna told me, last night.'

'You didn't know before?'

'I knew that the apartment would be broken into,' he answered. 'But you should tell Laurie that it was Elliot's computer they were after. Not hers.'

'And you know that because Franz Koehler was behind the break-in?'

'Yes. But no one was given any orders to harm her. They had no idea she was going to be there.'

'And you think that makes it all right?'

'No, of course not.'

'So what about Elliot? Do you know where he is?'

'No. But when it was discovered he was a reporter . . . I'm told that Patrice Bombola took care of things.'

'What the hell does that mean?' she murmured in horror.

'I'm repeating what I was told,' he said. 'And I can't go any further. I've trusted you with far too much already.'

Her eyes were glittering with angry confusion. 'And if you do go any further, what then? You'll be in danger yourself?'

His laugh sounded strangled as he said, 'Being around Franz Koehler you can never be anything else.'

'Especially,' she said, her heart starting to pound, 'if he were to find out you'd been planted in his life as some kind of informer.' She knew it was a desperate bid for him to be who she wanted him to be, but she was making it anyway. 'I'm right, aren't I?' she pressed, when there was no reaction from him at all.

Still he neither admitted nor denied it.

'We know about your father,' she said.

He glanced at her, then merely nodded, which she knew was probably as close to an admission as she was likely to get.

'OK. I know you can't discuss it,' she said, 'and I should know better than to ask. But just tell me this, did you have anything to do with Tim's murder?'

He turned to look at her as though shocked she might think so, then turning away again, he said, 'No, I didn't. In fact I probably don't know any more about it than you do, except that Franz

Koehler was involved somehow, and that he's desperate to find Katherine Sumner.'

She waited for him to say more, but he didn't.

'Chris, please,' she implored. 'You've got to understand how difficult this is for me, so whatever you know . . .'

'Koehler has never told me how your husband fits into the picture,' he said earnestly, 'and I'm afraid I'm not in a position to ask.'

'But you are in a position to pass on whatever I tell you,' she said bitterly.

He didn't respond.

'For God's sake, my husband's been murdered, don't you think I have a right to know what's going on?'

'Of course you have,' he responded, 'but I don't have the answers. I only have theories, which on the whole are the same as yours: that he got involved with Phraxos and something went wrong . . . It's that something we're trying to work out.'

'We being?'

He took a breath. 'You know the answer to that.'

Yes, she did, and maybe she should stop pushing him on it now, for as oblique as the admissions had been, she couldn't deny that he'd gone at least some way towards giving her the reassurance she needed. 'So it's generally believed that Katherine murdered him. Or set him up to be murdered?' she said.

'That's how it's looking, but since no one has spoken to Katherine, it's impossible to say for sure.'

'So what happens if you find her?'

'If Koehler finds her, I'm pretty sure he'll kill her.'

'But what about *you*? What if *you* find her?'

'I'm not looking. I just went with you to the Caribbean because I needed to know what you found out.'

'So you could pass it on to Koehler?'

He nodded.

'So you *are* his snoop?' This was like being in a house of crazy mirrors.

'On that occasion.'

'What about on others?'

Again he turned to look at her, and she was unsettled by how dense his eyes seemed. 'There's a lot I just can't tell you,' he said quietly. 'I wish to God I could, but I don't know what the consequences would be, so I can't take the risk.'

Feeling unsteady, she looked down at Romie slumbering peacefully in the midst of this madness. Then she lifted her head to watch the sun glinting on the sea, while shapeless white clouds scudded through the sky. When at last she turned back to look at him he was making Romie's ears twitch with a buttercup. 'You know, I can be trusted,' she said quietly.

'Yes, but it's not as simple as that.'

Her eyes fell to her hands as his words made her feel strangely bereft, shut out, and still resentful. 'Does your wife know about any of it?' she said shortly. 'Who you are? What you do? Whatever the hell that really is.'

'She knows some.'

She took a breath, not sure now how she was feeling, or what she was really believing. 'I saw the newspaper this morning,' she said.

He was gazing out to sea.

'My sister's very nervous about you and your wife breaking up.'

'I'm sure she is,' he said, 'but it's not going to happen.'

Unable to stop the pang of disappointment she felt, she turned her face away. 'So your marriage isn't "on the rocks",' she said, already wishing she hadn't.

'No, it's not, though right at this moment there's a good chance Stacey actually thinks I've left her.'

Her surprise showed. 'Why would she think that, if it's not true?'

'Because I'm here, with you.' His eyes remained straight ahead. 'She thinks I've . . . She thinks there's something between us.'

Rachel's face felt suddenly hot. 'But you told her there isn't?' she said.

'Of course, but she doesn't believe me.' He turned to look at her, and she had to lower her eyes for fear of betraying her own feelings. It was a while before he spoke, and when he did his voice was the gentlest it had been since he'd arrived. 'I really didn't expect this to happen,' he told her. 'I thought I was . . .' He tried again. 'I'm happily married.'

'Yes, you are,' she replied quietly, looking at her wedding ring, 'because nothing's happening. You wouldn't let it, remember?'

His eyes were still on her, and for one long, excruciating minute she was afraid he might touch her. Then, as though it might in some way stop her wanting him to, she picked up the shawl.

'Are you cold?' he said.

'No. Really, I'm fine.'

A few more seconds ticked by. 'I'm sorry,' he said.

'No, don't be,' she said. 'There's nothing to be sorry for.' She looked up at him and smiled. 'Stacey's a lucky woman that you love her enough to turn another woman down.'

'Maybe I'm the lucky one,' he said, 'that you came into my life and showed me certain things I don't think I'd realized before. Or perhaps not well enough.'

She looked surprised.

He swallowed. 'If circumstances were different,' he whispered. 'If I . . . Well, I think you know what I'm saying.'

She continued to look at him, thinking she probably did, and thinking too of what an extraordinary way the world sometimes had of bringing people into each other's lives, and how very capricious, or even cruel, the timing could be.

After a while he said, 'I should probably walk you back now.'

As he got to his feet she rolled her eyes up at him, and saw the familiar light of amusement spark in his own as he realized she needed some help.

'Thank you,' she said, as he pulled her up. Then she gasped as the baby delivered a ferocious kick. 'It's a monster,' she laughed, clutching her belly.

He looked down at her hands. 'Can I?' he asked.

Surprised, she parted her hands, then felt an unsteady beat in her heart as she watched him cover the mound that seemed to be getting livelier by the minute. 'OK. OK. He's showing off now,' she said as a series of somersaults started up inside her.

'So it is a boy?' he said, his tone taking on the tease they'd started in the Caribbean.

'She. I meant to say she,' she corrected, and putting her head to one side, she gazed up into his face. 'I'm sorry I've caused a problem between you and Stacey,' she said.

'We'll work it out,' he replied.

She smiled, then without really thinking, she reached up to put her arms round his neck and kissed him softly on the mouth. The feel of him kissing her back spread a warmth all the way through her. Then she pulled away and they stood gazing into each other's eyes, him still holding her belly, her with her arms linked behind his neck, until finally he took her hand and began walking her back across the meadow.

'We can talk more, if you like,' he said, 'but you understand how limited my answers have to be.'

'That's OK, I never did like garrulous men,' she quipped.

He smiled. Then as they reached the stile he said, 'Would it be acceptable to ask if you're free for dinner tonight?'

'Oh, I think so,' she answered. 'Though we should probably invite Beanie too, just to make sure we don't get out of control.'

Laughing, he vaulted over the stile then turned to help her. She shrieked and laughed as he swung her down, but as they continued walking back towards the village, with Romie trotting along beside them, the conversation became serious again as she returned to the subject of Elliot.

He wished there was more he could tell her, but there wasn't, for that was truly all Franz Koehler had told him, though right now he was much more troubled by the figure on horseback he'd spotted, at the far side of the meadow, when he'd swung her down from the stile. Though at this distance it was impossible to say for certain, he felt sure it was his wife's loyal servant, Elwyn, and if Elwyn had been there as long as he feared, then what he had to report back to Stacey was definitely not going to be anything Stacey wanted to hear.

Anna was upstairs getting the girls ready to go out for the evening when Cecily shouted up to let her know that Stacey Greene was on the line.

Anna's heart went into free fall. Robert had said he was going to see his agent, then might pop into the cutting rooms for an hour, so was she now going to discover she'd been wrong to trust him? Oh please God, don't let him have gone to Ernesto's to find out how the portraits were coming along. The party night run-in with Stacey had been bad enough, another this soon could prove disastrous. Her eyes closed as the night of the rape scene flashed through her mind, though if anything like that had happened, Stacey would surely be calling the police, not her.

All this was racing through her mind as she assured the girls that nothing was going to get in the way of their family night out, and yes of course Daddy was on his way home, and no, there were no reporters outside any more. Then leaving them to carry on with their own hair, and to try on every item of clothing they possessed, she went into her and Robert's bedroom and closed the door.

'OK,' she said down the line to Cecily. 'I've got

it.' She waited for the kitchen extension to go down, then with a violently pounding heart, she said, 'Hello, Stacey. I'm afraid if you want to talk to Robert –'

'No, it's you I want to talk to,' Stacey cut in sharply.

Anna's insides tightened at the tone of her voice. 'If it's about Friday night . . .'

'No, it's not about Friday night. It's about your bitch of a sister and the affair she's having with my husband.'

Anna was so stunned she couldn't speak.

'So, I should tell you,' Stacey went on, 'if you value your marriage, and I think we all know you do, then you'll make that whore stop seeing my husband, *now*, or I swear I'll do everything in my power to destroy yours. We both know I can do it, whether it means making him leave you, or publishing his disgusting poems for the world to see. So it's up to you, Anna. Tell her to *leave my husband alone*, or *you* and that perverted little creep you're married to, will pay the price.'

As the line went dead Anna blinked, so shocked that she didn't even know how badly she was shaking, until her knees buckled and the phone slipped from her hand. She sank on to the edge of the bed, trying hard to make herself think. It had never crossed her mind, when Stacey had screeched that ugly comment about keeping Rachel locked up, that she'd been referring to anything like this. Then her hands went to her face, as she remembered how interested Chris had seemed in hearing about Rachel. But surely to God they weren't having an affair.

Snatching up the phone she quickly dialled Rachel's number.

'Rachel! It's . . . Oh *no!*' she cried, realizing it was the answering machine.

'Mummy? Mum?' She spun round to see Justine's anxious little face peeping in the door. 'It's OK, darling,' she said, praying she didn't look as distraught as she felt. 'I'm just leaving a message for Aunty Rachel.'

Justine's big eyes showed her unease. 'Can I wear my new . . . ?'

'Yes. Whatever you like, darling,' Anna cut in. 'I'll be right there.' The beep was just sounding on Rachel's machine, but with Justine still hanging around she had to try and keep it light. 'Hi, it's me,' she said, hoping she sounded chatty to her daughter, but urgent to her sister. 'Call me as soon as you get this message. We're going to the theatre in the park, but should be home around ten. It doesn't matter how late it is, I nee . . . *want*, to talk to you.'

She put the phone down, then turned to Justine. 'There,' she said, smiling and getting up. Her legs were still weak but Justine couldn't see that. 'So where were we? Has Emily finished her hair yet?'

'I think so,' Justine answered, leading the way across the landing to her own room. 'When's Daddy coming back?'

'He's here,' Emily announced, climbing down from her windowsill. 'He's just pulled into the drive.'

Justine's face lit up. 'So we *are* going tonight?' she cried, looking up at her mother.

Anna's heart twisted, for she'd obviously

doubted it. 'Yes, of course,' she answered, stooping to hug her. 'And what was it you wanted to wear?'

'You already said I could,' Justine pouted, sulkily, just in case the decision was about to be reversed, then without waiting to find out she headed for the stairs. 'Daddy! Daddy!' she shouted, thundering down as he opened the front door. 'Mummy said I can wear my new dress, the one we bought at Top Shop, and I did all my piano practice, so you owe me a pound.'

As Robert responded with a mock groan, then what sounded like a whirling hug, Anna looked down at Emily.

'Are you all right, Mum?' Emily asked, attempting to sound grown up, but succeeding in seeming heart-rendingly young.

'Yes, of course,' Anna said, wanting to tear out her heart it hurt so much. Then she laughed in surprise as Emily suddenly embraced her. 'What's that for?' she said, trying not to cry.

'Nothing,' Emily said. 'I just wanted to do it.'

Anna carried on hugging her, keeping her eyes closed in a losing battle to hold back the tears. But she had to pull herself together, act normally and happily, because they needed tonight to go without a hitch, so that in some small way they could be reassured that everything was all right. The papers just got things wrong sometimes, she'd explained this morning, and no, of course Daddy wasn't thinking about leaving. He loved them all too much, and that was exactly what he'd told the reporters. And Anna knew it was true, for she'd never been in any doubt of it, despite the hellish nightmare of this obsession, and his failed attempts to overcome it. So no, he wasn't thinking about leaving, nor could Stacey make him, because Anna simply wouldn't allow it. This was her family and she was going to do everything in *her* power to keep it together. So Stacey Greene could just go straight to hell with her hysterical threats; even if there was something between Rachel and Chris Gallagher, which Anna simply couldn't believe, then Rachel was obviously on the rebound, so could easily be persuaded out of it.

However, that wouldn't solve the problem of the poems which, in their way, presented the biggest threat of all, for if they were ever to get into the wrong hands the shame and ridicule would be too much for Robert to bear. So as far as Anna was concerned, getting those poems back was every bit as much a priority as speaking to Rachel.

Franz Koehler was on board his private jet, talking to Chris Gallagher on the phone. 'So where are you now?' he said, taking the drink a steward was passing.

'Still in Cornwall,' came the reply.

'And Mrs Hendon?'

'She's still here too. There's been no approach, from Katherine, or anyone else.'

Koehler was puzzled. 'Mm, I felt sure there would be by now,' he responded. 'But after I've seen her it won't be a problem.'

'Where are you meeting?'

'Details,' Koehler chided. 'Now you can't hang around there any longer, you're needed back in Dubai. How soon can you get there?'

'I should be able to charter a plane from Bodmin, or Plymouth. Or if I leave tonight, I can pick one up closer to London.'

'Do it in the morning. We need you there in one piece.'

'What's happened to the money? Where is it now?'

'That's what you and Rudy need to find out,' he replied. 'He's already on his way over there. The place is crawling with police and press so don't do anything stupid. Just ask around, see what you can find out, and we'll take it from there.' He smiled and cocked an eyebrow. 'Maybe we'll send in the Marines,' he added, making a rare joke.

Chris said nothing in response.

'Is there someone you can ask to keep an eye on Mrs Hendon, while you're gone?' Koehler asked. 'Someone who'll tip you off, should Katherine stand me up, then show up unexpectedly on your fair shores.'

'I think so.'

'Good. See to it, then call me when you're en route.'

Xavier was pacing Katherine's hotel room, his lean, anxious face full of fear for the woman he considered almost a daughter.

Katherine was seated on the edge of the bed, the laptop computer open beside her, a brand new mobile phone next to it.

'I have to talk you out of this,' Xavier said, in his strongly accented English. 'I cannot let you do it. The risk is too great.'

'I really don't have a choice,' she responded

calmly. 'It's the only way we can bring this to an end.'

'No! Just give me time, I'll get you to Rachel Hendon. We just need to wait for the fuss to die down. We agreed, it would be six months, maybe more . . .'

'But I can't wait any longer, Xavier. I can't go on living like this, and Franz . . .' She swallowed. 'He'll find me, and if he does . . .'

'He'll kill you,' he said forcefully. 'And now you're going to walk straight into the lion's den. You'll never come out of there,' he cried, jerking an arm in the direction of Franz Koehler's secluded hilltop villa. 'Once you go through those gates, that's the end.'

'I agree it's a gamble,' she said.

'No, it's suicide! You can't trust him.'

'But I'm going to. And then we'll find out if he's prepared to trust me.'

Xavier turned angrily away, his tall, rangy body stiff with frustration and fear. He looked down over the slate grey and ochre rooftops of Locarno, to the treacly blue of the lake, where a scattering of boats rocked gently in the breeze, but he was seeing nothing beyond the disaster that was looming.

Behind him Katherine, a thousand times more afraid than she was showing, checked her small black purse for the handgun Xavier had brought with him. She knew he deeply regretted giving it to her now, but he wouldn't take it back, when it was her only means of protection.

'Did you hear anything from the actress, Stacey Greene?' she asked, knowing that if he had he'd have told her.

He shook his head. 'She was in the paper on Saturday, something about a fight with her husband.'

'I hadn't realized she was married,' she said. 'But I suppose it stands to reason. She's very beautiful, as I recall.'

'So are you, and you're not married,' he responded.

Her eyes went down. 'So she's obviously got other things on her mind, if she's fighting with her husband,' she said, after a while.

'It was never a good idea. You don't know enough about her.'

'It just felt right,' she said. Then looking at her watch, she said, 'Franz should be landing soon. Do you know why he was in London?'

'I imagine it was something to do with the journalist who's gone missing. Franz's name has been all over the papers in connection with it. Apparently the journalist was last seen in Paris, at a meeting of the Scientific Research Council for Central Africa. Franz was at the same meeting.'

'Well, we know what it was really about, don't we?' she said archly. 'And if the journalist is missing, we have to assume that he knows too.'

'Knew,' Xavier said.

She looked down at the gun and turned it over in her hand before sliding it back into its black leather pouch. 'Why don't we talk about what we're going to do *after* I've seen Franz?' she said.

It was so early in the morning when Rachel opened the kitchen door to let Chris in that the sunlight was no more than a honey mist spreading through the cove, where everyone else was still sleeping.

'Sorry about this,' he said softly, even though there was no one to wake. 'Did I frighten you?'

'Not really,' she answered, stifling a yawn. 'Well, maybe a little. Is everything all right?'

'I have to leave,' he told her, as she closed the door. 'I knew it might happen, I just wasn't expecting it this soon.'

She stood looking at him, awkwardly, wanting to object, but knowing it would embarrass them both. In the end, she merely said, 'Where are you going?'

His lips pressed together as his eyes showed regret.

Standing back, she gestured for him to go on inside, and closing the kitchen door she followed him down into the sitting room, pulling her dressing gown tighter as she shivered. Then looking up into his unshaven face she felt an unsteady beat in her heart. Their close proximity at a peculiarly intimate hour, especially while she was in her nightclothes, was having an unsettling effect, and she didn't think it was just on her.

'I wanted to see you before I left,' he explained. 'I know I could have called, but . . .' He pulled a hand over his face. 'I'm glad we've had this time to talk.'

'Me too.'

'I know I haven't been as expansive as you'd like . . .'

'It's all right,' she said. Then swallowing, 'You're making it sound as though you might not be coming back.'

His eyes held hers. 'I will be back,' he said, 'I'm

just not sure when, or how much might have changed by then.'

'Now you've got me really worried,' she chided.

His smile was too faint to be reassuring.

'Actually,' she said, turning towards the table, 'I'm glad you came, because I need to tell you about a call I had from Anna.' She looked back, glad there was this small distance between them now, considering what she was about to say. 'She's heard from Stacey and . . .'

His eyes closed in dismay. 'Please tell her I'll do everything I can to stop this . . . thing she's got going with Robert,' he said.

'It wasn't really about that,' Rachel said. 'It was more about us, and what Stacey's prepared to do to stop us having an affair.'

The word fell into the air between them, charging it with a potency that just seemed to get stronger as neither of them attempted to deny it.

'She's threatened to try and break up Anna's marriage if I don't stop seeing you,' she said, looking away. 'And she's got certain poems that Robert's written, which she's threatening to make public.'

He waited for her eyes to come back to his. 'You told Anna the truth about us, I take it?' he said.

'Yes, of course,' she answered, though her throat was dry and her chest felt tight. 'I told her there was nothing, that Stacey's got it wrong.'

His eyes were still locked on hers, and a long moment passed as the wish for more freedom to speak the truth stole between them. 'I'll speak to her again,' he said.

'It's the poems Anna's most concerned about,'

she explained. 'She needs to get them back, and we were hoping you might be able to help.'

He appeared irritated and impatient, though she guessed more with Stacey than with her. 'I'm not going to London,' he said. 'But I'll speak to her on the phone.'

She braced herself, for there was more, and she wasn't at all sure how he was going to take this. 'I told Anna about Stacey's smuggling enterprise,' she said. Then quickly added, 'I was so incensed when she told me how Stacey had threatened her, that I didn't really think it through. I just wanted to give her something to hit back with, some leverage to get the poems.'

'You did the right thing,' he assured her. 'But my advice to Anna is, don't go to Stacey, go to Petey, her assistant. He'll be a lot more concerned about saving his skin than Stacey will, so he's your man for getting the poems back.'

Rachel smiled with relief. 'Thank you,' she said. 'I told Anna you'd know what to do.'

His eyes shone with irony, but a moment later he was serious again. 'I have to go,' he said.

She waited, not sure what to do, for he'd made no move to leave.

'Take care of yourself,' he murmured. 'You've got my number. If you need to call.'

'Then don't forget to answer,' she responded.

'*Touché*, and OK it won't be switched on all the time, so just keep your wits about you, and if you're not sure about anything, trust your instincts.'

'A very unreliable set of tools,' she commented drily.

He smiled. 'I'll call Nick from the road,' he said,

'tell him to keep an eye out for anyone strange hanging around.'

Though her heart tightened at the prospect, she tried to make light of it, saying, 'Well that's a nice comforting thought to leave me with.'

'Everything'll be OK,' he told her. 'All you have to do if Katherine calls, or anyone on her behalf, is either refuse to see her, or, if you want to, set up the meeting, then call and let me know where it's supposed to be.'

She nodded.

Lifting a hand he brushed a thumb lightly over her cheek. 'Go back to bed,' he said softly, 'then get up at a decent hour and treat the boy to a man-size breakfast.'

For a moment she thought he was going to kiss her, but then he was gone, leaving her walking over to the window to watch him jog down the footpath to where he'd left his car, blocking hers in. She waited as he reversed back down towards the pub, then drove up over the hill, and vanished from sight. She'd already half turned back inside when a movement on the opposite headland caught her eye. At first she couldn't quite make out what it was through the mist, but as it moved again she realized it was someone on horseback. Since it wasn't such an unusual sight, even at this hour, she thought no more of it, as folding her arms over the baby she started back upstairs to bed.

Chapter 27

Four days had passed since Elwyn had reported seeing Chris with Rachel Hendon, putting his hands on her pregnant belly, kissing her, swinging her from a stile like lovers, and still it made Stacey feel violent just to think of it. The image was so abhorrent, so painful, that she almost wanted to beat her own head as though to crush the thoughts that gave it power. But it hadn't ended with that nauseating little scene on the hillside, because he'd apparently visited the pregnant bitch's cottage at five in the morning, presumably to say goodbye, before he left. Had Stacey been able to reach either of them when she'd heard about that little early morning tryst she'd have smashed them with all the might her fury, but she hadn't, so once again she'd had to make do with his belongings, which didn't exclude his valuable collection of paintings.

Since then, there had been nothing to report, but if he thought his absence was going to make her believe Anna Maxton's frantic phone calls, swearing there was no affair, then he could think again. No man put his hands on a woman's pregnant belly, then kissed her, without there being something to it, so Anna could just forget having her warped little husband's poems back, because they were staying right where they were. And attempting to use Chris to get them for her wasn't going to do her any good either, because his phone call, warning her to stop playing games or she'd have him to answer to, hadn't impressed her at all.

'And just what kind of threat is that?' she'd screamed at him.

'Stacey,' he'd replied curtly, 'give the damned things back, then leave the Maxtons alone. There's nothing between me and Rachel Hendon, and I have no intention of leaving you, but the way you're going about this might just change my mind.'

He'd cut the line then, and obviously turned off the phone, for she'd been unable to get through again, so she'd been left alone with her rage and fear – and the sick, pornographic poems, that *just no way was she giving back*. They were all she had to fight Rachel Hendon with, because that last comment of his, that he might change his mind about leaving, had told her, more clearly than anything, that the sly, conniving bastard was already planning it. He probably just didn't want to cause his precious Rachel any distress while she was pregnant, so he was waiting until the child was born to make the break from his rash and unpredictable wife. She could even hear him saying it!

Well, the hell was she going to let that happen, either then, or now. He was *her* husband, *her* lover, *her* future, and if he thought she was stupid enough to believe there was no affair, when the sheer intimacy of putting his hands on the *woman's pregnant belly, when it wasn't even his baby* . . . Jesus Christ, just because he hadn't spent the night with her last weekend didn't mean he hadn't screwed her in the Caribbean, or that he didn't want to now, or wasn't planning to in the future. Maybe she was too pregnant now, or the baby was in the wrong position. What the hell did she know? She'd never been pregnant, because *he wouldn't allow it*. Yet there he was, down there in Cornwall, fussing over the dead man's widow, as though it was his child she was carrying. And maybe it was. Anything was possible, because he was such a lying, cheating, duplicitous son-of-a-bitch, that for all she knew even his name was a lie.

Throwing more clothes into a suitcase, she stormed back across the bedroom and into the bathroom. Spotting his shaving brush and razor hooked on a stand, she picked up the whole lot and hurled it into the shower. Then with a growl of rage, she sank to her knees, seething and sobbing and pleading with God for this not to be happening. She'd given him everything, didn't he understand that? Fantastic sex, a great social life, his independence, his freedom; she was beautiful, intelligent, she made no demands, never asked questions . . . What more did he want? How could Rachel Hendon be any better? How could she even begin to understand what kind of man he really was? She had no idea what it took to satisfy him, or to understand his complexities. Surely to God he must know that, but even if he did, it was still

614

Rachel Hendon he'd rushed off to after a terrible scene with his wife; Rachel Hendon he'd spent the weekend with, and Rachel Hendon he hadn't been able to leave without seeing, while his own wife had only been worthy of a phone call that had ended with a threat that was driving her into a frenzy of fear.

Still shaking and sobbing, she picked herself up from the floor, wiping her eyes with the backs of her hands, then gathered together what she needed. After packing, she went to the phone and tried again to call Petey. She'd neither seen nor heard from him since the night of the party, which was adding another frightening dimension to her despair, for apart from him she had no real friends. Certainly no one she could trust, so where was he, for God's sake? She'd never needed him more, yet he'd disappeared from the face of the earth, and wasn't even returning her calls.

Getting his voice mail again, she cleared her throat and in a voice still thick with tears, she said, 'Petey, I don't know what I've done, but whatever it is, I'm sorry. *Please* call me back. I need the number I asked for. My agent's lost it, but if you still have it . . . If you don't want to speak to me then text it. *Please*. But call me.'

Seconds after she'd hung up, the phone rang.

'Stacey. It's Anna. Please can we talk –'

'Forget it,' Stacey snapped, and slammed the phone down.

A few hours later she was at the wheel of her car en route to Cornwall. Professional to the last, that was what they'd say about her, for she hadn't let Ernesto down, or anyone else that she knew of.

615

She'd made sure everything was taken care of, before leaving London, and now she was already halfway to the house, with no idea of what she was going to find when she got there. Secretly, she was terrified, for since Elwyn and Felicity had left for a fortnight's holiday, she'd had no one to keep her informed of what was going on, so there was a chance Chris might have returned. Damned mobile phones that made it impossible to know where someone was, for he could so easily be lying when he insisted, impatiently, each time she asked, that no, he wasn't even in England. If he was telling the truth, then she just hoped to God that she wasn't going to find Rachel Hendon was missing too, because if she was . . . Well, she didn't even want to think about what she'd do, she only wanted to keep believing, at least for now, that wherever either of them were, they weren't together.

'Hello,' she said, answering her mobile.

No one responded, then realizing the ring was alerting her to a text, she quickly pressed in the code. With her eyes flicking between the read-out and the road she started to frown, puzzled by the message. Then she realized it was the number she'd asked Petey for. So he really was avoiding her, for there was no other message, nothing to say where he was or why he wasn't getting in touch. She wondered what she'd done to offend him so much. Then a quick surge of venom stopped her caring. Fuck him! She didn't need him. If anything it was the other way round, which he'd find out when she turned him in to the police for the smuggling and dealing of illegal substances, which, she'd just discovered, he'd been carrying out in her name. Oh yes, she had the little shit well and truly stitched up over that, and herself well covered, so maybe he, like a lot of other people she knew, was about to find out just how big a mistake it was to cross Stacey Greene.

Not until she was as far as Devon did she pull off the road to write down the number Petey had left. Then taking out her mobile she began punching it in. Her heart was tight with nerves, for she wasn't at all sure what to expect from this call, or even if making it was a good idea. In fact, she probably had it all wrong, and was about to make a total fool of herself . . .

After four rings a male voice said, 'Hello.'

Stacey took a breath. 'Uh, I had a message to call Lee Krasner.'

There was a pause at the other end, then he said, 'Who's calling, please?'

'Stacey Greene.'

Again a pause, then he said, in a voice that was noticeably more accented than before, 'Yes, Miss Greene, thank you for getting back to me. We have a mutual friend . . . Are you aware of whom I am speaking?'

Ten minutes later, stunned, yet buzzing with adrenalin, Stacey put the phone back on the seat next to her and clutched her hands to her mouth as though to hold back a hysterical urge to laugh. So it was Katherine Sumner who'd been trying to get hold of her, though not in a million years would she ever have guessed the reason why. It was still making her light-headed just to think of it, even slightly queasy, for what they were asking her to do

. . . What she could end up getting involved in . . . But if this wasn't Providence calling then nothing was, for the timing, the person, even the locale, now she herself had suggested it . . .

She remained as she was, eyes closed, hands bunched in front of her face. Her mind was moving so fast it was scaring her, for what she was thinking now was crazy, even for her. She must make herself calm down, think rationally and clearly, because it wasn't just any crime Katherine Sumner was wanted for, it was murder, which meant the risk involved in getting her into the country was going to be far greater than any Stacey had ever taken before – though it wouldn't be her taking it, it would be Nick and Zac. She'd have to make sure that they had absolutely no idea who their passenger was, and somehow convince them that she didn't either: it was just a favour she was doing someone, no questions asked. Lee Krasner, or whoever he was, had said there was no shortage of cash, so that would help, and Katherine herself would take care of a false identity.

For a moment, as the thrill of it yielded to unease, and even fear, she almost turned the car round and headed straight back to London. After all, what she was planning might, by some horrible quirk, end up hurting Chris in a way that would have far more disastrous results for them both than she was able to imagine. But then the image of his hands moving over Rachel Hendon's pregnant belly sent such a malicious urge for revenge through her heart that she resolved to do it, because nothing else, not even Robert Maxton's poems, could ever offer such a foolproof way of getting Rachel Hendon out of

Chris's life, and, ultimately, that was all that mattered.

Anna's dread was already turning to panic as Petey came into the coffee bar. From his expression she could see it wasn't going to be good news, and though it probably wasn't his fault she wanted to strike him with all the might of her frustration.

'They weren't there,' he said, sliding into the seat facing her and looking none too happy about it himself. 'The place is a mess, though. She must have been going all out ballistic to have smashed it up like that.'

Alarmed by the idea of such violence, Anna said, 'Do you know where she is?'

'No sign of her. It wouldn't surprise me if she's gone to Cornwall. I tried calling Elwyn who manages the estate, but he turned out to be in Wales, so he couldn't tell me whether she's there or not.'

Anna's thoughts were going in too many directions. 'Do you think she'll have the poems with her?' she said, forcing herself to stay focused.

He looked up as a waitress approached. 'Tall decaff latte,' he ordered. 'I expect so,' he said to Anna.

'Then you have to get them,' she said urgently. 'I've got to have them back. If she publishes them, or even if she doesn't, she could hold them over us and God knows what she might try to blackmail out of us . . .'

He nodded in agreement. 'It's a horrible thought,' he said. 'I'm afraid your sister's really hit where it hurts, because Stacey's always been very precious about her husband.'

'I know, but what are we going to do?' Anna interrupted.

He shrugged. 'I guess first, we need to find out if she is in Cornwall,' he said. 'I take it your sister's there. Can you call her?'

'She's at the clinic this morning,' she answered, 'but I don't want to get her any more involved than she already is. She's pregnant, and if Stacey's in such a state that she's smashed up the flat . . .' Her mind reeled away from the thought. 'Isn't there someone else you can call, besides this Elwyn? One of the fishermen who's been doing the smuggling?'

Alarmed, he glanced around to make sure no one had heard. 'I don't have direct contact with them,' he answered quietly. 'Elwyn does all that, but I'll speak to him again, see what he can find out.'

She waited as he dialled Elwyn's number. 'OK,' he said, after telling Elwyn what he needed, 'he's going to make a couple of calls and ring back. There's a chance he'll call Stacey though, you should be aware of that, and if he tells her I'm trying to find out where she is . . . Well, she'll definitely find that odd when I could call her myself and ask.'

Anna's eyes were showing her despair. 'Then why don't you?' she implored.

'I've already explained,' he replied. 'Call it instinct, or survival, whatever you like, I just know this is a time to keep my distance. She's got too much on me, and frankly I'm afraid she'll try and use it to make me do something – well, a lot worse than smuggling pot, now I know all this is going on.'

Anna wasn't going to allow herself to think about what he was implying, because she *had to stay focused*. It should have been such a simple operation for him to go in there and get those poems, but now it turned out he was more afraid of Stacey shopping him than he was of her, and she couldn't think what to do next.

She started as her mobile rang. Recognizing Robert's number on the read-out, she clicked it on. 'Hello, darling,' she said brightly. 'How's it going?'

'Not bad. We're about to take a quick break for lunch. The editors are going to the pub, but I don't feel like it. Any chance you might be free?'

'Of course.' She wondered how he was handling having to look at Stacey over and over and over, but she wouldn't ask in front of Petey. 'I'll have to bring the girls,' she told him. 'Cecily's got a yoga class at two.'

'Perfect,' he responded. 'Get here as soon as you can.'

By the time she rang off Petey was talking on his own phone.

'OK, thanks, sweetie, I owe you,' he said, ending the call. 'Elwyn,' he told Anna. 'Apparently she is at the house.'

Dismay and fear burned like ice in Anna's chest at the idea of the woman being so close to Rachel. 'Will you go down there?' she said, plaintively, already knowing the answer.

'Sorry,' he said shaking his head. 'No can do.'

She bit back her frustration. There was no point threatening him again, when Stacey obviously had the edge over her on that. 'OK,' she said, forcing herself to be pleasant. 'If you can just tell me where the house is, and where exactly you think she'd keep them.'

His surprise showed, though if she was intending to try to get them herself it seemed he wasn't going to stand in her way. 'Well, the house itself you can't miss,' he told her. 'You can't see it from the road, but it's the only set of gates on the way to Kynance, about a mile off the main road on the left. And my guess is, she'll either put them in one of the drawers, next to her bed in the master suite, which is on the first floor, or somewhere in her desk in the studio, which is where she tends to keep most of her personal papers and things. My money's on there, actually. They're in a big white envelope, by the way.'

'And the studio's where?'

'There's a new wing. Garages on the ground floor, studio above. There's even an outdoor staircase leading up to the studio, and the door's not always locked.'

Feeling faintly breathless, Anna thanked him, then taking out her purse to put some money on the table, she got up to go. 'If you happen to find out anything else . . .' she said.

'I'll be in touch,' he promised, pushing the money back. 'But I should warn you, I probably won't be around much longer. I've got this friend in LA, he reckons I should find it easy to get work over there, plenty of egos to be pampered and starry whims to indulge, and you know me, nothing if not the perfect fag-totum.'

Anna smiled weakly at the pun, then turned and

walked out of the door, feeling alone, and afraid, but still fully focused on ending this nightmare.

It was absurd to be feeling nostalgic about a place she hadn't even left yet, or had barely even gotten to know, but that was how Katherine was feeling, as she took a last look around the small but comfortably furnished room of the three-star hotel in the beautiful old town of Locarno. She'd never see it again, she knew that, and after so hating being cooped up here, and being driven half crazy by the bump and grind of the noisy elevator outside, it seemed almost perverse to be feeling this sorry. But it was like saying goodbye to a stranger who'd provided calm in a crisis, for this room had allowed her to feel safe for a while – it might even be the last place that ever would.

The thought caused her a jolt of nerves, despite the inner calm she'd spent the past hour trying to summon through Vedic meditation and chants. She was unpractised in the skills, but even so they helped, and she was likely to need them a lot over the next few hours.

Letting the door swing to behind her, she crossed the shadowy landing to the elevator, and pressed to go down. Xavier had left two days ago, and now, strangely, she wished he were still here to stop her. But he had arrangements to make, and his own safety to think of. She'd received a hotmail from him late last night, telling her to start making her way towards the north-west coast of France as soon as she could. It had been no more specific than that, but she knew he'd contact her again, perhaps by morning, to tell her which airfield or seaport she should be heading for, and where to go and whom to contact once there.

He hadn't actually said so, but by signing off his email as Lee Krasner, he'd let her know that Stacey Greene, the woman she'd bonded with so briefly at that party, was coming through. She could hardly dare believe that someone who had so much to lose would put herself on the line like this. Silently and fervently, she transmitted her thanks to the beautiful redhead she remembered, and prayed to God that she'd do nothing to jeopardize Stacey's integrity as a law-abiding citizen, or, most of all, to endanger her life. But there should be no reason for that; just as long as she got into the country, and into a safe house, there would be no need to impose on Stacey any further. Until a few weeks ago she'd have been equally concerned about getting out of the country again, but things had changed since then, so now that particular issue was no longer a problem.

After settling the bill, she allowed the driver to take her bag out to the taxi, while carrying the briefcase and laptop herself. With a pang of wistfulness she looked across to where an old man was walking his grandson around the wall of a fountain, then getting into the taxi she put her head back and closed her eyes. In a moment or two Locarno old town would already be a memory. She took several quick breaths, in-out, in-out, in-out, as though it might speed her mind towards her goals. She'd get through this, she was certain of it. By taking each step at a time, and keeping herself totally centred, everything she was setting out to accomplish would be accomplished, including the crossing of the Swiss/French border with a gun. She'd already managed it from France into Italy, and Italy into Switzerland, in spite of the increased security – being a blasé Caucasian American, with ample cleavage and thigh on show, helped a lot, especially when she threw out her arms in a blatant invitation to be groped.

It took almost no time at all to wind up through the wooded hillside, and drive along a much narrower stretch to a set of tall, black iron gates where she asked the driver to stop. Then she waited to see if anyone was watching the security camera. A few moments later the gates swung open, telling her that someone was.

Slowly they moved along a drive that curved through opulent palms and succulents, immaculate lawns and vivid splashes of colour. The Italianate villa at the end was the colour of sand, with tall blue shutters at the windows and flowering ivy clinging to the walls. There was no sign of anyone.

When the taxi stopped she got out, waited for the driver to put her luggage on the ground, paid him and watched him drive away. Then turning towards the house, she looked up at the vast, imposing front door. Now she would find out if Franz, like her, was prepared to take the ultimate gamble, and meet her alone.

'So are those cops we just left tighter than clams, or am I just an idiot who doesn't understand British English?' Max said, as he and Laurie boarded a Circle Line train at Victoria station.

'The former,' Laurie answered, forcing her way through an intransigent clutch of people who were blocking a path to the seats. Not that any were vacant, but she'd spotted a couple of straps that would allow them to stand together. 'Bastards,' she growled. 'They're bound to have spoken to Bombola by now – it's been four days since we told them he was supposed to have "taken care of things".'

'What about this Gallagher guy? They must have been checking him out too.'

'You'd think so, wouldn't you, but if they are, they're not telling us.'

'So do you think the guy's genuine?'

'Rachel does, but even the toughest woman finds it hard to be objective when her heart's involved, and though hers might not be fully engaged I can tell you this much, he's a real charmer. But I suppose it doesn't seem likely that he'd pass on this kind of information about Bombola if he's really in bed with Koehler, does it?'

They continued discussing the frustrating interview they'd just come from with the police, while changing trains at Bank to take the Docklands Light Railway to Laurie's office.

'So what's on for the rest of the day?' Laurie asked, as they finally handed in their tickets at Westferry station.

'Well,' he said, 'I'm flying out of here in –' he glanced at his watch – 'about four hours from now.'

'To go where?' she said, the bruises on her face seeming to stand out more vividly as her natural colour blanched.

'Dubai,' he said. 'I told you the other day, something's cooking over there, and from the rumblings I'm hearing it's tied in to Phraxos. So at best, it could give us some kind of lead on what's happened to Elliot, at worst, it'll be a waste of an air fare. My guess is, it'll be somewhere in the middle, giving us more information on some strategic links in the supply and demand show our friend Koehler is running, so don't get your hopes up too much.'

Laurie's eyes showed her dismay. 'How long will you be gone?' she asked, continuing down the steps to the street.

'Hard to say right now, but you've got my number, so if he shows up this end, don't forget to call.'

She smiled at the way he'd managed to turn that back on her. Then leaving the station, they began walking along Narrow Street, towards her office.

'So,' he said, changing the subject, 'has Rachel heard anything from Katherine Sumner?'

Laurie slanted him a cynical glance. 'I don't think that's going to happen, do you?' she said. 'I think it's just a ruse on Franz Koehler's part to stop us trying to find her.'

'Total bullshit,' he agreed, 'because I can't think of a single reason why Katherine Sumner would want to contact, or even see, Rachel Hendon, unless she has a damned good excuse as to why the good minister was in her bed at that hour of the morning, not to mention his semen being all over her sheets. Then there's the little question of the bullet that ended up in his head . . . And that's before we even get started on the four million bucks that managed to turn up in a Swiss bank account bearing the good minister's name – or number, I believe it was. So, no way do I think Katherine Sumner's in any hurry to get reacquainted with Mrs Hendon. However, I've been known to be wrong before.'

Laurie's tone was dry, as she said, 'But it's rare that you are, Max. Anyway, the search goes on, though we're drawing blank after blank with it now. No one's come up with anything around Europe, and I've exhausted all our contacts – mine, Rachel's, yours, Elliot's – so much for six degrees of separation, eh?'

'How did you get on with your Iranian exiles? Did any of them come up with anything on this Xavier character?'

'Tighter than a drum,' Laurie responded, peering in the office window as they passed. 'If they know who he is, they're definitely not going to tell me. Great, Gino's back, I need him to hold the fort while I'm in Cornwall.'

As they reached the door Max stopped, and put a hand on her arm. 'I'm going to leave you here,' he said, as she turned round in surprise. 'Ellie's over at Elliot's office, so I'm going to pick her up and take her for lunch before I go.'

Swallowing her emotions, Laurie put her arms round his neck and hugged him tight. 'You will take care, won't you?' she said, her voice muffled by his shoulder.

'Of course.'

'And call me, if there's anything to report? Anything at all.'

'I promise.'

She looked up at him, then forced a smile as he kissed her gently on the forehead, before turning to carry on down Narrow Street.

Feeling horribly as though she was letting go of a

last link to Elliot, she watched him until he'd disappeared through the gap near Rhona's apartment, where the river path would take him on to Elliot's office. Then praying hard that he would come back safely, and with Elliot, she pushed the door open and went into the office.

'Shit! What timing!' Gino cried excitedly. 'You are *so* going to want to see this. Look!' he demanded pointing at the TV. 'Look who the fuck it is.'

Laurie frowned at the face in the caption behind the news presenter, then realizing who it was her heart turned over. 'What are they saying?' she cried, grabbing the remote to turn up the volume.

'Listen, they'll tell you,' Gino said, almost breathlessly.

As the newscaster continued the story Laurie stared dumbfounded at the screen, so stunned by what she was hearing, she could barely take it in. The instant the report ended and Gino went on line to find out more, she snatched up the phone to call Rachel.

'Oh no!' she cried, when she got the machine. 'Rachel! Call me!' she shouted. 'Franz Koehler's been shot. It's on the news. Oh my God! Call me.'

Chapter 28

It had been a long time since Stacey had actually set foot in the cove, and even now she was only on one of the headlands overlooking it, shrouded by drizzle and tousled by a sharp but fitful breeze. Despite the mist created by the rain, she could easily make out the two fishermen winching their boat up on to the beach, and an old woman in a headscarf, scurrying past the pub with her dog, then popping something into the letterbox that was set into the wall of the gig house. Otherwise the place could be deserted, for there was no smoke idling from a chimney stack, or even the glow of a light shining through a set of open curtains. The phone box was empty, the cars seemed abandoned; the thatched roofs looked damp and sad, and the centuries-old stone worn down by too many battles with the sea. Yet even on a dreary day like this, it still managed to emanate the kind of cosiness and charm that inspired poets and painters alike. But not her, for as undeniably picturesque as the cove was, it had always given her the chills, and even now, as she gazed down on it, she was experiencing the uneasy sensation of someone walking over her grave. She knew Chris occasionally experienced it too, but he'd spent a lot of his childhood here, so was less unnerved by the eerie atmosphere than she was. He wasn't even put off by the ghosts that everyone, including him, claimed to have seen, on the beach, in the pub, around the headlands, and in the hidden caves of the cliffs. Robert Maxton was right, she thought, there was a taint of wickedness to the beauty of Killian Cove – or was it the other way round?

As the horse shifted restlessly under her, she looked across to Rachel Hendon's cottage nestled on the other headland, pretty and perfect with its whitewashed walls and trellises of pink roses. She'd seen the bitch come out a while ago, huddled under an umbrella as she ran awkwardly down the footpath to get into a rusty old car. She'd been too far distant for Stacey to make out the swell of her pregnancy, but it would explain the ungainliness of her run. Just to see it had sent a rush of blood to Stacey's head. That *her* husband's hands had touched that woman, that he'd kissed her, held her and shown her any affection at all, filled her with such a raging jealousy her entire body might explode with it.

Too able to picture them together, she turned her eyes towards a horizon that had become blurred and purpled by cloud. Everything was so bleak and belligerent. She hated these cliffs, and the waves that boiled around them. She felt threatened here, as though the seething undertow of a past, riddled with disaster, could at any moment suck her into its invisible inferno. She was always cold here, no matter the weather, yet the moment she rode back across the moorland, to a point where the cove could no longer be seen, she invariably became warm again, despite the wind and rain.

Turning the horse around she spurred her to a canter and began heading back to the house. It was strange being there alone, with no one to talk to, except Anna Maxton, who was still calling for the poems – and Chris, though most of that was inside her head. He had been in touch though, a quick check to make sure she was OK. She hadn't told him where she was, or asked where he was either, she'd just accused him, bitterly, waspishly, of hiding out with Rachel Hendon, or being on the phone to the bitch morning, noon and night. She couldn't help herself, it just came blurting out of her, like venom. Of course he denied it but she didn't believe him, and just to think of that woman, daring to trespass on her life, made her want to smash up everything around her, most of all the bitch who had no damned right to her husband, just because she'd lost her own.

Instead of returning to the house, she circled back, and broke into a fierce gallop down towards the southern tip of the Lizard. The grass was soft and springy underfoot, the thistles dulled by the rain. The wind felt stronger when she rode like this, but not so strong that it could restrain, or even distract her. Soon the sea was visible either side of the peninsula, spreading like the huge leaden wings of a mythical beast. As she galloped along its spine tears of rage mingled with the rain on her cheeks, while steel and purpose blotted the fear

632

from her heart. Spotting the small barn up ahead, she reined the horse in, and sat looking at it, afraid to go any further, yet not ready to turn back.

Nick had told her about it only last night, though she'd seen it plenty of times before, while out riding, or even from one of the guest bedroom windows at the back of the house. But this was the first time she'd ever taken the time to pause and look at the seemingly innocuous, half-dilapidated structure that she'd now learned was locally referred to as the Hatch. She wouldn't go any closer, she'd merely sit here and imagine, from the few details Nick had given her, what it was like inside. Damp and mouldy, he'd said. Full of old junk, like rusted fish wire and damaged buoys, and crushed, fraying crab pots. Half of the roof was missing, and apparently there was an abandoned set of wheels too, that had once been used to tow a small boat. Most significant was the trapdoor that gave the barn its name, 'because it's that little trapdoor', Nick had told her, 'that covers the entrance to the tunnel we used to play in as boys, and that leads all the way down through the cliffs to a cave that no one can see, not even if they're out on a boat.'

Being so nervous of the sea herself, Stacey didn't envy Katherine the journey she would be making tomorrow, across this widest stretch of the Channel from France. She should arrive here some time after midnight, having been transferred from the French boat into Nick's some seven or so miles offshore, then he and Zac would bring her in, under the cover of what they'd said was going to be a moonless night. The only part she, Stacey, would play in the transfer would be to lend Nick the Range Rover, to drive his smuggled cargo from the Hatch across country to the house.

Her heart was thudding with apprehension at the thoughts in her head. Wheels within wheels, mysterious ways, cause and effect – call it what you will: as far as she was concerned there had to be some divine, or universal, power at work to have brought her this opportunity at a time when she so desperately needed it. So she had no misgivings about what she was doing, only a vague and occasionally disturbing flutter of conscience, but that was soon trampled by images of his trip to a Caribbean island, his eagerness to get down here in spite of his wife's protests, him saying that he might change his mind about leaving her, his brutal pronouncement that the house wasn't hers, but his; his hands on a pregnant belly . . .

Turning her horse, she started back towards the misted outline of the house. Did he have any idea how much he had hurt her, when he'd said that the house was his, not hers? Surely he must have, for he'd never been in any doubt about how much of their marriage, and love, she felt to be wrapped up in the place. She had reconstructed every wall, every room, every staircase, every nook and cranny, with as much love as she felt for the man who had provided it. He'd said he wasn't intending to move Rachel in, but she knew he was lying. She could already see them there, making love on her bed, throwing parties on her terrace, lighting a fire in her hearth, decorating a tree at Christmas, inviting people into *her* home as though she'd never even existed. She could hear his stories of Picasso's disdain for Matisse, of Modigliani's tragic wife. She could feel his passion, smell his skin, see his eyes, turbulent, troubled and heart-rendingly tender. To live without him would be like a musician having to survive without ears; an artist without eyes, or an actor without words. Her life would be incomplete, inconsequential, impossible – which was why it simply wasn't going to happen.

'So, unlike his role model, Maurice Conchis,' Rachel was saying, as she and Laurie climbed up the sodden, narrow trail that snaked to the top of the opposite headland, 'Franz Koehler appears to have been outsmarted.' She lifted a branch to clear the path. 'You know, even though I never met the man, it still seems incredible to think of him dead. He was shot, how many times?'

'Three, they said,' Laurie answered, wiping the drizzle from her face. 'Once in the head, twice in the chest. The chauffeur found him, apparently, when he went to pick him up to take him to the airport. They're questioning him now, but I think they're more interested in finding the blonde woman who took taxis to and from the house around the time of the murder.'

Rachel felt a jolt of unease. 'Do you really think it was Katherine?' she said.

'Don't you?'

Rachel nodded. 'I just can't work out where that takes us. Is she some kind of mad vigilante going round ridding the world of corrupt men in high places, or is she . . . Is she what? Why would she do it?'

'To clear the field, so that she can see you without Franz Koehler being a threat to either of you?' Laurie suggested.

'But why would it be so important to see me?'

'We can only guess at that,' Laurie replied, 'but we're pretty certain Franz Koehler didn't want it to happen. The question is, does she pose some kind of threat to you too?'

Sobered by the prospect, Rachel said, 'Do they have any idea where she is now? No, obviously not, or they wouldn't be saying they want to question her.'

'Gino and Dan are over there at the moment,' Laurie said. 'We'll know more when we speak to them later.'

Rachel slipped in the mud and slithered back a couple of steps.

Catching her and pushing her gently on, Laurie said, 'If she does get in touch, don't, whatever you do, agree to see her alone, will you?'

Rachel started to answer, but then deciding not to voice what she was thinking, she pushed open a five-barred gate and led the way through. 'You know, you're extremely tolerant,' she said, changing the subject, 'to indulge a hormonal woman's whim like this, especially in this weather.'

'It's only drizzle,' Laurie responded, 'and I came prepared.'

Rachel turned to give her a quick once-over. 'Barbour and Wellies, typical London garb for the country,' she commented. 'Just don't try it here, by the coast, in December and January.'

'It's a promise.'

Rachel smiled, then walking on she suddenly

clenched her fists and gave a howl of frustration. 'I feel so . . . *gullible*,' she cried. 'But honestly, I really believed him when we were together. It all seemed to make sense then, but now . . .' She shook her head in annoyance. 'I just don't know what to believe.'

'Well, if we keep his father in the equation, it's definitely plausible,' Laurie reminded her. 'So I don't know why you're giving yourself such a hard time over it.'

'But do *you* believe he's an informant? Some kind of mole?' Rachel challenged, turning to look at her from the depths of a cavernous rain hood.

'I was the one who thought so in the first place,' Laurie laughed. 'But I have to admit, I'd be happier if *he'd* told *you* that he's working for the Government, rather than the other way round. Except, he wouldn't tell you, because he can't, so that just gets us back where we started.'

'Or this plucky little expedition does,' Rachel said, gingerly pushing aside another bramble.

As they pressed on up the trail, Laurie said, 'I suppose you'd have told me if you'd heard from him again.'

'Of course,' Rachel replied. Then realizing Laurie's real reason for asking she felt a pang of guilt, for though she'd repeated what Chris had said about Patrice Bombola, she hadn't added how pessimistic Chris had been when she'd asked if he thought Elliot was still alive.

'So after he came to say goodbye at dawn,' Laurie said, 'what then?'

Rachel's heart fluttered. 'Nothing,' she said, recalling how intimate it had felt, and how much

637

the whole weekend had dominated her thoughts since. 'Just that he'd be back soon, and I should call if I needed to.'

'No mention of where he was going?'

'No.'

They walked on quietly, huddled into their jackets, until Rachel began climbing the stile.

'Can you manage there?' Laurie said, holding out a hand, just in case.

'Yes, I'm fine. Just watch your foot on that stone, it wobbles.'

After clearing the stile, and taking a quick breather for Rachel to work up more steam, they forged on across the wide open meadow towards the edge of the cliffs.

'So Stacey Greene's around,' Laurie said, wondering if Rachel felt as unnerved by that as she would were she in her position.

'Mm,' Rachel responded. 'Apparently she arrived a couple of days ago.'

'She hasn't tried calling, or coming to see you?'

'No, thank God. An hysterical Stacey Greene I can definitely do without.'

A minute or two later they were standing several feet from the edge of the Devil's Frying Pan, gazing at the intimidating blackness of the rim and the thunderous sky beyond. Though they couldn't see the gushing cauldron of waves at the bottom of the abyss, or the jagged rocks that encircled it, the noise was so ominous that to Laurie it easily explained the Devil's ownership.

'We shouldn't go any closer,' Rachel warned, 'the grass is incredibly slippery when it's raining like this.'

Happy to stay where she was, Laurie continued to look around, taking in the leaden darkness of the sky, the strange undulation of the sea that seemed to make the land roll in its wake, and the grim chasm that yawned before them.

Rachel said, 'It glowers and growls and does all sorts of things to your nerves when it's like this, doesn't it? But I love it all the same.'

Laurie shivered. 'Isn't this spot supposed to be haunted?' she said, going up on tiptoe to try to see into the abyss. 'You're right, it does do things to your nerves,' she agreed, coming back down again, 'but more importantly, what's it doing to your instincts? Anything?'

Rachel inhaled deeply. 'Nothing,' she confessed. 'I hoped coming back here might help clear my head, get me remembering why I found him so convincing on Saturday, but the weather's so different, the whole atmosphere has changed, and now it's starting to feel like a pretty ludicrous mission altogether.'

Laurie's eyes narrowed against the wind as she continued to look around. 'Going back to Stacey Greene,' she said, 'does she have something to worry about where you and Chris are concerned? I mean after last weekend.'

Feeling her cheeks colour, Rachel said, 'No. At least not in the sense you're meaning it. It's so soon after Tim and with me being in this condition . . . I'm sure it's only rebound on my part . . .' She looked at Laurie, then turned to gaze absently down at the sea. 'I wonder where he is now,' she said. 'What he's doing?'

'Why not try calling when we get back?' Laurie

639

suggested, turning to see who Rachel was waving to.

'I think it's Nick,' Rachel said, watching the small fishing boat battling the swell as it motored out to sea. 'Hard to tell from here. Anyway, time we were going back. I could do with a cup of tea, and Beanie baked some muffins this morning.'

'Oh, don't you just love Beanie?' Laurie enthused, her mouth already watering.

Ten minutes later they were kicking off their Wellies by the back door, still talking, while drying their hair with towels, both completely oblivious now to Nick's boat, as it chugged on over the far horizon.

'Jesus Christ!' Chris swore, jabbing off the phone and turning to Rudy. 'First Franz is dead, and now Katherine's on her way to England. At least we have to presume it's her.' He threw out his hands. 'Who the bloody hell else could it be?'

Rudy glanced over at him, then quickly returned his eyes to the busy coast highway.

'I don't believe this! I just don't fucking believe it!' Chris growled, banging his fist on the dashboard. That his own wife was facilitating Katherine's trip was too mind-blowing for words.

'You're going to have to get yourself over there,' Rudy told him. 'Franz might not be with us any longer, but there are a lot of others who don't want Katherine Sumner anywhere near Mrs Hendon.'

'Tell me about it,' Chris muttered, wincing as a motorbike zoomed past and cut too close in front.

'They could be a pair of sitting ducks, if you get there in time,' Rudy said glibly, then suddenly he braked hard and made a dangerous U-turn right in front of the Jemeirah Mosque.

'What are you doing?'

'Getting you to the airport. I've got plenty of back-up here, we should have that cash released by the end of the week. You just get yourself back there.'

They travelled the next few minutes in silence, plunging back into the scorched and teeming city streets of Dubai, heading for the Al Maktoum Bridge.

'You can do it, can you?' Rudy said.

Chris glanced at him. 'Are you kidding?' he cried. 'Of course I can do it. What the hell other choice do I have?'

Everything had gone according to plan. The two boats had rendezvoused in the Channel, more or less on time, the transfer had been made with no questions or mishaps, and Katherine had arrived at the house, just after two in the morning, windswept, and as white as the handkerchief she was still dabbing to her lips. Obviously the journey had not been easy, which made her earnest thanks for Stacey's help in getting her here all the more touching. Stacey had brushed it aside, insisting it was the least she could do, as though she were offering refuge to a friend caught in a storm, rather than a virtual stranger who was wanted for murder.

Once inside, though Katherine had appeared ready to talk, Stacey could see she was exhausted, so she'd shown her straight to one of the guest suites, where she'd already laid out clean nightclothes, fresh towels and toiletries and had even run a hot bath ready for her to step into. She'd left her then, and gone downstairs to make sure everything was all right with Nick. After that, she returned to her own suite, to pass an unsteady night thinking about the woman along the hall and praying that Chris wouldn't choose tonight or tomorrow to make an unexpected return. But if he did, she had her defence ready, for Katherine had quite genuinely assured her that she meant no one any harm, least of all Rachel Hendon. She merely wanted to talk to Rachel, explain what had happened, then accept the consequences, whatever they might be. Stacey had no idea how much of that was true, but it was the story the mysterious Lee Krasner had told her on the phone, and would work perfectly for Stacey to claim that she'd been taken in by Katherine's sorry tale of how she'd been maligned, misunderstood and turned into a virtual exile from the world for something she hadn't done – or maybe hadn't meant to do, Stacey still wasn't too clear on that. Nor did she want to be, for the more hazy that particular issue remained, the more convincing she could be later, when it inevitably came out that she had played a part in Katherine Sumner's visit to Tim Hendon's widow.

It was now almost midday, and with still no sign of Katherine, Stacey was sitting at her desk in the studio Chris had had built specially for her. At the time it had been designed to satisfy her desire to dance; later it had been the perfect place to practise her newfound passion for singing; then had come her most recent urge, to paint. He'd never balked at her fads, had willingly indulged them, no matter the cost or how vague the talent. In fact the only thing he had ever refused her was a child, but she'd been so sure she could change his mind about that, that she'd actually started making plans for the studio's next conversion into a nursery. The designer's drawings were right there, stored on the computer in front of her, though masked right now by other business. If only she could block out his refusal to make her pregnant so easily, as it was another sign that he had no plans for a future with her.

An untidy pile of printouts littered the desk, all concerning Tim Hendon's murder, but Stacey had stopped reading a while ago, and was now sitting quietly, resting her head in her hands, all but oblivious to the rain hammering against the windows. She was getting herself ready for the role she was to play for the rest of the day, and possibly into the night. The lines would necessarily have to be improvised, as would most of the action, for much depended on Katherine, but the motivation was unwavering and a thousand times more forceful than any she'd ever known before. However, this was only a brief, stabilizing exercise, for there was still plenty to do, or more particularly questions to be asked, of Katherine, that might help her to decide exactly how she was going to play this.

Upstairs, in one of the most comfortable rooms she'd stayed in for a while, Katherine was currently checking her email to see if anything new had come in from Xavier. Nothing had, but she sent him a message to let him know she'd got here safely. There was no need for him to come, he should just stay where he was safe now and leave the rest to her.

Though she was still shaken by the godawful journey, and the back-breaking climb up through the cliffs to the barn, when she'd slipped and stumbled, cracking her head against the walls, and torn the skin on her hands and knees – not to mention the disgusting insects and rodents that had scurried over her feet or clung to her face – she was feeling much calmer and more centred now than she had since leaving Locarno. A great deal had happened since then, too much to think about now, when she needed her mind clear and alert to carry out this final move in the game that she had wrested from Franz's control.

Looking up as someone knocked on the door, she remembered too late the gun that should be in her pocket book, instead of on the bed next to it. But Stacey didn't seem to notice, as she told her in a vague, friendly way that there was plenty to eat downstairs if she was hungry. 'I'm just popping out for an hour,' she said, 'help yourself to whatever's there.'

Katherine thanked her graciously, and felt curious to know why *she* wasn't curious, or even nervous, when it couldn't be every day she harboured a known murderer in her home; and even if she hadn't heard about Franz, she'd certainly know about Tim.

By the time Stacey came back Katherine was downstairs in the kitchen, eating a sandwich she'd prepared and flicking through the parish magazine. Stacey was impressed by how calm she seemed, as though nothing untoward was occurring or there was nothing at all unusual about keeping a gun right next to her plate. That was what Stacey presumed was inside the black leather purse she'd spotted earlier on the bed, but she could be wrong.

'Does it usually rain like this?' Katherine asked, still gazing at the french windows Stacey had just come in through.

'Sometimes,' Stacey answered, glancing at the doors too. Every now and again they rattled in the wind, and through their partially steamed up panes she could see a bundle of tumbleweed blowing across the stable-yard. 'It's forecast to stay like this for a few more days.' Peeling off her gloves, she turned back to Katherine. 'Does it affect your plans?'

Katherine shook her head. 'Not really,' she answered, picking up her milk. Then seeming to understand the question, she added, 'Please don't worry, I'll be out of here by this time tomorrow.'

Stacey removed her riding hat and jacket, then freed her hair from the net and shook it loose.

Katherine bit into her sandwich and watched as Stacey took a joint from a cigarette box and lit it. 'Is Rachel Hendon's house far from here?' Katherine asked.

Stacey exhaled slowly. 'No distance,' she answered. 'I'll draw you a map, but you can't miss it.'

'Will I need a car?'

'There's one in the garage you can use. Shall we go into the drawing room? It's cold in here.'

After hooking the black purse on to her wrist,

Katherine picked up her sandwich and milk, and followed Stacey across the spacious flagstoned hall towards an extremely grand set of double doors. She couldn't say she felt uneasy here, or unwelcome, but there was a strangeness to the atmosphere that perhaps came less from the historic fabric of the house than from the peculiar mood of her hostess. However, they'd only met once before, so perhaps Stacey was always like this – or, of course, it could be her own presence that was causing the weird sense of dislocation.

'You have a beautiful home,' she said, as Stacey waved her to one of the large, comfy sofas in the drawing room. 'Can I guess early eighteenth century?'

'That's right,' Stacey said. 'But it's only been in my husband's family for three generations,' she said, sitting down too. 'Before that it was something of a ruin. It used to belong to one of the wealthy mine owners of the region, when it was first built.'

'Tin, I presume,' Katherine said.

Stacey nodded, and took a generous pull on the joint. 'When were you thinking of going to see Rachel Hendon?' she asked, after a while.

Katherine glanced at her watch. 'Not until it gets dark,' she answered. Then watching Stacey's strange show of indifference, as she hooked her legs over the arm of the chair and smoked her pot, she said, 'Can I assume you mentioned nothing to her about me coming?'

Stacey blew a smoke ring and watched it float into the air. 'You can,' she confirmed.

Katherine wondered if she needed to explain the

request, but since Stacey wasn't asking, there seemed no reason to offer an answer. 'Are you here alone?' she asked, looking around. 'Your husband's an art dealer, is that right? Is he travelling?'

Stacey nodded. Her eyes had narrowed slightly, and beneath her cool exterior her heart rate was increasing. 'Of course, you didn't meet him that night, did you?' she said, getting to her feet. 'He wasn't at the party.'

'All I recall from that evening was the extremely stimulating conversation between us two,' Katherine said, smiling, and wondering if she'd imagined the rapport now.

Stacey smiled too, then lifted a photograph from the piano and carried it back to Katherine. 'This is my husband,' she said, handing it over. 'I think you may have met him.'

Katherine took it, still smiling, then as her eyes registered the face looking back at her, the blood started a thunderous rush through her head. She glanced up at Stacey, to see how closely she was watching her, then looked back at the picture. Through the shock, and panic, she was trying to gauge what was really going on, for there could be no coincidence here – this man was too close to Franz, and she was too close to Rachel Hendon now for it to be anything other than a set-up. So she'd walked into a trap, and the fact that she only had herself to blame, for failing to check out who the hell Stacey Greene was married to, was not going to get her out of it.

'You have met, haven't you?' Stacey prompted.

'Of course,' Katherine answered. She handed the photograph back and got to her feet. Though her face was ashen, her voice was steady as she said, 'Is he here?'

'No. He's travelling,' Stacey reminded her.

Katherine's eyes were harsh, yet confused. 'Why did you show me the picture?' she said. 'There was a reason, so please tell me why.'

'I want you to tell me what you know about him,' Stacey said.

'If he's your husband, how could I know more than you?' Katherine countered.

'I just think you do,' Stacey said. 'And let's call it my price for helping you.'

Though Katherine's eyes were still hostile and cautious, she was beginning to recover now, and could see that Stacey Greene might just have an agenda all her own here. Indeed, it was entirely possible, for why demand information about her husband, if she already had it? And since there were few in a better position to give it, there was no doubt she'd come to the right place. The question now was, how much did Stacey Greene already know, and how much was she, Katherine, prepared to tell?

Giving her a helpful lead-in, Stacey said, 'I know he's sold paintings to Franz Koehler, and that he occasionally acts as pilot-chauffer to Franz, so we could start there. Or,' she continued, 'we could discuss the blonde woman, early forties, who they're looking for in connection with the shooting of Franz Koehler.' She smiled. 'What I'd rather discuss though, is how my husband fits into the picture of Tim Hendon's murder.'

At last Katherine was managing to get something of a handle on this, and drawing a mental line down her centre to steady herself, she sat back down. 'There's probably quite a lot I can tell you about your husband,' she began, 'but as to how he was involved in Tim Hendon's murder, I'm afraid I can't help.'

'But you were there,' Stacey reminded her.

'And he wasn't, that much I do know,' Katherine responded. 'But there are other ways to play a part in a murder without actually being at the scene.'

Despite the display of nonchalance, Stacey was becoming extremely tense now, and vaguely disappointed too. 'So tell me what you do know,' she said.

Katherine watched her return to her chair and fold one jodhpured leg over the other. She was still holding the photograph, balancing it between her fingers, but her eyes were fixed on Katherine.

'What I know,' Katherine said, 'is that your husband's association with Franz began about three years ago, with a Modigliani nude. There were other paintings after the Modigliani, valuable, but not to compare with the nude, all brokered by your husband, to hang in one or more of Franz's homes. I'm not sure exactly when Franz began to use Chris's remarkable skills as a broker, and shipper, in other more . . . confidential areas of his business, but certainly it was happening within a year of them first meeting.'

Stacey's eyebrows went up, for she'd never quite seen Chris as a broker or shipper, though she had to concede it was, in its baldest terms, what he did.

'It turned out later,' Katherine said, 'that for the entire time Chris had worked exclusively as Franz's art dealer, he'd been feeding whatever information he could find out about Franz to a couple of British intelligence agents who were part of an investigation into certain Phraxos business practices, which were thought to relate to a highly confidential project.'

Stacey frowned.

'It's a project intended to fuel civil and military unrest in various African nations in order to step up the need for arms on the one hand, and military action, or intervention by the West, on the other. What you might call a win-win if you're a part of Phraxos.'

Stacey's heartbeat seemed to slow.

'I honestly believe,' Katherine continued, 'that your husband had no idea, when he was first approached by these agents, just how much was going to be expected of him. Obviously he'd have known that Phraxos is a defence-focused investment group, because that's no secret, but it's doubtful he expected to get involved in that side of Franz's life. Needless to say, that's all the agents were interested in, so whether it was anger, or revenge, or just plain opportunism, that motivated Chris to tell Franz exactly who he was and how he'd been double-crossing him, I've no idea, all I know is that Franz took him totally under his wing after that, and ever since they've worked an extremely complex but efficient system of feeding information to the interested parties that keeps them at just the right distance for business to carry on as normal.'

Though shocked, Stacey was quietly thrilled by this unexpected and extraordinary twist to her husband's mystique, which under any other circumstances would be making her passion burn hotter than ever. However, right now, it was more welcome for other reasons entirely. 'So what exactly does he do now?' she said.

'These days mainly he ships,' Katherine answered.

'Arms?'

'Cash. He's part of a select group that organizes the transportation of enormous sums of money around the world, to avoid the all-incriminating paper trail.'

Stacey's eyes moved to the middle distance, then after taking a long, thoughtful draw on her cigarette, she said, 'So essentially, what you're saying is, he's a traitor to his country.'

Katherine cocked an eyebrow. 'That would be one way of putting it,' she said.

Stacey absorbed the answer as though swallowing an elixir. 'Is there any more?' she said.

'If you want there to be,' Katherine replied.

Stacey looked down at Chris's photograph. Did she? 'No,' she said. 'I think I've heard enough.' Her eyes came up to Katherine's. 'Thank you,' she said earnestly.

Katherine's expression was sceptical. 'I doubt it's what you wanted to hear about your own husband,' she responded.

Stacey only smiled, because actually, she couldn't have wanted to hear it more.

Chapter 29

Rachel was sitting at the dining table, staring down at a mind-numbing printout of defence budgets and expenditure for the past three years. Laurie was at the table too, assessing which British arms manufacturers had links with Phraxos, while Beanie dozed in a chair over by the fire with Romie at her feet. Everything was still and quiet, a warm, tranquil haven secure from the rain hammering down outside, and the more distant roar of the tide raging up into the cove.

Beanie suddenly snorted herself awake. Rachel glanced at Laurie, they exchanged a smile, then went back to their work as Beanie picked up her knitting. A few minutes later they looked up again as the hoot of an owl bleated down through the chimney.

'No, please don't tell us what that means,' Rachel protested, before Beanie could speak, 'because I just know it's not going to be good.'

Clucking softly to herself Beanie carried on knitting, while Laurie returned to her computer and a couple of minutes later Rachel got up to go and sit in the window seat behind Beanie's chair.

'God, it's so gloomy out there,' she said, rubbing a circle in one of the steamed up panes and peering through the driving rain towards the cove. 'It could almost be night already.'

Laurie glanced at her computer clock. 'The news is about to start,' she said. 'Shall we watch?'

Rachel nodded, but made no move to get up. They'd been on line most of the day, so it was unlikely anything had developed that they didn't already know about. So she stayed where she was, only half listening to the headlines as they came up, and experiencing no surprise when Franz Koehler's murder and Elliot's disappearance failed to get a first mention, for they'd lost top billing yesterday to other breaking news. However, that didn't mean one of the stories, or even both, wouldn't feature somewhere later in the bulletin, and she knew Laurie was eager to hear anything at all about Elliot, even if she'd heard it a dozen times before.

Continuing to gaze out at the dark, angry sky, Rachel suddenly felt a twinge of alarm as she realized she hadn't heard from Anna all day. She knew the whole family was going to spend the weekend with friends in Dorset, but it was unlike Anna not to call at all. Then a baleful feeling entered her heart as she thought of how easily the car could go off the road in this sort of weather . . . But no, she wasn't going to torment herself like that. She'd just wait till the news was over, then try Anna's mobile to make sure everything was all right. And at least she knew that for once poor

653

Anna wasn't having to worry about Stacey Greene, because Stacey was apparently still here in Cornwall.

Trying to settle a little more comfortably on the bench seat, she pushed a cushion behind her back while wondering what Stacey was doing now, all alone in that big house up there on the thinly wooded stretch of the moor. A part of her was almost tempted to go over there to reassure her that there really was nothing between her and Chris, but it would probably end up making matters worse. Besides, could she really, in all good conscience, face the wife of a man she had so many conflicting emotions about, and swear there was absolutely nothing going on, when her thoughts, if not her actions, made her every bit as guilty as Stacey feared?

Closing her eyes, she ran a hand absently over the baby as it stirred, and tried to disentangle herself from the confusion she felt about him and his life. She'd spent too many hours this past week going over and over everything they'd talked about, not just that day on the clifftop, but in the Caribbean, and here at the cottage, and she was still no closer to knowing whether she should trust him or not. She wondered where he was now and what he might be doing. He hadn't called at all since he left, which had caused her far more concern than it should, not only about his honesty and integrity, but about his safety and what thoughts he might be having about her.

Sighing restlessly, she returned her gaze to the thickening fog of rain. It was still only just after five o'clock, far too early to be completely dark, but the gloom was hanging there like a malevolent shadow. Then becoming aware of the story that was being read on the news she tuned in to listen to how the search was continuing for Katherine Sumner, who police wanted to interview in connection with the murders of Franz Koehler and Tim Hendon. At the mention of her husband's name a surge of intense longing rose up in her, as she wished to the very depths of her soul that they could turn the clock back. She still missed him so much, and never stopped wanting him, even when she was hating him. He'd turned her life inside out, left it shattered and empty, then filled it with so much doubt that it was hard to imagine ever being able to trust anyone again. Yet still she couldn't help loving him.

'Max must be having a field day over there,' Laurie commented, switching off the TV as the commercials came on.

'Sorry?' Rachel said, turning round.

'Max,' Laurie repeated. 'He's in Dubai, where they've seized all that cash. Apparently they made some arrests today.'

Rachel's eyes drifted to the middle distance, not because she had no interest in the story, but because she was so tense and on edge that she was actually willing the thunder to explode overhead if only to break the awful expectancy in the atmosphere, and prove that *it* was the only storm brewing.

Anna's car was parked in tight to the hedge, lights off and wipers still. The road was narrow and twisted, but she was tucked into the overhung niche of a passing space, so other vehicles could get by, possibly without even seeing her. From where she was she could see the open gates that marked the entrance to Stacey's drive, but the house itself wasn't visible from here, so it was impossible to tell if anyone was home. Certainly no one was answering the phone because she'd tried, several times, on the way here. She'd called Robert several times too, to give him a progress report of her journey in the bad weather, and a few minutes ago she'd told him she'd arrived safely at Rachel's, and would be back at their friends' house in Dorset around lunchtime tomorrow. Now she only had to call Rachel to let her know she was coming, which she should have done hours ago, but with so much else on her mind, she'd forgotten.

She shuddered with nerves as she thought of what she had to get through before she could go to Rachel's, but if luck was on her side, it shouldn't take long. It was probably naive to think that a face-to-face encounter would intimidate Stacey into giving her the poems back, but she was intending to try it. And if it didn't work, she was even prepared to fight Stacey for them. What a mercy it would be to find that Chris had arrived home unexpectedly, so that he could add his weight to her side, but since she knew that wasn't very likely, she'd decided that the next best scenario was to find no one at home at all, so that she could creep in, search out the poems and steal them back without anyone even knowing she'd been there.

Her hands tensed on the wheel as the draught of another car speeding by rocked her own. Whoever it was must be a lunatic to drive like that on a night like this, but they were gone now, hurtling off towards Helston, and she could only hope for their sake that they made it in one piece.

She looked at the gates again. Any minute now she would find the nerve to restart the engine and begin the journey along the drive to the house. She couldn't think why she was so afraid, when it was only another woman she was facing and she had every right to be doing this.

Her hand was on the ignition key now, her foot on the clutch. Then noticing a set of headlights coming down the drive towards her, she froze. *Please God let it be Stacey going out,* she prayed fervently. *Please give me the chance to get in there without having to face her.* There was so much rain on the windscreen that it was impossible to make out who was at the wheel of the other car as it turned in front of her and started towards Roon Moor, but as the tail lights vanished round a bend, she was daring to hope that God might actually be on her side. She'd just give it another few minutes, then she'd make herself go in.

Stacey was in her studio, sliding the printouts on Tim Hendon into a drawer with Robert Maxton's poems. She liked the idea of the two husbands being shut up there together like that, it felt symbolic of the power she had over their wives, though of course Tim Hendon needed no symbol of being shut in a drawer, when he already had the reality of a grave. As for Rachel Hendon's power over her . . . She paused a moment, allowing herself to see Chris's hands on that pregnant belly again, the hands that had now, in her imagination, moved up to the big, milky breasts, stroking and teasing them, while Rachel Hendon ran her fingers through his tousled dark hair and they laughed softly together . . . She slammed the drawer closed, and turned sharply away from the desk. Anger was good, it helped keep her focused.

The room was in semi-darkness as she wove a path through the easels, paints and canvases that had hardly been touched. Every now and again jagged forks of lightning flashed the place alight, showing how benign everything was when the shadows were lifted. Catching her foot on something, she stooped to pick up a chiffon scarf that she sometimes used to tie back her hair. Draping it over a smock that was hanging near the door, she clicked off the lamp on the table beside it, then walked on along the hall towards the arch that connected the studio to the first floor landing of the house. On reaching her bedroom she was tempted to light another joint, but she'd already had two today; any more and she'd be at risk of losing control.

Since her talk with Katherine earlier she'd more or less avoided her, keeping to her studio or bedroom as she ran through the various options that were now open to her. Of course if Katherine were lying about meaning Rachel Hendon no harm, then all decisions would be taken for her, and the only problem she'd face then was explaining to Chris why she'd allowed Katherine to come here. But that was already worked out, and now, thanks to the extra information Katherine had given her, Chris was hardly in a position to make too much of a fuss about anything.

A growl of thunder rumbled through the rafters, but she barely heard it as going into her dressing room she began removing her clothes. Her face was blotched and pale, but her eyes were vivid and staring hard as she thought of how she needed to dress. Going to her wardrobe she pulled out one of the long white shifts she frequently wore and slipped it over her head. If she needed to go out in the storm, she didn't want it to look as though she'd prepared for it, so casual evening attire was called for now – boots and a raincoat would raise no eyebrows later, would in fact prove that she'd rushed out in a panic. As she walked back into the bedroom she could feel herself being assailed by all the painful emotions that made her feel so vulnerable and helpless and afraid of what to do. But she'd managed to fight them off earlier, and she would again, for she only had to think of a future without Chris, of being alone while he made a life with Rachel Hendon, and the anger would return to drive her. Then she'd stop caring which scene she had to play out, and remember that either one would lead to the right denouement – though if pressed, she had to confess that she'd prefer it if no one actually did get killed, at least not by her hand. However, once again, much depended on Katherine, and as she'd heard her go out a while ago, she guessed now would be a good time to go to her room to find out if she'd taken the gun.

'All right,' Beanie sighed, rolling up her knitting, 'time I went to put some dinner on. Though the way these lights keep flickering, I don't know about lamb chops, we could be in for a salad.'

'I'll get you the torch,' Rachel said, unplugging her computer. 'I think it's upstairs, on the bookshelf under the attic hatch.'

'I'll go,' Laurie said, standing up and stretching. 'I need a warmer sweater.'

'You should find some candles up there too,' Rachel told her, as she opened the stairwell door. 'In a box under my bed. Better bring them down, just in case.'

As Rachel stepped up into the kitchen and unhooked Beanie's raincoat from the alcove, she looked around curiously, wondering why the storm seemed so much louder up here. It unnerved her slightly, but then noticing that one of the windows over the sink wasn't quite shut, she went to tighten the catch, remembering that it had been faulty for a while.

'So what time do you want us to come round?' she said, helping Beanie into her coat.

'In about an hour,' Beanie answered, patting her pocket. Pulling out a small torch she said, 'Here, this'll do us. Forgot I had it.' She grimaced as the overhead lights shuddered and dimmed again. 'OK, Romes, ready?' she said, starting to open the door. 'Let's make a run for it, cabbage.'

As they disappeared into the night, Rachel quickly closed the door behind them, then remained where she was, trying to think why this storm should be unsettling her so much. It wasn't as if it was the worst she'd experienced, for it was nowhere near as terrifying as the big seas that crashed up over the headland in winter, and flooded the whole village. Yet there was something almost wilfully portentous about this one; it even seemed to be making the baby fidgety, for it had hardly stopped moving all day.

Deciding to go and put something soothing on the CD, she chose Satie's piano solos and as she pushed the button to start, was hoping that the lightning wouldn't send it into meltdown. Hearing the first, tenderly romantic bars of 'Je te veux', she quickly turned it off again, unwilling to deal with the memories of Paris that it instantly evoked.

'It might be a good idea to set these up ready,' Laurie said, holding up the candles, as she came back down the stairs. 'Where're the matches?'

'Here,' Rachel said, taking them off the mantelpiece. Then she promptly dropped them as the phone startled her. 'God, I'm a nervous wreck,' she grumbled, going to answer it as Laurie picked up the matches. 'Hello?' she said into the receiver.

'Rachel. It's me,' Anna cried. 'Surprise! I've dumped Robert and the kids in Dorset, and I'm on my way to spend a night with my sister.'

Rachel's face lit up. 'That's fantastic,' she said. 'Where are you now?'

'Not far. The weather's terrible, but I should be there soon.'

'Great. I'll tell Beanie we'll be one more for dinner. Laurie's here, so you'll have to have the small bedroom.'

'No problem. See you in about half an hour.'

Ringing off, Rachel was about to start dialling Beanie when the back door suddenly flew open. Despite the sudden jolt to her heart, she realized it must be Beanie, back for something she'd forgotten. 'I was just ringing you,' she called out. 'Anna's on her way.'

When there was no reply Laurie turned to look over her shoulder, a lit match still burning in her fingers. Shaking it out as she heard the door close, she was about to go and investigate when someone in a yellow hooded raincoat appeared in the arch. Laurie's eyes dilated with shock as the woman lowered her hood, and she realized who she was looking at. 'Oh my God,' she murmured.

Behind her, Rachel's face had turned completely white. For a moment she could neither speak nor move, then so much emotion rushed through the barrier of shock that she became light-headed, almost faint. A thousand thoughts were speeding through her mind, but most dominant of all was the fact that it was because of this woman that Tim was no longer alive. Hatred and anger welled up so forcefully that she was almost blinded by an urge to lash out, then she was remembering the warnings from Franz Koehler, and Chris . . .

'Please, don't be afraid,' Katherine said, seeming to read her expression. 'I'm sorry to barge in like this. I was afraid you wouldn't see me . . . I just want to talk. I swear, I'm not here to hurt you.'

Laurie was watching her closely. 'Why should she think you'd want to hurt her?' she challenged, unable for the moment to detect anything more menacing than the voluminous coat – which could, in fact, be hiding anything. 'I'd have thought it was you who had more to fear.'

Katherine's eyes moved from Rachel to Laurie. 'I do,' she said simply. Then turning back to Rachel she said, 'I didn't know you were pregnant. No one told me . . .' She stopped, briefly seeming to lose her composure. Then in a level tone, she said, 'It's hard to find the right words to tell you how sorry I am. It'll never make up for what's happened, I know that, but –'

'Stop!' Rachel cried, putting a hand to her head. 'Just stop. I don't want to hear how sorry you are, I don't even care how sorry you are, all I want to know is *why*? Why did you do it? What did you get him involved in?' Tears were suddenly starting from her eyes, as emotion choked off her words.

Laurie moved to her side and put a steadying hand on her shoulder.

'It's OK, I'm fine,' Rachel said pulling herself together. But her legs were buckling and she sank into the armchair behind her.

Katherine was still watching her, seeming to understand her confusion, and that she needed some time to adjust, so she said no more until Rachel finally looked up at her again. 'I don't know how much you've managed to piece together for yourself,' she said, 'but I'm sure you know about Phraxos, and Franz Koehler . . .'

'What I don't know is why Tim was murdered,' Rachel said through her teeth. 'Or how you've got the gall to come here now.'

'I'd have come before,' Katherine said. 'I wanted to, but I'd have put your life in danger if Franz thought, even for a minute, that I'd told you what he was doing and who was involved. '

'Is that why Tim was murdered?' Rachel broke in. 'Because you told him your odious secrets?'

Katherine shook her head. 'No,' she answered bleakly. 'That's not why it happened.'

Rachel's heart sank, as the brief glimmer of hope

that he hadn't been any more involved than that was extinguished. She wished, desperately, that this didn't have to go any further, that she could live the rest of her life without ever knowing what he'd done, but looking at Katherine again, she said, in a voice that was as cold as she could make it, 'You'd better come in.'

Katherine glanced at Laurie as she stepped down into the sitting room. No one had invited her to take off her coat, which had left a small puddle on the kitchen floor, so she kept it on, and went to perch on the edge of a dining chair, while Laurie sat on the arm of Rachel's chair.

'You understand, don't you,' Rachel said, 'that whatever you tell me now will go straight to the police. I don't intend to get involved in any of your secrets. '

'It's why I'm here,' Katherine assured her. 'I know you'll do the right thing, and I know what it'll mean for me. But I've come to terms with it. I just want to make sure that the truth is delivered into the right hands, before I face the consequences of what I've done.' She looked at Laurie. 'I'm sorry, we've never met. Obviously you know who I am . . .'

'Laurie's a friend,' Rachel said, 'and a reporter who's been helping me piece this together. She knows as much as I do. There are no secrets.'

Katherine's eyes widened a little. 'Laurie Forbes? The Ashby case?' she said.

Laurie nodded.

Katherine murmured quietly under her breath, and gave an incredulous shake of her head. 'Well at least you managed to get a few of the infamous billionaire syndicate behind bars,' she said. 'Marcus Gatling, Abe Kleinstein . . . There were a lot, as I recall, but no one ever managed to make the connection to Franz. He's just too smart. He knows how to take advantage of every complex business stratagem . . .'

'Just tell me about Tim,' Rachel cut in.

Katherine swallowed, but though her face was pale, and showed the strain she was under, her eyes remained steady as she said, 'I didn't kill him. I just need you to know that I didn't kill him.' She cast a quick glance at Laurie, then to Rachel she said, 'I believe it was someone by the name of Gustave Basim who did it. I was there when it happened, but I didn't actually see . . .' She took a breath. 'It was a mistake. It was me he was supposed to kill, not Tim.'

Rachel went very still, then abruptly she sat forward. Her mind was refusing to accept what she'd just heard: it was unthinkable. It couldn't be true, because if it were then there was no justice, no reason, no anything that made sense any more. 'Are you telling me,' she said, her voice shaking with horror, 'that his only crime was fucking *you*! That if he hadn't been there, this would never have happened?'

'I had no idea . . .' Katherine said.

'I don't believe this!' Rachel cried, clasping her hands to her head. 'I just can't make myself accept that he's lost his life for something *you* did. This hell I've been putting myself through, this terror of what we were going to turn up, and now you tell me that it's *you* who should be dead. *So why the hell aren't you?*'

665

Laurie's hand was on her back, trying to soothe her, but she started shouting again.

'But that's not the whole truth, is it?' she spat. 'It can't be, because there's the four million dollars that turned up in a Swiss bank account. So what was that about? How did he get it, if he was so innocent and you so guilty! *I thought you were here to tell me the truth*,' she screamed, *'and you're just fucking with my mind!'*

'No, I swear that's not true,' Katherine cried, earnestly. 'I can explain everything. If you'll just hear me out . . .'

Laurie's hand tightened on Rachel's shoulder, as though lending her strength, while Rachel, knowing she had to pull herself together, took several breaths in an effort to calm down. It was just so hard trying to deal with this rationally when she was so emotionally, and even physically, involved, for it was Tim's baby that was kicking inside her, and Tim's house they were all sitting in now, while he never would again. She felt so aware of his photograph on the table next to the lamp, and all at once she wanted to sob and scream, and beg him with all her heart to come back and turn this around so that none of it had happened. He couldn't have died as a mistake. He just couldn't.

But in the end her eyes only fell away, as a dull, chilling numbness crept over her heart. He was dead. For whatever reason, he would never be coming back, and now all she could do, for herself and the baby, was listen to why he'd been taken from them.

Katherine's eyes were troubled as she watched her, seeming to understand how hard this must be for her, but there was nothing she could do to make it easier. It had all happened the way it had, and now all she could offer was the truth.

'The four million dollars,' she said. 'I don't even know if Tim knew it existed, because it had only been there for a few days by the time he was killed. Franz, or someone from Phraxos, had set up the account as an incentive to Tim to join the Group. No one had actually got to the point yet of inviting him in – he and Franz had only met once, and it wasn't really a success, but first meetings often weren't. In Tim's case it was different, because I'd already told him all about the secret Phraxos project to create a demand for arms and military action. Naturally Franz wasn't aware I'd told him, he just thought Tim was going to need some of the normal persuasion, so he was starting to put the irresistibles in place. And if, in the end, Tim decided not to play ball and threatened to expose anything about the project, or the incentive, Franz and his lawyers had already drawn up paperwork to show that Tim had a shareholding in Phraxos, and that the four million dollars was an accumulation of profits, bonuses and dividends. It was normal practice to have all this prepared, in case a subject proved difficult, because the fact that the money actually existed, combined with the documents . . . Well, it would make it very hard for Tim to prove he *wasn't* involved in the Group, and even if he succeeded, the scandal alone would ruin him politically.'

Laurie was stupefied. 'So whichever way he turned, he'd have no choice?' she said.

Katherine looked at her. 'That's generally the

way it's set up,' she answered. 'But it's rarely needed. People are very easily seduced by such large sums of money.'

'And you act as the bait to lure them in?' Rachel said.

Katherine's eyes moved back to her. 'When I talked to Tim about Franz Koehler and Phraxos,' she said, 'it was to ask for his help in exposing what was really going on. Believe me, by then I was as guilty as everyone else, I'd conspired and profited and helped set up numerous senators or Pentagon insiders. I had my reasons for doing it, but then . . . September 11th was like, well like some kind of an epiphany for me . . . I started to see how blind and insanely dangerous I had become. I had a lot of anger left over from my childhood, a resentment towards my own Government. Basically, I was trying to punish the world for what had been done to me and my family.' Her eyes dropped. 'But then I was made to realize that it had gone too far. I was making the wrong people pay, so somehow I needed to make it stop. It was already too late in many ways, but if I left America I could at least lessen the chance of making it any worse. Franz couldn't keep using me for introductions the way I'd encouraged him to in the past.' She looked at Rachel again. 'I'd already made plans to come to Europe, I think you knew that when you invited me to run Tim's campaign. Franz immediately saw it as a golden opportunity to start tying the Brits into the Phraxos Special Project too. Of course a lot of British arms manufacturers have links to Phraxos already, it's too big an industry investor for them not to, but I don't think any of them are actively engaged in the project to create demand for their own product. Certainly there's no top-level government involvement, which was why Franz was keen to reel Tim in. Believe me, Franz was unshakeable in his belief that every man has his price, and though he might be right, I'm not convinced that Tim would ever have gone for it, had he been given the chance. But he never was, because instead of making the approach Franz wanted, I went to Tim and asked for his help in getting me out of it.' Her eyes were fully on Rachel's now as she said, 'Tim was the first politician I'd ever worked for that I felt comfortable about trusting, and I'd wanted out of Phraxos for a very long time. The trouble was I knew too much. Franz was never going to let me go, and there were so many powerful people involved in the US that I didn't dare to trust anyone there.'

'What about the media?' Laurie said. 'Didn't you think of going to them?'

'Of course, but Patrick Landen, an ex-senator . . .'

'We know who he is,' Laurie said.

'Then you know we had an affair, and you know how the media treats women who have affairs with politicians. They're ridiculed and verbally abused in a way that totally shoots any credibility they might have. And that's the spin it would have got, I know that, because I know the men I'd have been going up against, and they'd have made sure it did.' She turned back to Rachel. 'To me, Tim and his integrity seemed to offer a way out. I knew it was a risk, that I could be wrong about him and find that he too would be willing to be seduced by the incredible sums of money, but I've got to tell you that not once did he ever show an interest in becoming involved. His only concern was to help me get out of it, then do whatever it took to expose, or bring down, the entire operation. He started by agreeing to meet with Franz, and one of his senior field associates, a man by the name of Patrice Bombola. They were to discuss the opportunities, the benefits – political and financial – the various manufacturers Franz wanted an introduction to, the kind of government documentation that would be required to set the specialized arms shipments on their way, and so on. Basically, Tim wanted to hear it all for himself, which he did, then he ended the meeting by saying he'd go away and think about it. It was the answer he'd already told me he'd give, and Franz wouldn't have expected any more, because these things don't happen overnight. But he was already making his contingency plans, with the four million bucks, while Tim and I, in total secrecy, were putting together as much as we could for Tim to take to the Prime Minister, who Tim was utterly convinced we could trust. In the end, he never got that far, but I still have all the documents . . .' Her eyes were burning sincerity into Rachel's. 'You're the only person I know who has direct access to the PM, and who I can trust to make sure the documents get there.'

Rachel stared back at her, assimilating all she'd heard, and feeling the utter frustration and tragedy of the fact that Tim clearly hadn't been informed that an intelligence unit was already looking into the Phraxos Group's covert operations. The PM must have known, though, which would be why he had distanced himself after Tim's death, afraid that his friend, and trusted colleague, was going to turn out to be in bed with the Group. Indeed, the very fact that Tim had hired someone so close to the Group's chairman to run his campaign had probably already put him under close observation, if not outright investigation.

'So why did Franz order you killed?' Laurie said. 'Did he know about these documents?'

'Not exactly, but I know he'd sensed for a long time that I wasn't with him any more. And if you're not with Franz . . .' She shook her head. 'Knowing him as I did, he'd have found the idea of having me killed at a time when I'd become so close to the British Establishment an extremely pleasurable experience. He despises the British, and would relish nothing more than to see them squirm – which would have happened if someone so close to a senior Cabinet member was murdered. So I think he'd hoped to make Basim's mission look like some kind of burglary, or just one of those mysteries that never gets solved. I can only begin to imagine what a shock it must have been when he found out that Basim had managed to make such a monumental mistake.'

Hardly able to believe the sheer cruelty of a fate that had chosen its victim so randomly, so utterly pitilessly, or the blinding arrogance of a man who had set it all in motion, Rachel could only feel glad that he had lost his own life now, even though it seemed a very small price to pay for the one he had taken away. 'So the phone calls, during the build-up to the election?' she said. 'The accented voice, was that Franz Koehler?'

671

'Sometimes. And sometimes it was Xavier, an old friend of my father's. He's been helping me. I wouldn't be alive now, if it weren't for him.'

'We've been trying to track him down,' Laurie confessed.

'You wouldn't be able to. Xavier's a name only I use. No one else knows him as that. But please stop looking for him. He's a good man, and if you should happen to find him you'll only put him in danger, not so much from this, but from his own government.'

Rachel and Laurie looked at each other, clearly both thinking the same thoughts: that if Xavier Lachère was Iranian, and a one-time supporter of the Shah or Amir Hoveyda, then that wasn't so hard to believe.

'What about the four million dollars?' Rachel said, looking at Katherine again. 'Was it him who called my lawyer about it?'

Katherine frowned. 'No,' she said. 'That would more likely have been Franz. He'd have wanted it out of there before I could tell you, or anyone else, how it had got there.'

'And the tip-off about Gustave Basim?' Laurie said.

'That was me. I knew about Basim because Franz had used him before. It was pure chance that I happened to catch the story in a local paper in France, otherwise I'd never have known he was dead. In fact, I had no idea if it was the right man, but when I saw the name, and the manner of his death . . . The coincidence was enough to make me pick up the phone.'

'So how can you be so certain,' Rachel said, 'that

it was you he should have killed, when obviously Tim posed a threat too, knowing what he did?'

Katherine's eyes were unblinkingly earnest as she said, 'First of all, they didn't know that Tim knew as much as he did, and secondly, there was absolutely no way anyone could have known that he was going to be at my apartment that morning. Even we didn't know until it happened, and the killer was already there, though we didn't know that when we went in. Besides, I can't believe even Franz would order the killing of someone in such a high position as Tim. It would be insane, the risk too great, because the investigation, the publicity, would all be much too intense, and there were already too many roads that could lead to Franz.' She shrugged. 'You only have to look at how things have unfolded to see how much focus Tim's death has put on Phraxos, and believe me they won't be enjoying it, particularly now the share price has started to suffer.'

Laurie was regarding her closely. 'It's also cost Franz Koehler his life,' she said bluntly.

Katherine didn't even flinch. 'I had to do it,' she said, 'or he'd have killed me, and then it would just have gone on and on, because there would have been no one to stop him. He's too well connected, too protected to be reached, and even if anyone could, he's played the system so brilliantly that there would never be any question of bringing him down. There are too many others who stand to fall with him, so they just won't let it happen.'

'So how did you manage to do it?'

'He was a consummate gambler,' she answered, 'a game-player, a puppet-master, a stager of events, a manipulator. He believed himself indestructible, so when I threw him a challenge to meet me alone, in typical Franz style he treated it like some kind of contest, a kind of Russian roulette. As it turned out, I held the gun, and he . . . didn't.'

Rachel's eyes went down as the scene played itself out all too clearly in her head, while she was painfully aware that Tim's death was an event she still couldn't picture, nor was she entirely sure she ever wanted to. But there was nothing to be gained from shying away any longer, so steeling herself, she said, 'I'd like to hear the details of how my husband died.'

Though Katherine's cheeks paled slightly, as she glanced down at her hands, she merely said, 'Yes, of course.' Then lifting her head she warned, as gently as she could, 'A lot of this isn't going to be easy for you to hear . . .'

'Don't patronize me, just tell me.'

Katherine paused, then after pushing a stray strand of wet hair from her face, she said, 'Well, I guess I should start with when we got back to my apartment, after the celebrations . . . We had no idea, either of us, that anyone else was there. I guess we were too . . . wrapped up in the euphoria of it all, and we'd had a lot to drink. We went straight through to the bedroom, and well, it wasn't until I got up, later, to go to the bathroom . . .' She paused again, and took a breath. 'I didn't turn on any lights,' she said. 'Tim was sleeping . . . Or I think he was. He didn't move when I got up, so I crept into the bathroom so's not to wake him. But I was thinking that I'd have to soon, because he'd have to go home. Then I heard a noise in the bedroom. I guess I assumed it was him, getting up, but then there was this kind of fast whooshing sound, and . . .' She swallowed. 'I knew right away what it was. I guess it must have been instinct, because I'd sure never heard it before, except in movies, but I knew it was the sound of a gun with a silencer attached. I was so darned terrified I didn't dare move. I just stood there in the darkness listening, convinced someone was going to burst in at any second. But no one did. Then I heard someone coming out of the bedroom, going down the hall. After the front door closed everything just stayed silent.

'I don't know how much longer I stood there, it might have been seconds, it might have been minutes, then when I felt sure no one was coming back I rushed into the bedroom, not daring to turn on the lights. Tim was lying face down on the bed. I could hardly see him, but there was blood on the pillow . . . I was calling his name, shaking him, like it might bring him round. I tried his pulse, I even attempted CPR, but it was already . . .' She swallowed hard, as though forcing back tears. 'Please understand, I was in a state of shock, I hardly knew what I was doing I was so afraid . . . I remember I even ran back to the bathroom to throw up. I guess some kind of survival instinct kicked in, because I suddenly realized I had to get out of there. The killer had obviously assumed it was me in the bed, and Tim who'd gone to the bathroom. And if Tim had heard anyone coming in the room, he'd probably thought it was me coming back.

'All this was rushing through my head so much, it's hard to remember now . . . But mainly I was just thinking that I had to get away. Time had run out. Franz had sent someone to kill me. I'd been living in terror of it for months, which was why Xavier had helped me to prepare an escape. I had false documents, open-dated airline tickets with half a dozen airlines, various safe-houses lined up from Morocco to Singapore, a laptop, pay-as-you-go cellphones and half a million dollars in cash. So I grabbed it all, used one of the cells to call Xavier, and then I ran. I didn't contact the police until I got to the airport, and was about to board a flight to Marrakesh. Then I called and told them to go to my apartment. Maybe I should have gone to them. It's all a lot easier and clearer in hindsight, but at the time I was so scared, and Franz's contacts reached into so many high places . . .' She looked at Rachel. 'Tim was so suspicious of the people in his own department, I know you know that, so maybe you'll understand how afraid I was to trust anyone. They're so powerful in that Ministry, I just had to get away, but I swear, if he hadn't already been dead, I'd have called the emergency services even before I left the apartment.' She glanced down at her hands, then back to Rachel. 'If it's any consolation,' she said, 'I believe the bullet killed him instantly. I don't think he knew anything about it.'

Rachel lifted a hand to her eyes, then pushed it back through her hair. It was suddenly so very hard not to cry that she didn't even attempt to speak. She just kept seeing him lying there, asleep and unknowing, in the bed of a woman that *she* had brought into their lives. Dear God, if she'd only known what she was doing, how malicious the fates were going to be . . . She'd berated and tormented herself so often for not staying at the celebrations that night, and for not telling him on the phone that he was going to be a father. He'd still be alive now if she had. She'd made so many mistakes, and none would ever be put right now. She could never tell him about the baby, and he would never be able to explain about Katherine. As the thoughts circled painfully, her hands covered the mound of her belly. To the very depths of her soul she wished she could hug the baby now, for she felt so in need of the contact with Tim, and so utterly wretched inside, that she almost couldn't bear it.

Finally she took a breath to ask the only question left that really mattered to her now, but at that moment the lights went out, leaving them in the soft glow of the candles that Laurie had already lit. Then Laurie was asking about Gustave Basim, the man who had been hired to kill, then had been killed himself, as much, Katherine thought, for bungling the job, as for having to be disposed of anyway. They went on to discuss where Katherine had been all this time, moving from one country to the next, always looking over her shoulder, expecting any minute to feel the shock of a bullet going into her back.

It was barely sinking in, though Rachel knew it was all important detail for Laurie, and she wanted her to have it, but she also wanted her to leave them alone for a while so she could ask Katherine, in private, that still lingering but vital question about Tim that she so desperately needed, yet dreaded, an answer to.

*

In the semi-light of Stacey's studio Anna was staring down at the computer printouts she'd found with Robert's poems. They all seemed to be about Tim, which was making her extremely uneasy. What had Stacey hoped to find in all these media reports? How was she intending to use them? And was there any reason why they should have been shut up in the same drawer as the poems? It felt strange to the point of sinister. She shivered, and looked around. Even the normality in here seemed oddly malign tonight, though the weather was oppressive, and her nerves were as sharp as wire. She wondered where Stacey had been going just now, in such a hurry that she hadn't even seemed to notice Anna's car about to turn into the drive. It had completely thrown Anna to see her, when she'd assumed she was in the car that had left earlier; so much so, that Anna had very nearly just driven on and gone straight to Rachel's. But in the end she'd sped up the drive, parked round by the side of the garages, and finding the door to the back stairs unlocked, she'd run straight up here to the studio.

Now, unable to decide whether to take the printouts with her as well, she was still hovering in front of the desk when the sound of a car speeding up the drive sent a chill of panic right through her. She looked at the door, wondering if she should just make a dash for it, but the skid of tyres coming to a halt, and the heavy tread of footsteps running into the house, threw her into even greater confusion. Then the sound of Chris's voice, thundering up through the stairwell, calling his wife's name, almost made her cower.

Knowing that the light made it certain he would come here, she glanced frantically around for somewhere to hide. With the terrifying tread of his footsteps storming along the hallway outside, she dived under the desk and pulled the chair in front of her.

'Stacey!' he raged, throwing open the door.

Anna was trembling, and so afraid it could have been her his fury was focused on. She flinched as an easel crashed to the ground, and drew herself in tighter. Then to her unutterable relief, he left.

Not until she heard the car engine starting up again did she dare to creep out of her hiding place. Frantic now to get out of there, she ran straight to the door, closed it quickly behind her, and dashed down the stone steps to the car. It was still raining heavily, and the wind was as wild as Hallowe'en demons, but all she was thinking about now was getting to Rachel's, with the poems, as fast as she could.

Throwing the car into reverse, she backed round in a semicircle, then lurched off down the drive at a reckless speed, not even thinking to look back at the house. But even if she had, she wouldn't have been concerned about leaving the lights on, not when Chris had come back in such a rage that he probably wouldn't remember how they'd been anyway. But it wasn't just the lights that were a problem, it was the pale blue chiffon scarf that had floated in the draught she'd created closing the door, down on to a hot light bulb beneath.

Chris was at the wheel of Nick's Toyota Cruiser, his eyes blazing, his knuckles white from the grip.

Nick was next to him, having driven to the airfield to get him. It was a miracle he'd been able to land in this weather, and he'd seriously upset the controllers for insisting. But to hell with them now, he hadn't had any choice in the matter, and were he able to consider them his only problem he sure as hell wouldn't be risking life and limb right now to find out if the woman Nick had called him about really was Katherine Sumner.

Downshifting hard, he rounded the bend at Roon Moor, narrowly avoided the post office, then accelerated again, heading for the brink of the hill. On the back seat his mobile kept ringing, but he was in no position to answer. This had to come first. No matter that Franz Koehler was dead, it had to take priority. Rudy would understand that. He knew from the radio that arrests were happening by the hour in Dubai, and were it not for Nick's call he'd be right in the thick of it, probably even in handcuffs himself by now. So maybe he should be thanking Katherine Sumner for this maniacal race through the night, instead of wishing her to any place with a gag, lock and key. As for his damned wife who had orchestrated this nightmare turn in events, may God help her, wherever the hell she was, for if he got his hands on her tonight he might not want to be held accountable for what happened.

The lights had come back on so Rachel could see Katherine's face more distinctly again now. She still looked sad, and concerned, and nervous too, since Laurie had gone upstairs to give them some time alone.

Hearing the wind whistling around the walls, and the windows rattling in their frames, Rachel felt the poignancy of them being here together like this, as though trapped by the stormy fate that had tied them together. She wondered how Katherine felt, surrounded by everything that was Tim's, including his wife and unborn child. Then she looked away, knowing that no amount of reflection, or distraction, was going to make it any easier for her to ask the question that she was still finding so hard to summon. The problem was that whatever answer Katherine gave, she would have to live with it for the rest of her life, and if it turned out not to be what she wanted to hear, then she didn't really want to hear it at all.

'I think I know what's on your mind,' Katherine said eventually. She was still sitting at the table, rain continuing to drip randomly from the ends of her hair down into her neck, while her hands were pressed loosely together on her lap. Her eyes seemed very blue and deep, her beauty somehow more vivid in the redness of her mouth and honey tone of her skin. 'You want to know if that was the only time that Tim and I slept together,' she said.

Rachel's heartbeat started to slow. She almost wished the power would fail again now, for if Katherine's face were in shadow she might, if she needed to, be able to convince herself later that she was lying. 'Was it?' she said quietly.

Katherine's eyes lowered, then came up again. 'I knew, before coming here,' she said, 'that you would want an answer to that question. That even if it was going to break your heart, you'd need to hear how it had been between us. So I thought

681

about it a lot, trying to find the words that would help you to understand that, even though it wasn't the only time, he never once betrayed you in a way that mattered. By that I mean he never loved me, or even pretended to. He only ever loved you, and he never made any pretence about that either. All there was between us was an attraction that was extremely powerful, and that maybe we should have done more to try to control. But in hindsight, that's always easy to say, because unless you're actually in the grip of an attraction like that . . . It's not very rational . . .' She paused, then after taking a breath, she said, 'You meant everything to him. He didn't want or need anyone else, because his life with you was fulfilled and happy and just about perfect in every way. So it didn't make any sense to him that he couldn't keep away from me, when he loved you so much. For a man like Tim, who was always so in control, it was anathema. But there was never any question of him leaving you: in fact until the morning he was killed, we'd been success-fully managing to avoid being alone together for a while, and it wouldn't have happened then, had the opportunity not arisen when we were in the thrall of victory. It was the first time he'd ever been to my flat, which is how I know that Franz would never have sent someone there to kill him. We'd always avoided going there before in case anyone recognized him, so there was no pattern, no established routine, no reason to expect him to be there.

'I guess it was drink that made us reckless that morning, and the fact that we knew it really would be the last time. The campaign was over, I was on my way out of your lives, and as far as helping me with Franz, he'd already told me that he was ready now to hand everything over to the PM and intelligence services, and would keep it monitored from a distance.' She swallowed hard and pressed her hands in under her chin. 'He suffered a lot for what he was doing to you,' she said. 'I know, because I could see how much he loved you. I don't know if you understand what it's like to want someone sexually, or to have feelings for someone else, when you ought not, but if you do then you'll know it's not something you have control over. It just happens. You don't have any choice, in the person, the timing, in anything, it's just there. It's how you feel, and even if you try to deny it, work round it, ignore it, it's still there, and the more you try to resist it, the more powerful it seems to become. So please, try not to judge him, or me, just know that your memories are safe, and intact, because he truly did love you, and I was . . . I was nothing.'

Except the person who cost him his life, Rachel thought. But she didn't say it, she merely looked away, took a breath, then let it go slowly, shakily as she tried to accept the reality. Her head was heavy with the pain of knowing he could have felt such a passion for somebody else, such an irresistible desire that he'd put both his career and his marriage at risk for it. Yet as hurtful and even repellent as the images of them together were, how could she say she didn't understand, when she only had to think of Chris to feel all the guilt and shame of an untimely attraction, that try as she might she still couldn't deny. But not for a minute had it ever stopped her loving Tim – it was just something that seemed to exist separately, or maybe laterally, it was hard to say. Would she ever have felt that way if they'd met while Tim was alive? She'd never know now, but she thought it was likely, though how far it might have gone, or how forgiving Tim would have been had he found out, could never be an issue now, so there was no point in imagining.

Lifting her eyes back to Katherine's she was about to speak when the sound of footsteps running up the path to the kitchen door stopped her. She frowned, curiously, then jumped as someone knocked loudly. Realizing it must be Anna, she got to her feet. 'It'll be my sister,' she said. 'Did you lock the door?'

'I'm not sure,' Katherine answered. 'Does it lock itself?'

Pushing the door to the stairs closed as she passed, Rachel stepped up into the kitchen, and looked at the latch. No, it wasn't locked, so why was Anna knocking? She started at another thump on the door, then, staying where she was, she called out,

'Who is it?'

'Is Katherine in there?' a female voice called back. 'She left something behind.'

Rachel turned to look at Katherine.

'It's the woman I'm staying with,' Katherine said. 'Stacey Greene.'

Rachel's eyes opened wide in alarm. She was staying with Stacey Greene?

'We should let her in,' Katherine said. 'It's filthy out there.'

For a moment Rachel panicked, unable to think of an objection, then standing aside, she said, 'You go. She obviously has something for you.'

As Katherine passed, Rachel returned to the sitting room and went to stand in front of the hearth. She was trying hard to make herself understand why Katherine would be staying with Stacey, and how it linked to Chris, who'd been so adamant she shouldn't see Katherine, and now here she was, a guest in his house. So was Stacey really here just because Katherine had forgotten something? Feeling almost dazed, she listened to their voices, and hoped against hope that Katherine would just take whatever Stacey had brought, and not invite her in. But then she heard the stomping of Stacey's feet on the doormat as the door closed behind her, and a moment later Katherine came back into the sitting room, her eyes seeming to ask if it was all right, as behind her Stacey appeared in the arch, wearing a long black raincoat and nothing over her hair.

'Hello,' she said, smiling pleasantly at Rachel.

Rachel looked at her, her heart pounding with unease. What did she want? What was this really about?

'Katherine forgot her key,' Stacey explained, 'so I thought I should bring it.'

Rachel's eyes darted to Katherine, then straight back to Stacey, as she said, 'Oh dear, you forgot this too.' She pulled a small black purse out of her pocket and held it up for Katherine to see.

To Rachel's confusion, Katherine's face instantly paled.

Stacey was unbuttoning her coat. 'You don't

mind, do you?' she said to Rachel. 'It's so chilly and wet out there, and you know what they say, I won't find the benefit later.'

'Stacey, I don't know what this is about,' Katherine began, glancing anxiously at Rachel.

'No, but you will,' Stacey assured her, shrugging her coat off and draping it over a chair back. She was wearing a white crêpe dress and thick, heavy boots, while her wet hair clung like tangled seaweed to her neck and shoulders. 'I've been going over and over this, all day,' she said, turning back, and pantomiming confusion, 'and frankly I'm still not sure what to do. Incidentally, you have told her about my husband, haven't you?' she said to Katherine. 'She does know all about him now?'

Katherine looked at Rachel.

Rachel's heart was thudding.

'Oh! Does this mean you haven't?' Stacey said, frowning. 'So I don't suppose she's told you about their affair either.'

Katherine's lips parted in shock. 'Oh God, Rachel, please tell me that's not true,' she implored.

Rachel's eyes were frightened and angry as she turned them on Stacey. 'For your information Chris and I –'

'*Don't* pair yourself with my husband,' Stacey spat. 'There is no Chris and you. Do you hear me? There is *no* Chris and you.'

'Then we can't be having an affair, can we?' Rachel said cuttingly.

Stacey turned to Katherine. 'I hope you didn't let her put you through it for what you did with her husband,' she said scathingly, 'not after what she's been doing with mine.'

686

'I've done *nothing* with your husband,' Rachel shouted.

'Oh dear, a faulty zip,' Stacey said, tugging at the black purse. 'But no, it's OK now.'

'Stacey, for God's sake,' Katherine cried, as she took out the gun. 'Just give it to me.' She was holding out her hand and glaring angrily. 'I said *give it to me.*'

Stacey dropped the purse then pointed the gun at Rachel.

Rachel's heart twisted with terror, as she took a step back.

'Stacey, for God's sake,' Katherine cried again. 'I don't know what's been going on here . . . She's *pregnant*, for Christ's sake. You're scaring the hell out of her.'

'I can see that,' Stacey responded. 'But it's going to scare her a whole lot more when you shoot her, don't you think?'

Katherine balked in amazement. 'Are you crazy?' she gasped.

Stacey shook her head. 'No, just undecided,' she answered.

Rachel's hands were clasped over the baby. Adrenalin was pumping so fast through her veins it was making her giddy. This was the first time in her life she'd ever even seen a gun at such close quarters, much less had one pointed at her, and she didn't know what the hell to do. Panic was rushing through her mind like a tornado, ripping out strange, unreal thoughts . . .

'I'm just not sure *why* you would kill her,' Stacey was saying to Katherine, still looking as though she was trying to figure it all out. 'So that means it would have to be a murder/suicide situation, where you kill her first, then yourself, so no one ever gets to question why you did it.'

Katherine's eyes were wide with shock as she started to back off. 'You really are crazy,' she murmured.

'Or,' Stacey continued, 'since she has every reason in the world to want to kill you, as we all know, I could do it for her, then swear that she was the one who pulled the trigger. After all, it's only us here, and since you won't be in much of a position to call me a liar . . .' She nodded towards Rachel. 'She's the one with the motivation, so it would stand to reason that she did it, and plenty of babies are born in prison.' She looked puzzled again, and put a finger to her lips as she thought. 'It's a difficult choice,' she said in the end, 'but either way, Katherine, I'm afraid you don't get to tell the tale. And as for you . . .' Her eyes became suddenly hard as she turned them on Rachel, 'I'd have thought you'd have had the common decency, never mind human compassion, to keep your *hands off someone else's husband*, when you know how it feels to be the wife. What's the matter with you? Don't you have any feelings for anyone but yourself? What kind of mother is that going to make you? What kind of life is that child going to have when your only consideration is for yourself?'

'Stacey, please,' Rachel said shakily. 'I haven't slept with Chris . . .'

'You spend eight days in the Caribbean with him, and you think I'm going to believe you never slept with him?' Stacey cut in, mockingly. 'Would you?' she said to Katherine. 'If it were your husband she'd been with? Would you believe nothing happened? And if you did, think how everyone would laugh, the way they're laughing at me!'

'Her husband's only just died,' Katherine answered. 'And if she says there's nothing going on with yours . . .' She looked at Rachel. 'Do you know that her husband works for Franz?' she said.

Rachel nodded.

'Are you aware of what he does?'

Rachel's eyes were wide as she looked at her, for it was obvious Katherine would know a lot more than she did, but maybe she didn't know the entire truth either. 'More or less,' she said. 'Do you?'

'Oh sure, I know what he does,' she answered, 'and you've got to face it,' she said, turning back to Stacey, 'he's going to jail. We all are.'

'Oh but not me,' Stacey corrected. 'I'm not involved. But I'm prepared to wait for my husband.'

'Then it'll be for a good long time,' Katherine snapped, 'because the kind of double-dealing he's been pulling off isn't going to sit well with any jury, never mind the judge.'

'He's got money. He'll have the best lawyers,' Stacey said. She smiled at Rachel. 'Are you getting the drift?' she said sweetly. 'Do you understand what she's telling you? Chris started out as an informer, a sneak, working for the Government, but he switched sides when the money got big enough, and started feeding them false information.'

Rachel's face was white as she looked at Katherine.

In the stairwell, Laurie was listening hard, watching Stacey's distorted image through the small porthole in the door.

'So is that enough to make you back off?' Stacey enquired silkily. 'Do you feel quite so keen now? Or do I still need this?' She poked the gun forward, and slid a finger into the trigger guard.

'Stacey, please understand,' Rachel began, 'there's nothing going on.'

Seeing Stacey's finger start to tighten, Laurie's heart contracted, then hurling the door open, she smashed it hard into Stacey.

Stacey shrieked.

The gun went off.

The explosion blasted through the room as though to blow out the walls.

There was a moment's awful silence as time seemed to stand on the edge of a precipice – then Rachel slumped to the floor.

'Oh my God!' Laurie cried, running to her, as plaster showered down from the ceiling.

'It ricocheted. It must have been a ricochet,' Katherine panicked as she threw herself to the floor beside Rachel.

Behind them Stacey was backing away in horror. 'I didn't mean to do it,' she was mumbling. 'I was only trying to frighten her. Oh God, no!'

Laurie and Katherine weren't listening. Katherine was going for the phone as Laurie tried to find the bullet.

'It wasn't my fault!' Stacey cried. 'I didn't mean to do it!'

Chris had just leapt out of the car, leaving Nick to

park it when the sound of a gunshot reverberated around the cove. Immediately he started to run, harder than he ever had in his life, oblivious to the wind and rain as he raced past Tom Drummond's cottage, around Rachel's and Beanie's parked cars, and on up the footpath towards the last house. He was almost there when a woman came running out.

It was Stacey.

'No! No!' she screamed, struggling to get away as he grabbed her. 'I didn't mean to do it. It wasn't my fault.'

'What the hell are you talking about? What's happened?'

'It wasn't my fault,' she sobbed, and wrenching herself free she ran on down the footpath.

Willing Nick to catch her in the village, he dashed through the gate and through the open back door.

Katherine looked up, and her eyes dilated. 'Oh my God, no,' she murmured, seeing his gun. 'Please, no,' she begged.

Laurie turned round, and she too gaped at him in horror. 'Chris, no, you can't,' she said, moving to shield Rachel.

He stared back at them, his eyes as hard as granite as they moved from one to the other then blazed into Katherine. 'What happened?' he demanded.

'Nothing. The gun went off, but she's . . . *she's dead.*'

Realizing she was lying, he shouted, 'What the fuck happened? What did you tell her?'

'Nothing,' Katherine shouted back.

'For Christ's sake, I'm not going to hurt you,' he said angrily.

Laurie's fingers were inching towards the gun Stacey had dropped.

Noticing, Chris moved his aim to her. 'Don't do that,' he barked. Then to Katherine, 'I don't know how close anyone is behind me, so whatever you told her, just for God's sake stay with her – and if you need to use that,' he said to Laurie, 'do it.' Spinning round he began running back down to the village, trying to catch up with his wife.

He'd just reached the pub when he saw Nick coming off the beach where he'd left the car. 'Did you see her?' he shouted. 'Did you see Stacey?'

'Was that her? Yeah. She ran up that way, towards the top cottages.'

Chris sprinted in the direction Nick had pointed, speeding past the gig house and crab shop, around a tractor and up the small incline towards the cottages at the near end of the todden. Then he saw her, about fifty yards in front, starting up towards the other headland. He called out, but the wind whipped away his voice. Knowing she could get home that way didn't stop him; instead he urged himself to a killing pace, leaping over the boulders at the bottom of the footpath, skidding in the mud, then righting himself, before charging on in the direction of the five-barred gate. He could see her again now, climbing over it.

Moments later he was vaulting over it himself. He dropped the gun, left it and ran on, pumping his arms and pushing his legs to propel him on through the rain. She was almost at the stile now, but he was closing in.

'Stacey! Wait! Just wait!' he yelled.

Her hair and dress were flying in the wind. She was slithering and stumbling in the mud, but she kept on going. She was over the stile, jumping down and taking off across the meadow, heaving herself into the wind, and ignoring the rain.

He was less than ten feet behind her now. 'Stacey!' he shouted again, his lungs burning, his heart pounding. 'Stacey!'

She was getting too close to the edge. She had to turn, *now*!

'Stacey!'

Then quite suddenly she stopped.

Instinctively he stopped too as she spun round to face him.

For several moments there was only the sound of the storm, and their eyes trying to connect through the rain.

'It was an accident,' she shouted.

'I know,' he shouted back.

The wind was whipping at her hair, and tearing at her dress. It was too dark to see her expression, too treacherous to try and grab her.

He took a step forward. 'You're too close to the edge,' he told her, still having to shout.

'You love her, don't you?' she cried shrilly.

'It's not about that . . .'

'You're a liar.' She was still watching him, her hair blowing wildly around her head. She lifted a hand to clear her face.

Quickly closing the distance between them, he grabbed her shoulders and tried to pull her to him.

'You had a choice,' she hissed, knocking him away. 'Just now, when I came out of her house. You

693

could have come after me, but you chose her.'

'I thought she'd been shot!'

'And that mattered more. No *don't!*' she snarled, as he tried to get hold of her again.

'Stacey, you've got to listen to me . . .'

'To your lies? I don't want to hear them.' Her eyes were blazing into his.

He glared back.

All at once the ground began sinking beneath her. 'Oh my God!' she gasped. She made a grab for his hand. 'Chris!'

'It's OK, I've got you.'

'Oh God! Don't let me go.'

The rain was lashing at them, the sea foaming like a hungry beast over the rocks below. He could feel the ground going under him now.

'Chris!' she pleaded. She looked up at him, her face ravaged with fear.

'I'm here,' he said. 'I've got you.' But they both knew it wasn't true.

Nick was halfway up the trail when Chris came charging towards him like a madman.

'Call the lifeboat! *Call the lifeboat!*' he shouted. Then dashing on to the beach, he began dragging one of the boats towards the sea.

Nick ran into the pub. 'Lifeboat!' he yelled, then sped down to the beach.

'You'll kill yourself,' he shouted at Chris. 'You can't go out there in that.'

But Chris wasn't listening.

'I'm not going to let you,' Nick cried, wrestling him away from the boat.

Knocking him aside, Chris grabbed the boat

again. 'The lifeboat's got too far to come,' he raged.

'For God's sake, look at it out there, man!' Nick yelled. 'You'll never make it.'

The boat was sliding into the waves now, but as Chris made to leap in Nick caught him about the waist and threw him to the ground. Seconds later they were fighting furiously, rolling over the pebbles, into the surf, banging up against boats, crashing over buoys and crab pots, until finally they were pulled apart by the locals who'd come running out of the pub.

Breathless, soaked to the skin, and with blood running from his nose, Chris dropped to his knees and pushed his hands into his hair. His pain was almost palpable for those who stood quietly watching him. Then looking up at the foul, misty night, where the sea was churning with a sickening might, and the rain was slicing like blades through the darkness, he spoke to her silently from his heart, so that only she could hear.

No one had noticed the red glow on the horizon yet, like the small fan of a rising sun coming up over the wrong headland, but later they would all say what a curse, and a blessing, that storm turned out to be, for it was mainly due to the easterly gale and torrential rain that his house was saved from the fire.

Chapter 30

It had been a dreadful week, for everyone. The police inquiries had been so intense that they'd become almost more unnerving than the death itself, which was giving rise to so much speculation that Laurie had lost track now of how many theories there were as to what had really happened on that clifftop. Then there was the mystery of how the fire had started, the shock of Katherine Sumner's arrest, and the small handgun that one eagle-eyed police officer had spotted on the trail up to the Frying Pan. The gun's ownership had still not been made official, but everyone locally knew that it belonged to Chris.

With so much food for gossip, and so many reporters around, the press was having a field day. Most of the information must have been coming from surrounding villages, for Laurie knew very well that the locals had closed ranks round each other, and around Chris. They weren't talking to anyone unless they had to, and then they only said the absolute minimum.

Now Laurie was on the train back to London, still dazed by the sheer weirdness and trauma of it all. Letting her head loll to one side she gazed blankly out at the passing countryside. It all seemed so prosaically grounded and normal after the turbulence of the past week, yet it was calming too, which she welcomed, for she'd probably never felt so exhausted or drained in her life. The funeral, this morning, had probably been the worst, when Stacey had been laid to rest with Chris's parents in the small graveyard at Roon Moor. As far as Laurie knew, no one but Chris had viewed the body, except the lifeboatmen who'd found her, of course, and those at the coroner's office, so at least for most the memory of her beauty remained intact. For some reason that had seemed important, because several had mentioned it, especially those who'd come down from London, such as Petey, her assistant, Ernesto Gomez the famed artist, and the gossipy actress Gloria Sullivan, whom Laurie had given a very wide berth.

When the service was over, Chris and Rachel, heedless of gossip, had got into his car and travelled back to his house together. As far as Laurie knew it was the only private time they'd shared since that awful night, though it had been just a few minutes, because the others were right behind them, arriving for the wake that Beanie and Jenny had arranged. It hadn't seemed appropriate to ask Rachel then what they'd talked about, though she guessed Rachel would tell her when they got together later in the week. There would be a lot to discuss then, not least of all the question of why Stacey had set fire to her studio. They would

697

probably never know for certain, though it seemed to be the fire that had started the gossip that her death was a suicide, rather than an accident. In killing herself she'd wanted to destroy Chris's life too and had thought she might achieve that by burning down his house. Laurie didn't think anyone had said that to Chris, but since few had seen or spoken to him, after the lifeboatmen had brought in her body, it wasn't possible to know. The way he'd cut himself off had cast an even greater pall of sadness over the village, though that was almost nothing compared to the outrage they were all feeling towards the police who wouldn't leave him alone. According to the rumour mill they were trying to find out if he'd killed her, which was insane, because they all knew him, and there was absolutely no way he'd ever do anything like that. But the police weren't letting up; they'd even been there at the funeral, in their grey suits and clubby ties, fooling no one, and the villagers had considered it a disgrace. On today of all days they could have shown some respect.

Laurie wondered how they were all going to react when he was finally arrested, which was certainly on the cards, though not for murder, which was all they were discussing, but for other offences entirely. Before her own arrest Katherine had told Laurie and Rachel everything she knew about him, which had been a lot harder for Rachel to hear than it had for Laurie, though Rachel was still insisting they keep open minds until they'd had a chance to speak to him themselves. That could be a while in coming, for he'd informed Beanie earlier that he'd be accompanying the police back to London once the funeral was over. From there it was really anyone's guess what would happen next.

Sighing, and letting her head fall back against the seat, Laurie closed her eyes, and wished the journey could be over. All she wanted was to get home now, away from too much time to think and back to Rhona's, where she might just creep under the blankets and never come out again. Chance would be a fine thing, for she'd already arranged to go and visit Katherine tomorrow, at the prison she'd been taken to, near Bristol, and as there was so much more to learn from her, she could see it turning into a fairly regular trip. What a horrible job she had, she thought, building her own success on the foundations of other people's tragedies. Though after the talk she'd had with her, during the few hours before her arrest, she knew now that she had to start facing up to her own tragedy, for what she'd learned about Patrice Bombola had left precious little room for hope. He was as big an egomaniac as Franz Koehler, Katherine had said, and twice as dangerous. Remembering those words now, Laurie felt her heart burn with the pain of still not knowing for certain, and the dread of someone mentioning a memorial. Of course it was still far too soon for that, but the funeral today had started her thinking it, and now she just couldn't get it out of her head.

Deciding at least to try and get some sleep, she'd just curled up in the corner of her first-class seat, when her mobile started to ring. Checking the read-out to see if it was a call she wanted to take, her heart gave a lurch, and clicking on quickly she said, 'Max. How are you?'

'Cool,' he answered. 'How about you? How was the funeral?'

'Gruelling,' she answered, shifting to make herself more comfortable. 'What's happening your end?'

'Things are starting to calm down a bit now,' he told her. 'About sixteen arrests so far, and more to come, they say. I don't know if you've seen the news lately, but they've seized about forty mill, all in cash. Final destination still not known, but there's a lot of speculation going on, as you can probably imagine. Where are you?'

'On a train between Swindon and Reading. If you don't know where that is, then I'm about an hour west of London. Where are you?'

'A similar sort of distance south,' he said.

Laurie's eyes widened. 'You're on your way back already?'

'Yep. There's not much more to be learned on the ground out there, at least not from my perspective, and after what you've been telling me about Katherine Sumner I'd kind of like to pay her a visit. Do you think she'll see me?'

'I'm sure she will,' Laurie replied. 'She's given me the exclusive, but I think that extends to you.'

'She could really help wrap this up for us,' he said. 'She'll know more about Bombola than anyone else, which could help lead us to Elliot, but there's some stuff I need from his computer before I see her. Is it still in his apartment?'

'As far as I know,' Laurie answered, bracing herself, for she knew what was coming next.

'Can you meet me there?' he said. 'I take it it's OK to go in now. Or is it still a crime scene?'

'No, they've given it the all-clear,' she told him, starting to sink back into despair. She didn't want to go in there, she just didn't. She was too emotional right now, and unable to cope.

'So can you meet me?' he said. 'It shouldn't take long.'

'OK,' she replied, reminding herself it was for Elliot. 'Then I should give you your own key, so you can come and go as you like.'

'Sure,' he answered. 'So I'll see you in about an hour. Maybe an hour and a half.'

As Laurie rode the lift up to Elliot's flat so much gloom and tiredness was enveloping her that she knew once she got inside she'd just want to curl up in a corner and cry. She wondered how many more times she might take this lift before she was forced to start clearing everything out of the flat, the way Rachel was planning with her house, now she was coming back to London. She wondered if Elliot had made a will. If she should sell the flat. If she had any right to, even. He had no immediate family, but there was a cousin in Ireland, and a great-uncle somewhere up north. Would his ex-wife have a say? She doubted it, but she didn't want to think about it; pushing it from her mind, she tried to concentrate on those blankets at Rhona's that she was planning to disappear under just as soon as she could.

As she stepped out of the lift, she looked along the hallway, and her heart sank. No sign of Max. She'd hoped he would get here first, so she could just let him in and leave. Now she would have to wait.

Putting her heavy bag down as she reached the door, she rummaged for the key, then let herself in. The familiarity of it all, the feel, the smell, the early evening sunlight pooling on the sofas, engulfed her, as though it had been waiting, almost expecting her to return. She looked around and almost couldn't stand it, for it all seemed so normal, so back together now the police had gone, that the past few weeks might never have happened – though she knew that a lot of the damaged furniture was piled up in the spare bedroom, awaiting repair. She'd hidden it there herself, after being allowed to clean the place up. She'd tried to arrange it just as he'd left it, ready for when he came back.

Leaving her bag by the door, she took a couple of steps into the room, then found she could go no further. It still smelt of him, and the ache in her heart was so huge, she just couldn't bear it. She took a breath, and tried to push herself on, then a jolt of fear caught at her heart, as someone stepped into the sunlight that was streaming in through the kitchen door.

'Hello,' he said.

Her heart stopped beating.

Folding his arms he leaned against the doorframe, moving out of the sunlight.

She continued just to stare at him, taking in the wonderfully familiar features, his amusement, his uninjured body . . . Joy and disbelief collided in her heart, while the rest of her seemed unable to move. Then it was just too much, and covering her face with her hands she started to sob.

Laughing, he came to her and pulled her into his arms. 'Sorry, I should have given you some warning,' he said, holding her tight. 'I just wanted it to be a surprise.'

She carried on crying, shuddering and gasping, as he stroked and kissed her hair, and gently shushed her. She didn't even try to speak. All she wanted was to stay right here in his arms and forget that the rest of the world even existed.

But at last she turned her ravaged face up to his and felt her heart melting all over again as his smile faded and his eyes darkened with love. Then his mouth was on hers and he was kissing her tenderly, then passionately, then lingeringly and lovingly. 'I've missed you,' he said gruffly, when finally he let her go.

She was still slightly blurred from the kiss. 'I thought you were dead,' she said. 'We all did.'

'You were supposed to,' he responded. 'It was part of the deal, and I had to go along with it.'

She blinked. 'What deal?'

He looked at her dubiously. 'Are you up for this now?' he said.

'Elliot!' she cried. 'I want to know what's been happening. Where you've been.'

He took a breath, then still holding her about the waist said, 'OK, well, when the SIS set me up with an entry into the Phraxos Special Project, I swore I'd go along with whatever they said. I had to for my own safety, as well as for those who were already in there, under cover. I didn't even know until after I'd been whisked out of Paris that Koehler had managed to find out who I was, or that Patrice Bombola had promised to 'take care' of me, which he did, splendidly, at a rather palatial home in Botswana, which is where I've been all this time.'

She gaped in astonishment. 'You mean Patrice Bombola is working for the British Government?' she said incredulously.

'I didn't say that,' he responded.

She looked at him.

He winked, then laughed as she crossed her eyes.

'Details later,' he promised, 'but for now all you need to know is that Bombola saved my life after Franz Koehler gave the order for it to be terminated, and that in order to maintain Patrice's cover, I had to stay out of sight and incommunicado, until I was given the all-clear.'

'Which they presumably gave because Franz Koehler's dead?'

He nodded.

'So how much of what you found out are you going to be able to use?'

'I still don't know. There's a lot of sorting out to do, and the operation's not over, so I'm still bound by the Official Secrets Act – and you should consider yourself bound with me.' Tilting her chin up he kissed her again. 'Max told me all about Katherine Sumner,' he said. 'So it sounds as though you've been busy too.'

'Yes,' she said. 'There's obviously so much overlap in our stories,' she went on, loving the feel of the kisses he was planting all over her face and neck, 'that I won't be letting you out of my sight too often over the next couple of months.'

'Mm, I could be happy with that,' he murmured, moving his hands to the buttons at the front of her shirt. 'In fact, I'm in need of seeing you fully in my sight right now, because of all the things I missed while I was at the luxury gaff, you came out on top every time.'

She could already feel the heat of her own desire, as she lowered her head to watch his fingers slip each button free. Then after pulling the hem from the waist of her jeans, he pushed the shirt down over her arms and let it fall to the floor. She looked up at his face, then her eyes fluttered in a wave of pleasure as he unhooked the front fastener of her bra and peeled it from her breasts.

'Oh yes,' he murmured, and scooping their fullness in his hands, he stooped to kiss the hard buds of her nipples.

'Elliot,' she said breathlessly, lifting his mouth back to hers, 'aren't we missing something?'

'Do we need it?' he asked, kissing her.

'I'm talking about an opera.'

'I know. But are you up to it, because the way I'm feeling right now it won't stop at the Ride of the Valkyries, it'll be the whole damned Ring.'

With a splutter of laughter, she said, 'Then since I've just got off a train, I'll go to the bathroom for a moment, and let you decide whether you really think you can live up to that.'

A few minutes later, after taking the fastest shower of her life, she was drying herself down and smiling as the opening bars of Wagner's masterpiece began filling the flat. It was still incredible to her that he was actually here, and alive, though in spite of the euphoria, she remained ludicrously close to tears. But that was tiredness, and nerves, because she desperately didn't want anything to spoil this homecoming, especially not her own urgency to get everything properly sorted. There would be plenty of time to deal with all the issues they still had, so she would just make herself forget them for tonight, even though it would make everything so utterly perfect if it did work out, and now she'd made up her mind to do it, did she really want to delay?

The bedroom was in semi-darkness when she stepped out of the bathroom, wearing no more than the perfume he liked best. He was lying on the bed, apparently naked, though a single sheet covered him to the waist and he had one arm thrown over his eyes. She waited for him to look up, but obviously the music had drowned the sound of her entrance, so she walked over to the bed and sat down next to him. To her surprise, he still didn't move, so sliding a hand across his chest, she leaned down to kiss him. When he didn't kiss her back she sat up again, and stared down at him in amazement.

'Are you asleep?' she demanded.

There was no reply.

'Elliot Russell, I don't believe you!' she laughed. 'The whole *Ring* indeed! You couldn't even make the overture.'

Still he didn't move, and as his lips parted, indicating that he'd just sunk to an even deeper level of sleep, she lay down beside him and snuggled in close. Then after a while, keeping her voice low, she decided to have a practice. 'Elliot. Will you marry me?' she whispered. Then, 'Will you marry me, Elliot?'

'I thought you'd never ask,' he replied.

She froze, then drew back to look at him.

He raised his arm, and cast her a roguish look.

'I thought you were asleep!' she cried.

'I was, but now I'm engaged.'

Laughing, she collapsed back on to the pillows. 'You know, I love you so much that I just can't find the words,' she said, as he turned on his side to look at her.

'You know, I was having the same problem,' he responded, reaching past her to the nightstand, 'so I thought this might do it for me.'

She looked down at the little box he was holding, and a shock ran through her. 'Is that what I think it is?' she said, turning to look at him.

'No,' he answered. 'And you only get one guess.'

'Don't you dare,' she cried, grabbing his hand, as he started to put it back.

Letting the box go, he watched her as she opened it, then felt an enormous swelling in his own heart, as hers obviously overflowed because she was crying again.

'Oh, Elliot, it's a diamond,' she wept.

'Is it?' he said, sounding surprised.

'It's perfect,' she laughed, lifting the small, perfectly round stone with its plain gold band from the velvet crease. 'Just perfect.'

Taking it from her, he waited for her to hold out her left hand, then sliding it on to the third finger he said, 'I love you, Laurie Forbes, and yes, I think it's about time you made an honest man of me.'

Petey was leaving in three days for Hollywood! He'd have gone sooner, but ever since the funeral the world had been calling him morning, noon and night to discuss all the rumours that were flying around, so he'd just had to delay his flight in order to assure them all that yes, of course he was utterly devastated, and no he didn't believe she'd committed suicide . . . Though actually, yes, he did think there was a teensy little chance she might just have been pushed. Well, no, it was true, he hadn't thought that until a couple of days ago, but since her husband had been arrested, OK, for currency smuggling, not murder, but really, it was enough to make anyone have second thoughts . . .

'After all, sweetie,' he said to Gloria when she called, 'we always knew he was up to no good, so heaven only knows what he's capable of.'

'So you *do* think he did it?' Gloria replied eagerly.

'How would I know, sweetie, I wasn't there. I'm just saying, anything's possible.'

'And what about the rumours that he was having an affair with Rachel Hendon? Are they true?'

'Well, darling, you saw them at the funeral. Closer than the cheeks of a virgin's bum, I'd say. So draw your own conclusions.'

'Mmm,' Gloria murmured. 'It makes you start wondering about all sorts of things that, doesn't it? I mean like Tim Hendon's death, and whose baby she's carrying. And then we get back to what really happened on those cliffs.'

'Ah well,' he chirruped, 'maybe we should be adhering to the sublime advice of the bard when he says, *"Things without all remedy, should be without regard: what's done is done."* '

Gloria hesitated.

'Lady Macbeth,' he told her, rolling his eyes.

A few minutes later they rang off, with Gloria for once having forgotten to mention the fire, and why Stacey might have started it; so he hadn't brought it up either. Indeed he was more than happy to forget that curious little part of the puzzle, which was really only a mystery to everyone else. However, provided no one ever told what they knew about those pretty little hand-made boxes and their precious sweet cargo, he would never tell what he knew about Anna.

Chapter 31

The traffic was always bad trying to get out of London at Christmas, even in the mornings, and today was proving no exception as Rachel battled her way down towards the M3, hoping to get at least as far as the Devon/Cornwall border before nightfall. With Beanie driving they'd almost certainly make it, but Rachel wasn't prepared to take the risk. So Beanie had been relegated to the back seat, along with the carrycot, nappies, sterilizing units and all the other paraphernalia no modern baby would dream of travelling without.

'Still asleep?' Rachel said, glancing in the rear-view mirror.

Beanie peeled back the edge of a downy white blanket, and melted. 'Still asleep,' she confirmed. 'What time's his next feed?'

Rachel grimaced; the weight of her breasts might suggest it was overdue. 'Another hour or so,' she answered. 'We can stop somewhere around Salisbury Plain. By the way, did you remember to call Dick at the farm, and ask him to keep us a Christmas tree?'

'He's staying open till we get there,' Beanie told her. 'Don't matter how late, he said. He's got us a nice one.'

Rachel's pleasure was stolen by a wave of sadness as she thought of Tim, and how very different this Christmas was going to be without him, yet with his son who had captured her heart in a way she simply hadn't been prepared for. Of course she'd often heard mothers talking about how a child changed their lives and perspective completely, but she'd never really understood then just how profound the change could be. It was as though nothing had the same importance any more, old grievances seemed petty, and ambitions necessary only to the extent that they would enrich and protect her son. He was so utterly and completely the focus of her life that even to think of him, with all his raspberries, fist boxing, kicking and peeing into the air, filled her heart with so much love she couldn't begin to contain it.

Pressing hard on the accelerator to get them past a slow-moving lorry, she turned the radio on low to listen to the news. The struggling economy was still holding the headlines, with the National Health Service making it to second place, while the Prime Minister's plans for Christmas ended the short bulletin. Turning it off again, she sped on down the middle lane, and wondered if the small role she'd played in recent events would ever be revealed. She hoped not, for certain elements of the press would almost certainly turn it into something salacious and self-serving, the way they'd turned her friendship with Chris Gallagher into a full-blown affair. Even worse had been the shameless media trial they'd conducted when Chris had failed to achieve bail: they'd found him guilty of all charges, including some he hadn't even been arrested for.

As it turned out, they did reach the border before nightfall, but only just, so it had long been dark by the time Rachel turned the Mercedes SUV that she'd traded for Tim's 500 into the lane leading up to Dick Lom's farm. By then everyone was starving, not just the baby, so leaving Dick and one of the farmhands to tie a hearty five-foot spruce on to the roof rack, Beanie and Rachel took off to the warmth of the kitchen, where they tucked into Mrs Lom's mince pies, while the baby guzzled greedily on his own personal supply.

Then it was all back in the car, to cover the final four-mile stretch to Killian, where to Rachel's delight and relief, Nick and Jenny were in the pub keeping an eye out ready to help carry everything up to the cottage.

'We got the fire going,' Jenny told her, as they lugged the carrycot and a heavy bag each up to the cottage. 'And the heating's on. It's been bitter. But no snow. Had a heavy frost this morning though.'

'Are there carols in the pub tomorrow night?' Rachel asked, going in first through the gate.

'Christmas Eve? Course there's carols,' Jenny answered. 'We'll all be there. And this one too, I hope,' she added, smiling down at the baby.

'That will be the loudest voice of all,' Rachel assured her. 'Are you OK there, Bean? Those groceries are heavy.'

'I can manage,' she said, puffing her way in through the back door and plonking the bags down on a draining board. 'Oooh, it's nice and warm in here. I hope you remembered to put my heating on too,' she said to Jenny. 'And the turkey's ordered, is it? We need a twenty-pounder for all of us.'

'Everything's been taken care of,' Jenny told her, with an affectionate hug. 'We got you a tree as well. It's already in there. We left Romie at the pub until you was all settled. Oh, look at him,' she crooned, gazing down at the baby. 'He's awake. Look at his blue eyes. He's so like his dad. Can I pick him up?'

'Of course,' Rachel smiled. 'Careful he's not sick though, he seems to find that a fun way of introducing himself,' and leaving Jenny and Beanie to it, she trotted back down the footpath to get more things from the car.

'Can you manage there?' she said to Nick, as he lifted the tree down from the roof rack.

'No problem,' he assured her.

She waited until the tree was balanced, ready for him to carry, then seizing the opportunity of these few moments alone, she said, 'Is he here?'

'Yep. Arrived two days ago.'

'How is he?'

Nick's expression was thoughtful as he tilted his face to the moon. 'You'll see,' he told her.

At that, Rachel's heart contracted, for the last time she'd seen Chris had been on the day of the funeral, when they'd travelled back to the house together. They hadn't had long to talk, but it had seemed important to him then to apologize for everything that had happened, and for all she was going to learn over the coming months. He hadn't elaborated, though he had warned her not to believe everything she heard.

713

'Is there anything I can do?' she'd asked him. 'Some way I can help?'

'Yes, you can distance yourself,' he'd answered. 'There'll be a lot of fallout, and you've already been through enough. So it would help me to know that you're standing as well back from it as you can. No, please don't argue,' he'd said when she tried to protest. 'This is not going to be an easy time. I'm going to need all my wits about me, so please don't make me worry about you too.'

So she'd done as he'd asked and kept her distance, at least physically, but ever since his arrest she'd been in daily touch with Laurie and Elliot, who visited him and his lawyers regularly, so she'd always known what was happening, and just how difficult and alarming everything was proving. In the end it was Elliot's frustration with the system that would not allow him, at this stage, to report the outrageous injustice of what Chris was being put through, that had prompted Rachel to act. It had taken a while for anything to happen, but then Laurie had called late last week, to let her know that her little chat with the PM had done the trick, and the doors were finally opening.

After learning he'd gone to Cornwall following his release, she'd hastily changed their Christmas plans in the hope she could persuade him to join them. Since he was alone and had no family, it surely wouldn't be hard to prise him out, but she had yet to learn just how much damage had been done during the past three months, for his experiences at the hands of his own government could very easily have made him bitter, even vengeful. On top of that there was the loss of his wife, for whom he'd hardly had the chance to grieve since everything had blown up within days of the funeral. And the shameless speculation that had been bandied about in the press since, such as 'Did she fall, or was she pushed?' must have turned the whole horribly painful ordeal into a nightmare of unimaginable proportions.

'Hi, we're here,' she said to Anna later on the phone, after everyone had gone. 'It feels strange, but I'm glad we came.'

'How's the baby?' Anna said.

'Wonderful. Sleeping at the moment, so I'm just about to get in the bath. God, I'm still so fat,' she grumbled, catching sight of herself in the mirror.

'It'll go,' Anna assured her. 'But not this side of Christmas. When are Laurie and Elliot arriving?'

'Tomorrow afternoon. And you'll be here Boxing Day?'

'Absolutely.'

'Are you sure you don't mind staying with Beanie?'

'Of course not. Does she mind having us, is the question? Now, tell me, have you seen Chris yet?'

Rachel's heart skipped a beat. 'No. I thought I'd go over in the morning, while Beanie babysits,' she said.

'You know how to make her day,' Anna smiled. 'By the way, did Robert tell you that Ernesto's been in touch with Chris, and the exhibition's going ahead?'

'That's great news,' Rachel cried, taking it as a sign that Chris was already making an effort to move on with his life.

'I thought you'd be pleased,' Anna responded. 'I

know Robert is. He's hoping it might coincide with the opening of the film.'

'Is that likely?'

'Could be. I hate to say it, but after all the publicity surrounding her death . . . Well, it's not going to hurt either the exhibition or the film, but for God's sake don't quote me, especially not to Chris.'

'He'll know that anyway,' Rachel said. 'He might even be seeing it as a tribute, something he can do for her that helps keep her memory alive.'

'That's what Robert said. Certainly that's how he's seeing it.'

Rachel paused for a moment as she wondered how Robert was really feeling about Stacey's death, though whatever it was, he'd certainly been behaving like a man totally in love with his wife and in full control of his film these past three months, so it was probably wise not to delve any deeper. After all, if Anna wasn't worried then there was no reason for her to be, and since there was something rather more immediate that was concerning her about Chris she said, 'Tell me honestly, Anna, is he going to think I'm throwing myself at him? Trying to push some kind of relationship on him, by rushing down here like this?'

Anna laughed and sighed. 'Darling, after what he's been through there's no knowing what he'll think, but as long as *you're* clear about your motives, that's all that matters.'

Rachel's heart dipped; it wasn't quite the answer she'd hoped for, especially when her motives weren't so much clear as opaque, or when she had no way of knowing if he might hold their friendship to blame for Stacey's death.

After putting the phone down, Anna wandered out of the kitchen and back to the sitting room where Robert and the girls were still trimming the tree. Rachel would be all right, she felt sure of it, and even if it turned out that Chris didn't want to see her, she, Anna, would be there in a couple of days to take charge.

For a while she stood in the doorway watching her husband and children and felt her heart fill with so much love she almost wanted to cry. Had they really made it this far? Were they really recovering as well as it seemed? Stacey Greene's vanity and Robert's obsession had been formidable foes, the worse she'd ever had to face in a marriage and career that were liberally and painfully chequered by Robert's passions and crises. She'd always brought them through before, and she would probably have to again, but she couldn't imagine anything ever being so bad as Stacey. Just thank God Robert was finally starting to get over it now, though she wasn't fooling herself here, there was still some way to go; and seeing Stacey's face, hearing her voice every day in an editing room, was, all too often, almost more than he could bear. But he was fighting it, and with Anna at his side there was no doubt he would win. Anna would make sure he did, just as she made sure of everything else in his life.

Smiling as he urged her to come and join them, she walked over to the tree and sank down on a bean-bag next to Justine, who was rummaging

717

through the box of ornaments that dated back to before either of the children were born. So many of them had broken or become damaged over the years, yet Anna unfailingly put them together again, unwilling to let any of her precious memories go, no matter how worn or faded they might be.

Raising her eyes to Robert she found him watching her. Then she began to smile, almost playfully, as he went to the CD and changed the music from a robust medley of carols to one of their favourite blues songs.

'Dance?' he said, holding out a hand.

Emily looked from her mother to her father, and seeing Anna about to accept, put a hand over her mouth. 'Oh, puhleeze,' she protested.

Laughing, Anna got to her feet and moved into Robert's arms.

'Just don't kiss, all right,' Emily told them hotly.

'I like it when they kiss,' Justine piped up.

'That's because you're weird,' her sister informed her.

Their eyes shining with laughter Robert and Anna looked at each other and swayed slowly to the beat. A few minutes later Emily marched out in disgust, leaving Justine as sole witness to a kiss that Anna knew was as full of apology as it was of love – as full of gratitude that they were here together now, as it was of fear that somehow he would lose control again. And of course he would, because he always did. That was simply the way it was for him, as a writer, an artist, a creator. Just thank God he had her, and that women like Stacey never came along twice in a lifetime. She experienced a momentary flicker of guilt that she could feel so relieved at someone's death, then she thought of Chris and Rachel, and how very confused and difficult their emotions would be to handle, or even to understand now, in this aftermath of tragedy and facing a strangely uncertain future.

The following morning, after making sure Beanie had everything she needed for a couple of hours, Rachel got into the car and drove the few miles to Chris's house, the other side of Roon Moor. It was a chill, dank day, with not a glimmer of sun making it through the cloud as she followed the sparsely wooded lanes that led to his gates. As she turned in she noticed how drab and barren everything looked, uncloaked for the winter and ravaged by the winds, yet there was a kind of dignity to the sombreness, and a stoicism that seemed almost hypnotic in its own peculiarly subdued way.

When it came into view the exquisite old house, nestling cosily on its own horizon, caused her a tremor of nerves. She'd never seen it while the east wing was still standing, though knew that it had been a more recent addition, which was now completely destroyed by the fire. The clean-up must have continued while he was away, for there was little evidence now of the fire, or even that another wing had existed, though a builder's skip stood in the front courtyard, with piles of sand and other equipment nearby. It didn't appear that anyone was working today; the only sign of life was the glossy black mare that was grazing in a nearby field.

Driving around the centre island of the

courtyard, she pulled up next to the skip and turned off the engine. She knew, from the column of smoke rising from one of the chimneys, that someone was at home, and the car in front of the stable told her that it was almost definitely Chris. She wondered if the housekeeper and manager were around, or if he'd invited some friends down from London, but everything seemed very quiet, and since there were no other cars in sight, she dared to hope that she was going to find him alone.

Unbuckling her seat belt, she stepped down on to the gravel. The air was perfectly still, and so cold it stung her face, so pulling her scarf up round her mouth, she hunched herself into her eider coat and started towards the house.

After knocking she stamped her feet and punched her hands together. Her heart tripped as the door opened, and turning round she looked up into his eyes.

'Hello,' she said, in a small cloud of white breath.

His surprise was evident, though there was more that she couldn't quite define. Resistance? Hesitance? 'I . . . thought you were in London,' he said.

'We arrived last night,' she told him, starting to fear that he wasn't even going to let her past the doorstep. 'How are you?'

For what seemed an eternity he simply continued to look down at her, then standing aside, he gestured for her to come in.

She waited for him to close the door, then smiled awkwardly, not sure what to say now.

'I was in here,' he said, directing her into the

sitting room where an enormous fire was roaring in the hearth, and the newspapers he'd obviously been reading were scattered around the sofas.

As she reached the fireplace he said, 'Can I take your coat?'

As she unwound her scarf she looked around the elegant yet cosy room, with its big comfy sofas and armchairs, the throw pillows surrounding the coffee table, and the bookshelves that filled the niches either side of the chimney breast. It was the same as it had been the day they'd come for the wake; less people now, of course, and not quite so sad.

'This is a beautiful room,' she murmured, passing him her coat. 'Did Stacey do it this way?'

'Yes, she did,' he answered.

Though the reply had been short, he hadn't seemed to flinch at the mention of Stacey's name, which gave her courage, for she'd been afraid he'd shy immediately from that particular hurdle. Then realizing he was watching her, she turned to look at him too.

'No one would confirm it,' he said, 'but I think I have you to thank for the intervention that speeded up my release.'

She raised her eyebrows comically. 'I'm sure I don't know what you mean,' she responded.

He was still watching her. 'Thank you anyway,' he said. 'And thank you for coming. It's good to see you.'

'And to see you.' She wanted to touch him, if only to squeeze his hands, but knew instinctively that it would be wrong.

He gestured with her coat. 'I'll go and hang this

up, then can I get you something? Tea? Coffee? There's mulled wine, if you fancy it.'

Surprised and impressed, she said, 'Why not? It's Christmas. Did you make it?'

He gave her a waggish sort of look, a hint of his old self. 'I could lie,' he said, 'but I'm sure I'll be found out, so no, Jenny brought it over, yesterday. She seems to have appointed herself as a replacement for Elwyn and Felicity, now they've gone back to Wales. After all the fuss, they were nervous of the police unearthing a certain cottage industry that wouldn't thrive on that kind of publicity.'

Her eyes narrowed. 'Yes, what's happened about that?' she asked.

'I don't know, and I don't ask.'

'Better not to know,' she agreed.

He went off with her coat, then came back a few minutes later with two tumblers of warm, spicy wine.

'Merry Christmas,' she said, tapping her glass to his.

'Merry Christmas,' he echoed.

They both drank, then realizing he was watching her slightly curiously now, and afraid she knew why, she put a hand to her middle. 'I promise you, it's not still in there,' she said, 'though I know it looks like it.'

He smiled and it almost reached his eyes. 'I hear it was a boy.'

'Laurie told you?'

'Yes. Congratulations. How is he?'

'Adorable, but then I would say that. His name's Charles. Charlie, actually. Tim's name was

Timothy Charles, so I've called the baby Charles Timothy.'

'Charlie,' he said. 'I like it. Will I be able to meet him?'

Feeling a small leap in her heart, she said, 'Oh, I think so. In fact I've signed you up for nappy-changing duty during the carols at the pub tonight.'

His eyebrows rose, then he shook his head. 'I don't think I'll be going,' he said. 'But certainly another time.'

Keeping her disappointment hidden, while wanting to kick herself for being so clumsy, she went to sit in the armchair he was indicating, and crossed one booted leg over the other, while he went to sit on the sofa.

After a while she said, 'I know it's been a difficult time, and you probably don't want to talk about it, but I just want to know, has it all been sorted out now? Are you home for good?'

Stretching an arm out along the back of the sofa, he said, 'Actually, if there's one person I would want to talk to about it, it's you, though I'm not sure I knew that until today.' From his expression he seemed genuinely surprised by the discovery, but she could tell he was still keeping a barrier between them. 'Yes, I'm home for good,' he said. 'But as for everything being sorted . . .' His eyebrows went up as he looked down at his glass and shook his head. 'Insofar as they've finally dropped the charges against me, I guess you could say that it is all sorted, but there's still a heck of a lot going on behind the scenes, as I'm sure you know, so it could be that I'll be called on to testify at various trials, or inquiries, that *might* come up over the next couple of years, though it's by no means certain they will. If they do, it won't be easy, because I actually struck up personal friendships with some of those involved, particularly Rudy Forester. Did Laurie tell you about him?'

'Yes she did.'

'God knows how he's taking it now, finding out that I was a fake,' he said, looking very troubled. 'That's exactly what he'll call me. I can hear him saying it. So I've no doubt I've made myself a serious enemy there, and he won't be the only one.'

She took another sip of her drink. 'Are you going to be provided with any kind of protection?' she asked.

His expression was droll. 'The protection I need is from men in grey suits who go round press-ganging art dealers into their murky business,' he responded, 'and from a mad moment right out of university when I underwent training to follow in my father's footsteps. I don't think they're willing to supply that.'

Smiling, she shook her head. 'So they seriously believed that you'd switched sides to work for Franz Koehler?' she said.

'They believed it enough to hold me for three months without bail,' he answered drily. 'I mean, I knew there was a good chance I'd be arrested and held until they could get the necessary information about who I really was to the relevant authorities, but I never expected to have to convince them first that I really hadn't double-crossed them.' He laughed, incredulously. 'Can you believe that? It was their idea that I should come clean to Franz Koehler about who I was, with the intention of getting him to trust me, then they accuse me of selling out and feeding them false information.'

Unable to imagine the frustrations he must have been through during the past three months, she said, 'I presume some of the information was false, though. It would have to be, or Koehler would have known he was being set up.'

'Blindingly obvious really, isn't it,' he responded. 'But they seemed to have a problem getting their heads round that, even though I tried to signal when I thought the information was false, because frankly I didn't always know. The trouble is, the whole thing becomes so ambiguous after a while, and they're such devious players themselves...' He shook his head, disbelievingly. 'What I've learned in the last three and a half years... Well, what I learned was never to trust any of them, because on too many levels they're as bad as each other.'

Already having some idea of why he was saying that, she said, 'Laurie told me that when they first approached you they claimed to be looking into a black market for modern art, which they thought Franz Koehler was involved in.'

'And I fell for it,' he responded. 'How's that for gullibility? And even though I kept telling them, as the months rolled on, that there was no funny business in the way Koehler was buying or selling his art, it still took me far too long to realize that it wasn't about that at all. They were setting me up royally, because what they wanted was to get someone into Koehler's inner circle who wasn't connected in any way to the Phraxos Group, and who had a thoroughly genuine background that would pass any check. So when they discovered he'd contacted me about a Modigliani nude that one of my clients might be interested in selling, they didn't waste a minute. In they swooped, intending to take full advantage of Koehler's passion for art, and of the famed Lance Gallagher's son who already had the basic field training, albeit twenty years out of date. So off they rush me for a refresher, then in they send me, encouraging me to nurture a friendship with this billionaire business-man, to a point where he would eventually feel comfortable enough to start trusting me, not just with his several million-dollar purchases, but with the shadier aspects of his dealings. Good thought, had it only been about art, and had there been any shady aspects to those dealings, but it had nothing to do with any of that. They just wanted to get me fully integrated, before telling me what it was really all about. That was quite a signal moment in my life, I can tell you, learning that I'd been seriously suckered by agents from my own Government. But it didn't stop there, because next came the revelation that my bosom pal Franz, chairman of the world-renowned Phraxos Group, had a rather inventive supply and demand project going – a kind of stirring up the ants' nest in order to create a market for the killer. And then I was told how I was expected to use my highly privileged position as one of Franz Koehler's trusted cohorts, to become actively involved in this delightful little project. My skills as a pilot would do it, they thought. And as it turned out they weren't wrong, because in encouraging Franz to use my air taxi services, we got to know each other even better, and then he started to use me to transport certain documents, a few unidentified trunks here and there that probably contained cash, but who knows; very dubious, as well as authentic looking businessmen, mercenaries, rebels, you name it . . . It was working a treat, we were baking up a dream, and then they revealed the final dazzling stage of their strategy. I was now to make a totally clean breast to my bosom pal of how British intelligence was using me to get information on the Phraxos Special Project.'

Rachel's eyebrows went up in amazement. 'Talk about sabotaging the soufflé,' she murmured. 'Why on earth did anyone think that would work? Weren't they just giving away their hand by admitting they knew the project existed?'

'I certainly thought so,' he responded, 'but as it turned out, Franz knew very well that at least a dozen intelligence agencies were keeping tabs on the project. So finding out that I'd been planted on him was no great surprise, nor did it faze him that I'd taken the decision to tell him who I was. There's so much money to be made, it stood to reason, in his mind, that anyone would switch sides. Agents are doing it all the time, or so he told me. So my confession got me exactly where they wanted me to be, in bed with Franz Koehler and the Phraxos Special Project.'

'But if both sides knew about each other, I don't understand why they needed to use someone like you. Why not put in one of their own people?'

'They're in there, in several different guises,' he replied, 'but even I didn't know who they were. The point was, they didn't have anyone in the inner circle and that was the hardest to penetrate. I seemed like a good option.'

Looking decidedly unimpressed by such blatant exploitation, she said, 'Didn't Koehler ever worry that you might still be feeding back information?'

'I'm sure he did, but he was an exceptionally brilliant operator, who never allowed anyone the full picture. So all I was ever told was one piece of the puzzle, or one leg of a financial journey. It was the same for everyone in the inner circle; no one ever got the full story. But he also knew how unlikely it was that anyone would go all out to try to kill the project, because it's just not in anyone's interests to. The destabilization of Phraxos would have worldwide economic repercussions that wouldn't be good for anyone. Whereas war, which is very big business, is good for everyone, particularly if your pockets are being lined by Phraxos dollars. So all anyone's really after is the low-down on what the project's currently up to, and some advance warning of where civil unrest, or revolution, or military coups might crop up next. Which means, in effect, that Britain's operating a kind of blind-eye policy, which serves their own extremely powerful arms manufacturers very well.'

Knowing what an incredibly strong lobby those manufacturers had, she said, 'Do you think any of those companies are actively involved in the Special Project?'

'I've no idea,' he answered. 'The very top executives are almost certain to know of its existence, and are undoubtedly behind the furtherance of the blind-eye policy, but as for playing an actual part . . .' He shook his head. 'All I know for certain is that the Prime Minister himself ordered the intelligence operation, and that he's putting intense pressure on the US, as well as the Phraxos board, to close the project down. How much luck he'll have, when he's facing so much resistance even from his own Defence Ministry, only time will tell. Have you spoken to Elliot since his meeting with the PM?'

She nodded.

'Then you know that the PM's working with him to use his inside knowledge of the project to exert some pressure of his own. It's going to be a tricky one, because no one wants to upset the Americans.'

'What about the US intelligence units, what purpose are they serving?'

'Basically the same as everyone else's, they're keeping tabs on the project, because a man like Franz Koehler could have really got out of control, and sometimes it was necessary to let him know that he couldn't have everything his own way. The Dubai operation was about that. When they seized all that money, it served a dual purpose. A reminder to Franz Koehler that he doesn't run the world, and a salve to the British and American public to let them know that their security services and armed forces are on the ball. But maybe I'm just being cynical. All I know for certain is that I should have been arrested myself in Dubai, then I was to be quietly let go some time later. Unlike Rudy and a dozen or so others, who really will be facing jail.'

Realizing again how difficult he was finding that to deal with, she said, 'Were you ever in any danger? I guess that's a silly question, you must have been.'

'Actually, it's hard to say, when I was never fully informed of what was going on, so if I was, no one ever told me, and whether my two recruiting agents would have acted to get me out, should anything ever have gone seriously wrong, is anyone's guess.'

'Did anything go wrong, ever?'

'Several times, but the worst was at an airfield just outside Zurich, when the British and Swiss authorities had collaborated in allowing a cash shipment to be flown in from Moscow and transported to a Swiss bank. One of Franz Koehler's men and one Swiss customs official ended up dead.'

'How? What happened?'

'It turned out that the right information hadn't been passed on to the right people, so no way was this one customs officer going to let all that cash into the country. It just wasn't legal, and he didn't care what his colleagues had to say about it, it wasn't coming in.'

'How much was it?'

'Sixteen million dollars, which was due for onward transhipment to an unknown destination – at least unknown to me. I just knew about the Swiss stopover. The authorities were happy to let it in, because they were tracking it. They wanted to know where it was heading next. Then this ridiculous shoot-out started and the next thing I knew two men were dead.'

'What happened to the money?'

'Koehler got it back, I know that, but where it

ended up I was never told. By then it would have been labelled dividends, bonuses, commissions, you name it, care of the Caymans, or Monte Carlo, or Mauritius. I imagine someone's got a track on it, but they'll probably never do anything about it, and it wasn't my department any more.'

'Surely there was an inquiry into that!'

'I'm sure there was, but it never touched Franz Koehler, or not that I know of.'

After a while, she said, 'Laurie and I are getting very involved in Amnesty International now, and Human Rights Watch. Knowing what we do, we have to, because we've got to do something to stop people just switching off when they hear about fighting or misery in Africa. They've got to be made to understand the role their own governments play in it, supplying all those arms and military training. It's already backfired terribly on the West once, as we all know only too well, and if we don't start changing our policies it'll happen again.' Her eyes moved to his, then softened sheepishly as she realized she was climbing up on her soapbox. So in an attempt to return the subject to him, she said, 'I find it amazing that you're still sane, considering all you've been through.'

'On that front, I'm offering no guarantees,' he said wryly. Then added, 'I should tell you that I agree with everything you just said, and I'll be happy to lend my support. And I should also tell you that it was actually when you came into the equation that my life really started to become difficult, because it seemed to make sense to everyone concerned that I should be the one to keep an eye on you – I sort of knew your family, I lived nearby, I was an amenable sort of a fellow, and your journalistic enquiries had to be monitored. Franz Koehler assumed I was doing it exclusively for him, and occasionally I did give him information that I knew he didn't already have, such as Katherine's little sojourn in the Caribbean.'

'You reported that to him and not to the authorities?' she said, perplexed.

'The authorities first, then Koehler, once I knew I could. At which point you decided you were going to carry out your own search, and I could hardly tell you that I already knew Katherine was long gone.'

'But it took us days to find the pilot,' she protested. 'If you already knew about him, why did it take so long?'

'Actually, he was a genuine find,' he responded in a sardonic tone, 'so we did manage to find out more than they did.'

As she digested that, she found she wasn't sure whether she wanted to laugh or not. 'What about the four million dollars?' she said. 'Did you tell the police about that?'

He nodded. 'I'm afraid it marked rather a black day for Tim's reputation, because that was definitely not what anyone wanted to hear. Until then it was generally believed that Phraxos had not yet bought its way into the hierarchy of the British Government, so for the PM's close friend and unofficial successor to be the first . . .' He sucked in his breath. 'Did the Prime Minister tell you about any of this when you saw him?'

'Yes,' she answered. 'He feels extremely bad about it now, because he'd deliberately held the intelligence operation back from Tim as a . . . well a kind of test, I suppose. He had big plans for Tim's future, so he needed to know that Tim was incorruptible, which means that in a way Tim was under scrutiny too, especially after Katherine joined our team. And that just makes it harder for us all to know that given another week Tim would have proven himself beyond even the highest expectations.' Her eyes went down as, not for the first time, she tried to deal with how tragic it was that her husband, a good and honest man, had been so cruelly cheated of his future.

'But instead,' Chris continued, 'that damned four million turned up in a Swiss bank account. The timing of it . . . The way it looked . . .'

'The chances are it would have ruined his career anyway,' she said solemnly. 'It was a real Catch 22 – you're either with us, in which case the four million is a starting bonus, or you're against us, in which case you can kiss goodbye to any kind of high office, because we'll use the four million to discredit, or even destroy you. And even though they might have had a very hard time actually proving anything, the scandal alone would have had the desired effect.' She was shaking her head in profound dismay. 'If only I'd known what I was doing the day I contacted Katherine,' she said, almost to herself. Then lifting her eyes back to his. 'Sorry. I suppose I'm still not finding it very easy to accept my own role in this.'

'But you didn't know,' he reminded her. 'You can't blame yourself.'

'I know, but I do. Anyway, tell me, why didn't the money get frozen when you told them about it?'

'Mainly because at that point no one was quite sure whether you might be involved with Phraxos too, so they were all waiting to see what happened, what you would do, though it became evident quite quickly that Franz Koehler was menacing you for the money, so you at least were off the hook, and it was considered better all round just to let him have the money back.'

She nodded thoughtfully, then staying with the subject of money said, 'Laurie told me how much Franz Koehler paid you – enough to buy most men's loyalties.'

'Especially when my other so-called employers never shelled out a bean,' he retorted, reaching over to the table behind him to answer the phone. 'Hello?' he said.

He listened for a while, then after saying, 'That's definitely good news, thanks for letting me know,' he rang off again. 'My lawyer,' he said. 'Apparently I can repay him the loan he advanced me, because my credit cards and bank accounts have been unfrozen.'

'They froze your assets?' she cried.

'Afraid so,' he said, his eyes simmering with laughter. 'This has definitely not been one of the best periods of my life.'

She smiled wryly. 'Then here's to moving past it,' she said, raising her glass.

He drank too, then kept his eyes lowered as they lapsed into silence.

Realizing that he might be thinking about Stacey now, and wondering if she'd just been rather tactless in suggesting he simply move on past this difficult period as though his wife were something to be forgotten too, she tried to think of a way of broaching the subject that would allow her to apologize. In the end, she said, 'I understand if I'm not the person you want to talk to about your wife, but I want you to know that I'm really sorry about what happened. I know I said it at the funeral, but I really do mean it. I wish there was something I could do . . .'

'You already have,' he told her, looking up. 'Just by coming here.' He glanced briefly away. 'I wasn't sure I'd find it very easy to see you,' he said, 'in fact I thought if you did come I'd have to tell you that we couldn't see each other. But now you're here . . .' He lapsed into silence again and she could see how hard he was struggling with his emotions. 'I keep telling myself that it wasn't done intentionally to hurt her, that neither of us expected to feel the way we did . . .' He broke off, as though unsure how much more he wanted to reveal.

'It's true, we didn't,' she said.

He sighed and looked down at his drink. 'I just don't know if it helps,' he responded. 'I was cruel the last time I saw her. I wasn't even nice on the phone after . . .' His eyes remained lowered as his voice gave out.

'It'll take time,' she told him gently.

He nodded.

After a while she said, 'We've both got a lot of healing to do, so maybe we could try, as friends, to be a strength for each other.'

He was quiet for a long time and she guessed he was thinking of how much Stacey would hate that. Already she more than half suspected that, in the end, her ghost would be too strong for them both.

Certainly, if she allowed it, Rachel felt sure she'd be able to feel her here now, trying to push her way between them, and she didn't imagine, if Chris was feeling it, that he was resisting very hard. But then he surprised her as he said,

'The shops are still open. I'd like to get you and Charlie something for Christmas. Is there anything you need?'

She smiled. 'What we really need is someone to come and help us decorate our tree,' she said. Then aware that it was too much, too soon, she said, 'Or maybe you could just come and say hello to him.'

'Actually, I'm pretty good at decorating trees,' he told her.

She smiled again.

His eyes were holding hers.

'What are you thinking?' she prompted after a while.

'I'm thinking what a sorry spectacle I'm going to make, all on my own, in a house this size, over Christmas.'

She said nothing, knowing that the suggestions, whatever they might be, had to come from him now.

'I don't suppose you and Charlie . . . ? No, you'll have other plans.'

'Nothing that can't be changed,' she told him. 'Though I happen to know that Beanie's just dying to invite you on Christmas Day. She's got a jumbo jet of a turkey.'

He laughed. 'She used to do a lot of cooking in this kitchen,' he said, sounding nostalgic.

It took another few minutes, then he said, 'Do you think she'd like to bring her jumbo jet here?'

736

'We'll have to ask her, but I think she'd probably like nothing better. But are you sure? There's quite a lot of us. Laurie and Elliot are arriving from London late today, then there's Nick and Jenny, and Jen's mother, and . . . I've lost track of who's coming.'

'Then it sounds as though you need to do it here,' he told her drily. 'Which means we should probably go and get a tree – after we've finished decorating yours.'

She sat quietly for a moment, loving him for the effort he was making, though still not sure if all this fuss was what he needed. 'You know, we all really want you to be part of Christmas, but if you feel . . . Well, if you'd rather we all squeezed into the cottage . . . Or if it was just me and Charlie . . .'

'No, I'd like you all to come,' he said. 'We used to have wonderful Christmases here when my mother was alive. Stacey always preferred it to be just us, but I like family and lots of activity. Gives me a chance to sing and make a fool of myself.'

Smiling as her heart filled up, for they both knew that he probably wasn't quite in the mood for it this year, she said, 'Then I guess we'd better put my tree on hold and go to get yours, because you'll need a pretty big one to make an impression in a house this size.'

He looked around, as though trying to visualize where a tree would go, then after returning his eyes to hers, he put down his empty glass and came to pull her to her feet. 'Merry Christmas,' he said, wrapping her in his arms. 'And thank you.'

'Merry Christmas,' she replied, hugging him back.

They stood together for a long time, experiencing a closeness that was real enough not to need words, but still awkward enough to require silence. She was thinking, not for the first time, of the very peculiar tides of the past few years that had never quite brought them together when they might have, then had when they perhaps ought not. Yet, when all the clutter and confusion of events and judgements, grief and everyday life, was chipped away from their small part of life's journey, there seemed something inherently right about their friendship, almost as though it was meant to be.

Finally he let her go and looked down into her eyes. 'Did you ever finish *The Magus*?' he said.

She nodded. 'I know you're not Conchis's main victim, Nicholas Urfe,' she said. 'And I'm not Lily or Julie.'

He smiled. 'I never thought you were. No duplicity from you. None from me now, either,' he promised.

'That's good to hear.' She thought of the character Allison who had come back to life, and then of Stacey. How hard, she wondered, had he willed that particular piece of fiction into fact.

'You know, I think I'm starting to get an idea of what my New Year's resolution might be,' he said.

'Oh?'

His eyes were teasing. 'I'll let you know if I manage to keep it,' he answered.

Laughing, she embraced him again, then taking his hand she walked with him to get their coats. Though she knew that the next few days were probably going to be harder for them both than either wanted to admit, in her heart she was quite certain now that though their feelings for each other were buried for the moment, beneath all the darkness and pain of their shared and separate experiences, they would, in time, maybe like the flowers of spring, start to find their own sun.

Intimate Strangers

Susan Lewis

Investigative journalist, Laurie Forbes, is planning her wedding to Elliot Russell, when she receives a tip-off that a group of illegally smuggled women is being held somewhere in the East End of London. During her search unexpected and devastating events begin throwing her own life into chaos, so fellow journalist, Sherry MacElvoy steps in to help. Taking on undercover roles to get to the heart of the ruthless gang of human-traffickers, neither reporter can ever begin to imagine what dangers they are about to face.

Neela is one of the helpless Indian girls being held in captivity. Her fear is not only for herself, but her six-year-old niece, Shaila. A disfiguring birthmark has so far saved Neela from abuse, but she knows it is only a matter of time before she is sent for – and worse, before Shaila is taken. Her desperate bids to seek outside help are constantly thwarted, until finally she, and the women with her, agree there is only one way out . . . *Intimate Strangers* is a rich and engrossing story of intense love, heart-break, terror and survival.

'Spellbinding – you just keep turning the pages, with the atmos-phere growing more and more intense as the story leads to its dramatic climax'
Daily Mail

'Mystery and romance par excellence'
Sun

'Susan Lewis strikes gold again . . . gripping'
Options

arrow books